Three Novels of Suspense

MADAM, WILL YOU TALK?

NINE COACHES WAITING

MY BROTHER MICHAEL

MARY STEWART

Three Novels of Suspense

Madam, Will You Talk?

Nine Coaches Waiting

My Brother Michael

M. S. MILL COMPANY and
William Morrow & Company
New York

Contents

Madam, Will You Talk?

FOR MY MOTHER AND FATHER

CHAPTER I

Enter four or five players.

THE WHOLE affair began so very quietly. When I wrote, that summer, and asked my friend Louise if she would come with me on a car trip to Provence, I had no idea that I might be issuing an invitation to danger. And when we arrived one afternoon, after a hot but leisurely journey, at the enchanting little walled city of Avignon, we felt in that mood of pleasant weariness mingled with anticipation which marks, I believe, the beginning of every normal holiday.

No cloud in the sky; no sombre shadow on the machicolated walls; no piercing glance from an enigmatic stranger as we drove in at the Porte de la République and up the sun-dappled Cours Jean-Jaurès. And certainly no involuntary shiver of apprehension as we drew up at last in front of the Hôtel Tistet-Védène, where we had booked rooms for the greater part of our stay.

I even sang to myself as I put the car away, and when I found they had given me a room with a balcony overlooking the shaded courtyard, I was pleased.

And when, later on, the cat jumped on to my balcony, there was still nothing to indicate that this was the beginning of the whole strange, uneasy, tangled business. Or rather, not the beginning, but my own cue, the point where I came in. And though the part I was to play in the tragedy was to break and re-form the pattern of my whole life, yet it was a very minor part, little more than a walk-on in the last act. For most of the play had been played already; there had been love and lust and revenge and fear and murder—all the blood-tragedy bric-à-brac except the Ghost—and now the killer, with blood enough on his hands, was waiting in the wings for the lights to go up again, on the last kill that would bring the final curtain down.

How was I to know, that lovely quiet afternoon, that most of the actors in the tragedy were at that moment assembled in this neat, unpretentious little Provençal hotel? All but one, that is, and he, with murder in his mind, was not so very far away, moving, under that blazing southern sun, in the dark circle of his own personal hell. A circle that narrowed, gradually, upon the Hôtel Tistet-Védène, Avignon.

But I did not know, so I unpacked my things slowly and carefully, while, on my bed, Louise lay and smoked and talked about the mosquitoes.

"And now—a fortnight," she said dreamily. "A whole fortnight. And nothing to do but drink, and sit in the sun."

"No eating? Or are you on a cure?"

"Oh, that. One's almost forgotten how. But they tell me that in France the cattle still grow steaks . . . I wonder how I shall stand up to a beefsteak?"

"You have to do these things gradually." I opened one of the slatted shutters, closed against the late afternoon sun. "Probably the waiter will just introduce you at first, like Alice—Louise, biftek; biftek, Louise. Then you both bow, and the steak is ushered out."

"And of course, in France, no pudding to follow." Louise sighed. "Well, we'll have to make do. Aren't you letting the mosquitoes in, opening that shutter?"

"It's too early. And I can't see to hang these things away. Do you mind either smoking that cigarette or putting it out? It smells."

"Sorry." She picked it up again from the ash-tray. "I'm too lazy even to smoke. I warn you, you know, I'm not going sight-seeing. I couldn't care less if Julius Caesar used to fling his auxiliaries round the town, and throw moles across the harbour mouth. If you want to go and gasp at Roman remains you'll have to go alone. I shall sit under a tree, with a book, as near to the hotel as possible."

I laughed, and began putting out my creams and sunburn lotions on what the Hôtel Tistet-Védène fondly imagined to be a dressing-table.

"Of course I don't expect you to come. You'll do as you like. But I believe the Pont du Gard——"

"My dear, I've seen the Holborn Viaduct. Life can hold no more. . . ."

Louise stubbed out her cigarette carefully, and then folded her hands behind her head. She is tall and fair and plump, with long legs, a pleasant voice, and beautiful hands. She is an artist, has no temperament to speak of, and is unutterably and incurably lazy. When accused of this, she merely says that she is seeing life steadily and seeing it whole, and this takes time. You can neither ruffle nor surprise Louise; you can certainly never quarrel with her. If trouble should ever arise, Louise is simply not there; she fades like the Cheshire Cat, and comes back serenely when it is all over. She is, too, as calmly independent as a cat, without any of its curiosity. And though she looks the kind of large lazy fair girl who is untidy—the sort who stubs out her cigarettes in the face-cream and never brushes the hairs off her coat—she is always beautifully groomed, and her movements are delicate and precise. Again, like a cat. I get on well with cats. As you will find, I have a lot in common with them, and with the Elephant's Child.

"In any case," said Louise, "I've had quite enough of ruins and remains, in the Gilbertian sense, to last me for a lifetime. I live among them."

I knew what she meant. Before my marriage to Johnny Selborne, I, too, had taught at the Alice Drupe Private School for Girls. Beyond the fact that it is in the West Midlands, I shall say nothing more about the Alice Drupe as it is virtually impossible to mention it without risking a heavy libel action. Louise was still Art Mistress there, and owed her continued health and sanity to the habit I have described, of removing herself out of the trouble zone. As far as it was possible to do this at the Alice Drupe, she did it. Even there, she saw life steadily. At any rate she saw it coming.

"Don't speak too soon," I warned her. "You may yet come across Lloyd-Lloyd and Merridew sipping their Pernod in the restaurant downstairs."

"Not *together,* my dear. They don't speak now. The Great Rupture paralysed the whole school for weeks. . . ." She paused and wrinkled her nose. "What a revolting metaphor . . . And *not* Pernod, Charity; Vichy water." She lit another cigarette.

"What happened?"

"Oh, Merridew put up a notice without asking Lloyd, or Lloyd put one up without asking Merridew, or something desperately frightful like that," she said indifferently. "I wasn't there."

Naturally not.

"Poor things," I said, and meant it.

Louise flicked her ash neatly into the bowl, and turned her gold head on the pillow.

"Yes, you can say that. You're out of it now for good, aren't you? You're lucky."

I didn't answer. I laid Johnny's photograph gently back in the case, where I had just come across it, and picked up a frock instead. I shook it out and laid it over a chair, ready to put on. I don't think my expression changed at all. But Louise happens to know me rather well.

She ground out her cigarette, and her voice changed.

"Oh God, Charity, I'm sorry. I forgot. I am a fool. Forgive me."

"Forget it," I said, lightly enough, "I do."

"Do you?"

"Of course. It's a long time now. I'd be silly and unnatural not to.

And I *am* lucky, as you said." I grinned at her. "After all, I'm a wealthy widow . . . look at these."

"My dear girl! What *gorgeous* undies. . . ."

And the conversation slipped comfortably back to the things that really matter.

.   .   .   .

When Louise had gone to her own room, I washed, changed into a white frock with a wide blue belt, and did my face and hair very slowly. It was still hot, and the late sun's rays fell obliquely across the balcony, through the half-opened shutter, in a shaft of copper-gold. Motionless, the shadows of thin leaves traced a pattern across it as delicate and precise as a Chinese painting on silk. The image of the tree, brushed in like that by the sun, had a grace that the tree itself gave no hint of, for it was merely one of the nameless spindly affairs, parched and dust-laden, that struggled up towards the sky from their pots in the hotel court below. But its shadow might have been designed by Ma Yüan.

The courtyard was empty; people were still resting, or changing, or, if they were the mad English, walking out in the afternoon sun. A white-painted trellis wall separated the court on one side from the street, and beyond it people, mules, cars, occasionally even buses, moved about their business up and down the narrow thoroughfare. But inside the vine-covered trellis it was very still and peaceful. The gravel between the gay little chairs was carefully raked and watered; shade lay gently across the tables, some of which, laid for dinner, gleamed invitingly with glass and silver. The only living thing in the court was a thin ginger cat, which was curled round the base of my spindly tree, like—who was it? Nidhug? —at the root of Yggdrasil.

I sat down by the half-shuttered window, and began to think about where I should go to-morrow.

Avignon Bridge, where one dances, of course; and after Avignon itself, the Pont du Gard—in spite of the fact that I, too, had seen Holborn Viaduct. I picked up the Michelin Guide to Provence, and looked at the sketch of the great aqueduct which is on the cover. . . .

To-morrow, I said to myself, I would take things easy, and wander round the ramparts and the Popes' Palace. Then, the day after . . .

Then fate, in the shape of Nidhug, took a hand.

My cue had come. I had to enter the stage.

The first hint I had of it was the violent shaking of the shadows on the balcony. The Chinese design wavered, broke, and dissolved into the image of a ragged witch's besom, as the tree Yggdrasil vibrated and lurched sharply under a weight it was never meant to bear. Then the ginger cat shot on to my balcony, turned completely round on a space the size of a sixpence, sent down on her assailant the look to end all looks, and sat calmly down to wash. From below a rush and a volley of barking explained everything.

Then came a crash, and the sound of running feet.

The cat yawned, tidied a whisker into place, swarmed in a bored manner up an impossible drainpipe, and vanished on to the roof. I got up and looked over the balcony railing.

The courtyard, formerly so empty and peaceful, seemed all of a sudden remarkably full of a boy and a large, nondescript dog. The latter, with his earnest gaze still on the balcony, was leaping futilely up and down, pouring out rage, hatred and excitement, while the boy tried with one hand to catch and quell him, and with the other to lift one of the tables which had been knocked on to its side. It was, luckily, not one of those which had been set for dinner.

The table, which was of iron, was very heavy, and the boy seemed to be having some difficulty in raising it. Eventually he let go the dog, and taking both hands to the job, succeeded in lifting the table almost halfway. Then the dog, who appeared to be a little slow in the uptake, but a sticker for all that, realized that his prey was gone from the balcony and leaped madly in several directions at once. He crashed into the boy. The table thudded down again.

"*Oh Rommel!*" said the boy, surprisingly enough.

Before I could decide what language this was, the boy looked up and saw me. He straightened, pushed his hair back from his forehead, and grinned.

"*J'éspère,*" he said carefully, "*que ce n'était pas votre chat, mademoiselle?*"

This, of course, settled the question of his nationality immediately, but I am nothing if not tactful. I shook my head.

"My French isn't terribly good," I said. "Do you speak English, monsieur?"

He looked immensely pleased.

"Well, as a matter of fact, I *am* English," he admitted. "*Stop* it, Rommel!" He grabbed the dog with decision. "He hadn't hurt the cat, had he? I just saw it jump for the balcony."

"It didn't look very worried."

"Oh, that's all right, then. I can't persuade him to behave decently, as —as befits a foreigner. It seems funny to *be* foreigners, doesn't it?"

I admitted that it did indeed.

"Have you just arrived?"

"At about four o'clock. Yes."

"Then you haven't seen much of Avignon yet. Isn't it a funny little town? Will you like it, do you think?"

"I certainly like what I've seen so far. Do *you* like it here?"

It was the most trivial of small-talk, of course, but his face changed oddly as he pondered the question. At that distance I could not read his expression, but it was certainly not what one might expect of a boy—I judged him to be about thirteen—who was lucky enough to be enjoying a holiday in the South of France. Indeed, there was not much about him at that moment, if you except the outward signs of crumpled shirt, stained shorts, and mongrel dog, to suggest the average boy at all. His face, which had, even in the slight courtesies of small-talk, betrayed humour and a quick intelligence at work, seemed suddenly to mask itself, to become older. Some impalpable burden almost visibly dropped on to his shoulders. One was conscious, in spite of the sensitive youth of his mouth, and the childish thin wrists and hands, of something here that could meet and challenge a quite adult destiny on its own ground, strength for strength. The burden, whatever it was, was quite obviously recognized and accepted. There had been some hardening process at work, and recently. Not a pleasant process, I thought, looking at the withdrawn profile bent over the absurd dog, and feeling suddenly angry.

But he came out of his sombre thoughts as quickly as he had gone in —so quickly, in fact, that I began to think I had been an over-imaginative fool.

"Yes, of course I like it. Rommel doesn't, it's too hot. Do you like the heat?" We were back at the small-talk. "They said two English ladies were coming to-day; that would be you—Mrs. Selborne and Miss Crabbe?"

"Cray. I'm Mrs. Selborne," I said.

"Yes, that's it." His grin was suddenly pure small-boy. "I'm bad at remembering names, and I have to do it by—by association. It sometimes goes awfully wrong. But I remembered yours because of Gilbert White."

Now most people could see the connection between cray and crab, but not many thirteen-year-olds, I thought, would be so carelessly familiar with Gilbert White's letters from his little Hampshire village, which go under the title of *The Natural History of Selborne*. I had been right about the intelligence. I only knew the book myself because one is apt to be familiar with most of the contexts in which one's name appears. And because Johnny——

"My name's David," said the boy. "David Shelley."

I laughed.

"Well, that's easy enough to remember, anyway. How do you do, David? I shall only have to think of the Romantic poets, if I forget. But don't hold it against me if I address you as David Byron, or——"

I stopped abruptly. The boy's face, smiling politely up at me, changed again. This time there could be no mistake about it. He went suddenly rigid, and a wave of scarlet poured over his face from neck to temples, and receded as quickly, leaving him white and sick-looking. He opened his mouth as if to speak, fumbling a little with the dog's collar. Then he seemed to make some kind of effort, sent me a courteous, meaningless little smile, and bent over the dog again, fumbling in his pocket for string to fasten him.

I had made a mistake, it seemed. But I had not been mistaken when I had sensed that there was something very wrong somewhere. I am not a person who interferes readily in other people's affairs, but suddenly, unaccountably, and violently, I wanted to interfere in this one.

I need not have worried; I was going to.

.   .   .   .

But not for the moment. Before I could speak again we were interrupted by a woman who came in through the vine-trellis, from the street. She was, I guessed, thirty-five. She was also blonde, tall, and quite the most beautiful woman I had ever seen. The simple cream dress she wore must have been one of Dior's favourite dreams, and the bill for it her husband's nightmare. Being a woman myself, I naturally saw the enormous sapphire on her left hand almost before I saw her.

She did not see me at all, which again was perfectly natural. She paused a moment when she saw David and the dog, then came forward with a kind of eye-compelling grace which would have turned heads in Piccadilly, Manchester, on a wet Monday morning. What it did in Provence, where men make a hobby of looking at women, I hesitated to think. I believe I had visions of the cafés along the Rue de la République emptying as she passed, as the houses of Hamelin emptied a different cargo after the Pied Piper.

She paused by the upturned table and spoke. Her voice was pleasant, her English perfect, but her accent was that of a Frenchwoman.

"David."

No reply.

"*Mon fils. . . .*"

Her son? He did not glance up.

She said, evenly: "Don't you know what the time is? And what on earth happened to the table?"

"Rommel upset it." The averted head, the sulky-sounding mumble which David accorded her, were at once rude and surprising. She took no notice of his manner, but touched him lightly on the shoulder.

"Well, put it right, there's a good boy. And hurry up and change. It's nearly dinner-time. Where have you been to-day?"

"By the river."

"How you can——" She laughed and shrugged, all at once very French, then reached in her bag for a cigarette. "Well, put the table up, child."

David pulled the reluctant Rommel towards a tree, and began to tie him to its stem. He said flatly:

"I can't lift it."

A new voice interrupted, smoothly:

"Permit me, madame."

The man who had come quietly out of the hotel was dark and singularly good-looking. His clothes, his air, no less than his voice, were unmistakably French, and he had that look of intense virility and yet sophistication—the sort of powerful, careless charm which can be quite devastating. It was all the more surprising, therefore, that the woman, after a glance of conventional thanks, ignored him completely, and lit her cigarette without glancing in his direction. I would have gone to the stake for my conviction that she, where men were concerned, was the noticing type.

The newcomer smiled at David, lifted the heavy table without apparent effort, set it straight, then dusted his hands on a handkerchief.

"Thank you, sir," said David. He began untying Rommel again from the tree.

"De rien," said the Frenchman. "Madame." He gave a little bow in her direction, which she acknowledged with a faint polite smile, then he made his way to a table in the far corner of the courtyard, and sat down.

"If you hurry," said David's mother, "you can have the bathroom first."

Without a word the boy went into the hotel, trailing a somewhat subdued dog after him on the end of the string. His mother stared after him for a moment, with an expression half puzzled, half exasperated. Then she gave a smiling little shrug of the shoulders, and went into the hotel after the boy.

The Frenchman had not noticed me either, his handsome head was bent over a match as he lit a cigarette. I went quietly back through my window, and stood for a moment in the cool shade of the room thinking over the little scene which, somehow, had hidden in it the elements of oddity. The exquisite film-starry creature, and the dilapidated dog . . . Christian Dior and Gilbert White . . . and she was French and the boy's accent was definitely Stratford-atte-Bow . . . and he was rude to her and charmingly polite to strangers.

Well, it was no affair of mine.

I picked my bag up and went downstairs for a drink.

CHAPTER II

*Ther saugh I first the derke ymaginyng
Of felonye . . .*

(CHAUCER)

WHEN I got down into the little courtyard, it was beginning to fill up. Louise was not down yet, so I found a table in the shade, and ordered a Cinzano.

I looked about me, resigned to the fact that almost everybody in the hotel would probably be English too. But the collection so far seemed varied enough. I began to play the game of guessing at people's professions—and, in this case, nationalities. One is nearly always wrong, of course, and it is a game too often played by those self-satisfied people who are apt to announce that they are students of human nature . . . but I played it, nevertheless.

The two men at the next table to me were Germans. One was thin and clever-looking, and the other was the fat-necked German of the cartoons. And since I heard him say *"Ach, so?"* to his companion, it didn't need any great insight to hazard the rest. There was a young couple, honeymooning at a guess, and, at another guess, American. Then there was the handsome Frenchman, drinking his Pernod by himself in the corner, and another man sitting alone near the trellis, reading a book and sipping a bright green drink with caution and distrust. I puzzled for a long time over him—he might have been anything—until I saw the title of the book. *Four Quartets,* by T. S. Eliot. Which seemed to settle it. There were two other parties who might have been anything at all.

At this point Louise joined me.

"I have been kept from my drink," she complained, bitterly for her, "by the *patronne*, who is convinced that I cannot wait to know the history, business, and antecedents, of everyone in the hotel. And who, incidentally, was panting to find out mine and yours."

Her vermouth was brought, and she tilted it to the light with a contented sigh.

"L'heure de l'apéritif. What a civilized institution. Ah, that must be M. Paul Véry." She was looking at the Frenchman in the corner. "Mad-

ame said he was handsome enough to suicide oneself for, and that hardly
applies to anyone else here. He's from Paris. Something to do with antiques."

"This is thrilling."

"The other lonely male is English, and a schoolmaster. His name is
John Marsden and he is almost certainly a Boy Scout and a teetotaller as
well."

"Why on earth?" I asked, startled.

"Because," said Louise drily, "any lonely male I ever get within reach
of these days seems to be both, and to eschew women into the bargain. Is
that the right word, eschew?"

"I believe so."

"At any rate, one would not suicide oneself for *that* one. I wonder
why he looks so solemn? Do you suppose he's reading *Whither England,*
or something?"

"It's T. S. Eliot," I said. *"Four Quartets."*

"Oh *well*," said Louise, who does not consider poetry necessary. Mr.
Marsden was dismissed.

"I suppose that couple are American?" I said.

"Oh yes. Their name is Cornell, or they come from Cornell, or something. My French had a breakdown at that point. And Mamma and Papa
under the palm tree are hot from Newcastle, Scotland."

"Scotland?" I said blankly.

"So Madame informed me. Scotland, zat is ze Norz of England, *n'est-
ce pas?* I like the daughter, don't you? The Young Idea."

I looked cautiously round. The couple under the palm tree might have
sat anywhere for the portrait of Suburban England Abroad. Dressed as
only the British can dress for a subtropical climate—that is, just as they
would for a fort-night on the North-East coast of England—they sat sipping their drinks with wary enjoyment, and eyeing their seventeen-year-
old daughter with the sort of expression that barnyard fowls might have
if they suddenly hatched a flamingo. For she was startling to say the least
of it. She would have been pretty in a fair English fashion, but she had
seen fit to disguise herself by combing her hair in a flat thick mat down
over one side of her face. From behind the curtain appeared one eye,
blue-shadowed to an amazing appearance of dissipation. Scarlet nails,
spike-heeled sandals, a flowered dirndl and a cotton jersey filled to
frankly unbelievable proportions by a frankly impossible figure . . .
Hollywood had come to Avignon by way of the Scotswood Road. And it
became apparent that this not inconsiderable battery of charm was
turned full on for someone's benefit.

"The man in the corner . . ." murmured Louise.

I glanced towards M. Paul Véry, who, however, appeared quite indifferent to the effort being made on his behalf. He had a slight frown between his brows, and he was tracing a pattern with the base of his glass on the table-top as if it were the only thing that mattered in the world.

"She's wasting her time, I'm afraid," I remarked, and, as if he had heard me (which was impossible) the Frenchman looked up and met my eyes. He held them deliberately for a long moment in a cool, appraising stare, then, just as deliberately, he raised his glass and drank, still with his eyes on me. I looked away to gaze hard at the back of the fat German's neck, and hoped my colour had not risen.

"She is indeed wasting her time," said Louise softly. She raised an amused eyebrow at me. "Here's metal more attractive."

"Don't be idiotic," I said with some asperity. "And control your imagination, for goodness' sake. Don't forget this is Provence, and if a woman's fool enough to be caught staring at a man, she's asking for it. That's what's called an *œillade,* which is French for leer."

"All right," said Louise tranquilly. "Well, that's all that Madame told me. I think the other lot are Swiss—nobody else except Americans could afford a gorgeous vulgar car like that—and are just *enpassant.* The only other resident is a Mrs. Bristol, who's either a widow or divorced. *Et voilà tous.* Shall we have another drink?"

Then the blonde appeared, threading her way between the tables, to sit down near the trellis, two tables away from Mr. Marsden. She crossed one exquisite nyloned leg over the other, took out a cigarette, and smiled at the waiter. There was a sort of confusion, which resolved itself into three separate movements—the fat German beat the waiter and Mr. Marsden by a short head—to light her cigarette. But Mr. Marsden won on points, because the German's lighter refused to work, and Marsden had a match. She flung a smile to Fat-Neck, an order for a drink to the waiter, and a look across the flame of the match to Marsden that made the flame look awfully dim. At any rate he read *Burnt Norton* upside down for quite some time afterwards. I had been right about the Pied Piper.

"Eschew," said Louise, "was definitely *not* the right word. I suppose that is Mrs. Bristol."

It was on the tip of my tongue to correct her when the waiter, travelling like a Derby winner, brought the drink.

"Madame Bristol's drink." He bowed it on to the table, and himself away.

She settled back in her chair, and looked about her. Seen at close quarters, she was as lovely as ever, which is saying a lot. It was a carefully tended, exotic loveliness, like that of a strange flower. That is a hackneyed metaphor, I know, but it describes her better than any other . . . her skin was so smooth, and her heavy perfume seemed part of her. Her eyes, I saw, were a curiously bright blue, and large. Her hands were restless, and at the corners of mouth and eyes I could see the faint lines of worry. These deepened suddenly as I watched her, and then I realized that David had come out from the hotel. He followed the waiter, who was bringing another drink for Louise, and, as he passed our table, saw me. He gave me a sudden little half-apologetic grin, which the waiter masked, I think, from the woman. Then the queer sullen look came down over his face again, and he sat down opposite her. She looked approvingly at his clean shorts and white shirt, and said something, to which he did not reply. She looked at his bent head for a moment, then resumed her casual scrutiny of the tables.

The place was filling up rapidly now, and the waiters were handing round the menus.

"Have you met that boy before?" asked Louise, "or was that just another leer?"

I said that I had spoken to him for a moment in the courtyard. For some reason which I could not analyse, I did not want to talk about it and I was glad when she dropped the subject without further question.

"We'd better order," she said.

We studied the menu with some enthusiasm. . . .

But when Louise asked me if I wanted *côte d'agneau* or *escalope de veau,* I replied "Shelley" in an absent sort of way, and between the *petites pommes de terre sautées* and the *tarte maison* I was still trying to fit the lovely (and French) Mrs. Bristol in with Gilbert White and that appalling dog and the expression on a child's face of something being borne that was too heavy for him to bear.

.   .   .   .

After dinner Louise announced that she was going to get her book, and sit over her coffee and cognac until bedtime. So I left her to it, and went out to explore Avignon alone.

Avignon is a walled city, as I have said, a compact and lovely little town skirted to the north and west by the Rhône, and circled completely by medieval ramparts, none the less lovely, to my inexpert eye, for having been heavily restored in the nineteenth century. The city is dominated from the north by the Rocher des Doms, a steep mass of white rock crowned by the cathedral of Notre Dame, and green with singing pines. Beside the cathedral, taking the light above the town, is the golden stone palace of the Popes. The town itself is slashed in two by one main street, the Rue de la République, which leads from the main gate straight up to the city square and thence to the Place du Palais, at the foot of the Rocher des Doms itself.

But these things I had yet to find. It was dusk when I set out, and the street was vividly lit. All the cafés were full, and I picked my way between the tables on the pavement, while there grew in me that slow sense of exhilaration which one inevitably gets in a Southern town after dark. The shop windows glittered and flashed with every conceivable luxury that the mind of the tourist could imagine; the neon lights slid along satin and drowned themselves in velvet and danced over perfume and jewels, and, since I have learned in my twenty-eight years to protect the heart a little against too much pity, I kept my eyes on them, and tried not to think about the beggars who slunk whining along the city gutters. I went on, carefully not thinking about those beggars, until I reached the end of the street, where the Rue de la République widens out and becomes the main square of the city, and where all Avignon collects at night, together with, one would swear, every child and every dog in France.

The square is surrounded with cafés, which overflow the narrow pavements with a froth of gay little tables and wicker chairs, and even cast up a jetsam of more little tables across the roads and into the centre of the square itself. Here, as I said, Avignon collects at night, and for the price of a cup of coffee, which secures you a chair, you may sit for an hour and watch France parade for you.

I paid for my coffee, and sat in the milk-warm air, marvelling, as one has to in Provence, at the charming manners of the children, and the incredible variety of shapes possible among the dogs, at the beauty of the half-naked, coffee-brown young men in from the fields, and the modest grace of the young girls. One in particular I noticed, an exquisite dark creature who went slowly past with downcast eyes. Her dress was cut low over her breasts, and gathered tightly to a tiny waist, but her face might have been that of a nun, and she walked demurely between her parents, stout, respectable-looking folk who made the girl as difficult of access, no doubt, as Danaë. And she was followed, I could see, by dark-eyed glances that said exactly what had been said to Bele Yolanz and fair Amelot, five hundred years before, when the troubadours sang in Provence.

"Excuse me," said a woman's voice behind me. "But didn't I see you at the hotel?"

I turned. It was Mamma from Newcastle, Scotland, and she was smiling at me rather hesitantly from a near-by table.

"I'm Mrs. Palmer," she said. "I hope you don't mind me speaking, but I saw you at dinner, and——"

"Of course I don't. My name's Charity Selborne." I got up and picked up my coffee-cup. "May I join you?"

"Oh, do." She moved her chair to make way for me. "Father and Carrie—they go off walking about the place, exploring they call it—only sometimes they seem to take so long, and——"

"And it seems longer when you don't know anyone to talk to," I finished for her.

She beamed as if I had said something brilliant. "That's exactly how I feel! Fancy! And of course it's not like home, and what with people talking French it's different, isn't it?"

I admitted that it was.

"Of course if I go in for a cup of tea at home," said Mrs. Palmer, "in Carrick's, you know, or it might be Fenwick's, there's always someone I know comes in too, and you can have a nice chat before you get the bus. That's why it seems kind of funny not knowing anybody here, and of course it isn't tea anyway, not *real* tea, as you might say, but I just can't seem to fancy this stuff they give you with lemon in, can you?"

I said on the whole, no, and how very brave of her to come all this way for a holiday.

"Well," said Mrs. Palmer, "it wasn't really me that suggested it, it was Carrie. I'd never have thought of a grand holiday like this, you know. But I just thought to myself, why not? You always read about the South of France and what's the good of just going every year to Scarborough and reading about the South of France? Well, I just thought, we can afford it, and why not? So here we are."

I smiled at her, and said why not indeed, and good for her, and what a splendid idea of Carrie's.

"Of course she likes to be called Carole," said Mrs. Palmer hastily. "I think it's these films, you know. She will try to dress like them, say what I will."

I said Carole was a pretty girl, which was true.

"Now that Mrs. Bristol, poor thing," said Mrs. Palmer. "She *does* look the part, the way Carrie never will. Of course she *was* on the stage or something, before It Happened."

I sat up straight.

"Before what happened, Mrs. Palmer?"

"Oh, didn't you know? I recognized her straight away. Her photo was in all the Sunday papers, you know. Before she married that dreadful man, I meant."

"What dreadful man? *What* happened?"

"The murderer," said Mrs. Palmer, lowering her voice to a whisper. "He was tried for murder, the Brutal Murder of his Best Friend, it said in the papers." The quoted headlines echoed queerly. "He thought his friend was carrying on with *her*—with his wife—so he murdered him. It was all in the papers."

I stared at her stupid, kindly, half-excited eyes, and felt a bit sick.

"David's father, you mean?" I asked numbly. "David's father a *murderer?*"

She nodded.

"That's right. Strangled with a blind cord. Horrible. An Act of Jealous Madness, it said."

I said, inadequately, looking away from her:

"Poor little boy . . . how long ago was all this?"

"The trial was in April. Of course, she's not the boy's mother, you know, she was his second wife. But of *course* she took the boy away: she couldn't leave David to *him*. Not after what happened."

"What do you mean? D'you mean he's still alive?"

"Oh yes."

"In prison?"

She shook her head, leaning a little closer.

"No. That's the awful part of it, Mrs. Selborne. He's At Large."

"But——"

"He was let off. Insufficient evidence, they called it, and they acquitted him."

"But perhaps he's not guilty. I mean, the courts of law——"

"Guilty," said Mrs. Palmer, tapping my arm. "Guilty as hell." She broke off and went rather pink. "That's what Mr. Palmer says, you understand, Mrs. Selborne. And it's my belief he was mad, poor soul, or he'd never have gone for the boy like he did, murder or no murder."

"Gone . . . for the boy?" I repeated, a bit shakily.

"Yes. Terrible, isn't it?" I could see the easy moisture start into her pale kindly eyes, and I warmed towards her. There was nothing of the ghoul about Mrs. Palmer; she was not enjoying the story, any more than I was. "They found David unconscious in the bathroom near the bedroom where the body was found. He'd been knocked on the head."

"Did he say his father had done it?"

"He didn't see who hit him. But it must've been the murderer. Caught in the Act, as you might say. Oh, it was an awful business; I'm surprised you don't remember it, really. The papers went on about it for long enough."

"No, I don't remember it." My voice sounded flat, almost mechanical.

Poor David. Poor little boy. "I don't remember hearing the name before at all. It's—it's terrible."

Mrs. Palmer gave an exclamation, grabbed her handbag, and rose.

"Oh, there's Father and Carrie, off down the other side of the square, they can't have seen me . . . I must run. It's been lovely having a little chat, Mrs. Selborne, really lovely." She beamed at me. "And don't take on about poor Mrs. Bristol and the little boy. She's divorced from that Man, you know. He can't do a thing. And children do get over things, they say."

Over some things, yes.

"I'm glad you told me," I said, "I might have said something . . . I had no idea."

"Well, if you didn't see the photos——" said Mrs. Palmer. "Of course, Bristol isn't their real name, so you wouldn't have heard it. The real name was Byron. Richard Byron, that was it. And now I must run. Good night, Mrs. Selborne."

She went across the square, away from me, and I sat there for a long time before I even realized she had gone.

CHAPTER III

Sur le pont d'Avignon
L'on y danse, l'on y danse
Sur le pont d'Avignon
L'on y danse, tout en rond.
(FRENCH NURSERY RHYME)

BY TEN the next morning it was already as hot as on the hottest day in England, but with no sense of oppression, for the air was clear and light. Louise, true to her word, retired with a book and a sketching pad to the little green public gardens near the hotel.

"You go and play tourist," she said. "I'm going to sit under a tree and drink grape juice. Iced."

It sounded a tempting programme, but to-morrow would be no cooler than to-day, and in any case the heat does not worry me unduly, so I set off for a gentle tour of exploration. This time I went out of the city gate, and turned along under the massive outer walls, towards the quarter where the Rhône races under the Rocher des Doms and then round the western fortifications of the city. It was a dusty walk, and not a very pleasant one, after all, I discovered. The verges of the narrow road were deep in dust and grit, the only vegetation, apart from the trees along the river, being thistles as dry as crumbling paper. Even along the flat edge of the Rhône itself, under the trees, there was no grass, only beaten dirt and stones, where beggars slept at night on the bare ground. A pair of enormous birds dipped and circled above the river.

But presently, round a curve in the city wall, the old bridge of the song came into view, its four remaining arches soaring out across the green water to break off, as it were, in midleap, suspended half-way across the Rhône. Down into the deep jade water glimmered the drowned-gold reflection of the chapel of St. Nicholas, which guards the second arch. Here, held by a spit of sand, the water is still, rich with the glowing colours of stone and shadow and dipping boughs, but beyond the sand-bank the slender bridge thrusts out across a tearing torrent. Standing there, you remember suddenly that this is one of the great rivers of Europe. Without sound or foam, smooth and incredibly rapid, it sucks its enormous way south to the Mediterranean, here green as serpentine, there eddying to aquamarine, but everywhere hard in colour as a stone.

And then I saw David, playing with Rommel beside the pool under the chapel. Both boy and dog were wet, David, since he was in bathing trunks, more gracefully so than Rommel, who looked definitely better when his somewhat eccentric shape was disguised by his wool. I was on the bridge, actually, before I saw them below me. They seemed absorbed, David in building a dam, Rommel in systematically destroying it, but almost at once the boy looked up and saw me sitting in the embrasure of the chapel window.

He grinned and waved.

"Are you going to dance up there?" he called.

"Probably not," I called back. "It's too narrow."

"What's in the chapel?"

"Nothing much. Haven't you been up?" I must have sounded surprised.

"No money," said David, succinctly.

"Tell the concierge I'll pay for you on my way down."

"I didn't mean that, you know."

"No, I know. But I did. Only for heaven's sake hang on to Rommel. There's no parapet, and he'd be at Marseilles by tea-time if he fell into this."

Boy and dog vanished into the concierge's lodge, and presently emerged on to the bridge, slightly out of breath, and disputing over Rommel's right to hurl himself sportingly straight into the Rhône.

But presently Rommel, secured by the inevitable piece of string, was reckoned as being under control, and the three of us cautiously went to the very end of the broken arch—cautiously, because the bridge is only a few feet wide and there is always a strong breeze blowing from the North—and sat down with Rommel between us. We sang *"Sur le pont d'Avignon"* in the style of Jean Sablon, and David told me the story of St. Bénézet who confounded the clerics of Avignon, and built the bridge where the angel had told him, and we watched the two big birds, which were kites, David said, and which soared and circled beautifully up in the high blue air.

Then we went down to the road, and I paid the concierge, and David thanked me again, and we set off back to the hotel for lunch.

It seemed impossible, on this lovely gay morning, that David's father might be a murderer, and that David himself had been struck down, for no reason, in the dark, by a hand that must surely have belonged to a madman.

"Where do you spend most of your days?" I asked.

"Oh, by the river, mostly. You can swim under the bridge at the edge, inside the sand-bank where there's no current."

"You haven't seen—well, the countryside? The Pont du Gard, and the arena at Nîmes, and so on? Perhaps you don't bother with that sort of thing?"

"Oh *yes*. I'd love to see the arena—do you know they have bull-fights every Sunday and one of the matadors is a woman?"

"Well I should hate to see a bull-fight," I said decidedly. "But I intend to go and see the arena to-morrow anyway, and if you'd like to come, there's plenty of room in the car. Do you think your mother would let you?"

"My step-mother," said David distinctly.

He shot me a little sidelong look and flushed slightly. "That's why we have different names, you see."

"I see. Would she let you come? That is, if you would like to come?"

He hesitated oddly for a moment, and once again I saw the mask fall across his face, and as before, for no reason that I could guess. It was as if he considered some grave objection, rejected it eventually, and finally shrugged it away.

"I should like it very much, thank you," he said formally. "And I don't think my step-mother will object at all. It isn't her kind of thing, you know," naïvely enough, "but she doesn't much mind what I do."

When we reached the hotel, people were gathering for *apéritifs* in the cool courtyard. I came down from my room to find Mrs. Bristol already installed at a table beside an orange tree. She smiled at me, and made a gesture of invitation, so I went over and sat down at her table.

"I hear you have been with David," she said to me, "so very kind of you to trouble."

"Not at all. We met by accident—I enjoyed the morning immensely." I murmured commonplaces, and she thanked me charmingly for what she called my kindness.

She bought me a drink, and we talked nothings about the heat, and the town, and the shops for some time. She was very charming and talkative, but I noticed that the worried lines round her mouth seemed rather more pronounced to-day, and that whenever David's name cropped up in the conversation, there seemed to darken in her eyes the same shadow—of wariness, was it?—that had crossed David's face when I spoke of the trip to the arena at Nîmes.

"I had thought of taking the car to the Pont du Gard to-morrow," I said at length, "and then on to Nîmes, to look round a bit. If you have no objection, I should like to take David with me? I don't know whether my friend will want to go, and I should very much like to have David's company."

She was lighting a cigarette when I spoke, and she paused with the flame of the lighter an inch from the cigarette-end, in the queerest, most exact repetition of David's own deliberation. I saw her assimilate the question, look at it carefully, hesitate, and then decide. For the life of me I couldn't understand why a proposal for a day's sight-seeing tour (which was surely what one came to Roman France for anyway?) should raise such problems as mine apparently did.

"It's so very kind of you," said Mrs. Bristol, and the lighter finally made contact with the cigarette. "I'm sure David will enjoy it." She made a charming grimace. "These antiquities—they are not for me; I am for Paris, the cities, the people—places where one amuses oneself . . . you understand?"

"Oh yes—but I rather like it both ways," I laughed. "And I'm afraid I adore sight-seeing. I'm a born tourist, but I don't like to go in a crowd. But what on earth do you find to do in Avignon if you don't like—er, antiquities?"

She hesitated again, and sent me a quick look from under her darkened lashes.

"We do not stay long—we pass through to Monte Carlo. We rest a few days in Avignon on the way."

"Well, thank you for the drink, Mrs. Bristol," I said, getting to my feet. I had caught sight of Louise, who had taken a corner table, and was looking at the lunch menu. We murmured more civilities, and I turned to go, but the strap of my bag caught on the back of the chair, and as I swung round again quickly to disentangle it, I saw Mrs. Bristol staring at me, with her lovely eyes narrowed against the smoke of her cigarette, and in them a look of half-pleased, half-apprehensive speculation that puzzled me considerably.

.   .   .   .

That evening, as Louise was no more inclined than formerly to go for a walk, I left her sketching in a café in the city square, and went alone up the little dark street that leads to the Popes' Palace and the gardens among the pines, high up on the Rocher des Doms.

Unlike the main square, the Place du Palais was almost empty, the buildings on three sides dark and blank, while on the right the great façade of the Palace soared up out of the living rock, shadowy yet luminous in the starlight. I lingered for a while gazing up at it, then went slowly up the sloping zigzag walk through the pines towards the high gardens, which lie at the very edge of the city, and are girdled in by the city wall itself. Very few people appeared to be up there that evening, and only occasionally, it seemed, I heard the murmur of voices and the soft scrunch of the gravel under someone's foot. The air was still, and the cicadas were quiet at last, but the pines kept up a faint continuous murmuring overhead, almost as if, in sleep, they yet gave back the sound of the wind that sweeps down the river all winter, and, in summer, lingers in them still.

Climbing slowly up through the winding alleys of evergreens, I came at length to the topmost edge of the gardens, above the Rhône, and leaned over the low battlemented wall to rest. Below me the wall dropped away vertically, merging into the solid cliff which bounded the river. The Rhône, beneath, slipped silently under the darkness on its wide and glimmering way.

It was very quiet.

Then suddenly, from somewhere behind me, came a man's voice, speaking low, in French.

"So this is where you are!"

Startled, I turned my head, but behind me was a thick bank of evergreen, and I could see nothing. I was alone in my little high corner of the wall. He must be on the lower walk, screened by the bushes. A woman's voice answered him.

She said: "You're late. I've been here a long time. Have you a cigarette?"

I heard the scrape of a match, then he said in a voice which sounded sullen: "You weren't here when I passed ten minutes ago."

"I got tired of waiting, and went for a walk." Her voice was indifferent, and I heard the gravel scrape, as if he made an angry movement.

I had no intention of letting myself be marooned in my corner while a love scene went on within hearing, and I determined at this point that, as I would have to pass them to get back to the main path, I had better emerge before anything passed that might make my appearance embarrassing. But as I turned to move, the woman spoke again, and I realized, suddenly, two things; one, that the voice was that of Mrs. Bristol, and secondly, that she was very much afraid. I suppose I had not recognized the voice immediately because I had previously only heard her speak in English, but as her voice rose, edged with fear, I recognized it.

She said: "It's happened. I knew it would happen. I knew. . . ."

His voice cut in sharply, almost roughly: "What's happened?"

"He's here. He's come. I had to see you, I——"

He interrupted again.

"For God's sake, pull yourself together. How do you know he's here?"

She spoke breathlessly, still with the tremor in her voice.

"I got a phone call to-night. His car's been seen. They traced it as far as Montélimar. He must be coming this way. He must have found out where we are——"

"Loraine——"

"What are we going to do?" It was a desperate whisper. I leaned against the wall in my little corner; not for anything could I have come out now. I could only trust they would not seek its greater privacy for themselves.

I heard the man (I think it was he) draw in a long breath. Then he spoke quietly and with emphasis.

"There is nothing that we can do, yet. We don't know for certain where he is, he may be anywhere in Provence. When was he seen in Montélimar?"

"Yesterday."

He exploded with wrath. "God in heaven, the clumsy fools! And they only telephoned to-night?"

"They weren't sure. It was a big grey car with a GB plate, and they think it was his. It was the first glimpse they'd had since Chartres."

"They should have been sure. What the hell are they paid for?" he said angrily.

"Can't we find out where he is? I—I don't think I can stand much more of this—this suspense."

"No, we must do nothing. We'll find out soon enough, I've no doubt." His voice was grim. "And for God's sake, Loraine, take hold of yourself. You shouldn't have got me up here to-night, you don't know who's about, and this is such a tiny place. Anybody from the hotel——"

Her voice was sharp with new alarm: "You don't think he's got someone planted in the hotel? Do you mean . . . ?"

"I don't mean anything," he returned shortly. "All I'm saying is, that we mustn't be seen together. You know that as well as I do. Anyone might see us, they might mention it to David, and he has little enough confidence in you anyway, as far as I can see."

"I do try, I really do."

"I know you do," he said more gently. "And I know David's not easy. But it's not David I'm thinking about, so much as *him*. If *he* ever got to know we were connected I'd be a hell of a lot of use to you, wouldn't I? He'd find a way to get me out of the road first, and then——"

"Don't, please!"

His voice softened: "Look, my dear, stop worrying. It'll be all right, I promise. I got you out of the mess before, didn't I? I got you away from England, didn't I? and the boy too?"

She murmured something I couldn't catch, and he went on: "And it'll be all right again, I swear it. I know it's hell just sitting around wondering what's going to happen, but I'm in charge and you trust me, don't you? Don't you?"

"Yes. Yes, of course."

"Here, have another cigarette." I heard him light it for her, and there was a pause.

"Those damned English police," she said bitterly. "If they'd known their job this would never have had to happen. He ought to be dead and done with." The way she repeated it made me shiver. "Dead and done with," she said.

"Well, he's not," said the man briskly, sounding as if he were dragging back the conversation, with an effort, on to a less dramatic and more practical level. "He's here, in France. And there's nothing to be scared of. He can't do a thing to you, after all. All you've got to do is keep your nerve and hang on to David. We ought to go back, I think. You go first—come down to the corner with me till we see if there's anyone about." He must have turned to go, for his voice grew suddenly fainter.

She stopped him for a moment. Her tone was calmer, and the note of fear was gone, but I could hear the tautness of her nerves through it, for all that.

"I meant to ask you—that girl, Selborne I think her name is—she offered to take David out in her car to-morrow. I suppose it's all right?"

There was another pause. I think he took her arm, because I heard them begin to move off together, but I heard his reply, faintly, before they went out of earshot.

"Quite all right, I imagine. In fact, it might be a good idea. . . ."

.   .   .   .

The palms of my hands, I found, had been pressed so hard against the stone of the parapet that they were sore. I stood perfectly still for some time after they had gone, slowly rubbing my hands together, and thinking.

It was not a particularly pleasant thought, that somewhere near at hand, possibly even in Avignon at this moment, was a man who was probably a murderer; a man vindictive enough, if I had understood aright what I had heard, to pursue the wife who had divorced him after the trial, and dangerous enough to frighten her as Loraine Bristol was being frightened. She was not, I thought, a woman who would frighten easily.

Why was he apparently following her? Did he want her back, was he hoping for reconciliation . . . no, that wouldn't do, she wouldn't be so afraid if that were all. Then was he angry at her action in divorcing him at such a time, was it revenge he was after? No, that was absurd; people just didn't behave that way at all, not rational people . . . that must be it, I thought, and went cold . . . he was *not* rational. Mrs. Palmer had said that he was mad, and no sane man, surely, would have struck down his own son. . . .

David.

It wasn't Loraine he was pursuing at all, it was David.

I pressed my now tingling hands to my cheeks, and thought of David and the dog Rommel, building dams under the Pont St. Bénézet, and as I thought, some of the loneliness of the child's situation dawned on me, and made me feel chilled. I knew a lot about loneliness. And I knew that, come murderers, come hell, come high water, I should have to do something about it.

I slowly descended the zigzag walk to the level of the Palace square, on the alert in case I should run into Mrs. Bristol, who might be waiting about somewhere to give her companion a start.

Her companion? I had not recognized the lowered voice, the rapid French. But that it was someone at the hotel I felt sure.

Then, in the narrow dark little street that skirts the foot of the rock where the palace is built, I saw someone standing, a man. He did not see me, but stood gazing in the direction of the main square, and, as I paused in the darkness under the palace steps, I saw him slip out of the shadows, and saunter down the street and into the light.

I recognized him all right.

It was Marsden.

CHAPTER IV

Old moniments . . .
(SPENSER)

TOWARDS MID-MORNING the next day I eased the Riley down the narrow main street of Avignon, and out on to the perimeter road. Louise sat beside me, and in the back were David and Rommel, wrangling as usual over the necessity of chasing every cat we passed. We skirted Avignon, following my route of the previous day, but before we reached the old bridge of St. Bénézet, I turned the car over the narrow suspension bridge which crosses the Rhône. We crept across swaying, resounding metal surface, then swung through Villeneuve-lès-Avignon and headed south for Nîmes.

The heart of Roman France . . . I thought of the legions, tramping behind their eagles through the pitiless heat and dust, across this barren and hostile country. The road was a white and powdery ribbon that twisted between slopes of rock and shrub. Whin I recognized, and juniper, but most of the shrubs were unfamiliar—dark green harsh foliage that sucked a precarious life from the cracks among the screes and faces of white rock. Here and there houses crouched under the heat, clinging to the edge of the road as if to a life-line; occasionally a grove of olives hung on the slopes like a silver-green cloud, or a barrier of cypress reared its bravery in the path of the mistral, but for the most part the hot and desert slopes rose, waterless and unclothed by any softer green than that of gorse and scrub.

"Mustn't they have felt hot in their helmets?" said David, breaking into my thoughts as if he had known exactly what I was thinking. "Though I suppose Italy's just as hot."

"And they fought all summer," I said. "In winter they retired——"

"To winter quarters—I remember that," said David, grinning. "In my Latin Grammar, if they weren't going to the city to buy bread, they were always retiring to winter quarters."

"I believe they went to the coast. There's a nice little place east of Marseilles where Caesar made a sort of spa for his veterans."

"Aren't the Michelin guides wonderful?" murmured Louise. "And incidentally, Charity—I hate to interfere, but you *have* seen that bus, haven't you?"

"I could hardly avoid it," I said drily. "It's in the middle of the road."

"Oh, I just thought—what's the French for 'breakdown'?"

"*Dépannage*. Or in this case, just plain *accident*. Haven't you got used to the French way of driving yet? You should have."

We were rapidly overtaking a bus which was indeed thundering along in the very centre of the narrow road. But I knew my stuff by now, after the hundreds of heartbreaking miles before I had discovered that the "courtesy of the road" means very different things in France and England. I swung to the left, bore down on the bus with every appearance of intending to ram it, and put the heel of my hand down hard on the horn. The bus, responding with an ear-splitting klaxon, immediately swerved to the left, too, straight into our path. I didn't even brake, but put my hand on the horn and kept it there. The bus, with an almost visible shrug, moved over about a foot to the right, and we tore by.

Louise let out a long breath. "I'll never get used to that!"

"If he'd seen the GB plates we'd never have done it. The British are despicably easy to bully on the roads."

"Did you see who was on the bus?" said David.

"No, I was busy. Who was it?"

"That man from the hotel. I think his name's Marsden. He sits at the table by the big palm."

"Oh. Yes, I've noticed him."

I eased my foot off the accelerator, and glanced at the bus in the driving-mirror. It might conceivably turn off at Pont du Gard for Tarascon, but I had the idea that the Avignon-Tarascon buses went another way. In which case, this must be the bus for Nîmes, and Marsden was on it. And after what I had heard last night up at the Rocher des Doms, I was not quite sure what I thought about the possibility of Marsden's following us to Nîmes.

I slowed down a little more. With a triumphant screech of its klaxon, the bus overtook the Riley, and demanded the road.

I glanced in the mirror as it loomed up behind the car. Yes, unmistakable, even in mirror-image: NIMES.

I put my foot down again, and we drew away. I was trying to think, but I had too little to go on. It was like groping for a window through curtains of spiders' webs, only to find that it was dark outside the window, and that when the webs were all torn down, the window would be still invisible.

I thrust the problem aside, and passed a small Citroën with concentrated care.

> .   .   .   .

At Pont du Gard we drew in under the shade of the trees, opposite the hotel. Louise began to gather her things together.

"David," I said. "Will you do something for me?"

"Of course. What?"

"Ask up at the hotel what time the bus gets here. How long it stays. What time it gets to Nîmes. Will your French stand up to that, do you think?"

David gave me a look, and scrambled out of the car with Rommel.

"Of course," he said again; then, with a sudden burst of honesty—"It's not so much *asking,* because you can practise on the way up, but it's understanding what they tell you—'specially when it's numbers. But I'll try." He gave me his swift engaging grin, and ran off through the gravel terrace of the hotel.

"Are you sure you don't want to come on to Nîmes, Louise?"

"Quite, thanks. I'll go down by the river and paint the bridge—oh, all right, aqueduct—I'll have lunch here first. What time are you coming back?"

"I'm not sure. When d'you want to be picked up?"

Louise looked through the trees towards the river, where could be seen a glowing glimpse of golden stone.

"I don't know, honestly. I'll tell you what, Charity—we won't tie ourselves down. You go on to Nîmes and look at your remains in your own time. If I'm sitting at one of those tables when you come back, pick me up. If not, I'll have gone back on the bus, so don't bother. You won't want to come back much before dinner-time, anyway, and I'll have finished painting long before that."

David came panting across the road to the door of the car.

"*Midi-vingt!*" he announced with triumph. "The bus gets here *midi-vingt*. It waits half an hour, and it gets to Nîmes at half-past one. Is that what you wanted to know?"

"That's fine," I said, glancing at my watch. "It's barely twelve now, and the bus doesn't get here till twenty past. We'll have time to look at the bridge—sorry, Louise, aqueduct—after all."

I took the ignition key out and dropped it into my bag.

"What *do* you mean?" asked Louise. She was looking at me curiously. "I thought that's one of the things you came for? What's the bus got to do with it?"

I felt the colour creep into my face. I had been thinking aloud, without realizing how queer it must have sounded.

"Nothing," I said, rather lamely. "I was thinking about lunch. We'll have lunch in Nîmes, so we won't stay here too long."

I need not have been afraid that Louise would pursue the subject. She was already rummaging for her pencils, and hardly listened to my reply. But as I turned from the car, I saw David looking at me. A long, unreadable look . . . and again I sensed that all those impalpable defences were up. Then Rommel gave an impatient tug to his string, and we all went down towards the bank of the river, under tall trees harsh with the shrilling of the cicadas.

CHAPTER V

O bloody Richard!
(SHAKESPEARE)

WHENEVER I look back now on the strange and terrifying events of that holiday in Southern France, I am conscious of two things which seem to dominate the picture. One is the continuous dry and nerve-rasping noise of the cicadas, invisible in the parched trees, the other is the Roman aqueduct over the Gardon as I first saw it that brilliant day. I suppose the ten or twelve minutes that David and Rommel and I spent gazing at those golden arches spanning the deep green Gardon were like the last brief lull before the thunder.

We stood near the edge of the narrow river, on the water-smooth white rock, and watched Louise settle herself in the shade of some willows, where the aqueduct soared above us, its steep angle cutting the sky. On the under-sides of the arches moved the slow, water-illumined shadows, till the sun-steeped stone glowed like living gold. Except for the lazy sliding silver of reflected light under the striding spans, nothing stirred. Not a leaf quivered; there was no cloud to betray the wind. You would have sworn that the gleaming river never moved. . . .

The sound of an engine on the road above recalled me abruptly. We said good-bye to Louise, who hardly heard us, and climbed the dusty track again to the car.

Not until we had swung out on to the road to Nîmes did either of us speak.

Then David gave a queer little sigh, and said:

"I'm glad I did come, after all." Then he flung a quick glance at me, and flushed. "I mean—I didn't mean——"

"It doesn't matter. I'm glad you're glad you came."

He glanced at me again, and I could sense, rather than see, a long and curious scrutiny.

"Mrs. Selborne——"

"Yes?"

He hesitated. I could feel his body beside me, tense as a runner's. I kept my eyes on the road and waited. Then he gave another odd, sharp little sigh, and bent his cheek to Rommel's shoulder.

"Oh, nothing. How far is it to Nîmes?"

And for the rest of the way we talked about the Romans. I was not to be allowed to help, after all. And I knew better than to force confidence from a boy of his age—a boy, moreover, who had so much the air of knowing exactly what he was up against, and what he was going to do about it. But stealing a look down at the childish curve of the thin cheek laid against the dog's fur, I wasn't so sure that he could deal with whatever queer situation he was in. And again, I knew that I wanted most desperately to help. It was irrational, and I can't explain it, even to-day. It was just the way David made me feel. I told myself savagely that I was a fool, I said unpleasant things under my breath about a frustrated mother-complex, and I kept my eyes on the road, my voice casual, and I talked about the Romans.

And so we drove into Nîmes, parked the car in a side-street just off the Cathedral Square, and had lunch in a restaurant nearby, well out of sight of the Square and the place where the buses stop.

.   .   .   .

"The Arena first!" said David. "I want to see where they keep the bulls!"

"Bloodthirsty little beast, aren't you? But there's no bull-fight to-day, you know. Sunday nights only. The better the day, the better the deed."

"Look, there's a poster—a Corrida, and this Sunday, too!" He looked at me wistfully. I laughed.

"No, David. I won't. And you wouldn't like it either, really. You're English—you'd be on the side of the bull. And think of the horses."

"I suppose so. Golly, look! Is that it?"

We climbed the sloping street towards the enormous curve of the Arena, and made our way round half its circumference until we found the way in through its massive and terrible arches. I bought tickets, and we went into the barred shadows of the lower corridor. There were a few other tourists there, staring, chattering, fiddling with cameras. We followed a little group of English people up the main steps, out into the sunlight of the Arena until we emerged in what must have been the ringside seats, looking down into the great oval where the beasts and the Christians used to meet in blood and terror under the pitiless sun. I went forward to the edge and looked down at the sheer sides of the Arena, just too high for a man to leap, even if he were in terror of his life. David came to my side. He, at any rate, was not haunted by the things that had been done here. His face was excited and a little flushed and his eyes shining.

"Golly, Mrs. Selborne, what a place! I saw a door down there labelled TORIL. D'you suppose that's the bull? Do they use Spanish names here? Where does the bull come out to fight?"

I pointed to the big double doors at the end of the oval, where, in white letters, the word TORIL stood again.

"*Golly!*" said David again. He leaned over the parapet and gazed down with concentration. "Do you suppose we could see bloodstains?"

I moved back into the shadow of the stairway. The heat reflected from the stones was almost unbearable. I heard, behind and below me, the monotonous voice of the concierge doling out tickets to a new batch of tourists. Two or three people came up the steps beside me, and another group, I noticed, went through a doorway near the foot of the steps, that apparently led out into the arena itself.

I leaned back against the cool stone in the shadows, and watched David idly as he sauntered along the ringside tier, periodically stopping to lean over—looking for bloodstains, I supposed. Well, at least that disposed of an idea that the boy was a neurotic—a healthy desire for bloodstains was, I knew, part of the normal boy's equipment.

I closed my eyes. The concierge's voice rose and fell. There was a murmur of talk in French, in German, in American. Somewhere near me a camera clicked. Some more tourists came up the steps beside me, talking vigorously in German. For once we seemed to be the only English people there. But no sooner had the idle thought crossed my mind than I was proved wrong, for down below, on the arena floor itself, I heard some people talking English. And suddenly, a man's voice, sharp, distinct, edged with bad temper:

"This is *not* the wrong blasted ticket. It was issued at the Maison Carrée."

Then someone passing on the steps jostled me, and my bag slipped from my lax fingers. Startled, I opened my eyes, and made a grab for it. The culprit—it was a pleasant-looking woman of about forty—stooped for the bag and handed it to me with a soft-voiced apology in a charming American drawl.

I stopped her. "No, please," I said quickly. "It was my own fault. I was half asleep."

"It's this terrible heat," she said. "You do better in the shade. Come along, Junior." As they turned to go, I became aware of David at my elbow. He spoke breathlessly:

"Mrs. Selborne!"

"What—why, what on earth's the matter, David?"

He had hold of my sleeve. His face was flour-white, and in the shadow his eyes looked enormous.

"Don't you feel well?"

"No—I—that is——" The hand on my arm was shaking. He began to pull me down the steps. "May we go now? I don't want to stay here—do you mind?"

"Of course not. We'll go straight away. I was only waiting for you."

He hardly waited for me to finish; he went down the steps as if his feet were winged, and out through the gate into the hot street, with Rommel close at his heels.

I followed, to find him heading back the way we had come.

"Why, David, don't you want to see the other things? This is the way back to the car."

He paused a moment as we rounded the street corner, and put out a tentative hand again.

"I—I don't feel too good, Mrs. Selborne. I suppose it's the heat. D'you mind if I don't see the other things with you? I—I can wait for you somewhere."

I took him by the arm.

"I don't mind at all. Of course not. I'm sorry you're not feeling well, though. Shall we go back to the car?"

We retraced our steps to the square, then he stopped and faced me again. He looked better now; he was still very pale, but he had stopped shaking, and even smiled at me.

"I'll be fine now, Mrs. Selborne. I'll sit in the Cathedral till you come back. It's lovely and cool in there. Please don't worry about me."

"What about a drink? An iced mint? Here's a café."

But he shook his head.

"I'll just go and sit in the Cathedral."

"What about the dog?"

"Oh——" he glanced uncertainly at the Cathedral door. "Oh. I expect it'll be all right. I'll sit near the back, and it's not the time for service. He could stay in the porch anyway. . . ."

In the end he had his way. I watched him into the cool shadow of the west doorway, then I turned away to look for the temple and the gardens.

At least nobody appeared to have forbidden Rommel's entry, and the church was the best place David could choose in this heat. I realized that, if he thought his indisposition had spoiled my day, he would be very embarrassed, so I decided to continue my sight-seeing tour of Nîmes, but to complete it as quickly as I could.

I saw the lovely pillared Maison Carrée, then I made my way along the stinking street beside the canal to the beautiful formal gardens which are the pride of Nîmes. The heat was terrific, and by the time I reached the gardens—so beautifully laid out around their stagnant and pestilential pools—even my enthusiasm for Roman remains had begun to waver.

I stood for a moment gazing up at the ranks of pine trees on the steep slope which leads up to the Roman Tower. It was very steep; the cicadas were fiddling in the branches like mad; the heat came out of the ground in waves.

"No," I said firmly.

I turned my back on the tower, and made like a homing bee for the little ruined Temple of Diana—which has a café just beside it, where one can drink long iced drinks under the lime trees.

After two very long, very cold drinks, I felt considerably better. I still could not face the Tour Magne, but out of self-respect, as a tourist, I must use up the part of my tourist's ticket dedicated to the Temple of Diana. I left my chair and went through the crumbled arches into the tiny square of the temple.

It was like being miles from anywhere. Behind me, back through the crumbled archway, was the hot white world with its people and its voices; here, within, was a little square of quiet and green coolness. Trees dipped over the high broken walls, shadows lay like arras in the pillared corners, fronds of ferns lent softness to every niche and crevice. And silence. Such silence. Silence with a positive quality, that is more than just an absence of sound. Silence like music.

I sat down on a fallen piece of carved stone, leaned back against a pillar, and closed my eyes. I tried not to think of Johnny . . . it didn't do any good to think of Johnny . . . I must just think of nothing except how quiet it was, and how much I liked being alone. . . .

"Aren't you well?"

I opened my eyes with a start.

A man had come into the temple, so quietly that I had not heard him approach. He was standing over me now, frowning at me.

"What's the matter? The heat?" He spoke with a sort of reluctant consideration, as if he felt constrained to offer help, but hoped to God I wasn't going to need it.

I knew there were tears on my eyelashes, and felt a fool.

"I'm all right, thanks," I said crisply. "I was only resting, and enjoying being alone."

He raised his eyebrows at that, and the corner of his mouth twitched sourly.

"I'm sorry."

I got up, feeling still more of a fool.

"I'm sorry too. I didn't mean that—I didn't mean to be rude. I—it was actually the literal truth. I wouldn't have said it, but you caught me a little off balance."

He did not answer, but stood looking at me; I felt myself flushing like a schoolgirl and, for some idiotic reason, the tears began to sting again behind my eyes.

"I'm not usually rude to perfect strangers," I said. "Especially when they have been kind enough to—to ask after my health. Please forgive me."

He didn't smile, but said, kindly enough:

"It was my fault for catching you—off balance. Hadn't you better have a cigarette to put you back on again before you go out?"

He handed me his case, and added, as I hesitated: "If you don't accept cigarettes from perfect strangers either, we had better remedy that. My name's Coleridge. Richard Coleridge."

I took a cigarette. "And mine's Charity Selborne. Though it ought to be Wordsworth, I feel."

He lit a match for me, and his look over it was sardonic.

"Don't tell me you feel a bond between us already?"

"No . . . though as a matter of fact I did wonder for a moment if we'd met before. There's something familiar——"

He interrupted, his voice rough again: "We haven't. I don't know any Selborne outside of Gilbert White."

I lifted my head, startled.

"Gilbert White?"

"Yes. You know the book——"

"Of course. It was just that somebody else the other day connected me with it too, and not so very many people read it now. And I was surprised at David, because he's only a boy."

I suppose I should have been more careful; I suppose I should have heard the way his voice altered then. But I was still embarrassed, wanting to get away, chattering aimlessly about nothing.

He said, very quietly: "David?"

"Yes. David Shelley. That's who I was thinking of when I said I should have been called Wordsworth. All the Romantic poets seem to be in——"

"Where did you meet this David Shelley?"

I heard it then. I stopped with my cigarette half-way to my lips and looked at him. His hand was quite steady as he flicked the ash from his cigarette, and his face showed no expression. But there was a look behind his eyes that made my heart jolt once, sickeningly.

He said again, softly, almost indifferently: *"Where did you meet this David Shelley?"*

And looked at me with David's eyes.

Shelley—Coleridge—Byron. I knew now. I was alone in that quiet little temple with Richard Byron, who had been acquitted of murder on the grounds of insufficient evidence, and who was looking at me now as if he would like to choke me.

He threw away his cigarette and took a step towards me.

CHAPTER VI

Escape me?
(BROWNING)

"Excuse me, monsieur."

Richard Byron stopped and swung around. The concierge stood just inside the doorway of the temple, looking at him with a sort of mournful reproach.

"Your ticket, monsieur. You nevaire show it." His limp moustache drooped with rebuke. His eyes were pale watery brown, and slightly bloodshot. I thought I had never seen anybody I liked better. I ground out my cigarette with shaking fingers, and started—oh, so casually!—for the door. But the concierge must have thought that Richard Byron and I were together, for he stood his ground.

As I fished hurriedly in my bag for my ticket, Byron handed over his paper slip with an abrupt gesture of impatience. The concierge took it, eyed it with the same spaniel-like reproach, and shook his head.

"It is torn, monsieur. It is defaced. It is perhaps not the right ticket. . . ."

Richard Byron spoke harshly: "I cannot help its being torn. It was torn when I got it."

"Where did monsieur get it?"

"At the Maison Carrée."

Something else jolted in my mind. The voice in the Arena, protesting about the same ticket in almost the same words; and David, who had been leaning over the parapet gazing into the Arena, coming flying down the steps to me, and dragging me away. David, white and shaking, going to hide in the Cathedral.

David had seen his father all right, and was even now hiding in the Cathedral like a rabbit in its burrow. At the thought of David, I was suddenly not afraid of Richard Byron any more. I held out my ticket again to the concierge, who took it, looked mournfully at it, and clipped it. Then I was out in the sunlight again walking past the café tables, back towards the canal. I was trying desperately to think of some way to get back to David and the car without Byron's seeing me. But the lovely gardens stretched ahead of me, open as a chessboard, and then there were the long, straight streets . . . I began to hurry; if only the concierge would keep him . . . but he must have squared the old man somehow, for I had hardly gone fifty yards towards the canal when I heard his step behind me, and he said:

"Just a minute. Please."

I turned to face him.

"Look," I said, pleasantly, casually, "it's been very pleasant meeting you, and thank you for the cigarette. But I must go now. Good-bye."

I turned to go, but he was at my elbow again.

"I just wanted to ask you——"

I tried to freeze him—to act as if I thought this was just the usual pick-up, and to get away before he could ask any more questions.

"Please allow me to go," I said icily. "I prefer to go alone, as I said to you before."

"I want to talk to you."

"I'm afraid I——"

"You said you knew a boy called David Shelley." He was scowling down at me, and his voice had an edge that I by no means liked. Against this direct attack I felt helpless, and in spite of myself, panic started to creep over me again. I wanted time to think—to think what to do, what to say. "Where did you see him?"

"Why do you want to know?" I must have sounded feeble, but I could only stall weakly for time.

"I know him," he said shortly. "If he's hereabouts, I'd like to look him up. He's—he's the son of an old friend. He'd want to see me."

Like hell he would, I thought, hiding away like a panic-stricken rabbit in the Cathedral, poor little kid.

I said: "I'm sorry, I don't really know him."

I could see people approaching up the long flight of steps from the gardens below, and I felt better. He could hardly detain me, make a scene, when there were people there. When they reached us I would break away from him, move off with them, lose myself among the other tourists. . . .

I looked candidly into Richard Byron's angry grey eyes: "I only met him casually on a sight-seeing trip—the way I met you. I couldn't tell you where he's staying."

"When was this?"

"Two days ago."

"Where?" The question was quiet, but somehow I could sense behind it some intolerable strain. I was reminded sharply again of David.

"In Tarascon," I said, at random, some memory of the morning's encounter with the bus no doubt still in my mind. The people were nearly up the steps now, were pausing on a landing to look back at the view. . . .

"Whereabouts in Tarascon? Did he say if he was staying there?"

"No. I told you I didn't know. I only met him for a short time when we were looking at——" Panic flooded me for a moment. What *was* Tarascon? What did one look at in Tarascon? I plunged on a certainty, which under the circumstances had an ironic ring of truth—"At the Cathedral."

I heard him take in his breath in a long hiss and looking up I saw his eyes narrowing on me in a look that there was no mistaking. It was not imagination this time to see violent intentions there. If ever a man looked murder at anyone, Richard Byron looked it at me on that bright afternoon between the flaming beds of flowers in the gardens of Nîmes.

Then the little group of tourists was round us, and I turned to go with them. Anywhere, so long as I was among people, safe in a crowd, safe from the danger of betraying David to this hard-eyed man who stood in the sunlight looking like murder.

"Why, hello," said a soft American voice. "Didn't I see you before—down at the bull-ring? It certainly is a quaint little place, isn't it? Where's your little boy?"

It was the woman who had picked up my bag. She smiled charmingly at me, but my mouth felt stiff. I just looked at her.

"Mom," came a plaintive voice, "Hi, Mom! Will you fix this film for me?"

She smiled at me again, and hurried towards Junior, who was wrestling with his Kodak at a café table. I started to follow, but a hand closed round my wrist, and gripped it hard.

"Just a minute," said Richard Byron again.

He pulled me round to face him. I turned as if I were a wax doll—I had no more resistance. His grip was hurting my wrist, and he pulled me close to him. The group of tourists, self-absorbed and chattering, moved by, paying no attention. He drew me behind a group of statuary.

"Let me go!"

"So you were in the Arena to-day with a boy?"

"Let go my wrist or I'll call the police!"

He laughed, an ugly little laugh. "Call away."

I bit my lip, and stood dumb. The police—the questions—my papers, my car—and I still had to get quietly out of Nîmes with David. Richard Byron laughed again as he looked down at me.

"Yes, you'd be likely to call the police, wouldn't you?" His grip tightened, and I must have made a sound, because his mouth twisted with satisfaction before he slackened his hold. "Now, where's this boy you were with?"

I couldn't think. I said, stupidly: "She's mistaken. He wasn't with me. I was just talking to him. It wasn't David."

He sneered at me.

"Still lying? So you were just talking to him, were you? The way you talked to David Shelley in the Cathedral at Tarascon?"

I nodded.

"Would it surprise you to be told," said David's father, "that Tarascon is a small and dirty village whose main claim to fame is a castle on the Rhône? And that, though I suppose there must be one, I have never even seen a church there?"

I said nothing. I might have known. Johnny always said I was a rotten liar.

"And now, damn you," said Richard Byron, "take me to David."

And he pulled my arm through his own, and led me towards the steps.

      ·   ·   ·   ·   ·   ·   ·   ·   ·

He did not speak as we went down the long shallow flight of stone steps to the lower gardens, and I was grateful for the chance to think. Why he was acting like this I could not imagine, and I did not intend to waste time thinking about it yet. I must think of nothing but how to shake him off, and get out of Nîmes and back to Avignon without his following me or seeing David.

One thing was certain, I thought, remembering the boy's panic-stricken flight from the Arena on hearing his father's voice, David was mortally afraid of meeting his father. So all that mattered for the moment was that David should get away. If only he had told me then, we could have left

Nîmes straight away. And after meeting Richard Byron, I knew that, sooner than let him get his hands on David, I'd murder him myself.

I stole a glance at his profile, with its expression of brooding bitterness, and the unpleasant set to the mouth. Then I remembered, with a queer cold little twist of the stomach, what Mrs. Palmer had said.

"He must have been mad . . . they ought to have locked him up . . . *he must be mad!*"

Panic swept over me again, and at the same time a queer sense of unreality that I believe does come to people when they are in fantastic or terrifying situations. This could not be happening to me, Charity Selborne; I was not walking along the canal-side in Nîmes, Provence, with my arm gripped in that of a man who might be a murderer. A man who had hurt me and cursed me, and looked as if he would like to kill me. These things didn't happen . . . my mind spiralled stupidly; I wonder if Johnny thought it couldn't be happening to him, when he came down over France with his wings in flames . . . ?

"Well?" said Richard Byron.

He had paused at the corner leading to the Arena, and looked down at me.

I said nothing, and his brows came down sharply into a scowl.

"Well?" he repeated with the sneer in his voice. "You beautiful little bitch, what about it?"

Then suddenly, gloriously, I was angry. Someone once described it as a "chemically useful reaction"; I believe it is. At any rate, my mind cleared at that moment and I forgot to be afraid of him, madman or no. And I knew what to do.

I looked up the street that leads to the Arena, and saw, parked at the extreme end of it, a big grey car, and I remembered Loraine's panicky whisper . . . "A big grey car with a GB plate . . ." I looked the other way towards the square; there was a bus standing there, and I could see its destination: MONTPELLIER.

Then I put a hand to my eyes, and my lip quivered.

"All right," I said. "I was lying to you, but you frightened me, and I wanted to get away. I *was* with David Shelley in the Arena."

His arm moved sharply under mine.

"That's better. Where is he now?"

"I don't know."

"Now look here, my girl——"

I shook my head impatiently: "Can't you see I'm telling the truth now? He didn't want to go up to the Tour Magne with me. He went off on his own."

"Where are you meeting him again?"

I hesitated, and I could feel him tensing.

"In the square," I said reluctantly. Oh, David, I prayed, if it doesn't work, forgive me!

"When?"

"In time for the bus. You're making me late."

He whirled round, his eyes on the square. There was no sign of David.

"The Montpellier bus," I said sulkily.

His eyes showed his satisfaction.

"That's the Montpellier bus standing there now," he said. "When does it go?"

I peered towards it, screwing up my eyes. "Is it? Yes, it is." I saw the drivers standing about in the sun, as if they had all the time in the world, and once again I took a chance. "It goes in about ten minutes." Then I looked up at him, and my eyes really did swim with tears. "And now, please may I go? I—I'm sorry if I annoyed you, but you scared me so."

He hesitated, and I tried not to hold my breath. Then he dropped my arm abruptly, and said: "Very well. I'm sorry I scared you, but I thought —well, you shouldn't have told me those lies. I'm a little anxious about David, you see, and I thought you were stalling me off. I'll see him at the bus."

He started quickly up the street towards the parked car. I walked as casually as I could to the corner, then, once out of sight, I broke and ran for the Cathedral as if hounds were out and I was the hare.

Luckily there was no one about in the porch to see me tear into the building as if I were bent on sacrilege. If David weren't there—I couldn't think beyond that possibility. But he was, curled up in a big pew in a side aisle with Rommel asleep at his feet. He straightened up with a jerk when he saw me.

"David," I said breathlessly. "Don't ask questions. He's looking for you. Come to the car—quick!"

He threw me one scared and wondering look, and came. As we reached the porch I hesitated for a moment and scanned the square, but could not see the big grey car. We turned right and tore across the open space, and as we ran I saw out of the tail of my eye the bus for Montpellier slide out of the rank and turn on to the Montpellier road.

Then we had found our side street and the car, and were threading a maze of narrow streets away from the square.

"Our luck's in . . ." I breathed. "The Montpellier bus . . . it left early . . . he'll follow it until he finds out, and by that time——"

Two minutes later the Riley slipped out of Nîmes and took the Avignon road.

CHAPTER VII

Never——
(BROWNING)

WE WERE some way out of Nîmes before either of us spoke. Then I said carefully: "You saw your father at the Arena, didn't you, David?"

"Yes." His voice was low and expressionless, and I didn't look at him; my eyes hardly ever left the driving mirror, where I was watching for a big grey car with a GB plate. "I heard him speak first, then I looked over and saw him. I didn't think he'd seen me."

"He hadn't. I gave you away by mistake. I met him up at the Temple of Diana. Up in the gardens."

"What happened?"

"Oh, he tried to make me tell him where you were. I told a few lies and got caught out in them—I never did have much luck that way. Then I managed to make him think we were getting the Montpellier bus."

"I suppose he'll follow it?"

"Yes, I'm hoping so," I said cheerfully. "And it's in quite the opposite direction from Avignon."

"Yes, I know."

Something in his tone made me glance quickly at him. He was sitting, hugging Rommel between his knees, and staring in front of him with an expression I found hard to read. He was still very white, and there was a look of strain over his cheek-bones, as if the skin were stretched too tight. His eyes looked enormous, and as he turned to answer my look I could see in them misery and a kind of exaltation, through the tears that were slipping soundlessly down his cheeks. My heart twisted uncomfortably, and I forgot to be casual any more. I put out my left hand and touched him on the knee.

"Never mind, David. Is it very bad?"

He did not answer for a bit, and when he did his voice was coming under control again.

"How did you find out about my father?"

"I'm afraid there was some gossip at the hotel. Someone who'd followed the—the case recognized your step-mother. Did you know he might be in Nîmes?"

"No. I thought he might be following us down here, but I didn't know . . . I thought it couldn't do any harm to have one day out. You—you didn't tell him we were staying in Avignon?" The terror was back in his voice as he half turned to me.

"Of course not. It's very important that he shouldn't find you, isn't it?"

He nodded hard over Rommel's head.

"Terribly important. I can't tell you how important. It—it's a matter of life and death." And somehow the hackneyed over-dramatic words, spoken in that child's voice with a quiver in it, were not in the least ludicrous, and were uncommonly convincing.

"David."

"Yes?"

"Would it help you to talk about it?"

"I don't know. What did they tell you at the hotel?"

"Not very much. Just what was in the papers at the time. You see, if you'd told me about your father when you saw him first in Nîmes, this needn't have happened. From what I had heard at the hotel, I gathered that it might be—undesirable—for your father to find you again, and then when I met him in Nîmes and realized that it was his voice that had frightened you in the Arena, I knew that whatever happened you didn't want him to catch you. That's all."

The driving mirror was still blank of anything but a narrow white road snaking away from the wheels.

"That's all there is," said David at length. "Except for one thing. Mrs. Selborne, there's one thing that's terribly important too."

"What's that, David?"

He spoke with a rush: "Don't tell anyone—*anyone,* what's happened to-day!"

"But, David—how can I help it? Your step-mother ought surely——"

I saw his hands move convulsively in the dog's fur, and Rommel whined a protest. "No! Oh, please, Mrs. Selborne, *please* do as I say. It would only worry her terribly, and it couldn't do any good. It won't happen again, because I won't go out, and anyway, we leave in a few days for the coast. So please keep it a secret! I wouldn't ask if it didn't matter."

I was silent for a moment, and the Riley sang up a steep rise in the road. A little way ahead I could see the deep trees and the golden arches of Pont du Gard.

"All right," I said. "I don't know why, but I'll do as you say. Though I still think I ought to tell your step-mother. But I won't."

"Cross your heart?" I don't suppose the childish oath had ever been administered with such an agony of urgency. I smiled at David.

"Cross my heart."

There was a little sigh beside me. "You're awfully nice, aren't you?" said David naïvely.

"Thank you."

"How—how did he look?"

I slowed down and pulled in behind a big brake van with a Vaucluse plate. Still nothing in the mirror. But in front of my eyes rose Richard Byron's face, dark and angry, with scowling brows and hard mouth, and I could feel the bruises on my wrist where he had hurt me.

"He looked well enough," I said carefully, "but of course he was pretty angry, and so he wasn't too pleasant. I don't blame you for being scared, you know; I was scared silly. I wondered——" I broke off abruptly.

"You wondered if he was mad?" said the small voice beside me. "Well, I think he is—I think he must be. Quite mad."

And we drove into Pont du Gard and drew up in front of the hotel.

.   .   .   .

A hasty look through the tables on the terrace satisfied us that Louise must have already gone home, so we set off once more for Avignon. On the second half of the journey we hardly spoke; I watched the driving mirror and drove as fast as I dared, while David sat crouched beside me holding the dog. We swung through Villeneuve-lès-Avignon shortly before six o'clock, and crawled over the suspension bridge. It was queer, after only two days, how much coming back into Avignon felt like coming home; I supposed that after the events of the day the hotel was a refuge, a bolt-hole, where one could hide and lock a door.

I took the car straight in through the Porte de l'Oulle this time, feeling that another ten minutes of exposed driving on the perimeter road was more than I could stand. We threaded the narrow streets as fast as a homing cat, and the Riley ran into the garage and stopped with a little sigh, just as the clock in the Place de l'Horloge struck the hour.

L'heure de l'apéritif. And Louise would be sitting in the quiet court-yard drinking her vermouth, just as she had done yesterday and the day before.

I smiled at David, and got out of the car.

"I think a bath before dinner, don't you? And we had a very pleasant, very ordinary day in Nîmes. You were very impressed with the Arena, I remember."

He managed a smile. "Thank you for taking me," he said.

I watched him through the court into the hotel, then I turned sharply, and went back into the street. I almost ran back to the gate which commanded the suspension bridge, and there, in a crowded little café, sitting well inside, against the wall, I had my drink—a cognac, this time. For half an hour I sat there, watching the narrow bridge that joined the city with Villeneuve-lès-Avignon.

But no big grey car with a GB plate crossed the bridge. So after a while I got up and went back to the hotel.

.   .   .   .

I found Louise, not in the courtyard, but in her room, thumbing through her sketch book. The inevitable vermouth stood on her dressing-table.

"I just came to make sure you were back. I thought you must be when we didn't see you at Pont du Gard."

"I came back after the light began to change," she said. "Did you have a good day, or were you broiled alive?"

I pushed the hair back off my forehead, and sat down on the edge of the bed.

"It was fearfully hot," I admitted. "I didn't finish the course, I'm afraid. I just could *not* climb the last long mile to the Roman tower. But the other things were well worth a visit. How did the sketches go?"

Louise knitted her smooth brow at her sketch book.

"Oh, so-so. The shapes are wonderful, but oh Lord, the light. It can't be got. If you leave out the reflections the arches look like American cheese, and if you put them in they look like fat legs in fish-net nylons. The colours just aren't there in the box."

She sipped her drink, and her eyes considered me. "Are you sure you haven't overdone it a bit, Charity? You look done up. Don't forget you're not quite as tough as you think you are."

"I'm all right."

"Well, be careful, that's all. This isn't the climate to take risks with——"

"I'm all right," I said again. "Or at least I shall be when I've had that dinner I'm beginning to dream up."

I went to my room to change. I hadn't time for a bath, but I took a quick cool sponge down, and put on my pale green dress. I looked in the mirror as I brushed my hair, and saw with a faint surprise that under their faint tan my cheeks were quite without colour. I leaned closer to the mirror. Something about the eyes and the corners of the mouth reminded me vividly of David's face as he had turned to me in the car, some trace seemed to be there of strain—and fear. I frowned at my reflection, and then fished in a drawer for some rouge, annoyed that my encounter with David's father, which I had been trying to put out of my mind until I could think it over without disturbance, should have apparently had such a profound effect on me. After all, what did it amount to? A bruised wrist and some abuse? The natural fear of a sane person confronted with the unreasonable? For certainly no sane man—even discounting David's terrible little confession to me on the homeward drive—would have behaved in that way to a strange woman, even if she were apparently obstructing him in his desire to see his son.

I smoothed the rouge faintly over my cheek-bones, back towards the hair-line, then dusted over with powder. That was better. My coral lipstick next, and the face that looked back at me was an altogether braver affair. Thank God for cosmetics, I thought, as I put them into my bag; one not only looks better, one *feels* better, with one's flag at the top of the mast again. I would not think about Richard Byron again this evening. He had not come to Avignon, of that I was sure. David had only to lie low for a few days more, then he was to go to the coast, and surely France was big enough for a small boy to get lost in? There was nothing more that I could do, and up to date, even if I was left with food for a nightmare, I hadn't done so very badly.

I picked up my bag, and as I did so, I caught sight of the blue marks on my wrist. I turned the arm over, and examined the dark prints where Richard Byron's fingers had bitten into the flesh. Then I remembered my wide silver bracelet, and, hastily searching for it, clasped it round my wrist, over those tell-tale bruises. To my fury, I found that I was shaking again.

"Oh *damn* everything!" I said aloud, with unwonted viciousness, and went to get Louise.

. . . .

The dinner that I had dreamed up proved to be every bit as good as the dream. We began with iced melon, which was followed by the famous *brandade truffée,* a delicious concoction of fish cooked with truffles. We could quite contentedly have stopped there, but the next course— some small bird like a quail, simmered in wine and served on a bed of green grapes—would have tempted an anchorite to break his penance. Then *crêpes Suzette,* and, finally, coffee and armagnac.

We sat over this for a very long time, and then we went up to the Place de l'Horloge and had more coffee and sat again. Louise talked a bit about light, and reflections, and a picture by Brangwyn of the Pont du Gard that she had seen in a Bond Street exhibition, but I was not listening very hard. I was not even thinking, at any rate not usefully. I just sat and drank black coffee and felt very, very tired.

We went back to the hotel at about half-past ten, to find the courtyard empty save for the thin cat at the foot of the tree Yggdrasil. I said good night to Louise and went to my room. The tired feeling still persisted, and it was with slow mechanical movements that I took off the green frock, creamed my face, brushed my hair, and went through all the motions of getting ready for bed. I was even too tired to think, and with the edge of my mind I remember feeling glad about this.

Finally I wrapped my housecoat round me, and went along the corridor to the bathroom, which was at the far end from my room.

I was in the bathroom, and was in the act of closing the door softly behind me, when I heard a quick tread in the corridor, a man's tread. A door opened, and I heard an urgent whisper:

"*Loraine!*"

I froze. It was the voice of the man I had overheard with Loraine Bristol on the Rocher des Doms.

"*Loraine!*"

"*You! What is it? What has happened?*"

"*Loraine, he's here! I saw him. To-day. In Nîmes.*"

There was a sound like a deep-drawn breath of terror. Then the door shut behind him, and I heard the click of a lock.

I shut the bathroom door and leaned against it for a moment, my brain revving up like a tired engine.

Marsden. On the bus to Nîmes. I had forgotten all about Marsden.

I must ask David where Marsden came into the picture. I crept out of the bathroom without a sound, and paused outside Loraine Bristol's door. There was the barest murmur inside, of voices. I tip-toed on, round the angle of the corridor, to David's door, and lifted my hand to scratch at the panel, wondering as I did so if Rommel slept in the room with him, and if he would bark.

Then I stopped, with my hand half-way to the panel, and froze again.

From inside the room came the sound of a child's desolate sobbing.

I stood there for a long moment, then my hand dropped to my side and I went back to my own room.

CHAPTER VIII

—While I am I, and you are you,
So long as the world contains us both . . .
While the one eludes, must the other pursue:
                                        (BROWNING)

ALL THINGS CONSIDERED, I did not sleep too badly. I was wakened at
about nine o'clock the next morning by Louise, who stopped to knock on
my door on her way down to breakfast.

I got up slowly, and dressed. The shadows under my eyes were still
there, and so were the marks on my wrist, but I put on my coffee-cream
linen dress and my silver bracelet, and felt pretty well able to face what
might come. I went down to the courtyard for breakfast.

David was there, looking as if he had not slept too well, but he gave me
a gay little smile of greeting, and Rommel, under the table, wagged his
silly tail. Loraine Bristol looked up from lighting one cigarette from the
half-smoked butt of another. She, too, looked as if she had not slept, and
the lines from nostril to mouth were sharply etched on her lovely face,
giving her suddenly an older, harder look. I felt sorry for her.

She said: "Good morning, Mrs. Selborne. It was so good of you to take
David yesterday. He has been telling me how much he enjoyed the day."

I said, lightly: "That's all right, it was a pleasure. Nîmes is a lovely
place, except for the smells. I hope David will be able to come with me
for another trip some day."

I saw David's swift upward glance, then Mrs. Bristol said: "It's so nice
of you. Perhaps. But we plan to leave Avignon soon, and we will go then
to Nice."

"I hope you enjoy it," I said, and we smiled at one another like two
mechanical dolls, and then I went to our own table and sat down.

Over the coffee and *croissants* I looked round me. Mamma and Papa
from Newcastle were there, and Mamma waved cheerfully when she
caught my eye. Carole, apparently, was not up yet, or perhaps it took her
a long time to complete her fearsome toilette. The young American couple, each-in-other-absorbed, sat with heads close together in their corner.
The Frenchman, Paul Véry, was nowhere to be seen. But Marsden sat at

his table beside the vine-covered trellis, imperturbably eating his *croissants,* and reading *Little Gidding.*

"At breakfast!" said Louise in an awed voice. "A man who can read poetry at breakfast would be capable of anything."

You're probably right at that, I thought, remembering the decisive voice in the dark . . . *I got you out of the mess before, didn't I?* . . . *I'm in charge, and you trust me, don't you?*

"More sight-seeing to-day?" came Louise's voice. I shook myself free of my thoughts, and poured another cup of coffee.

"I'll do what you do," I said.

"Sit in the shade and drink iced grape-juice?"

"Just that."

"Tired?"

"A bit. You were right. The heat did take it out of me yesterday. I'll stay at home to-day and think up something good for to-morrow."

Presently people began to move, the tourists discussing the day's programme. The Germans went off, arguing over a guide book, and soon afterwards the American couple strolled out into the Rue de la République, arm-in-arm. David got up then, and went into the hotel with Rommel, and in a few moments Marsden went in too. Loraine Bristol lit another cigarette and stared in front of her. I made some excuse and got out of my chair. Perhaps now I could get to David's room and ask him about Marsden,—why Loraine Bristol, if she did know Marsden, and if he had helped her and David in the first place, had not told David of the connection. Perhaps David would feel safer if he knew that there was a man on guard between him and Richard Byron.

It was possible, of course, I thought as I climbed the stairs, that David did know, but he had betrayed no such knowledge yesterday when we had seen Marsden on the bus, nor had any sign of recognition passed between Marsden and himself, beyond the casual recognition of fellow-guests in a hotel.

Marsden was in the upper corridor, so, without going near David's door, I went into my own room, and collected the things I should want for the morning, my sun-glasses, a book, my Michelin guide. Then, after a few minutes, I went out again into the corridor, only to find that my plan of having a private word with David would have to wait, for he and Rommel and Marsden were together, making for the stairs.

". . . So I thought I'd go up there this morning," David was saying, "instead of to the river."

"I'm walking up that way myself," said Marsden. "Mind if I come with you?"

"Not at all, sir . . ." The voices faded. I went back into my room, thinking that it certainly did not sound as though David knew of any intimate connection between Marsden and his own affairs. Then I heard them come out into the courtyard, below the balcony, and I moved towards the window.

". . . The tower at the north corner," said Marsden. "Though how he ever got a mule up it I don't know. Have you ever been in?"

"No," said David. I saw him stop beside his step-mother's table. "I'm going up to the Rocher des Doms," he told her. "Mr. Marsden's coming too. You get a marvellous view of the ferry-boat from there; it has to cross with a rope, in case it gets swept away."

Yes, I thought, watching them go together up the Rue de la République, and you also get a marvellous view of the suspension bridge that leads in from Nîmes and Montpellier. And I wondered just how much of his day David would spend up on the battlements, watching for a big grey car with a GB plate.

. . . .

The day dragged by. Louise and I spent the morning in the gardens, according to plan, drinking iced grape-juice and idly watching the circular sprays watering the vivid lawn. Then she got out her sketch book and began to make rapid clever little drawings—of the children, thin and brown, of the old women who sat squarely on the narrow seats, knitting and watching them, of the ragged-trousered half-naked men who raked the gravel, of the frocked priests moving to and from the church across the way. I took out my book and tried to read, but between my eyes and the page swam perpetually two angry grey eyes under their black brows, and a mouth twisting with sudden murderous fury. I blinked it away and began to read with steady concentration, only to find after several minutes that I had read the same page over and over again, and had not taken in a single word of it, and that my brain was mechanically repeating, like a damaged record . . . *you little bitch, you little bitch, you little bitch*. I pushed back my hair as if by the action I could brush my mind clean of memories, but I gave up the attempt to read after a while, and sat, fidgeting with my sun-glasses, and wishing I could draw—do anything to take my mind off the wheel that it was treading, over and over again.

"Louise."

"Mm?"

"Let's go and have lunch."

"Already?"

"It's time. We may as well go back to the hotel, don't you think?"

But though we sat for a long time in the court, over a leisurely lunch and cigarettes, David did not appear nor did Marsden. Paul Véry was in his corner, and smiled at me over his *apéritif*, but apart from him and ourselves, all the other residents, including Loraine Bristol, seemed to be lunching elsewhere. At length I got up.

"I think I'll go and rest," I said, and went up to my room.

. . . .

To my own surprise I slept deeply and dreamlessly for a long time, and woke in the late afternoon, feeling refreshed and in my right mind. As I washed and slipped into the pale green dress I felt singularly light-hearted, as if some heavy cloud had lifted off the landscape, and had left nothing but a shining prospect of sun upon the wet spring grass. I had had an unpleasant experience, which had upset me considerably; very well, now it was over, and the memory of Richard Byron's crazy furious behaviour could be thrust back with all the other nasty things into the woodshed. I sang as I clipped the silver bracelet on over the bruises, and I smiled at my reflection as I brushed my hair.

And as for David—the lifting cloud cast a momentary shadow there; but the fresh wind of common sense blew it away into rags. David's problem was a tragic one, certainly, but a comparatively simple one, after all. There were two adults to look after him, and, if the conversation on the Rocher des Doms meant anything, Loraine Bristol would eventually marry her helper. The only problem was to keep David out of his father's way, and surely that wouldn't be so very difficult to manage? And, whatever I felt about it, I could do nothing for David. It was Mrs. Bristol's problem, and I was a stranger. And I would see the last of them in a few days' time anyway. There was only one sane thing to do, and that was to forget the whole business.

I went lightly along to Louise's room, and found her doing her hair.

"Louise, I've had an idea. I'm feeling as restless as a gipsy, and I'm sick of doing nothing. I'm going to take the car and drive up to Les Baux for a night—or even a couple of nights. D'you want to come?"

"Les Baux? Where's that and what is it?"

"It's a ruined village, a hill village south of Avignon. I believe it's a queer wild sort of place—just ruins and a deserted village and an inn and a wonderful eerie view. It's just what I feel like, anyway, miles from anywhere."

Louise put away her brush and comb and began to do her face.

"Do you want me to come—I mean, do you *not* want to go alone?"

"I don't mind whether I go alone or not. That's not why I was asking. If you'd like the drive, come by all means. If not, I'll be perfectly happy."

She looked at me in the mirror. "Sure?"

"Perfectly. I take it you *don't* want to come?"

"Not particularly. I'd rather laze about here and draw. But if you——"

"Then forget it. It was a sudden idea, and it suits the way I'm feeling, but you needn't let it affect you. I'll go and ring up and see if they've a room at the inn, and I'll drive up there for dinner."

Louise sat down to put on her sandals. "You know," she said, with an upward look at me, "I was wondering last night—well, is anything up?"

"Not a thing," I lied cheerfully. "I was tired, but after that sleep this afternoon I feel wonderful. But I feel a bit stifled in Avignon, and I want to be off up to Les Baux to-night. You're sure you don't want to come?"

Louise shook her head.

"No. You go off and commune with nature and the ghosts in the ruined houses. It sounds terrible. I'll see you when I see you, I suppose."

So I went downstairs and telephoned the inn at Les Baux, where I was lucky in being able to secure a room for one night at least, with the probability of the next, if I should wish it. Feeling something like a released prisoner, I hurried back to my room, pushed a nightdress and a few toilet necessities into my big handbag, went down again and saw Madame, then said good-bye to Louise and went out to get the car.

It was all done so quickly, and I was out of Avignon and heading for Orgon, before I really had time to think what I was doing. But when I did think about it, pushing the car along at a comfortable speed in the evening light, it still seemed a good thing to do. I wanted, above all things, to be out of Avignon, out of that *galère,* even for a short time. And I wanted to be alone. I was glad Louise had elected not to come, though, knowing Louise, I had never really for a moment suspected that she might want to. Somehow, the picture I had formed of Les Baux, the empty little mountain village, where night was so quiet and dawn so beautiful, just represented the sort of thing I very much needed.

About David Byron I steadfastly refused to think, and about Richard, his father, I did not think at all, except for a little twist of wry amusement when I looked at the map and saw that soon I would be turning on to the Tarascon road.

The evening was drawing down, and the light deepened. Away behind me I caught a last glimpse of the towers of Avignon, like torches above the trees. Around me the landscape grew wilder and more beautiful, muted from the white and dusty glare of day to the rose and purple of evening. The sun set, not in one concentrated star of fire, but in a deep diffusion of amber light, till the sharp black spires of the cypresses seemed to be quivering against the glow, and flowing upwards like flames formed of shadows.

It did not seem long before the Riley climbed the last hill, and I berthed it outside the inn not long before seven o'clock.

CHAPTER IX

Oi deus, oi deus, de l'alba! tan tost ve.
(Ah God, ah God, but the dawn comes soon)
(MEDIÆVAL FRENCH LYRIC)

THE DESERTED TOWN of Les Baux, in medieval times a strong and terrible fortress, stands high over the southern plains. The streets of eyeless houses—little more than broken shells—the crumbling lines of the once mighty bastions, the occasional jewel of a carved Renaissance window, clothed with ferns, have an uncanny beauty of their own, while something of the fierce and terrible history of the "wolves of Les Baux," the lords of Orange and Kings of Arles, still seems to inhere in these broken fortifications. The prospect is wild enough, and strange enough, to satisfy anyone who, like myself that evening, felt so pressingly the need for quiet and my own company. With faint amusement I perceived slowly creeping over me the mood of melancholy in which the not-quite-romantics of the eighteenth century in England found such gentle pleasure.

I sat near the window of the little inn's dining-room, watching the evening light on the distant slopes, and enjoying my lonely dinner. I ate slowly, and the light was dying from the land when at length I took my coffee and chartreuse outside on to the little terrace, and prepared to let the past have its way with me.

I got out my book, and read the *chansons de toile* again, the songs of lovely Isabel, Yolande the beautiful, Aiglentine the fair, who had sat at their embroidery, singing, so very long ago, in this same land. Then I shut the book, and sat dreaming, with my eyes on the broken lines and ghost-filled terraces of the town, trying to pave the streets and cut back the vegetation and fill the empty ways with horses and men and the glint of armour and the scarlet of banners.

I sat there till darkness had drawn over the scene, and then I went down to the car and drove it away from the inn door, round the open sweep to face the road again. I left it parked there, two wheels on the verge. Then I went up to my room.

Where was it that I had read that to watch the dawn over the ruined town was one of the sights of the world? Looking out of my window into the darkness, tracing the imperceptibly darker shapes of rock and hill, I thought that whatever the book had said it was probably right. I would go out early and wait for the sun to rise, and see if the ghosts of the Kings of Arles really did ride at cock-crow. So I did not undress, but merely took off frock and shoes, and lay down on one of the beds. I was asleep almost at once.

I must have slept for three or four hours, because when I woke and turned my head to look at the window, I could see, not light, but a faint lifting of the darkness. I put a light on and looked at my watch, only to find that I had forgotten to wind it the night before. I put the light off again, got up, and went to the window to lean out. My room faced south-east, and away to my left I could see what looked like the beginnings of a rift in the night, a soft pencilling of light on the underside of a cloud. The air was chill and clear and silent.

I closed the shutters, put on the light again, and got into my frock and shoes. I rinsed my face and hands in cold water to wake myself up properly, then put on my coat, and went quietly out of my room and down the stairs.

I must have made some slight noise, but nobody seemed to hear, or at any rate to bother about it. I supposed the people at the hotel were used to dawn-watchers in Les Baux. The door of the inn was not locked, so apparently there was nothing tangible, at any rate, to fear from the ghostly princes of Orange. Wishing I had a torch, I let myself out with caution and moved carefully towards the deserted buildings. My feet made no sound upon the grass.

.   .   .   .

How long I sat out there, in a coign of carved stone and rough rock, I do not know. Long enough, I suppose, for my vigil did at length bring in the dawn. I saw the first light, forerunning the sun, gather in a cup of the eastern cloud, gather and grow and brim, till at last it spilled like milk over the golden lip, to smear the dark face of heaven from end to end. From east to north, and back to south again, the clouds slackened, the stars, trembling on the verge of extinction, guttered in the dawn wind, and the gates of day were ready to open at the trumpet . . .

oi deus, oi deus, de l'alba! tan tost ve . . .

Suddenly I was cold. The pleasant melancholy had faded, and in its place began to grow, unbidden, the little germ of loneliness which could,

I knew, mature in these dark and wild surroundings all too soon into the flower of desolation. I began to wish violently for a cigarette.

I got up, stretched, stood for a moment looking at the growing light. Waiting, perhaps, unconsciously, for the trumpet to blow its shrill aubade across the stars.

Something moved behind me.

Moved and spoke.

As I whirled, my heart stampeding, my hands to my throat——

"So I've found you again," said Richard Byron.

.   .   .   .

He was standing barely three yards away from me. In the darkness I could see him only as a looming shape on the slope above me, but I would have known that voice anywhere, hard, incisive, with an edge to it, and an unpleasant undertone of mockery. He stood where he was, above me in the dark, and I knew that I was as securely trapped in my corner of rock as if I had been in a locked room. To the left of me, and at my back, the rock wall and the remains of a towering buttress; to my right, the sheer drop to the southern plain; and before me, Richard Byron.

I stood still, and waited.

He lit a cigarette, and in the hissing flare of the match I saw again the face of my nightmare, the dark hair falling over the frowning brow, the hard eyes narrowed against the flame.

The match lit a brief arc over the cliff. The cigarette glowed red as he drew on it.

"How did you get here?" I asked, and was annoyed because my voice was not my own at all.

He said: "You stopped for petrol at St-Rémy. You went across the road and had a drink in a boulevard café while they put oil in and cleaned up for you."

"Yes, I did. Were—were you in St-Rémy?"

"I was. I was, like you, having a drink while they did something to my car. I went to your garage and waited for you, but when I heard you ask the man for the road up to Les Baux I knew you were safe, so I thought I'd wait. It isn't so public here as it was in St-Rémy, and you and I have something that we want to discuss, haven't we?"

"Have we?"

His voice was unemotional: "You god-damned little bitch, you know we have. Where's David?"

So there we were again, except that the issue, for me, was slightly clearer. I knew that I was not going to tell him where David was, but I also knew what before I had only suspected, that he was crazy, and would stop at nothing to get what he wanted.

"Where's David?"

"Asleep in bed, I hope," I said.

He made an impatient movement, and my throat tightened.

"You know what I mean. Where is he?"

"I'm not going to tell you," I said levelly. If it maddened him, I couldn't help it, but I judged it better to be downright than to prevaricate.

He was silent for a moment, and I saw the cigarette glow again, twice, in rapid succession.

The next question, when it came, took me completely by surprise. He said abruptly: "Is it money you want? If so, how much?"

"I've as much money as I want," I said, when I could speak. "What were you going to offer—thirty pieces of silver?"

I could feel him staring at me through the darkness. He dragged on his cigarette again.

"But I wouldn't refuse a cigarette," I said.

I heard him fumble for it, and again a match rasped and flared. This time his eyes were watchful on me across the flame. He lit the cigarette and, coming a step nearer, handed it to me.

"What's the matter?" I said contemptuously. "Are you afraid I'll push you over if you come any nearer?"

"Listen, my dear," said Richard Byron evenly. "This won't get either of us anywhere. I want to know where David is. You do know, and you refuse to tell me. Very well, then I shall have to make you tell me."

The cigarette wasn't much help after all; I threw it over the cliff. My brief moment of initiative was over, and he was attacking again.

I said, more bravely than I felt: "And how do you propose to do that? Torture? Be your age, Mr. Byron."

He said savagely: "My God, I'd like to try. If I lay hands on you again I'll not answer for myself. I'd like to wring your lovely neck."

"I see. Gestapo stuff." But my voice shook.

"And why not? I've seen it done, and to women. It works, as often as not."

"Don't be a fool," I said sharply. The nightmare terror was seeping into me again, cold, cold. I could see him a little better now, towering over me, silhouetted against the faintly glowing east, like some shadow of fear. "If you so much as moved a finger towards me, I'd scream the place down."

"Don't worry. I'm not going to hurt you. Not yet. But I think we'll get things plain and clear, you and I."

He flung away his cigarette, and at the sharp movement my inside twisted over with a little thrill of fear, and I began to feel sick. Cold and sick. I put a shaking hand backwards on to the firm stone, and the hand slipped a bit. It was clammy.

Richard Byron spoke without emphasis, but his voice beat at me with the wince of hammer on steel.

"I gather that you know who I am. I told you I was a friend of David's. That was not true, as presumably you know. I am David's father, and I have an idea that that gives me a right to know where David is."

I said nothing. I was leaning back against the stone, fighting off the same feeling of unreality and nightmare that I had experienced in the streets of Nîmes. And fighting off, too, waves of sickening blackness that kept washing over me out of the cold night.

"You've no doubt been told," said Richard Byron pleasantly, "that I did a murder once—and got away with it. They say it's even easier the second time. And I assure you, you stupid little fool, that I'd do murder to-day as easily as I'd stub out a cigarette, to get hold of my son."

The gates of the eastern sky were opening behind him; the aubade must have blown, and I had never heard it. . . . Pure and piercing, the first fingers of the dawn stabbed the sky. Then they were blotted out again by another wave of darkness which washed up from the damp ground at my feet. I was falling . . . I clawed at the stones . . . they were slipping sideways from me . . . the whole world was slipping sideways, away from the sun.

From a great way off, a voice spoke in the blackness.

"Nothing could be easier than murder, you know. . . ."

I put out my hands in a futile little gesture, and his shadow towered over me, then stooped like a hawk. . . .

And I fainted.

.   .   .   .

I was buried, and they had put a heavy stone on top of me. But I was not dead, and I was struggling to lift it, only they had tied my hands as well, and I could not move . . . I could not even open my eyes. Then, of itself, the stone lifted off me, and I could move my head and my hands a little, in the silence and the darkness. I must have been crying, or had I died of drowning? . . . my face was wet and cold.

I struggled back to the edge of consciousness, and opened my eyes, to find that the darkness, at any rate, was real, and so were the tears on my face. Tears? I slowly put up a hand, and found that not only my cheeks, but my forehead and hair were damp—someone had put cold water on me. That was it. I had fainted, for some reason, and someone had put cold water on my face to bring me round.

Hazily I turned my head. I was lying on a bed beside a window whose slatted shutters were barring out the faint grey light of early morning. I looked into the room. In the darkness I could see the shape of a chest of drawers . . . another bed. . . . Someone was lying on the other bed, smoking. I saw the cigarette glow and fade, glow and fade.

I murmured: "Johnny?"

The voice that answered me dispelled the dream, and brought reality back with a rush. It said: "So you're round again. Who's Johnny? Is he in this too?"

I didn't answer for a bit. Then I said: "You can't get away with this, you know."

"With what?"

"What are you doing in here? Why won't you leave me alone?"

He said, lazily: "This is as comfortable a way of keeping an eye on you as any. And I've told you why I won't leave you alone. You're my link with David, and I'll keep my hand on you till I get what I want."

I said: "But this is my room. Don't you imagine the folk at the inn will want to know who you are? You can't get away with this sort of thing, even in France. What if I start to scream?"

The cigarette glowed placidly, and I could hear the smile in his voice, as he said: "Scream away."

I bit my lip. Of course I couldn't scream; I could see in my mind's eye the result if I did—the fuss, the explanations, the recriminations, perhaps the police—then names . . . and addresses. No, I couldn't scream.

He laughed in the darkness. "I'm your husband, anyway. I got here late last night, and didn't want to disturb them. After all, I don't imagine you specified a single room, did you? And all the rooms here are double, which was lucky."

"What are you going to do?" I said again.

"Stick to you like a leech, my dear, like a lover." He settled himself comfortably on his bed. I stared into the dark, somehow too exhausted to be afraid; I felt empty and tired. I remembered to be glad that I had not told Madame where I had come from, and that I had registered merely "en passant". He would get no information either from the inn or from the register.

"Won't they think it a bit odd that we each arrive in our own cars?"

"I didn't bring mine up," he said. "I left it a couple of hundred yards down, round the bend out of sight. I wasn't going to let you see it, if by any chance you happened to be about when I arrived. Don't worry about that."

I did not bother to explain how little I was worrying. I turned away towards the window, and turned the pillow over, so that the dry side was against my cheek. This would have to wait till morning. I could do nothing, and common sense told me that if Richard Byron wanted information out of me, at least he would not murder me in my sleep. Neither, I thought, would he risk trying anything approaching violence, now that people were within call, and now that, if I were frightened enough, I would risk police investigation. I was still in coat and shoes, of course, so I slipped the latter off and wrapped the former warmly round me, and curled up with my back to the other bed.

Richard Byron said: "Who's Johnny?"

I said shortly: "I don't want to talk to you. I'm going to sleep."

I heard a faint scrunching sound as he ground out his cigarette in a tray between the beds. He said nothing. The springs of the other bed creaked heavily, and I tensed myself unconsciously. But he was only settling himself down and relaxing.

After a while, to my own vague surprise, I drifted off to sleep.

CHAPTER X

And Charity chased hence by Rancour's hand.
(SHAKESPEARE)

I AWOKE to an empty room, dredged with sunlight through the shutters, and the comforting sounds of breakfast on the terrace below the windows. For a long drowsy moment I wondered why I should be lying so uncomfortably curled up on the top of the quilt, wrapped in my coat. Then I remembered, and sleep fled incontinently as I turned over to look at the other bed. It had not been a nightmare, that strange interview among the dark ruins, my fainting, the implacability of the man who was going to stick to me like a lover—I could see the impression where he had lain on the other bed, the dent left by his head in the pillow, and a little pile of cigarette-butts in the ash-tray between the beds.

I sat up and swung my legs over the side of the bed. I felt a little stiff from sleeping curled up, and as if I had not slept long enough, but otherwise the night's adventures did not seem to have affected me physically to any great extent. But mentally I was in a turmoil. Where was Richard Byron now? What did he propose to do to-day? And how, how, *how* was I going to get away from him?

I crossed to the door, locked it, then took off my coat and frock and washed, afterwards patting cold water into my cheeks till the skin tingled and I felt fresh and invigorated. I brushed my hair hard, then shook out the green dress, thanking heaven and the research chemists for uncrushable materials, and put it on again. The familiar routine of doing my face and hair did a good deal to restore my confidence. Somehow I would get away from him, get back to Avignon, make some excuse to Louise, and we would drive off somewhere else for our holiday, at any rate until Loraine and the boy had left for the coast. Or at worst, if I could not shake my enemy off, I could lead him astray, away from Avignon . . . though I felt a little cold quiver of the familiar fear to think what he might do if I thwarted him again.

At any rate I would get ready for whatever opportunity might come. I put my book, my dark glasses, my toothbrush, all the small things I had brought for the night, into my bulky handbag, glanced round the room to see that nothing was forgotten, then put my coat round my shoulders and unlocked the door and went out into the corridor.

Richard Byron was waiting for me at the foot of the inn's single flight of stairs. He was leaning against the newel-post, smoking the inevitable cigarette, and as I came hesitantly down the stairs he looked up and gave me a sardonic good morning.

"I hope you slept well?" he said, straightening up.

"If we are husband and wife," I said, "you ought to know. And I should like a cigarette, please."

He gave me one, and we went out on to the terrace. One or two people were still breakfasting, but I had slept late, and most of the guests had already gone into the ruined town, or had left in their cars.

He followed me to a table near the edge of the terrace, and held a chair for me.

I sat down in the shade without looking at him or speaking, and watched the smoke from my cigarette curling up in delicate blue fronds towards the hanging vines that clothed the terrace wall. We sat for some minutes in silence, but it was not the comforting silence of companionship; I could feel his eyes on my face, and was intensely conscious of his presence on the other side of the little table, and between us the air positively sizzled with unasked questions and ungiven answers.

So I watched the tip of my cigarette, and then the waiter came with the coffee and *croissants*.

The coffee was smoking hot and delicious, and smelt wonderful in that sunny still air. I put one of the flat oblongs of sugar into my cup, and stirred it slowly, enjoying the smell and the swirl of the creamy brown liquid in the wide-mouthed yellow cup.

"Have a roll," suggested Richard Byron, and handed me the flat basket where the new hot *croissants* reposed on their snow-white paper napkin. There was something in the ordinary familiar little gesture over the breakfast table that made me suddenly still more sharply conscious of the queer and uncomfortable situation that I was in now, deeply in. I took a roll, still without looking at him, but memory stirred queerly . . . Johnny passing me the toast-rack, the marmalade . . . I bit my lip. Johnny had never seemed so far away, so utterly gone. I said it to myself, deliberately: so dead.

I was alone. Any help I got now would only come from myself, and I was well aware that I am not the stuff of which heroines are made. I was merely frightened and bewildered, and deeply resentful of the situation in which I found myself.

Which is why I sat eating my rolls without really tasting them, and staring at the golden distance of the southern plain beyond the rocks, without really making any plans at all. With every mouthful of hot and fragrant coffee, I felt better, but my brain was numb, and I dared not look at Richard Byron, in case he should see how afraid of him I was. Though, I told myself, if he doesn't know by now that you panic every time he comes near you, my girl, he must be mad.

Mad. The coffee suddenly tasted vile, and I put down my cup unsteadily on the saucer. That was the root of the matter, of course—even a heroine might legitimately be afraid of a mad-man, and a mad-man who had cheerfully, not very long before, threatened to murder her. I had to get away. I didn't know how, but I had to get away.

Then my eyes fell on my car, which was standing where I had left it, facing down the hill, about fifty yards from the terrace steps. And I remembered something Richard Byron had said last night . . . something about leaving his car a short way down the road, parked off the track. If I could somehow get to my car without him, get a start, I might get away. The Riley was fast and utterly reliable; I had not seen, in Nîmes, what make of car he drove, but I knew the Riley could be depended upon to give the average touring car a run for its money. And I had filled up last night with petrol and oil. Everything I had brought with me was in my handbag . . . I had only to go.

And if Richard Byron had posed as my husband, then Richard Byron could do the explaining, and pay the bill.

My heart was beginning to thump again, and I dared not look at him. I fumbled in my bag, ostensibly for a handkerchief, but in reality to make sure of my car keys. I took out my book of Provençal poetry, and laid it on the table, while I rummaged beneath my nightdress in the bag. My fingers closed over the keys, and I slipped them into a top compartment where I would be able to reach them easily, then I took out my hand-kerchief and a cigarette, put the book back, and closed the bag.

Richard Byron struck a match and held it for me across the table. I tried not to look at him, but something drew me to raise my eyes across the flame, and I saw that he was watching me with a curious expression on his face.

"What did you come up here for anyway?" he asked.

I tried to speak lightly: "What does anyone come up here for? To see the lair of the wolves of Orange."

"I can't help wondering," he said slowly, "just where you come into all this. And who is Johnny?"

My fingers tightened on my bag. "Do you mind?" I said. "I don't particularly want to talk to you. And I don't feel too good this morning."

I saw his hand make an abrupt movement of impatience, and he bit back something he had been going to say. We were alone on the terrace now, and the waiter had vanished. A couple of sight-seers came out of the inn, paused for a moment in the shade of the terrace roof, then stepped out into the blinding morning sun. The girl was wearing white, and swung a scarlet bag in one hand. The man, in khaki shorts and a loose linen jacket, carried an enormous camera. They were laughing. They strolled past us, below the terrace, and away towards the ruins, and disappeared round a high wall of rock, and as they went, the normal safe and happy world seemed to go with them and suddenly I was, again, alone with Richard Byron, caught in the dark circle of his little personal hell.

For a short while we sat there, in the hot silence, while the sunlight moved a fraction, and laid its slanting glare across the toe of my sandal. Somewhere, a cicada started to rasp, dry and rhythmic.

I dropped my half-smoked cigarette and ground it out gently on the floor. I leaned my forehead on my hand.

"Is there any more coffee?" I said, as if with difficulty.

I felt him glance sharply at me.

"No. It's finished. What's the matter?"

I shook my head a little. "It's nothing. It's only——" My voice trailed away, and I said nothing.

There was another short silence, while I could feel him staring at me. I sensed the puzzlement and suspicion that must be in his glance, but this time I had an advantage I had not had in Nîmes—there must have been no possible doubt about the genuineness of my faint last night, and I must be looking quite definitely the worse for it this morning. I lifted my head and looked at him, and I know my eyes were strained and shadowed, and my lips, under the brave coral paint, were dry.

"I'm all right, thanks," I said, "but would you ask the waiter for some water—or a cognac; yes, a cognac?"

I don't know quite what I was planning to do. I had some general idea of establishing the fact that I was too rocky to make any violent attempt at escape; I think, too, that with hazy memories of thrillers I had read, I toyed with the idea of throwing the cognac into his eyes and making a run for it before he could recover.

But suddenly the opportunity was there, and for once, like every other heroine, I took it, and took it fast.

Richard Byron called the waiter, called again. I drooped in my chair, indifferent. But the waiter, whether because he did not hear, or because he was busy and we were so late—I suspect he helped in other ways in that little inn besides waiting at table—at any rate, the waiter did not come. After calling, and going up to the inn door to peer into the empty lobby, Richard Byron, with a long backward look at me, went into the inn.

It was all the start I needed.

As I ran the fifty yards between the terrace and the car, I snatched out the keys. It took three seconds to open the door and slip into the driving seat, leaving the car door silently swinging. That blessed engine came to life at a touch, and the Riley slid forward on the slope as I lifted the brakes.

As she gathered way I saw, out of the tail of my eye, Richard Byron, with the *patronne,* emerging from the inn door. He started forward, and I slammed the car door and went into gear. As the car rounded the first bend, gathering speed, I saw the *patronne,* gesticulating wildly, catch Byron's sleeve, so that he had to turn and speak to her. . . .

Well, let him do the talking, I thought grimly, then I began to laugh. Let him explain why his wife bolts without a word, let him get out of the silly mess of his own making—*and* pay the hotel bill into the bargain.

The Riley sighed down the curling hill, round another sweeping bend, and there, by the verge, parked in a bay of rock, stood a big grey car. A Bentley.

A Bentley, I thought savagely, braking hard. It would be. Something that could give me a fairly alarming chase, unless I did something drastic to it first. I slipped out of the car, with thoughts of tyre-slashing, taking sparking-plugs, and other acts of thuggery storming through my mind. But there was a garage at the hotel, and who knew what spares might be available? As I stumbled across the stones to the grey car I thought wildly. Not the rotor-arm, for the same reason—and I had nothing to slash tyres with anyway. . . . The hood was unlocked, and I lifted it, with half an eye on the road behind me.

It came automatically after all; it was the way Johnny had taught me to immobilize the car during the war, when we had to leave it parked for hours at the R.A.F. Station dances, and when the young officers, after about one in the morning, thought nothing of "winning" someone else's car for a joy-ride with a girl in the blackout. Not a usual method at all, but one very difficult to detect, and which could give an awful lot of trouble. . . . And so simple. I whipped off the distributor-cap, gave one of the screws a turn and a half with the end of my nail-file, to break the electric contact, put back the cap, closed the hood, and raced back to the Riley, all in less time than it takes to tell.

My hands were shaking and slippery on the wheel, but when the car leaped forward again down the slope, I began to feel steadier. Down a bank, with a rush like a lift, along an uneven stretch of flat, round another high walled bend . . . and we were out of sight and well away . . . and it might take him some time to find out why the Bentley spluttered and would not start, with everything, apparently, intact.

Presently we dropped gently round the last bend, and swung on to the good surface of the Tarascon road. I turned to the right in St-Rémy, twisted through back streets till I thought I might have confused my trail a little, then, still keeping generally eastwards, hummed along the narrow country roads with elation in my heart.

CHAPTER XI

Exit, pursued by a Bear.
(SHAKESPEARE)

ANYWHERE but Avignon. I might have given him the slip altogether, I hoped at any rate that I had delayed him considerably, but I could not risk leading him straight back to Avignon, and to David. Or, for that matter, back on to my own trail, which from Avignon, wherever I went, would be an open book. I sent the car at what speed I dared over the rough narrow roads, between their blinding high hedges of thorn and cypress, while I thought of where to go and what to do.

I would get clear away, if I could, then I would telephone Louise, tell her as much as I knew, and ask her to pack up and come to meet me.

She could hire a car; I would pay for it, and it would save her having to
wrestle on the crowded trains with two people's luggage. But where would
she meet me? I puzzled over it as the Riley crept cautiously over a narrow and manifestly unsafe river-bridge. Then I made up my mind,
taking the simplest solution as being also the best. Marseilles. I had always heard, and indeed it was reasonable enough, that a big city was
the easiest place to hide in, and here was I within fairly easy reach of
one of the biggest cities in France. Another thing, Louise and I had
originally intended to visit Marseilles for a day or so, so the obvious thing
to do was to ask her to leave Avignon to meet me in Marseilles.

Even as I made the decision, the Riley ran into a small country town
—a large village, by English standards—and a glance at a road sign
showed me that it was Cavaillon. I turned off the road into a straight
little alleyway and berthed the car. Then after I had lowered the top and
made it fast, I got back into my seat and took out the map.

For Marseilles, I saw, I should not have crossed the river, but have
turned sharp south at Orgon on to the main Marseilles road. That much
of my way, at any rate, I must retrace. I sat biting my lip, gazing down
the narrow alley, which gave at the far end on to the main street of the
town, and wondering what to do next. If I went back the way I had
come, by the side-roads, and Richard Byron had picked up the trail, I
would run straight into his jaws. If, on the other hand, he had not followed my actual tracks, he would be on the main road, and if I took
that way I should deliver myself neatly into his hands. He had only the
two alternatives, I knew, and, now, so had I.

I sat gripping the wheel, in an agony of indecision. Two alternatives
. . . and I was wasting time. I looked at the map again, desperately
tracing out with my finger the possible routes to Marseilles. There were
three things, it appeared, after all, that were possible. I could take a
chance, and go back by one of the two ways across the river Durance,
on to the main road for Marseilles, or I could go east through Apt, on
Route 100, by an involved and roundabout way; or I could go back to
Avignon.

The last did not count so I dismissed it straight away. And I was
through with taking chances; I was through with trusting my luck. I was
not going back across the Durance, to meet Richard Byron. I would go
east, and take the long road to the coast. With a heavy heart I folded the
map, and started up the Riley. We crept along the alley, which was barely
car-width. It was roughly cobbled, and gleamed with stinking puddles
where thin cats prowled and rummaged in the gutters. The plaster on the
houses was peeling, the shutters hung crookedly on rusty hinges. We
crawled along towards the main road.

Then stopped dead as I jammed on all the brakes and sat shaking.

In the slash of vivid sunlight which was the main road at the alley's end, a big grey car flashed past, heading east for Route 100.

It was the Bentley.

. . . .

My first thought was, absurdly enough, a sort of admiration for the speed he had made, even with my spanners in the works. My second was a sharp elation for myself. At any rate, the road to Orgon was now clear, and I could double on my tracks. I pushed the Riley forward to the brink of the alley, then braked again, and getting out of the car, ran forward to peer up the main street of Cavaillon.

The sun was blinding. The street was narrow, and crowded with the usual French country market crowd. There were women with baskets and string bags clustering round the street-stalls piled high with melons and beans and oranges and sleek purple aubergines. There were mule carts and lorries and big gleaming cars. There were dogs and children and half-naked brown men in berets and faded blue trousers.

But the Bentley had disappeared. I fancied I could see its dust still hanging in the hot quivering air at the east end of the street.

I ran back to the Riley, and in a flash we were out of the alley and scudding west for the river-bridge and Orgon, where one turns south-east for Marseilles.

. . . .

Now that the Riley had her top down, I was grateful for the breeze which, with our speed, fanned my cheeks and lifted my hair. But for the wind of our movement, the day was utterly still; under the pitiless sun of late morning the leaves of the planes that lined the road hung heavy, in thick lifeless clusters of yellow-green. The lovely stems of the trees with their dapple-work of silver and russet-peeled bark, shone in their long colonnades like cunningly worked pillars. The blinding road was barred by their shadows.

Regular as the pulse of a racing metronome, the shadow-bars flicked along the hood and back over my shoulder. We sailed out of Cavaillon on the verge of the speed-limit, tore through a dusty section of untidy ribbon-building, then suddenly the road writhed out from the plane-trees, and there, in the full glare of the sun, was the Durance and the long river-bridge.

And a queue of vehicles waiting to be allowed to pass over it.

With a sinking heart I took my place in the queue. The bridge, it appeared, was only a temporary one, three hundred yards of wooden boarding, narrow and unsteady, between the newly erected iron spans. At each end was a sentry-box, from which a man in uniform controlled the passage of traffic. At the moment, the stream from the opposite end of the bridge was being given the way, and cars, lorries, and carts crawled slowly and painfully across the narrow boards, while the white baton of the *agent de police* stretched implacably in front of us.

The heat poured down. I could feel it striking up in waves from the upholstery of the car, and gently prickling out in sweat on my body. I could not relax; I sat rigid, with my eyes switching like a doll's eyes from that forbidding white baton to my driving mirror, and back again.

And still the baton held us back, and the opposite stream of traffic crept forward, and all round me, before, behind, and edging forward to the left, impatient French drivers hooted and raced their engines and stamped on their klaxons, and got ready for a mad rush for first place on the narrow bridge. . . .

Behind me, in the tiny mirror, a gigantic lorry quivered and roared, almost on my rear bumper; behind him again I could see a mule cart with a round canvas top. To my left a yellow Cadillac had edged up and was ready to slip in ahead, between the Riley and the brake van in front of me.

My nerves began to stretch. The roaring exhausts, the heat, the klaxons, the undisciplined traffic of the French highways . . . would the white baton never drop? The impatient racing of motors round us suddenly became feverish, and again the imperceptible movement forward began; I saw that the other end of the bridge was now barred, and only three or four vehicles were still coming across; presumably as soon as the way was empty we would be allowed to go.

I gripped the wheel tighter, with an eye on the white baton, and another on the yellow Cadillac.

The last lorry lumbered off the reverberating boards. The white baton dropped, and a hand waved us on. The brake van leaped at the gap, and the yellow Cadillac, with a triumphant blare, cut across the Riley's bows and roared in behind it.

I was third in line on to the bridge, when I looked in the mirror again.

And saw the grey Bentley nosing out from behind the covered mule-cart.

.   .   .   .

At the far side of the bridge stood the other queue now, with windscreens flashing like morse in the sun. We crawled towards it. Behind me the green lorry edged on to the boards, shaking the whole contraption in a hair-raising manner. And the Bentley——

Richard Byron had reckoned without the Frenchman's utter lack of anything that might be called conscience or courtesy on the road. For as the Bentley drew out to pass the mule-cart, the driver glanced round and saw him, and immediately, with what looked like an imprecation, lashed at his mule, and hauled at its head, so that the cart swung drunkenly across the Bentley's path. The Bentley checked abruptly, and the driver, lashing his mule again, crammed into the vacant place behind the lorry.

I reckoned afterwards that it gave me a good five miles' start. When I slipped off the bridge on to the western bank, the mule-cart was still plodding, only a third of the way over, with the grey car, held fuming, at less than a walking pace behind it.

I put my foot down and kept it there. The Riley tore up the straight good road like a storm. We passed the brake van as if it were standing, and then I put a thumb hard down on my horn and left the yellow Cadillac blinding through my dust at fifty miles an hour.

The needle flicked up . . . sixty . . . seventy . . . seventy-three . . . and ahead in the glare I could see trees across the way . . . A turn sharp to the left. I lifted my foot off the accelerator. . . .

Mercifully there was nothing coming. We took the turning on the wrong side, and the back of the car skidded round it in the dust. There was a protesting scream from the tires, and then the car straightened out and roared along the crown of the road. I felt no fear any more, I could not afford to think of anything but my driving . . . the world had narrowed down to the blinding straight ribbon of the *route nationale,* and the shadow-flecks across it that blurred now into one long flicker of shadows, like an old film.

I don't even remember Orgon. I suppose I must have slowed down for it, and gone through it with some care, but we were through it before I knew, and out on the road again, with my blessed good engine pulling like the horses of the sun.

We flashed by a little farmstead, set among its bronzed rye-fields, swung out for a cruising car, and passed a cart as if it did not exist. A long white hill loomed up, between slopes of baking scrub, and then we were up the hill with the smooth rush of a lift, and dropping down the other side as if the hill had never been.

A little hamlet, pink-painted among dark cypress, hurtled towards us, closed in on us, was gone. Two oncoming cars went by, with a smack like the rattle of a drum.

And the long road writhed and turned and rose and fell beneath the roaring tyres to whip back and away in the driving mirror like a flying snake. And in all the world there was nothing but the racing engine and the rushing air and the road that streamed and streamed towards us.

CHAPTER XII

And southward aye we fled.
(COLERIDGE)

THEN, SUDDENLY, we were not alone any more. Out of the tail of my eye, to the right, I saw the plume of white smoke that meant a railway engine. The line was running parallel to the road, about fifty paces away, and an express came steaming out of a wooded defile, placidly heading south, like a pompous and attendant sprite.

My mind leaped ahead; I tried vainly to envisage the map. Would there be a railway bridge, or would it be one of those level crossings so common in southern France? So common, and so slow. Dear God, I thought to myself, *so slow*. I had waited before now a full twenty minutes for the bar of a crossing-gate to lift on an apparently quite empty line. And I might have grabbed a good start, but I had had some taste of the speed Richard Byron could make. I couldn't lose him on this road, and my only chance was to get into Marseilles with sufficient start to lose him there. Five minutes would do in those swarming streets, I thought grimly, and, with a hunted glance at the train, I put my foot down again.

To this day I do not know whether the driver of that train really did try and race my car or not. It seems impossible that he should have done so, and yet it really seemed to me, pelting along beside the rattle of the express, that the train gave a lurch and a sharp wail, and thereafter really entered into the spirit of the thing. The engine and I had it neck and neck for perhaps four hundred yards, while the driver and his mate leaned out of the cab and waved, and I sat over the wheel and looked neither to right nor left. Then we began to gain. The engine, panting, fell behind, and its pursuing rattle was deadened and then lost round a wooded bluff. For another span of minutes that seemed like hours, I held the car to its speed, then suddenly we slashed up a swift hill between two banks of olive-trees, and away ahead, two miles off down a straight stretch of road, I saw, like a brightly painted toy in the distance, the sentry-box and the red and white bars of the level crossing.

It was still open.

But someone, a tiny figure dim in the quivering heat of the distance, was moving out to lower the bars.

I heard myself give a little sound like a groan, as the Riley hurtled down that road like a rocket-bomb.

The sentry-box came towards us with the sickening speed of a hangar towards a homing aircraft. The man lifted his arm to the crank that would release the bars. I put the heel of my hand down hard on the horn, and kept on.

I saw the startled jerk of his head, the white blur as his face turned towards us, his instinctive leap further out of the way.

Then with a roar and a rush and a sickening jerk and sway of springs, we were through.

I heard the bar crash into its socket behind us.

We had come down that two-mile stretch in one-and-a-half minutes dead.

.   .   .   .

We ran into Salon at a decorous pace, and threaded the main street with innocent care. In my mind's eye I saw the grey Bentley, fuming, stuck behind that maddening red and white bar until long after the train had passed.

I warned myself, through my relief, that I couldn't count on it. Richard Byron was quite capable of bribing the official to lift the bar as soon as the express was through, and the official was no doubt quite capable of obliging him.

So I did not pause in Salon, but held straight on.

But I had begun to feel tired.

.   .   .   .

So far, I thought, as I held the car at a comfortable fifty between the flickering avenues of plane-trees, so far the breaks had been about even. And the last good break had been mine. I began, I think for the first time, seriously to believe that I might be able to get clean away, lose myself where Richard Byron could not catch up with me, go right away with Louise until the storm-centre moved, and resume our disrupted holiday elsewhere.

Later on, perhaps, when I had time to think about it, I should begin to be angry at the way my time, my liberty—yes, and my person (I smiled wryly at the out-dated phrase) had been tampered with. I had got embroiled in the affair through no fault of my own, but through an impulse I still could not fully understand, the impulse that had led me in the first place to seek David's company, and in the second, to attempt to protect him. But I had certainly not deserved the kind of thing that had

recoiled upon me. I ought to be angry, but just at present I was too preoccupied with my immediate problem to indulge in righteous indigna-
tion. The fact that Richard Byron was a murderer, and possibly of
unsound mind, rendered null and void any prospect of talking reasonably with him. I had to escape, and then, perhaps, I could think.

The road was climbing steadily, towards the band of hills that lies
between the Etang de Berre and Marseilles. It was unbearably hot, and
I was hungry, but I put the thought aside, and pressed on through that
deserted landscape, in a slow steady climb towards the crest of the
rocky hills.

Towards the top the air grew fresher, and clumps of pines, looking
cool and northern and beautiful, grew here and there beside the road.
Then, some way ahead of me, I saw a little *bistro,* just a small yellow-
washed house with three Continental pines to the back of it, a red petrol
pump, and some small tables outside under a striped awning. Suddenly
I felt unbearably thirsty. I tried to persuade myself that my lead from
Richard Byron was such that I could afford ten minutes—no, five—with
a long cold drink under that gay awning; that I had at any rate time to
stop and buy some rolls and a bottle of red wine. But it was no use; I was
definitely through with taking chances; it was Marseilles first stop. So I
went relentlessly up the last hundred yards of that hill without looking
at the *bistro* any more.

Then the decision was taken rudely out of my hands, because I was
barely twenty yards short of it when I felt the Riley swerve across the
road. I told myself that I must be more tired than I knew, and I straightened her up and crept on towards the crest of the long rise. Then I felt her
pull and veer again, and once again I got her into line. It was only as I
actually topped the rise that the dismal truth filtered through into my
preoccupied and tired mind.

The breaks were even again, and this one was against me. I had picked
up a puncture.

.   .   .   .

But not so badly against me, after all. The Riley, true as ever, had
chosen to have her puncture within a hundred yards of an outpost of
civilization, so, grateful for this unlooked-for fortune, I backed her
slowly in on to the little flat stretch of gravel in front of the *bistro.*

A big stoutish man in shirt-sleeves and a white apron was rubbing
glasses behind the bar in the shady interior. I leaned over the door of the
car.

"Monsieur. . . ."

He put down the glass he was polishing, and came out into the sun
with a grin.

"Please, monsieur, I have a puncture as you see. Is there by any chance a garage? I see you sell petrol. Is there anyone here who could change my wheel while I have something to eat?"

He looked a little doubtful.

But he was French, and I gambled on that. I laid a hand on his arm, looked desperately up at him, and said, with a quiver in my voice that was not entirely assumed: "Monsieur, it's very urgent. I—I'm running away from someone, and he isn't far behind me. I daren't let him see me, and if I'm stuck here with a puncture he——"

The most complete comprehension flashed across his face.

"Your husband?"

"Yes, my husband. He's following me, and—and, oh, monsieur, *do* help me!"

He was wonderful. In two minutes we had the Riley parked round at the back of the house, in two more he had routed out a lanky and capable youth from (I think) his afternoon siesta, and started him jacking up the car. Within seven at most I was inside the house, in a cool little room at the back, and he was asking me what I would have to eat.

"And madame need have no fear," he said largely, with gestures, "for to-night she will sleep with her lover in safety."

I didn't argue, but I asked for an iced mint drink, a long, long one, and whatever food he could manage in the time it would take to change the tyre.

"An omelette? A herb omelette? It will only take five minutes. We will find something for madame. Madame is tired? She should have something reviving with her omelette, yes?"

In a very little more than five minutes it was there, a fluffy fragrant omelette, flanked with fresh rolls, butter, honey and coffee. I swallowed down my cold drink and started on it. I don't think I have ever tasted anything so wonderful as that perfect little meal that I ate hastily in the little back room of that *bistro*, while Jean-Jacques, outside the window, was yanking off my wheel.

I was actually getting up to go, gulping the last of my coffee, when I heard the whine of another car coming up the hill outside, and the check and deepened note as she changed gear. Then the swish of gravel under her tyres as she turned off the road and stopped in front of the *bistro*.

I stood frozen, with the cup half-way to my mouth.

His voice came quite clearly through the nearly shut door. After the conventional greetings——

"No, nothing to drink, thank you," he said, but I heard the rustle of notes, "I haven't time. I stopped to ask you if you had seen an English car pass here within the last half-hour, a dark green car with the top down. Did you happen to notice?"

There was another rustle.

"A dark green car . . ." repeated the *patron* slowly. I heard the clink of a glass, and could imagine him picking it up and deliberately starting to polish it again while he considered.

"A dark green car, English . . ." he paused, and I don't know which must have waited in the most tension, I or Richard Byron, one on either side of the door. "With a young demoiselle driving?" asked the *patron*.

"Yes." I could almost see the flicker in Richard Byron's eyes as he leaned forward.

The *patron* said, indifferently: "A young woman driving a dark green open car went by here some time ago. She was going fast. Would that be the one monsieur means?"

"That's the one. How long ago?"

In a voice that sounded like a shrug: "About twenty minutes, twenty-five, half an hour—who knows, monsieur? I paid no attention, but I remember the car you speak of because of the speed . . . and the pretty girl."

Something passed with a rustle, I heard a mumble of thanks from the *patron* and then, almost immediately, the roar of the Bentley's engine and the sound of rapidly engaged gears. The engine sang across the crest of the hill, and dwindled and died, so that soon the only sound was the rustle of the pines in the little hill-top breeze, and the clink of a glass from the bar.

The *patron* came back grinning.

"He was not far behind you, that one," he said. "But if you give him time now he will lose himself ahead of you. Madame cannot go back now the way she came?"

I thought for a moment, then shook my head. I would not lead the chase back into the Avignon area, come what might.

I would wait here, smoke a couple of cigarettes, then drive into Marseilles by the side road, and go to ground and call Louise. And I would tell Louise everything, when I saw her again; I was tired of playing this alone. I didn't feel that David would hold me to my promise of not speaking, after what had happened.

I said: "Is there another way into Marseilles besides by the main road?"

"Yes, there are many. After one has passed Les Assassins——"

"*Les Assassins?*" I asked, startled.

"It is a place at the top of these hills, where one begins to go down into Marseilles. The road goes between walls of rock, a little gorge."

"But why is it called Les Assassins?"

"Because much rock has fallen there, and the old road used to wind in among the cliffs and boulders, and it was the place where brigands waited, in ambush, for the coaches and the carts of merchants."

"And after that?"

"Then there is the long run down into Marseilles, and before one reaches the suburbs there are roads which branch and which, if one has a map, will take one into the city by a different way. There is no need to go down the main road into the town." He smiled suddenly. "He is to meet you there, *hein?*"

"He—who? Oh, yes, of course," I said. I had momentarily forgotten that I had a date with a lover in Marseilles that night. "You have been more than kind," I told the *patron,* and he shrugged expansively.

"It is nothing, nothing at all. If one cannot help a *belle demoiselle* in distress—what would you? One might as well be dead."

He went out, beaming good-will, and I sat for a while, quietly smoking, while time passed softly. I felt, gradually, a sense of peace descending on me, a feeling that this was a safe little harbourage that I should be sorry to leave. I sat, relaxed, and I believe I even dozed a little, for over an hour longer. And then, when I saw by my watch that it was nearly three o'clock, I rose reluctantly, and prepared to go.

I found the *patron,* and paid for what I had had, renewing my thanks, and including a thousand-franc note, over and above what I owed him, and a substantial tip for Jean-Jacques.

I found that the latter had occupied his time not only in changing my wheel, but, when told there was no need to hurry, in finding and mending the puncture in the discarded wheel. This, mended now and serviceable, was strapped in place as spare. I thanked him gratefully, and, pursued by good wishes, and frank promises of joy to come from the *patron,* I drove the Riley back round the house and out again on to the road.

Soon the little *bistro* was lost to sight behind us, round a bend in the track, and we were off on our travels again, with the sun for company, and the tall pines whispering above the humming engine. I did not hurry. For one thing, there was now no need, and I would not unnecessarily abuse the car on the rather stony road, and risk picking up another puncture—which I would have to deal with myself. For another, the strain of the previous night, and of the hectic and nerve-racked morning, were beginning most definitely to tell on me. My head was aching a little, and a sort of lassitude, an almost don't-care-ishness, bred of fatigue and lack of sleep, was making itself felt. I knew that, even if the occasion should arise, I would be quite unequal now to the sort of demands that had been made on me that morning. If suddenly called upon for

headlong speed, I would probably drive the car off the road at anything
over fifty miles an hour.

So I nursed the engine up the long inclines, and took the car gently over
the rough surface, with half of my mind on my driving, and the other
half trying to recall the street plan of Marseilles and the way I had
planned to take.

The white rocks gave way, as we climbed higher, to red. The country,
deserted before, was here desolate, stripped even of its olives and its
vines. The red rocks, slashed with hard cobalt shadows, rose sheer from
the road on either hand, and the only green was the dark cresting of the
pines, swaying richly against the dazzling blue. As we approached what
appeared to be the summit of the hill, I could see how the cliffs had split
and crumbled, till on either side of the road were bare boulders and
pylons of rock. Among the strewn red fragments to the left I saw where
the old track had wound tortuously across the hill-crest behind the pines
and fallen rocks. But the new road went through the sheer red cliff like a
white slash.

Les Assassins.

And, in the blue distance, the Mediterranean.

As the Riley gained the summit, I changed up, and she slipped into the
long descent with a sigh. Before me the road sank in an interminable
and gentle hill towards the enormous untidy sprawl of Marseilles, set on
the edge of the loveliest shore in the world.

We started slowly down the last stretch. To the left of the road, several
yards ahead, I saw where the old track emerged again on to the road,
behind a knot of pines. We slid past it and down.

I suppose I should have seen it coming, but I confess I had not. There
was no reason I could see why Richard Byron should not believe the
patron of the *bistro*, and race on towards Marseilles in the hope of catching me. But of course, he had not believed him.

The grey Bentley glided out of that knot of pines, and closed in behind my car without a sound.

CHAPTER XIII

Re-enter Murderer.
(STAGE DIRECTION)

THERE WAS nothing to be done, of course.

Even if I had not been so tired, I still could not have hoped to drive away from him with no start, and no advantage. I was beaten, and I knew it. I would go quietly.

Without thinking very much of anything at all, except that my head ached and I would be glad to stop driving and get out of the sun, I went on down the long stretch towards Marseilles as if there were no grey car behind me, and no angry man in it who had, by this time, quite a big account to settle with me.

In a very short time we were in the suburbs of Marseilles. The main road runs for perhaps two miles or more through streets of tattered houses and little grubby shops, where the plaster and the paint hangs in peeling festoons, and where beautiful ragged children and hideous mongrel dogs play together among the refuse of the gutters. Soon the tram-lines begin, and the traffic of the city begins to close in. Lorries, mules, carts of all shapes and sizes, cars of assorted vintages and nationalities—all the world on wheels seems to drive through the narrow streets of Marseilles, hooting, shouting, pushing for places, in a rich and strange confusion.

I steered mechanically through it all, changing gear, stopping, swerving, going through all the rapid actions necessary to getting a vehicle more or less undamaged through that incredible *tohu-bohu*. Behind me, like a shadow, the big grey Bentley swerved and checked and swept forward again on my track, never more than ten yards behind me, never less than four.

I didn't even bother to watch it, except as I would watch anything so close on my tail, in order to give it the necessary signals.

I was finished. I wasn't trying any more. My temples throbbed and I felt as if a heavy weight were pressing down on my shoulders. My mind, even had I tried to make it, would have refused to contemplate what was going to happen after this.

Which is why, when the miracle happened, I did not even notice it.

The first I knew of it was when it gradually filtered through to my stupid senses that there was no grey car reflected in the driving mirror. There was only a mule-cart, and nothing behind that that I could see.

I stared stupidly for three seconds, then I stole a look back over my shoulder. I had come about a hundred yards from where it had happened. A lorry, emerging from a blind side street, had swung across the path of the Bentley, and grazed a passing tram. The Bentley, caught between the two, had had to stop, but whether it was touched or not I could not, of course, tell. But it was stuck fast enough, that much was apparent. Already the beginnings of a crowd had gathered, and excitement was mounting. . . . And there were the police. . . .

It might take him minutes, or even hours, to get himself out of that.

Like a fainting man who makes a last desperate conscious effort before he goes under, I turned the Riley down a side street, and trod on the accelerator . . . left, right, right, left again—no, that was a cul-de-sac— right, in and out like a twisting hare . . . then before me was a garage, where behind a row of pumps yawned the dark cave of an enormous shed, half filled with lorries, cars, buses, in varying stages of repair. I turned in, ran the car as deep into the shadow as I could, and berthed it finally behind a solid rank of wagons.

Still mechanically, I switched off the engine, collected my bag, maps, glasses and coat, and got out of the car.

I cannot remember what instructions I gave to the proprietor, who had hurried up, but I paid him something in advance, and only just retained enough wit to ask for his card with the address of the garage. I tucked this inside my bag, and went slowly out into the sunshine of the back street.

I turned right, away from the city centre, towards where I imagined the sea to lie, and walked for some way through shabby streets that nevertheless seemed moderately respectable. And soon the name of a little hotel caught my eye, a name I had seen in the Michelin guide. It would, in that case, be clean and comfortable, so I went into its cool tiled lobby, signed my name, and climbed a steep spiral of marble steps to a stone landing on the third floor, where Madame showed me a small and spotless room.

The door clicked shut behind me. I sat down slowly on the bed, and for a full five minutes I don't suppose I even moved an eyelash. The shutters were closed against the sun, and so were the windows, so that the hum and clash of traffic from Europe's noisiest city surged up, muted and drowsy, into the high little room. There was a wash-basin, a foot-bath, a narrow comfortable bed with a snow-white cover, a carafe of water on the table beside the bed. . . .

I drank deeply. I stood up, and after I had locked the door, I slowly undressed, shaking out my clothes one by one, and laying them neatly on the bed. I had a leisurely cool wash, bathing and drying my whole body, standing on the warm floor with the slatted sunlight barring me from head to foot. Then I slipped on my nylon nightdress, and brushed my hair thoroughly.

I moved my clothes to the back of a chair, had another long drink, and lay down on the bed.

The day began to recede, grow confused, grow dim, as the sound of the traffic blurred with distance . . . Richard Byron might be miles away, he might be in jail, he might be just outside the door . . . it didn't matter at all.

I slept.

.   .   .   .

It was just before six when I awoke, and at first, swimming up from the warm depths of sleep, I could not tell where I was, lying on a strange bed with the deepening rays of the sun slanting through the shutters. The light had mellowed from gold to amber, and the sound of the traffic below, too, seemed to have mellowed its note to a subdued rushing like the rushing of an underground sea.

I lay still for a while, enjoying the relaxed warmth of my body and the softness of the bed. Then I got up and began leisurely to dress again in the green frock. It looked fresh enough, considering the wear and tear of the last night and day, I thought, as I buckled the wide belt round it, and slipped into my shoes.

I was hungry, and the first problem I intended to face was that of finding a meal. I toyed with the idea of buying food and wine, and locking myself safely in my room to eat, but, since I had to go out anyway to buy food, the risks were equal. And Marseilles was a big and crowded city, not like Nîmes, or Avignon. I would go out, avoiding the main streets, and dine in some small restaurant where I was not likely to be seen. But first I must telephone Louise.

As I went downstairs I was recalling what I had read of Marseilles—that the city was sliced in two by the straight line of the Canebière, the busiest street in Europe, where, sooner or later, all the world passed by. It was said that if you sat in the Canebière long enough, you would see passing by you every soul that you knew. If I were Richard Byron, I thought, that's where I'd go. I'd select a table in a boulevard café on the Canebière, and sit and watch for the girl in the pale green dress.

So the girl in the pale green dress would go elsewhere.

There was a telephone booth in the hotel lobby, a tiny cupboard in the darkest corner under the stairs. I shut myself in and addressed myself to the alarming intricacies of the French telephone exchange.

The call went through quickly enough. I leaned against the chilly wall of the booth, listening to the steady thresh of the Tistet-Védène's telephone bell, and wondering what on earth to say to Louise.

But Louise was not there. The tinny voice of the telephone assured me of that, stonewalling my stupidly repeated queries with demonstrably diminishing patience. Miss Cray was not there. Yes, Miss Cray had gone out straight after lunch, and was not yet in. Definitely not. Quite sure. No . . . The receiver went dead in my hand, leaving me in mid-sentence—leaving me also, with the unmistakable impression that whoever had answered the call had been driven into positive rudeness not only by my desperate reiterations but by some private and overpowering trouble of her own. At least, I thought, as I lowered the receiver, my informant's preoccupation had prevented her from asking who or what I was. And I had found out, dismally enough, all that I needed to know. Louise wasn't in the hotel. I was in this thing alone for a little longer. . . .

I found that my hand was still tight over the cradled receiver. I pulled it away and went out into the foyer. I handed my key to Madame at the desk, stepped carefully over the marmalade cat in the doorway, and went down the three stone steps into the street.

The exhausted feeling had passed, leaving only, as an aftermath of that deep sleep, a profound sensation of unreality, as if I were moving, effortless and bodiless, through a dream. People passed me, traffic rattled by, but these movements seemed to have no connection with the world in which I found myself; men were "like trees walking," without character or feature or sound, irrelevant creations in the background of my nightmare. The only living person was myself, Charity Selborne, to whom none of these things could possibly be happening. . . .

I walked fairly rapidly to the end of the street and glanced to right and left. To the right a vista of still meaner streets and warehouses met my eyes, so I turned left through a narrow way towards the sea. After a while I realized that I was making for the harbour—I could see masts and the gleam of a gull's wing and a flash of early neon lights at the end of the street.

I hesitated. One had heard such tales of Marseilles, the wicked city . . . and was it not near the harbour that the wickednesses congregated? A street led off to my left, and I paused in my walk, and glanced up it.

Then made for the harbour without another second's hesitation. For he was there, my enemy, hesitating like myself at the far corner of that street, which, I found later, gave straight on to the Canebière:—I had been right, as far as it went. I did not think he had seen me, but the hunt was up again, and I made for the Old Port of Marseilles without another thought of the wickednesses there abounding. I believe I would have almost welcomed the offer of a free trip to Buenos Aires at that moment.

When the street led into the harbour I hesitated again. It was so open. The Old Port was a vast open space, criss-crossed by tram-lines and railway tracks, bounded on three sides by houses and restaurants all flashing their gaudy neon signs in the face of the sunset, and open on the fourth side to the sea. The harbour waters were crowded with boats of all shapes and colours, and in the amber light the forest of masts swayed and bobbed amid the glancing web of their ropes.

I only hesitated for a second, then made across the open square towards the nearest crowd of people, hoping to lose myself among them, and get somehow to the other side of the square. There were about twenty or thirty people standing there, talking and laughing, between the railway tracks and the edge of the quay. I reached them and joined the crowd, ignored a pressing invitation from a couple of sailors obviously ashore for the evening, and took refuge behind what appeared to be a family party, papa, mamma, and two little boys in sailor suits with red pom-poms on their bonnets. I threw a cautious glance at the mouth of the street I had just left. He was not there.

Then I discovered why the crowd had collected there on the quay.

An old boatman, with scarlet cheeks, a quantity of white whiskers, and a liquid and lascivious eye, suddenly appeared up a short gangplank which led from the quay beside us to the stern of a motor-boat moored below.

"This way!" he yelled. "This way for the Château d'If!"

Simultaneously, another old man, with whiskers slightly less white, and an eye proportionately more lascivious, shot up in rivalry in the next boat.

"This way," he screamed. "*This* way for the Château d'If!"

The crowd, showing neither fear nor favour, turned as one and began to file down the twin gangplanks. It looked as if, my cover gone, I was going to be left high and dry on the edge of the Old Port.

I flung a look at the street corner, just in time to see Richard Byron emerge, glance once back over his shoulder, then turn to scan the square, but he was not looking at the quay; he was looking the other way towards the din of the Canebière.

I scuttered down the nearest gangplank and sat down under the awning, as far forward as I could get. The boat lay well below the level of the quayside, and I knew he could not see me from where he stood. But it looked as if, barring Buenos Aires, I was going on a trip to the Château d'If.

The boatman, with a good deal of quite unnecessary noise, cast off, and soon we were churning through the milky waters of the bay towards the harbour mouth.

.   .   .   .

I cannot pretend that I enjoyed any part of that trip to the Château d'If. I was caught again in the noose of the old fear, and now it was worse, threaded through as it was with the drab strands of hopelessness. It seemed that I literally could not get away from him, almost as if there were something so linking this dark and dangerous man with myself, that wherever I went, he was there. In the whole of Marseilles, to meet him the first moment I ventured out: in the whole of Provence, to meet him in the ruins of Les Baux. To whatever shifts I resorted, he found me: whatever falsehoods my brain devised, he knew the truth behind . . . this, at any rate, is how I was thinking, and how much was due to hunger and how much to inescapable fate I was in no fit state to judge. . . .

I sat on the low parapet of the turret of the Château d'If, watching the white stone slowly flush to a tender rose. I watched the softly breaking water of the tideless sea wash and wash across the whispering white pebbles, aquamarine rippled through with liquid gold.

I saw it all in a kind of dream; and the whisper of the sea came like a dream's echo.

The boat went, and I sat where I was. Another came, and discharged its noisy cargo of sightseers, who streamed chattering into the castle, and crowded through the prison-cells and across the wide flat roof where I was sitting. I got up suddenly, and went down to the boat which was waiting. My watch told me I had been on the island already over an hour: he would have gone, I said to myself, without conviction. With rather more conviction, and a good deal more common sense, I told myself that this state of numbed fatalism was the result of hunger and fatigue, and the sooner I got back and got a meal the better I should be.

The journey back seemed much shorter than the outward trip. It was almost dark by now, and along the shore the lights were strung out like a necklace. There were no waves, but bars of darkness slid softly towards the land to lap against the dim rock.

We shut off our engine and drifted towards the quay followed by our arrowing wake. The port was gemmed with neon lights, white, scarlet, green and amethyst, and under the more subdued orange glow of the street lamps the evening crowds were gathering. The city of the night-time was waking up. I sat in the silently moving boat, relaxed now, still in the trance-like drifting state of acute reaction from strain. I scarcely bothered to scan the quay in the twilight, to see if this last absurd bid for escape had worked. I knew it could not. I knew that there was something far stronger than anything I had known before, that would lead Richard Byron straight to the gang-plank to wait for me.

We were tying up at the quay-side. The boatman yelled to a boy on shore, and between them they threw out the gangway. The other people in the boat got up, calling to one another and laughing, and trod awkwardly up the plank. I followed.

I hardly even looked at Richard Byron as he took my arm and helped me on to the quay.

CHAPTER XIV

Fate, I come, as dark, as sad
As thy malice could desire;
Bringing with me all the fire
That Love in his torches had.
(MARVEL)

I WALKED across the quay beside him, his hand under my elbow. People passed us, walked at our shoulders, even jostled us, but we might as well have been alone. I saw the crowd vaguely, darkly through a glass, and the sounds of them were remote, in an anaesthetized distance. The only sound I heard in all the clamour was the tread of our feet on the cobbles, and the breathing of Richard Byron beside me.

He said, not ungently: "We still have to have our little talk, you know."

Something deep inside me seemed to snap. The anger I had been too scared, too tired to feel, suddenly jetted up. I stopped abruptly, and swung to face him. People streamed past us, but they were not there at all; there was only myself and my enemy, in a little circle of anger.

I looked him straight in the eyes. I said furiously: "We can have as many little talks as you want, since you seem prepared to make such a damned nuisance of yourself to get them. But I can tell you one thing now, and it's the most important thing of all, and it's this. *I am not going to tell you anything about David*. I know perfectly well where he is, and you can bully me and threaten me as much as you like, but you'll find out nothing. Nothing."

"But I——"

I swept on as if he hadn't spoken: "You've as good as admitted you're a murderer. Do you think I am going to be a party to handing a child over to you, a child who, for all I know to the contrary, you *did* bash over the head in the dark the night you murdered your friend? Think again, Mr. Richard Byron. David is a darling, even if he *is* your son, and I—I'd murder you myself if you laid a finger on him!"

The hot tears were welling up in my eyes, tears of anger, anxiety and strain. I felt them spill over and begin to run down my cheeks. I could not see his face through them, and he did not speak for a long moment.

"My God," said Richard Byron at length in a curious voice. But I hardly heard him.

"Apart from which," I finished, "you—you've ruined my holiday, and I've been looking forward to it for ages."

After which remarkably silly speech I suddenly broke; I began to cry helplessly, with my hands to my face, and the tears dripping out between my fingers. I turned blindly away from Richard Byron, stumbled over a rail-track, and would have fallen, but that his hand caught me again by the elbow and steadied me.

Then he said, in the same curious voice: "You'll feel better when you've had something to eat. Come along."

The neon-lighted cafés were a blur. I felt him piloting me along the sidewalks, and I fought for self-control, groping in my bag for a hand-kerchief. Then suddenly we were in out of the street, in a little, beautifully appointed restaurant where the tables were set back in alcoves, lit softly by wall-lights. I caught a confused glimpse of napery and glass and silver, and a great spray of yellow flowers, then I was comfortably settled on a deep wall-seat upholstered with wine velvet, and Richard Byron was putting a glass into my hand. My own was shaking, and his hand closed on it, holding it steady until I regained sufficient control to raise it to my lips.

I realized, as from a great distance, that his voice was very gentle. He said: "Drink it up. It'll make you feel better."

I gulped some of it down. It was spirit of some kind, and it seemed to burst and evaporate inside my mouth and throat in an immediate aromatic warmth, so that I gasped and choked a little, but my breath came more evenly afterwards, and I found I could control the little shaking sobs that were racking me.

"All of it," urged Richard Byron. I obeyed him, and lay back against the deep cushions with my eyes closed, letting my body relax utterly to the creeping warmth of the drink and the smell of food and wine and flowers. My bones seemed to have melted, and I was queerly content to lie back against the yielding velvet, with the soft lights against my eyelids, and do nothing, think of nothing. I was quiet and utterly passive, and the awful beginnings of hysteria were checked.

Still from that same dimensionless distance, I heard him speaking in French. I supposed he was ordering food. And presently at my elbow I heard the chink of silver, and opened my eyes to see the big glittering trolley of *hors d'œuvre* with its hovering attendant.

Richard Byron said something to him, and without waiting for me to speak, the man served me from the tray. I remember still those exquisite fluted silver dishes, each with its load of dainty colours . . . there were anchovies and tiny gleaming silver fish in red sauce, and savoury butter in curled strips of fresh lettuce; there were caviare and tomato and olives green and black, and small golden-pink mushrooms and cresses and beans. The waiter heaped my plate, and filled another glass with white wine. I drank half a glassful without a word, and began to eat. I was conscious of Richard Byron's eyes on me, but he did not speak.

The waiters hovered beside us, the courses came, delicious and appetizing, and the empty plates vanished as if by magic. I remember a red mullet, done somehow with lemons, and a succulent golden-brown fowl bursting with truffles and flanked by tiny peas, then a froth of ice and whipped cream dashed with kirsch, and the fine smooth caress of the wine through it all. Then, finally, apricots and big black grapes, and coffee. The waiter removed the little silver filtres, and vanished, leaving us alone in our alcove.

The liqueur brandy was swimming in its own fragrance in the enormous iridescent glasses, and for a moment I watched it idly, enjoying its rich smooth gleam, then I leaned back against the cushions and looked about me with the eyes of a patient who has just woken from the first long natural sleep after an anaesthetic. Where before the colours had been blurred and heightened, and the outlines undefined, proportions unstable, and sounds hollow and wavering, now the focus had shifted sharply, and drawn the bright little restaurant into sharp dramatic outline.

I looked across at Richard Byron.

He was sitting, head bent, watching the brandy swirl in the bottom of his glass, the light of the subdued wall-lamp falling upon him from behind and to the left. I found myself for the first time really looking at him without any underlay of fear and suspicion to colour my picture of him. The light lit sharply the angles of cheek-bone and jaw, and the fine line of the temple, throwing a dramatic slant of shadow from his lowered lashes—David's lashes—across the hard line of his cheek. And the first thing that struck me was the deep unhappiness of that face; it was unhappiness rather than harshness that had driven those furrows down his cheeks, and given the eyes such sombre shadowing. As he sat with his head bent, obviously toying with his brandy-glass, the angry lines of brow and mouth were smoothed away, and instead there was a withdrawn and brooding look, an aspect harsh and forbidding enough, until it was betrayed by the unhappiness of the mouth.

His lashes lifted suddenly and he looked at me. I felt my heart jolt once, uncomfortably, then I met his gaze squarely.

"How do you feel now?"

I said: "Much better, thank you. It was good of you to salvage the wreck—I must look like——"

He laughed, and it was suddenly like coming face to face with a complete stranger, where you had been talking to someone you thought you knew.

He said: "You must be feeling better, if you're beginning to worry about how you look. But don't let it distress you. You'll pass, indeed you will."

He lit a cigarette for me, and suddenly his eyes were grave over the flame, and very intent. He said, quietly: "There are only two things I want to ask you just at this moment——"

My face must have changed, because he added sharply: "Don't look like that. Please. I've been every kind of a damned fool, and I'm sorry, but for God's sake don't look at me like that any more. They're very harmless questions, but if you'll tell me the answers, I'll leave you alone till you feel like telling me the rest."

He paused, and all of a sudden it was as if the room were as still as the pole.

Here it comes again, I thought. He looked down at his glass, so that I could not see his eyes, but under the non-committal voice I could feel the urgency that had frightened me before.

He said: "How is David? Does he seem well—and happy?"

I looked at him in surprise; I had expected a very different question. I said: "As far as I could see, he is very well indeed. But I don't imagine that he's happy. For one thing, he's lonely, and for another, he's too scared."

"Too scared?" He looked at me this time. He set his glass down so sharply that the brandy splashed and sparkled, and then his hands came down to grip the table's edge, the whites of the knuckles showing. From the ash-tray, where his cigarette burned unheeded, a pencilled blue line of smoke spiralled up between us. Richard Byron stared at me through the smoke, and he repeated, very softly: "Too scared—of what?"

I raised my eyebrows. "Of you, of course."

There could be no doubt about his first reaction to that uncompromising reply; it was stupefaction, sheer, speechless stupefaction. He stared at me across the table, and his eyes widened. Then, suddenly, as if he had understood or remembered something, the old bitter look was back in his face, and he seemed to withdraw once more into himself. He said, in a curiously flat voice:

"Of me? Are you sure it's of me? Did he say so?"

Then suddenly, I knew. I felt my own eyes widening as his had done, and I sat staring at him like an owl.

"Why," I whispered, "why, I don't believe you killed your friend. I don't believe you ever hurt David in your life. I believe you love him. Don't you. *Don't you?*"

Richard Byron gave me a queer little twisted smile that hurt. Then he picked up his cigarette again and spoke lightly.

"I love him more than anything else in the world," he said, quite as if it didn't matter.

. . . .

Then suddenly, the bubble was broken, and the illusion of privacy dispelled. The head waiter came hovering, his face split with a smile, his hands fluttering before him like large pursy moths.

"Madame has enjoyed her dinner? Monsieur has fed well? The *Chapon marseillais,* he is good, yes? He is the *specialité de la maison,* you understand, Madame. . . ."

We assured him that everything had been perfect, and, wreathed in smiles and mothlike swoops of the hand, he bowed himself off, and another waiter, with the faint air of apology that is worn by a man committing an act in questionable taste, sidled up with the bill.

Richard Byron glanced at it, put a quite staggering amount of money down on the salver, and waved the bowing waiter aside. Then he hesitated oddly, and looked at me.

"I know it's useless saying I'm sorry for what has happened," he said, "but as far as the inadequate phrase can go, I *am* sorry. I've been a damned fool and a blind one. I should have known that someone like you wouldn't have been mixed up in this thing. I promise not to pester you again—but could we go somewhere, take a walk or something, and will you let me explain? It's quite a long story, and somehow I'd rather you knew it."

His face looked white and strained in the subdued light. I had a sud-

den sharp memory of David's face, wearing much that same look, and of
a hesitating childish voice asking me: *"How did he look?"*

I said: "If it concerns David, I'd like to hear it. And as for what's in
the past, shall we forget it for a while? It looks as if you're not the only
one who's made mistakes—and mine, perhaps, were the bigger."

"You had the more excuse."

He smiled his sudden warm smile, and to my own amazement, I
smiled back, and rose.

"If I promise not to climb out of a back window, may I go and powder my nose?"

"You——" he bit off something he had been going to say. "Yes, of
course."

As I went I saw him get out another cigarette, and settle back in his
chair to wait for me.

.   .   .   .

We went out into the dark streets that ray from the Old Port, and
turned, instinctively and as if by mutual consent, towards the sea. Presently we found ourselves in a cobbled street which slanted along the sea
front, with tall houses to the left of us, and a low sea-wall to the right.
Away ahead, floating in the starlit air like a vision, glimmered the gold
statue of Our Lady who stands on the high summit of Notre Dame de
la Garde.

The houses were dark and secret, and the occasional lamps cast only
a furtive light on the cobbles. Boats bobbed and curtseyed at the
water's edge, rubbing each other's shoulders, the sea lipping at them with
small sucking sounds. Where the shamefaced lamplight let fall a reflection on the water, the shifting surface cast a pattern of light upwards on
to the bellies of the boats, so that they seemed to be swimming, netted in
a wavering luminous mesh. Further out in the bay, the green and red
and golden riding-lights of the bigger ships drowned themselves in long
liquid shadows. The ropes looked as fragile and as magical as gossamer.

We stood looking over the sea-wall. A group of sailors, noisily talking
and laughing, went past, then a man and a girl, absorbed. Nobody
seemed to pay any attention to us, and once again I felt the beginnings
of that strangely dream-like feeling I had experienced before, only this
time it was not brought about by weariness, but by something else I
could not quite understand. It was as if Richard Byron and I were alone
in a bubble of glass, enclosed in its silence, into which nothing could
break, and out of which we might not go. People, like the dim denizens
of some under-sea-world in which our bubble was suspended, came and
went, floating, soundless, amorphous, outside the glass, peering in perhaps, but having no power to intrude upon the silence that enmeshed

us. To this day I still remember Marseilles, the noisiest city in the world, as a noiseless background to that meeting with Richard Byron, a silent film flickering on a screen in front of which we two moved and stood and talked, the only living people there.

I turned to face him.

"You said there were two questions you were going to ask me, and you've only asked one. What was the other?"

He looked at me without speaking, and in that dim light his expression was unreadable, but I got the impression that he was oddly at a loss.

I said: "I think I know; in fact, I can hardly help knowing, can I? It should have come first, shouldn't it?—it's the more important."

I saw the corner of his mouth lift in a smile.

"Possibly."

I said, deliberately: "David is at the Hôtel Tistet-Védène, Avignon."

For a long moment he was motionless, then suddenly his body swung round to face me, and his hands shot out to grip my wrists. Again, as in Nîmes, his grip hurt me, but this time I made no attempt to get away. I could feel his heart beating in his hands.

"Charity," he said roughly, "why did you tell me that? Why—suddenly? I haven't told you the story yet—haven't explained. I haven't even told you I was lying when I played the murderer to scare you into giving David up. You've no reason on earth to think you can trust me— I've bullied you and hurt you and abused you and all but made you ill. Why the hell should you suddenly make me a present of this before I've even started to say my piece?"

It was as if his heart was an engine, and its pounding was driving mine as well. It started to race.

"I—I don't know," I said lamely, and tried to pull my hands away.

He shifted his grip, and his eyes fell on my bruised wrist. For a second or two he stood with his head bent, staring at the ugly dark mark, then his mouth suddenly twisted, and he pulled me into his arms and kissed me.

After a long while he let me go, and I leaned back against the low parapet, while he turned abruptly and gazed out to sea.

"I suppose that was why," I said shakily.

"The hell of it is," he said, "that I've wanted that ever since I walked into the Temple of Diana and saw you sitting there, with tears on your eyelashes. And all the time I thought you were a crooked little——"

"Bitch."

He grinned a little. "Quite," he said. "Yes, all that time, when I thought you were in with them, a cheap little crook mixed up in a particularly filthy game of murder—the sort of game that plays with a child's life and sanity as if it were a—a plastic counter you could lose, and never miss it."

He looked away from me suddenly.

"Your refusing to tell me where to find David—was it because *David* wanted you to?"

"Yes," I said gently.

"And I thought you were helping them to keep him away from me. You looked so guilty, so guilty and scared, and of course I'd no idea that David himself——" He broke off sharply.

"I'm sorry, but that's how it was. He wanted to—to avoid you, so I helped. I thought I was doing the right thing."

He gave me a little smile. "Yes, I see that now. But you must see how all the evidence went against you, even while every instinct I've ever had rose up and screamed that the evidence was wrong. . . . It was just one more thing, after all those that had happened, one more thing which could shake one's values to smithereens, and make yet another safe road as shifty as sand. Another thing that *couldn't* be, but *was*."

"I know," I said. "How does it go——?"

> Sith there is yet a credence in my heart,
> An esperance so obstinately strong,
> That does invert the attest of eyes and ears;
> As if those organs had deceptious functions,
> Created only to calumniate. . . .

Isn't that what you mean?"

He smiled again, more naturally. "Yes, exactly, though I can't say it puts it much more clearly. Poor Troilus—he says it better later on, you know——

> If beauty have a soul, this is not she . . .
> If there be rule in unity itself,
> This is not she. . . .

But I was luckier than Troilus, wasn't I? For me, the rules did hold good —that no one who looks and moves and speaks as you do *could* be the bitch you seemed to be. But it was hell while it lasted, reason and instinct at war, and both violated." He turned his head. "You do understand, don't you?"

"Of course. Didn't it happen to me too? I thought you were a beast and a murderer, I was scared of you, and yet—this happened."

"This happened," he repeated, "and reason goes out of court—for both of us."

"Yes."

He said slowly, looking down at the dark opaque shifting of the water: "But you got the question wrong, Charity. You didn't really think I was going to throw that one at you again, did you, before I'd explained why I still had the right to an answer?"

"I got it wrong? You weren't going to ask where David was?"

"No."

"What were you going to ask, then?"

He stood, watching the water, leaning on his elbows on the low wall. He said, heavily, for the fourth time:

"Who's Johnny?"

CHAPTER XV

Madam, will you walk——?
(OLD SONG)

THE DARK WATER heaved below the wall, oily looking, webbed with a flotsam of straws and pieces of cork. It was strangely fascinating, as well as soothing, to watch the lift and fall and sway of the drifting fragments in the shallow gleam of the street-lamp.

I said: "Johnny was my husband."

"Was?"

"Yes," I said.

"Oh, I see. I'm sorry."

I turned, like him, to face the sea, leaned my elbows on the wall and concentrated on the moving water.

"He and I were married in the war—he was in the R.A.F. We had two years, so I suppose we were lucky. Then he was killed over Pas de Calais."

"Bomber?"

"No. Fighter escort." Away out over the sea the milky haze had begun to withdraw from the moon. The horizon swam up out of darkness to meet her faint light.

"Some day," I said, "I'll tell you about Johnny. But not now."

He glanced at me quickly.

"Because of this—because of what's happened?"

"Because you kissed me, do you mean?"

"Because I love you, Charity."

"No," I said. "Not because of that. What happens to me now doesn't alter what happened to me before. What was between me and Johnny was a real thing that we built very carefully for ourselves, and, when we built it, it was perfect and satisfying. But because it was blasted to bits by a German shell, that doesn't mean I'm never to try and build anything else among the ruins. Johnny isn't a ghost, you know, tagging along at my elbow, reminding me to mourn."

"When I first saw you," he said softly, "you were crying."

"I know," I said. "And it's true I was thinking about Johnny. But the memory of my life with him isn't likely to get up and forbid me to live any more, or any differently. . . . One ought to build even better the second time, and I can still build. And Johnny——" I said, turning to Richard Byron, "why, Johnny would have egged me on."

He straightened up, and his arms went round me, this time very gently. He was smiling, and his eyes had a little steady flame deep in the grey. He held me a little away from him and looked at me, his lips curving.

"I love you, Charity," he said again. "You're so sweet and you're so sane. My God, I think you could almost make the world seem a sweet, sane place again, the way it used to be. . . . Am I to take it that you're telling me to go ahead and kiss you again?"

"Why, no, I——"

"Because I'm planning to," said Richard Byron.

And did.

.   .   .   .

It seemed hours later, and the moon had laid her trail of silver out to sea, when we stood again, side by side, elbows on the wall again, and began to talk.

". . . Enough of this side-tracking," said Richard. "I've got to think, and you've got to help me, so you've got a right to know the story. It's a pretty filthy one to drag you into——"

"It seems to me," I said mildly, "that I'm in fairly deep as it is, and entirely through my own efforts."

He mused a little, and I could see the lines etch themselves again deeply round his mouth, those bitter little lines that made his face suddenly harsh and frightening.

He began to talk. . . .

It was certainly not a pretty story, and as I listened, I could feel some of the anger that burned even now in Richard's voice, licking along my own veins.

Briefly, it was this.

Richard Byron, who was reasonably well-to-do, lived at Deepings, in Surrey, and had acquired some reputation among those who knew, as a dealer in various kinds of antiques. "It started in a strictly amateurish sort of way," he said. "I bought things I liked, and occasionally sold again to people who saw them and wanted them; then bit by bit I came into it as a business, because I got interested. I didn't have to make a living that way, but I gradually learned more about it, and began to travel after stuff, and in time became really keen on certain aspects of the business—old silver and jewellery particularly. I'm supposed to know quite a lot about it now."

The war had put a stop to it, of course, and he had joined the Air Force—"Flying a ruddy great Lanc. over the Ruhr," said Richard. "That was where I got to know Tony."

"Tony?"

"Tony Baxter. The lad I'm supposed to have murdered."

"Oh."

"He was my navigator, and one of the nicest chaps you could ever know. The idea that he could ever have fallen for Loraine——"

"You did, yourself," I reminded him. "After all, you married her."

He shot me a look from under his brows. "Yes, I married her. David was twelve and Mary had been dead seven years, and I thought——" he broke off. "Well, hell, you've seen her, and if you don't know why I married her you ought to."

I had a sudden vivid memory of Loraine Byron's lovely face and blue eyes, of her long white throat and the full breasts outlined by the silk of her dress.

"I can guess," I said.

He sent me another look. "I met her in Paris," he said. "I opened my Paris office in the spring of last year, and I was over there several times during the year. In September I went over to attend a big sale of silver, and I took Tony with me, with some idea of showing him the ropes and persuading him to come in and work for me. Loraine was at the sale—I didn't see who with. Then I met her again soon afterwards at a party; she was there with a man I knew, Louis Meyer, the London representative of a big Paris dealer. He introduced me to Loraine. We met again, several times. I was at a horribly loose end, just then, and I——" he paused. "Anyway, I married her about a month later, and took her back to Deepings at the end of October."

His mouth twisted, and his voice took on the hard unpleasant undertone I had first heard in it.

"It didn't work," he said shortly. "Naturally. As soon as we were mar-

ried I knew I'd been a fool. In the first place, she hadn't wanted to go to
England at all: she wanted me to settle in France, in the South. But
there was Deepings—and David—and I insisted. Then of course there was
trouble. And—again of course—it just didn't work with David; she
couldn't be bothered with him, and he had no time for her. He's a courteous little devil, and he said nothing to me, but I could see he was unhappy
about it. . . . We had a highly unpleasant few weeks, and then Tony
came to stay for Christmas." His voice went flat and dead. He might have
been reading out of the police report. "He was found dead in his bed at
three o'clock on the morning of January 19th. He had been strangled.
There was a thin cord knotted tightly round his neck. It was the cord
from my window-blind, and my finger-prints were on the little acorn
gadget that you pull the blind down with."

"Of course they were," I said. "I expect you'd pulled the blind down
at some time or other, hadn't you?"

"Yes. That's the sort of thing that saved my neck in the end. They
could think what they liked, but there was an innocent reason as well as a
guilty for most of the things they found. Then ten minutes after Loraine
discovered the body——"

"Loraine found him!" I exclaimed.

"Yes," he said, with the edge back on his voice. "She went to his
room—at three o'clock in the morning. She was quite open about it,
all in the cause of justice. The police were impressed. She admitted
she'd been there before—often: it was a lovely motive for me to kill
him, handed to the police on a plate. What do you think about that?"

"I think that three o'clock on a January morning's an awfully funny
hour to be waking your lover up," I said.

He gave a hard little laugh. "You're right at that, sweet Charity. It's
a hell of a funny hour. But she did, and then when she had fainted with
the shock, and someone went to the bathroom to get some water, they
found David there; my little David, unconscious and as cold as ice.
When I got there, I thought for a minute that he was dead too."

The hard voice stopped, and he stared at the sea. But I knew he was
not seeing the white path the moon paced across the water, but a small
body huddled on a cold tiled floor.

"He couldn't remember much about it," he said at length. "When he
was fit to talk he told them that he'd woken with the tooth-ache, and
gone along to the bathroom to fill a hot-water bottle. He didn't remember the time. But as he switched on the bathroom light somebody struck
him from behind."

"He had no idea at all? He didn't hear anything—a skirt swishing,
or high heels? Nothing to tell him whether it was a man or a woman?"

He gave a wry smile. "Believe me, if there'd been the faintest scrap of evidence that could have pinned it on Loraine, I'd have pinned it," he said viciously. "Because she was in it, all right. You can't live with a woman for half a year, even the way we lived, and not know when she's lying in her teeth. She knew all about it. But she didn't hit David. It was a man. David was facing the bathroom mirror—it hangs opposite the door, and he just saw the arm raised over him, for a fraction of an instant, before it happened. It was a man's arm, in a navy sleeve."

"Not a dressing-gown?"

"No, not a dressing-gown." He grinned a little, and his hand moved till it covered mine. "You're very quick on the evidence in my defence, aren't you? Yes, that was one small thing; I'd been wearing a grey suit that day, as well. And I don't possess a navy one."

"Well, why——?"

"They didn't attach much importance to David's testimony, you see. He's only a child, he'd had a bad shock, the glimpse he'd had was too slight and might have been imagined, and besides, he might be expected to be a pretty partial witness, of course. He insisted from the very beginning that it couldn't possibly have been me—not for any reason, except that it just couldn't."

"And so you were arrested?"

"After a bit, yes. Oh, the police were very thorough and really very decent over the whole thing. It was all done by kindness. But one thing and another mounted up, and everything pointed the same way—so I was arrested."

He regarded the water sombrely.

"I'll spare you the next part. Standing your trial for murder, even when you get off, isn't a thing to go back to, even for a moment, in your mind. It's like having a filthy and contaminating disease—degrading, exhausting, leaving pock-marks on your spirit that never smooth out. Again, everybody was very decent—surprisingly decent. And though I got to hate the prosecuting Counsel more than anyone else on earth, it was a fair trial. The fact that I'm here proves that . . . oh, I've nothing against the police, even if she did lead them right up the garden path and back again. Other mugs had taken that walk before them."

"But, Richard, did *she* do it? The murder, I mean? And *was* there a man in a navy suit? Who was he?"

"I wish I knew," he said heavily, "I wish I knew. They never traced him. But I think there was a man there with her, an accomplice, whom she let in to do the job. He may have come in through the bathroom window—it was open, by the way—and have hidden behind the door when he heard David coming. It was he who knocked David out, to prevent his seeing him. Then either he or Loraine killed Tony. I myself think that he, not she, did it—or why did she have him there at all?"

"Her lover?"

"Possibly. But even if he were spending the night with her—you'll have gathered that she and I had stopped sharing a room—and even if Tony had found out, that's hardly a motive for murder. No, she let him in to do the job."

"Burglary, perhaps? And Tony——"

"Nothing was touched. And Tony had never moved from his bed. They said he was strangled as he slept."

"But why——?"

"That's it, Charity, that's the big thing. Why?" His voice exploded suddenly. "My God, *why?* Night after night after night I've spent wondering *why?* If I only knew that . . . he was one of the decentest souls God ever sent, Charity. An ordinary, decent boy that nobody on this earth would want to kill, you'd think. They must have meant to do it, planned to do it, quite deliberately, but what the motive was I do not know. That was the strongest thing against me, of course—the fact that there wasn't a shadow of motive for anyone else to do it. And when Loraine confessed to being Tony's mistress that gave me the strongest motive there is."

He was silent for a moment, his brows drawn. Then he gave his head a little shake, as if to rid it of the thoughts crowding through his brain.

"Try as I will," he said, "I can't see why Loraine should either do it herself, or connive at its being done."

"What if he'd turned her down?" I suggested. "It can take women that way, can't it?"

"*Hell hath no fury?* I suppose it could . . . but then what about the other man? Why should he help in that situation?"

"You seem very sure there *was* a man."

"Yes," he said. "David may be only a kid, but he's intelligent, and he doesn't get rattled easily. If he said there was a man's arm then there was a man's arm."

"Couldn't he have been trying to divert suspicion from you?"

"He told them the story as soon as he was fit to talk, and he had no idea what had happened, or that I'd even be remotely suspected. No, he told the truth. He thought he'd surprised a burglar."

There was a pause.

"It's a stinker, isn't it?" said Richard.

"It certainly is."

"And that's only half the story. I don't know yet why Tony was murdered, or why, apparently, Loraine should be so very anxious to see me dead."

"But how can you be sure——?" I interrupted, then broke off as, like a whispering echo, I remembered her voice repeating in the frightened dark: *he ought to be dead and done with, dead and done with, dead and done with.* . . . What was it they did to murderers? Buried them in quicklime, so that there was nothing of them left?

I shivered in the still warm air, and his hand closed sharply over mine, warm and strong and very much alive.

His voice was sombre, and he spoke with a conviction that chilled me again.

"Because," he said, "I'm next on the list. She couldn't get me hanged, but she staged another murder. And the second time, I was the victim."

CHAPTER XVI

Madam, will you talk——?
(OLD SONG)

"IT WAS after the trial," he went on. "I was allowed to go, of course, and someone handed me a note as I was leaving the court, to say that Loraine wanted to see me at Claridge's, where she had a room. I got a taxi and went to see her. She was alone, and she had some news for me. Good news. She told me, quite plainly, that she was going back to France, and that there was no need for me to institute divorce proceedings."

"No need? What did she mean?"

"She had just discovered, she said, that her previous husband, who had been missing and presumed dead since 1943, was still alive. Our marriage, therefore, was never valid."

"But—was this true?"

"She showed me her marriage certificate—naturally, I knew she had been married before—and then a letter from a Paris lawyer. The certificate, of course, was genuine; about the letter I don't know yet."

"What was his name—the husband's, I mean?"

"Jean Something-or-other, I think." He reached for a cigarette. "To tell you the truth I hardly bothered. I'd come straight from the dock, I hadn't even had a chance to wash the prison smell off my hands, I felt as if I never wanted to see her or speak to her again—and I wanted most damnably to get home and see David. He was still at Deepings, of course, and I imagined he must be half out of his mind."

I must have made some inarticulate sound.

He said: "Yes, I know. Well, I slammed the papers down and snarled that I hoped to God it was true, and that I didn't care what she did as long as she kept out of my way, and she could leave it to the lawyers because I didn't particularly want to stay and talk to her. And a few other things. It wasn't pretty, I can tell you."

"I don't blame you. I'd have wrung her neck."

"She wasn't frightened. She knew I wasn't the neck-wringing sort."

I said drily: "You don't give a bad imitation of it, at times."

He grinned a little at that, then seemed suddenly to recollect the cigarette-case in his hand. We lit cigarettes.

"Well, our loving talk finished with Loraine throwing the car keys at me, and telling me she'd left the Rolls at Redmanor station and would I *ficher le camp*—only the phrase she used was more—direct, shall I say? —than that."

I laughed. "I get it."

"You shock me. Well, I did as she suggested; I got the hell out of it, and, what with one thing and another, by the time I got down to Redmanor I was half sick with worry and reaction, and in a flaming temper into the bargain. The Rolls was there, all right, and I went off at the hell of a lick, with only one thought in my head: David."

"And there was an accident?"

"Right first guess; there was an accident. There's a place where you turn off the main road, about a mile from my house, where the road skirts a quarry. There's a sharp bend about half-way down, with the quarry on your left, and a bluff of rock to the right—the road swings right-handed round it. In general it's safe enough, because above the bluff it's open, and before you reach the bend you can see if anything's on the road below. Well, as I say, I was going the hell of a lick. I could see the chimneys of Deepings through the trees in the valley, and there was nothing on the road, so I took a run at that hill. And just half-way round that bend I met another car, on its wrong side. I was well over to the left, but there wasn't time, and he held on. . . . There was just room, only just, if I went into the verge; and he kept coming. I yanked the wheel over, something snapped with a crack like a gun, and we went clean over the edge."

"Richard!"

"Oh, they had no luck," he said grimly. "The off-side door wasn't caught—I'd been in such a hurry that I hadn't noticed—and it fell open as we went over. I fell out. The car dropped to the bottom of the quarry and went on fire, but some bushes broke my fall, and I only got concussed on a ledge."

"But—are you sure—couldn't it have been a real accident?"

"I told you I'd seen there wasn't a car on the road. He must have had it parked, waiting for me. I've had plenty of time to think about it, there in hospital, and this is what I think happened. There's a phone box a mile or so along the road, and he could have been waiting there as soon as he heard the trial was over. They must have known I'd make straight for Deepings."

"But, Richard, why bother to tell you about the marriage business, if they'd planned to kill you?"

"She had to know just when I started for Deepings, and besides, she wanted to give me the keys and make sure I'd take the car. Then, when I left her, I think she must have phoned him. He had his car parked behind the barn near the foot of the hill, and waited for me with field glasses. It was a cream-coloured Rolls coupé, and pretty unmistakable. He had only to time himself, so that he'd meet me on the bend, and he could reckon it would happen just like that, if the steering had been damaged beforehand. I tell you, it went with a crack like a gun, and the wheel just spun in my hands."

"Wasn't he taking a big risk of being hurt himself?"

"You have to take risks to get away with murder," returned Richard grimly. "But, after all, the risk wasn't so very great. He may have meant to swerve at the last minute, if I didn't try to crowd into the edge, but he could be pretty well certain that I'd pull as far to the left as I could, and of course, with the steering column damaged, it was a hundred to one I'd go over."

"Didn't the police find what had been done to the steering column?"

"No. That was Loraine's one piece of luck. The car burned right out —there was hardly a piece left recognizable, they told me."

"I suppose her accomplice had damaged the steering while the Rolls was in the station yard?"

"I imagine so. I found the car unlocked, anyway, and my own keys inside it. But that proved nothing. No, my story was more than the police could swallow, I think; after all, motiveless murders, and an invisible, elusive murderer—it was too much. They were quite right, of course, it *was* too much. I'd started by insisting I was being framed for Tony's murder—*why?* Then I'd talked of an attempt on my own life—*why?* It wouldn't wash, Charity. We're back where we were—where is the motive for these attempts?" He gave a sharp little sigh, and threw his cigarette-

stub out into the water. "The police were very patient, all things considered, but I could see their minds were beginning to run in all sorts of
curious channels, so eventually I shut up and allowed them to write it off
as accident."

"What sort of curious channels?"

"Oh . . . suicide, for instance."

"Richard!" I cried again.

"Oh, yes. Disgraced Man's Mind Unhinged by Trial . . . you know.
The papers got it, of course, and said as much as they dared. But again,
there was no proof."

"And David?"

"The last time I saw David," he said slowly, and with great bitterness, "was when they arrested me and took me away. I wouldn't let
him visit me in prison, of course. Then, when I was in hospital after the
smash, Loraine did as she'd promised. She went back to France. But
she did more, as you know. She took David with her. He never even
came to see me in the hospital before he went. . . ."

He stopped, apparently absorbed in watching the floating butt of his
cigarette discolour, split, and disintegrate into a little mess of sodden
tobacco, among the débris floating below the wall. I said nothing.

"As soon as the doctors would let me, a fortnight ago, I came over. I
traced them as far as Lyons, heading south . . . and the rest you know."

"But, Richard, I don't understand. David didn't believe all that about
suicide, did he? And he thought you were innocent of murder; you said
so. Why did he go with Loraine?"

Richard's voice tautened. "I don't know. I suppose, if she never told
him she wasn't legally my wife, he'd assume that, as his step-mother, she
had the right to look after him when I was ill. And he's only a child.
He'd do as he was told."

"But why didn't he *write?* Why did you have to 'trace' them? Why
didn't——?"

He turned to look at me, and the slanting lamplight slid over his
face, sharpening the finely drawn angles of cheek and jaw-bone, and
setting his face into a mask of great unhappiness. His eyes were full of
such misery and uncertainty that I looked away.

He said, heavily: "I don't know, Charity. I don't know. Don't you
see, that's what's such a hell for me? I've stopped giving one single
damn about Loraine or her precious confederate, or her shots at killing
me, or even poor Tony's death. I want to see David again, and get things
straight with him. I want to find out what lies they've told him to make
him go off like that without a word. Perhaps, in the end, they got him

to believe it all . . . that I was a murderer, I mean . . . and he didn't dare to wait and see me——" He broke off.

His voice, when he spoke again, was very quiet.

He said, his head bent low, watching the water:

"But you know that side of it, don't you, Charity? You said he *was* afraid of me, didn't you?"

I saw the sudden gleam and shift of his knuckles as he clenched them, and a wave of compassion went over me, so real—I mean so physical—that it left me shaking. I could not speak.

He looked at me sharply. "Well?"

"Oh, Richard," I said miserably, "I don't want to hurt you any more. It's all such a muddle, and I don't know what anything means, or what to believe at all."

His face softened a little, and he touched my hand again, a feather-light touch.

"We can't work the muddle out until we get all the facts, my dear. Tell me your end of it—tell me everything he said, what both he and Loraine have been doing and saying. Don't worry about my feelings—they should be pretty tough by now. Just tell me what you know, from the first moment you met him."

I saw, as if a brush had suddenly sketched it in across the moonlight, the slight delicate branches and paper-thin leaves of the tree Yggdrasil . . . that shook and swayed as the cat clawed up the stem, then dissolved again into moonlight. I said suddenly: "Do you know a man called Marsden?"

He frowned, thinking.

"Marsden? No, I don't think so. What's he like? Why?"

"I remembered something," I said abruptly. "I think David was perfectly right about there being a man in the house that night." I began to tell him about the conversation I had overheard up at the Rocher des Doms. "And I remember his very words," I finished. "He said: *I got you out of the mess before, didn't I? I got you out of England, didn't I, and the boy too?*"

Richard had turned sharply as I spoke, and his eyes were very intent. When I had finished he was smiling, with a kind of grim satisfaction.

"So we were right. So far, so good. It's only a very little, Charity, but it's something. I wonder just where this man Marsden could tie in with Loraine's missing husband, Jean-Something-or-other, who appeared so providentially?"

"If he did appear."

"If, as you say, he did appear." He straightened up suddenly. "We'll soon know if *that* part of the story's true: I've got someone investigating it in Paris. It's beginning to matter, rather, too."

He grinned.

"Well, who knows what else you've seen and heard? We'll have it cleared up before dawn at this rate—long before dawn, my dear, because you look tired, and no wonder. Come and get a drink, and we'll find somewhere to sit while you tell me your story."

CHAPTER XVII

Madam, will you walk and talk with me?
(OLD SONG)

"I SHALL probably get it very muddled," I said, "because of course a lot happened before I began to notice things particularly. And I doubt if I have the gift of narrative. But I'll do my best."

So I began to tell him what I could remember: David and the dog, Mrs. Palmer and her account of the Byron trial, the trip to Nîmes, and David's reactions to his father's presence. The drive home, and David's half-confidence and strange childish insistence that I should tell Loraine Byron nothing at all. The snatch of conversation heard in Loraine's bedroom that night. And everywhere, the presence of the man Marsden —lighting Loraine's cigarette, loitering in the dark at the foot of the Rocher des Doms, driving to Nîmes in the bus, going up to the gardens with David next morning. . . .

Richard Byron listened in silence, tracing little patterns in spilt wine on the table-top, his head bent, his brows frowning.

"So you see," I said finally, "why I behaved in the silly way I did. I didn't even tumble to the fact that David hated her when he insisted that his name wasn't the same as hers. I just thought I had to keep you away from him. I—I rather fell for David," I finished lamely.

He shot me a look that brought the blood to my cheeks, then returned to his drawing on the table-top.

"Yes, David," he said slowly. "We always come back to David. And the old questions: why he went away like that without a word; what he believes, now, about that horrible night; why he's afraid to meet me.

. . . Why, d'you know, I even thought they might have done away with him, too, until I got the anonymous letter from Paris."

"Anonymous letter?"

"I got dozens," said Richard briefly. "The usual filth that always starts flowing when a murder trial opens the sewer. This one was posted in Paris, and whoever wrote it apparently knew me, and knew David, and had seen him there. It included, of course, a lot of abuse about—oh, well, that doesn't matter, does it?"

"Richard, how beastly!"

"But it gave a clue, you see. My housekeeper had told me that David went off with Loraine, and Loraine had told me she was going to France. This gave me a start. So I raised heaven and earth and the R.A.C. and shipped the car across on the next boat. And at my *appartement* in Paris —I have a room over my office—there was another letter waiting."

"But who on earth——?"

"Loraine," he said, grimly. "Dear Loraine. This time it was signed, and it was written, not typed, but there was something about the style that made it just a continuation of the first one."

"Was it still about David?"

"It was. She and I, it said, must have a long talk, some time, about his future. But, as David didn't want to see me, and she herself didn't feel like facing me yet, she was taking him away from Paris, and would get in touch with me later. That wasn't all, but that was the gist of it."

"What did you do?"

"The letter was postmarked Lyons, so of course I went down there. I hunted about for a couple of days, café-haunting, and asking questions, until I picked up what looked like a clue. Loraine's pretty conspicuous, as you know, and the barman at one of the hotels remembered seeing her, and remembered too, that she'd spoken of going south. I won't bore you with the rest of it, but I traced them fairly easily as far as Bollène, and then I went wrong. They had been seen on the road to Pont St. Esprit, and that, as you know, is across the Rhône from Bollène, and on the way to Nîmes. Well, I followed my nose, and landed in Nîmes on a chance. It was a wrong chance, as it happened, but it turned out to be near enough."

I said: "No wonder you wanted to kill me when you got so near to David, and I got in the way."

He said, remorsefully: "I thought you must be in with them. You see, I didn't believe for a moment that David himself didn't want to see me. I thought she—they—must be keeping him under some sort of duress so that he couldn't write. I thought you were part of it, and I wanted to kill you." He smiled. "Poor little Charity, did I scare hell out of you?"

"You did. Is that why you tried to make me think you were a murderer?"

"Of course. I didn't know how much they'd told you of the truth, and I wanted to frighten you. And I did. I made you faint. I want whipping for that."

"It's done with," I said. "I was really scared because I thought you were——" I stopped abruptly.

"You thought I was what?"

"Nothing."

"Come on. All the facts. You promised."

"I thought you were mad," I said, not looking at him.

He did not speak, but I saw his hand arrested in the middle of drawing a circle on the table.

"I only knew what Mrs. Palmer had told me," I said quickly. "And then when you—you were so violent, and David was so frightened, I thought you must be mad. I thought you'd have to be mad to have hit David that night. . . . After I'd met you in Nîmes," I finished miserably, "I thought you'd done it, you see."

There was a little pause.

"Charity."

"Oh, Richard——"

"Charity, tell me something."

"What?" I asked. Here it comes, I thought, here it comes.

"Did David say anything that led you to believe that I was mad?"

"I—I don't know," I floundered.

"You're lying, Charity. You ought to know by now that you can't lie to me. Did David tell you I was mad?"

"Yes," I said.

When I looked at him at last, he was smiling.

"You silly little owl," he said. "Don't worry so. It makes it reasonably simple."

"Simple?" I echoed stupidly. "But I thought you'd——"

"I mean, it's something definite," he said. "Something we can fight. He did say it himself?"

"Yes."

"In so many words?"

"Yes."

"I see. Well, that means simply this: they've persuaded him to believe that it was I who bashed him on the head and/or tried to commit suicide with the Rolls. That's all that could be construed as mad, unless they threw in the actual murder for good measure. And, since I'm morally certain that they couldn't get him to believe either that I killed Tony or attacked David himself, then it's probably the attempted suicide."

"So?"

"Well, as I see it, we're now in a fairly strong position to fight this belief. He trusts you, doesn't he?"

"I think so. Yes, I'm sure he does, after the way I helped him at Nîmes —to get away from you."

"Don't look so rueful. You'll have to go back and talk to him, convince him, somehow, that I'm as sane as you are, and get him to meet me somewhere and talk to me. Then we'll get this thing straight, and have done with it once and for all."

"You mean, take him straight away?"

"Of course. D'you think I'd let him go back to her? She and her lover —husband, what you like—can go their way, and David and I will go ours. . . ." His glance met mine. "And yours."

"It sounds easy when you put it like that," I said. "But, Richard, if they *are* determined somehow to kill you—well, will Deepings be any safer now than it was before?"

He put a hand to his head, in a gesture at once indescribably weary and very youthful.

"It's the same old answer, Charity," he said. "I don't know. My own home . . . and for some strange reason it's no longer safe for me or for my son . . . *for some strange reason:* that's the centre of the matter. This whole crazy story—it's like a tale told by an idiot, held together by some lunatic logic that we can't follow till we've delved back through his mad past and found——"

"Freud in the woodshed?"

He grinned a little at that, and finished his drink at a gulp. "If you put it that way, yes."

By now the café was almost empty, and the steady flow of people on the broad pavement had dwindled perceptibly. A few Negro sailors went by, arm in arm with brightly dressed girls. An Arab boy, slim and golden-brown, who might have sat to Polyclites as Hylas, slipped between the tables, begging. People flung him lumps of sugar, which he caught with quick, greedy, graceful fingers, while his monotonous degraded voice mumbled for more.

"Sometimes lately I've thought I really would go mad," said Richard suddenly. "The murder and the trial, then the car-smash and the weeks in hospital, and the appalling headaches I still get. And David. A sudden and complete disruption of my whole life, and David's life, out of the blue. And it's the basic unreason of the business that's getting me down; certain facts are there, but they can't *be* facts; there's no sane pattern to which they fit. That's what I meant before, Charity, that's what made me behave like a devil; I find my values slipping till my brain —how does it go?—*suffers then the nature of an insurrection.* Nothing makes sense; things have turned upside down."

"And nothing is," I quoted softly, *"but what is not."*

He said quickly, half eagerly: "Yes, that's it. That's what *Macbeth's* about, isn't it? Nothing keeping to the rules any more?"

I said: "But you forget. Macbeth broke the rules first and upset the balance. There was a logic in it, after all; and Richard, there still is. There must be an explanation, a reason, for your idiot's tale, only we just haven't hunted deep enough in the woodshed."

He did not speak, but his eyes lifted to mine for a moment, and something in them made me speak urgently.

"Richard. I *know* I'm right. Don't you remember, only an hour ago, on the quay, when you said the same thing—about me—and you said that the rules *did* hold good, no matter what the evidence to the contrary seemed to be? It's *true,* my dear. You'll find there *is* a pattern that'll fit the facts. There always is."

"But if it's an idiot's tale—if you're dealing with the borderland of sanity——"

"You're not," I said flatly. "And even if you were . . . why, in Looking-Glass Land itself they kept to the rules of chess. The rules don't break themselves, Richard."

"In fact——"

"In fact," I repeated, "there is no such thing as 'basic unreason'."

His eyes were on me, and they were suddenly very bright. He said, softly: *"Charity never faileth.* Yes, you're right. You're right. How very right you are. . . ." He laughed then, and straightened in his chair. "Forgive me, my darling. I've been living so long on the edge of nothing that it's addled my wits. Let's have some coffee, shall we? What'll you take with it this time?"

"The same, please."

"Garçon. Deux cafés-cassis. No"— the vigour was back in his voice as he spoke to me—"nothing really matters except David, and that part of it'll soon be straightened out. Once I've seen him. . . . How tired are you, Charity?"

The abrupt turn startled me. "Tired? I don't feel tired now."

"Sure?"

"Quite."

He smiled his sudden, devastatingly attractive smile. "Then, on your quite unwomanly assumption that there's a logic in everything, we'll begin again at the beginning, rake over the ashes till we discover what makes them tick, probe every avenue to the bone——"

"I get you," I said. "Leave no hole and corner unturned. All right. I'm on."

CHAPTER XVIII

The mordrynge in the bedde . . .
(CHAUCER)

HALF AN HOUR and two coffees later, our minds were almost as mixed as our metaphors had been. We had taken out every fact we knew, aired it, shaken it, and set it in its place, and, while certain things had become clearer, the centre of the mystery remained dark.

"The motive," said Richard for the twentieth time. "Tony murdered, and two attempts to murder me—and no motive."

"Murder needs a pretty strong motive," I said stoutly. "There's one somewhere, if we knew where to look. What do they say are the recognized motives—gain, passion and fear? It's not murder for money, or for love, apparently, but the third motive's the strongest of the lot."

"Fear? But who's so afraid of me that they've got to kill me?"

"Obviously someone is, because they've tried. Is that logic, Richard?"

He smiled, though the smile was a little strained. "All right. Go on from there. You're not going to tell me that Loraine's sufficiently afraid of me to want to murder me?"

"No. I thought we'd decided she was working for somebody else."

"Our old friend X; the man in the car. Yes?"

"X tries to kill you," I said, "not for gain, not for jealousy, but because of something you can do to him. You, alive, constitute a threat to him, to his liberty—or livelihood—or life."

The glint of amusement in his eyes was genuine enough. "In fact, we've arrived at another hoary old friend; there's something I know that I don't know I know?"

"Well, it happens," I said stubbornly. "Don't try to muddle me. There's something else that struck me, too, about your chase after Loraine and David."

He shot me a quick look. "Yes?"

"It was too easy, Richard. If they had really wanted to hide——"

He gave a little nod, as if of satisfaction. "Exactly. That's one of the things that puzzled me. It was too easy by half. She told me she was going to France, she sent me the letters, clearly postmarked as she knew they must be . . . she left a trail, in fact, up to a point."

"You see what it means?" I said. "She—or X—wanted you over here. You told me she tried to get you to come here after you were married. She still wanted that. That's why she took David in the first place. You'd never have followed Loraine herself, would you? If she'd written to ask you to meet her again you'd have left it to a lawyer——"

"I certainly should," he remarked grimly.

"So, to make sure of you, she took David to act as bait, and headed you neatly to the South of France."

"Towards X, I suppose? You're implying, are you, that, having failed to kill me in England, X is getting ready to have another shot over here? Laying a trap?"

"Granted they brought you over here deliberately," I said uneasily, "and it looks as if they did, then I don't see why else they should have done it."

"All right, we'll grant that. They lead me to the South of France, but lose me at Pont St. Esprit, either by accident or design."

"Which do you think it was?"

He said slowly: "I rather think it was an accident. The wrong trail that I followed to Nîmes was genuine enough; another couple had been seen setting out for Nîmes, a couple that might have been Loraine and David from the description I got. I must have gone tearing off after them before Loraine's clue, whatever it was, had a chance to reach me." He laughed shortly. "So there they were, marking time in Avignon, while I lost myself chasing red herrings!"

"No wonder she began to lose her nerve," I said. "She sounded really frightened that night at the Rocher des Doms."

"And no wonder they were quite pleased to let you take David about," returned Richard. "With me loose in the vicinity, looking for him, there was quite a chance I'd see him, and pick up the trail again."

I objected to this. "What was to stop you talking to David, putting things straight with him, and just taking him away?"

"Mr. X," said Richard simply.

I looked at him, startled. He nodded. "Loraine, who had lost her nerve, was better out of the way in Avignon. But where David went, you may be sure Mr. X went too."

I drew a long breath. "On the Tarascon bus," I said.

Richard nodded again, and his eyes gleamed. "D'you know, I believe we're getting somewhere! If we're right, it must have been a bitter moment for Mr. X when you so neatly scooped David out of my reach again, sweet Charity—and incidentally led me right away from X and all his works! It seems I may owe you quite a lot."

"But what could he possibly hope to do in Nîmes?" I protested.

He shrugged. He sounded almost indifferent. "God knows. It's a wild half-deserted country. Anything could happen. A body could lie in that scrub for months, and the kites would——"

"Don't!"

"Well, there it is. It's a good part of the world for a quiet murder; and that, no doubt, is why I'm being decoyed here." He smiled without mirth. "I wonder where the trap was to be sprung originally? Avignon? It seems unlikely."

"Loraine said they were going south in a day or so," I said quickly. "Nice and Monte Carlo."

"Did she indeed? If that was true, it could mean anything . . . there's some lovely lonely country down here, with nice dangerous cliffs——"

"And a nice dangerous city," I put in.

He lifted an eyebrow. "Marseilles? Well? Why not? X fails twice in law-abiding Surrey, so he——"

"Gets you on to his own ground," said I.

"You're jumping at this thing, aren't you?" said Richard, amused. "So Mr. X lives in Marseilles now?"

"He may call himself Marsden," I said doggedly, "and read T. S. Eliot—which, incidentally, I saw him doing upside down—but I'll bet he's French, and I'll bet he's Loraine's first husband Jean Something-or-other, and I'll bet he has some definite reason for wanting you down in this part of the country!"

The amusement in his eyes deepened. "So it's all solved, is it? If only I could remember what I know that I don't know I know!"

"Well, try, Richard!" I said, hopelessly. "No, don't laugh at me. I thought this was serious! Think!"

"My dear child, certainly. But what about?"

I hesitated. "Tony's murder. Murder's the only thing serious enough to make X go to such lengths, isn't it? I mean—if you knew something that would hang him?"

But Richard shook his head. "That horse won't run, Charity dear. There's nothing there, I'm certain of it. The police went into everything, and I—God knows I've had long enough to turn it all over in my mind, every grain, every particle, every atom of fact in my possession. You get a lot of time to think in prison, you know."

"Yes, I suppose so. I'm sorry I reminded you."

"Don't worry; it doesn't matter nearly so much as it did half an hour ago." He gave me a brief smile. "But we're forgetting one thing, you know. Tony was murdered too, and also without apparent motive. What if X wants, not me for anything connected with Tony's murder, but *both Tony and me* for something we were in together?"

"The antique trade?" I said hopelessly. "Here we go round the prickly pear."

He shrugged again, and reached for his cigarette-case. "Well, there it is. That's all the connection Tony and I ever had, except the War."

"Had you flown together for long?"

"Not really. It was fairly near the start of my third tour that I pranged. Tony had been with me since half-way through the second."

"That, and your meeting after the War—that was absolutely all?"

"Absolutely."

"No shady dealings in Paris?"

"Not more than usual."

"No witnessing a grisly crime in Montmartre?"

"No."

"But you must have done," I insisted. "Think again. You and Tony must at least have witnessed a murder."

He grinned. "No."

"Not even a very small one?"

"Not even a——" He checked suddenly in the act of striking a match, and his voice changed. "How very odd!"

"What?" My voice must have sounded excited, because he shook his head quickly and struck the match.

"It's nothing; nothing to do with this affair. But, oddly enough, Tony and I did once see murder done." He held a match to my cigarette, and smiled at my expression. "No, really, it's nothing to do with this. It was during the War; part of the general frightfulness."

"You don't mean the bombing?"

"Lord, no. I wasn't young enough to class that as murder; that was just a job. No, this was cold-blooded murder, rather particularly beastly."

"Tell me about it. It might, after all, have something to do——"

"I very much doubt it. And it's not a nice story."

"Never mind that. Tell me, just the same."

"Very well. It was when Tony and I were being taken up to Frankfurt for interrogation after the crash—we were the only two commissioned in the air-crew—and there'd been some bomb-damage on the main line, so we were hitched on to a little goods train that went by another route, up the Lahn valley. We had to stop in a siding to let an express go past. It was a filthy grey winter's afternoon, with snow everywhere, and a sky like a dirty dish-cover clamped down over it. God, it was cold. . . ."

He was staring at the cigarette between his fingers, talking more to himself than me. I think, indeed, that he had forgotten me completely, and was back in that desolate little siding beside the Lahn.

". . . There was another train waiting, too—a lot of boarded-up trucks, with some chalk-marks scrawled across them. We didn't tumble to it until we saw a little bunch of S.S. guards standing about, and then we realized what was going on. It was a train-load of Jews going East to the slaughter-houses."

He drew on his cigarette, and expelled the smoke almost fiercely. "For a long time, nothing happened, and then, everything seemed to happen at once. We heard the express whistle a short way off. Then there was a yell, a shot, a whole babel of shouts, and the S.S. guards seemed to be running in all directions. All, that is, but the officer; he never even turned his head. I heard two more shots, and a man screaming. Then the screaming stopped, as if he'd bitten his tongue, and the guards were dragging him out from between the trucks of the other train. I suppose he'd made a break for it, poor little bastard. Just a little chap he was, a little thin scarecrow of a man, bleeding a bit, and scared silly. He was crying when they dragged him up to the officer, and they hit him in the face to stop him." He shifted in his chair. "It was all so quick—far quicker than I've been able to describe it: There were we, hardly grasping what was going on, stuck with our guard behind the carriage-windows, and outside—that, all over as quickly as a curse. There wasn't a sound but the screech of the express, and the little chap crying. And the officer hadn't even bothered to turn round."

"What happened?" I was feeling sick, but I had to know.

"Oh, one of them spoke, and he turned and looked at the little man, and smiled. Quite a pleasant smile. Then he just moved a hand, idly enough, and said something. We couldn't hear what it was, because the express was coming up, roaring between the sheds, but the little Jew screamed again, and began to struggle."

"Oh God," I said.

"They threw him down across the line," said Richard. "He seemed to lie there for ever, like a little black broken golliwog in the snow, then that damned great express engine burst out from behind the sheds and went by like a shrieking guillotine. I—I don't know what we were doing. Our carriage was locked, of course, but I remember battering at the door and cursing like a fool and our guard trying to stop me, because he knew the officer and was afraid of him—and of course we weren't supposed to have been there at all."

"Did the officer see you?"

"Yes. After the express was gone he heard the racket we were making, and he turned and saw us. We were hauled up in front of him then and there, and I think we'd have been shot out of hand if we hadn't been on our way to being interrogated by General von Lindt, who was a bit more important even than Herr Oberfürer Kramer."

"That was the officer's name?"

"Yes. Max Kramer. A great big blond handsome brute with eyes like slate. He stood there, staring at Tony and me, and I think it was the worst couple of minutes I ever had in my life. He wanted to shoot us—my God, how he wanted it! His mouth went wet, and his gun-hand was shaking a little." He shook his head sharply, as if to dodge a memory. "I can see it at this moment—that gun pointing at us like a wicked little eye, and that hideous hand curled round the butt; there was an ugly scar running right down the forefinger, and the nail was twisted and deformed. I remember how the scar showed white, and the whole thing, hand and gun, shook with a kind of lust. . . ."

I broke across it. "But he had to let you go."

"Oh yes. We went. I never saw him again. Our train moved off straight away, and we ended up, conventionally enough, in Oflag XIV. But Charity——"

"What is it?" The shadow was deep in his eyes. I wanted to tell him to forget it all, to stop talking about it, but I knew that the time had not yet come when he would be able to forget. "What is it?" I said.

"The little Jew. I recognized him."

I stared back in a kind of horror. "You mean, you *knew* him?"

"Oh no, not like that. I'd met him once, that's all, in a Bond Street gallery. He was a painter—a good painter, too. His name was Emmanuel Bernstein."

"I see. Yes, that does make it worse."

Richard's mouth twisted as he stabbed out his cigarette in the ashtray. "One of the best things he'd done," he said, "was called *Landscape under Snow.*"

CHAPTER XIX

I say, there is no darkness but ignorance; in which thou art more puzzled than the Egyptians in their fog.
(SHAKESPEARE)

IT WAS getting late. It seemed absurd that it was only a few hours since I had stepped on to the Marseilles quay straight into Richard Byron's arms. Then he had been my enemy, my nightmare, and now . . .

"I seem to have been sitting talking to you over café tables all my life," I said inconsequentially.

He looked up at that, and seemed all at once to come out of his dream. He smiled, "And I've been talking too much," he said. "I shouldn't have told you that beastly story. It's over and done with, and, as you see, it has nothing to do with this affair."

"It certainly doesn't seem to," I agreed. "And there's one thing certain, that Mr. X is not Kramer—at least Marsden isn't Kramer. He was never a big blond in his life."

"So that's that." Richard looked at his watch. "Time for bed. More coffee?"

"I couldn't drink another drop."

"I'm with you there. Now we're going to decide what's the next thing to do, and then I shall see you back to your hotel."

His plan was very simple. I was to return next day to Avignon, tell Louise what had happened, and get David to go sightseeing with me once more. I was to deliver him into his father's hands, and then Louise and I were to remove ourselves quietly from Avignon, to a hotel Richard knew in Aix. Here we were to lie low for a day or so. Richard would take David to some friends of his, the Dexters, who were spending the summer at Hyères, further along the coast, and then would get in touch with me again.

"Now that I'm forewarned to some extent," he said, "I should be able to deal with Mr. X, or whoever is following David about, providing he's on the job alone. And then, when I've put things straight with David, and got him tucked safely away with Bill Dexter, I'll be able to work out what to do. With David still in the open, my hands are tied."

"It's all nice and clear and simple when you put it like that," I said, "if only it works. Where shall I take David sightseeing to meet you?"

He gave me a grin of pure malice. "What about the Cathedral at Tarascon?"

"Beast!" I said, with feeling. "I wish I was a good liar. Don't remind me of it!"

"Well, what about Arles—the arena, above the main gate? I'll be there by ten-thirty, and I'll wait all day if necessary. Of course, if you could lose Mr. X on the way . . . but don't take any risks. If anything should go wrong, you can ring up the *Légionnaire* at Nîmes, and leave a message—for Richard Coleridge, remember. Right?"

"Right."

We stood up, and he paid the waiter. Then we moved out into the bustling throng of the Canebière. There was still, for me, something dreamlike in the teeming, sparkling, roaring streets of Marseilles. The crowd flowed round us, jostling and chattering, the buses clanged past, the cafés were hives of laughter and music, but for me, still, the only real thing in all that glittering pageant was the feel of Richard's hand on my arm.

"This way," he said, and we were suddenly out of the throng and walking up a dark, half-empty street. "Where did you leave your car?"

I fished in my bag for the little paste-board slip, and read it aloud: "*Bergère Frères, 69 Rue des Pêcheurs.* But I haven't the foggiest idea where it is, I'm afraid."

"I know it. I'll call at your hotel in the morning, say eight-thirty; we'll have breakfast somewhere, and I'll take you to get your car. Then we'll go in procession again up the road to Avignon." He grinned. "And don't try running away again, my girl."

"I won't."

"You nearly foxed me at Cavaillon, you know. Who on earth taught you to drive, by the way? You're pretty good."

"Johnny."

"Oh, of course. It would be."

"It was his hobby," I said. "It had been his job, before he joined the R.A.F. He'd raced cars practically ever since he'd had a license. He was wonderfully good."

"He certainly taught you a thing or two."

"Did you pay my bill at Les Baux?" I asked suddenly. "Because I ought to ring up——"

"I had to," said he, with wry amusement. "I'd asked for it, after all, hadn't I, after spending the night in your room? I managed to avert arrest by some story about your being ill recently, and a bit unstable——"

"Dash it——!"

"Don't worry, you're getting better rapidly, but you're still prone to sudden impulses: it was quite a good story, anyway, and she believed it, mainly because it was less trouble to believe it than otherwise, and I was paying anyway. The French are realists; so don't you bother about Les Baux."

"I'll never dare go back again."

"One of the things that really began to puzzle me about you," said Richard, "was why the devil you should go up there at all; and why you should go armed with a book of medieval French poetry in any case. I somehow couldn't see an accomplice of Loraine's sitting alone up there reading the *chansons de toile*. And there you were, admiring the dawn like any tourist. . . . You're a woman of parts, aren't you, Charity? Did Johnny teach you to read Middle French as well?"

"I taught French before I was married," I said, "and there are translations in the book anyway."

"Well, I thought——" Then his voice broke off, and I heard his breath drawn sharply between his teeth. His hand gripped my arm, and I felt him stiffen. He stopped.

"What on earth——?" I said startled.

There was no one to be seen. We were half-way down a narrow, badly lit street, which curled its seedy way to join two wider thoroughfares. It was a street of tallish, faintly furtive-looking houses, which had seen better days, and now masqueraded as offices, garages, warehouses, and even shops. It was at one of the latter that Richard was staring now. I followed his gaze. The shop-window we had been passing was the only lighted one in the street, but apart from that I could, at first, see nothing remarkable about it. It was long and low, and was crammed with an artful and rather attractive confusion of chairs and tables, faldstools, jugs, and ivory chessmen.

I read the legend above the window: *"Werfel et Cie, Paris et Marseille, Objets d'art.* . . . Antique dealers!" I said reproachfully. "Richard, you shop-hound——"

And then I saw it, too.

It was lying, beautifully placed on the sweep of a velvet drape, glittering in the light of the single lamp. It was a silver bracelet, where the arms of a noble house were wrought about with lilies and griffins and the wings of birds. And I had seen it before.

Richard's arm had relaxed under mine, and he gave a little sigh. "How odd to see it there!" he remarked. "I gave that bracelet to Loraine before we were married. She must have sold it in Paris, and it's found its way here. It startled me to see it, I don't know why." He turned away. "Let it lie," he said.

I said: "If she sold it, then she sold it to-day in Marseilles."

He swung round at that. "What d'you mean?"

"I mean I've seen it before, too—or one very like it."

"It's unique," he said shortly. "Fifteenth-century Italian. It was made for Lucrezia di Valozzi, and there isn't another like it."

"Then Loraine was wearing it yesterday morning," I said.

There was a pause. I was angry to find myself beginning to shake. Richard's hand, hard and excited, gripped my arm. His voice was apprehensive, but I knew the fear in it was not for himself. "David," he said. "We've got to find out what's happened to David. This means Loraine's in Marseilles already."

"The trap," I said shakily. "The trap . . ."

"Trap be damned," said Richard curtly. "They'd take a shorter chance to catch me than this. They've none of them seen me since Nîmes, I'll be bound, and Marsden wasn't on the road to-day. Now listen——" He had drawn me back from the lighted window, and his voice was low and urgent: "I'm going in to see who hocked that bracelet, and when. Your hotel is in the street at the end of this one, the Rue Mirabell; turn to the right, and it's about fifty yards along. Go straight there, and telephone your friend Louise at the Tistet-Védène. Find out from her when Loraine left, if Marsden's with her, and David—anything she can tell you. You know what to ask. Then come back here. Got any change?"

"Plenty. But, Richard, I don't want——"

He loomed over me in the darkness. His face was all at once grim, remote, frightening, the face of my enemy. His voice, too; it was hard, and the edge was back on it.

"You'll do as I tell you," he said, and pulled me towards him and kissed me hard upon the mouth.

Then I was half walking, half running up the dark street, and, as I went, I heard the shop-door open and shut behind him.

.   .   .   .

Louise's voice, across ninety-five kilometres of crackling French telephone-wire, sounded surprisingly clear, and blessedly unruffled.

"Why, Charity! I'd been wondering if you meant to come back to-day. How's the ghastly village with the ghosts?"

"Not too bad," I said. "Louise, can anyone hear you?"

"Only the concierge, and he's as deaf as a post," said Louise very sensibly.

"Well, listen: I'm speaking from Marseilles——"

"From *where?*"

"Don't repeat it aloud, for goodness' sake; Marseilles. Listen, Louise, I haven't time to explain now, but I just want you to answer me a few questions; it's terribly important. I'm in a bit of a jam, and——"

Louise's calm voice spoke in my ear. "Is David with you?"

So it was true. She had taken David away. The damned woman had taken David away.

". . . Charity? Are you there?"

"Yes."

"Are you all right? You sound a bit odd."

"I'm all right. Are you trying to tell me that the Bristols have left the hotel?"

"Yes indeed. Such a flap," said Louise placidly, "as you ever saw. Mrs. Bristol screaming and throwing hysterics and swearing you'd abducted him, and Mr. Palmer and the Germans and that handsome Paul Véry out searching——"

"Louise! Do you mean that David's *run away?*"

"This morning. He left a polite note for his mamma, and moved out, complete with dog. They found out at lunchtime. So he's *not* with you?"

"Of course he's not!"

"Well, I just wondered," said Louise reasonably. "You've been so thick with him, and then you suddenly announced that you wanted to go to Les Boos, or whatever it is, which seemed an odd thing to do. However, I'm glad you're not a kidnapper."

I was thinking furiously. "Louise, I suppose it's all genuine? I mean, he really *has* run away?"

"My Lord, yes! There was nothing phoney about the way Mrs. B. went for me to-day and demanded to know where you'd gone. She was as white as a sheet, and——"

"Did you tell her?"

"No," returned Louise calmly. "I didn't imagine you'd kidnap anyone without due cause, and I don't like the woman anyway. What's the matter?"

"Nothing," I said. "Nothing at all. Louise, you are the most wonderful woman in the world."

"Well, it wasn't anything to laugh about. In fact, the hotel was so awful that I just went away for the rest of the day. Naturally."

Naturally. "Go on. Tell me what's happened. Is Mrs. Bristol still there?"

"No. Apparently she champed around all day while the various men hunted about in cars and things, and then she left just before dinner."

"Alone?"

"As far as I know. I didn't get in till after dinner. I must say I was glad to find everyone gone."

"Everyone?" I asked sharply. "Has Mr. Marsden gone too?"

"Yes. He left this morning. And the Germans——"

"Before David disappeared or after?" My hand was sticky on the receiver."

"Nobody knows. He checked out at about ten, but of course no one saw David go."

"I—see." I leaned against the wall of the telephone booth, with my free hand pressed to my brow, trying to sort it out. David had vanished. And Marsden too. That didn't look so good. But then, I thought confusedly, Marsden couldn't have gone *with* David, or Loraine Bristol wouldn't be so upset that she had gone to the lengths of accusing me of kidnapping.

"Was there any suggestion of going to the police?" I asked.

"Well, there was, of course," said Louise. "Madame wanted to, but Mrs. Bristol wouldn't hear of it. She quietened down after a bit, and said she'd been hysterical with shock—which was true—and she apologized for what she'd said about you. Then, apparently, she said she thought she knew where he might have gone, and that no one was to worry further about a boy's prank, and she herself would go to find him. So she packed up, according to Mrs. Palmer, and left on the seven o'clock train for Marseilles. If I were you, I'd come straight back to Avignon, Charity, my dear."

"I shall, very soon. Has anyone else left the hotel?"

"I wouldn't know. I wasn't in to dinner, and the Palmers were the only people in the court when I got back. I can't say I was sorry; it's been a trying day, on the whole. I say, Charity?"

"Yes?"

"Do you know anything about this business?"

"A little," I acknowledged, "but I didn't know David had bolted; and I don't know where he is. I wish I did. Had he any money, d'you know?"

"That's just it," said Louise's tranquil, faraway little voice. "He hadn't. That's why he took Mrs. B.'s bracelet. He pinched that *and* his passport. He explained in the note that he needed the money and he'd send her the pawn-ticket."

"I—see," I said again. My heart had begun to jolt, painfully. Two facts: David was in Marseilles, and Loraine was on her way. And Mr. X. . . .

"Louise, I must go. One more thing—did David say anything else in the note?"

"No. I saw it. She was brandishing it all over the place. It just said he was going, he was taking the bracelet because she'd never liked it anyway, and good-bye. Charity, tell me——"

"Dear Louise," I said rapidly, "be the utmost angel that you always are and forgive me, but I can't explain now. Don't ask me about it; I've got to go. I'll ring up later on. Angel. Good-bye."

The voice in the telephone rose the barest fraction of a tone. "I wasn't going to ask you about it, whatever it is. But please just tell me where you're staying. "If," finished Louise on the faintest note of interrogation, "that's not a secret too?"

"No. The Belle Auberge, Rue Mirabell. Got it?"

"Yes, thank you. Good-bye."

And she rang off.

CHAPTER XX

By the pricking of my thumbs,
Something wicked . . .
(SHAKESPEARE)

WHEN I came out of the telephone booth I found, in spite of the warmth of the night, that I was shivering. I hesitated, wondering if I dared spare the time to fetch my coat. I looked at my watch. The call had taken less than ten minutes. My room was on the second floor, and the lift was standing empty; it was the work of three more minutes to go to my room, pick up my coat, and reach the lobby again. I said a polite and, I hope, normal, good night to the concierge, and ran out into the Rue Mirabell, hugging the comfort of my coat close round me as I turned the corner and plunged once more into the dimness of the narrow street. Round the next bend in the road, past the shuttered Boucherie Chevaline, past the double warehouse doors and the heap of sand and stone where the pavement was being repaired, and there, across the street, was the long low window of the antique shop, with the bracelet on its velvet drape under the lamp. My steps faltered, slowed, and stopped. I stood in the shadows, staring across the road, while the night seemed suddenly colder.

The bracelet was still there. I could see it, pale against the velvet. But the lamp was out, and the shop had the still, deserted look of emptiness. Richard was nowhere to be seen.

I don't know how long I stood there, stupidly staring at the shop, gazing up the street and down the street, alternately, as if somehow I could conjure his presence out of empty air. I even started back the way I had come, as if I could have passed him unseen on my way from the hotel, but I told myself sharply not to be a fool, and went back to my post in the shadows. Firmly I thrust back the stupid, formless fear that was fumbling at me with chilly fingers. I was over-excited, I told myself; I had had an exhausting day, and, before that, a shocking night. There was no reason to suppose that anything untoward had happened at all. I must simply wait. It was only fifteen minutes since I had left him, and after all—with a lovely wave of relief the simple explanation burst over me—after all, Richard had probably gone through to the back of the shop, into the proprietor's office. I bent forward, peering, and then smiled to myself. There was, indeed, a line of light on the floor at the rear of the shop, that seemed to come from under a door.

I hesitated for a moment. Richard had told me to come back here. Should I wait where I was till he came out, or go across into the shop myself? I stood in the shadows, undecided.

Streets away, the traffic's roar sounded like the surging of a distant sea. Twenty yards off, on business or pleasure bent, a scrawny cat slunk purposefully across the pavement. Somewhere near at hand an engine coughed, and a car moved away with a roar and a shocking gear-change. I realized that I was shivering again, whether from apprehension, or nerves, or cold, I did not know. But I was not, I decided, going to stand in the street any longer.

Sometimes, even now, I dream of that moment, of what would have happened if I had walked across the road, and of what it might have meant. And sometimes, in my dream, I do actually walk out of the shadows, over the road, into the shop . . . then, if I am lucky, I wake up screaming. . . .

I was actually beginning to move forward when the blare of a car's horn, as it swung into the little street, startled me, and made me take an instinctive backward step. The oncoming car was a taxi, and it shot down the narrow road, skidding to a stop beside me. Almost before it had stopped the far door opened, and a woman got out. She thrust money into the driver's hand, and hurried across the pavement into the antique shop. The taxi jerked forward and roared away. I heard the shop door slam behind her, and the tap-tap-tap of her heels across the shop. I saw the door at the rear of the shop open, and she stood for a second, as brightly lit as if she had been on the cinema screen. It was Loraine.

I no longer had any desire to move out of the shelter of my doorway. Thankful for my dark coat, I crouched back, my mind racing, wondering how Loraine had traced David so quickly, wondering if Richard was still in the office, and, if so, what sort of a scene was taking place in there at this moment.

I was to know soon enough. The office door opened again, and swung wide. There were three people in the room. I saw Loraine quite clearly; she was standing gesturing furiously with a cigarette, talking to a man who sat in an arm-chair with his back to the door. I could see his arm in a short blue shirt-sleeve, and one navy-blue trouser-leg. It was certainly not Richard. There was another man, whom I took to be the owner of the shop; he it was who had opened the door, and now he paused for a moment to fling a remark at Loraine before he moved out of the lighted office towards me. He was big and broad, and, though his hair was grey, he did not walk like an elderly man. He closed the office door behind him, and came forward to the shop-front.

Really frightened now, I pressed myself back, closer into the shadows. But he did not come out into the street; he was only locking up. I heard the sharp *click* of the door-lock, and then he moved to the window and reached for the blind to pull it down. It came slowly and quietly, hiding his head, his chest, his body, until the whole shop-window was a blank, but for the big white hand that gripped the edge of the blind. In that uncertain light the hand, disembodied, looked like some monstrous white sea-beast, a squid or an octopus, floating in the nebulous murk behind the glass. A monstrous, deformed creature of the dark . . . *deformed*.

I pressed the back of one shaking hand to my mouth, as I leaned against the wall, cold and sick. Even at that distance, and in that light, it showed quite clearly. The hand was crooked, and an ugly, puckered scar ran across the back of it, and down to the twisted finger-nail.

The blind clicked down.

It was the trap.

CHAPTER XXI

Will you walk into my parlour?
(NURSERY RHYME)

I DON'T believe I thought at all. There was certainly no plan in my head. I just stood there, in the dark doorway, looking at the shop. It did not occur to me that I had exactly no chance at all against them, that I was a woman, alone, unarmed; that even if I had had a weapon I would not have known what to do with it. It did cross my mind, since I am a normal law-abiding person, to go to the police, but imagination quailed before the prospect of explaining, in a foreign tongue, an incredible situation to a sceptical officialdom. And there was not time. Richard and David were in there, and they must be got out.

I walked quietly across the road towards the shop.

The street was luckily still deserted, and no sound came from within the locked and shuttered shop. I had noticed, two doors from it along the street, a broken door which seemed to give on to a narrow tunnel running through the block of buildings to the back. I pushed this open. It creaked slightly, and I slipped through, groping my way down the tunnel into what seemed to be a warehouse yard. The dark shapes of buildings loomed up to right and left; there were piles of old boxes, and an orderly stack of crates; ahead of me I could make out a pair of solid double gates, and, beside them, the darker cavern of an open garage.

I waited for a moment in the mouth of the alley, until I had got my bearings, and in a very few seconds I found that I could see fairly clearly. The moon that Richard and I had watched rise was dispensing a faint light from somewhere beyond the roof-tops, and, in rivalry, the glow of the city streets threw the same chimneys into warmer silhouette. One lighted window on my left cast a line of light like a yellow bar across the blackness, but it was a smallish window, about ten feet up, and the shaft of light went high, to be lost among the deeper shadows of the open garage.

I threw one apprehensive glance at this window, which I guessed to be that of the antique-dealer's office, and then I started on a hurried tiptoe search of the yard buildings. The garage offered the only real hiding-place, and I slid into its black cave like a ghost. Save for some boxes and a few drums of oil, it was empty. But a smell of stale exhaust still hung in the air, and with a flash like the springing open of a door I remembered the car I had heard drive off only a few minutes ago. I bit my lip in an agony of indecision and frustration. Perhaps Richard was no longer on the shop-premises. Perhaps he—his body . . . I thrust the thought back into the limbo whence it peered and grimaced, and tried to discipline my thoughts. *He was not dead: he could not be dead* . . . with a little sob of a prayer that was not so much a supplication as a threat to the Almighty, I turned to leave the garage, and found myself staring down at a dark stain that spread hideously on the concrete floor.

It gleamed faintly under the oblique light from the office window. Its surface was thick and slimy. I don't know how long it took me to realize that it was only oil. My flesh seemed to shrink on my bones as I bent down, put a testing finger into the viscous pool, and sniffed at it. Oil. Nothing worse. I was straightening up when, out of the corner of my eye, I saw something on the floor of the garage. It had fallen behind an oil-drum, and, if I had not stooped, I should not have seen it. It showed squarish and pale in the shadows.

Now was the time, I thought, with the tiny remnant of irony that insisted on denying the realities of my situation—now was the time to discover the monogrammed handkerchief with the message scrawled in blood—or oil, amended the other part of my mind, rather hurriedly. I picked up the pale object, which was, at any rate, certainly not a handkerchief, because it was hard, oblong, and about a quarter of an inch thick. It felt as if it could be a book.

It was a book. It was a smudged and ruffled copy of T. S. Eliot's *Four Quartets*.

. . . .

In something less than twelve seconds I was across that yard, and crouching in the shelter of some crates under the lighted window, with Marsden's book thrust deep into the pocket of my coat. Suspicion, then, was certainty. Marsden had been in that garage; Marsden, in fact, might have been driving the car that I had heard.

But in this last supposition, it soon appeared, I was wrong, for, quite clearly from some four feet above my head, came the voice I had heard that night on the Rocher des Doms.

". . . Why you had to behave as if all hell was let loose, Loraine. Couldn't you——"

I had not missed much. They were still discussing Loraine's outburst at the hotel. Her voice cut in, petulant and brittle: "It *was* all hell. That hotel . . . you don't know what it was like——"

"Don't I? I was staying there myself."

"Yes, but you had something to *do*. Following that damned kid around. I hadn't. I tell you——"

"You still needn't have lost your nerve to quite that extent, my dear." He spoke cuttingly, and she flared back:

"It's all very well for you, blast you. What d'you think I've been through, this last few months? You were sitting pretty while I—I've had nothing; no fun, nothing to do except cope with that—that bad-tempered iceberg, damn him. Then *l'affaire Toni,* and the police, and now this last business . . . all that waiting: d'you wonder it's got me down? I tell you, *I couldn't help it.* I've done my best, and for God's sake, Jean, leave me alone."

Jean. Jean Something-or-other, the husband. John Marsden.

A new voice cut across the interchange, a deep voice, speaking a guttural French that I found hard to follow.

"Stop it, both of you. Loraine, pull yourself together; and you, Jean, leave her alone. She's behaved like a fool, but there's no harm done; what's happened to-day has cancelled out any mistakes either of you may have made."

Jean spoke soberly: "My God! we've been lucky! When I think of it— the kid walking in here as large as life, and his father after him!"

The antique dealer was curt: "All right, we've been lucky. Then it seems my luck has got to make up for your carelessness."

"Damn it, Max——"

Max. Max Kramer; John Marsden. The pieces fitting smoothly into place. The rats in the woodshed.

There was a crash as a fist hit the table. Kramer shouted: *"Lieber Gott,* will you listen to me? This isn't the time to wrangle over what's past. We've got those two to dispose of, and it isn't until I see them officially reported as accidental deaths that this thing's over. *When* that happens, and not before, you'll get your money."

"And the papers," put in Loraine sullenly.

"And the papers; and we'll cry quits, and you two can go to perdition in your own way, and leave me to go mine. Is that understood?"

"All right. What do we do?" This from Jean.

Loraine said, still sullen: "I don't even know what's happened yet. Are they dead?"

"No," said Kramer, and I felt a muscle jump and tighten in my throat. "The boy's asleep; he should stay that way for quite a time; I gave him enough to keep him quiet till it's over." He laughed. "I've always had a kind heart. His father's had something to keep him quiet, too; perhaps it wasn't administered quite so gently, but then Jean and I were hardly prepared. . . . He'll be out for a bit—quite long enough, unless we waste any more time."

His voice dropped, and I strained closer. "Now listen. I've been thinking hard since this happened, and I've seen how we can use things the way they've played themselves. It works out pretty well with what we planned before. The boy and his father will be found dead at the foot of the cliffs—at our arranged spot. They'll be together in the wreck of Byron's car."

"Have you got it?"

"His keys were in his pocket, along with the garage chit. It's in one of Blériot's lock-ups."

"And the story," said Jean, with triumph lighting his voice, "will be that the boy bolted to meet his father; the two of them set off—for Italy, perhaps; and *pff*—an accident in the darkness!"

"Exactly," said Kramer, with satisfaction. "The child really played into our hands by running away. He even stole his passport to take with him. There'll be no reason why anyone should think about—murder. No one will look in that boy's body for drugs."

"And any signs of violence on the man will be accounted for——"

"Exactly," said Kramer again.

Then the purr of satisfaction faded, and his voice went hard and precise: "André's taken the two of them, tied up in the van. He's been gone about fifteen minutes. We should be there almost as soon as he is. He's a bit of a fool, as you know, and he's afraid of trouble; I told him we'd have to wait for you, Loraine, but that one of us would go after him as soon as possible. Jean——"

"What?"

"My car's in the garage on the other side of the street. Here are the keys." I heard the jingle as he threw them. "You get straight after André. See that he parks well out of sight."

"Right. And you?"

"I've got to get Byron's car; it won't take me long. If either of them wakes up and makes trouble——"

"I'll know what to do."

"*So,*" said the German.

Loraine said: "What about me? Can't I come? I want to watch."

Jean sounded amused. "Chief mourner? What on earth did the poor sod do to you, *ma belle?*"

"You'll go with me," said Kramer flatly. "I want Jean's mind on his job. Get going, Jean."

"Okay. Throw me my coat."

I heard the chair-springs creak as he got up. I heard the small jingle of the car keys as he dropped them into his pocket. He was going. He took three steps, and the door opened. They were on their way to kill Richard and little David, and there was nothing I could do. Nothing. Somewhere out in the night, along that cruel coast, Richard and his son would hurtle to their deaths, and I would not even know where they lay, until I saw the headlines in the morning papers.

I suppose I was praying. I only know that my cheeks and lips were wet, and my hands were gripping the edge of a crate until the bones seemed to crack. *Dear God, don't let them die* . . . not Richard, not little David; there must be something I can do . . . perhaps, even now, the police . . . there must be something I can do. There must be. If only I knew where they'd been taken, I'd find something, somehow . . . if only I knew where they were. *Dear God, won't you tell me where they are?*

"Max," said Jean's voice above me, half laughing, half casual, "I'm damned if I can remember whether it's the first fork right after Aiguebelle, or the second."

"*Lieber Gott!* The second!" said Kramer. "The first only goes to a cottage on the cliff. The track you want drops steeply away from the road just beyond those big parasol pines on the left. This is a hell of a time to ask a question like that!"

"Isn't it?" said Jean insolently, and went out, whistling, into the shop.

I heard Kramer say: "Loraine. Quickly now. Get on the telephone to that hotel of yours——" and then I was across the yard and fumbling for the catch of the double gates that opened on to the back alley. With Jean at the street door I dared not go that way. I must chance finding my way through the alley, back to the Rue Mirabell, and thence to locate my car. The road to Italy, the coast road, past Aiguebelle . . . I found myself whispering frantically as my hands clawed at the heavy catch of the gate: "*Bergère Frères, 69 Rue des Pêcheurs . . . 69 Rue des Pêcheurs* . . . my car, please, quickly . . . the second on the right after Aiguebelle; on the left the parasol pines." And then, again, like a refrain: "*Bergère Frères. . . .*"

The bolt was rusty, and my fingers slipped and strained. There was sweat on my hands. I thought I heard the outer door of the shop open and shut in the distance. I thought I heard a soft whistle in the street. I couldn't move the bolt. I strained and tugged to move it, and it would not come, and something inside me strained too, and stretched to snapping-point. I couldn't get out. They were going to murder Richard, and I couldn't get out.

In another moment I'd have broken: I'd have been caught by Kramer screaming in his warehouse yard and beating the gates with my hands, but, just as the panic inside me swelled to bursting-point, a little door in the gate swung open like magic in front of me, and I was free. It was one of those little man-doors they cut into bigger ones, to save having to haul the latter open every time somebody wants to get out; and it swung wide in front of me, creaking ever such a little.

I bent down and stepped through it into the narrow back alley-way.

As I straightened up, something hit me. It caught me full on the chest, and I staggered back against the gates, pinned there by my assailant's weight, and with his breath on my cheek.

CHAPTER XXII

Needs must when the Devil drives.
(PROVERBS)

BEFORE I had time to do more than draw breath for the scream I dared not utter, my attacker gave a little snuffling whine and began licking my face.

"*Rommel!*" Relief made me weak. My legs shook, and I wanted, insanely, to laugh. I pushed the delighted dog down with a warning whisper and a hand over his muzzle, while my other hand groped for his collar. The inevitable piece of string was there, about two feet of it, the end snapped and frayed. David must have tied the dog up when he went into the shop, and the poor beast had eventually broken the string and come wandering in search of him. As I ran down the back alley in the direction of the Rue Mirabell I was busy with the new and minor problem; what on earth could I do with the dog?

I could abandon the poor beast, of course, if he would let me, but something in me shrank from such an action. I could leave him in my hotel, but the thought of the fuss, the explanations, the waste of time, was more than I dared face. He was running happily beside me, panting with the pleasure of having at last found a friend, and it occurred to me, too, that I was in no position to reject help of any sort. I might yet be glad, even, of Rommel's friendship.

I was proved right about thirty seconds later, as we plunged across the Rue Mirabell into another dark little alley, and a drunken Lascar rose straight out of the shadows to lurch across my path. I tried ineffectually to dodge him and slip by, but, even as he gripped my sleeve, Rommel gave a snarl, and leaped for him, hitting him in the groin. The man doubled up and staggered back with a curse, reeling against the wall. I fled by, and Rommel with me, the pleasure on his silly face greatly enhanced by the satisfactory little episode. For me, remembering suddenly the reputation of the city through whose dubious streets I was adventuring alone, the sound of the dog's lollopping feet and excited panting were now enormously comforting. I gripped the frayed string more tightly, and we ran out of the alley into a street that I vaguely remembered.

This was a main street, well lighted, the road, in fact, down which I had come from Avignon into Marseilles. I had turned off it some way further west, in my attempts to dodge Richard, so the garage of Bergère Frères must lie somewhere in the maze of streets between this one and the docks. It couldn't be far, I thought hopefully, as Rommel and I crossed the street and hesitated on the further pavement; I remembered that I had not walked a great distance before recrossing this street and finding the hotel in the Rue Mirabell.

I looked round me. It was not a street of cafés, and there were surprisingly few people about. The newspaper kiosk at my elbow was shut, so was the *boulangerie* in front of me, but thirty yards away was an open garage, the lights of its petrol-pumps glowing like beacons. Someone there would certainly know the way to the garage in the Rue des Pêcheurs. I tugged Rommel in that direction.

One garage-hand was busy at the pumps, attending to a car, but as I hurried forward another emerged from the garage door, carrying a bucket. He put this down, and, at my breathless query, pushed the beret back on his head and scratched his hair.

"Rue des Pêcheurs, mam'selle? Why, yes, but——" he eyed me dubiously. "It's no sort of place for you to be going, this time of night."

"But I must!" My insistence was such that his stare became curious. "It's most urgent. Which is the way?"

He rubbed his ear, still staring. "I'll point the way out to you, sure enough. But I tell you——"

"I must!" I cried again. He meant kindly, no doubt, but my heart was hammering in my throat, and the engine of every car that passed was like the whining hum of a minute-gong. I took a step towards him. "Please, m'sieur!"

His stare was all over me now, taking in my smudged hands, my dusty sandals, the plaster-marks on my coat, the desperation in my face. There was a glint in his eyes now that was more than curiosity. "I'll tell you what I'll do." He passed his tongue over his upper lip, and smiled quite pleasantly. I wondered if he were thinking of telephoning the police. "I'm off in ten minutes," he said. "If you like to wait I'll take you there myself."

I grabbed at the edges of my patience and politeness. "M'sieur, you are kindness itself. But I repeat, this is urgent; I cannot wait. I have to leave Marseilles immediately, and I must have my car. So——"

"Car?"

"Yes. At Bergère's garage. It's in the Rue——"

"I know that. But it's shut." He spoke curtly; he was losing interest. He half turned away and picked up his bucket.

"*Shut?*" The world stood still, then began to spin. "Are you sure?" He shrugged slightly. "*Mais certainement.* It's a repair garage: it shuts at eight."

"Perhaps someone—it's so very important . . . where do they live?" I found myself beginning to stammer; I was groping for words, my French slipping from me as my brain panicked again: "I could go to the house——"

He spoke a little more gently: "I don't know where they live. You could perhaps ask at the houses near the garage."

A tram bucketed down the street behind me, the noise of its speed mocking me. A car turned in beside the petrol pumps, and the swish of its tyres on the gravel made the hairs prickle along the nape of my neck. I dropped Rommel's string on the ground, set my foot on it, and began to grope in my handbag with shaking hands.

"No, that's no use. I've no time. I must go now. I must hire a car. Please get one out immediately and fill it up. How much——?"

"There is no car." Interest, curiosity, perhaps even compassion, these were still in his eyes, but deepening there, too, was suspicion. Heaven knows I didn't blame him: if he could read my face as I read his, he must be able to see something sufficiently out of the ordinary. My whole bearing must speak my fear. I dragged at a handful of notes and held them out. "A car, m'sieur, for God's sake——"

He eyed the notes, but made no move to take them. "It is the truth. We have no car for hire. I am sorry." His shrug of regret was genuine, and final. He turned away.

I just stood there, numbly, clutching the notes, and in me, the hope that had never been a hope at all, drooped and died. It was no use. Richard was dead. I could go to the Rue des Pêcheurs, I could knock from door to door, breathless, hurrying, desperately fumbling for words.

I could find M. Bergère; I could explain to him: I could persuade him to open his garage. I could get my car out, and drive along the coast road to Aiguebelle and the parasol pines, I and this silly fluffy dog of David's. And when I got there there would be nothing to see except the moonlight on some car-tracks in the dust, and nothing to hear except the grating roar of the sea on the shingle at the foot of the cliff. I was too late. . . .

Rommel turned his head and wagged his ridiculous tail. Someone spoke behind me.

"Mrs. Selborne!"

I turned, as in a dream. A tall man in a dark suit was standing by the petrol-pumps, looking at me. He spoke again, in English, and took a step towards me.

"It *is* Mrs. Selborne, isn't it?"

I knew him now: it was the handsome Frenchman from the Tistet-Védène. I smiled mechanically. "Monsieur—Véry?"

He smiled back and gave a charming little bow. "I never expected to see you here, madame; this is indeed a pleasure." Then as I, at a loss, stammered something, his eyes fell on Rommel. They widened, and he turned on me a look half amazed, half quizzical, and wholly amused.

"So it *was* you?" he said. I did not reply, but he appeared to notice nothing odd in my demeanour. He laughed. "Tell me, where have you hidden him—the little boy you stole?"

"I–I––"

He made a gesture. His dark eyes were alight with amusement. "Figure to yourself, madame, what it was like at the *hôtel,* this morning! The cries, the tears––"

"Tears?" I repeated the word dully. I was not taking this in. All my attention was on the trivial task of folding the notes very neatly, and putting them back into my bag.

"We—ell, perhaps not tears." He grimaced slightly. "There is no love lost there, *hein?* But *you"*—his eyes were dancing—*"you* the criminal! Tell me, why did you do it? He was unhappy, the little one? Did he tell you, perhaps——?"

"No, no. I didn't——"

"You haven't been caught yet, anyway?" He chuckled. *"Bon.* You caused a lot of trouble, you know, but it was *fort amusant,* just the same. I thought I was going to have to miss the end of it; I had to leave to-day for Nice, and I was *désolé* that I should never know what happened. And now, by the purest chance, I pull in here"—he gestured to the pumps—"and here you are, with the evidence of the crime, red-fingered . . . or is it red-handed?"

But I was not listening. My eyes had followed his gesture, and for the moment my whole world was filled with what they saw.

The mechanic was just screwing the cap back into the petrol-tank of Paul Véry's car. And what a car! Long, low, and open, with *power* written along every gleaming line of her, the Mercedes-Benz lay along the garage-front like a liner at a fishing-jetty. From where I stood she looked about thirty feet long.

"Monsieur Véry——" It stirred in me, that crazy little hope that wouldn't die. My heart began to thud.

At something in my face his expression changed. The amusement dropped like a peeled-off mask. His eyes scanned me. "I am sorry. I shouldn't have jested about it. You are in trouble."

"Yes. Great trouble." I came close to him and put out a hand that was not steady. "You're going to Nice, you say . . . could you, *would* you, take me with you part of the way?"

"But of course. The boy——?"

"It's to do with the boy," I said shakily. "I know where he's gone. Please understand—it's terribly important to hurry; let me explain as we go. I—it's so urgent——"

His hand closed over mine for a brief, reassuring moment. "Don't worry, *ma belle;* we shall hurry. That car—it is difficult, with her, to do anything else."

Two minutes later, with Rommel safely tied in the back seat, the Mercedes flicked through the traffic in the Canebière, and turned her nose to the east.

CHAPTER XXIII

Tyger, Tyger——
(BLAKE)

ALMOST AT ONCE, it seemed, the glare and rattle of the Marseilles streets thinned around us, and we were threading the tree-lined suburbs, whose ever-sparser street-lamps and high shuttered houses flickered past in a gathering darkness. If there was a speed-limit here, Paul Véry ignored it. He drove fast, cutting dangerously through the remaining knots of traffic in a manner that made me at one moment feel glad of the speed we were making, and at another wonder if he reckoned the risks he took. If we should be stopped by the police . . . for the Mercedes made no secret of her speed; it did not need the klaxon blaring at the crossing to advertise her coming: on a rising snarl she swept through the last of the thinning streets, and roared down the tunnel of her own undimmed lights, racing like a homing tiger for the forests of the night.

The gleaming tram-lines of Marseilles vanished from under our wheels: the lights of the last house flickered through its cypresses and were gone; and we were in the open country. A wind had risen. The wind of our own speed beat against us, whining along the great hood and clawing at the wind-screen, but I could tell from the drift of the high clouds against the starlight that the upper air, too, was alive. The moon had vanished, swallowed by those same clouds, and we raced through a darkness lit only by faint stars, save where the car's great lights flooded our road for what seemed half a racing mile ahead. And down that roaring wedge of light she went, gathering speed, peeling the flying night off over her shoulder as a comet peels the cloud. Along that rushing road the pines, the palisaded poplars, the cloudy olives, blurred themselves for an instant at the edge of vision, and were gone. The night itself was a blur, a roar of movement, nothing but a dark wind; the streaming stars were no more than a foam in our wake.

The road whipped wickedly under us like a snake. The world swung in a sickening lurch as the tyres screamed at a bend. Then we were straight again, tearing hell-bent down our long tunnel of light.

Paul Véry glanced at me with a little smile. "Is this fast enough for you?"

"No," I said.

In the glow of the dashboard I saw him look momentarily disconcerted, and I realized that, in taking so literally my demand for speed, he had expected me to be scared. Even at that moment I could feel a wry twinge of amusement at the idea that anyone who had lived with Johnny could ever be afraid of speed again: this bat-out-of-hell flight through the roaring darkness had been Johnny's normal way of driving home. But then, Johnny had been—Johnny: I admitted to myself, on a second thought, that I had had several qualms to-night already as we had bullied our way out of Marseilles. I had been in this kind of car too often not to know just what she could do with half-a-second off the chain.

"Nevertheless," said Paul Véry, decelerating, "it is as fast as is safe." He, too, then, felt that moment at the bend when the tiger had nearly got away from him.

"I'm sorry," I said. "I was worrying. I'm watching all the time for their tail-light, and I spoke without thinking. I'm most terribly grateful to you for taking me at all."

"It's a pleasure." He accompanied the formal words with a smile so delightful that, in spite of my heart-aching fear and apprehension, I smiled back. I found myself watching him as he leaned back in his seat, and settled the car down to a steady sixty-five, his eyes narrowed on the extreme arrow-tip of light ahead. In its reflected glow his face was a handsome mask of concentration.

The road tore towards us. Once my heart jumped and fluttered in my throat as a red light appeared in the blackness ahead, but it was only a small car, stationary, with a couple in it, a man and a girl. I sank back in my seat, and the blood seemed to seep back from my tingling finger-tips and slowly start to feed my heart again.

Paul Véry had glanced sideways at me, and now he spoke.

"That is not the tail-light you are looking for, I take it?"

"No." I smiled a little uncertainly at him. "I suppose you must be wondering what it's all about?"

His gaze was back on the road. "But naturally. You talk of urgency, and you are anxious and afraid. Who would not wonder, madame? Believe me, I am eager to help . . . but there is not the least need to tell me your affairs if you would rather not."

"You're very good. I—I told you it was something to do with the boy David."

"*Eh bien?*"

"I *didn't* take him away, you know. But I do know where he is now. That's where I'm going."

His hands moved a little, as if with surprise, on the steering-wheel, and the car gave a wicked swerve. He cursed it under his breath.

"Sorry," I said. "I didn't mean to startle you. But the rest of my story's a good deal more startling than that. I told no more than the truth when I said I was in trouble. I am: desperate trouble." My voice wavered as the spectre of that desperation once more gibbered at me out of the dark. "Life-and-death trouble," I said, on a little sob.

"And you need help—badly." It was almost a question, spoken very softly, without looking at me. There was a curious lilt to his voice, and I turned my head to look at him, the sob caught in my throat. Help . . . of course I needed help. Up to this moment, stupid with weariness and dazed by my terror for Richard, I had thought of Paul Véry only as a miraculous means of my reaching the little road beyond Aiguebelle. Further than that I had not gone. But now . . . the miracle was complete: I and Rommel were alone no longer, we had an ally, and our immediate objective was apparent. André was ahead of us, with Richard and David, and he was alone on the job. It was by no means probable that Jean, also, was before us: he would have had little, if any, start of us, and, at the rate we were going, we would almost certainly by now have caught any car going at a more normal speed.

André was alone, and there were two of us—and Rommel.

My heart lifted, and I turned gratefully to my companion. He was smiling; he looked extremely handsome, and also, I realized, entirely formidable.

"And where are 'they' taking this little boy, *hein?* And who are 'they'?" The strange note was back in his voice, and all at once I knew it for what it was. It was enjoyment. He sounded amused, excited, and not at all apprehensive. He had, of course, no idea yet of the real danger of the situation: it was the unusualness of it, the lady-in-distress touch, the mad speed through the dark—all this must be appealing to some sense of adventure in him. But I knew, too, as I looked at him as it were with new eyes, that no threat of danger to come would damp that enjoyment.

I found myself heartened by his demeanour, the lift of excitement, almost gaiety, in his voice and look. It was catching, and it was certainly, to anyone in my desperate plight, heartening, to be suddenly given an ally at once so eager and so redoubtable.

And redoubtable was by no means too strong a word. There was about him an impression of force, of energy leashed in only precariously . . . the whole personality of the man was, at such close quarters, almost overwhelming. I had, I realized, failed to estimate Monsieur Paul Véry. It was not only the headlong speed of the car that snatched at my breath as I began the explanation that was his due.

"It's a long story, and a nasty one," I said quickly, "and I mayn't have time to tell it all to you before things happen. But the main thing is that David, whose real name is David Byron, is going to be murdered to-night, along with his father, if we can't do something to prevent it."

He shot me a startled look. "But——"

"I know!" I cried. "It sounds fantastic! But listen: I'll try to tell you a little about it. . . ."

I began, stumbling a little in my haste, to tell him what I knew about Kramer and Richard and Loraine. He listened in silence, but when at length I came to Marsden's part in the affair, he interrupted me with an exclamation that sounded amused.

"Monsieur Marsden? *That* one? The rest, yes; I will believe it because you tell me so, and because I think you really are in bad trouble. But *this* I cannot think, that the good Monsieur Marsden is a murderer. Besides, he is English."

"He *says* he's English," I said sharply. "But I tell you he *is* her hus-

band, and he's in Kramer's pay. You've *got* to believe me. The good
Monsieur Marsden, as you call him, is on his way at this moment to
murder both Richard and David Byron, unless we can do something to
stop him!"

I could see his face in the dim light. He was smiling a little still, but
his brows were drawn with bewilderment.

"Mais, ma belle——"

So I was to be spared none of the nightmare. The ordeal by unbelief
was to be part of it . . . and in my own bewildered terror I must try
and sort out the affair's lunatic logic, so that this man might believe and
help me. I clutched my shaking hands together, and fought to marshal
my knowledge. I remember that the only clear thought in my head was a
wish that Paul Véry would stop calling me *"ma belle."*

"Listen, monsieur," I said carefully, "I am telling you no more than
the truth, as I know it. There is no time to go back to the beginning. I
can only tell you what is happening now, to-night, and beg that you will
believe me. I'm not quite sure of this man Kramer's reasons for employ-
ing Loraine and Marsden to do murder for him, but I *think* it's because
of something that happened during the War, Richard and a friend of his
witnessed a—an atrocity, I suppose one would call it—in which Kramer
was concerned."

"That does not matter." He spoke all of a sudden with sharp impatience. "I have said that I will believe you. All this talk of the War . . .
there is no time. Tell me now what you think this man plans to do—
what *you* plan to do, now, to-night."

The relief was so sharp, so intense, that the darkness blurred round
me, and I shut my eyes and pressed the palms of my hands against
them. I felt the car slow down, and took my hands away, to find that
we were threading a decorous enough way between walls and houses. A
festoon of street lamps swung up into the darkness, a lighted tram rattled
out of a side-street, and suddenly we were plunged into a brilliance of
neon-lights and cafés and the impatient blare of traffic.

"Toulon," said Paul Véry. "Go on. Tell me your plan."

"Very well," I said. "Here it is, without trimmings. Somewhere along
this road is a village called Aiguebelle. A little way beyond it, on the left,
there is a group of parasol pines, and opposite them a lane branches
right-handed off the road, along the cliff top. There, unless we overtake
it on the road, a van will be waiting, in the charge of a man called André.
In that van are Richard and David Byron, unconscious and, I believe,
tied up. André has orders to wait there for the others, then they're going
to stage an accident. Kramer's bringing Rich—Byron's own car, and
Loraine's with him. But Marsden left before them. And at the rate we've

been travelling, he's hardly had a chance to overtake us, but he won't be
so very far behind." I drew in my breath. "He'll hurry a bit, of course,"
I added, "as André's alone on the job, and a bit of a fool into the bargain."

I stopped. There was a pause, filled with the rushing wind. The town
was behind us, and once again we were plunging down our lighted tunnel into the lonely night. I did not look at Paul Véry: I had pleaded my
cause abominably, I knew, but weariness, bewilderment, and agony of
mind were my excuse. I bit my lip, and waited.

His reaction, when it came, was unexpected. I heard him give a long-
drawn whistle of stupefaction, then he swore softly, and laughed. But
even as I opened my mouth to speak he moved one hand off the wheel
to drop it lightly over mine.

"Forgive me, I did not mean to laugh . . . but you seem to be so deep
in the confidence of this murderer. How do you know all this?"

I slid my hand from under his, and began to fumble in my bag for a
cigarette. At least he was not alarmed, I reflected. I said: "Does that
matter now? You said we'd got to think of what to do."

"Yes indeed." He removed his hand at that, and reached in a pocket
to produce a flat silver case. He handed it to me without looking at me.
He seemed all at once to withdraw into his own thoughts; it was as if he
had forgotten me, forgotten all but the immediate problem of action.
When he spoke, his voice was abstracted, and he used his own language
for the first time.

"Why did you not . . . light me one too, will you, *ma belle?* . . .
why did you not go to the police?"

I answered in the same tongue: "I hadn't time." I took a cigarette
from the case, and bent low behind the wind-screen, shielding my face
from the draught as I flicked my lighter.

"And the dog . . . how did you come by the dog?"

The lighter went out, and I had to flick it two or three times to relight
it. I huddled lower in the car, making a little draught-proof cave, and
tried again. I did not reply, but he hardly appeared to notice; he was
talking almost to himself, still in that preoccupied, almost absent voice.

"And the man Marsden; why should you be so certain that the man
Marsden is the husband of Loraine?"

The lighter flared, and burned steadily. I lit the cigarette, and
handed it up to him out of my cave. I fumbled in the open case on my
knee for another. "Does it matter?" I said again. "Have you by any
chance got a gun?"

"As it happens, I have," said Paul Véry, and I could tell by his voice that he was smiling again. "But tell me, how do you come to be in Marseilles anyway? And what is your connection with this Byron?"

I held the lighter to my cigarette, and drew at the flame. Then I froze, crouched there under the dashboard of the car, while the flame of the lighter, illuminating my tiny cave of blackness, flickered over the open lid of Paul Véry's cigarette-case.

There was an inscription there, beautifully tooled in the silver. It was only his name, and a date.

It read:

> Jean-Paul.
> A jamais,
> L.   17.8.42

The lighter went out. Above me in the darkness, his voice said, ever so slightly mocking: "Don't worry about it any more, *ma belle*. It'll be all right, I'll see to that. And you trust me, don't you?"

That phrase, softly spoken in French in the darkness . . . the voice of the Rocher des Doms; the voice I had heard less than an hour ago in Kramer's office. . . . And, like another echo behind it, too late, whispered the ghost-voice of Louise: *"Paul Véry . . . something to do with antiques. . . ."*

"You do trust me, don't you?" repeated Jean, smiling into the darkness above me.

CHAPTER XXIV

Who rides the tiger cannot dismount.
(CHINESE PROVERB)

IT WAS COLD. The Mediterranean night-wind, pine-scented, sea-scented, sang past my cheek in a warm dark tide, but I was shivering as I hugged myself deep into my coat and fought down the rising hysteria of hopelessness.

Fool that I was! I had heard Loraine's husband—I still thought of him as Paul Véry—go for his car. In the time it had taken me to escape from Kramer's yard and run as far as the garage he could just have got his car out and driven across to fill her up. In spite of his connection with the Tistet-Védène, in spite (I told myself savagely) of his now obvious eligibility for the rôle of Loraine's husband, I had not tumbled to it. I had run to him in thankfulness, like a fool, putting our last pitiful little chance straight into his hands. Murderer's hands.

The lights of Hyères swam up in front of us; they swooped by, and were engulfed in our dark wake. I huddled deeper into my seat, and stole a glance at him. Now that I knew . . . oh, yes, now that I knew, it was plain to see, the glint of amusement below the insolent lids, the arrogant tilt of the chin, the whole formidable confidence of the man. And I was aware again, sharply, of the impression of excitement that I had received before: somehow, it was there, banked and blazing, under the smoothly handsome exterior: the faint gleam of sweat over his cheekbones betrayed it, the nostrils that flared to a quicker breathing above a rigid upper lip, the hands, too tight upon the wheel. Murderer's hands.

The dim road hurtled towards us. A village, a huddle of houses, flickered by like ghosts. Ahead two eyes gleamed: they stared, then darted like fireflies as the rabbit turned to run. Paul Véry gave a little laugh, and deliberately thrust down his foot. I heard the rabbit squeal as we hit it: behind me Rommel whined, sharply. Paul Véry laughed once more.

"Frightened?" The question came again; he must have heard me make some sound. This time I could honestly give him the satisfaction he wanted.

"Yes. Do we have to go as fast as this?"

He smiled at the tremor in my voice, but, to my surprise, slackened the car's headlong speed.

"And did you have to do that?" I said.

"Do what?"

"Kill that wretched rabbit."

He laughed again, a charming, gay little laugh. He looked extraordinarily handsome. "You don't like killing?"

"Of course not." I hoped there was nothing in my voice but an austere disapproval, nothing of the cold creeping terror that was shaking me.

The car slowed still further. The speedometer, under its masked light, showed a decorous fifty as Paul Véry took a hand off the wheel and dropped it over mine. The contact, warm, vital, and wholly mocking, sent a new shock through me: it was as if the man were giving off tangible waves of excitement.

"Do you?" I asked, knowing the answer.

"If something gets in the way, *ma belle,* it's asking to be killed, isn't it?" Warm and strong, his hand tightened over mine. The car's speed dropped further, and he turned his head to smile down at me. "Not afraid any more?"

I said "No," cooly enough, but I drew on my cigarette as if for succour, and my lips were unsteady. For I knew now what I was in for. I would have to be killed along with Richard and David; that much was obvious. Like the rabbit, I had got in the way. I knew, too, that Paul Véry was a real killer, who enjoyed the act of killing, and that this mad ride through the dark towards his dreadful objective had touched in him some ghastly stop of pure excitement. And my presence was the final titillation. Darkness, speed, danger, murder . . . and a girl. Nothing was to be missing from Mr. Véry's white night.

The Mercedes sang down to thirty, twenty-five, twenty. . . . We were crawling at ten miles an hour down a sloping black tunnel of trees, and Paul Véry had thrown away his cigarette; his arm had slid round my shoulders and his handsome face was bent close to mine. I leaned back against the arm but it was like a bar of steel. At my involuntary movement of resistance it tightened brutally, and I saw something begin to blaze in the eyes above me.

I suppose real terror is mercifully paralysing. I shut my eyes as he pulled me to him, only vaguely wondering if he would kill me here, or send me over the cliff with Richard. I even found myself wishing that he would watch the road when he was driving.

His rapid breathing was hot on my cheek. His voice said, with something ruffling its deep velvet caress: *"Ma belle. . . ."* I felt his mouth searching for mine, and jerked my head away. He said again, on a note of surprised reproach: *"Ma belle. . . ."*

And even as I wondered half hysterically why a victim should be expected to want to kiss her murderer, the cobwebs of terror blew aside for one moment, and I remembered that he still had no idea that I knew him for what he was. His pained reproach held no hint of mockery: passion had left no room for that. He was simply so damned handsome that no woman had ever refused him a kiss before.

My knowledge was my only weapon: it was a pitiful enough tool, a despicable tool if you like, but it was all I had. I didn't hesitate a second. I opened my eyes, and smiled Delilah-wise into his. "It's only . . . do *please* watch the road," I whispered.

I heard his little soft laugh of triumph as he turned his head away to glance at the road. I relaxed against his shoulder, and the arm tightened round me as the Mercedes drew to a sliding halt at the side of the road.

I threw away my cigarette with my free hand.

"Oh damn!"

The car slid to a stop.

"What's the matter, *chérie?*"

"My bag," I said crossly. "It went overboard when I threw my cigarette out." I sat up and made as if to pull away from him.

He pulled the handbrake on with a sharp movement, and turned to prevent me, taking me in both arms and drawing me back towards him. "Does it matter?" It was the brown velvet voice, irresistibly caressing, flatteringly urgent. He had forgotten to switch the engine off.

I hung back, pouting like a chorus starlet: "Silly! Of course it matters! Get it for me, there's a dear."

"Later," he said, his voice roughening. His mouth came down on mine, and I sighed tremulously, and slid my arms round his neck. I began to wonder how soon we might expect Kramer in the Bentley. . . .

It seemed an age, a ghastly crawling age, before he relaxed his embrace a little and spoke again: "Trembling, *ma belle?*"

I managed a breathless little laugh, which became half genuine as I saw the satisfied vanity in his face. It never occurred to him to doubt my surrender. I hastened to make him even surer of me.

"Paul."

"*Chérie?*"

"You like me?"

"A silly question, *ma belle!*"

You're telling me, I thought. I said: "Even looking the way I do now?"

He laughed complacently. "Any way, madame. Tell me—what is Richard Byron to you?"

He must have felt me jump in his arms, but he put it down to startled recollection. "Oh!" I cried. "How *dreadful* of me! I'd actually forgotten!" I tried to push him away. "Monsieur Véry, hadn't we better go on? I can't imagine what I was thinking about!"

"Can't you?" He was laughing again, and I had to control a sharp impulse to strike him across his beautiful complacent mouth. "Answer me, *ma belle*. This Richard Byron——"

"I don't know Richard Byron," I said quickly. "It's the little boy I care about, little David—let's go on, Monsieur Véry!"

"You called me Paul a minute ago."

"Paul, then. If we're not in time——"

"There is plenty of time." He pulled me close again, and I went as if in spite of myself. I knew he had no intention of going on yet. I was afraid of pushing my hand and making him suspicious. I relaxed against him for another long, agonizing minute, while I strained my ears for the sound of Kramer's car, and the darkness pressed in around us. The silence seemed thick and heavy under the trees. Only by the faintest quivering of her body did the Mercedes betray that her engine still ran. Paul Véry either did not care, or he was too preoccupied to notice. I wondered just how long it would be before things got beyond me, and guessed that it would not be very long now. Would I be strangled, like Tony, or——

I gave another long sigh, and drew away. "We must go," I said huskily. "The little boy, Paul, *chéri*—we mustn't forget him. I'd never forgive myself if anything happened to him because we'd——" I stopped and put up a hand to his cheek. "Let's go on, Paul."

He was as taut as a wire, and breathing fast. There was a queer look in his eyes, a kind of cold blaze that was uncanny, a blank look that I knew, suddenly, was the look of a killer. His hands moved, blindly. Things would be beyond me any moment now.

I pushed his hands away gently. "Please!" I said. "Get me my bag and then we'll go."

He didn't move, but sat there still with his eyes on me.

I smiled at him. "All right, handsome," I said. "We don't go. But get it for me anyway. I feel a fright and I want my mirror."

I leaned forward quickly and kissed him, as earnest of good intentions, then reached across him and opened the door. He hesitated, then with a little shrug he got out of the car. *Humour the victim; she'll come quietly.* . . .

I had dropped the bag before the car stopped, and I judged it to be about twenty yards back.

He walked back up the road, peering at the dark verge.

I counted his steps, and put my hand on the handbrake, releasing the ratchet. I held it there, waiting.

Five, six, seven . . . he paused and I thought he glanced back.

"Can't you find it?" I called. "Shall I come?"

"It's all right." He moved on slowly.

Eight, nine. . . .

I reached a foot over to the left and threw out the clutch. We were on a slope; I eased the gear-lever into second.

Ten, eleven. . . .

"Here it is," he said, and stooped to pick it up.

In a flash I was in the driver's seat. I shoved the brake off, opened the throttle with a roar, and let in the clutch. Behind me, I heard a shout and a curse. The Mercedes jerked forward sharply—too sharply. For a moment I feared I would stall her, and threw out the clutch again. Then she caught hold as a racehorse takes the bit, and we were away.

But my moment of fumbling with the unfamiliar controls had cost me dear enough.

As I swung her out to the crown of the road and changed up, I heard his hoarse breathing and the thud of feet, and felt the lurch as he flung himself on to the running-board of the car.

"*Rommel!*" I screamed, above the rising snarl of the engine. "*Get him, Rommel!*"

I heard the dog give an excited bark, but there was no movement of attack. After all, the dog had seen me kissing the man only a few seconds before. Then I remembered that Paul Véry had a gun, and called, for the dog's sake, even more urgently: "*Down, Rommel!*" and heard Paul Véry's ugly little breathless laugh.

The Mercedes gathered speed with a roar. The man was cursing behind me as he clung to the rear door. We plunged out of the tunnel of trees, and went up a hill with the sickening swoop of a swing. Ahead of us, once more, our great floodlights made a funnel into the dark, and we hurtled down their narrowing glare.

In control now, my hands on the wheel, I felt suddenly, beautifully, icily cool. The needle began to creep over to the right of the dial. We slashed through a tiny village. The name Euzès swam up for a second into the light, and vanished, while I knitted my brows and tried to remember the map.

The Mercedes roared on, and out of the corner of my eye I saw Paul Véry, clinging like a remora, give a heave of his muscles and lift a leg to climb inboard. I waited till the leg was just about to slide over the door, then I gave the wheel a jerk that sent the car across the road in a sickening, screeching swerve.

I heard him scream, saw him lurch outwards, but somehow he managed to retain his grip. He clung there, huddled together, yelling God knew what blasphemies at me.

I gave him a moment or so, and then I did it again. The tyres tore at the road, and I listened indifferently enough. If I had a burst, it would be just too bad, but unless I could get rid of Paul Véry and his gun, then I might just as well die this way as any other. I drove my foot down and dragged at the wheel again. The rear wheels skidded savagely, and the car bucked like a mad stallion. The lights careened dizzily across the night, and the darkness swung in a great arc round us. For a moment I thought I had done it too violently, and had lost control. Paul Véry was yelling again, and I heard the frightened dog give a sharp howl as he was flung down. The car, rocking madly, lunged forward again at the same wicked pace. The beam swung ahead, swung and steadied like a searchlight. Two fir-trees flickered by like ghosts, and then the lights met —nothing.

The road ahead had switched sharp left. I saw the verge of it leap towards our wheels, and beyond it a yard of dusty ground where thin grass waved spectral antennae against an immensity of darkness. Stars and wind, and a strange shifting luminous abyss of darkness. The edge of the sea.

This time I skidded the Mercedes in earnest. The wheel kicked like a live thing, and the dust mushroomed up behind us in an atomic cloud. We only missed hitting a rock with our off-front wheel because both off-side wheels were a foot from the ground.

Then we were round. There was blood on my bottom lip, but I was feeling good.

Then I realized that the left-handed swerve had helped Paul Véry to heave himself inboard at last. Cursing, half sobbing, he flung himself into the car, and, almost before I knew what had happened, he had scrambled into the front seat and was crouched beside me, thrusting a shaking hand into the pocket of his coat.

CHAPTER XXV

In this heedless fury
He may show violence to cross himself.
I'll follow the event . . .

(TOURNEUR)

"COME ON, you——," he said, in an ugly voice. "Pull her up, or you'll get it! I warned you I carried a gun!"

I didn't even glance at him. The second turning past Aiguebelle, I was thinking . . . by the big parasol pines. . . .

"In the belly," said Paul Véry, and added a filthy word.

I laughed. I was as cool as lake-water, and, for the moment, no more ruffled. The feel of that lovely car under my hands, in all her power and splendour, was to me like the feel of a sword in the hand of a man who has been fighting unarmed. The Mercedes was my weapon now, and by God! I would use her. I knew just how frightened Paul Véry was: I had watched it all, the gradual stretching of his nerves . . . the savage excitement of his murderous assignment, the acute pleasure of baiting me, the speed, the anticipation of the final thrill . . . and then, this. The man's nerves were rasped naked. I had realized, watching him driving, that he was more than half afraid of his own speed. The delicious excitement of frightening himself, of terrifying me, had been half the thrill. No first-rate driver—I could hear Johnny telling me yet again—no first-rate driver is ever excited at speed. Driving, he would add, is just a job, and you can't afford to let your brain revv up along with your engine. Then he would give that little smile of his, and the hedges would accelerate past us into a long grey blur. *When you let excitement in,* Johnny would add, in a lecture-room sort of voice, *fear will follow.*

And fear was in the car with us now. I could hear it raw in his voice. I could smell the sweat of it.

And I had in my hands the weapon to break him with. If I could smash his nerve completely before we reached the parasol pines . . . if I could get that gun away from him. . . .

So I laughed, and drove my lovely shining sword slashing through the night.

"Put the thing away," I said contemptuously. "If you shoot me, what d'you suppose would happen to the car—and you?"

I heard his breath hiss, and thought for a moment that he was far enough gone to shoot without thinking. But he didn't. He merely cursed again, and moved up to me until I could feel something hard pressing against my body through my coat. It was shaking a little.

"I mean it," he said hoarsely. "I'll do you, you——! Pull in, I tell you, or I'll blow a hole in your guts and take the chance of stopping the car myself!"

We were on a long straight stretch of road. I drove my right foot hard down, and the Mercedes tore up the straight with a rising scream. The needle swung hard to the right and held there.

"Some chance," I said derisively, "but go ahead. It's Kramer's car, after all; and he's a fool to lend it you when he must know you're a lousy driver."

The gun wavered. I heard him let out a quivering breath.

"If you tickle me with that thing at this speed," I added, "I can't answer for the consequences."

The gun withdrew. Ahead, the road curved, and I let my foot up a bit. Above the roar of the overdrive I heard him begin to curse again. . . . "If I'd guessed you knew, you –, if I'd guessed——" he said between his teeth, and told me what he would have liked to do to me. He was speaking in French, and gutter-French at that, so I missed a good deal of it, but I had to stop it somehow, before it took my mind off the road.

I cut across the stream of filth. "But it was obvious that I knew, monsieur."

That shook him. "How?"

My voice dripped contempt like an icicle. "Do you really imagine that I'd have let you maul me about like that because I *liked* it? My dear Monsieur Véry, as a lover you'd hardly even pass the first test——"

Then he lurched at me. In lashing his precious vanity, I had gone too far. I thought he was going to shoot me and damn the consequences, but instead he lunged savagely at the wheel. I thought he had it, and that we would all go over the cliff; but he missed his grab, and fell against me, clawing at my legs.

I jerked the wheel, stamped on the brake, and sent the rear of the car round again in a left-handed skid. He was flung away from me against the side of the car.

"Keep your hands off me, please," I told him, rather breathlessly, and straightened the Mercedes up.

He did not answer. He stayed slumped against the right-hand door of the car, breathing noisily through his throat. Poor Rommel, behind us, was whining with fear. I began to wonder just how much more assault and battery the tyres would stand.

And at that moment we roared by a fork in the road.

The first fork to the right. Not far to go. For the first time I glanced briefly at Paul Véry, and experienced a sense of shock at what I saw.

He, at least, had had as much assault and battery as his nerves could take. Gone was the immaculate Frenchman of the Tistet-Védène, gone the velvet-voiced Don Juan of the Mediterranean night; in their place huddled a man with twitching hands and a face shining with sweat. Nothing, not even fear, could strip Paul Véry of his extraordinary good looks, but, somehow, they had cheapened in front of my eyes; the man who sat there, staring in fascinated horror at the hurtling road, might have been brought up in any Paris gutter.

Formidable no longer. The power and competence that had seemed the very essence of the man had vanished: defeat—defeat by a woman—had knocked the props from under him. But he was still dangerous. The menace had not disappeared, it had only changed in quality. I was facing, instead of a powerful and relentless executioner, a mean and unpredictable thug.

What was more, I thought, a stupid thug. Only a stupid man, knowing how much I knew, would have talked to me as he had, taken the risks that he had taken, all for a moment's self-gratification. The significance of his final exchange with Kramer suddenly struck me: only a conceited fool would have forgotten, or pretended to forget, such information at such a moment. Paul Véry was a tool, and, up to a point, a good tool. But shake him out of his master's grip, and he was lost.

These speculations, flashing through my mind in the brief moment before I turned back to watch the road, effectively silenced any further attempts on my part to bait Paul Véry. In deliberately trying to crack his nerve, I had been running a far graver risk than I had known. He was, actually, quite stupid enough, in a moment of blind rage, to have shot me as I drove. The last incident had proved it, when, maddened by my mockery, he had flung himself at the wheel. If, at that moment, he had had his gun in his hand . . .

My heart gave a jerk in my breast, then seemed to tip over, sickeningly, and spill chilled blood down all my veins, so that even my fingers tingled.

If he had had his gun.

Clearly, in imagination, I heard his voice again, as I had heard it in Kramer's office. *"Throw me my coat."* Would he have spoken so carelessly if there had been a gun in the pocket? I remembered him standing, dark and handsome in his well-fitting suit, by the petrol-pumps in Marseilles. No bulging pocket had spoiled the fit of that coat. . . .

I flashed a look at him as I lifted my foot a little. His eyes were fixed on the road.

I drew my left hand softly off the wheel, and, with a breath that was a prayer, felt down beside me. There was a pocket on the car door. I slipped my hand into it.

Cold, deadly, and infinitely comforting, the gun slid into my grasp.

And at that moment, like great grey clouds billowing in the furthermost tip of our beam of light, I saw the parasol pines.

CHAPTER XXVI

We will die, all three.
(SHAKESPEARE)

LIKE A FLASH, I cut out the headlights, but Paul Véry had seen them. I saw him stiffen, and shoot his neck out like a bird of prey.

There was only one thing to do. I must drive straight on past the turning, ditch my companion some way beyond, and then return to deal with André alone. It seems odd that it never occurred to me to shoot

Paul Véry—though perhaps not; I had never handled a gun in my life.

"Listen to me," I said rapidly. We were nearly there. The pines stood back from the road, making a great grove like a tent. "I've got——"

But I was too late. Even as I spoke the first of the great trees loomed over the car, shutting out the stars, and our dimmed lights had picked out the shape of a van, parked on the beaten dust a little way ahead, and, beside the van, the figure of a man. André, who was a bit of a fool, had not parked out of sight.

Paul Véry let out a yell: *"André Ici Jean! Au secours!"*

I switched the headlamps full on, and trod on the accelerator. The beam of light shot out, catching the man who ran forward under the cover of the pines.

It was Marsden. He had a gun in his hand.

"A moi! André!" yelled Paul Véry. He was standing, leaning forward, half out of the car.

Marsden had reached the edge of the road. Was in the road. I put a fist down on the klaxon, and my foot hard down on the boards, and, with a little sob of pure terror, I drove that ton or so of murderous, screaming metal straight at him.

I saw him jump; at least, I think I did, but the next few seconds were just a terrifying blur. I remember Marsden's face, white in the roaring light; his mouth was a gaping hole; he was yelling. There was a scarlet stab of flame: another. Then the car hit something, and the whole world heeled over in the rocketing, exploding skid. The Mercedes seemed to rear straight up in the air, and her headlights raked a dizzy arc of sky. Then they went out, and darkness stamped down on us as a man stamps on a beetle. Clinging to that crazily kicking wheel, blinded, half-stunned, wholly automatic, I fought the car. For a moment I thought I had her, then she swept into a bucketing turn. The night split, wheeled, hung suspended for a million years, then shattered into splinters of flame. Then silence, broken only by the tiny tinkle of falling glass.

There was a shout, a thud of feet running. The door of the Mercedes was wrenched open, and hands seized me out of the darkness.

There was a roaring in my ears. The night, the stars, were spiralling down an enormous, narrowing funnel. Somewhere, far down the gyroscope, I heard a rough exclamation, then another shout—voices, urgent, sharp with something that might have been fear. Hands moved over me, patting, searching. Someone had hold of my head, and was forcing liquid between my teeth.

I choked, gasped, stirred, and the gyrating universe whirred slowly to a standstill, re-focusing itself around me. The stars steadied themselves, and hung, only faintly tremulous, in a still pall of sky. There were two

men beside the car. One was holding me; the other bent over me in
the darkness, peering down. His face blurred palely in front of me; it
was Marsden. I was conscious, first of all, of a tremendous wave of pure
relief; I hadn't killed him after all. Then I began to struggle feebly
against the arms that held me.

"I've got a gun," I said firmly.

Amazingly, somebody laughed, and the arms tightened.

"Lie still, you little fire-eater. Haven't you done enough for one
night?"

I turned my head and blinked stupidly.

"*Richard!* But—but you're tied up in the van. I was going to rescue
you."

He laughed again, a little shakenly. "Yes, I know, my darling. But
there's no need to run over the police in the process."

"*Police?*"

Marsden was grinning down at me. "Strictly unofficial, madam. But
Scotland Yard in person!"

"I—I'm awfully sorry," I said feebly. "I thought you were André. One
of *them,* anyway. And you shot at me, didn't you?"

"We both did," said Marsden ruefully. "I knew it was Kramer's car,
and I thought he'd seen me and was getting away."

"But he was yelling for help."

"My French isn't all that good," said Marsden simply, "and I couldn't
really hear him anyway. There wasn't a great deal of time to think, you
know."

Richard spoke. "Can you move all right, Charity? You'd better get
out of the car. It's in a rather uncertain position, to say the least."

I sat up out of his arms and felt my limbs gingerly.

"I think I'm all right." With their assistance I climbed out of the
Mercedes. Now that my eyes were accustomed to the darkness I could see
quite clearly in the starlight. The car had skidded clean off the main
road, and had ended up some yards down the track on the right, facing
the way I had come. She was standing, decorously enough, on the sea-
ward verge of the track, and for a moment I could not see what Richard
meant. Then I saw. The night swayed perilously, and I was glad of the
support of Richard's arm. The edge of the little road was the edge of the
cliffs. A yard beyond the near-wheels of the car, the ground dropped
sheer to the sea, three hundred feet below.

"I—I had some luck, didn't I?" I said shakily. "What did we hit?"

"Nothing. Marsden got one of your front tyres. You turned round twice
and skated backwards down here. The car's not even dented—except for
a headlamp. I did that."

I pushed my hair back from my forehead, and took a deep breath of the sweet night air. Things had steadied round me, and I felt a good deal more normal. Richard and Marsden were gently urging me across the road and under cover of the trees.

"It sounds like some very pretty shooting," I said, then memory flooded back. "David!" I cried. "Where's David?"

"He's all right; he's still asleep. He's safe in a ditch a hundred yards or so away; we moved him from the danger zone."

"And—and Paul Véry?"

"Alive," said Marsden grimly. "He's unconscious, and of course I don't know how badly he may be hurt. I haven't looked yet. He didn't look too good. Byron got him out of the car; he's lying behind it. I'll go back and have a look at him in a minute."

"Right," said Richard, "but we'd better let Charity put us in the picture quickly, in case things start to move again. What were you doing in Kramer's car with that man? And where's Kramer? Marsden said Kramer was going to follow the van out."

"Kramer's coming," I said. "He and Loraine are following in your car. It was to be sent over the cliff with you and David in it, Richard."

"My car, eh?" His voice was hard. "We might have thought of that, Marsden. And I suppose that thug I laid out just now is Loraine's real husband?"

"Yes."

"The man who murdered Tony and hit David. . . ." His expression was ugly, but it changed as we reached the shelter of the trees and he spoke to me again: "Are you sure you're all right?" He made me sit down behind an enormous double-trunked tree, with the van between me and the road.

"Yes, perfectly. Don't worry about me. Go and—oh!" My hand flew to my mouth. "Rommel!" I said, aghast.

"What?" Richard's voice was blank.

"Rommel, the dog. He was in the back of the car. I'll never forgive myself if he's hurt."

"There wasn't any dog in the back of the car."

"But there must have been——"

"I assure you there wasn't."

I was on my feet, steadying myself by the trunk of one of the trees.

"He must have been thrown out. He'll be lying around somewhere. Perhaps he's hurt——"

His hand steadied me. "We'll look presently. Now sit down again. Have some more brandy."

"No, thank you."

"Come on; do as you're told."

I obeyed him. "You seem to spend a lot of time forcing spirits down my throat, Richard."

He corked the flask and put it down beside me. "You seem a lot more worried about this dog than you do about friend Paul."

"It's David's dog. Besides, Paul Véry ran over a rabbit," I added, as if that explained everything.

"What——" began Richard, then checked himself and spoke rapidly: "Now listen. Only Kramer and Loraine are coming in my car?"

"As far as I know."

"How far behind you?"

"I don't know. He had to go to your garage first to get the car."

"I see . . . well, that wasn't very far. You came fast, I take it?"

"Pretty fast, yes. We did stop once on the road; that wasted about five minutes, I'd say."

"Did you indeed? What for?"

"A spot of love-making," I said levelly.

"I—see." He was silent for a moment. "Of course. That was when you changed places, I suppose?"

"Yes. But Richard, tell me what's happened? This man Marsden——"

"Later. Listen; as things have turned out, we've every chance of winning. They'll stop when they see the van and the Mercedes, and we're two men armed, with surprise on our side. It'll be all right in a very short time, you'll see."

"What are you going to do?"

He gave a little laugh. "I've no idea. No doubt inspiration will come in the moment of crisis."

"Where's Mr. Marsden?"

"Gone to take a look at our friend Paul . . . *listen, is that a car?*"

We froze, straining our ears through the myriad noises of the night's silence. I became conscious of the whispering of the sea; not the breathing, bell-tolling, ebbing-and-flowing sorrow of the northern tides I knew, but the long, murmurous *hush-hush* of the land-bound waters. And above us sang the pines.

"No," I said presently in a low voice. "I can't hear a car."

He stayed for a while with his head cocked to listen, then he relaxed, and I saw the faint gleam of a gun as he turned it over in his hand.

"There was a gun in the car," I said quickly. "I had it on my knee when we skidded. If we can find it that makes three of us——"

"No." His voice was flat. "Indeed it doesn't. You'll stay behind the lines, lady—in the trenches, in fact." I saw his arm lift, and point inland.

"About forty yards back of these trees there's a rocky bank, with a dry gully beyond it. David's there. You'll wait with him, please."

I opened my mouth to protest, but at that moment Marsden interrupted us, looming suddenly out of the darkness.

"He's still unconscious," he said in a rapid undertone, "but nothing seems to be broken. We'll bring him over here, to be on the safe side, and tie him up in the van. We don't want to take the risk that they'll see him lying there, and be warned before they stop that there's something wrong. Is there any rope left?"

"I doubt it." Richard was on his feet, and the two of them were moving about the van. "I think we used all there was."

I felt an absurd desire to laugh. "On André?"

"Mmm?" Marsden's voice was muffled. He seemed to be investigating a tool-box. "André? Who's he?"

"The driver of the van."

"Oh. Yes. He's tied up in there. He's all right."

Richard spoke softly from inside the van: "Nothing here. Charity, is there a belt on your coat?"

"No."

"Oh hell." He landed beside me, soft-footed on the pine-needles. "This is beginning to have all the elements of farce, isn't it? Too many villains, and nothing to tie them up with. And for the life of me I daren't give you my trouser-belt."

"I doubt if he'll give much trouble," said Marsden, "but I'd rather be sure. There may be a rope in the boot of the car. Coming, Byron? We'll go and get him."

"O.K.," said Richard. "Charity, if you hear a car, get back to that gully and stay with David till we come for you."

"Yes, Richard," I said meekly.

But Marsden was made of sterner stuff. "I found a gun in the Mercedes. Perhaps she——"

"No," said Richard once more, finally. "Both you and I have had a pot at her to-night, and Kramer might be luckier."

"Beautifully put," I said, and Marsden laughed.

"Let's go."

They had barely taken two paces when I was on my feet, backed against my tree, all my brittle self-confidence in fragments.

"There it is!" I said hoarsely. "Listen!"

Through the ghostly song of the pines, through the secret breathing of the sea, we heard it, faint but unmistakable; the throb of an engine.

"Blast!" said Marsden softly.

"And coming at a wicked pace," said Richard, and listened a moment longer. My heart was beating to suffocation. "That's my car all right, damn him . . . Charity, please."

"I'm going." My voice, like my body, was shaking. I had to push myself away from the solid comfort of the pine-tree's bole. I was vaguely aware of the two men, moving like shadows in the cover of the van. I ran away from the road, through the trees. The Bentley's engine cut through the silence in a rising drone, urgent, *crescendo*. I was free of the pines, and dodging through head-high scrub. In front loomed a dark mass that might be the rocky bank. The Bentley was coming fast, her engine snarling on a wasp-note of anger . . . I reached the foot of the rocky bank, and stopped. I could not go on. I suppose it was delayed shock, or something, but I know that I was stuck there, shaking and sweating and cold as ice, staring back through the leaves and the pine-trunks, towards the road.

I saw the glare of the Bentley's lights, cutting along the darkness of the cliff-top. The sound of her engine swelled suddenly as she rounded the curve half a mile away. The parasol pines soared again like great thunderhead clouds in the moving light.

The headlamps went out, and the Bentley swooped towards us in the little glow of her side-lights, confident, menacing—the tiger coming in to kill. He had seen the parasol pines; I heard his brakes grip momentarily as he swept into the last stretch of road. Any minute now he would see the van, and stop. The Bentley's snarl deepened. She was on us, moving fast. She was swinging right-handed into the track.

Then the night was ripped, unbelievably, by the roar of another engine. The Mercedes.

I don't remember moving at all, but I must have run towards the road like a mad thing. I only knew that Paul Véry had come round; had somehow got into the Mercedes, and was giving his warning.

I saw the Bentley veer into the track on the cliff-top, I heard the shriek of her brakes. I saw the Mercedes, roaring like a bomber, leap forward, then lurch on to her burst front tyre, and plunge broadside on across the road.

The Bentley never had a chance.

There was a yell, a dreadful scream, and then the cars met in a sickening crash of rending metal and shrieking tyres. Some hideous freak of chance knocked the Bentley's switch as she struck, so that, for one everlasting moment, as the two cars locked in a rearing tower of metal, her headlights shot skywards like great jets of flame. The cars hung there, black against the black sky, locked on the very brink of that awful cliff, then the beam swung over in a great flashing arc, and the locked cars dropped like a plummet down the shaft of light, straight into the sea.

And after that last appalling impact, silence, broken hideously by echo after echo of the sound, as the disturbed sea washed and broke, washed and broke, against the cliff below. For an age, it seemed, the agitated waves beat their terrible reiteration on the rock, till, spent at last, they sank and smoothed themselves to their old whispering.

The last clouds shifted, parted, broke under the wind, and the moonlight fell, infinitely pure, infinitely gentle, to whiten the moving water.

CHAPTER XXVII

O most delicate fiend!
Who is't can read a woman?
(SHAKESPEARE)

DAVID WAS still asleep. I had gone to find him, leaving the two men looking for a way down the cliff. They had driven the van across the road on to the track, switched on its lights, and turned it to face the sea. There was not a chance in a million, Marsden said, that any of the three in the cars were still alive, but we could hardly leave the place without attempting to find out.

With a shudder, I left them to it, and made my way back through the trees to look for David. As I emerged at the top of the rocky bank, I found that I could see my way plainly in the moonlight. Below me, in sharply shadowed monochrome, lay the gully; under a jut of rock and leafage, a darker shadow stirred. I scrambled down hurriedly, to be met by a shapeless shade that whined a little and wriggled with a somewhat subdued delight.

"Rommel!" I went down on my knees in the dust, and hugged him. "Oh Rommel! Did I nearly kill you, poor boy?"

Rommel lavished me with generous but damp forgiveness, and then ran, with a yelp of excitement, into the shelter of the rock. I followed.

David lay curled up, wrapped in a coat. He looked very young and touching, and the sweep of his dark lashes over his cheek was so like Richard's that I felt a sudden rush of some emotion stronger than any I had ever felt before. I knelt down again, beside him, and felt his hands; they were cold. I put a hand to his cheek, and was horrified to feel it wet

to the touch, as if with sweat, but immediately Rommel, feverishly licking the other cheek, provided the clue. I pushed him off.

"It was very clever of you to find him," I told him, "but wait a minute,
will you?"

I gathered David up close to me, and began to rub the cold hands.
Rommel, pressing close with quivering body, watched eagerly.

And presently the dark lashes stirred, and lifted. He stared at me
blankly, and his hands moved a little under mine.

"Hullo, David," I said.

The wide gaze flickered. "Mrs.—Selborne?"

"Yes. How d'you feel?"

"Pretty foul." He moved his head gingerly, and blinked up at the
moonlit bank with the great pines billowing beyond. "Where am I?"

"Some way east of Marseilles. But don't worry. Everything's all right
now."

His eyes were on me again, with a look in them I couldn't quite
fathom. I felt him move away from me a little. "I remember now . . .
Marseilles. How did you get here?"

I understood then. I reached out a hand and took hold of his. "David,
I tell you it's all right. I'm *not* one of them; you can trust me. I followed you out here—Rommel and I did, that is——"

"Rommel?"

He turned at that, and his eye fell for the first time on the dog, who,
belly to earth, shivering with delight in every hair, was waiting to be
noticed.

"He found you all by himself," I said. "Tracked you down."

"Oh, *Rommel!*" said the boy, and burst into tears, with his head buried deep in the dog's fur, and his arms round its neck. I let him cry out
his fright and loneliness and distrust, while Rommel administered comfort, but presently the sobs changed to hiccups, and a voice said un-
compromisingly from Rommel's neck: "I feel beastly sick."

"I'm not surprised," I said. "It'll do you good. Don't mind me. . . ."

Some short time later, after a nasty little interlude, he came back and
sat down beside me. I put my coat round him, and held him close. I was
wondering how on earth to begin telling him about Richard.

"You'd better have a drop of this."

"What is it?"

It was Richard's flask. "Brandy."

"Oh!" He was palpably pleased. "*Real* brandy? . . . ugh, it's horrible!"

"I know, but it's fine when it gets a bit further down. Have some more."

"No, thanks. I feel all right, only hungry."

"Great heavens!"

"What are we doing here anyway?" he demanded. "What happened? I want to *know*. Are we——?"

"One thing at a time. We're waiting here for—for transport back to Marseilles."

He spoke quickly, apprehensively: "Marseilles? That shop? I don't want——"

"Not to the shop," I said reassuringly. "That's all over. The owner of that place has been dealt with. Will you tell me what happened there, or don't you want to talk about it?"

"I hardly remember. I took the bracelet in, and he looked at it, and then asked me where I got it. He looked so queerly at me that I thought he guessed I'd pinched it, and so I made up a few lies. He seemed all right then, and asked me into the office. He went to a drawer; I thought he was getting the money. But he turned round with a towel or something in his hand. I—I don't really remember what happened then."

"Chloroform, I think." The smell was still there very faintly, sweet and horrible. Kramer must have recognized him at once, I thought. Probably Loraine had rung up as soon as he was missing, and told her employer about the bracelet. My arm tightened round him. "What on earth made you choose *that* shop, of all the shops in France?"

"Well, I had no money," said David, "and that beastly bracelet was all I could find. I thought Marseilles was the only place hereabouts where I could sell a thing like that and no questions asked, so I hitch-hiked here. It took *ages*. I took the bracelet into two or three places, but they wouldn't buy it. In the end one chap told me to go to that shop. He said the man was a dealer in silver and he'd probably take it." He gave a little shudder, and burrowed his head against my shoulder.

"What were you planning to do after you'd got the money?"

"Eat." The answer was prompt and emphatic.

I looked down at him. "You poor wretch! D'you mean to tell me you've had nothing all day?"

"I had lunch with some lorry-drivers, but nothing since then."

"Oh dear! And I had some chocolate in my bag, but I lost it. The only consolation is that you'd have been a lot sicker if you'd been chloroformed on top of a good meal. I dare say it won't be very long before you'll get something." I lifted my head to listen, but there was no sound except the sighing of the pines. "And after you'd eaten, David, what were you going to do then?"

"I was going back to Nîmes to look for Daddy."

I was startled, and showed it. "To look for *your father?*"

He gave me a slightly shamefaced look. "Yes. It was really because you went away from the hotel that I decided to go."

"I don't get it."

"That day in Nîmes—you remember?—when we ran away from my father, and I told you I was afraid of him. . . . Well, it wasn't true."

I began to sort out my ideas all over again. "You never really thought he was mad? You weren't ever really afraid of him at all?"

David said, with scorn: "Of course not. Afraid of *him?* I'd never be afraid of him as long as I lived!"

I said, helplessly: "Then for heaven's sake explain! I can't get this straight. You *said* you didn't want to meet him; you *said* it was a matter of life and death, and you said he was mad. And you did look afraid; you looked scared stiff. Now, what's it all about?"

"I was afraid," he said sombrely, "terribly afraid, but *for* him, not *of* him. I'll try and tell you. . . . Shall I just begin at the beginning?"

"Please."

He began to talk, in a clear little voice completely empty of emotion. It was a queer experience to hear the same beastly story of the night of murder and treachery, so soon retold in the voice of a child. It differed from Richard's in nothing but point of view.

". . . And when I heard he'd been acquitted, I knew he would come down to Deepings straight away. But he didn't. I waited and waited, and then the police telephoned Mrs. Hutchings—that's the housekeeper— that Daddy'd had an accident, and was badly hurt. He'd been taken to hospital, they said. Of course I wanted to go and see him, but they said he was still unconscious, and I must wait. Then, quite late, *she* came."

The pitch of his voice never changed, but suddenly, shockingly, I was aware of the cold hatred underneath it. Then, as he went on, I began to realize that David's story was more terrible, even, than Richard's.

"She came to my room. I wasn't asleep, of course. She told me she'd been to the hospital. She broke it ever so gently, you know, but—she told me Daddy had died. What did you say?"

"Nothing. Go on. *She told you your father was dead?*"

"She did. She also told me it was no use going to the hospital; she said I'd not be able to see him, because he'd been too badly burned. Of course," said David, his mouth half buried somewhere near Rommel's right ear, "I wasn't exactly *thinking* straight, you know. I didn't really want to go away with her, but I couldn't stick Deepings just then, and anyway, what could I do? Daddy was dead, and she was my step-mother, and I more or less thought I had to do as she said. There's not much you can do if you're only a boy, and besides, I'd not had much practice in thinking things out for myself, *then.* I have now."

"I know that," I said bitterly.

David went on: "She'd taken a flat up near the Bois, and we lived there. She was quite decent to me, as I thought, and I was so dashed unhappy anyway that I didn't care what happened. I suppose I just moped around the place. I found Rommel one day in the Bois, with a can tied to his tail. After that it was better."

I said, a little grimly: "What happened next?"

"About three weeks ago, she told me Daddy was still alive."

"How on earth did she explain away her lie about his death?"

"She told me she'd done it for my sake." The grey eyes lifted to mine for a moment: they were quite expressionless. "She said that, according to the reports she'd had from the doctors and the police, Daddy had tried to commit suicide."

"David!"

"Yes. She implied, of course, that he *had* done that awful murder, and that it had been preying on his mind. Oh," said David, with a large gesture, "she spared me all she could. She said that he'd been going queerer and queerer for some time, and that he must have killed Uncle Tony—*and* knocked me down—in a sort of blackout. She prescribed it to —is that the word?"

"Ascribed."

"Oh. She ascribed it to his terrible experiences during the War. Why did you laugh?"

"There's a certain irony in that," I said, "but it doesn't matter."

"Well," said David, "that was her story. He was batty, and he was dangerous, so she'd removed me from the trouble zone."

"Did you believe it?"

"No. I knew he wasn't mad; I knew he hadn't killed Uncle Tony; and of course I knew he hadn't hit me. I also knew for certain that he hadn't meant to crash his car and commit suicide, because he'd rung me up from London as soon as he got out of Court, and told me he was coming straight down."

"Did you tell her that?"

"No." He looked at me. "I can't quite explain it, Mrs. Selborne, but I began to get more and more strongly the feeling that I ought to keep things to myself. There was something so—well, sort of queer and *wrong* about the whole set-up. Some of the things she said, the way she looked at me sometimes—the very fact that she'd taken me away with her when I was certain she disliked me anyway—oh! lots of things seemed odd. And now all this talk about father: I was certain that she didn't think he was mad, either. And of course nothing could excuse the lie she'd told about his death." He paused.

"Why didn't you write to your father? Surely that——"

"It was the first thing I thought of, of course. But there was a catch in it, Mrs. Selborne. There were two chaps in the flat below—she said they were her cousins—and they were with us all the time. I never got a minute to myself. I couldn't have got a letter to him without them knowing, and reading it. What's more, she seemed to *want* me to write to him, and that was quite enough, at the time, to make me think twice about it."

"She wanted you to ask him to come and see you?"

"Exactly." His tone was a quaint echo of Richard's. "She said she couldn't possibly let me go back to England till we saw how he was, and she suggested I write and ask him to come to France. She'd have read the letter; there was no question of my being able to tell him what the set-up was, and ask him what had really happened at his end. She went on and on about my writing to invite him, and in such a funny way that I got suspicious again, and just refused. I pretended that I'd believed her story about his being mad, and that I was frightened to see him." He gave a dry little chuckle. "Gosh! she was furious, being hoist in her own juice like that. Is that right? It sounds a bit odd."

"I rather think you mean stewing with her own petard. But let it pass. I get it. She wrote to him herself in the end, you know."

He shot me another look. "Yes, I did know. I telephoned him one night."

"You did? But——"

"He wasn't there. I—I was pretty disappointed. I managed to sneak down one night and phone from the cousins' flat while they were with *her*. Mrs. Hutchings answered. She said Daddy'd had a letter marked *Paris* that morning, and he'd left straight away. I said how was he, and she told me he was all right, but just worried to death, and only just out of hospital anyway. . . . The cousins caught me on the way up from the phone. I spun them a lie, but they didn't believe me, and after that I was never left alone. Next morning we all went to Lyons, and then, stage by stage, down here. It puzzled me no end, till I began to think they wanted Daddy down here, instead of in Paris. And I could only think that it was still something to do with that murder, and that they'd harm him."

"A trap," I said, "with you as bait."

"Exactly," he said again. "So I wasn't going to get into touch with Daddy just to lure him in; I wanted to be quite sure, first, that it was safe. The queer thing was that the cousins left us at Montélimar, and when we were in Avignon, she let me go round alone. . . ."

"She didn't," I said, thinking of Paul Véry. "Someone else had taken over. You were accompanied all the time."

"*Was* I? Then I was right to run away in Nîmes?"

"Very probably."

He spoke slowly, in an unconscious echo of his father's own bewilderment: "It was pretty awful, not knowing what to do—not knowing whether people were enemies, or just ordinary people. It was as if"—he gave a little shiver—"as if everything was upside down." He shivered again.

"It's over now," I said firmly. "If you're cold, come under my coat again."

"I'm not, really. I want to know what's happened, and how you know all this. I say, do we *have* to stay here, Mrs. Selborne? This 'transport' you mentioned——"

"Is here now," I said, and got to my feet. I could hear footsteps scrambling up the further side of the bank. David jumped up, looking a little scared, and Rommel bristled.

"Who——?"

Richard swung himself down the slope, and stood there in the moonlight, looking at his son. He hesitated a little, then put out a hand.

There was a rush of feet past me, and David hurtled into the moonlight like an arrow going into the gold. I saw his father's arms close round him, and the dark heads close together.

I went quickly past them, and Marsden's hand reached down to help me up the bank.

I looked a query at him.

He shook his head. "Not a sign," he said quietly.

We walked through the trees, towards the road where the van stood waiting, her nose towards Marseilles.

CHAPTER XXVIII

Two loves have I . . .
(SHAKESPEARE)

I WOKE to bright sunlight and a most delectable smell of coffee. Swimming up through the billows of a deep and dreamless sleep, I found myself blinking drowsily at the white walls and red-tiled floor of a room that was vaguely familiar. The sun blazed in bright bars through a closed shutter: the other had swung open, letting in a flood of gold. From out-side the cries and clangs of the city rose musically, as if muted by the light.

The door had opened softly, letting in the lovely coffee-smell that had roused me. I turned my head, then sat up, fully awake.

"Louise!"

Immaculate as ever, she was standing just inside the door, looking speculatively at me across a loaded tray.

"So you are awake? Or did I disturb you? I thought it was high time——"

"Oh, Louise, how nice to see you! How did it happen? And what *is* the time?"

She set the tray on my knees, and went to open the shutter. "High noon, my child."

"Good Lord, is it really?" I poured coffee. "When did you get here?"

"About an hour and a half ago. I got the first train." She added, rea-sonably: "You said you were in a jam, and I knew you hadn't any clothes with you."

"My *dear*," I said gratefully, "don't tell me you've brought my clothes! I knew you were the most wonderful woman in the world."

She laughed. "No one can face a crisis unless they're suitably clad. How do you feel?"

"Fine—I think." I stretched a few muscles gingerly, and was relieved. "A bit stiff, and a bruise here or there, but otherwise"—I smiled at her— "on top of the world."

"Mmmm. . . ." Louise eyed me as she pulled an unsteady-looking wicker chair to the bedside. "Ye-es. Your ghastly village seems to have been a pretty exciting place after all. What happened to you?"

I chuckled through a bite of *croissant,* aware of a miraculous spring-time lift of the heart, a champagne-tingling of the blood: the nightmare had gone; this fresh sun of morning rose on a different world where the last gossamer rag of fear and uncertainty must shrink and vanish in the superfluity of light. I said: "I was—translated."

"Yes. You look it. I suppose you met the Wolf of Orange?"

"In person," I said happily.

"I thought so." Her tone was bland. "He rang up about half an hour ago. If you're feeling fit, we are to meet him for lunch at the Hôtel de la Garde. On the terrace, at one-fifteen. And now," said Louise, settling herself in the wicker chair and regarding me placidly, "I am dying by inches of curiosity, and I want to be told every single thing that has hap-pened, including why this Richard Byron who is David Bristol's father and who I thought was a murderer anyway should be ringing you up in

Marseilles and asking you to lunch, and why he should feel it necessary to inform me that neither he nor Mr. Marsden was in jail as yet and that Rommel had bitten André in the seat of the pants and that I was to let you sleep late and then take you some coffee and see you took a taxi to lunch as if"—finished Louise on a faintly accusing note—"he had known you all your life instead of—how long?"

I said, in simple surprise: "Three days . . . off and on."

"And rather more off than on, at that," said Louise. "A dictatorial gentleman, I'd have said, at a guess."

"He is a bit." I stirred my coffee absorbedly.

"And you like it," she accused me.

"I'm—well, I got used to it, you know. Johnny——"

"I know. No wonder you keep getting married and I don't," said Louise, without rancour.

I coloured, and laughed a little. "He hasn't asked me, as it happens."

She merely raised a beautifully groomed eyebrow and handed me a cigarette.

"Well, come along, my girl. Tell me all about it."

"It's a long story——"

"We've got an hour before we meet the Wolf. Go on: begin at the beginning, go on to the end, and then stop."

"—and an utterly fantastic one."

"I am all ears," said Louise contentedly, and leaned back in her chair.

So I told her, lying back on the pillows in my little hotel room at the Belle Auberge, with the peaceful sunlight slanting across the coverlet, and the smoke from our cigarettes winding in placid spirals between us. I told her everything just as it had happened, and, like Paul Véry, she listened silently, only staring at me with a kind of shocked disbelief.

"We—ell," she said at length, on a long note of amazement. "What an extraordinary tale! Not, of course, that I believe a word of it, only——"

"You'd better ask the others," I told her. "Mr. Marsden said——"

Louise sat up. "Yes! Now *that* I don't follow at all. What the dickens is John Marsden doing in this *galère* at all?"

It was my turn to raise an eyebrow. "John?"

"After you left for Les Boos," she said calmly, "we got acquainted."

"Well I'll be dashed," I said. "If I'd known that I'd have stopped suspecting him at once."

"On the principle that all my men friends turn out to be Boy Scouts or curates on holiday," agreed Louise. "It certainly shook me to hear he's a great detective. Marsden of the C.I.D. Well, well. And he's very nice, even if he does read poetry. Go on. Did he tell you how he got to this awful place on the cliff?"

"Yes. He made it sound awfully simple. Apparently he was helping at first, this spring, in the investigation of Tony Baxter's murder. Richard, it turns out, had actually met him a couple of times, but didn't remember the name when I described Marsden to him. Well, Marsden was taken off to work on another big case, but he was interested in the Baxter murder, and the man in charge of it, Inspector Brooke, wasn't at all satisfied with the way the case finished. He came at length to believe, himself, that Richard hadn't done it; the murderer, therefore, must be still at large, possibly active, and the motive undiscovered. Richard's so-called car-accident shook him a good bit. Richard was safe in hospital, but Brooke began to wonder about Loraine, and to worry quite a lot about David."

"Good for him."

"Yes indeed. Well, Marsden was due for leave, and offered to do a spot of unofficial guardianship. He has friends at the Sûreté, and they said right, go ahead, so he came over to France to locate David."

"Well, well," said Louise. "Then that's why he disappeared from the Tistet-Védène when David did."

"Quite. I'd noticed him hanging round where David was, and imputed sinister motives to him. Well, to cut it short, he managed, with a good deal of difficulty, to get on to David's tail south to Marseilles. Apparently it took the poor child nearly all day to get here, as he felt obliged to hide at sight of every car, and the lorries were slow, and few and far between. But he got here, with Marsden faint but pursuing, and eventually landed in Kramer's beastly little shop."

I glanced at my watch. "I must get up soon. . . . Well, poor David was chloroformed—pretty heavily, too—while Marsden skulked about outside not knowing what had happened. I imagine that Kramer got busy on the telephone, then, to Avignon, and told Loraine to get on to the next train. Paul Véry must have left long before——"

"He did," said Louise. "He took his car out soon after lunch, ostensibly to look for David. The American couple did the same, and so did those two Germans. But Paul Véry didn't come back for dinner."

"I've no doubt he did look for David," I said, "and probably passed him hiding in a ditch. He must either have telephoned Kramer later, and heard of David's capture, or have driven straight down here for orders; at any rate, Marsden says, Véry got here a good hour or so before Loraine. I saw him myself in the office when she landed in a taxi, Marsden was still hanging about waiting for David to leave the shop, when Paul arrived, and turned into the garage opposite, just as if he'd lived there all his life. Marsden recognized him, and began to wonder just what was going on, so, when Paul Véry walked into the shop, and straight through into the office, Marsden, like me, found his way through to the back, and listened under the window. It must have been just about then," I said meditatively, "that Richard and I were sitting talking about four streets away. . . ."

"There seems to have been quite a procession into Kramer's parlour," remarked Louise.

"Yes indeed." I shuddered. "Well, Marsden heard quite a bit under his window. He could tell that there were at least three men—Kramer and Jean-Paul and André—in the office, so, even when he learned what had happened to David, he couldn't do very much about it. His French was just good enough for him to realize they were planning to move David, so he didn't dare risk losing track of him by going to the police. He simply stuck around and hoped for a chance to grab David."

"Poor John," said Louise.

"He said it was hell," I told her. "He waited and waited, and they talked and talked, and then the door opened, and Richard walked in."

"That must have been quite a moment."

"Mustn't it? Richard, of course, remembers nothing but the sight of David lying on a sofa. He started for him, and the three of them set on him straight away. Marsden, under the window, didn't see a thing, but he heard Richard say 'David!' in English, and then the hullabaloo. Then Kramer said something about 'putting them both in the van,' so Marsden slipped across to the garage. He says he imagined they'd all three go with the van, and since his one thought was not to be left behind, he got inside it and hid under some sacks. But they dumped Richard and David in, locked the door on them, and Kramer told André to get out to that place on the coast, park under cover, and wait for him. Then he and Paul Véry went back to wait for Loraine. Marsden was furious. If he hadn't been locked in, he could have dealt with André then and there, and driven Richard and David straight off to the police-station. But he was stuck, so he lay low, untied Richard, and set about bringing him round."

Louise sighed with satisfaction. "So when poor André stopped the van and went to get the bodies——"

"Exactly. They knocked him cold, tied him up, and took his gun. They even took his coat to wrap David in. On the whole," I said, "I'm a little sorry for André. Kramer said he was a bit of a fool."

Louise laughed. "And now Rommel's bitten him. Poor André."

I pushed back the coverlet and got out of bed. "Poor Rommel, you mean. He's had a lot to bear. David left him outside the shop, and the poor dog must have waited for centuries. He found his way round to the back streets in the end, and that's where I picked him up. Did you say something about bringing me some clothes?"

"They're in my room. I'll get them; I didn't want to wake you before."
She smiled at me as she rose. "What a good thing I brought your very
nicest dress!"

"*Not* the Mexican print?" I said gratefully. "Dear Louise, you shall
be my bridesmaid *again*."

"Not on your life," said Louise. "It's unlucky, and anyway, I'm too
old. I'll wait and be godmother."

"You're a little premature," I said.

"So I should hope," said Louise, making for the door. She turned, and
her sleek brows mocked me again. "So are you, aren't you?"

"I?"

"Yes. He hasn't even asked you."

The door shut gently behind her.

.   .   .   .

As I lifted my dress from the case Louise had brought, I saw the silver
photograph-frame underneath. Johnny's eyes smiled up at me.

I picked up the photograph, and was looking down at the pictured
face, when the fading bruise on my wrist caught, as it were, at the edge
of my vision.

I smiled back at Johnny. Then I held my wrist very lightly against my
cheek. Any hesitations I had had, all the doubts that my intellect had
been placing in front of my heart, seemed, with the rest of the nightmare
adventure, to resolve themselves and fade away. Past and future dove-
tailed into this moment, and together made the pattern of my life. I
would never again miss Johnny, with that deep dull aching, as if part of
me had been wrenched away, and the scar left wincing with the cold;
but, paradoxically enough, now that I was whole again, Johnny was
nearer to me than he had ever been since the last time that we had been
together, the night before he went away. I was whole again, and Johnny
was there for ever, part of me always. Because I had found Richard, I
would never lose Johnny. Whatever I knew of life and loving had been
Johnny's gift, and without it Richard and I would be the poorer. We
were both his debtors, now and for ever.

I lifted Johnny's photograph and kissed it. It was the last time I
should ever do so. Then I laid it gently back in the case, and picked up
my dress again.

A short time later I opened my door, called Louise, and went out into
the sunshine to meet Richard.

CHAPTER XXIX

O frabjous day!
(CARROL)

THE TERRACE of the Hôtel de la Garde almost overhangs the edge of the sea. It is wide, and flagged with white stone, with beautifully formal little orange-trees in pots to give it shade, and a breeze straight off the Mediterranean to cool it. The bright little boats bob, scarlet and green and white, just below your table, and the *bouillabaisse* is wonderful.

We were a gay enough party. Richard and Marsden had spent the greater part of the night and morning with the police, and both looked tired, but about the former I noticed something I had not seen in him before; he was relaxed. The last of the strain had been lifted, and though his eyes were weary, they were clear, and his mouth had lost its hardness. As for David, he was in tearing spirits, and kept us all laughing until coffee and cigarettes came round.

Marsden got out his pipe and settled back in his chair with a long sigh of satisfaction. He, too, looked as if some strain were lifted, but with him it was rather a slackening of concentration, a putting, so to speak, of his intelligence into carpet slippers for a while. He had come off duty.

His blue eyes studied me over the match-flame as he held it to his pipe. At last this was going nicely.

"If I may say so, Mrs. Selborne," he said, "you've come out of this affair looking remarkably fit. How do you feel to-day?"

"Fine, thank you," I said. "Nothing to show but a few bruises." I caught Richard's rueful grin, and smiled back. "How restful it is, isn't it, now that everybody knows whose side they're on?"

"It certainly is," agreed Marsden. He cocked an eye at Louise. "I take it you've put Louise in the picture?"

"She told me the whole story," said Louise, "except for the most important thing—the reason for it all. That was just guesswork. Have you found out anything further about *why* Kramer employed those two to do the murders?"

"Our guesswork was right," said Richard. "The police searched Kramer's premises this morning, and there's evidence galore. The whole thing is clear enough now."

"Tell us, please," I said.

"I'll try." He flicked the ash from his cigarette into the sea, then stared thoughtfully at the tip of it for a moment, before he spoke.

"We were right," he said, looking at me. "It all began on that beastly January day in 1944, when Tony Baxter and I, on our way to a prison camp, were witnesses to Kramer's murder of Emmanuel Bernstein—and, incidentally, to his connection with the mass-murder of the Jews." He glanced at Louise. "Did Charity tell you about that?"

"Yes. What a beastly affair! I don't wonder you lost your temper and blew up."

Richard's eyes met mine. "I do, sometimes," he admitted. "It's a fault I have. But this time Tony did as well. I'm glad of that, because if I'd been solely responsible for attracting Kramer's notice I'd feel a very heavy burden of guilt for Tony's death. As it is"—his face darkened for an instant, but he resumed in a normal tone: "Well, you know what happened; we were eventually permitted to go, but Kramer had occasion to remember us, and his memory was excellent."

He paused. "That wouldn't have mattered at all, of course, if it hadn't been for the next connection between us: both Kramer and I were in the same line of business, the trade in antiques, and both, as it happens, particularly interested in old silver. When the War finished, and the Nuremberg witch-hunt started, Kramer somehow or other managed to disappear. He got out of Germany, and appeared in France as an Austrian refugee, one Karel Werfel. He had managed to salt away a pleasant little fortune in money and loot, and before long he was doing very nicely, with his headquarters in Paris, and branches in Lyons and Marseilles. I should mention here, perhaps, something that we found out this morning. Loraine was his"—his gaze fell on David, wide-eyed and absorbed—"Loraine was with Kramer for a time immediately after the War." Richard's voice was sombre, tinged with a kind of pity. "She had a bad record; she was suspected of collaboration, and of having a hand in the murder of two French officers. Kramer helped her to avoid the consequences, but kept the proof himself and used it to gain a hold over her."

He stubbed out his cigarette. "By the time Tony and I appeared again on his horizon, Max Kramer had a lot to lose. He had this perfectly genuine and lucrative business, but he also had other business, even more lucrative, and highly criminal, for which the antique trade was a cloak. His real headquarters for that was here, in Marseilles. I'm not quite sure just what rackets he was concerned in, but at the moment the Marseilles police are having a fine old time rounding up some of the people whose names were in Kramer's safe. There hardly seems to be any pie he didn't have a finger in—smuggling, dope-running, and so forth, but the most important thing that came to light when his premises were searched is definite evidence that he's been mixed up in some of these underground movements to upset the present German government and bring back the National Socialists."

"You mean those gangs of Neo-Hitlerites? Were-wolves, or whatever they called themselves?" asked Louise.

"Something like that." It was Marsden who answered her. "His genuine business, with its wide trade contracts, and the necessity for a good deal of foreign travel, made an excellent mask for the centre of a widish organization. The police think now that Kramer—or Werfel—was at the back of a good deal of organized thuggery, sabotage, and what-have-you, in Germany and Northern France shortly after the end of the War. Go on, Byron."

"Well, into this comfortable and prosperous picture," resumed Richard, "came, suddenly, Tony and myself. There was a big sale in Paris, for the disposal of the Lemaire collection of silver, and naturally I was there. Kramer, apparently, was there too, and must have seen us, though neither of us noticed him. But he made enquiries, and discovered that I was in the same business as himself, and had, in fact, opened an office in Paris. We were bound to meet. And if Tony or I recognized him, well" —his gesture was eloquent—"even if he escaped a war crimes tribunal, there would be enquiries, and he couldn't afford the least investigation. It would be the end of Karel Werfel. . . ."

"It was a pretty frightful coincidence, wasn't it," said Louise, "that David should have gone to *Kramer's* shop to sell the bracelet?"

"Frightful," agreed Richard, "but not so much of a coincidence, if you think it over. The thread that runs through the whole story, after all, is the antique-business: if Kramer and I hadn't happened to be in the same line of country, we would probably never have met after the War —and certainly the danger of our meeting more than once would have been slight. But we were both interested in the same thing, and would in all likelihood be thrown together again and again: and *that* Kramer dared not risk. Yes, the whole *raison d'être* of the affair, you might say, was 'old silver', and the bracelet would almost inevitably act as a link. I bought it for Loraine; Loraine bought it—and David and me—down into Kramer's country: once David tried to sell such a thing hereabouts it was almost certain to come to Kramer's notice pretty soon. And that's what happened; David was advised to take it to him to get an opinion on its value. No, the coincidence lies in the fact that I saw the thing in the shop-window when I did; but that was just Kramer's luck. I was supposed to be got into his den sooner or later, it just happened to be sooner."

"Paul Véry," I said, as he stopped. "Where did he come in?"

"He had a criminal record as long as your arm," said Marsden cheerfully, "and half a dozen aliases. Kramer had enough tucked away in his safe to send Paul Véry to Devil's Island for several lifers."

"He must have promised to hand the papers over to Loraine and Paul after Richard was safely out of the way," I said. "I heard him tell them they'd be free of him once the job was over."

"Was she really Paul Véry's wife?" asked Louise.

"Indubitably. They were married in 1942, then he was posted missing the following year. She picked up with Kramer in the autumn of 1945. When Paul Véry turned up again he appears to have accepted the situation (to some extent, I imagine, under pressure), and stayed on to work for Kramer. He seems to have taken a pretty—what shall I say?—liberal view of his wife's activities. When Kramer saw Byron and Baxter at the Lemaire sale, and decided they would have to be eliminated, he picked Paul Véry for the job."

"Greatly helped," said Richard bitterly, "by the fool Byron, who, seeing Loraine at the sale, began to show signs of interest that made it easy for the precious trio to commit the first murder."

"If you hadn't 'married' her and taken her to Deepings," said Marsden, "they'd have managed some other way."

"I dare say," said Richard, "but you can't say I didn't help. At least it's a comfort of a sort to know she was never legally my wife. . . . It was Paul Véry, of course, who killed Tony and knocked David out. It was Paul Véry who tried to ram my car. And when the attempt at double murder failed, they took David to France. I doubt if they had a plan worked out at all, but David was an obvious trump card."

"I don't quite see why, you know," said David.

"Don't you?" said his father. "Loraine knew very well that I'd never willingly see her again. Kramer wanted me over here, but if she'd tried to get me to see her I'd either have ignored her or put my lawyers on to it. But you"—he flicked David's cheek with a casual finger—"I can't afford to let you go. You're a rebate on my income-tax."

"Talking of income-tax," I said, "your insurance company——"

"Oh God, yes," said Richard. "Two cars in four months! I know. I'm going to have a gay time explaining when I get back. . . . Anyway, that's the story. You know the rest. They planned to get me down here, where there were better facilities for disposing of me, and, heaven knows, their plan might have worked, if they hadn't left two important things out of their reckoning."

"What two things?" demanded David.

Richard said soberly, looking at Marsden: "The integrity and human-kindness of the English police, for one. I shan't forget it, Marsden, and neither will David. I'll write to Brooke to-night. We're deeply in your debt."

Marsden looked acutely uncomfortable, and muttered something, then turned and began to tap out his pipe on the balustrade between the table and the sea.

"And the second thing?" asked David.

Richard smiled at me suddenly, so that my heart turned a silly somersault in my breast.

"The spanner in the works," he said, and laughed.

"The what, Daddy?"

"Chance, my dear David, in the shape of Charity."

David looked from him to me, and back again. "Charity?"

I said: "It's my name, David," and blushed like a fool.

"Oh, I see." His bright gaze rested on me for a speculative moment, then returned to his father, but all he said was: "I thought you meant that stuff in the Bible about *Charity suffereth long and is kind.*"

"That, too," said Richard, and laughed again.

"Your father exaggerates," I told David. "The only thing I did of real practical value was to find Rommel, and then I nearly killed him."

"Your idea of practical value," said Richard drily, "is a distorted one, to say the least. That ill-favoured mongrel——"

David shot up in his chair. *"Mongrel?* He's not! Anyone can *see* he's well-bred! Can't they?" He appealed to Marsden, who grinned.

"Let us say that a good deal has gone into his breeding," he said tactfully. "I'm sure he's highly intelligent."

"Of course he is!" David was emphatic. "Look how he found me! Why, he's practically *police-trained!"*

Richard said dampingly: "I suppose that means you've trained him to sleep on your bed?"

"The police," began Marsden, "don't as a rule——"

But David hadn't heard him. He was eyeing his father with some caution. "As a matter of fact, I have."

"And a very good habit too," I said promptly. "He can keep the—the mice away."

Across David's look of gratification, Richard's eyes met mine.

"I—see," he said. "Collusion. Conspiracy against me in my own home. I seem to be letting myself in for——"

"Daddy!" David's eyes were round. He looked at me. "Mrs. Selborne! Are you going to marry Daddy?"

"Yes," I said.

David got to his feet. "I'm terribly glad," he said simply, and kissed me.

Above the general babel of question and congratulation the smooth voice of the *maître d'hôtel* insinuated at Richard's ear: "Champagne for m'sieur?" They didn't miss much at the Hôtel de la Garde. Then the magnificent bottle arrived, all gold-foil and sparkling ice and bowing attendant acolytes, and Marsden, on his feet, was making a very creditable speech, unaware of—or unconcerned by—the broad smiles and palpable interest of the people at the other tables. Behind him the blue sea danced, diamond-spangled, and in his uplifted glass a million bubbles winked and glittered.

". . . The only correct ending," he was saying, "to adventure. *So they lived happily ever after.* I give you the toast: Richard and Charity!"

He sat down among quite a small storm of clapping and general laughter.

"When's it to be?" he asked me.

Richard took a folded paper from his breast-pocket. "In ten days' time," he said. "That's the very soonest you can do it in France. I made enquiries this morning when I got the licence."

I heard Louise murmur: "Dictatorial . . ." just beside me, and then David demanded:

"But when did all this *happen?*"

Richard was laughing at me across his glass of champagne, with devils in his eyes. I said: "Actually, it hasn't happened. I mean, he hasn't asked me to marry him at all."

"Hasn't *asked* you——?"

Richard said: "Will you marry me?"

"Yes," I said.

David grabbed his glass again. "Well, then," he said, in briskly practical tones, "that's settled, isn't it? All in front of witnesses, too. He'll not find that easy to wriggle out of, Mrs. Selborne. I'll see he gets held to it. And now may I have some more champagne?"

"It seems to me," I said austerely, "that you've had quite enough."

He grinned at me. "It was a very nice proposal," he admitted. "No words wasted, no beating about the bush. . . ." He reached for the champagne-bottle.

"No!" said Richard firmly, as I moved the bottle beyond David's reach.

"Collusion!" said David bitterly. "Conspiracy! I can see——"

"I've had a lot of practice," I told him, "and I'm a very managing woman."

Richard was grinning. "Did Johnny always do as he was told?"

"Always," I said composedly.

Louise laughed. "Some day," she told him, "I'll tell you the truth about that." She got to her feet, and smiled at the others, who had risen too.

"Well, thank you for my lunch and the champagne. Don't let me keep you from the police and the other joys in store. Will they want David? No? Then perhaps he could spend the afternoon with me?"

"Thanks very much," said Richard. "If the dog'll be in the way——"

"On the contrary," said Louise, "I wouldn't dream of leaving the dog behind. What do you suggest I do with the pair of them?"

Richard's hand slipped under my arm as we all turned to make our way out of the restaurant.

"Most people," he said gravely, "begin their sightseeing in Marseilles with a trip to the Château d'If."

CHAPTER XXX

EPILOGUE

Upon the Islands Fortunate we fall,
Not faint Canaries but Ambrosiall.
(DONNE)

IT WAS LATE the following afternoon, and the sun slanted a deepening gold through the boughs that arched the avenue where Richard and I were walking. The columns of the planes were warm in their delicate arabesques of silver and isabel and soft russet-red. Over our heads the leaves, deepening already towards the sere time, danced a little to the straying wind, and then hung still.

"At least," said Richard, "we have nine days to get to know each other in before it's too late. Are you sure you don't mind being rushed into it like this?"

"Quite sure."

"The least I can do is to leave it to you to choose a place for a honeymoon."

I said: "The Isles of Gold."

"Where's that? Ultima Thule?"

"Not quite. It's another name for Porquerolles. You sail from Hyères."

"Wonderful. We'll have a fortnight there—and perhaps Corsica, too. The Dexters say David can stay as long as he likes and we can pick him up——"

"Oh, Richard, look!" I cried.

We were passing a shop window, and, backed against a neutral screen of porridge-grey, a single picture on a little easel was standing.

Richard turned and glimpsed it. He stopped.

"Oh," was all he said, but it was said on a long note of discovery.

The picture was small, but against the flat background of the screen the colours in it glowed like jewels, so placed that they vibrated one against the other, until you could have sworn the boy in the picture smiled. He was standing against a shadowed ground of leaves and rock, very straight, with his dark head high, and a gallant look to him.

"It's David!" I said.

"It *is* David," said Richard. "See the sling in his hand? He's just setting off to face Goliath and the Philistines."

"It's the first time I saw him," I said, and gazed down at the pictured face, so young, and with that look I remembered so well of the brave acceptance of a burden too heavy for his shoulders. David, alone among his enemies, had faced them with just this same gaiety and temper that was written in the bearing of the young champion of Israel.

"May I have it for a wedding-present?" I asked.

"You certainly may. What a glorious bit of painting! And the man who painted that meant it with every stroke of the brush. Young Israel, up against the enemy . . . I—I wonder——"

He broke off suddenly as he leaned forward to peer at the narrow strip of brass along the base of the frame.

At the look in his face I cried out: "Richard, what is it?"

"Look for yourself," he said.

I peered through the plate glass. In tiny letters on the brass I made out the legend:

LE JEUNE DAVID

and below this the name of the artist:

EMMANUEL BERNSTEIN

．　　．　　．　　．　　．　　．　　．　　．　　．

And so it ended, where it had begun, with the little Jewish painter whose death had been so late, but so amply avenged. And, ten days later, with *The Boy David* carefully boxed in the back of the Riley, my husband and I set our faces to the South, and the Isles of Gold.

Nine Coaches Waiting

FOR ELIZABETH MANNERS

CONTENTS

CHAPTER I

First and Second Coaches

O, think upon the pleasure of the palace!
Securèd ease and state! The stirring meats
Ready to move out of the dishes, that e'en now
Quicken when they are eaten. . . .
Banquets abroad by torchlight! music! sports!
Nine coaches waiting—hurry, hurry, hurry—
Ay, to the devil. . . .

Tourneur: The Revenger's Tragedy.

I was thankful that nobody was there to meet me at the airport.

We reached Paris just as the light was fading. It had been a soft, gray March day, with the smell of spring in the air. The wet tarmac glistened underfoot; over the airfield the sky looked very high, rinsed by the afternoon's rain to a pale clear blue. Little trails of soft cloud drifted in the wet wind, and a late sunbeam touched them with a fleeting underglow. Away beyond the airport buildings the telegraph wires swooped gleaming above the road where passing vehicles showed lights already.

Some of the baggage was out on the tarmac. I could see my own shabby case wedged between a brand-new Revrobe and something huge and extravagant in cream-colored hide. Mine had been a good case once, good solid leather stamped deeply with Daddy's initials, now half hidden under the new label smeared by London's rain. Miss L. Martin, Paris. Symbolic, I thought, with an amusement that twisted a bit awry somewhere inside me. Miss L. Martin, Paris, trudging along between a stout man in impeccable city clothes and a beautiful American girl with a blond mink coat slung carelessly over a suit that announced discreetly that she had been to Paris before, and recently. I myself must have just that drab, seen-better-days shabbiness that Daddy's old case had, perched up there among the sleek cabin-class luggage.

But I was here, home after ten years. Ten years. More than a third of my lifetime. So long a time that now, pausing in the crush beside the Customs barrier, I felt as strange as I suppose anybody must feel on their first visit abroad. I found I even had to make a conscious effort to adjust my ears to the flood of French chatter going on around me. I even found myself, as all about me people uttered little cries of recognition, excitement and pleasure, and were claimed by waiting friends and relations, scanning the crowd of alien faces for one that I knew. Which was absurd. Who would there be to meet me? Madame de Valmy herself? I smiled at the thought. It was very good of Madame de Valmy to have provided me with the money for a taxi into Paris. She was hardly likely to do much for the hired help. And that was what I was. I had better start remembering it, as from now.

The *douanier,* chalk in hand, was pausing over my shabby case. As I stepped forward to claim it an airport official, hurrying past, bumped against me, sending my handbag flying to the floor.

"Mille pardons, mademoiselle. Excusez-moi."

"Ce n'est rien, monsieur."

"Je vous ai fait mal?"

"Pas du tout. Ce n'est rien."

"Permettez-moi, mademoiselle. Votre sac."

"Merci, monsieur. Non, je vous assure, il n'y a pas de mal . . ."

And to my repeated assurances that nothing was lost and that I was not irretrievably damaged, he at length took himself off.

I stared after him for a moment, thoughtfully. The trivial little incident had shown me that, after all, that ten-years' gap had not been so very long. Ear and brain had readjusted themselves now with a click that could be felt.

And I must not let it happen. It was another thing I must remember. I was English. English. Madame de Valmy had made it very clear that she wanted an English girl, and I hadn't seen any harm in letting her assume that my knowledge of France and things French was on a par with that of the average English girl who'd done French at school. She had made rather a lot of it, really . . . though probably, I thought, I'd been so anxious to get the job that I'd exaggerated the importance of the thing out of all measure. After all, it could hardly matter to Madame de Valmy whether I was English, French or even Hottentot, as long as I did the job properly and didn't lapse into French when I was supposed to be talking English to young Philippe. And I could hardly be said to have deceived her, because in fact I *was* English; Daddy had been English and Maman at least a quarter so . . . and even to me those early years were faded and remote. The years when Maman and I lived out at Passy with Grand'mère, and the Boche was in Paris, and Daddy was away somewhere unspecified but highly dangerous and we never allowed ourselves to speak or even think in English . . . even for me those years had sunk well back into the past, so far back that now they

seemed hardly to belong to me at all. Infinitely more real were the last
ten years in England—seven of them spent at the Constance Butcher
Home, an orphanage in North London, and the last three in a qualified
independence—a travesty of freedom—as general help and dogsbody at a
small prep school for boys in Kent. Those endless green-linoleum corridors, the sausage on Mondays and Thursdays, the piles of dirty sheets
to count, and the smell of chalk and carbolic soap in the classroom . . .
these were a very much more present memory than the lovely old house
at Passy or even the top flat in the Rue du Printemps, where we had
gone after the war was over and Daddy came home. . . .

The *douanier* said wearily, *"Vous n'avez rien à déclarer?"*

I started and turned. I said firmly, in English, "Nothing to declare.
No, none of those things. Nothing at all. . . ."

There were taxis waiting outside. To the driver I said, "Hôtel Crillon,
please," and derived my third twinge of amusement from the slight air
of surprise with which he received the august address. Then he heaved
the old brown case in beside me; the car door slammed, the gears raced,
and we were off.

If there had been any strangeness left in me, it would have vanished
now. The taxi swung around into the main road with a screech of
brakes, skidded as a matter of course on the wet tarmac, and roared
toward Paris. I sat back in the familiar reek of Gauloises, disintegrating
leather, and stale exhaust, and the old world closed around me in a cloud
of forgotten impressions which seemed in a moment to blot out the last
ten years as if they had never been. The taxi was Pandora's box, and I
had not only lifted the lid, I was inside it. These sweet, these stinging
memories . . . things I had never before noticed, never missed, until
now I saw them unchanged, part and parcel of that life that stopped ten
years ago. . . .

The driver had been reading a newspaper; it was thrust into a compartment beside the dashboard. I could see the familiar black blurred print,
and the corner of an out-of-focus picture. A bus approached, its direction
board already lighted: SENLIS. I saw the crowd of girls and workmen
standing on the rear platform, crushed together and lurching with the
movement against rails and rope. And now the ugly suburbs were closing
in; tall houses with wrought-iron balconies and slatted shutters; hoard-
ings with their peeling posters, Bonbel, Sunil, Ancre Pils; shabby little
tabacs with their lights reflected orange and gold in the damp pavements; in a café-bar, bright light on rows of glittering bottles and a
huddle of metal tables behind steamy glass; Dubo, Dubon, Dubonnet

. . . and there ahead of us, down the long straight stretch of the Route de Flandre, Paris was lighting up.

My eyelids stung suddenly, and I shut my eyes and leaned back against the shabby upholstery. But still through the open window Paris met me, assailed, bombarded me. The smell of coffee, cats, drains, wine and wet air . . . the hoarse voices shouting *France-Soir, Paris-Presse* . . . someone selling lottery tickets . . . the police whistles . . . the scream of brakes. Something was missing, I thought vaguely, something had changed . . . but it was only when the taxi swerved violently and I opened my eyes to see it miss a pack of cyclists by inches that I realized what it was. He wasn't using his horn; the incessant blare of Paris was gone. I found myself looking about me all at once as if I were a stranger and this were a new town and a new experience.

Something inside me welcomed the change. Quite deliberately I turned my thoughts away from the easy path they were treading, and made myself think about the future. I was back in France; that much of the dream of the past ten years had come true. However prosaic or even dreary my new job might be, at least I had come back to the country I had persisted in regarding as my home. If I had deceived Madame de Valmy, I had done so under a pressure that was to me a necessity. Well, here I was. This was France. The lighted suburbs that were swimming past me were those of my home. Not very long now and we would be in the heart of Paris, thrusting our way down the confusion of the Rue Royale to shoot out into the great glittering spaces of Concorde, where the windows of the Crillon look out through the still-bare chestnut branches toward the Seine. Then tomorrow we would set off again, deeper into France, across her pastures and vineyards and hills and high Alps till we reached the Château Valmy, perched above its forests by the little village of Soubirous in High Savoy. . . . I could see it in my mind's eye now, as I had pictured it a hundred times since the journey started —the fairy-tale castle of a dream, something remote and romantic and impossible—a sort of Walt Disney advertisement for Gibbs Dentifrice. Of course it wouldn't be like that, but all the same. . . . The taxi checked, then ground to a reluctant halt behind a stationary bus. I clutched my handbag tightly on my knee and leaned forward, staring out of the window. Now that I was here, even this tiny delay became suddenly intolerable. The bus moved a yard or so and pulled to the right. The taxi shot past with three centimeters to spare, did a quick in-and-out between two terrified pedestrians, and tore on its way. *Hurry.* . . .

Suddenly, unbidden, verses were spinning in my brain.

Nine coaches waiting—hurry, hurry, hurry— But here, surely, the quotation was desperately inappropriate? What was it, anyhow? I racked my brain, remembering. . . . Something about *the pleasures of the palace, securèd ease and state . . . banquets abroad by torchlight! music! sports! nine coaches waiting—hurry, hurry, hurry* . . . some tempter's list of pleasures, it had been, designed to lure a lonely young female to a luxurious doom; yes, that was it, Vendice enticing the pure and idiotic Castiza to the Duke's bed. . . . (*Ay, to the devil*). . . . I grinned to myself as I placed it. Inappropriate, certainly. This particular young female was heading, I hoped, neither to luxury nor the devil, but merely to a new setting for the same old job she'd abandoned in England. Miss Linda Martin, nursery-governess to Philippe, Comte de Valmy, aged nine.

In a few minutes now I would be there. Madame de Valmy, silver and elegant and so upright in her chair that you thought a draft would sway her—Madame de Valmy would receive me. I abandoned fairy tales, dragged a mirror from my bag, and began to tidy my hair, making myself recall, as if it were a lesson, what I could remember of my new employers.

Madame de Valmy, when I had talked to her in London, had not told me a great deal about the family I was to serve, but I had gathered the essentials of what seemed to have been a fairly complicated story. The old Comte de Valmy, Philippe's grandfather, had been enormously wealthy, and on his death the property had been divided between his three sons, the new Comte Étienne, Léon, and Hippolyte. To Étienne went the bulk of the fortune, the Château Valmy, and the Paris house; to Léon, among other things, a lovely little estate in Provence called Bellevigne, and to Hippolyte a large property on the edge of Lac Léman, a few kilometers below the Valmy estate. At the time of the old Comte's death the eldest son, Étienne, had not been married, and had been thankful when his brother Léon offered to stay on at Valmy and run the estate for him. Étienne preferred Paris, so to Paris he went, while Léon stayed on at Valmy and managed it, running his own Midi property from a distance. The younger brother, Hippolyte, who was, I gathered, an archaeologist of some standing, lived quietly at his house in Thonon-les-Bains, in between bouts of traveling and "digging" abroad.

So things had gone on for some years. Then, long after anyone had ceased to expect him to do so, Étienne had married, and within a couple of years Philippe had been born. The family had stayed on in Paris until last year, when Philippe was almost nine years old, tragedy had struck at him even as it had struck at me. His parents had been killed together in an air crash on their way back from a holiday in Spain, and Philippe had left Paris to live with his uncle Hippolyte in Thonon. Hippolyte was still unmarried, "but," said Madame de Valmy to me, poised in that silver elegance of hers beside a Regency mirror in her sitting room at Claridge's, "but the child had seen a lot of him, and is very fond of him. Hippolyte —my brother-in-law—wouldn't hear of his coming to us at Valmy, even though, officially, Valmy is Philippe's home. . . ." She smiled then, that remote sweet smile of hers that was about as cosy as an April moon, so that I thought I saw Hippolyte's point. I couldn't exactly picture the exquisite Héloïse in a romp with a nine-year-old boy. Philippe was certainly better off at the Villa Mireille with Uncle Hippolyte. Even an archaeologist, I thought, must be more approachable than Madame de Valmy. At least he would share the normal small boy's passion for grubbing in the mud.

But an archaeologist must occasionally grub to order. Philippe had been only a few months at the Villa Mireille when Monsieur Hippolyte had to fulfill an engagement which took him to Greece and Asia Minor for some months. The Villa Mireille was perforce shut up, and Philippe went up to Valmy to stay with his other aunt and uncle for the duration of Hippolyte's tour. And his Paris-bred nanny, restless enough in the little town of Thonon, had struck at the prospect of perhaps half a year's sojourn in the remote Savoyard valley, and removed herself, with tears and reproaches, back to Paris. . . .

So here was I. And it was curious that, in spite of the familiarity with which Paris invaded me, I didn't yet feel at home. I was a stranger, a foreigner, going to a strange house and a strange job. Perhaps loneliness was nothing to do with place or circumstance; perhaps it was in you, yourself. Perhaps, wherever you were, you took your little circle of loneliness with you. . . .

The taxi swerved across the Rue Riquet and swung right-handed into streets I knew. Away on the right I could see the dome of Sacré Coeur sharp against the daffodil sky of evening. Somewhere below it, in the spangling blue dusk of Montmartre, was the Rue du Printemps.

On an impulse I leaned forward, my hands tight on the clasp of my shabby handbag.

"Do you know the Rue du Printemps? It's off the Avenue Verchoix, Eighteenth Arrondissement. Take me there, please. I—I've changed my mind."

I stood on the damp pavement outside the open door and looked up at Number 14, Rue du Printemps. The paint was peeling off the walls; the wrought-iron of the balconies, that I remembered as a bright turquoise, showed in this light as a patched and dirty gray. A shutter hung on one hinge beside the first-floor window. Monsieur Bécard's canaries had long since gone; there wasn't even a patch of darker color on the wall where the cage had hung. The top balcony, our balcony, looked very small and high. There were pots of straggling geraniums arranged around its edge, and a striped towel hung over the railing to air.

How stupid to have come! How unutterably stupid to have come! It was like finding the glass empty when you lifted it to drink. I turned away.

Someone was coming down the stairs. I could hear the click of high-heeled shoes. I waited, perhaps still in some faint hope that it might be somebody I knew. It wasn't. It was a young woman, cheap and smart, with that tight-black-sweater-and-skirt smartness made to look very Place Vendôme with ropes of improbable pearls. She was blonde, and chewed gum. She eyed me with slight hostility as she crossed the lobby to the concierge's desk by the door and reached to the rack for a bundle of papers.

"You looking for someone?"

"No," I said.

Her eyes went beyond me to my suitcase on the pavement. "If you're wanting a room—"

"I wasn't," I said, feeling suddenly foolish. "I was just—I used to live hereabouts, and I thought I'd just like to look at the place. Is—is Madame Leclerc still here? She used to be the concierge."

"She was my aunt. She's dead."

"Oh. I'm sorry."

She was leafing through the papers, still eying me. "You look English."

"I am English."

"Oh? You don't sound it. But then I suppose if you lived here. . . . In this house, you mean? What name?"

"My father was Charles Martin. The poet Charles Martin."

The blonde said, "Before my time," licked a pencil, and made a careful mark on one of the papers she held.

I said, "Well, thanks very much. Good evening," and went back to where my case stood on the pavement. I looked up the now darkening street for a taxi. There was one coming, and I lifted a hand, but as it came nearer I saw that it was engaged. A street lamp shone into the back as it passed me. A middle-aged couple sat there—a wispy woman and a stoutish man in city clothes; two girls in their early teens sat on the drop seats. All four were laden with parcels, and they were laughing.

The taxi had gone. The street was empty. Behind me I heard the blonde's footsteps receding up the stairs of Number 14. I glanced back over my shoulder once at the house, then turned back to the street to watch for another taxi. Neither house nor street looked even remotely familiar any more.

Quite suddenly I ceased to be sorry I had come. It was as if the past, till then so longed after, so lived over, had slipped off my shoulders like a burden. The future was still hidden, somewhere in the lights that made a yellow blur in the sky beyond the end of the dark street. Here between the two I waited, and for the first time saw both clearly. Because of Daddy and Maman and the Rue du Printemps I had made myself a stranger in England, not only bereaved, but miserably *dépaysée,* drifting with no clear aim, resenting the life I had been thrust into with such tragic brutality; I had refused to adapt myself to it and make myself a place there, behaving like the spoiled child who, because he cannot have the best cake, refuses to eat at all. I had waited for life to offer itself back to me on the old terms. Well, it wasn't going to. Because of my childhood I had rejected what England had for me, and now the Paris of my childhood had rejected me. Here, too, I had been dispossessed. And if I was ever to have a place, in whatever country—well, nobody ever wanted you anyway unless you damned well made them. And that was what I would have to do. I had my chance in front of me now, at the Château Valmy. As yet I knew nothing of the family but their names; soon those names would be people I knew, the people I lived with; the people to whom I would matter. . . . I said their names over slowly to myself, thinking about them; Héloïse de Valmy, elegant and remote with that chilly grace that would—surely—melt in time; Philippe de Valmy, my pupil, of whom I knew nothing except that he was nine years old and not very strong; his uncle, the acting master of the château, Léon de Valmy. . . .

And then a queer thing happened. Whether it was because now for the first time I said the name over to myself, coupled with the fact that I was standing in the street where a million unconscious memories must be stirring, I don't know; but now, as I said the name, some trick of the subconscious drew some of those memories together as a magnet draws pins into a pattern so that, clear, and till now unrecollected, I heard them speak. "Léon de Valmy," Maman was saying, and I think she was reading from a newspaper, "Léon de Valmy. It says he's crippled. He's cracked his back at polo and they say if he recovers he'll be in a wheel chair for the rest of his life." Then Daddy's voice, indifferently: "Oh? Well, I'm sorry to hear it, I suppose, though I can't help feeling it's a pity he didn't break his neck. He'd be no loss." And when Maman said, "*Charles!*" he added impatiently, "Why should I be a hypocrite about the man? You know I detest him." And Maman said, "I can't think why," and Daddy laughed and said, "No. You wouldn't. . . ."

The memory spun away into silence, leaving me tingling with something that might have been apprehension, wondering if I had really remembered it at all, or if it were some new trick of that romantic imagination of mine. A taxi had appeared and I must have signaled it because here it was swerving in toward the curb with a screech of brakes. Once again I said, "Hôtel Crillon, please," and climbed in. The taxi moved off with a jerk, swung left out of the Rue du Printemps and accelerated down a dark, shuttered street. The sound of the engine swelled and echoed back from the blind houses. *Nine coaches waiting, hurry, hurry, hurry. . . . Ay, to the devil . . . to the devil. . . .*

It wasn't apprehension, it was excitement. I laughed to myself, my spirits suddenly rocketing. To the devil or not, I was on my way. . . .

I rapped on the glass.

"*Hurry,*" I said.

CHAPTER II

Third Coach

> *. . . his form had not yet lost*
> *All her original brightness, nor appeared*
> *Less than Archangel ruin'd . . .*
> MILTON: *Paradise Lost.*

> *My first thought was, he lied in every word,*
> *That hoary cripple, with malicious eye*
> *Askance to watch the working of his lie*
> *On mine. . . .*
> BROWNING: *Childe Roland.*

THE LITTLE TOWN of Thonon-les-Bains lies some twenty miles northeast of Geneva, on the southern shore of Lac Léman. Our plane had been met at Geneva by the big black Daimler from Valmy, which wafted us smoothly through the expensive streets of the city toward the French frontier and Thonon.

Madame de Valmy had talked very little to me on the journey from Paris, for which I was grateful, not only because my eyes and mind were busy with new impressions, but because—although she had been kind and pleasant in the extreme—I could not yet feel quite at ease with her. There was that curious remoteness about her which made her difficult to approach, or even to assess. Conversation with her had an almost long-distance touch about it; far from feeling that she had come halfway to meet you, you found her suddenly abstracted, all contact withdrawn. I wondered at first whether she was deliberately keeping me at a distance, but when she had twice asked me a question, only to lose interest before I had answered, I decided that she had graver matters on her mind than Philippe's governess, and myself retired contentedly enough into silence.

The car was purring along through prosperous, densely-cultivated country. To our left, through thickets of poplar and willow, the gleam of water showed and hid and showed again. On the right the country rolled green and gradual to wooded foothills, then swooped dramatically up to the great ranges of the Alps and the dazzle of the colossal snows. One of them, I supposed, was Mont Blanc itself, but this, I thought, stealing a glance at Héloïse de Valmy beside me, was not the time to ask.

She was sitting with shut eyes. I thought as I looked at her that I had been right. She looked both tired and preoccupied, though nothing, it seemed, could impair her rather chilly elegance. She was, I supposed, about fifty-five, and was still a beautiful woman, with the sort of beauty that age seems hardly to touch. Bone-deep, that was the phrase; it was in the shape of her head and temples and the thin-bridged, faintly aquiline nose with its fine nostrils; it was only at another glance that you saw the fine wrinkles etching eyes and mouth. Her skin was pale and clear, and expertly tinted; her brows delicately drawn and arched with a faint arrogance above the closed lids. Her hair was sculptured silver. Only her mouth under the curve of its expensive rouge, and the hands which lay gray-gloved and still in her lap, were too thin for beauty. She looked expensive, a little fragile, and about as approachable as the moon.

I sat back in my corner. In front of me were the square shoulders of Madame's chauffeur. Beside him, equally square and correct, sat Madame's maid Albertine. If I—as the classic tales of governessing led me to expect—was to be insecurely poised between the salon and the servant's hall, at least I was now at what might be called the right end of the car. For which I was grateful, as I didn't much like what I had seen of Albertine.

She was a dark sallow-faced woman of perhaps forty-five, with a sullen, secretive expression and ugly hands. Although she had been most of the time about Madame de Valmy's rooms last night when I had been there, she had not once spoken to me and I had seen her watching me with a sort of stony resentment which had surprised me, but which I now realized was probably habitual and without meaning. She sat rigidly beside the chauffeur, gripping Madame's jewel case tightly on her lap.

Neither she nor the man spoke. Neither, as far as I could tell, was remotely aware of the other's presence. They seemed so admirably suited
that I found myself wondering, quite without irony, if they were a married couple (I found later that they were, in fact, brother and sister).
Bernard, the chauffeur, had impeccable manners, but he, too, looked
as if he never smiled, and he had the same dark-visaged, almost resentful air as the woman. I hoped it wasn't a common Savoyard characteristic. . . . I stole another look at Madame's still face. It didn't look as
though, for gaiety, there was going to be much to choose between the
drawing room and the servants' hall. . . .

We had crossed the frontier, and were climbing now toward Thonon,
where our road would turn south toward the mountains. As we climbed,
the ground fell sharply away to the left, spilling a huddle of bright roofs
and budding fruit boughs down toward the belt of trees that bordered the
water. Through the mist of still-bare branches showed, here and there,
the chimneys of some biggish houses. One of these—Madame de Valmy
surprised me by rousing herself to point it out—was the Villa Mireille,
where the third Valmy brother, Hippolyte, lived. I could just see its
chimneys, smokeless among the enveloping trees. Beyond, mile upon
glimmering mile, stretched Lac Léman, lazily rippling its silk under the
afternoon sun, with here and there a slim sickle of white or scarlet sail
cutting the bright field of water.

It was a warm afternoon, and the little town through which we drove
was gay in the sun. Pollarded trees lined the streets, linking trained
branches where buds were already bursting into green. Shops had spilled
their goods onto the pavements; racks of brightly printed dresses swung
in the warm breeze; red and green peppers shone glossy among last season's withered apples; there was a pile of gaily-painted plant pots and a
small forest of garden tools in brilliant green. And at the edge of the
pavement there were the flowers; tubs of tulips and freesias and the
scarlet globes of ranunculus; box after box of polyanthus, vivid-eyed;
daffodils, sharply yellow; the deep drowned-purple of pansies; irises
with crown and fall of white and ivory and blue and deeper blue . . . oh,
beautiful! And all packed and jammed together, French-fashion, billowing and blazing with scent as thick smoke in the sunlight.

I must have made some exclamation of pleasure as we slid past them
and into the square, because I remember Madame de Valmy smiling a
little and saying, "Wait till you see Valmy in April." Then we had swung
to the right and the road was climbing again through a sparse tree-
crowded suburb toward the hills.

Very soon, it seemed, we were in a narrow gorge where road, river, and railway, crossing and recrossing one another in a fine confusion, plaited their way up between high cliffs hung with trees. After a few miles of this the railway vanished, tunneling away on the right, not to reappear, but the river stayed with us to the left of the road, a rush of green-white water that wrestled down its boulder-strewn gully. The cliffs closed in. Above, the gray March-bare trees hung in clouds. The road began to climb. Away below us the water arrowed loud and white between its boulders.

A grim little valley, I thought, and a dangerous road . . . and then we rounded the bend called Belle Surprise, and away in front of us, like a sunlit rent in a dark curtain, lay the meadows of Valmy.

"That's Soubirous," said Madame de Valmy, "there in the distance. You'll lose sight of it again in a moment when the road runs down into the trees."

I craned forward to look. The village of Soubirous was set in a wide, green saucer of meadow and orchard serene among the cradling hills. I could see the needle-thin gleam of water, and the lines of willows where two streams threaded the grassland. Where they met stood the village, bright as a toy and sharply focused in the clear air, with its three bridges and its little watch-making factory and its church of Sainte-Marie-des-Ponts with the sunlight glinting on the weathercock that tips the famous spire.

"And Valmy?" I said, as the car sailed downhill again and trees crowded thickly in on either side of the road. "We must be near it now?"

"Those are the Valmy woods on your left. They stretch most of the way back to Thonon. The Merlon—that's the name of the river—marks the boundary between Valmy and Dieudonné, the estate to the right of the road. We cross the river soon and then—" she smiled faintly—"you'll see Valmy."

She spoke as usual in that cool flute-clear voice, with nothing ruffling the silvery surface. But I thought, suddenly, she's excited—no, perhaps nothing so strong as that, but there's anticipation there and something more. . . . I had been wrong in my judgment of her a while back; in spite of the rather fragile urban charm, she loved this lonely valley, and came back with pleasure to it. I felt a little rush of warmth toward her, and said impulsively, "It's lovely, Madame de Valmy! It's a beautiful place!"

She smiled. "Yes, isn't it? And you're lucky, Miss Martin, that spring has come early this year. It can be bleak and grim enough in winter, but it's always beautiful. At least, I think so. It has been my—our home for many years."

I said impetuously, "I shall love it here! I know I shall!"

The gloved hands moved in her lap. "I hope you will, Miss Martin." The words were kind, but formally spoken, and the smile had gone. She was withdrawn again, cool and remote. She looked away from me. I might be at the right end of the car, but it seemed I must keep to my own side.

I threw her a doubtful little look that she didn't see, and turned again to my own window. And at that moment I saw the château.

We had been running for a little time along the bottom of the valley, with the Dieudonné plantations—tall firs with the sun and wind in their crests—on our right, and beyond the river the steep woods of Valmy, a wild forest where holly gleamed among oak and birch, and great beeches rose elephant-gray from a tangle of hawthorn and wild clematis. Above these banked and raveled boughs hung a high plateau; and there, backed by more forest and the steep rise of another hill, stood the Château Valmy, its windows catching the sunlight. I had only a glimpse of it, just enough to show me that here was no romantic castle of turrets and pinnacles; here was the four-square classic grace of the eighteenth century, looking, however, wonderfully remote, and floating insubstantially enough up there in the light above the dark sea of trees. It also looked inaccessible, but I had barely time to wonder how it was approached when the car slowed, turned gently off the main road onto a beautiful little stone bridge that spanned the Merlon, swung again into a steep tunnel of trees, and took the hill with a rush.

The Valmy road was a zigzag, a steep, rather terrifying approach which the big car took in a series of smooth upward rushes, rather like the movement of a lift, swooping up through woodland, then open hillside, and running at last under the high boundary wall that marked the end of the château's formal garden. At the top was a gravel sweep as big as a small field. We swung effortlessly off the zigzag onto this, and came around in a magnificent curve to stop in front of the great north door.

The chauffeur came around to open Madame de Valmy's door and help her to alight. Albertine, without a glance or a word for me, busied herself with wraps and hand luggage. I got out of the car and stood waiting, while my employer paused for a moment talking to Bernard in a low rapid French that I couldn't catch.

I did wonder for a moment if her instructions could have anything to do with me, because the man's little dark eyes kept flickering toward me almost as if he weren't attending to what his employer said. But it must only have been a natural interest in a newcomer, because presently he bent his head impassively enough and turned without a further glance at me to attend to the luggage.

Madame de Valmy turned to me then. "Here we are," she said unnecessarily, but with such grace that the cliché took on almost the quality of a welcome. She gave me her sweet, fleeting smile, and turned toward the house.

As I followed her I got only the most confused impression of the size and graciousness of the place—the great square façade with the sweep of steps up to the door, the archway on our left leading to courtyard and outbuildings, the sunny slope beyond these where orderly kitchen gardens climbed toward another tree-bounded horizon. . . . I saw these things only vaguely, without noticing. What met me with the rush almost of a wind was the sunlight and space and the music of the trees. Everywhere was the golden light of late afternoon. The air was cool and sweet and very pure, heady with the smell of pines and with the faint tang of the snows.

A far cry, certainly, from North London.

I followed my employer up the wide flight of steps and past a bowing manservant into the hall of the château.

At first I did not see the woman who waited for us a few paces inside the great door.

The hall seemed immense, but this was mainly because it was very high and full of shadows. The floor was a chilly chessboard of black and white marble, from which, opposite the door, a staircase rose to a wide landing lit by a window whose five tall lancets poured the sun downward in dazzling shafts. At the landing the staircase divided, lifting in twin graceful curves toward a gallery. So much I saw, but the light, falling steeply through the speartips of the high windows, threw all but the center of the hall into deep shadow.

I was still blinking against the glare when I heard a voice greeting Madame de Valmy, and then a woman came toward us in welcome. I supposed she was the housekeeper. She was a stout body of sixty-odd, with a fat comfortable face and gray hair worn neatly in an old-fashioned bun. She was dressed in severe black, her only ornament—if it could be called that—being a pair of gold-rimmed pince-nez which stuck out of a pocket high on her bosom, and was secured by a chain to a plain gold pin. Her pleasant face, her plodding walk, her whole appearance were solid respectability personified. This was no secret dark Savoyard, at any rate.

She looked at me curiously as she greeted Madame de Valmy. She had a cheerful voice that sounded perpetually a little out of breath, and surprisingly, her French, though fluent, was atrociously bad.

Madame answered her greeting absently. In that merciless cascade of light the lines in her face showed up clearly. She said abruptly, her eyes sliding past the woman in black toward the dimmer background of the hall, "The Master—he's well?"

"Oh yes, madame. He's been—oh, quite his old self the last few days, madame, if you'll forgive my saying so . . . interested in what's going on, the way he hasn't been for long enough, and full of plans. Oh, quite like old times, madame."

She spoke with the ease of an old servant, and her faced showed her very real pleasure in the good news she could give her employer. More pleasure, indeed, than Madame de Valmy's own face reflected. I thought I saw a shadow pass over it as she said, "Plans?"

"Yes, madame. I don't rightly know what they are, myself, but he and Armand Lestocq were talking it over for long enough, and I do know there's extra hands busy in the garden, and a man came today to look round the place and give his estimate for the jobs the Master was talking about last winter. He's here now, as it happens, madame. He went up to take a look at the stonework on the west balcony, and I think the Master went with him. The Master's lift wasn't at the ground floor when Seddon made up the library fire."

Madame de Valmy was pulling off her gloves with quick nervous movements. She said abruptly, "Do you know if he has heard from Monsieur Hippolyte?"

"I think so, madame. There was a letter a week ago, on Tuesday . . . no, it was Wednesday; it was your letter came from London on Tuesday about the young lady." She paused, puffing a little, and then nodded. "That's right. The one from Athens came on the Wednesday, because I remember Armand Lestocq was up here that very day, and—"

"Very well, Mrs. Seddon, thank you." Madame de Valmy might hardly have been listening. "You said the Master was upstairs? Please send someone to tell him I'm here with Miss Martin."

"I've already done that, madame. He most particularly asked to be told the minute you arrived."

"Ah, thank you." Madame de Valmy turned then toward me, still with those abrupt, slightly nervous movements, and spoke in English. "Now, Mrs. Seddon, this is Miss Martin. I wrote to you about her when I informed the Master. Miss Martin, Mrs. Seddon is the housekeeper here. She is English, so you need not feel too much alone. Her husband is our butler, and he and Mrs. Seddon will do what they can to help you."

"That we will," said Mrs. Seddon warmly. She beamed at me and nodded, so that the gold chain on her bosom bobbed and glittered. "You're very welcome, I'm sure."

"Miss Martin's rooms are ready?"

"Oh, yes, madame, of course. I'll take her up now, shall I, and then show her round myself, seeing that perhaps she's a little strange?"

"Thank you, yes, if you will, but not straight away. She will come upstairs presently. Perhaps you will wait for her?"

"Of course, madame." Mrs. Seddon nodded and beamed again, then retreated, puffing her way steadily up the stairs like a squat determined tug.

Madame de Valmy turned as if to speak to me, but I saw her eyes go past my shoulder, and her hands, which had been jerking her gloves between them, stilled themselves.

"Léon."

I heard nothing. I turned quickly. Even then it was a second or so before I saw the shadow detach itself from the other shadows and slide forward.

Though I had known what to expect, instinctively my eye went too high, and then fell—again by instinct, shrinkingly—to the squat shape that shot forward, uncannily without sound, to a smooth halt six feet away.

Pity, repulsion, curiosity, the determination to show none of these . . . whatever feelings struggled in me as I turned were swept aside like leaves before a blast of wind. The slightly dramatic quality of his entrance may have contributed to the effect; one moment a shadow, and the next moment silently there. . . . But, once there, Léon de Valmy was an object for no one's pity; one saw simply a big, handsome, powerful man who from his wheel chair managed without speaking a word to obliterate everyone else in the hall—this literally, for almost before the wheel chair stopped, the servants had melted unobtrusively away. Only Mrs. Seddon was still audible, steaming steadily up the right-hand branch of the staircase toward the gallery.

It was a tribute to Léon de Valmy's rather overwhelming personality that my own first impression had nothing to do with his crippled state; it was merely that this was the handsomest man I had ever seen. My experience, admittedly, had not been large, but in any company he would have been conspicuous. The years had only added to his extraordinary good looks, giving him the slightly haggard distinction of lined cheeks and white hair that contrasted strikingly with dark eyes and black, strongly-marked brows. The beautifully-shaped mouth had that thin, almost cruel set to it that is sometimes placed there by pain. His hands looked soft, as if they were not used enough, and he was too pale. But for all that, this was no invalid; this was the master of the house, and the half of his body that was still alive was just twice as much so as anybody else's. . . .

He was smiling now as he greeted his wife and turned to me, and the smile lit his face attractively. There was no earthly reason why I should feel suddenly nervous, or why I should imagine that Héloïse de Valmy's voice as she introduced us was too taut and high, like an overtight string.

I thought, watching her, she's afraid of him. . . . Then I told myself sharply not to be a fool. This was the result of Daddy's intriguing build-up and my own damned romantic imagination. Just because the man looked like Milton's ruined archangel and chose to appear in the hall like the Demon King through a trap door, it didn't necessarily mean that I had to smell sulphur.

It was disconcerting to reach downward to shake hands, but I hoped I hadn't shown it. My self-command, as it happened, was a mistake. He said gently, "You were warned about me?" The dark eyes, with a question in them, slid to his wife standing beside me.

I felt rather than saw her small movement of dissent. A glance passed between them and his brows lifted. He was too quick by half. With a guilty memory of my own secret I said uncertainly, "Warned?"

"About Lucifer's fall from heaven, Miss Martin."

I felt my eyes widen in a stare. Was the man a thought-reader? And was he determined I should smell sulphur? Or . . . did he really see himself as the thunder-scarred angel he quoted? Oddly, the last thought made him more human, more vulnerable.

Before I could speak he smiled again, charmingly. "I'm sorry. I shouldn't have tried to be so cryptic. I was referring to the accident that, as you see—"

I said hastily and a bit too ingenuously, "I know. I was only surprised because that's what I was thinking myself."

"Was it indeed?" His laugh held a tiny note of self-mockery, but I thought he looked pleased. Then the laugh died and his eyes were on me, intent, appraising. I remembered perhaps rather late that I was a servant and this was my employer. I felt myself color, and said quickly, almost at random, "Someone told me about your accident—someone I met on the plane from London."

"Oh? An acquaintance of ours, perhaps?"

"I think so. We talked. When I told her I was coming here she remembered having met you."

"She?" said Héloïse de Valmy.

I said, "I never knew her name. She was elderly, and I think she came from Lyons or somewhere like that. I don't remember."

Léon de Valmy abandoned the catechism abruptly. "Whoever it was, it's just as well she told you." He hesitated a moment, looking down at his hands, then went on slowly, "You must think this very odd of us,

Miss Martin, but I believe my wife does not care to speak of my . . .
deformity. Consequently it is apt to meet people with a shock. And I myself—even after twelve years—am absurdly sensitive of meeting new people and seeing it in their eyes. Perhaps both my wife and I are foolish
about this. . . . Perhaps already you are condemning me as a neurotic.
. . . But it is a very human folly, Miss Martin. We all of us spend some
of our time pretending that something that *is,* is not—and we are not
grateful to those who break the dream."

He looked up and his eyes met mine. "One day, perhaps, it will cease
to matter." He shrugged, and smiled a little wryly. "But until then. . . .

He had spoken quite without bitterness, only that small wryness
touched his voice. But the speech was so little what I would have expected from him that I found myself, embarrassed and disarmed, shaken
into some stupid and impulsive reply.

I said quickly, "No, please—you mustn't mind. Deformity's the wrong
word, and it's the last thing anybody'd notice about you anyway . . .
honestly it is."

I stopped, appalled. From Linda Martin to Monsieur de Valmy the
words would have been bad enough. From the new governess to her
employer they were impossible. I didn't pause then to reflect that it was
the employer who had—deliberately, it seemed—called them up. I stood
biting my lip and wishing myself a thousand miles away. Through my
sharp discomfort I heard myself stammering, "I—I'm sorry. I shouldn't
have said that. . . . I only meant—"

"Thank you, my dear." His voice was still grave, but I saw the unmistakable flash of amusement in his eyes. Then he was saying easily,
"It seems, Héloïse, that your excessively silly friend Lady Benchley has
justified her existence at last in recommending Miss Martin to us. We
were indeed lucky to find you, Miss Martin, and we're delighted to welcome you to Valmy. I hope we'll manage to make you feel at home."
He paused. That gleam again. "Not perhaps quite a felicitous expression.
Shall I say rather that I hope Valmy will become a home for you?"

I said rather stiffly, "Thank you. You're very kind. I was happy to have
the chance to come, and I'll try my best to—"

"Endeavor to give satisfaction? That's the usual bromide, isn't it?
What are you staring at?"

"I'm sorry. It was impertinent of me. It was just—your English is so
frightfully good," I said lamely. Damn the man; was I never to regain my
lost poise? I finished the sentence coldly—"Sir."

He laughed outright then, a quite delightful laugh that at once conceded a point and abandoned the game, whatever it was. He began then
to inquire quite naturally and very kindly about the journey and my

impressions of the valley; Madame de Valmy joined in, smiling, and soon, under their renewed phrases of welcome, I found my embarrassment relaxing into naturalness once again. More, into liking. The man's charm was palpable, and he had taken the trouble to turn it on full blast . . . and I was all the more vulnerable for being tired, lonely, and a bit bewildered. By the time the three of us had talked for a few minutes longer I was back on top of the world again with my shattered poise restored and all the tensions and uneasinesses of the past half-hour dismissed as figments. Monsieur and Madame de Valmy were a handsome and delightful couple and I was going to like them and love living at Valmy and belonging even in this humble sort to a family again.

Sulphur? Poppycock.

But all the same, I reflected, it hadn't taken me long to see what had been implied in that remembered snatch of conversation. *"You wouldn't,"* Daddy had said, and I saw what he meant. The man was damnably attractive, no doubt of that . . . and I used the adverb deliberately; it was the *mot juste*. And, charm or no, the faintest of resentments still pricked me. Léon de Valmy had played a game with me, and I hadn't liked it. I had been shaken into offering pity and comfort where none was needed . . . and he had been amused.

Nor did I attempt to explain, even to myself, why I had launched so unerringly on that sea of lies about the elderly lady from Lyons, or how I knew I would never, never have the courage to tell Léon de Valmy that I spoke French even better than he spoke English, and had understood perfectly well what he said to Héloïse when, at length dismissed, I had gone upstairs to meet Mrs. Seddon on the gallery landing.

He had said softly, and I knew he was staring after me, "All the same, Héloïse, it is possible that you've made a very great mistake. . . ."

CHAPTER III

The castle hath a pleasant seat; the air
Nimbly and sweetly recommends itself
Unto our gentle senses. . . .
       SHAKESPEARE: *Macbeth*

The raven himself is hoarse
That croaks the fatal entrance of Duncan
Under my battlements. . . .
       IBID.

MY ROOMS were lovelier than anything I had imagined, certainly than any I had ever been in. They had tall windows facing west, which gave onto a balcony and the view across the valley.

This drew me straight away. I stood leaning on the stone balustrading and looked out over that incredible view. So high-perched we were that I seemed to be looking level at the crest of the Dieudonné forest beyond the Merlon; below, along the zigzag, the bare tree tops moved like clouds. The balcony was afloat in a golden airy space. Soubirous, to the south, glinted like a jewel.

I turned. Mrs. Seddon had followed me to the window, and waited, smiling, plump hands clasped under plump bosom.

"It's . . . wonderful," I said.

"It's a pretty place," she said comfortably. "Though some don't like the country, of course. Myself, I've always lived in the country. Now I'll show you the bedroom, if you'll come this way."

I followed her across the pretty sitting room to a door in the corner opposite the fireplace.

"These rooms are built in a suite," she said. "All the main rooms open onto this corridor, or the south one. You saw how the balcony runs the whole length of the house. These rooms at the end have been made into the nursery suite, and they open out of one another as well. This is your bedroom."

It was, if possible, prettier than the sitting room. I told her so, and she looked pleased. She moved to a door I had not noticed, half-concealed as it was in the ivory and gold paneling. "That door's to the bathroom and Master Philip's bedroom opens off it the other side. You share the bathroom with him. I hope you don't mind?"

At the Constance Butcher Home we had queued for baths. "No," I said, "I don't mind. It's beautifully up to date, isn't it? Baths behind the paneling. Did all the ghosts leave when the plumbing was put in, Mrs. Seddon?"

"I never heard tell of any," said Mrs. Seddon, sedately. "This was a powder closet in the old days; it runs the whole way between the two rooms. They made half of it into a bathroom and the other half's a little pantry with an electric stove for making nursery tea and Master Philip's chocolate at night. Here's the pantry." The door she opened showed a small immaculate room which seemed to share the functions of pantry and broom closet. Beside the door was an orderly stock of housemaid's tools—vacuum cleaner, step-ladder, brushes, mops—and beyond these was a small electric stove in what looked like a very efficiently planned nest of fitted cupboards and gleaming shelves. I must have looked surprised, because she added, "This was always the schoolroom wing; the Master and his brothers were brought up here, you see, and then these altera-tions, with the electricity and all that, were done when Mr. Rowl was born."

"Mr. . . . Raoul?" I queried.

"The Master's son. He lives at Bellyveen. That's the Master's place in the Midi."

"Yes, I knew about that. I didn't know there was a son, though. Mad-ame de Valmy didn't—well, she didn't talk to me much. I know very lit-tle about the family."

She gave me a shrewd look, and I thought she was going to make some comment, but all she said was: "No? Ah well, you'll find every-thing out soon enough, I dare say. Mr. Rowl isn't Madame's son, you understand. The Master was married before. Mr. Rowl's mother died twenty-two years ago this spring, when he was eight. It's sixteen years ago now that the Master married again and you can't blame him at that. It's a big place to be alone in, as you may well imagine. Not that," said Mrs. Seddon cheerfully, chugging across the room to twitch a curtain into place, "the Master was ever one in those days for sitting alone in the house, if you take my meaning. Fair set Europe alight between them, him and his oldest brother, if all tales be true; but there, wild oats is wild oats, and the poor Master'll sow no more of them even if he wanted to, which I doubt he doesn't, and poor Mr. Étienne's dead, God rest him, and long past thinking of the world, the flesh and the devil, or so we'll hope. . . ." She turned to me again, a little out of breath with these re-markable confidences; it appeared that Mrs. Seddon, at any rate, didn't

share Madame de Valmy's habit of reticence: "And now would you like
to see over the rest of the place, or will you wait till later? You'll be tired,
I dare say."

"I'll leave it till later, if I may."

"It's as you wish." Again the shrewd twinkling glance. "Shall I send
Berthe to unpack for you?"

"No, thank you." That look meant that she knew quite well that I
wouldn't want a maid exploring my meager suitcase. Far from resenting
the thought, I was grateful for it. "Where's the nursery?" I asked. "Beyond Master Philip's bedroom?"

"No. His bedroom's the end one, then yours, then your sitting room,
then the nursery. Beyond that come Madame's rooms, and the Master's
are round the corner above the library."

"Oh, yes. He has a lift there, hasn't he?"

"That's so, miss. It was put in soon after the accident. That'd be, let's
see, twelve years ago come June."

"I was told about that. Were you here then, Mrs. Seddon?"

"Oh, yes, indeed I was." She nodded at me with a certain complacency.
"I came here thirty-two years ago, miss, when the Master was first married."

I sat down on the edge of the bed and looked at her with interest.
"Thirty-two years? That's a long time, Mrs. Seddon. Did you come with
the first Madame de Valmy, then?"

"That I did. She was from Northumberland, the same as me."

"Then she was English?" I said, surprised.

"Indeed, yes. She was a lovely girl, Miss Deborah. I'd been in service
at her home ever since she was a little girl. She met the Master in Paris one
spring, and they was engaged in a fortnight, just like that. Oh, very romantic it all was, very romantic. She said to me, she said: 'Mary—' that's
my name, miss—'Mary,' she said, 'you'll come with me, won't you? I won't
feel so far from home then,' she said." Mrs. Seddon nodded at me, with
an easy sentimental moistening of the eye. "So, seeing as I was courting
Arthur—that's Mr. Seddon—meself at the time, I married him and made
him go along, too. I couldn't let Miss Debbie adventure all by herself to
foreign parts, like."

"Of course not," I said sympathetically, and Mrs. Seddon beamed,
settling her arms together under the plump bosom, obviously ready to
gossip for as long as I would listen. She gave the appearance of one indulging in a favorite pastime whose rules were almost forgotten. If I had
been delighted to see her pleasant English face after the secret coun-
tenances of Albertine and Bernard, it was obvious that Mrs. Seddon had
been equally pleased to see me. And the governess, of course, was not

on the proscribed list: this could not be called Gossiping with the Servants. I supposed that, for me, Mrs. Seddon was hardly on the proscribed
list either. At any rate I was going to gossip all I could.

I prompted her. "And then when your Miss Debbie . . . died, you
didn't go back to England? What made you stay on, Mrs. Seddon?"

As to that, it seemed that she was not quite sure herself. Miss Debbie's
father had died meanwhile and the house in England had been sold,
while here at Valmy Mrs. Seddon and her husband had excellent jobs
which "the Master" seemed quite disposed to let them keep. . . . I also
gathered that Miss Debbie's interest had lifted them into positions which
in another house they might never have filled; Seddon himself had been
on my one sight of him impeccably polished, neutral and correct; Mrs.
Seddon, too, had all the trappings of the competent and superior housekeeper; but her voice and some of her mannerisms had, gloriously defy-
ing gentility, remained the homely and genuine voice and ways of Mary
Seddon, erstwhile second-gardener's daughter.

I listened to a long description of Miss Debbie, and others of Miss
Debbie's home, father, pony, clothes, jewelry, wedding, wedding presents and wedding guests. When we appeared to be about to launch (via
how much Miss Debbie's mother would have liked to be at the wedding
if only she had been alive) on a description of Miss Debbie's mother's
clothes, jewelry, wedding, and so on, as observed by Mrs. Seddon's
mother—then I thought it was time to prod her gently back to foreign
parts.

"And there was Miss Debbie's son, wasn't there? Of course you
wanted to stay and look after him?"

"Mr. Rowl?" She primmed her lips a little. "French nurses they had
for him. Such a quiet little boy as he was, too—a bit like Master Philip
here, very quiet and never a mite of bother. You'd never have thought—"
But here she stopped, sighing a little wheezily, and shook her head. "Eh,
well, miss, he's half foreign, say what you will."

There was all rural England in the condemnation. I waited, gravely
expectant, but she merely added, maddeningly, "But there, I never was
one to gossip. And now, if you'll excuse me, I'll have to be getting about
my work and leaving you to unpack. Now, miss, if there's anything you
want you've only to ask me or Seddon and we'll do our best to help you."

"Thank you very much. I'm awfully glad you're here, Mrs. Seddon,"
I added naïvely.

She looked pleased. "Well, now, that's very nice of you, miss, I'm sure.
But you'll soon feel at home and pick things up. I couldn't speak a word
of French when I came here first, and now I can talk it as fast as they
can."

"I heard you. It sounded wonderful." I stood up and clicked back the locks of my suitcase. "As you say, thirty years is a long time, especially when one's away from home. You didn't feel tempted to go back to England, say, when Monsieur de Valmy married again?"

"Oh, we talked of it, Seddon and I," she said comfortably, "but Seddon's that easygoing, and we liked the new madame, and she was satisfied, so we stayed. Besides, I've had the asthma terrible bad since a girl, and, say what you like, none of these new-fangled things they give you, anti-hysterics and suchlike, seem to do me any good. I used to get it terrible bad at home, but up here it cleared up something wonderful. It still comes now and again, but it soon goes off. It's the air. Wonderful healthy it is up here, and very dry."

"It's certainly lovely."

"And then," said Mrs. Seddon, "after the Master had his accident, she wouldn't hear of us going. He couldn't stand changes, you see."

"I did gather that from what he said to me in the hall. Does he—does he have much pain, Mrs. Seddon?"

"Pain? No. But he has his days," said Mrs. Seddon cryptically. "And you can't blame him, the way things are."

"No, of course not. He's bound to get depressed at times."

"Depressed?" She looked at me blankly. "The Master?"

I was still trying to equate the self-confessed "neurotic" with the impression of easy and competent power that Léon de Valmy gave. "Yes. Does he get sort of sorry for himself at times?"

She gave a sound suspiciously like a snort. "Sorry for himself? Not him! Mind you, this last few years he's not been just as sweet-tempered as he might be, but he's all there, miss, you may be sure. He'd never be the one to give up because of a little thing like being crippled for life!"

"I think I can see that. In fact you never think of that when you talk to him." (I didn't add "unless he reminds you," but the thought persisted.)

"That's so." She nodded at me again. "And he forgets it himself, most times. What with that electric chair of his, and the lift, and the telephone to every corner of the place, and that there Bernard to be the legs of him, there's nothing he can't do. But now and then, just like *that*, something'll bring it home to him, and then. . . ."

I said, still thinking of the scene in the hall, "What sort of thing?"

"Dear only knows. It might be a bad night, or a report coming in that something's gone wrong or been neglected in some place he can't get to himself to see to it, or something that needs doing and no money to do it with, or Mr. Rowl—" As before, she stopped abruptly.

I waited. She pulled unnecessarily at a chair cover to straighten it. She

said vaguely, "Mr. Rowl runs the other estate for him, Bellyveen, in the
Midi, and there's always trouble over money, and it upsets the Master,
and besides . . . ah, well, he's not often here, which is as it should be,
seeing he's the one that reminds the Master most often that he's a helpless
cripple for all the powerful ways he has with him."

I stirred. "Reminds him? That's rather beastly."

She looked shocked. "Oh, not on purpose, you understand. I didn't
mean that! It's only that he—well, Mr. Rowl might be the Master like he
was twenty years ago, you see."

"Oh, I see what you mean. He does all the things his father used to like
doing. Polo, for instance?"

She shot me a surprised look. "Did they tell you about that?"

"No. I heard it from someone who knew them—someone I met on the
plane."

"Oh, I see. Yes, that sort of thing. He could put his hand to anything,
the Master." She smiled reminiscently and a little sadly. "Miss Debbie always did say he'd break his neck one day. He was such a one for sport—
all sorts, motorcars, horses, speedboats . . . fighting with swords, even.
He's got a shelf of silver cups for that alone."

"Fencing?"

"That's it. But cars and horses were the chief thing. I've often thought
he'd break his own neck and everyone else's, the way he'd come up that
zigzag from the Valmy bridge. Sometimes," added Mrs. Seddon surprisingly, "you'd think a devil was driving him . . . like as if he had to be
able to do everything—*and* do it better than anybody else."

Yes, I thought, I can believe that. And even crippled he has to be a
crippled archangel. . . .

I said, "And now he has to sit and watch his son riding and driving
and fencing . . . ?"

"As to that," said Mrs. Seddon, "Mr. Rowl hasn't got the money . . .
which is just as well, or maybe he'd go the same way as his father. And
like I said, he's not here very often anyway. He lives at Bellyveen. I've
never been to Bellyveen myself, but I've heard tell it's very pretty."

I said "Oh?" with an expression of polite interest as she began to tell
me about Bellevigne, but I wasn't really listening. I was reflecting that if
Raoul de Valmy was really a younger copy of his father it was probably
just as well he visited Valmy only rarely. I couldn't imagine two of Léon
de Valmy settling at all comfortably under the same roof. . . . I stirred
again. There was that same damned romantic imagination at work still.
. . . And what had I to go on, after all? A vague snatch of memory
twelve years old, and the impression of an overwhelming personality in
some odd way playing with me for its own amusement, for some reason

concerned to give me a picture of itself that was not the truth. . . .

It struck me then, for the first time, that there had been a notable omission from my welcome to the Château Valmy.

And that was the owner of all this magnificence, the most important of the Valmys, Monsieur le Comte, Philippe.

And now Mrs. Seddon was preparing to go about her own affairs.

She plodded firmly away to the door, only to hesitate there and turn. I bent over my case and began to lift things out onto the coverlet. I could feel her eying me.

She said, "You . . . the Master . . . he seemed all right with you, did he? I thought I heard him laugh when I was waiting upstairs for you."

I straightened up, my hands full of folded handkerchiefs. "Perfectly all right, Mrs. Seddon. He was very pleasant."

"Oh. That's good. I'd like to have been able to have a word with you first and warn you what he sometimes was like with strangers."

I could well understand her slightly anxious probing. It was obvious that the emotional temperature, so to speak, of the Château Valmy, must depend very largely on Léon de Valmy and "his days."

I said cheerfully, "Thanks very much, but don't worry, Mrs. Seddon. He was awfully nice to me and made me feel very welcome."

"Did he now?" Her eyes were anxious and a little puzzled. "Oh, well, that's all right, then. I know he was very pleased when Madame's letter came about you, but as a rule he hates changes in the house. That's why we were so surprised when Master Philip's Nanny was dismissed after being with the family all those years, and they said a new girl was coming from England."

"Oh, yes, Madame de Valmy told me about her." I put the handkerchiefs down and lifted some underwear out of the suitcase. "But she wasn't dismissed, surely? I understood from Madame that she didn't want to live in the wilds at Valmy and, as Madame was in London at the time, Monsieur de Valmy wrote urgently and asked her to find an English governess while she was there."

"Oh, no." Mrs. Seddon was downright. "You must have misunderstood what Madame said. Nanny was devoted to Master Philip, and I'm sure she broke her heart when she had to go."

"Oh? I was sure that Madame said she'd left because the place was so lonely. I must have been mistaken." I found myself shrugging my shoulders, and hastily abandoned that very Gallic gesture. "Maybe she was just warning *me* what it would be like. But she did seem very anxious to engage someone to teach him English."

"Master Philip's English is excellent," said Mrs. Seddon, rather primly.

I laughed and said, "I'm glad to hear it. Well, whatever the case, I suppose if Philippe's nine he's old enough to graduate from a Nanny to a governess of sorts. I gathered from Monsieur de Valmy that that was the idea. And for a start I'm going to try and remember to call the nursery the 'schoolroom.' I'm sure one's too old for a nursery when one's nine."

"Master Philip's very young for his age," she said, "though there's times when he's too solemn for my liking. But there, you can't expect much after what's happened, poor mite. He'll get over it in the end, but it takes time."

"I know," I said.

She eyed me for a moment and then said, tentatively, "If I might ask —do you remember your own folks, now?"

"Oh, yes." I looked across the room and met the kindly inquisitive gaze. Fair was fair, after all. She must be every bit as curious about me as I was about the Valmys. I said, "I was fourteen when they were killed. In an air accident, like Philippe's. I suppose Madame told you I'd been at an orphanage in England?"

"Indeed, yes. She wrote that she'd heard of you through a friend of hers, a Lady Benchley, who comes up every year to Évian, and Lady Benchley thought very highly of you, very highly."

"That was very nice of her. Lady Benchley was one of the governors at the orphanage for the last three years I was there. Then when I left to be assistant at a boys' school it turned out she had a son there. She came up to me on Visitors' Day and talked to me, and when I told her I hated the place she asked me if I'd ever considered a private job abroad, because this friend of hers—Madame de Valmy—was looking for a governess for her nephew and had asked her if she knew of anyone from the Home. When I heard the job was in France I jumped at it. I—I'd always fancied living in France, somehow. I went straight up to London next day and saw her. Lady Benchley had promised to telephone about me, and—well, I got the job." I didn't add that Madame must have taken Lady Benchley's recommendation to be worth a good deal more than it actually was. Lady Benchley was a kindly scatterbrain who spent a good deal of her time acting as a sort of private labor-exchange between her friends and the Constance Butcher Home, and I doubt if she had ever known very much about me. And I had certainly got the impression that Madame de Valmy had been so anxious to find a suitable young woman for the post during her short stay in London that she hadn't perhaps probed as far back into my history as she might have done. Not, of course, that it mattered.

I smiled at Mrs. Seddon, who was still eying me with that faintly puz-

zled look. Then all at once she smiled back, and nodded, so that the
gold chain on her bosom glittered and swung.

"Well," she said, "well," and though she didn't actually add "You'll
do," the implication was there. She opened the door. "And now I really
will have to be going. Berthe'll be up soon with some tea for you; she's
the girl that looks after these rooms and you'll find she's a good girl,
though a bit what you might call flighty. I expect you'll make yourself
understood to her all right, and Master Philip'll help."

"I expect I shall," I said. "Where is Master Philip, Mrs. Seddon?"

"He's probably in the nursery," said Mrs. Seddon, her hand on the
door. "But Madame particularly said you weren't to bother with him
tonight. You were to have a cup of tea—which I may say is *tea,* though
it took near thirty years to teach them how to make it—and settle yourself
in before dinner and you'll be seeing Master Philip tomorrow. But not to
bother yourself tonight."

"Very well," I said. "Thank you, Mrs. Seddon. I shall look forward
to that tea."

The door shut behind her. I could hear the soft plod of her steps
along the corridor.

I stood where I was, looking at the door, and absently smoothing the
folds of a petticoat between my hands.

I was thinking two things. First that I was not supposed to have heard
Mrs. Seddon mentioning the lift in her conversation with Madame de
Valmy, and that if I was going to make mistakes as easily as that I had
better confess quickly before any real damage was done.

The second thing was Mrs. Seddon's parting admonition: "not to
bother with him tonight." Had that really been Héloïse de Valmy's
phrase? *"Not to bother with him."* And he was "probably" in the nursery . . . I laid the petticoat gently in a drawer, then turned and walked
out of my pretty bedroom, across the roses and ivory sitting room, toward the schoolroom door. There I hesitated a moment, listening. I
could hear nothing.

I tapped gently on the door and then turned the gilded handle. It
opened smoothly.

I pushed it wide and walked in.

My first thought was that he was not an attractive little boy.

He was small for his age, with a thin little neck supporting a round
dark head. His hair was black, and cut very short, and his skin was
sallow, almost waxen. His eyes were black, and very large, his wrists and
knees bony and somehow pathetic. He was dressed in navy shorts and a

striped jersey, and was lying on his stomach, reading a large book. He looked small and a little drab on the big luxurious rug.

He looked around in inquiry and then got slowly to his feet.

I said, in English, "I'm Mademoiselle Martin. You must be Philippe."

He nodded, looking shy. Then his breeding asserted itself, and he took a short step forward, holding out his hand. "You are very welcome, Mademoiselle Martin." His voice was small and thin like himself, and without much expression. "I hope you will be happy at Valmy."

It came to me again, sharply, as I shook the hand, that this was the owner of Valmy. The thought made him, oddly enough, seem even smaller, less significant.

"I was told that you might be busy," I said, "but I thought I'd better come straight along and see you."

He considered this for a moment, taking me in with the frankly interested stare of a child. "Are you really going to teach me English?"

"Yes."

He said, "You do not look like a governess."

"Then I must try and look more like one, I suppose."

"No, I like it as you are. Do not change."

The de Valmys, it seemed, started young. I laughed. *"Merci du compliment, Monsieur le Comte."*

He gave me a swift look upward. There was glimmer in the black eyes. But all he said was, "Do we have a lesson tomorrow?"

"I expect so. I don't know. I shall probably see your aunt tonight, and no doubt she'll tell me just what the program is."

"Have you seen . . . my uncle?" Was there, or was there not, the faintest of changes in that monotonous little voice?

"Yes."

He was standing quite still, small hands dangling from their bony wrists in front of him. It came to me that he was in his own way as un-get-at-able as Héloïse de Valmy. My task here might not be a very easy one. His manners were beautiful; he was not, it was patent, going to be a "difficult" child in the sense of the word as usually used by governesses; but would I ever get to know him, ever get past that touch-me-not electric fence of reserve? That, and his unchildlike habit of stillness, I had already met in Madame de Valmy, but there the resemblance ended. Her stillness and remoteness was beautiful and poised; this child's was ungraceful and somehow disturbing.

I said, "I must go and unpack now, or I'll be late for dinner. Would you like to help?"

He looked up quickly. "Me?"

"Well, not help, exactly, but come and keep me company, and see what I've brought you from London."

"You mean a present?"

"Of course."

He flushed a slow and unbecoming scarlet. Without speaking, he walked sedately past me through my sitting room toward my bedroom door, opened it for me, then followed me into the room. He stood at the foot of the bed, still in silence, staring at my case.

I stooped over it, lifted a few more things out onto the bed, then rummaged to find what I had brought.

"They're nothing very much," I said, "because I haven't much spare cash. But—well, here they are."

I had brought him, from Woolworth's, a cardboard model of Windsor Castle—the kind that you cut out and assemble, together with a box, as big as I could afford, containing a collection of men in the uniform of the Grenadier Guards.

I looked a little uncertainly at the silent owner of the Château Valmy, and handed him the boxes.

"An English castle?" he said. "And English soldiers?"

"Yes. The kind they have at Buckingham Palace."

"With the fur hats, to guard the Queen. I know." He was still looking raptly at a picture of a full regiment of Guards, drilling in an improbable fashion.

"They're—they're not much," I said. "You see—"

But I saw he was not listening. He had opened the lid, and was fingering the cheap toys inside. "A present from London," he said, touching one crudely-painted toy soldier. It came to me, suddenly, that it would not have mattered if they had been homemade paper dolls.

I said, "I brought you a game, too, called Peggitty. You play it with these pegs. Later, I'll show you how. It's a good game."

From the schoolroom a girl's voice called, *"Philippe? Où es-tu, Philippe?"*

He started. "It's Berthe. I have to go." He shut the boxes and stood up, holding them tightly to him. He said, very formally, "Thank you. Thank you, mademoiselle." Then he turned and ran to the door. *"Me voici, Berthe. Je viens."* On the threshold he stopped and swung around. His face was still flushed, and he clutched the presents hard.

"Mademoiselle."

"Yes, Philippe?"

"What is the name of the game with the pegs?"

"Peggitty."

"Peg-it-ee. You will show me how to play it?"

"Yes."

"You will play this Peg-it-ee when I have had my supper before I go to bed?"

"Yes."

"Tonight?"

"Yes."

He hesitated as if he were going to say something else. Then instead he went quickly out, and shut the door gently behind him.

CHAPTER IV

> *O my prophetic soul!*
>
>   *Mine uncle?*
>
>   SHAKESPEARE: *Hamlet.*

HOWEVER STRANGE and luxurious my new surroundings, life at Valmy soon settled itself into a simple and orderly routine. Every morning Monsieur Bétemps, Philippe's tutor, arrived, and the two were closeted together till lunchtime. Once my various morning jobs about the schoolroom suite were finished I could count myself free, and for the first few days I occupied myself happily in exploring the gardens and the nearer woods, or in reading—hours and hours of reading, a luxury so long denied me at the Home that I still felt guilty whenever I indulged in it.

The library at the château almost certainly contained English books, but since it was Léon de Valmy's private study-cum-office, I could not —or would not—ask permission to use it. But I had brought as many of my own books as I could carry, and in the schoolroom there were shelves to the ceiling full of an excellent miscellany—children's books thrust cheek by jowl with English and French classics and a good deal of lighter reading. I wondered a little at the odd collection until I saw in some of the volumes the name *Deborah Bohun*, or the message *"To Debbie,"* and once I took down a battered old copy of *Treasure Island* to find it inscribed in a flamboyant young hand *Raoul Philippe St. Aubin de Valmy* . . . of course, Léon's son was half-English and had used these very rooms. I found Buchan, too, and Conan Doyle, and a host of forgotten or never-known books that, gratefully, I devoured—forcing myself to ignore the irrational feeling drilled into me in the seven years at the Home that Reading was a Waste of Time.

On one occasion my guilty feeling was justified. When I read French, I read it in secrecy, and once I was nearly caught out over *Tristan et Iseut*. I was devouring it, rapt and oblivious in my bedroom, when Berthe knocked and, receiving no reply, came in to dust the room. She noticed nothing, but I cursed myself and vowed yet again to be careful and wished for the hundredth time that I had never embarked on the silly deception that had seemed at the time to matter so much, and became daily more difficult to confess.

I no longer imagined seriously that anyone would mind; Philippe and I got on well together, and Madame de Valmy, in her aloof way, seemed to like me; I was certainly very completely trusted with Philippe's well-being. But I didn't particularly want her to know that I had deceived her —systematically, as it were, schemed to deceive her. And, as with all deceptions, the thing grew bigger daily. I had to make myself understood to Berthe, the schoolroom maid, and did this in elementary schoolgirl French which amused her and even made Philippe smile. Luckily, I never had to do this with my employers; invariably in my presence they spoke in their flawless and seemingly effortless English. And so the days went by and I said nothing. I dared not risk their displeasure; I loved the place, I could easily cope with the job, and I liked Philippe.

He was a very quiet, self-controlled child, who never chattered. Every afternoon, unless it rained too hard, we went for a walk, and our "English conversation" mainly consisted of my comments on the country or the gardens where we took our walks. That electric fence of his was still up: it was not a consciously erected barrier—the gift of the toys had won his alliance if not his heart—but it was there, the obstruction of a deep natural reserve. I imagined that his naturally undemonstrative nature had been made even more so by the sudden loss of his parents, to whom he had never referred. This was not a child one could readily "get to know." I soon stopped trying, and kept both his and my own attention on things outside ourselves. If I was ever to win his confidence, it would only be done by very gradual and natural degrees: by custom, as it were. And there was, indeed, no reason why I should push my way into his fenced and private world; I had suffered so much from lack of privacy in the Home that I deeply respected anybody's right to it, and would have looked on any attempt at intimacy with Philippe as a kind of mental violation.

His reserve showed itself not only toward me. Each evening, at half-past five, I took him down for half an hour to the small salon where his aunt sat. She would politely put aside her book or writing paper, pick up her exquisite and interminable petit point, and hold conversation with Philippe for the half-hour. I say "hold conversation" advisedly, because that phrase does perfectly imply the difficult and stilted communication that took place. Philippe was his usual quiet and withdrawn self, answering questions readily and with impeccable politeness, but asking none and volunteering nothing. Madame de Valmy was the one, it seemed to me, who had to violate her personality here; she, also naturally withdrawn, had to unbend, almost to chatter.

I suppose, though, that it was I who loathed those half-hours most, and who suffered the most. Madame de Valmy and Philippe talked, naturally, in French, and this exchange I was supposed not to understand. But occasionally she would revert to English, either for my benefit or to test my pupil's knowledge of that tongue, and then I was drawn into the conversation, and had the awkward task of betraying no knowledge of the exchange in French to which I had just been listening. I don't remember if I made any mistakes; she certainly appeared to notice none, but then, she never gave the appearance of more than the most superficial attention to the whole routine; it was, for her, the discharge of a duty to a charge she hardly knew. Madame de Valmy, certainly, could not be accused of trying to violate anybody's confidence.

Her husband was never there. His only meeting with Philippe seemed to be the purely chance ones of encounters in corridors, on the terrace, or in the gardens. At first I found myself blaming Philippe's uncle for his lack of interest in a lonely and recently bereaved little boy, but soon I realized that it wasn't entirely Léon de Valmy's fault. Philippe systematically avoided him. He would only go down the library corridor with me when we had seen the wheel chair safely out beyond the ornamental ponds or at the far side of the rosery; he seemed to have the faculty for hearing the whisper of its wheels two corridors away, when he would invariably drag at my hand, persuading me with him to vanish out of his uncle's sight.

There seemed to be no good reason for this steady aversion; on the two or three occasions during my first week when we did, unavoidably, meet Monsieur de Valmy, he was very nice to Philippe. But Philippe was, if possible, more withdrawn than ever; in front of his uncle the child's reserve appeared to be little more than the sulks. This was natural enough in a way; in Léon de Valmy's overwhelming presence anyone as awkward and unattractive as Philippe was bound to be made to feel doubly so, and, consciously or not, to resent it. Moreover his uncle's tone toward him was kind with the semi-indifferent indulgence he might have accorded to a not-very-favorite puppy. I could never make out

whether Philippe noticed or resented this; I know that on one or two
occasions I found myself resenting it on his behalf. But I still liked Léon
de Valmy; Philippe, on the other hand—and this I came only gradually
to realize—disliked his uncle very much indeed.

That this was irrational I tried on one occasion to tell him.

"Philippe, why do you avoid your uncle Léon?"

The stonewall expression shut down on his face. *"Ne comprends pas."*

"English, please. And you do understand quite well. He's very good
to you. You have everything you want, don't you?"

"Yes. Everything I want I have."

"Well, then—"

He gave me one of his quick, unreadable looks. "But he does not
give it to me."

"Who then? Your aunt Héloïse?"

He shook his head. "It is not theirs to give to me. It was my father's
and it is mine."

I looked at him. This, then, was it. Valmy. I remembered the little
gleam in the black eyes when I had laughingly addressed him as Count
de Valmy. This was another thing at which it seemed the de Valmys
started young. "Your land?" I said. "Of course it's yours. He's keeping
it for you. He's your trustee, isn't he?"

He looked puzzled. "Trustee? I do not know trustee."

"He takes care of Valmy till you are older. Then you have it."

"Yes, until I am fifteen. Is that trustee? Then my Uncle Hippolyte is
also trustee."

"Is he? I didn't know that."

He nodded, with that solemn look that sat almost sullenly on his
pale little face. "Yes. *Tous les deux*—both. My uncle Léon for the property and my uncle Hippolyte for me."

"What do you mean?" I asked involuntarily.

The gleam in the look he shot me might have been malice or only
mischief. "I heard Papa say that. He said—"

"Philippe," I began, but he wasn't listening. He was wrestling with a
translation of what papa had said, only to abandon it and quote in
French in a rush that spoke of a literal and all-too-vivid memory.

"He said, 'Léon'll keep the place going, trust him for that. God help
Valmy if it was left to Hippolyte.' And Maman said, 'But Hippolyte
must have the child if anything happens to us. Hippolyte must look after
the child. He is not to be left to Léon.' That's what Maman—" He
stopped, shutting his lips tightly over the word.

I said nothing.

He slanted that look at me again and said in English, "That is what they said. It means—"

"No, Philippe, don't try and translate," I said gently, "I don't suppose you were meant to hear it."

"N—no. But I wish I had not had to leave my uncle Hippolyte."

"You're fond of him?"

"Of course. He has gone to *la Grèce*. I wanted to go with him but he could not take me."

"He'll come back soon."

"Yes, but it is a long time."

"It'll pass," I said, "and meanwhile I'll look after you for him, and your uncle Léon'll look after Valmy."

I paused and looked at the uncommunicative little face. I didn't want to sound pompous or to alienate Philippe, but I was after all in charge of his manners. I said, tentatively, "He does it very well, Philippe. Valmy is beautiful, and he cares for it, *ça se voit*. You mustn't be ungrateful."

It was true that Philippe had no cause to complain of his uncle's stewardship. Léon seemed to me to spend his whole time, indeed, his whole self, on the place. It was as if the immense virility that was physically denied its outlet was redirected onto Valmy. Day after day the wheel chair patroled the terraces and the gravel of the formal gardens, the conservatories, the kitchen gardens, the garages . . . everywhere the chair could possibly go it went. And in the château itself the hand of a careful master was everywhere apparent. No plan was too large, no detail too small, for Léon de Valmy's absorbed attention.

It was also true that, as Comte de Valmy, Philippe might legitimately claim that he was a cypher in his own house, but he was only nine, and moreover a Paris-bred stranger. His uncle and aunt did ignore him to a large extent, but his daily routine with its small disciplines and lack of what one might call cosy family life was very much the usual one for a boy in his position.

I added, rather lamely, "You couldn't have a better trustee."

Philippe shot me one of his looks. The shutters were up in his face again. He said politely and distantly, "No, mademoiselle," and looked away.

I said no more, feeling myself unable to deal with what still seemed an unreasonable dislike.

But one day toward the end of my second week at Valmy the situation was, so to speak, thrust on me.

Philippe and I had, as usual, been down for our five-thirty visit to Madame de Valmy in the small salon. Punctually at six she dismissed us, but as we went she called me back for some reason that I now forget.

Philippe didn't wait, but escaped without ceremony into the corridor.

A minute or so later I left the salon, to walk straight into as nasty a little scene as I had yet come across.

Philippe was standing, the picture of guilt and misery, beside a table which stood against the wall outside the salon door. It was a lovely little table, flanked on either side by a Louis Quinze chair seated with straw-colored brocade. On one of the chair seats I now saw, horribly, a thick streak of ink, as if a pen had rolled from the table and then across the silk of the chair, smearing ink as it went.

I remembered, then, that Philippe had been writing to his uncle, Hippolyte, when I called him to come downstairs. He must have come hurriedly away, the pen still open in his hand, and have put it down there before going into the drawing room. He was clutching it now in an ink-stained fist, and staring white-faced at his uncle.

For this time of all times he hadn't managed to avoid Monsieur de Valmy. The wheel chair was slap in the middle of the corridor, barring escape. Philippe, in front of it, looked very small and guilty and defenseless.

Neither of them appeared to notice me. Léon de Valmy was speaking. That he was angry was obvious, and it looked as if he had every right to be, but the cold lash of his voice as he flayed the child for his small-boy carelessness was frightening; he was using—not a wheel, but an atomic blast, to break a butterfly.

Philippe, as white as ashes now, stammered something that might have been an apology, but merely sounded like a terrified mutter, and his uncle cut across it in that voice that bit like a loaded whip.

"It is, perhaps, just as well that your visits to this part of the house are restricted to this single one a day, as apparently you don't yet know how to behave like a civilized human being. Perhaps in your Paris home you were allowed to run wild in this hooligan manner, but here we are accustomed to—"

"This is my home," said Philippe.

He said it still in that small shaken voice that held the suggestion of a sullen mutter. It stopped Léon de Valmy in full tirade. For a moment I thought the sentence in that still little voice unbearably pathetic, and in the same moment wondered at Philippe, who was not prone to either drama or pathos. But then he added, still low, but very clearly, "And that is my chair."

There was a moment of appalling silence. Something came and went in Léon de Valmy's face—the merest flick of an expression like a flash of a camera's shutter—but Philippe took a step backward, and I found myself catapulting out of the doorway like a wildcat defending a kitten.

Léon de Valmy looked up and saw me, but he spoke to Philippe quietly, as though his anger had never been.

"When you have recovered your temper and your manners, Philippe, you will apologize for that remark." The dark eyes lifted to me, and he said coolly but very courteously, in English, "Ah, Miss Martin. I'm afraid there has been a slight contretemps. Perhaps you will take Philippe back to his own rooms and persuade him that courtesy toward his elders is one of the qualities that is expected of a gentleman."

As his uncle spoke to me, Philippe had turned quickly, as if in relief. His face was paler than ever, and looked pinched and sullen. But the eyes were vulnerable: child's eyes.

I looked at him, then past him at his uncle.

"There's no need," I said. "He'll apologize now." I took the boy gently by the shoulders and turned him back to face his uncle. I held him for a moment. The shoulders felt very thin and tense. He was shaking.

I let him go. "Philippe?" I said.

He said, his voice thin with a gulp in it, "I beg your pardon if I was rude."

Léon de Valmy looked from him to me and back again.

"Very well. That is forgotten. And now Miss Martin had better take you upstairs."

The child turned quickly to go, but I hesitated. I said, "I gather there's been an accident to that chair, and that Philippe's been careless; but then, so have I. It was my job to see that nothing of the sort happened. It was my fault, and I must apologize too, Monsieur de Valmy."

He said in a voice quite different from the one with which he had dismissed Philippe, "Very well, Miss Martin. Thank you. And now we will forget the episode, shall we?"

As we went I was very conscious of that still, misshapen figure sitting there watching us.

I shut the schoolroom door behind me, and leaned against it. Philippe and I looked at one another. His face was shuttered still with that white resentment. His mouth looked sulky, but I saw the lower lip tremble a little.

He waited, saying nothing.

This was where I had to uphold authority. Curtain lecture by Miss Martin. Léon de Valmy had been perfectly right: Philippe had been stupid, careless, and rude. . . .

I said, "My lamb, I'm with you all the way, but you are a little owl, aren't you?"

"You can't," said Philippe very stiffly, "be a lamb and an owl both at the same time."

Then he ran straight at me and burst into tears.

After that I did help to keep him out of his uncle's way.

CHAPTER V

Ay, now the plot thickens very much upon us.
BUCKINGHAM: *The Rehearsal.*

THE SPRING WEATHER continued marvelous. There was still snow on the nearer hills, and the far high peaks that unrolled below the clouds were great dazzling beds of white as yet untouched by the spring. But the valley was green, and yet greener; the violets were out along the ditches, and all the urns and stone tubs that lined the château terraces held their constellations of narcissus and jonquil that danced with the wind.

Philippe and I went out every afternoon, coated and scarved against the breeze that blew off the snow. The mountain air seemed to be doing him good; color came into the sallow cheeks: he even, occasionally, laughed and ran a little, though for the most part he walked stolidly at my side, and answered in his slow but excellent English my dutiful attempts at conversation.

One of our walks was a steep but easy track down through the meadows toward the village. At the foot of the slope a narrow wooden bridge crossed the Merlon, deep here and placid in its wandering from one wide and gleaming pool to the next. From the bridge the track led straight through water meadows and budding orchards to the village.

On the occasions when it was known that our walk would take us to Soubirous, we were given small commissions to execute there, usually for Mrs. Seddon or Berthe, and sometimes for Albertine, but occasionally for Madame de Valmy herself.

One morning—it was the first of April—Philippe and I set out for the village soon after breakfast. It was Monday, and as a rule on Monday morning Monsieur St. Aubray, the curé of Soubirous, came up to the château to instruct the young Comte in Latin, Greek and the Roman Catholic religion. But M. le Curé had twisted an ankle, and, since it did not seem desirable for Philippe to miss his instruction, I took him down to the presbytery beside the church and left him there.

It was the first time I had been on my own in the village, with time to spare. I stood in the little square outside the church and looked about me.

The day was warm, the sunlight as it beat up from flags and cobbles was bright and almost hot. There was a white cat sunning itself on top of a low wall below which someone had planted primulas. The single *bistro* had put out its red-and-black striped awning, and in spite of faded paint and peeling walls the houses looked gay with their open doors and the colored shutters fastened back from the windows. A canary in a small cage hanging outside a shop sang lustily. Some small children, black-haired and brown-limbed, were intent on something in a gutter. Outside a food shop cabbage and cheeses and tired-looking oranges made a splash of color. A boy on a bicycle shot past me, with a yard or so of bread under one arm.

It was a pleasant, peaceful, lighthearted little scene, and my own heart was light as I surveyed it. It was a lovely morning; I was free to do as I wished with it for two hours; I had some money in my pocket; the shadow of the Constance Butcher Home for Girls dwindled and shrank to nothing in the warm Savoyard light. It was also—as a stray warm breeze stirred fragrance from the primulas and brought a shower of early cherry blossom floating out over the presbytery wall—it was also spring.

I walked slowly across the square, made sure that it was only marbles, and not a frog or a kitten, that was occupying the children in the gutter, then turned into the pharmacy beside the *bistro* to carry out what commissions I had for the day.

"Mademoiselle Martin?" The apothecary came out of his dark cave at the back. He knew me well by this time. Mrs. Seddon, in the intervals of antihistamine, seemed to live exclusively on aspirin and something she called Oh Dick Alone, while I (after half a lifetime of White Windsor) had developed a passion, which had to be satisfied frequently, for the more exotic soaps.

I said gaily, in my most English French, "Oh, good morning, Monsieur Garcin. It is a fine day, is it not? It was a fine day yesterday. It will be a fine day tomorrow. Not? I am looking at the soaps, as usual."

I said *par usuel,* and the chemist's thin lips pursed. It was his weekly pleasure to correct my French, always with that pained, crab-apple face, and I didn't see why I should deny him anything.

"*Comme d'habitude,*" he said sourly.

"*Plaît-il?*" I said, very fluently. He had taught me that one last week.

"*Comme d'habitude,*" said Monsieur Garcin, raising his voice as to the slightly deaf.

"*Comme quoi?* I do not understand," I said carefully. I was behaving badly and I knew it, but it was a heavenly day and it was spring, and Monsieur Garcin was prim and dry and a bit musty, like herbs that have been kept too long, and besides, he always tried to put me in what he thought was my place. I raised my voice, too, and repeated loudly, "I said I was looking at the soaps, *par usuel.*"

The chemist's thin nose twitched, but he restrained himself with an effort. He looked at me dourly across a pile of laxatives. "So I see. And which do you want?" He heaved up a box of Roger and Gallet from behind the counter. "There is a new box this week. Rose, violet, cologne, sandalwood, clove pink—"

"Oh, yes, please. The clove pink. I love that."

A slight gleam of surprise showed in the oyster-like eyes. "You know what flower that is? *Oeillet mignardise?*"

I said composedly, "The name is on the soap. With a picture. *Voilà.*" I reached across to pick the tablet out, sniffed it, smiled at him, and said kindly, "*C'est le plus bon, ça.*"

He rose to that one. "*Le meilleur.*"

"*Le meilleur,*" I said meekly. "Thank you, monsieur."

"You are doing quite well," said Monsieur Garcin, magnanimously. "And have you any little commissions for your employers today?"

"Yes, if you please. Madame de Valmy asked me to get her medicine and the tablets—her pills for sleeping."

"Very well. Have you the paper?"

"Paper?"

"You must give me the paper, you understand."

I puckered my brows, trying to remember if Albertine had given me a prescription along with the shopping list. The chemist made a movement of ill-concealed impatience, and his mouth drew up and thinned till it disappeared. He repeated very slowly, as to an imbecile, "You—must—have—a paper—from—the—doctor."

"Oh," I said evilly, "a prescription? Why didn't you say so? Well, she didn't give me one, monsieur. May I bring it along next year?"

"Next *year?*"

"I mean next week."

"No," he said curtly. "I cannot give you the drugs without the prescription."

I was already regretting having teased him. I said distressfully, "Oh, but Madame asked specially for the medicine. I'll bring the paper as soon

as I can, or send it or something, honestly I will! Please, Monsieur Garcin, can't you trust me for a day or two?"

"Impossible. No." His bony fingers were rearranging the tablets of
soap. "And what else do you want?"

I glanced down at the list in my hand. There were various things on
it, listed—luckily for Monsieur Garcin's patience and my own ingenuity
—in French. I read them out to him carefully: someone wanted tooth
powder and Dop shampoo: someone else (I hoped it was the sour-faced
Albertine) demanded corn plasters and iodine, and so on to the end,
where came the inevitable aspirin, Eau de cologne, and what Mrs. Seddon simply listed as "my bottle."

"And Mrs. Seddon's pills," I said finally.

The chemist picked up the packet of aspirin.

"No," I said, "the others." (I wouldn't know the word for asthma,
would I? And I genuinely didn't know the word for antihistamine.) "The
pills for her chest."

"You got them last week," said Monsieur Garcin.

"I don't think so."

"I know you did."

His voice was curt to rudeness, but I ignored it. "Perhaps," I said
politely, "she has need of more?"

"She cannot have, if she got them last week."

"Are you so sure she did, monsieur? She put them herself on the list
today."

"Did she give you the paper—the prescription?"

"No," I said.

He said impatiently, "I told you she got them last week. You took
them yourself. You were in a hurry and you handed me a list with a
prescription for Madame Sed-don. I sent the tablets. Perhaps you forgot
to give them to her. I have an excellent memory, me; and I remember
handing them to you. Moreover, I have a record."

"I am sorry, monsieur. I just don't remember. No doubt you're right.
I thought—oh, just a minute, here's a paper in my bag! Here it is, monsieur, the prescription! *Voyez-vous*. Is this it?"

I handed him the paper, carefully keeping anything of I-told-you-so
out of my voice. Which was just as well, because he said tartly, "This is
not for Madame Sed-don. It is the paper for Madame de Valmy's heart
medicine."

"Oh? I hadn't realized I had it. It must have been with the list. I came
out in a hurry and didn't notice. I'm so sorry." I smiled winningly at
him. "Then you can give me the medicine after all, monsieur. I'll get the
tablets in Thonon on Friday."

He shot me a queer look out of those oyster eyes, and then, by way of teaching me, I suppose, that servants shouldn't argue with their betters, he proceeded to put on his spectacles and read the prescription through with exaggerated care. I watched the sunlight beyond the doorway and waited, suppressing my irritation. He read it again. You'd have thought I was Madeleine Smith asking casually for half a pound of arsenic. Suddenly I saw the joke and laughed at him.

"It's all right, monsieur. It's quite safe to let me have it. I'll see I deliver it promptly where it belongs! I don't often eat digitalis, or whatever it is, myself!"

He said sourly, "I don't suppose you do." He folded the paper carefully and pushed my purchases toward me. "There you are then. I'll give you the drops, and perhaps you will also see that Madame Seddon gets the tablets I sent up on Wednesday?" As I gathered the things up without replying I saw him throw me that queer, quick look yet again. "And I must congratulate you on the way your French has improved, mademoiselle," he added, very dryly.

"Why, thank you, monsieur," I said coolly. "I try very hard and study every day. In another three weeks you won't even guess that I'm English."

"*Anglaise?*" The word was echoed, in a man's voice, just behind me. I looked round, startled. I had heard nobody come in, but now realized that a newcomer's large body was blocking the door of the pharmacy, while his enormous shadow, thrown before him by the morning sun, seemed to fill the shop. He came forward. "Excuse me, but I heard you say '*Je suis anglaise.*' Are you really English?"

"Yes."

"Oh, I—that *is* a relief!" He looked down at me half shyly. Seen properly now, and not just as a colossal silhouette framed in the shop door, he still appeared a very large young man. He was dressed in khaki shorts and a wind-breaker. His head was bare, and covered with an untidy thatch of fair hair, very fine and thick. His eyes were blue in a tanned face. His hands and legs were tanned, too, and on them in the sunlight the fair hair glinted, pale as barley in September.

He groped in an inner pocket and produced a tattered old envelope. "I wonder—could you possibly help me, d'you think? I've got a whole list of stuff to get, and I was wondering how on earth to ask for it. My French is nonexistent, and yours seems terribly good—"

I said firmly, "My French may sound wonderful to you, but it sounds like nothing on earth to Monsieur Garcin."

I sent a bright smile to the chemist, who still watched me, sourly, from behind the stack of laxatives. No response. I gave it up and turned back to the Englishman, who was saying, unconvinced, "It seems to get results anyway." He gestured toward my purchases.

I grinned. "You'd be surprised what a fight it is sometimes. But of course I'll help—if I can. May I see your list?"

He surrendered it relievedly. "This is awfully good of you to let me bother you." He gave his disarmingly shy grin. "Usually I just have to beat my breast like Tarzan and point."

"You must be very brave to come holidaying here without a word of French."

"Holidaying? I'm here on a job."

"Paid assassin?" I asked, "or only M.I.5?"

"I—I beg your pardon?"

I indicated the list. "This. It sounds a bit pointed." I read it aloud. "Bandages; three, one-and-a-half, and one-inch. Sticking plaster. Elastoplast. Burn-dressing. Boracic powder. . . ." I looked at him in some awe. "You've forgotten the probe."

"Probe?"

"To get the bullets out."

He laughed. "I'm only a forester. I'm camping off and on in a hut at four thousand feet, so I thought I'd set up a first-aid kit."

"Do you intend to live quite so dangerously?"

"You never know. Anyway I'm a confirmed hypochondriac. I'm never happy till I'm surrounded by pills and boluses and thermometers marked in degrees centigrade."

I looked at his six-feet odd of solid bone and muscle. "Yes. One can see that you should take every care. Do you really want me to struggle with sticking-plaster and burn-dressings for you?"

"Yes, please, if you'd be so good, though the only item I'm really sure I shall need is the last one, and I could ask for that myself at a pinch."

"Cognac? Yes, I see what you mean." Then I turned to Monsieur Garcin and embarked on the slightly exhausting procedure of describing by simple word and gesture articles whose names I knew as well as he did himself. Monsieur Garcin served me reservedly, and as with Philippe, his reserve sometimes bore a strong resemblance to the sulks. I had twice tried the *amende honorable* of a smile, and I was dashed if I would try again, so we persevered in chilly politeness to the last-but-one item on the Englishman's list.

At last we had finished. The Englishman, weighed down with enough pills and boluses to satisfy the most highly-strung *malade imaginaire,* stood back from the doorway and waited for me to precede him into the sunlight.

As I picked up my own parcels and turned to go the chemist's voice

said, as dry as the rustle of dead leaves, "You are forgetting the drops
for Madame de Valmy." He was holding out the package across the
counter.

When I reached the sunny street the young man said curiously,
"What's biting him? Was he being rude? You're—forgive my saying so
—but you're as pink as anything."

"Am I? Well, it's my own fault. No, he wasn't rude. It was just me
being silly and getting what I deserved."

"I'm sure you weren't. And thank you most awfully for being such a
help. I'd never have managed on my own." He gave me his shy grin. "I
still have to get the cognac. I wonder if you'd help me to buy that too?"

"I thought you said you could ask for that yourself."

"I—well, I rather hoped you'd come with me and let me buy you a
drink to thank you for taking all that trouble."

"That's very nice of you. But really, there's no need—"

He looked down at me rather imploringly over his armful of packages. "Please," he said. "Apart from everything else, it really is wonderful to talk English to someone."

I had a sudden vision of him up in his lonely hut at four thousand feet,
surrounded by pills and boluses and thermometers in degrees centigrade.

"I'd like to very much," I said.

He beamed. "That's fine. In here? It's Hobson's choice anyway—I
think this is the only place apart from the Coq Hardi half a mile away."

The *bistro* with its gay awning was next door to the pharmacy. Inside
it looked dim and not very inviting, but on the cobbles outside there
were two or three little metal tables, and some old cane chairs painted
bright red. Two small clipped trees stood sentinel in blue tubs.

We sat down in the sun. "What will you have?" He was carefully
disposing his life-saving parcels on an empty chair.

"Do you suppose they serve coffee?"

"Surely." And it seemed, indeed, that they did. It arrived in large
yellow cups, with three wrapped oblongs of sugar in each saucer.

Now that we were facing one another more or less formally across a
café table, my companion seemed to have retreated once more behind a
rather English shyness. He said, stirring his coffee hard, "My name's
Blake. William Blake." On this last he looked up with a trace of defiance.

I said, "That's a good name to have, isn't it? Mine's only Belinda Martin. Linda for short—or for pretty, my mother used to say."

He smiled. "Thank you."

"For what? Making you free of my name?"

"Oh—yes, of course. But I meant for not making a crack about the
Songs of Innocence."

" 'Little lamb, who made thee?' "

"That one exactly. You'd be surprised how many people can't resist it."

I laughed. "How awfully trying! But me, I prefer tigers. No thank you, Mr. Blake—" this to a proffered cigarette—"I don't smoke."

"Mind if I do?"

"Of course not."

Across the spluttering flare of a French match he was looking a question. "If one may ask—what are you doing in Soubirous? Not a holiday, I take it?"

"No. I'm here on a job, too. I'm governess."

"Of course. You must be the English girl from the Château Valmy."

"Yes. You know about me?"

"Everybody knows everybody else hereabouts. Anyway I'm a near neighbor, as things go round here. I'm working on the next estate, in the plantations west of the Merlon."

"Oh," I said, interested. "Dieudonné?"

"That's it. The château—it's only a country house really, a quarter the size of Valmy—lies in the valley a bit beyond the village. The owner's hardly ever there. His name's St. Vire. He seems to spend most of his time in Paris or down near Bordeaux. Like your boss, he gets a lot of his money from his timber and his vineyards."

"Vineyards? Valmy?"

"Oh, yes. They own chunks of Provence, I believe."

"Of course," I said. "Bellevigne. But that's Monsieur de Valmy's own property, and Valmy isn't. Even he wouldn't spend its income on Valmy."

"*Even* he?"

To my surprise my voice sounded defensive. "I believe he's an awfully good landlord."

"Oh, that. Yes, second to none, I imagine. He's pretty highly thought of hereabouts, I can tell you. And the gossip goes that most of the Bellevigne income did get diverted up here until a few years back; there used to be plenty money, anyway."

"There still is," I said, "or so it seems."

"Yes. Things are waking up again, I gather. Two good vintages, and you get the roof repaired. . . ." He laughed. "Funny how everyone in these places minds everyone else's business, isn't it?" He looked at me. "Governessing. Now that's a heck of a life, isn't it?"

"In story books, yes; and I suppose it could be in real life. But I like it. I like Philippe—my pupil—and I love the place."

"You're not lonely—so far from home, I mean, and England?"

I laughed. "If you only knew! My 'home in England' was seven years in an orphanage. Governessing or not, Valmy's a wild adventure to me!"

"I suppose so. Is that what you want, adventure?"

"Of course! Who doesn't?"

"Me, for one," said Mr. Blake firmly.

"Oh? But I thought all men saw themselves hacking their way with machetes through the mangrove swamps and shooting rapids and things. You know, all hairy knees and camp fires and the wide wide world."

He grinned. "I got over that pretty young. And just exactly what is a machete?"

"Goodness knows. They always have them. But seriously—"

"Seriously," he said, "I don't know. I'd like to get around, yes, and I like travel and change and seeing new things, but—well, roots are a good thing to have." He stopped himself there and flushed a little. "I'm sorry. That was tactless."

"It's all right. And I do see what you mean. Everybody needs a—a center. Somewhere to go out from and come back to. And I suppose as you get older you enjoy the coming back more than the going out."

He gave me his shy, rather charming smile. "Yes, I think so. But don't listen to me, Miss Martin. I have a stick-in-the-mud disposition. You go ahead and chase your tigers. After all, you've done pretty well up to now. You've found one already, haven't you?"

"Monsieur de Valmy?"

His eyebrows lifted. "You were quick onto that. He *is* a tiger, then?"

"You did mean him? Why?"

"Only that he seems a little fierce and incalculable by reputation. How do you get on with him? What's he like?"

"I—he's very polite and kind—I'd even say charming. Yes, certainly he's charming. He and Madame seem terribly anxious that I should really feel at home here. I don't see an awful lot of them, of course, but when I do they're awfully nice. . . ."

I looked away from him across the square. Two women came out of the boulangerie, and paused to glance at us curiously before they moved off, their sabots noisy on the stones. Someone called, shrilly, and the group of children broke up, chattering and screaming like jays. Two of them raced past us, bare feet slapping the warm cobbles. The clock in the church tower clanged the half-hour.

I said, "And what made you come here? Tell me about your job."

"There's nothing much to tell." He was drawing little patterns on the table top with the handle of his spoon. And indeed, the way he told it, his life had taken a very ordered course. A pleasant, reasonably well-to-do suburban home; a small public school; two years in the Army, doing nothing more eventful than maneuvers on Salisbury Plain; then the University—four years' hard work, with holidays (more or less of the busman variety) in Scandinavia and Germany; finally, a good degree and the decision to go on to a further two years' research on some conifer diseases, which he proceeded to explain to me very carefully and with much enthusiasm. . . . Far from lacking adventure, it appeared that (what with butt rot, drought crack, larch canker, spruce bark beetle, and things with names like *Phomopsis* and *Megatismus* and even *Ips*) life in a conifer forest could positively teem with excitement. I gathered that Mr. Blake himself was seriously involved with the Pine Weevil . . . there was a magnificent infestation of these creatures (*Hylobius,* mark you, not *Pissodes*), in a plantation west of the Merlon. . . .

But here he recollected himself and flushed slightly, grinning at me. "Well, anyway," he finished, "that's why I'm here. I'm busy getting the best of both worlds—thanks to Monsieur de St. Vire, who's a remarkably decent chap for a Frenchman." He added, seeming to think this phenomenon worth explaining, "My father knew him in the War. He's given me a job here of a sort—at any rate I'm paid a bit for doing what's really my own research program anyway. I'm getting some valuable material as well as experience, and I like working in this country. It's small-scale stuff hereabouts, but those people—at any rate the Valmys and St. Vires —really do care about their land. But there's a lot to learn." He looked wistful. "Including the language. It seems to escape me, somehow. Perhaps I've no ear. But it would be a help."

"If you're living alone, with thermometers," I said, "I can't see why."

"Oh, I'm not up at the hut all the time. I work up there mostly, because it's near the plantation I'm 'on' at present, and it's quiet; I keep all my stuff up there, and I sleep there when I'm short of cash." He grinned. "That's quite often, of course. But I do come down to the Coq Hardi pretty frequently. It's noisy, but the boss speaks English and the food's good . . . ah, is that your little boy?"

From where we were sitting we could see the high wall of the presbytery garden, and now the gate in it opened, and Philippe appeared in the archway, with the broad figure of the curé's housekeeper behind him.

"Yes, that's Philippe," I said. "I'll have to go."

I got to my feet, and the child saw me, said something over his shoulder to the woman, and then ran across the square in our direction.

"I'm glad you waited. I told Madame Rocher you would go—would have gone for a walk. But here you are."

"Here I am. You're early, aren't you, Philippe? Did Monsieur le Curé get tired of you?"

"I do not know tired *of*."

"*Ennuyé.*"

He was solemn. "No. But he is not very well. He is tired, but not at—of—me. Madame Rocher says I must come away."

"I'm sorry to hear that," I said. "Philippe, this is Monsieur Blake, who works for Monsieur de St. Vire. Mr. Blake, the Comte de Valmy."

They shook hands, Philippe with the large gravity that sat on him rather attractively.

"What do you work at, monsieur?"

"I'm a forester."

"Forest—oh, yes, I understand. There are foresters at Valmy also."

"I know. I've met one or two of them. Pierre Detruche, Jean-Louis Michaud, and Armand Lestocq—he lives next door to the Coq Hardi."

"As to that," said Philippe, "I do not know them myself yet. I have not been here very long, *vous comprenez.*"

"Of course not. I—er, I suppose your uncle manages these things."

"Yes," said Philippe politely. "He is my trustee."

The look he shot me was merely one of minor triumph that he should have remembered the word, but it tinged the reply with a sort of smug stateliness that brought the beginnings of amusement to Mr. Blake's face. I said hastily, "We'd better go, I think, Mr. Blake, thank you so much for the coffee. I'm awfully glad we met." I held out my hand.

As he took it, he said quickly, "I say, please—don't just vanish. When can we meet again?"

"I'm not a very free agent. Sometimes I've a morning, but I don't often get as far as this."

"Are you free in the evenings?"

"No, not really. Only Fridays, and a Sunday here and there."

"Then that's no good," he said, sounding disappointed. "I've arranged to meet some pals of mine this week end. Perhaps later on?"

Philippe had given a little tug to my hand. "I really must go," I said. "Let's leave it, shall we? We're sure to meet—the valley isn't all that big. And thank you again. . . ."

As we crossed the bridge I glanced back, to see him laboriously gathering up the bandages and the sticking-plaster and all the homely remedies which were to reassure life at four thousand feet.

I hoped he would remember to get the cognac.

CHAPTER VI

*Something will come of this. I hope it
mayn't be human gore.*
DICKENS: *Barnaby Rudge.*

THAT EVENING the quiet run of our existence was broken. Nursery tea
was over; the early April dusk had drawn in against the uncurtained windows where lamp and firelight were cheerfully reflected. Philippe was on
the hearthrug playing in a desultory fashion with some soldiers and I
was sitting, as I often did at that time, reading aloud to him, when I heard
a car climbing the zigzag. It was a mild evening, and one of the long
balcony windows was open. The mounting engine roared, changed,
roared again nearer. As I paused in my reading and glanced toward the
window, Philippe looked up.

"Une auto! Quelqu'un vient!"

"English," I said automatically. "Philippe, what are you doing?"

But he took no notice. He jumped up from the rug, while his toys scattered unheeded. Then he flew out of the window like a rocket and vanished to the right along the balcony.

I dropped the book and hurried after him. He had run to the end of
the balcony where it overlooked the gravel forecourt, and was leaning
over eagerly and somewhat precariously. I stifled an impulse to grab
him by the seat of his pants and said instead, as mildly as I could, "You'll
fall if you hang over like that. . . . Look, the dashed thing's loose anyway—this coping moved, I'm sure it did. This must be one of the bits they
were talking about repairing. Philippe—"

But he didn't seem to be listening. He still craned forward over the
stone coping. I said firmly, "Now come back, Philippe, and be sensible.
What's the excitement for, anyway? Who is it?"

The car roared up the last incline, and swung with a scrunch of tires
across the gravel. She had her lights on. They scythed around, through
the thin dark thorns of the rose garden, the flickering spear points of the
iron railings below us, the carefully-planted pots on the loggia, came to
rest on the stableyard archway, and were switched off.

A door slammed. I heard a man's voice, low-pitched and pleasant.
Another voice—I supposed the driver's—answered him. Then the car

moved off slowly toward the stableyard, and the newcomer crossed the gravel and mounted the steps to the great door.

I waited with mild curiosity for the door to open and the light from the hall to give body, as it were, to the voice. But before this happened Philippe ducked back behind me and retreated along the balcony toward the schoolroom windows. I turned, to see in the set of the thin back and shoulders the suggestion of some disappointment so sharp that I followed him in without a word, sat down again in my chair by the fire, and picked up my book. But Philippe didn't settle again to his toys. He stood still on the hearthrug, staring at the fire. I think he had forgotten I was there.

I leafed through a few pages of the book and then said very casually, "Who was it, did you know?"

The thin shoulders lifted. "Monsieur Florimond, I think."

"Monsieur Florimond? Do you mean the dress designer?"

"Yes. He used to visit us a lot in Paris and he is a friend of my aunt Héloïse. Do you know of him in England?"

"Of course." Even in the Constance Butcher Home we had heard of the great Florimond, whose 'Aladdin' silhouette had been the rage of Paris and New York years before and had, it was rumored, caused Dior to mutter something under his breath and tear up a set of designs. I said, impressed, "Is he coming to stay?"

"I do not know." His voice sufficiently also expressed that he did not care. But the general impression of poignant disappointment prevailed so strongly that I said, "Did you expect someone else, Philippe?"

He glanced up momentarily, then the long lashes dropped. He said nothing.

I hesitated. But Philippe was my job: moreover, he was a very lonely little boy. Who was it who could expect that headlong welcome from him?

I said, "Your cousin Raoul, perhaps?"

No answer.

"Is anyone else supposed to be coming?"

He shook his head.

I tried again. "Don't you like Monsieur Florimond?"

"But yes. I like him very much."

"Then why—?" I began, but something in his face warned me to stop. I said gently, "It's time we went down to the salon, *petit*. I haven't been told not to, so I suppose, guests or not, that we'll have to go. Run and wash your hands while I tidy my hair."

He obeyed me without a word or look.

I went slowly across to shut the balcony window.

In a small salon a log fire had been lit, and in front of it sat Madame de Valmy and Monsieur Florimond on a rose-brocaded sofa, talking.

I looked with interest at the newcomer. I don't know what I expected one of fashion's Big Five to look like; I only know that the great Florimond didn't look like it. He was vast, baldish, and untidy. His face in repose had a suggestion of tranquil melancholy about it that was vaguely reminiscent of the White Knight, but no one could ever doubt Monsieur Florimond's large sanity. Those blue eyes were shrewd and very kind: they also looked as if they missed very little. He wore his conventional, superbly cut clothes with all the delicate care one might accord to an old beach towel. His pockets bulged comfortably in every direction, and there was cigar ash on his lapel. He was clutching what looked like a folio-society reprint in one large hand, and gestured with it lavishly to underscore some story he was telling Madame de Valmy.

She was laughing, looking happier and more animated than I had seen her since I came to Valmy. I realized sharply how lovely she had been before time and tragedy had drained the life from her face.

On the thought, she turned and saw myself and Philippe by the door, and the gaiety vanished. The boredom and annoyance that shut down over it were humiliatingly plain to see. I could have slapped her for it, but then realized that Philippe had probably not noticed. He was advancing solemnly and politely on Florimond, who surged to his feet with noises indicating quite sufficient delighted pleasure to counter Héloïse's obvious irritation.

"Philippe! This is delightful! How are you?"

"I am very well, thank you, m'sieur."

"H'm, yes." He tapped the boy's cheek. "A little more color there, perhaps, and then you'll do. Country air, that's the thing, and the Valmy air suits you, by the look of it!" He didn't actually say "better than Paris," but the words were there, implicit, and Philippe didn't reply. It wasn't easy to avoid mistakes just then with him. Florimond registered this one, I could see, but he merely added amiably, "Mind you, I don't wonder that Valmy's good for you! When one is lucky enough to have a beautiful young lady as one's constant companion, one must expect to flourish!"

The perfect politeness of Philippe's smile indicated how completely this gallant sally went over his head. It had perforce, since they were speaking French, to go over mine too. I looked as noncommittal as I could and avoided Florimond's eye.

Héloïse de Valmy said from the sofa, "Don't waste your gallantries, Carlo. Miss Martin's French improves hourly, so I'm told, but I don't think she's reached the compliment stage yet." Then, in English: "Miss

Martin, let me introduce Monsieur Florimond. You will have heard of
him, I don't doubt."

I said composedly as I shook hands, "Even in my English orphanage
we had heard of Monsieur Florimond. You reached us perhaps some six
years late, monsieur, but you did reach us." I smiled, remembering my
own cheap ready-made. "Believe it or not."

He didn't pretend to misunderstand me. He made a largely gallant
gesture with the book which was, I saw, *The Tale of Genji,* and said,
"You, mademoiselle, would adorn anything you wore."

I laughed. "Even this?"

"Even that," he said, unperturbed, a twinkle in the blue eyes.

"The size of that compliment," I said, "strikes me dumb, monsieur."

Madame de Valmy said, sounding amused now, and more naturally
friendly than I had yet heard her, "It's Monsieur Florimond's constant
sorrow that only the old and faded can afford to be dressed by him, while
the young and lovely buy dresses *prêtes à porter* . . . there's a phrase—
my English is slipping in the excitement of talking to you, Carlo—what's
the phrase you have for 'ready-made'?"

" 'Off the peg?' " I suggested.

"Yes, that's it. You buy your dresses off the peg, and still show us up."

"Your English *is* slipping, madame," I said. "You're getting your pro-
nouns all wrong."

As she lifted her eyebrows Florimond said delightedly, "There, *chère
madame,* a real compliment! A compliment of the right kind! So neat
you did not see it coming, and so *subtil* that you still do not see it when
it has come."

She laughed. "My dear Carlo, compliments even now aren't quite so
rare that I don't recognize them, believe me. Thank you, Miss Martin,
that was sweet of you." Her eyes as she smiled at me were friendly, almost warm, and for the first time since I had met her I saw charm in
her—not the easy charm of the vivid personality, but the real and irresistible charm that reaches out halfway to meet you, assuring you that you
are wanted and liked. And heaven knew I needed that assurance. . . . I
was very ready to meet any gesture, however slight, with the response
of affection. Perhaps at last . . .

But even as I smiled back at her it happened again. The warmth
drained away as if wine had seeped from a crack and left the glass empty,
a cool and misted shell, reflecting nothing.

She turned away to pick up her embroidery.

I stood with the smile stiffening on my lips, feeling, even more sharply
than before, the sense of having been rebuffed for some reason that I
couldn't understand. A moment ago I could have sworn the woman liked

me, but now . . . in the last fleeting glance before the cool eyes dropped to her embroidery I thought I saw the same queerly apprehensive quality that I had noticed on my first day at Valmy.

I dismissed the idea straight away. I no longer imagined that Madame de Valmy feared her husband; on the contrary. Without any overt demonstration it was obvious that the two were very close; their personalities shared a boundary as light and shadow do; they marched. It was probable, I thought pityingly and only half comprehendingly, that Héloïse de Valmy's keep-your-distance chilliness was only a by-product of the sort of Samurai self-control that she must have learned to practice elsewhere. With the inability of youth to imagine any temperament other than my own, I felt that life must be a good deal easier for Léon de Valmy himself than for his wife. . . .

And her attitude to me—to Philippe as well—must only be part of the general shutdown. . . . It would take time for the reserve to melt, the door to open. That look of hers wasn't apprehension; it was a kind of waiting, an appraisal, no more. It would take time. Perhaps, she was still only wondering, as I was, why Léon de Valmy thought she'd made "a very great mistake. . . ."

She was setting a stitch with delicate care. There was a lamp at her elbow. The light shone softly on the thin white hand. The needle threaded the canvas with moving sparks. She didn't look up. "Come and sit by me, Philippe, on this footstool. You may stay ten minutes . . . no, Miss Martin, don't slip away. Sit down and entertain Monsieur Florimond for me."

The mask was on again. She sat, composed and elegant as ever over her needlework. She even managed to appear faintly interested as she put Philippe through the usual catechism about his day's activities, and listened to his polite, painstaking replies.

Beside me Florimond said, "Won't you sit here?"

I turned gratefully toward him, to find him watching me with those mild eyes that nevertheless seemed to miss nothing. He may have noticed the ebb and flow of invitation and rebuff that had left me silent and stranded; at any rate he now appeared to lay himself out to amuse me. His repertoire of gently scandalous stories was extremely entertaining and probably at least half true, and—as I knew his Paris better than he realized—I was soon enjoying myself immensely. He flirted a very little, too—oh, so expertly!—and looked slightly disconcerted and then delighted when he found that his gallantries amused instead of confused me. He would have been even more disconcerted if he'd known that, in a queer sort of way, he was reminding me of Daddy: I hadn't heard this sort of clever, oversophisticated chatter since I'd last been

allowed in to one of Daddy's drink-and-verses jamborees ten years before. I may be forgiven if I enjoyed every moment of the oddly nostalgic
rubbish that we talked.

Or would have done, if every now and again I hadn't seen Héloïse de
Valmy's cool eyes watching me with that indefinable expression which
might have been appraisal, or wariness, or—if it weren't fantastic—fear.

And if I hadn't been wondering who had reported on the "hourly" im-
provement of my French.

The entry of Seddon with the cocktail tray interrupted us. I looked
inquiringly at Madame de Valmy, and Philippe made as if to get to his
feet.

But before she could dismiss us Florimond said comfortably, "Don't
drive the child away, Héloïse. Now he's said his catechism perhaps you'll
deliver him over to me."

She smiled, raising her delicate brows. "What do you want with him,
Carlo?"

He had finally put down *The Tale of Genji* on the extreme edge of a
fragile-looking coffee table, and was fishing in one untidy pocket with
a large hand. He grinned at Philippe, who was watching him with that
guarded look I hated to see, and I saw the child's face relax a little in
reply. "Last time I saw you, my lad," said Florimond, "I was trying to
initiate you into the only civilized pastime for men of sense. Ah, here
we are. . . ." As he spoke he fished a small board out of one pocket.
It was a traveler's chess set, complete with tiny men in red and white.

Madame de Valmy laughed. "The ruling passion," she said, her cool
voice almost indulgent. "Very well, Carlo, but he must go upstairs at a
quarter past, no later. Berthe will be waiting for him."

That this was not true she knew quite well, and so did I. Though the
conversation was now in French, I saw her give me a quick glance, and
kept my face noncommittal. It was interesting that I wasn't the only one
who schemed to keep Philippe out of his uncle's way.

Philippe had dragged his stool eagerly enough across to Florimond's
chair and the two of them were already poring over the board.

"Now," said Florimond cheerfully, "let's see if you can remember any
of the rules, *mon gars*. I seem to recollect some erratic movements last
time you and I were engaged, but there's a sort of wild freshness about
your conception of the game which has its own surprising results. Your
move."

"I moved," said Philippe demurely, "while you were talking."

"Did you, *pardieu?* Ah, the king's pawn. A classic gambit, monsieur . . . and I, this pawn. So."

Philippe bent over the board, his brows fiercely knitted, his whole small being concentrated on the game, while above him Florimond, leaning back vast in his chair, with cigar-ash spilling down his beautifully-cut jacket, watched him indulgently, never ceasing for a moment the gentle, aimless flow of words, of which it was very obvious that Philippe, if indeed he was listening at all, would understand only one in three.

I sat quietly and watched them, feeling a warm, almost affectionate glow toward this large and distinguished Parisian who, among all his other preoccupations, could bother to make a lonely small boy feel he was wanted. From the couturier's talk you would suppose that he had nothing to do for the past year but look forward to another game with Philippe.

I noticed then that Madame de Valmy wasn't sewing. Her hands lay idle in the tumble of embroidery in her lap. I thought that she was interested in the game until I saw that she wasn't watching the board. Her eyes were fixed on the back of Philippe's down-bent head. She must have been deep in some faraway thoughts, because when Philippe made a sudden exclamation she jumped visibly.

He gave a little whoop of glee and pounced on the board. "Your queen! Your queen! *Regardez* monsieur, I've got your queen!"

"So I see," said Florimond, unperturbed. "But will you kindly tell me, Capablanca, by what new law you were able to move your piece straight down the board to do so?"

"There was nothing in the way," explained Philippe kindly.

"No. But the piece you moved, *mon vieux,* was a bishop. I'm sorry to be petty about it, but there is a rule which restricts the bishop to a diagonal line. Nugatory, you will say; trifling . . . but there it is. Medes and Persians, Philippe."

"A bishop?" said Philippe, seizing on the one word that made sense.

"The ones with the pointed hats," said Florimond tranquilly, "are the bishops."

"Oh," said Philippe. He looked up at his opponent and grinned, not in the least abashed. "I forgot. You can have your queen back then."

"I am grateful. Thank you. Now, it's still your move and I should suggest that you observe again the relative positions of your bishop and my queen."

Philippe concentrated. "There is nothing between them," he said, uncertainly.

"Exactly."

"Well—*oh!*" The small hand hastily scooped the lawless bishop out of the queen's path. "There. I move him there."

Florimond chuckled. "Very wise," he said. "Very wise." From the way he leaned forward to scan the board through a thoughtful cloud of tobacco-smoke you would have thought he was matched with a master instead of a small boy who didn't even know the rules.

I glanced at the clock. Sixteen minutes past six. I looked in surprise at Madame de Valmy, whom I had suspected of a clock-watching nervousness almost equal to my own. She had dropped her hands in her lap again and was staring at the fire. She was a hundred miles away. I wondered where . . . no pleasant place, I thought.

I said, "Madame."

She started, and picked up her embroidery so quickly that she pricked her finger. I said, "I'm sorry, madame, I startled you. I think it's time I took Philippe upstairs, isn't it?"

I had my back to the door so I neither saw nor heard it open. It was the quick turn of Philippe's head and the widening of the black eyes that told me. Léon de Valmy's beautiful voice said, "Ah, Philippe. No, don't move. Carlo, how delightful! Why don't we see you more often?"

The wheel chair glided silently forward as he spoke. For such a quiet entrance the effect was remarkable enough. Philippe jumped off his footstool and stood staring at his uncle like a mesmerized bird, Monsieur Florimond hoisted himself again to his feet, Héloïse de Valmy dropped her embroidery and turned quickly toward her husband, while I slid out of my place as his chair passed me and retired toward my usual distant window seat.

I didn't think Léon de Valmy had noticed me, but Philippe had. He, too, made a movement as if to escape, but was netted, so to speak, with a word.

"No, indeed, Philippe. It's all too rarely that I get a chance to see you. We must thank Monsieur Florimond for bringing me in early. Sit down."

The child obeyed. The wheel chair slid up beside the sofa and stopped. Léon de Valmy touched his wife's hand. "Your devotion to duty touches me, Héloïse. It does really."

Only an ear that was tuned to it could have detected the taunt in the smooth voice. I saw their eyes meet, and Héloïse de Valmy smiled, and for the second time that evening I felt the scald of a little spurt of anger. Did they find even half an hour out of the day intolerably much to give to Philippe? And did they have to make it plain? This time Philippe didn't miss it. I saw the swift upward slant of his lashes at his uncle, and the too-familiar sullenness settle on the pale little face, and thought: why don't you pick someone your own weight, damn you . . . ?

The next second the incident might have been illusion. Léon de

Valmy, obviously in the best of spirits, was welcoming Monsieur Florimond almost gaily. "It's very nice of you to look us up, Carlo. What brought you to Geneva?"

Florimond lowered himself once more into his chair. "I came on the track of a material." He made another of his large gestures, this time toward *The Tale of Genji,* which promptly fell onto the floor. "Take a look at those pictures some time, Héloïse, and tell me if you ever saw anything to touch that elegance, that courteous silverpoint grace just on the hither side of decadence. . . . Ah, thank you, *mon lapin.*" This to Philippe, who had quietly picked up the book and was handing it to him. "Give it to your aunt, *p'tit. C'est formidable, hein?*"

She glanced at it. "What's this, Carlo?"

"A threat to your peace of mind and my pocket," said Léon de Valmy, smiling. "The 'mandarin' line, or some such thing, I don't doubt, and just on the hither side of decadence at that. I confess I can't see you in it, my dear. I doubt if I shall permit it."

Florimond laughed. "Only the material, I do assure you, only the material! And that's as much as I shall tell you. Rose Gautier and I have concocted something between us that ought to flutter the dovecotes next November, and I came up to keep a father's eye on it in the making." He grinned amiably at his host. "At least, that's the excuse. I always try to desert Paris at this juncture if I possibly can."

"How's the collection going?" asked Madame.

Florimond dropped a gout of ash down his shirt front, and wiped it placidly aside across his lapel. "At the moment it's hardly even conceived. Not a twitch, not a pang. I shall not be in labor for many months to come, and then we shall have the usual lightning and half-aborted litter to be licked into shape in a frenzy of blood and tears." Here his eye fell on Philippe, silent on his stool, and he added, with no perceptible change of tone, "There was thick mist lying on the road between here and Thonon."

Léon de Valmy was busy at the cocktail tray. He handed his wife a glass. "Really? Bad?"

"In places. But I fancy it's only local. It was clear at Geneva, though of course it may cloud up later along the Lake. Ah, thank you."

Léon de Valmy poured his own drink, then as his chair turned again into the circle round the hearth he caught sight of the chessboard on the low table.

The black brows rose. "Chess? Do you never move without that thing, Carlo?"

"Never. May I hope you'll give me a game tonight?"

"With pleasure. But not with that collection of dressmakers' pins, I beg of you. I don't play my best when I've to use a telescope."

"It's always pure joy to play with that set of yours," said Florimond, "quite apart from the fact that you're a foeman worthy of my steel—which is one way of saying that you beat me four times out of five."

"Hm." Léon de Valmy was surveying the board. "It would certainly appear that Red was playing a pretty shortsighted game in every sense of the word. I knew you were not chess-minded, Héloïse, my dear, but I didn't know you were quite that bad."

She merely smiled, not even bothering to deny it. There was no need anyway. He knew who'd been playing, and Philippe knew he knew.

"Ah, yes," said Florimond calmly. He peered at the miniature men. "Dear me, I have got myself into an odd tangle, haven't I? Perhaps I need spectacles. You're quite right, my dear Léon, it's a mistake to underrate one's opponent. Never do that." The big hand shifted a couple of men with quick movements. The mild clever face expressed nothing whatever except interest in the Lilliputian maneuvers on the board.

I saw Léon de Valmy glance up at him swiftly, and the look of amusement that came and went like the gleam on the underside of a blown cloud. "I don't." Then he smiled at Philippe, silent on his stool. "Come and finish the game, Philippe. I'm sure your aunt won't drive you upstairs just yet."

Philippe went, if possible, smaller and more rigid than before. "I— I'd rather not, thank you."

Léon de Valmy said pleasantly, "You mustn't allow the fact that you were losing to weigh with you, you know."

The child went scarlet. Florimond said, quite without inflection, "In any case we can't continue. I disarranged the pieces just now. The situation wasn't quite as peculiar as your uncle supposed, Philippe, but I can't remember just what it was. I'm sorry. I hope very much that you'll give me the pleasure of a game another time. You do very well."

He pushed the board aside and smiled down at the child, who responded with one quick upward look. Then he leaned back in his chair, and, smiling amiably at his host, launched without pausing straight into one of his improbable stories, thus effectively forcing the general attention back to himself. Philippe remained without moving, small on his stool, the picture of sulky isolation. I watched him, still feeling in my damn-them mood. He must have felt my glance, because eventually he looked up. I winked at him and grinned. There was no answering gleam. The black lashes merely dropped again.

Then the door opened, and Seddon, the butler, came in. He crossed the floor to Madame de Valmy's side.

"Madame, a telephone message has just come through from Monsieur Raoul."

I saw her flash a glance at her husband. "From Monsieur Raoul? Yes, Seddon?"

"He asked me to tell you he was on his way up, madame."

The base of Léon de Valmy's glass clinked down on the arm of his chair. "On his way? Here? When? Where was he speaking from?"

"That I couldn't say, sir. But he wasn't at Bellevigne. He said he would be here some time tonight."

A pause. I noticed the soft uneven ticking of the lovely little clock on the mantel.

Then Florimond said comfortably, "How very pleasant! I don't know when I last set eyes on Raoul. I hope he'll be here for dinner?"

Seddon said, "No, monsieur. He said he might be late, and not to wait for him, but that he would get here tonight."

Léon de Valmy said, "And that was all the message?"

"Yes, sir."

Madame de Valmy stirred. "He didn't sound as if there was anything wrong . . . at Bellevigne?"

"No, madame. Not at all."

Florimond chuckled. "Don't look so worried, my dear. They've probably had a week of the mistral and he's decided to cut and run for it. The original ill wind."

"He doesn't usually run in this direction," said his father, very dryly. "Very well, Seddon, thank you."

Madame de Valmy said, "Perhaps you'll be good enough to see Mrs. Seddon straight away about a room?"

"Of course, madame." Seddon, expressionless as ever, bent his head. I saw Héloïse de Valmy glance again at her husband. I couldn't see his face from where I sat, but she was biting her bottom lip, and to my surprise she looked strained and pale.

A nice gay welcome for the son of the house was, it appeared, laid on. Him and Philippe both. . . . As a cozy family home the Château Valmy certainly took some beating. The Constance Butcher wasn't in it.

Then the central chandelier leaped into a lovely cascade of light. Seddon moved forward to draw curtains and replenish drinks. Glasses clinked, and someone laughed. Philippe moved cheerfully to help Florimond pack away the tiny chessmen . . . and in a moment, it seemed, under the bright light, the imagined tensions dissolved and vanished. Firelight, laughter, the smell of pine logs and Schiaparelli, the rattle of curtain rings and the swish as the heavy brocades swung together . . .

it was absurd to people the lovely Château Valmy with the secret ghosts of Thornfield.

The Demon King turned his handsome gray head and said in English, "Come out, Jane Eyre."

I must have jumped about a foot. He looked surprised, then laughed and said, "Did I startle you? I'm sorry. Were you very far away?"

"Pretty far. At a place in Yorkshire called Thornfield Hall."

The black brows lifted. "So we're *en rapport?* No wonder you jumped." He smiled. "I shall have to be careful. . . . And now will you take your charge away before Monsieur Florimond corrupts him with vermouth? No, Philippe, I do assure you, you won't like it. Now make your adieux—in English, please, and go."

Philippe was on his feet in a flash, making those adieux correctly, if rather too eagerly. I think I was almost as thankful as he was when at length, his hand clutching mine, I said my own quiet good nights and withdrew.

Léon de Valmy's "Good night, Miss Eyre," with its wholly charming overtone of mockery, followed me to the door.

Philippe was a little subdued for the rest of the evening, but on the whole survived the ordeal by uncle pretty well. After he was in bed I dined alone in my room. It was Albertine, Madame de Valmy's sour-faced maid, who brought my supper in. She did it in tightlipped silence, making it very clear that she was demeaning herself unwillingly.

"Thanks, Albertine," I said cheerfully, as she set the last plate down just a shade too smartly. "Oh, and by the way—"

The woman turned in the doorway, her sallow face not even inquiring. She radiated all the charm and grace of a bad-tempered skunk. "Well?"

I said, "I wonder if you can remember whether I got Mrs. Seddon's tablets for her last week, or not?"

"*Non,*" said Albertine, and turned to go.

"Do you mean I didn't or do you mean you don't remember?"

She spoke sourly over her shoulder without turning. "I mean I do not know. Why?"

"Only because Mrs. Seddon asked me to get the tablets today and Monsieur Garcin said he gave them to me last week. If that's the case you'd think I must have handed them to her with her other packages. I've no recollection of them at all. D'you know if there was a prescription with the list you gave me?"

The square shoulders lifted. "Perhaps. I do not know." The shallow black eyes surveyed me with dislike. "Why do you not ask her yourself?"

"Very well, I will," I said coldly. "That will do, Albertine."

But the door was already shut. I looked at it for a moment with com-
pressed lips and then began my meal. When, some little time later, there
came a tap on the door and Mrs. Seddon surged affably in, I said, almost without preamble—

"That Albertine woman. What's biting her? She's about as amiable as
a snake."

Mrs. Seddon snorted. "Oh, her. She's going about like a wet month
of Sundays because I told her to bring your supper up. Berthe's helping
Mariette get a room ready for Mr. Rowl seeing as how Mariette won't
work along with Albertine anyhow and she's as sour as a lemon if you
ask her to do anything outside Madame's own room. Her and that Bernard, they're a pair. It's my belief he'd rob a bank for the Master if
asked, but he'd see your nose cheese and the rats eating it before he'd
raise a little finger for anybody else."

"I believe you. What I can't understand is why Madame puts up with
her."

"You don't think she has that sour-milk face for Madame, do you?
Oh, no, it's all niminy-piminy butter-won't-melt *there,* you mark my
words." Conversation with Mrs. Seddon was nothing if not picturesque.
"But she's like that with everyone else in the place bar Bernard, and it's
my belief she's as jealous as sin if Madame so much as smiles at anybody besides herself. She knows Madame likes you, and that's the top
and bottom of it, dear, believe you me."

I said, surprised, "Madame likes me? How d'you know?"

"Many's the nice thing she's said about you," said Mrs. Seddon comfortably, "so you don't have to fret yourself over a bit of lip from that
Albertine."

I laughed. "I don't. How's the asthma? You sound better."

"I am that. It comes and goes. This time of year it's a nuisance, but
never near so bad as it used to be. I remember as a girl Miss Debbie's
mother saying to me—"

I stopped that one with the smoothness of much practice. "I'm afraid
Monsieur Garcin wouldn't give me the antihistamine today. He said I
got it last week. Did I give it to you, Mrs. Seddon? I'm terribly ashamed
of myself, but I can't remember. D'you know if it was with the other
things I got for you? There was some Nestlé's chocolate, wasn't there,
and some buttons, and some cotton-wool—and was it last week you got
your watch back from the repairers?"

"Was it now? Maybe it was. I can't mind just now about the pills, but
I know there were a lot of things and the pills may have been with them."
She laughed a little wheezily. "I can't say I took much notice, not want-
ing them till now, but Mr. Garsang's probably right. He's as finicky as

the five-times-table, and about as lively. I'll have a look in my cupboard tonight. I'm sorry to give you the bother, dear."

"Oh, that doesn't matter. I did get you the aspirins and the eau de cologne. They're here, with your change."

"Oh, thanks, dear—miss, I mean."

I said, "Is Monsieur Florimond staying, or is he only here for dinner?"

"He only came for dinner, but I dare say he'll stay on late to see Mr. Rowl. It might yet be they'll ask him to stay the night if the fog gets any thicker."

I got up and went over to the balcony windows.

"I don't see any fog. It seems a fine enough night."

"Eh? Oh, yes. I think it's only down by the water. We're high up here. But the road runs mostly along the river, and there's been accidents in the valley before now in the mist. It's a nasty road, that, in the dark."

"I can imagine it might be." I came back to my chair, adding, with a memory of the recent uncomfortable session in the drawing room, "Perhaps Monsieur Raoul won't get up here after all tonight."

She shook her head. "He'll come. If he said he was coming he'll come." She eyed me for a moment and said, "Did they—was there anything said downstairs, like?"

"Nothing. They wondered what brought him, that was all."

"They've not much call to wonder," she said darkly. "There's only one thing'll make him set foot in the place and that's money."

"Oh?" I said, rather uncomfortably. There were limits to gossip, after all. "I thought—I got the impression it might be some business to do with Bellevigne."

"Well," said Mrs. Seddon, "that's what I mean. It's always Bellyveen and money." She sighed. "I told you, Mr. Rowl manages it for him and now and again he comes up and talks to him about it and then—" she sighed again—"there's words. It's trouble every time, what with Mr. Rowl wanting money for Bellyveen and the Master wanting it for Valmy and before you know where you are it's cat and dog, or maybe I should say dog and dog because nobody could say Mr. Rowl's like a cat, the horrible sneaking beasts, but a dogfight it's always been, ever since Mr. Rowl was big enough to speak up for himself and—"

"He—he must be a careful landlord," I said hastily.

"Oh, I don't deny he makes a good job of Bellyveen—he's too like his father not to, if you see what I mean—but they do say he rackets about the place plenty between times. There's stories—"

"You can't believe everything you hear," I said.

"No, indeed, that's true," said Mrs. Seddon, a shade regretfully, "and especially when it's about Mr. Rowl, if you follow me, miss, because he's the sort that'd get himself talked about if he lived in a convent, as the saying is."

"I'm sure you're right," I said.

"And where does he get the money, I ask you that?" Mrs. Seddon was now fully and enjoyably launched. "Where did he get the car he was driving last time he was here? As long as the Queen Mary and a horn like the Last Trump, and you can't tell me he got anything out of the Master so I ask you, where?"

"Well," I said mildly, "where?"

"Ah," said Mrs. Seddon darkly, "you may well ask. I heard the Master ask him that very question, sharplike, the last time he was here. And Mr. Rowl wouldn't tell him; just passed it off in that way he has with something about a lucky night and a lucky number."

I laughed. "It sounds to me as if he won it at roulette. Good luck to him."

She looked a little shocked. "Well, miss! I don't say as how I think a little flutter does any harm and I'm as partial to a nice game of whist as anyone, but—well, many's the time I wonder what Miss Debbie would have said. Many's the time she said to me, 'Mary,' she said—"

"Forgive me," I said quickly, "but it's time for Philippe's chocolate. I left him reading in bed and I must put his light out."

"Eh? Oh, yes, to be sure, how time goes on, doesn't it? And it's long past time I ought to be seeing if Berthe and Mariette have put that room properly to rights. . . ." She heaved herself onto her feet and plodded to the door, which I opened for her. "Have they remembered the milk?"

"It was on the tray."

"Ah, yes. That Berthe, now, do you find she does her work all right, miss? If there's anything to complain of, you must be sure to let me know."

"I've no complaints," I said. "I like Berthe very much, and she keeps the rooms beautifully. You've only to look in the pantry here."

She followed me into the tiny pantry, where the light gleamed on the spotless enamel of the little stove, and saucepan, beaker and spoon stood ready. I poured milk into the pan, set it on the stove and switched on. Mrs. Seddon ran a practiced eye over the tiny room, and an equally practiced finger over the shelf where the tins of chocolate, coffee and tea stood, and nodded her head in a satisfied manner.

"Yes, Berthe's a good girl, I must say, if she'll keep her mind on her work instead of running after that there Bernard. . . . The sugar's here, miss."

"No, not that. I use the glucose for Philippe, you remember—that's his special tin, the blue one. Oh, thank you. D'you mean to tell me there's something between Berthe and Bernard? I hope it's not serious? It would be an awful pity. He's too old for her, and besides—"

I stopped, but she took me up.

"Well, miss, you never said a truer word. A pity it is. If that Albertine wasn't his sister born, I'd have said why not them, they wouldn't spoil two houses, and them as alike as two hogs in the same litter. A sour-faced, black-a-vised sort of chap he is and all, for a bonny young girl like Berthe to be losing her head over. But there, human nature's human nature, believe it or not, and there's nothing we can do about it. What are you looking for now?"

"The biscuits. They've been moved. Ah, here they are." I put three into Philippe's saucer, looking sidelong at Mrs. Seddon. "Extra rations tonight. It was a slightly sticky session in the drawing room."

"That's right. He could do with a bit of spoiling, if you ask me. And now I'll have to go, really. I've enjoyed our little chat, miss. And I may say that Seddon and me, we think that Philip's a whole lot better for having you here. He likes you that's plain to see, and it's my belief that what he needs is somebody to be fond of."

I said softly, half to myself, "Don't we all?"

"Well, there you are," said Mrs. Seddon comfortably. "Not but what his other Nanny wasn't a very nice woman, very nice indeed, but she did baby him a bit, say what you will, which was only natural, seeing as how she'd brought him up from a bairn in arms. Maybe the Master was right enough like you said in thinking he ought to have a change, especially after losing his Mam and Dad like that, poor bairn. And you're making a grand job of him, miss, if you'll excuse the liberty of me saying so."

I said with real gratitude, "It's very nice of you. Thank you." I lifted Philippe's tray and grinned at her over it. "And I do hope all goes well downstairs. At least there's one person who'll be pleased when Mr. Raoul arrives."

She stopped in the doorway and turned, a little ponderously. "Who? Mr. Florimond? Well, I couldn't say—"

"I didn't mean him. I meant Philippe."

She stared at me, then shook her head. "Mr. Rowl hardly knows him, miss. Don't forget Philip only came from Paris just before you did, and Mr. Rowl's not been over since he was here."

"Then Monsieur Raoul must have seen something of him in Paris, or else when he was with Monsieur Hippolyte."

"He didn't. That I do know. And I'd go bail him and Mr. Rowl hardly saw each other in Paree. Paree!" said Mrs. Seddon, reverting to form,

"Paree! He'd not be the one to bother with Philip *there*. He had other kettles of fish to fry in Paree, you mark my words."

"But when we heard the car coming up the zigzag tonight with Monsieur Florimond, Philippe flew out onto the balcony like a rocket—and he certainly wasn't hoping to see *him*. He looked desperately disappointed . . . more than that, really; 'blighted' would almost describe it. . . . Who else could he be looking for if it wasn't his cousin Raoul?"

Then I looked at her, startled, for her eyes, in the harsh light, were brimming with sudden, easy tears. She shook her head at me and wiped her cheeks with the back of a plump hand. "Poor bairn, poor bairn," was all she would say, but presently after a sniff or two and some action with a handkerchief, she explained. The explanation was simple, obvious, and dreadful.

"He never saw them dead, of course. Nor he wasn't allowed to go to the funeral. And it's my belief and Seddon's that he won't have it they're really gone. They were to have driven back from the airport, you see, and he was waiting for them, and they never came. He never saw no more of them. It's my belief he's still waiting."

"That's dreadful." I swallowed. "That's . . . dreadful, Mrs. Seddon."

"Yes. Every car that comes up, he'll fly out yonder. I've seen him do it. It's lucky there's not more coming and going than there is, or he'd do it once too often, and end up on the gravel on his head, or else stuck on those spikes like a beetle on a pin."

I shivered. "I'll watch him," I said.

"You do," said Mrs. Seddon.

CHAPTER VII

Fourth Coach

> *A Being, erect upon two legs, and bearing all the outward semblance of a man, and not of a monster.*
>
> DICKENS: *Pickwick Papers.*

PHILIPPE was already asleep, curled in an extraordinarily small bundle under the bedclothes. The light was still on, and his book had slid to the floor. Something was clutched in his hand, and I drew the sheet aside to see what it was—one of the Queen's soldiers with the fur hats.

I picked up the book, straightened the bedclothes, turned off the light, and went softly out, taking the unwanted chocolate back to the pantry.

Back in my room, I walked straight through it onto the balcony, letting the curtains fall behind me to cut off the light. The night was calm, and unexpectedly warm. There was still no sign of fog, but I thought that I could see a paler darkness away in the valley's depths. The damp of spring hung in the air. An owl called below me, down in the woods; called again. Its muted melancholy found too ready an echo in me. I felt tired and depressed. Too much had happened today; and the pleasant things—the morning's encounter with William Blake, my gay little flirtation with Florimond in the salon—had somehow faded back out of mind and left me with this queerly flattened feeling.

I know what it was, of course. I'd lived with loneliness a long time. That was something which was always there . . . one learns to keep it at bay, there are times when one even enjoys it—but there are also times when a desperate self-sufficiency doesn't quite suffice, and then the search for the anodyne begins . . . the radio, the dog, the shampoo, the stockings-to-wash, the tin soldier. . . .

I bit my lip and took myself sharply to task. Just because I had had two pleasantly off-duty encounters—not to mention a cozy and entertaining gossip with the housekeeper—I didn't have to feel let down and left out when they were over and I had to put in the evening by myself. I didn't have to stand here glooming at the spring dusk and picturing myself for the rest of my life relegated to the edge of the room, the frame of the conversation piece.

And what did I want, for heaven's sake? To retreat on the illusion that Florimond's courtesy had created, that he and I and Madame de Valmy could share a fireside on equal terms? To be where Madame de Valmy was? Where I might still have been if the thing that happened ten years ago hadn't happened? Well, *that* was out, and the sooner I accepted once and for all the fact the jamboree was over, the sooner I would stop riding this uneasy seesaw of moods and memories.

I turned deliberately and walked along to the southern end of the balcony until I stood above the salon.

The light from the long windows, muted by gold curtains, streamed softly across the loggia and onto the terrace. The bare rose bushes stood out, thorn and twig in a naked mesh netting the light. Their shadows raked away like besoms over the freshly-dug beds. One window had been opened to the mild night, and here the light streamed out boldly, and with it the sound of talk and laughter. I could imagine the spurting glow of the log fire, the gleam of rummers, the smell of coffee and brandy and cigars. . . .

Good night, Miss Eyre . . . amusement supervened and with it sanity. I grinned to myself as I walked softly back to my own window. If I did have to spend the rest of my life sitting in the corner of someone else's drawing room, knitting and wearing black bombazine—whatever that was—then by God it would be the best bombazine. The very best bombazine.

Ignoring the anodynes of book, radio and stockings-to-wash, I got my coat and went out.

I went down the zigzag very slowly, for in the faint moonlight the slope was deceptive, and the slight dampness made the surface slippery. There was a way down through the wood itself—a steep track of alternate step and slope that short-circuited the zigzag—but it would have been too dark under the trees, so I avoided it and kept to the road.

The air was very still. Below me, in the valley depths where the river ran, I could see, quite distinctly now, the pale drift of mist. The owl cried again once, very sadly, from the wood. There was a strong wet smell of earth and growing things; the smell of spring . . . not softness, not balm-and-blossoms, but something harsh and sharp that pierced the senses as the thrust of new life broke the ground . . . *the cruelest month, breeding/Lilacs out of dead land* . . . yes, that was it. That was *it*. Not for the first time I was sharply grateful to Daddy for making poetry a habit with me. *The best words in the best order* . . . one always got the same shock of recognition and delight when someone's words swam up to meet a thought or name a picture. Daddy had been right. Poetry was awfully good material to think with.

Something rustled in last year's beech leaves and poetry fled as, absurdly, I remembered that there were still bears in France. And boars. And probably wolves. And werewolves and vampires too, no doubt . . . by mocking myself I got at length safely down to river-level and the bridge to the main road.

The bridge was an elegant affair of the eighteenth century, with carved balustrading that opened in graceful curves toward the river banks. The mist was thick here, but only in patches. Where I stood it was waist-high, but beyond the parapet to my right it slanted down like a snowbank to lie low over the water, pinned through here and there by spikes of bulrush and the black spars of dead boughs.

The water itself was invisible. The sound of it was dark and deep, a lovely liquid undertone to the night. The owl's breathy call fell less sadly now, less hollowly through the dim boughs.

I stood still in the center of the bridge, my hands deep in my pockets, and gazed up at the steeply wooded slope on the other side of the main road. Rank upon rank of pines, I knew, crowded up those rocky heights, with here and there a bare crag jutting through, where in daylight the hawks mewed and circled. Now, in the faint moonlight, the forest was no more than a looming darkness, a towering cloud faintly luminous where the crescent moon feather-edged the rims of the pines. The scent drifted down, spicy and sharp and somehow dark like the pines themselves.

A car was coming up the valley. I heard the sound of the engine grow and fade and grow again as the curving road and the mist cut off and distorted the sound. It came round Belle Surprise, high above the mist, before I saw its lights. I saw them turn then, tilt, and drive down into the darkness, to bend this way and that among the trees, brightening and then blurring as the fog clouds blunted them. I watched the stems of the trees outline themselves sharply against the light, to reel away like logs tumbling over a waterfall, then swoop back and up into the towering shadow behind the glare where still the tree stems blanched, drifted, and darkened. . . .

Only a late truck driving up to Soubirous . . . The headlights went steadily past the end of the bridge, and the mist tossed and whirled in the red of the tail lamp.

I was turning to go back up the zigzag, when my eye was caught by a tiny light high up among the Dieudonné trees. A minute before it had not been there, but now it pricked through the cloud of pines like a small yellow star.

I stopped and looked up at it. The trees along the roadside were busy in their ghostly dance as another truck roared up the valley, but that tiny light hung there high above them, warm and steady. No, not a star: a planet, and lived on at that. It might very well not be William Blake's little hut at four thousand feet, but somehow I thought it was. I smiled to myself picturing him sitting up there with his bandages and boluses (what *was* a bolus?) and thermometers in degrees centigrade.

The second truck thundered past the end of the bridge.

And the cognac—had he remembered the cognac?

I hadn't noticed the car traveling quietly behind the enormous truck. I didn't see it until it turned sharp onto the narrow bridge and came at me like a torpedo.

It was an easy corner, and he took it fast. The main beam leaped out and pinned me full in the glare. I heard his brakes shriek as they bit metal. I jumped for the edge of the road. The lights lurched and tires screeched and ripped the tarmac. One yard: that was all the leeway he had. Something grabbed at me; tore. I slipped on the greasy road and fell flat in the gutter under the parapet as the car went by with a foot and a half to spare and screamed to a skidding halt beyond the bridge.

The engine cut. The door slammed. Léon de Valmy's voice said, "Where are you? Are you hurt? I didn't touch you, did I?" Quick footsteps sounded on the tarmac. "Where are you?"

I had risen to my knees in the wet gutter, and was holding rather hard to the parapet. At the sound of the footsteps and that familiar voice I thought I must have been hit and gone mad. I was blind, too. I couldn't see anything, anyone. I was blinking in a dazed sort of panic as I pulled myself shakily to my feet. . . .

I wasn't blinded after all; the mist sank and dwindled and swirled waist-high again as I turned, leaning back for support against the parapet.

Nor was I mad. The man who was striding toward me in the moonlight was not Léon de Valmy, though thirty years ago Léon de Valmy had probably looked exactly like him. As with his father, my first impression of Raoul de Valmy was that he was remarkably good looking; but where age and illness had given the older man's looks the fine-drawn, fallen-angel quality he had mocked to me on our first meeting, there was nothing in the least fine-drawn about Raoul. He merely looked tough, arrogant, and, at the moment, furious. It wasn't exactly the time to judge whether he possessed the charm which his father could apparently radiate at will, though his personality certainly made—this without irony—as strong an impact. But the difference was there again: where Léon de Valmy kept himself banked down, so to speak, and burning secretly, Raoul was at full blaze. And just now he was blazing with something more than personality. He was as shaken as I was, and it had made him angry.

I sat down suddenly on the parapet, and waited. He loomed over me, tall and formidable looking in the misty moonlight.

Tall, dark and handsome . . . the romantic cliché repeated itself in my head—so automatically and irresistibly that I braced myself to dislike him on sight.

He said sharply, "Are you hurt?"

"No."

"Did I hit you?"

"No."

"Not even touch you?"

I was smoothing my coat down with unsteady fingers. "N—no."

"You're sure you're all right?"

"Yes. I—yes. Thank you."

I heard his breath expelled in quick relief. He relaxed and his voice warmed then into anger. "Then will you kindly tell me what the bloody hell you were doing standing in the middle of the road in a fog? You came damned near being killed and if you had you'd have deserved it!"

Shock was reacting on me too, and I wasn't used to being sworn at. I stopped fussing with my clothes and lifted my head to glare straight back at him. "It's not a public road and I've a perfect right to stand in the middle of it or sit in the middle of it or lie in the middle of it if I want to! I wasn't expecting you—at least I'd quite forgotten you were coming and in any case you've no business to come at that speed, whether it's a private road or not!"

There was a fractional pause, during which I had the impression that he was distinctly taken aback. Then he said mildly, "I was only doing fifty, and I know the road like the back of my hand."

"*Fifty!*" I heard my voice rise to a squeak, and was furious. "Why, that's—oh, kilometers, of course."

"What else?"

"It's still too fast and there was mist."

"I could see the way quite well and that car sits down on the corners like a broody hen." He was beginning to sound amused, and that made me angrier.

I snapped, "Broody hen or no, it very nearly ran me down!"

"I'm quite aware of that. But I would hardly expect to find anyone standing on the bridge at this time of night—"

He stopped and then went on, the amusement now clear in his voice, "I'm damned if I see why I should have to stand here defending myself for not having run you over! Perhaps now you'll be good enough to tell me why you consider you've a perfect right to stand—or was it lie down?— in the middle of this particular private road? This is my—this is the Valmy estate, you know."

I was busy wiping my muddy hands on a handkerchief. "Yes," I said, "I live here."

He made a little movement of surprise, and I saw his eyes narrow on me in the moonlight. "Surely," he said, "you're not one of the, er—?"

"Servants? In a way," I said. "I'm Philippe's governess."

"But," said Raoul de Valmy, slowly, "they told me she was to be an English girl."

I felt as if he had dealt me a sharp blow in the stomach. For the first time I realized that the whole of the exchange had been in French. Literally thrown off my balance as I had been, I had answered him without thinking in the tongue that he had first used.

I said feebly, "I—I forgot."

"You are English?" he said, in a tone of great surprise.

I nodded. "Linda Martin, from London. I've been here three weeks."

His voice was a little dry. "Then allow me to congratulate you on your progress, Miss Martin."

But this second shock had shaken me quite out of all composure. The dry note in his voice was so like Léon de Valmy's that I found myself saying, in a taut little voice that was pitched a shade too high, "You must know perfectly well that I haven't learned all my French in the last three weeks, Monsieur de Valmy, so don't add insult to injury by baiting me as well as knocking me down!"

This was palpable injustice and I half expected the annihilation I deserved. But he merely said, "I'm sorry. And now do you feel recovered enough to move? I shouldn't keep you here talking any more. You must have had a nasty shaking. We'll get you into the car and I'll drive you up to the house."

Like his father, he knew how to disarm. . . . I found myself obediently sliding off the parapet to my feet, while he put a steadying hand under my elbow.

"I'm all right," I said.

But when I tried to move toward the car I found that my knees were very shaky still, and I was thankful for his support.

He said quickly, "You're limping. You *are* hurt."

I found myself reassuring him. "Not by you. I slipped and fell when I tried to jump out of the way. It's only a bumped knee or something. Honestly, that's all."

He said, sounding worried, "Well, I think the sooner I get you up to the château and find you a drink, the better. You'll have to get in by the driver's door, I'm afraid. The other one's rather difficult of access just at present."

This was, I saw, only too true. The big car, in swerving to avoid me, had skidded slightly on the damp tarmac, and run up onto the right-hand verge of the road beyond the bridge. The verge at this point was a muddy grass bank, mercifully not very steep, but quite steep enough to cant the car at a crazy-looking angle.

I looked at it guiltily, and then up at Raoul de Valmy's impassive face. "I—it isn't damaged, is it?"

"I don't think so. Would you rather wait on the road while I straighten her out, or had you better get in and sit down?"

"I think if it's all the same to you I'll sit down."

"Of course." He opened the nearside door. I got in—with just a little difficulty, as my knee was undoubtedly stiff, and got myself somehow past the wheel and into the passenger's seat. He leaned into the car and groped in the darkness under the dash. There was a click, and the headlamps flashed on, so that just in front of the car the first bend and slope of the zigzag strode forward at us, a ragged white wall of tree and rock, not six feet from the front bumper.

He didn't even glance at it. "Just a minute," he said. He slammed the door and went around to the back of the car.

I closed my eyes to shut out the sight of that looming rock-wall, and lay back in the deep seat, relaxing as well as I could. The car was very big and very comfortable, even tilted as it was at that odd angle. It smelled faintly of cigarettes and expensive leather. I opened my eyes again. In the light reflected back off the rock ahead the bonnet gleamed long and black—plenty horses under that, I thought, and remembered Mrs. Seddon's description, *"As long as the Queen Mary and a horn like the Last Trump."* I wondered what Raoul de Valmy's lucky number was. . . .

I settled my shoulders back in the luxurious seat. The shaky feeling had almost gone. Suddenly out of nowhere I remembered something I had once heard at the Constance Butcher—a piece of servant girls' lore which had amused me at the time and now came back with an added point. *If you ever get run over, be sure and pick a Rolls-Royce.* . . . Well, there was something in that, I reflected . . . and a Cadillac was perhaps not a bad second choice, especially when it had as good a driver as Raoul de Valmy at the wheel. Now that the first shock had subsided I realized perfectly well how near I had been to being badly hurt, through my own silliness. Moreover it was no thanks to me that Monsieur Raoul's expensive Cadillac hadn't smashed itself against the parapet.

I became aware that Raoul de Valmy was still behind the car. I peered back through the swirls of mist to see him bending over a rear wing, while a flashlight moved slowly over the metal. I bit my lip, but before I could speak he had straightened up, switched off the torch, and come swiftly around to the driver's door.

He slanted a quick look at me as he slid in beside me. "All right?" I nodded. "We'll soon get you home. Hold tight."

He touched the starter button and the engine snarled to life. He thrust the big car very gently forward and to the left; she moved, jerked, hesitated, and then the front wheels swooped down with a plunge to the level of the road. The back wheels seemed to mount for a moment, then slid down after them, and the car rolled onto the level road and stopped there, rocking gently on her superb springs.

"Et voilà," said Raoul de Valmy, and smiled at me.

As his hand moved on the handbrake I said, in a small voice, "Monsieur de Valmy."

The hand paused. "Yes?"

"Before you take me back I—I'd like to apologize. I'm most awfully sorry, really I am."

"Apologize? And for what? My dear ma'am—"

I said, "Don't be so *nice* about it, *please!* I know it was really my fault and you're making me feel a *worm!*" I heard him laugh, but I went on doggedly and not very clearly, "I had no business to be in the road and you saved my life by doing what you did and then I went and was rude to you and you were nothing but nice to me when ninety-nine drivers out of a hundred would have blasted me from here to Madagascar, and it's true, I do feel a worm. An utter *crawling* worm! And—" I took breath and finished idiotically—"if you've damaged your car you can stop it out of my wages!"

He was still laughing at me. "Thank you. But it's not damaged, as it happens."

"Is that the truth?" I asked suspiciously.

"Yes. Not a scratch. I thought I heard something as she skidded, but it was only a bit of a fallen branch hitting the wheel. Not a mark. So no apologies please, Miss Martin. If anybody should apologize, it's I. I believe I swore at you. I'm sorry."

"That's all right," I said a little awkwardly. "We were both a bit shaken up, I suppose. I didn't quite know where I was or what I was saying."

He said nothing. He seemed to be waiting. He made no move to start the car. I stole the sidelong look at him and saw that he was watching me steadily, with the amusement gone from his face. It was an oddly daunting look, and, though he had been much nicer to me than I deserved, I found that I was gripping my hands between my knees to give myself courage to go on.

I said, "I knew so little about what I was saying that I'm afraid I gave myself away to you."

"When you spoke to me in French." It was not a question.

"Yes."

His hand moved to the ignition, and the engine died. He cut off the headlights, so that the car stood islanded in the little glow of side and tail-lamps. He half-turned toward me, his shoulder propped back against the door. I couldn't see his face now, and his voice told me nothing. He said, "This is interesting. So I was right?"

"That they didn't know I was partly French when I got the job? Yes."

He said, "I'm not your employer, you know. You don't have to explain. But as a matter of curiosity, do I understand that you did deliberately deceive my father and Madame de Valmy over this?"

"I—I'm afraid so."

"Why?"

"Because I wanted the job."

"But I don't see why—"

I pressed my hands tightly together, and said carefully, "I *needed* the job. I—I'll try and tell you why, though I don't suppose you'll understand. . . ." He started to say something but I went on quickly and not very coherently, "I'm partly French and I was brought up in Paris. When I was fourteen Maman and Daddy were killed in a plane crash. Daddy was writing a script for a film to be made in Venice, and Maman went with him for the holiday. The—oh, the details don't matter, but I finished up in an orphanage in London. . . . I don't know if you've ever been inside an orphanage?"

"No."

"Well, the details don't matter there, either. They were very kind to me. But I wanted—oh, to *live,* to find some place in the world that was mine, and somehow I seemed to be getting nowhere. My schooling was all to blazes, what with the war and—and everything, so I can't do much, but I got a job at a small private school. I—I wasn't very happy there, either. Then when one of our governors heard that Madame de Valmy wanted an English governess it seemed like a gift from heaven. I told you I'm not qualified to do much, but I can look after children and I knew I could make a good job of Philippe's English and I thought it would be so wonderful to be in France and living in a real home again."

He said, very dryly, "So you came to Valmy."

"Yes. That's all."

There was a pause. He said, "I do understand, I think. But there was no need to explain all this to me, you know. I've no right to question you."

I said shyly, "I felt I sort of owed you something. And you did ask me why I wanted the job."

"No. You misunderstand me. I asked you why you had deceived my father and Héloïse about it."

I began, rather stupidly, "I told you—"

"I should have said, rather, why you *had* to deceive them. I'm not concerned in the least with the fact that you did do so." I caught the glimmer of a smile. "I merely find myself wondering why it was necessary. Are you trying to tell me that you concealed the fact you were partly French because you wouldn't in that case have got the job?"

"I—yes, more or less."

A little silence. "Indeed."

"It wasn't put like that," I said hastily, "not said in so many words. But—but I honestly did get the impression that it might have mattered.

I mean, once we had got past the point where I should have told Madame de Valmy I couldn't very well go back and confess or she'd have thought there was something queer about me and she'd never have looked at me. And she'd made rather a lot of the fact that I wouldn't be tempted to lapse into French when I was talking to Philippe—I'm supposed always to talk to him in English, you see. I didn't really see that it mattered, myself, because I could have taken care to speak English with him anyway, but—well, she was so emphatic about it that I—oh, I just let it slide. I know I was silly," I finished miserably, "and it's such a stupid little thing, but there it is."

"And I suppose I'm to understand," he said, still rather dryly, "that they still don't know."

"Yes."

"I see." To my relief he was beginning to sound amused again. "Haven't you found that such a deception—I'm sorry I started by using such a harsh term for it—has its socially embarrassing moments?"

"You mean overhearing things I'm not meant to? No, because Monsieur's and Madame's manners are too good." Here he laughed outright, and I said rather confusedly, "I mean—when I meet them without Philippe they always talk English, and when I take Philippe to see them they talk about his lessons, which I know about anyway; and in any case I don't listen."

He said, "Well, I should stop worrying about it. As far as I can see it can hardly matter one way or the other." He turned in his seat and started the engine. The lights sprang up. I could see him smiling. "And I certainly didn't mean to add insult to injury by turning this into an inquisition! Forgive me; it's not my affair."

"Monsieur," I said quickly, in a rather small voice.

"Yes?"

"I—I wonder if you'd not—I mean—" I floundered and stopped.

He gave me a quick glance. "You wondered if I'd not give you away?"

"Yes. Please," I added, feeling even smaller.

There was a fractional pause. "For what it's worth," said Raoul de Valmy, slowly, "I shan't. . . . And now I think we'd better make tracks. . . ."

The car moved forward and took the first slope at a decorous speed.

He drove in silence, and I had time to reflect with wry surprise that shock produces some very odd aftereffects. What on earth had impelled me to blurt out that naïve and stumbling betrayal on my pathetic needs to Raoul de Valmy's no doubt hard-bitten sophistication? *Daddy and Maman . . . they were very kind to me at the orphanage. . . .* What did it matter to him? A dreary little fool, that was what he'd think of me. And that's what I was, anyway, I thought, remembering my depression of earlier that evening. I bit my lip. What did it matter anyway? He probably hadn't even been listening. He had more important things than Philippe's governess on his mind. Bellevigne, for instance, or whatever had driven him up to see his father in the face of what appeared to be his normal welcome at the Château.

I found myself remembering Florimond's presence with a species of relief, and then felt amused. Raoul de Valmy would hardly need the same kind of protection as Philippe.

I said, "Monsieur Florimond's here this evening."

"Oh? Is he staying long?"

"I think he only came to dine, but if the mist gets thicker he'll probably stay."

"Ah," said Raoul, "that's something else to put down to the fog's account. It's an ill wind, they say."

I was still working that one out when the Cadillac swung off the last rise and came to a whispering halt at the foot of the steps.

Seddon was crossing the hall as we came in. He turned when he saw Raoul and came hurrying to meet him, then his eye fell on me, and a slight twitch of dismay crossed his impassive features.

"Mr. Raoul! Miss Martin! Has there been an accident?"

"I nearly ran Miss Martin over on the Valmy bridge. I suggest that you get her some brandy now, and send someone upstairs—"

"No, please," I said quickly, "I don't want any brandy. I'm all right now, Seddon. Mr. Raoul never touched me; I slipped and fell as I was getting out of the way. It was all my fault. I'll just go upstairs and have a bath then make some tea in the pantry."

Seddon hesitated, glancing at Raoul, but I said firmly, "It's all right, really it is. I don't want a thing."

"Well, miss, if you're sure. . . ." He looked at Raoul. "I'll have your things taken straight up, sir. You're in your usual room."

"Thank you. How are you, Seddon? And Mrs. Seddon? The asthma keeping away?"

"Yes, thank you, sir, we're both well."

"That's fine. I'll come upstairs in a moment. Where's everyone? The small salon?"

"Yes, sir. Monsieur Florimond is here, sir, and he's staying the night. Shall I tell Madame you've arrived?"

"If you will. Say I'll join them in a few minutes."

"Very good, sir." And, with a final glance at me, he went.

As I turned to follow him, Raoul said, "You've torn your frock."

I looked down, unable to suppress a movement of dismay. My coat was open. At the hem of my frock a tear showed.

"Oh, yes. I remember now. I felt it catch on something. But it's nothing much. It'll mend."

He was frowning. "The bumper must have caught you. I really am most—"

"Raoul?"

The voice came from behind me. I jumped and spun around. Raoul must have been inured to his father's methods of approach, for he merely turned, said, "How d'you do, sir?" and held out a hand. As Léon de Valmy took it his brilliant dark gaze turned to me.

"What's this? Did I hear something about a bumper catching you?"

I said, "It's nothing."

"Miss Martin and I," said Raoul, smiling, "met—rather abruptly—down on the Valmy bridge."

His father's eyes went to the torn hem of my frock; went lower to a laddered stocking and the stain of a muddy graze on my leg. "You mean you knocked her over?"

I said quickly, "Oh, no, nothing like that! I fell down and bumped my knee, that's all. Monsieur Raoul didn't touch me. It—"

"That tear wasn't done by falling down. That stuff's been ripped. Was that done by that damned great car of yours, Raoul?"

Temper flicked suddenly, patently, through the words, like a whip. For a moment I was reminded of the way I had heard him speak to Philippe, pilloried beside the yellow-brocaded chair, and, damn it, Raoul was—what? thirty? I felt myself going hot with embarrassment, and glanced at him.

But this was not Philippe. He merely said, unruffled, "I imagine so. I had only just noticed it. I was abasing myself when you came in." He turned back to me. "Miss Martin, I really am most terribly sorry—"

"Oh, please!" I cried. "It was nothing. It was my own fault!"

Monsieur de Valmy said, "What were you doing down on the bridge at this time of night?"

"I went out for a walk," I said. "It was damp in the woods so I went down the road."

"What happened?"

Raoul began to speak but I said hastily, "I stopped in the middle of the bridge. I was going to turn back and I stood for a minute or two listening to the water. It was a silly thing to do, because there was a drift of mist there over the river, and Monsieur Raoul ran slap into it. But I'd forgotten he was coming."

"Forgotten?"

I looked at him in faint surprise. Then I remembered that the conversation in the salon had been in French. I said steadily, hoping my color hadn't risen, "Mrs. Seddon told me this evening that he was coming."

"Ah. Yes." The dark eyes were unreadable under the heavy black brows. He looked at Raoul. "And then?"

I said quickly, "So of course Monsieur Raoul didn't see me—he couldn't have seen me till he was just about running me down. It was entirely my own fault and I'm lucky to get away with a bruise and a torn frock. If it was the car that tore it that's all it touched, honestly. The bruise I got myself by slipping and falling in the gutter."

Léon de Valmy was still frowning. "That's a bad corner . . . as we all know." The cutting edge was back on his voice. "Raoul, if you must come up that road on a night like this—"

Raoul said gently, "I have already told Miss Martin how sorry I am."

Something sparked inside me. My employer had a perfect right to catechise me, but not to make his son look a fool in front of me. And I'd seen a little too much of his tactics tonight already. I said hotly, "And I have explained to Monsieur Raoul that the fault was mine and mine only. So please may we drop the subject? It isn't fair that he should be blamed. If he'd been any less brilliant a driver I'd have been killed!"

I stopped. I had seen the faintest, least definable shade of amusement in Raoul's face, and in his father's something that was, less mistakably, anger. He said smoothly, but with the edge still on the carefully pedantic words, "A brilliant driver should not have to call upon his skill to that extent at such a dangerous corner."

Raoul smiled at him and said, very pleasantly, "The corner was relaid last autumn . . . by the Bellevigne estate, remember? And are you sure you're qualified to criticize my driving? You forget that both roads and cars have altered considerably since you were last able to drive."

In the sharp little silence that followed I saw the lines around Léon de Valmy's mouth deepen, and the white hands moved on the arms of the chair. He said nothing. Raoul smiled lazily down at him. No, this was not Philippe. No wonder he'd been amused when I wildcatted to his defense. I thought, with an absurd rush of pleasure: *that for Philippe, Monsieur the Demon King!*

Raoul turned to me and said easily, "Are you sure you won't have something sent up to you, Miss Martin?"

"Quite sure." I looked from one to the other a bit uncertainly. "Good night, Monsieur de Valmy. Good night, Monsieur Raoul."

I went quickly upstairs, leaving the two of them together.

CHAPTER VIII

Fifth Coach

Thou art more deep damn'd than Prince Lucifer.
There is not yet so ugly a fiend of hell
As thou shalt be, if thou didst kill this child.
SHAKESPEARE: *King John.*

NEXT DAY all traces of mist had gone, and the trees moved lightly in their Lenten green. Since the winds of March had whipped some of the buds into tiny leaf, our favorite walk had been the way through the woods that stretched northward down the valley, and this afternoon we went that way again.

We started down the path that short-circuited the zigzag. For all its steepness it was not bad walking, as the path itself was ribbed across with sunken logs to give a foothold, and the occasional flights of steps were in good repair, with wide flat treads scored and clear of moss. Here and there the path crossed a trickle of water; sometimes the bridge was only a step, a slab of stone over a mossy trough where water chuckled; but in places some streamlet had cut deeply through the rock into miniature cascades, spanned by sturdy little bridges no more than two planks' width, with a single handrail of untrimmed pine.

It was on these bridges that Philippe loved to linger, gazing down at the ferns and grasses swaying in the wind of the cascade, and counting what he fondly imagined to be the fish attempting to leap up the spray. This morning we hung happily together over the biggest of the pools where fingers of bright sunlight probed the ferns and made an iridescent bloom of fine spray.

"Three," said Philippe, triumphantly. "*Voilà,* did you see her? Beside the stone there, where the waves are!"

I peered down at the whirling pool some fifteen feet below us. "I can't see anything. And it's not *her,* Philippe."

"It was. Truly it was. I am seeing her—"

"I'm sure you are. But a fish isn't *her,* it's *it.*"

"A trout is her in French," said Philippe firmly. It was a great source of pride to him that my French was worse than his English.

"No doubt," I said, "but not in English. Oh, look, there's one, Philippe, definitely! I saw her—it jump!"

"Four." Philippe knew when to pursue his triumphs and when to hold his tongue. "Four and a half, because I do not know if that shadow is a *truite*—trout, or a shadow." He gripped the rail and leaned over, peering eagerly down.

"Let's go on," I said. "If it's still there when we come back, it's a shadow. Let's go down into the big wood again."

He turned obediently off the bridge onto the wide level path that led along the hillside deeper into the trees. "All right. To look for wolves?"

"Wolves?"

He was trotting ahead of me. He turned, laughing. "Mademoiselle, you sounded quite frightened! Did you think there were really wolves?"

"Well, I—"

He gave a crow of laughter and a comic little skip that shuffled up last year's dead leaves. "You did! You did!"

"Well," I said, "I've never lived in a place like this before. For all I know Valmy might be crawling with wolves."

"We have got bears," confided Philippe, in the tone of one inviting congratulations. He looked earnestly up at me. "We truly have. This is not a *blague*. Many bears of a bigness incredible." His scarlet-gloved hands sketched in the air something of the dimensions of an overgrown grizzly. "I have never seen one, *vous comprenez,* but Bernard has shot one. He told me so."

"Then I hope to goodness we don't meet one today."

"They are asleep," said Philippe comfortingly. "There is no danger unless one treads on them where they sleep." He jumped experimentally into a deep drift of dead leaves, sending them swirling up in bright flakes of gold. The drift was, fortunately, bearless. "They sleep very sound," said Philippe, who appeared to find it necessary to excuse this failure, "with nuts in the pocket, like an *écureuil.*"

"Squirrel."

"Skervirrel. Perhaps you prefer that we do not look for bears?"

"I would really rather not, if you don't mind," I said apologetically.

"Then we will not," he said generously. "But there are many other things to see in the woods, I think. Papa used to tell me of them. There is chamois and *marmottes* and the foxes, oh, many! Do you think that when I have ten years—"

" 'When I am ten.' "

"When I am ten years I can have a gun and shoot, mademoiselle?"

"Possibly not when you're ten, Philippe, but certainly when you're a bit older."

"Ten is old."

"It may be old, but it's not very big. You wouldn't be of a bigness—I mean you wouldn't be big enough to use the right gun for a bear."

"Skervirrels, then."

"Squirrel."

"Skervirrel. I could have a small gun for skervirrel when I am ten?"

"Possibly, though I should doubt it. In any case, it's what they call an unworthy ambition."

"*Plaît-il?*" He was still jigging along slightly in front of me, laughing back over his shoulder, his face for once flushed and bright under his scarlet woolen ski cap. He said cheekily, "English, please."

I laughed. "I meant that it's a shame to shoot squirrels. They're charming."

"Char-ming? No, they are not. They eat the young trees. They cause much work, lose much money. The foresters say it. One must shoot them."

"Very French," I said dryly.

"I *am* French," said Philippe, skipping gaily on ahead, "and they are *my* trees, and I shall have a gun when I am older and go out every day to shoot the skervirrels. Look! There's one! *Bang!*" He proceeded, with gestures, to shoot down several squirrels very loudly, singing meanwhile an extremely noisy and shapeless song whose burden was something like:

> *Bang, bang, bang,*
> *Bang, bang, bang,*
> *Got you, got you,*
> *Bang, bang, bang.*

"If you don't look where you're going," I said, "it'll be you who'll— look *out,* you silly chump!"

Then three things happened, almost simultaneously.

Philippe, laughing back at me as he jigged along, tripped over a tree root and fell headlong. Something struck the tree beside him with the sound of a hand smacking the back, and, a fraction later, the sharp crack of a rifle split the silence of the woods.

I don't know how long it took me to grasp just what had happened. The unmistakable crack of the gun, and the child's body flat in the path . . . for one heart-stopping moment terror zigzagged like pain through my blood. Then even as Philippe moved the significance of that sharp smack on the tree's bole struck me, and I knew he was not hit.

I found myself shouting into the silent woods that sloped above us, "Don't shoot, you fool! There are people here!" Then I was beside Philippe, bending over him, making sure. . . .

The bullet had not touched him, of course; but when I looked up and saw the hole in the tree just above where he lay, I realized how nearly he had been hit. The silly little jiggling song that had tripped him up had saved his life.

He lifted a face from which all the bright gaiety and color had gone. There was mud on one thin little cheek and his eyes were scared.

"It was a gun. Something hit the tree. A bullet."

He spoke, of course, in French. This was no moment to insist either on his English or my own false position. In any case he had just heard me shouting in French at the owner of the gun. I put my arms around him and spoke in the same tongue. "Some silly fool out with a rifle after foxes." (Did one shoot foxes with a rifle?) "It's all right, Philippe, it's all right. A silly mistake, that's all. He'd hear me shout and he'll be far more scared than we were." I smiled at him and got up, pulling him to his feet. "I expect he thought you were a wolf."

Philippe was shaking, too, and I saw now that it was with anger as much as fright. "He has no business to shoot like that. Wolves don't sing, and in any case you don't shoot at *sounds*. You wait till you can *see*. He is a fool, an imbecile. He should not have a gun. I shall get him dismissed."

I let him rage on in a shaken shrill little voice, a queer and rather touching mixture of scared child and angry Comte de Valmy. I was scanning the slopes of open wood above us for the approach of an alarmed and apologetic keeper. It was quite a few seconds before I realized that the wood was, apparently, empty. The path where we walked ran between widely-spaced trees. Above us sloped some hundred yards of rough grass—an open space of sunlight and sparse young beeches, where brambles and honeysuckle tangled over the roots of felled trees. At the crest of the rise was a tumble of rock and the dark ridge of a planted forest. Nothing moved. Whoever was at large there with a rifle had no intention of admitting the recent piece of lunatic carelessness.

I said, my jerking heart shaking my voice a little, "You're right. He shouldn't be allowed out, whoever he is. You wait here. Since he won't come out I'm going to see—"

"*No!*" It was no more than a breath, but he caught hold of my hand and held it fast.

"But Philippe—now look, son, you'll be all right. He's miles away by now and getting further every second. Let me go, there's a good chap."

"*No!*"

I looked up through the empty wood, then down at the small pinched face under the scarlet cap.

"All right," I said, "we'll go home."

We were hurrying back the way we had come. I still held Philippe's hand. He clutched at me tightly. I said, still shaken and angry, "We'll soon find out, Philippe, don't worry, and your uncle'll dismiss him. Either he's a careless fool who's too scared to come out, or he's a lunatic who thinks that sort of thing's a joke, but your uncle can find out. He'll be dismissed, you'll see."

He said nothing. He half trotted, half shuffled along beside me, silent and sober. No skipping now, or singing. I said, trying to sound calm and reasonable above the blaze inside me, "Whatever the case, we're going straight to Monsieur de Valmy."

The hand tucked in mine twitched slightly. "No."

"But, my dear Philippe—!" I broke off, and glanced down at the averted scarlet cap. "All right, you needn't, but I must. I'll get Berthe to come and give you some five-o'clock and stay with you till I get back to the schoolroom. I'll ask Tante Héloïse if she'll visit you upstairs instead of making you go down to the salon, and then we'll play Peggitty till bedtime. How's that?"

The red cap merely nodded. We trudged on in silence for a bit. We came to the bridge where we had counted the trout, and Philippe walked straight over it without a glance at the pool below.

The blaze of anger licked up inside me again. I said, "We'll get the stupid criminal fool dismissed, Philippe. Now stop worrying about it."

He nodded again, and then stole a queer little look up at me.

"What is it?"

"You've been talking French," said Philippe. "I just noticed."

"So I have." I smiled at him. "Well, I could hardly expect you to re-member your English when you were being shot at like a *skervirrel*, could I?"

He gave the ghost of a little smile.

"You say it wrong," he said. "It's *squirrel*."

Then, quite suddenly, he began to cry.

Madame de Valmy was alone in the rose garden. Early violas were already budding beside the path where she walked. There were daffodils out along the edge of the terrace. She had some in her hands.

She was facing in our direction, and she saw us as soon as we emerged from the woods. She had been stooping for a flower, and she stopped in mid-movement, then slowly straightened up, the forgotten daffodil trailing from her fingers. Even at that distance—we were still some hundred yards away—she must have been able to see the mud on Philippe's coat and the general air of dejection that dragged at him.

She started toward us.

"Philippe! What in the world has happened? Your coat! Have you fallen down? Miss Martin—" her voice was sharp with real concern— "Miss Martin, not another accident, surely?"

I was breathless from the hasty ascent, and still angry. I said baldly, "Someone shot at Philippe in the wood down there."

She had been half bending toward the little boy. At my uncompromising words she stopped as if she had been struck.

"Shot . . . at Philippe?"

"Yes. They only missed him because he tripped and fell. The bullet hit a tree."

She straightened up slowly, her eyes on my face. She was very pale. "But—this is absurd! Who could . . . did you see who it was?"

"No. He must have known what had happened, because I shouted. But he didn't appear."

"And Philippe?" She turned shocked eyes to him. *"Comment ça va, p'tit? On ne t'a fait mal?"*

A shake of the red cap and a quiver of the hand in mine were the only answers. My own hand closed on his.

"He fell down," I said, "but he didn't really hurt himself. He's been very brave about the whole thing." I didn't feel it necessary to insist in front of the child that, but for the tumble, he would probably now be dead. But Madame de Valmy understood that. She was so white that I thought she would faint. The pale eyes, watching Philippe, held a look, unmistakably, of horror. So she did care after all, I thought, surprised and a little touched. She said, faintly, "This is . . . terrible. Such carelessness . . . criminal carelessness. You . . . saw nothing?"

I said crisply, "Nothing. But it shouldn't be too hard to find out who it was. I'd have gone after him then and there if I'd been able to leave Philippe. But I imagine Monsieur de Valmy can find out who was in the woods this afternoon. Where is Monsieur, madame?"

"In the library, I expect." She had one hand to her heart. From the other the daffodils fell in an unheeded scatter. She really did look dreadfully shocked. "This is—this is a dreadful thing. Philippe might have—might have—"

"I think," I said, "that I'd better not keep him out here. Will you excuse us from coming down tonight, madame? Philippe had better have a quiet evening and early bed."

"Of course. Of course. And you, too, Miss Martin. You have had a shock—"

"Yes, but I'm angry, too, and I find it helps. I'll go and see Monsieur de Valmy as soon as I've taken Philippe in."

She was nodding in a shocked, half comprehending way. "Yes. Yes, of course. Monsieur de Valmy will be terribly . . . annoyed. Terribly annoyed."

"I hope," I said grimly, "that that's an understatement. Come on, Philippe, let's go and find Berthe. Madame . . ."

As we left her I glanced back to see her hurrying away, toward the corner of the terrace. To tell Léon de Valmy herself, no doubt. Well, the sooner the better, I thought, and swept Philippe into the house and upstairs to the haven of the schoolroom.

Berthe was in the pantry, busy with some cleaning. After a swift explanation that shocked her as much as it had Héloïse, I would have left Philippe with her, but he clung to me, and looked so suspiciously like crying again that I stayed with him. Madame de Valmy had certainly taken the tale straight to her husband, who would, no doubt, put the necessary machinery in motion to discover the culprit. For me, Philippe was the first concern.

So I stayed with him and talked determinedly lighthearted nonsense to distract him till at length, fresh from a hot bath, he was safely ensconced with a book on the rug by the schoolroom fire. He made no objection when Berthe brought in her mending and prepared to keep him company while I went down to see his uncle.

Léon de Valmy was alone in the library. I had not been in the room before. It was a high room, lit by two long windows, but warmed and made darker by the oak bookshelves lining it from floor to ceiling. Above the fireplace a huge portrait glowed against the paneling; my first glance told me that it was a young portrait of Raoul de Valmy, looking very handsome in riding clothes, one hand holding a whip, the other the bridle of a gray Arab pony with large soft eyes and a dark muzzle. I wondered why his father kept it there. Below the portrait a log fire burned in the open hearth, which was flanked by a single armchair. The room contained, apart from its thousands of books and a big desk beside one window, very little furniture. I realized the reason for this as Léon de Valmy's wheel chair turned from a side table where he had been leafing through a pile of papers, and glided toward the fire, there to stop in the vacant place opposite the single arm chair.

"Come and sit down, Miss Martin."

I obeyed him. The first rush of my anger had long since ebbed, but nervousness tightened my throat and made me wonder a little desperately how to start.

Not that there was anything even slightly intimidating about him today. His voice and face were grave and friendly as he turned toward me. It came to me then, with a sense of almost physical shock, that the portrait above the mantel was not of his son, but of Léon himself.

He must have caught my involuntary glance upward, for his own followed it. He sat in silence for a moment, regarding the picture somberly, then he turned to me and smiled. "It seems we are an ill-starred race, we Valmys."

There was the same wryness in voice and smile that I remembered from our first encounter. The slightly dramatic phrasing, no less than the repeated and deliberate reference to a state he ostensibly wanted ignored, jarred on me sharply. Did he see everything then, purely in relation to his own misfortune? I said nothing, but looked away from him to the fire.

He said, "I am told we have barely escaped another tragedy this afternoon."

I looked up. (*Another tragedy.*) I said stolidly, "Has Madame de Valmy seen you?"

"She came straight to me. She was very much shocked and upset. It has made her ill. Her heart, I am afraid, is not robust." He paused and the dark eyes scanned my face. There was nothing now in his own but gentleness and concern. "You, too, Miss Martin. I think you had better have a drink. Sherry? Now supposing you tell me what happened." He reached a hand to the tantalus at his elbow.

"Thank you." I took the glass gratefully. My nervousness had gone. I was left with an empty feeling of reaction and fatigue. In a voice drained of any emotion I told him briefly of the afternoon's events. "Do you know who was out with a gun today?" I asked in conclusion.

He lifted his sherry glass. "Off-hand, no. Armand Lestocq told me— no, that won't do. He went to Soubirous this afternoon to the sawmill. In any case Armand is never careless with a gun."

"But you'll be able to find out, won't you? He shouldn't be allowed—"

"I am doing my best." A glance. "My active work is mainly done by telephone. And when I do find out he'll be dismissed."

He was turning the glass around and around in his long fingers, watching the gleam and shift of the firelight in the amber liquid. Behind him the mellow brown and gold of the books glinted in the firelight. Outside the dusk fell rapidly; the windows were oblongs of murky gray. Soon Seddon would come to draw the curtains and turn on the lights. Now in the flickering glow of the logs the room looked rich and pleasant, even —in this book-lined bay where the fire burned—cozy.

I said, "Someone's been out already to look around?"

He glanced up. "Of course. But the chances are that the culprit would make straight back when he saw what he had done—or nearly done. He wouldn't want to be caught out with the gun." He gave a little smile. "You do realize that whoever it is is going to take quite a bit of trouble to cover his tracks, don't you? Good jobs aren't as easy to get as all that around here."

"If he'd been going to come forward he'd no doubt have come running when he heard me shout," I said. "But I quite see why he's scared to. It might even be a question of police proceedings."

The dark brows rose. "Police? If there had actually been an accident —yes. But as it is—"

"I don't think it was an accident."

He looked considerably startled. "What in the world are you suggesting, then?" Then, as I made no immediate reply, he said in a voice where anger flickered through derision and disbelief, "What else, Miss Martin, what else? Deliberate murder?"

Mockery—but through it I felt anger meeting me, palpable as the beat of a hot wind. The words bit through the air between us. I merely gaped at him, surprised.

Then it drew off. He said, his voice smooth and cold, "You're being a little hysterical, aren't you? Who would want to kill a child? Philippe has no enemies."

No, I thought, and no friends either. Except me. I sat up and met Léon de Valmy's hard stare. I said coolly, "You take me up too quickly, Monsieur de Valmy. I wasn't suggesting anything quite as silly as that. And I am not hysterical."

His mouth relaxed a little. "I apologize. But you gave me a shock. Go on. Explain yourself."

I drank sherry, regarding him straightly. "It's only that I can't quite see how it could have been pure accident. The place was so open and he *must* have been able to hear us fairly easily. I think it was some silly prank—some youth, perhaps, showing off or trying to startle us. And he got nearer than he meant to, and then was so scared of what he'd done that he made off."

"I see." He was silent for a moment. "You had better fill in the details for me. Exactly where were you?"

"We went down the path that short-cuts the zigzag toward the Valmy bridge. We left it about halfway down, where you cross a deep ravine and turn right down the valley."

"I know it. There's a cascade and a trout pool."

Some fleeting surprise must have shown in my face, for he said quietly, "I have lived at Valmy all my life, Miss Martin."

It was an almost physical effort to keep from looking at the picture above our heads. I said quickly, "Of course. Well, you know how the path runs along the hillside down the valley? After about half a mile it's quite wide, and flat, and there are thick trees on the left going down toward the river, but on the right, above you, they thin out."

"I know. An open ride, with grass and beech rising to a ridge of rock. Above the rock is the planted forest."

I nodded. "The pines are about twenty feet high now, and very thick. We were going along the path; Philippe was singing and hopping about ahead of me, not looking where he was going."

"Fortunately, it seems," said Léon de Valmy dryly.

"Yes. Well, just as he tripped and fell flat, a bullet went slap into the tree that had tripped him, and I heard the report from above us, to the right."

"From the ridge?"

"I suppose so. It was the best cover, and where it happened there was nothing between us and the ridge except brambles and a few stumps covered with honeysuckle."

"You saw nothing?"

"Nothing. I shouted, and then, of course, I had to attend to Philippe. I suppose I assumed that whoever it was would have had a bad fright, and would come pelting down to see if we were hurt. But he didn't. I'd have gone up to investigate, only I thought I ought to get Philippe straight home."

He was watching me curiously. "You would have done something as dangerous as that?"

"Of course. Why not?"

He said slowly, "You are a courageous young woman, are you not?"

"Where's the courage? We both know it couldn't have been deliberate. Why should I be afraid of a fool?"

A pause, then all at once his face lighted with that extraordinarily charming smile. "A young woman might well be afraid to approach a fool armed with a rifle. Don't be angry with me, mademoiselle. It was meant as a compliment."

"I'm sorry." I swallowed, and said as an afterthought, "Thank you."

He smiled again. "Tell me, just how much do you know about guns?"

"Nothing whatever."

"I thought as much. You seem, when you talk of an 'accident,' to be picturing a singularly unlikely one. You think, in fact, that this fool with the gun fired more or less at random through the trees at a barely-seen target, or even at a sound?"

"Yes. And I can't quite see how he didn't know—"

"Exactly. The place was open and you said Philippe was shouting or singing."

"Yes. That's why I thought it must have been meant as a joke."

"Some unauthorized youth with a talent for excitement? Hardly. No, the explanation's far simpler than that. An 'accident' with a gun usually only means one thing—a carelessly-held gun, a stumble (as Philippe stumbled) over a stone or a root . . . and the gun goes off. I think, myself, that he must have seen Philippe fall, and have thought he had hit him. So . . . he panicked, and ran away."

"Yes, of course. That does seem to be the answer."

"Well, you can be sure it'll be looked into. The culprit may even come forward when he hears that no damage was done—but personally, I don't think he will." The long fingers toyed with the glass. He said, kindly—it could surely not be amusement that so faintly warmed his voice?—"My poor child, you've had a strenuous couple of days, haven't you? We're very grateful to you, my wife and I, for your care of Philippe. I'm sorry it's been such a frightening burden today."

"It's not a burden. And I'm very happy here."

"Are you? I'm glad. And don't worry any more about this business. After all, whether we find the man or not, it's not likely to happen again. Has Philippe got over his fright?"

"I think so."

"There's no need to call a doctor, or take any measures of that kind?"

"Oh, no. He's perfectly all right now. I doubt if he really knows how —how near it was. He seemed quite happy when I left him, but I did have to promise to go back and play a game before bedtime."

"Then I won't keep you. But finish your sherry first, won't you?"

I obeyed him, then set the glass down and said carefully, "Monsieur de Valmy, before I go, I have a confession to make."

An eyebrow lifted. I was right. It was amusement.

I said, "No, I'm serious. I—I've been deceiving you and Madame de Valmy, and I can't do it any longer. I've got to tell you."

The glint was still there. He said gravely, "I'm listening. How have you deceived us?"

I said, in French, "This is how I've deceived you, monsieur—ever since I came into the house, and I think it's high time I came clean."

There was a short silence.

"I see," he said. "Not just good French, either; the French of France, Miss Martin. Well, let's have it. Come clean."

The murder was out. It was over. My useless deception was confessed, and nothing had happened except that Léon de Valmy had laughed rather a lot—not only at the shifts I had been put to, but at the idea that my job should be contingent on an ignorance of French. Shamefacedly, I laughed with him, only too ready, in my relief, to admit my own folly. But . . .

Somewhere, deep inside me, something was protesting faintly. But . . .

But now the Demon King laughed good-temperedly, and, thankfully, I laughed with him.

It was into this scene of hilarity that Raoul de Valmy came a few moments later. I didn't hear him come in until he said from the door, "I'm sorry. I didn't know you were engaged."

"It's all right," said his father. "Come in."

With a click, the lights sprang to life. Raoul came around the bookcase into the bay where we sat. "I've just got in—" he began, then saw me sitting, sherry glass in hand, and paused.

"Good evening, mademoiselle." He glanced from me to his father. "I believe you wanted to see me, sir?"

I put down my glass and got quickly to my feet.

"I was just going," I said. I spoke in French, and I saw Raoul's brows lift, but he made no comment. Then I paused, glancing back diffidently at my employer. "Perhaps Monsieur Raoul has found something about the shooting? Has he been out to look for this man?"

"No," said Monsieur de Valmy. He nodded a pleasant dismissal. "Well, Miss Martin, thank you for coming. Good night."

"Shooting?" said Raoul sharply.

He was speaking to me. I hesitated and looked uncertainly at Monsieur de Valmy. Raoul said again, "What's this about shooting? Who should I have been looking for?"

"Oh," I said awkwardly—I had, after all, been already dismissed from the library—"I thought perhaps . . . then you don't know what happened this afternoon?"

Raoul had moved between his father's chair and the fireplace and was reaching for the sherry decanter.

"No. What did happen?"

Léon said coldly, "Some fool out with a rifle in the woods has narrowly missed killing your cousin."

Raoul's head jerked up at that. Some sherry splashed. "*What?* Philippe? Someone shot at Philippe?"

"That's what I said."

"Was he hurt?"

"He wasn't touched."

Raoul straightened, glass in hand, his shoulders back against the mantel. He looked from one to the other of us. "What did the chap think he was doing?"

"That," said his father, "is what we would like to know." He tilted his head back to look at his son. "You've been out, you say. Did you see anyone?"

"No."

"Which way did you go?"

"East. I told you I was going up through the new plantations. I went up from the kitchen gardens. I never saw a soul. Where did it happen?"

"On the track through the beechwood, half a mile north of the bridge."

"I know the place." He looked at me. "This is . . . shocking. He really wasn't hurt at all?"

"Not at all," I said. "He fell down, and the bullet missed him."

"And you? I take it you were there?"

"I was with him. It didn't go near me."

He stood looking down at the empty glass between his fingers, then set it carefully on the mantelpiece beside him. "Don't go yet, please. Sit down again. D'you mind telling me just what happened?"

Once more I told the story. He listened without moving, and his father leaned back in his chair, one hand playing with the stem of his empty glass, watching us both. When I had finished Raoul said, without turning his head, "I assume you have the matter in hand?"

For a moment I thought he was speaking to me, and looked up, surprised, but Léon de Valmy answered, "I have," and proceeded to outline the various instructions he had given by telephone. Raoul listened, his head bent now, staring into the fire, and I sat back in my chair and watched the two of them, wondering afresh at the queer twisted relationship that was theirs. Today all seemed quite normal between them; last night's perverted cut and thrust might never have been. The two voices, so alike; the two faces, so alike and yet so tragically different . . . my eyes lifted to the devil-may-care young face above the mantelpiece, with the pictured smile and the careless hand on the pony's bridle. No, it wasn't Raoul; it could never have been Raoul. There was something in his face, something dark and difficult that could never have belonged to the laughing careless boy in the picture. I had the feeling, watching Raoul as he talked to his father, that the young man of the picture would have been easier to know. . . .

I came back to reality with a jerk. Léon de Valmy was saying, "We seem to treat our employees a little roughly. I would have liked to persuade Miss Martin to take the evening off, but she feels it her duty to entertain Philippe."

"I must," I said. "I promised."

"Then go out afterward. Not—" that flash of charm again— "for a walk, as we seem so determined at Valmy to dog you with malice, but why not shake our dangerous dust from your feet, Miss Martin, and go down to Thonon? It's not late. A café, a cinema—"

"By the time she has put Philippe to sleep there'll be no buses to Thonon," said Raoul.

"It doesn't matter," I said quickly, surprised at the desire to escape that had swept over me. An evening outside Valmy—supper in a crowd, lights, voices, music, the common comings-and-goings of café and street —suddenly I longed desperately for these. I had had enough of drama this last two days. I got to my feet, this time decisively.

"It's very kind of you, but I did promise Philippe, and he's been upset. . . . I mustn't disappoint him. I'll rest after dinner."

"Tea alone in your room again and an early bed?" Raoul straightened his shoulders. "Are you sure you won't go?"

"Well I—" I hesitated, laughing. "I can't, can I?"

"There are two cars at Valmy, and the requisite number of people to drive them." He glanced down at Léon. "I think we owe Miss Martin her escape, don't you?"

"Assuredly. But I'm afraid Jeannot has the big car in Geneva on my business, and the shooting brake isn't back yet from the sawmill."

"Well," said Raoul, "there's mine." He looked at me. "Do you drive?"

"No. But look, you mustn't think—I wouldn't dream—"

"You know," said Raoul to the ceiling, "she's pining to go. Aren't you?"

I gave up. "It would be heaven."

"Then take my car." He looked at his father. "You can spare Bernard to drive it?"

"Of course."

"Where is he?"

"Out. I sent him straight away to look for traces of this fool with the gun, but it's dusk now so he should be back. No doubt he'll be in soon to report. . . . That's settled, then. Excellent. It only remains for me to wish you—what, Miss Martin? A pleasant evening, an evening to remember?"

I said, thinking of Philippe's face streaked with mud and tears, "I thought it was to be an evening to forget."

Léon de Valmy laughed.

Raoul crossed the room and opened the door for me.

"At eight, then?"

"Thank you. Yes."

"I'll see he's there. I—er, I gather we now speak French?"

I said, low voiced, "I told him just now."

I didn't add that I was pretty sure my confession had been quite unnecessary. The Demon King had known already.

Punctually at eight the lights of the car raked the darkness beyond the balcony rail. Philippe was already sound asleep, and Berthe sat sewing beside the fire in my sitting room. It was with a light step and a light heart that I ran downstairs toward my unexpected evening of freedom.

The Cadillac was standing there, its engine running. The driver, a tall silhouette against the lights, waited by the off front door. I got in and he slammed it after me, walked around the front of the car, and slid into his seat beside me.

"You?" I said. "That wasn't in the bond, was it?"

The car glided forward, circled, and dived smoothly into the zigzag. Raoul de Valmy laughed.

"Shall we talk French?" he said in that language. "It's the language I always take girls out in. Construe."

"I only meant that I don't see why you should chauffeur me. Couldn't you find Bernard?"

"Yes, but I didn't ask him. Do you mind?"

"Of course not. It's very nice of you."

"To follow my own inclinations? I warn you," he said lightly, "I always do. It's my *modus vivendi*."

"Why 'warn'? Are they ever dangerous?"

"Sometimes." I expected him to smile on the word, but he didn't. The light mood seemed to have dropped from him, and he drove for a while in an abstracted, almost frowning silence. I sat there rather shyly, my hands in my lap, watching the road twist and swoop up to meet us.

The car dropped down the last arm of the zigzag, turned carefully off the bridge and gathered speed on the valley road.

He spoke at length in a formal, almost cool tone. "I'm sorry you should have had such a bad two days."

"Two days?"

"I was thinking about last night's episode on the bridge back there."

"Oh, that." I gave a little laugh. "D'you know, I'd almost forgotten it."

"I'm glad to hear it. But perhaps that's only because what happened this afternoon has overridden it. You seem to have got over your scare now." He threw me a quick glance and said abruptly: "Were you scared?"

"Today? Ye-es. Yes, I was. Not of being shot or anything, because that part was over before I knew anything about it, but somehow—just scared." I twisted my fingers together in my lap, thinking back to that heart-stopping point of time, trying to explain. "I think it was the moment when I heard the shot and there was Philippe flat on the path . . . the moment before I realized he wasn't hurt. It seemed to last forever. Just the silence after the shot, and the world spinning round out of gear with no noise but the tops of the trees sweeping the air the way you hear a car's tires when the engine's off."

We were sailing up the curve toward Belle Surprise. The trees streamed by, a moment drenched in our flowing gold, then livid, fleeing, gone. I said, "Have you ever thought, when something dreadful happens, 'a moment ago things were not like this; let it be *then,* not *now,* anything but *now'?* And you try and try to remake *then,* but you know you can't. So you try to hold the moment quite still and not let it move on and show itself. It was like that."

"I know. But it hadn't happened after all."

"No." I let out a long unsteady breath. "It was still *then.* I—I don't think I'll forget the moment when Philippe moved as long as I live."

Another of those quick glances. "And afterward?"

"Afterwards I was angry. So blazing angry I could have killed someone."

"It takes people that way," he said.

"Because they've been scared? I know. But it wasn't only that. If you'd seen Philippe's face—" I was seeing it myself a little too clearly. I said, as if somehow I had to explain, "He's so quiet, Philippe. It's—it's all wrong that he should be so quiet. Little boys shouldn't be like that. And today was better; he was playing the fool in that silly maddening way children have, shouting rubbish and hopping about, only I was so pleased to see him like that that I didn't mind. And then . . . out of the blue . . . that beastliness. And there was mud on his face and he didn't want to stop to look at the trout and then he—he cried." I stopped then. I bit my lip and looked away from him out of the window.

"Don't talk about it any more if you'd rather not."

"It . . . gets me a bit. But I feel better now I've told someone." I managed a smile. "Let's forget it, shall we?"

"That's what we came out for." He smiled suddenly, and said with an abrupt, almost gay change of tone, "You'll feel quite different when you've had dinner. Have you got your passport?"

"What?"

"Your passport. I suppose you carry it?"

"Yes, it's—here it is. This sounds serious. What is it, a deportation?"

"Something like that." We were approaching the outskirts of Thonon now. Trees lined the road, and among them globed lamps as bland as melons made fantastic patterns of the boughs. "What d'you say," said Raoul, slowing a little and glancing at me, "shall we make a night of it? Go across into Geneva and eat somewhere and then dance or go to a cinema or something like that?"

"Anything," I said, my mood lifting to meet his. "Everything. I leave it to you."

"You mean that?"

"Yes."

"Excellent," said Raoul, and the big car swept out into the light and bustle of Thonon's main square.

I am not going to describe that evening in detail though, as it happens, it was desperately important. It was then, simply, one of those wonderful evenings. . . . We stopped in Thonon beside a stall where jonquils and wallflowers blazed under the gas jets, and he bought me freesias which smelled like the Fortunate Isles and those red anemones that were once called the lilies of the field. Then we drove along in a clear night with stars aswarm and a waxing moon staring pale behind the poplars. By the time we reached Geneva—a city of fabulous glitter and strung lights whose reflections swayed and bobbed in the dark waters of the Lake— my spirits were rocketing sky-high; shock, loneliness, the breath of danger all forgotten.

Why had I thought him difficult to know? We talked as if we had known each other all our lives. He asked me about Paris and I found myself, for the first time, talking easily—as if memory were happiness and not regret—of Maman and Daddy and the Rue du Printemps. Even the years at the orphanage came gaily enough to hand, to be remembered with amusement, more, with affection.

And in his turn Raoul talked of his own Paris—so different from mine; of a London with which it seemed impossible that the Constance Butcher Home for Girls could have any connection; of the hot brilliance of Provence, where Bellevigne stood, a little jewel of a château quietly running down among its dusty vines. . . .

Anything but Valmy. I don't think it was mentioned once.

And we did do everything. We had a wonderful dinner somewhere; the place wasn't fashionable, but the food was marvelous and my clothes didn't matter. We didn't dance there, because Raoul said firmly that

276 NINE COACHES WAITING

food was important and one must not distract oneself with gymnastics, but later, somewhere else, we danced, and later still we drove back toward Thonon, roaring along the straight unenclosed road at a speed which made my blood tingle with excitement, yet which felt, in that wonderful car, on that wonderful night, like no speed at all. The frontier checked us momentarily, then the big car tore on, free, up the long hill to Thonon. Along the wide boulevard that rims the slope to the Lake, through the now-empty market place, past the turning that led up to Soubirous. . . .

"Hi," I said, "you've missed the turning."

He glanced at me sideways.

"I'm following one of my dangerous inclinations."

I looked at him a little warily. "Such as?"

He said, "There's a casino at Évian."

I remembered Mrs. Seddon, and smiled to myself. "What's your lucky number?"

He laughed. "I don't know yet. But I do know that this is the night it's coming up."

So we went to the casino, and he played and I watched him, and then he made me play and I won and then won again and then we cashed our winnings together and went out and drank café-fine and more café-fine, and laughed a lot and then, at last, drove home.

It was three in the morning when the great car nosed its way up the zigzag, and—whether from excitement or sleepiness or the fines—I might have been floating up it in a dream. He stopped the car by the side door that opened off the stableyard, and, still dreamily and no doubt incoherently, I thanked him and said good night.

I must have negotiated the dark corridors and stairways to my room still in the same trancelike daze. I have no recollections of doing so, nor of the process by which eventually I got myself to bed.

It wasn't the brandy; the coffee had drowned that effectively enough. It was a much more deadly draught. There was one thing that stood like stone among the music and moonfroth of the evening's gaieties. It was stupid, it was terrifying, it was wonderful, but it had happened and I could do nothing about it.

For better or worse, I was head over ears in love with Raoul de Valmy.

CHAPTER IX

Sixth Coach

Never seek to tell thy love,
Love that never told can be . . .
WILLIAM BLAKE: *Poem from MSS.*

IT WAS to have been expected. It would be a very odd Cinderella indeed who could be thrown out of such dreary seclusion as the orphanage had offered me, into contact with Raoul de Valmy, without something of the sort happening. A man whose looks and charm were practically guaranteed to get him home without his even trying, had exerted himself to give a very lonely young woman a pleasant evening. *An evening to remember.*

That it was no more than that I was fully aware. In spite of a quantity of romantic reading and a great many wistfully romantic (and very natural) dreams, I had retained a good deal of my French common sense. That, along with the nastily-named English quality called phlegm, would have to help me to control the present silly state of my emotions. I had had my evening. Tomorrow would be another day.

It was. Soon after breakfast the big Cadillac disappeared down the zigzag; Raoul, I supposed, gone back to Bellevigne. I tore my thoughts resolutely away from a Provençal idyll where he and I drove perpetually through moonlit vineyards with an occasional glimpse of the Taj Mahal and the Blue Grotto of Capri thrown in, and concentrated rather fiercely on Philippe.

Nobody owned to the rifle incident, and there was little hope of tracing the culprit. But Philippe seemed to have got over his fright so the matter was allowed to drop. Life fell back into its accustomed pattern, except for the exciting prospect of the Easter Ball, which now provided a thrilling undercurrent to conversation below stairs. This function had for many years been held at Valmy on Easter Monday. Mrs. Seddon and Berthe, when they were about the schoolroom domain, delighted to tell me of previous occasions when the Château Valmy had been *en fête*.

"Flowers," said Berthe (who seemed to have taken serenely for granted my sudden acquisition of fluent French) "and lights everywhere. They even used to string lights right down the zigzag to the Valmy bridge. And there's floodlights in the pool, and they turn the big fountain on, and there are little floating lights in the water, like lilies. Of course," pausing in her dusting to look at me a little wistfully, "it isn't as grand as it used to be in the old days. My mother used to tell me about it when the old Comte was alive; they say he was rolling in money, but, of course, it's not the same anywhere now, is it? But mind you, it'll be pretty grand, for all that. There's some as says it's not quite the thing to have a dance this Easter seeing as Monsieur le Comte and Madame la Comtesse were killed last year, but what I says is them that's dead is dead (God rest their souls)—" crossing herself hastily—"and them that's alive might as well get on with the job. Not wanting to sound hardhearted, miss, but you see what I mean?"

"Of course."

"Anyway, Madame says it'll be just a small private party—not but what *they* call a small private party'd make your eyes stand out on stalks, as the saying is . . . if you'll excuse the expression, miss. But—" here she brightened, and picked up a brass tray which she began to polish with vigor—"We'll have *our* dance just as usual."

"You have one, too?"

"Oh yes. All the tenants and the château staff. It's the night after the château dance, on the Tuesday, down at Soubirous. Everybody goes."

This not unnaturally, left me wondering which dance I would be invited to attend, but it was very soon made clear to me by Madame de Valmy that for this occasion at any rate I was above the salt. . . . So I, too, succumbed to the universal feeling of pleased anticipation, a pleasure shot through with the worry of not having a dance frock to wear.

I didn't worry about this for long. I am French enough where my needle is concerned, and I had been—there was nothing else to do with it—saving the greater part of my salary for the last weeks. I didn't doubt that I could achieve something creditably pretty, even though it might not stand comparison with the Balmains and Florimonds with which the ballroom would probably be crowded. It would be pretty enough to sit out in, I told myself firmly, thrusting back a vision of myself *en grande tenue,* dancing alone with Raoul in a ballroom about the size of Buckingham Palace. But it would *not* (this with a memory of Jane Eyre's depressing wardrobe and Léon de Valmy's mocking eye) it would *not* be "suitable." I wasn't down to bombazine yet.

My next halfday off fell some three days after the incident with the rifle, and I went down to Thonon on the afternoon bus, with the object of buying stuff and pattern for a dance frock. I didn't think it would be much use looking for a ready-made in so small a place as Thonon, and Évian or Geneva prices were beyond me. So I hunted happily about for the best material I could afford, and at last was rewarded with a length of some pretty Italian stuff in white, webbed with gossamer silver threads, at what the saleswoman called a bargain price, but to me represented a horrifying proportion of my savings. I fought a swift losing battle with the remnants of my common sense, and firmly planted the money down on the counter with no trace of regret. Then, clutching the parcel to me, I pushed my way out through the shop door into the windy street.

It was almost five o'clock, one of those dark, rain-laden April days with a warm gusty wind blowing. There had been showers earlier, but now a belated gleam from the west glissaded over the wet housetops and etched the budding chestnuts of the square in pale gold against a slaty sky. Many of the shop windows were bright already, harshly lighted grocery stores and *boucheries* mirrored to soft orange and copper in the damp pavements. Over the flower stall where Raoul had bought me the freesias a naked gas jet hissed and flared in the gusty wind, now a snake-long lash of brilliant flame, now a flattened mothswing of cobalt and sulphur-yellow. The tires of passing cars hissed softly on the wet tarmac. Here and there among the bare chestnuts an early street lamp glowed.

I was longing for a cup of tea. But here my sense of economy, subconsciously outraged, no doubt, by the recent purchase, stepped in to argue the few francs' difference between tea and coffee. A *salon de thé* would be expensive, while coffee or an apéritif were at once far better quality and half the price.

I abandoned the tea and walked across the square toward a restaurant where a glass screen protected the tables from the fitful wind.

As I gained the pavement and paused to choose a table, a diffident voice spoke beside me.

"Miss Martin?"

I turned in some surprise, as the voice was unmistakably English. It was the fair young man of my encounter in Soubirous. He was dressed in a duffel coat supplemented by a shaggy scarf. His thick fair hair flopped in the wind. I had forgotten what an enormous young man he was. The general effect was that of a huge, shy blond bear, of a bigness incredible, as Philippe would have said.

He said, "D'you remember me? We met in Soubirous."

"Of course I remember you, Mr. Blake." I could have added that I was hardly likely to have forgotten him—the one English lamb in my pride of French tigers—but thought it was, perhaps, not tactful. . . . "I hope you haven't had to use any of those bandages and things?"

He grinned. "Not yet. But I expect to daily. Were you—were you thinking of going in here for a drink? I wonder if you would—may I—I mean I'd be awfully glad if—"

I rescued him. "Thank you very much. I'd love to. Shall we sit out here where we can watch what's going on?"

We settled ourselves at a table next to the glass screen, and he ordered coffee in his laborious English-French. His look of triumph when in actual fact coffee did arrive, made me laugh. "You're coming on fast," I said.

"Aren't I? But really, you know, it's hard to go wrong over *café*."

"Are you managing your shopping all right today?"

"Oh, yes. You can usually find someone who understands English in Thonon. Besides," he said simply, "it's cheaper. I usually shop in the market. I don't need a lot."

"Are you living up at the hut now?"

"For the time being. I sleep at the Coq Hardi in Soubirous a couple of nights in the week, and I have the odd meal there, but I like the hut. I get a lot of work done, and I can come and go and eat and sleep when I like."

I had a momentary and irresistible vision of him curling up in straw, nuts in the pocket, like a bear, for the winter. This made me think of Philippe. I said, "Does anyone from your side of the valley ever bring a gun over to Valmy?"

"Only if invited. There are shooting parties in the autumn, I believe."

"I didn't mean that. Would the foresters or keepers or anyone ever go stalking foxes or chamois or something with a rifle?"

"Good Lord, no. Why?"

I told him in some detail just what had occurred on Tuesday afternoon with Philippe. He listened with great attention, shocked out of his shyness by the end into sharp expostulation.

"But that's frightful! Poor kid. It must have been a beastly shock—and for you, too. The best you can say of it is that it's bl——er, criminal carelessness! And you say they've found no trace of the chap?"

"No one admits it, even now it's known that nobody was hurt. But that's easy to understand; he'd lose his job just like *that,* and jobs aren't all that easy to come by up here."

"True enough."

"What's more," I said, "when Monsieur de Valmy sent a couple of men down to look at the place where it happened, they found that the bullet had been dug out of the tree."

He whistled. "Thorough, eh?"

"Very. D'you see what it means? Those men were sent down there as soon as Philippe and I got back to the house. It means, first, that the chap with the gun knew what had happened when he loosed it off; and, second, that he didn't run away. He must have sat tight waiting for Philippe and me to go, then skated down to remove the evidence." I looked at him. "The thought of him hiding up there in the wood watching us is rather—nasty, somehow."

"I'll say. What's more, the man's a fool. Accidents do happen, and if he'd done the decent thing and come tearing down to apologize and see you both home the odds are he'd have got off with just a rocket from the boss. He must have lost his head and then not dared own up. As it is, I hope they do get him. What's de Valmy doing about it?"

"Oh, he's still having inquiries made, but I don't think they'll produce anything now. All we've got so far is lashings of alibis, but the only two I'm prepared to believe are Monsieur de Valmy's and the butler's."

William Blake said, "The son was here, wasn't he?"

His tone was no more than idle, but I felt the blood rushing hotly to my cheeks. Furious with myself, I turned away to look out through the glass at the now twilit square. If I was going to blush each time his name was mentioned, I wouldn't last long under the Demon King's sardonic eye. And this sort of nonsense I couldn't expect him to condone. I fixed my gaze on the brilliant yellows and scarlets of the flower stall, and said indifferently, "He was; he went away the morning after it happened. But you surely can't imagine—" In spite of myself my voice heated. "It certainly couldn't have been *him!*"

"No? Cast-iron alibi?"

"No. It—it just couldn't!" Logic came rather late in the wake of emotions: "Dash it, *he'd* have no reason to sneak about digging bullets out of trees!"

"No, of course not."

I said, rather too quickly, "How are the weevil traps?"

That did it. He was the last person to see a reference to his work, however abruptly introduced, as a mere red herring. Soon we were once more happily in full cry. . . . I listened, and asked what I hope were the right questions, and thought about the Valmy dance. Would he be there? Would he? *Would* he?

I came out of my besotted dreaming to hear William Blake asking me prosaically which bus I intended to take back to Valmy. "Because," he said, "one goes in about twelve minutes, and after that you wait two hours."

"Oh Lord, yes," I said, "I mustn't miss it. Are you getting the same one?"

"No. Mine goes just before yours. I'm sloping off this week end to meet some friends at Annecy." He grinned at me as he beckoned the waiter. "So forget you saw me, will you, please? This is A.W.O.L. but I couldn't resist it. Some pals of mine are up in Annecy for the week and they want me to go climbing with them."

"I won't give you away," I promised.

Here the waiter came up, and Mr. Blake plunged into the dreadful struggle of The Bill. I could see all the stages; understanding the waiter's total, translating it mentally into English money, dividing by ten for the tip, reckoning to the nearest round number for simplicity, slowly and painfully thumbing over the revolting paper money, and finally handing over a sheaf of it with the irresistible feeling that so much money cannot possibly be the fair amount to pay for so little.

At last it was over. He met my eyes and laughed, flushing a little. "I'm all right," he said defensively, "until they get to the nineties, and then I'm sunk. I have to make them write it down."

"I think you're wonderful. By the time you've been here another month you'll talk it like a native." I stood up. "Thank you very much for the coffee. Now you'd better not bother about me if you want to dash for that bus."

"You're right. I'm afraid I'll have to run." But he still hesitated. "It was—awfully nice meeting again. . . . Could we—I mean, when do you have your next afternoon off?"

"I don't quite know," I said, not very truthfully. Then I relented. "But I'm often in Thonon on a Friday afternoon and—look, for goodness' sake . . . isn't that your bus? The driver's getting in! Go on, run! Is this yours? And this . . . ? Good-by! Have a good week end!"

Somehow he dragged his paraphernalia up from the floor, lurched, with rope and rucksack perilously swaying, between the crowded tables, thrust his way through the swing door I grabbed and held wide for him, then waved a hand to me and ran. He reached the bus just as the driver's door slammed and the engine coughed noisily to life. Then wedged—it seemed inextricably—on the narrow steps of the bus, he managed to turn and wave again cheerily as the vehicle jerked and roared away.

Feeling breathless myself, I waved back, then turned hurriedly to cross the road to where my own bus waited. But before I could step forward a big car slid to a halt beside me with a soft hush of wet tires. A Cadillac. My heart, absurdly, began to race.

The door was pushed open from inside. His voice said, "Going my way?"

He was alone in the car. I got in beside him without a word, and the car moved off. It swung around the corner of the square where the Soubirous bus still stood beside its lamp, and turned into the tree-lined street that led south.

It was odd that I hadn't really noticed till now what a beautiful evening it was. The street lamps glowed like ripe oranges among the bare boughs. Below in the wet street their globes glimmered down and down, to drown in their own reflections. *He hangs in shades the orange bright, like golden lamps . . .* and on the pavements there were piles of oranges, too, real ones, spilled there in prodigal piles with aubergines and green and scarlet peppers. The open door of a wine shop glittered like Aladdin's cave with bottles from floor to roof, shelf on shelf of ruby and amber and purple, the rich heart of a hundred sun-drenched harvests. From a brightly lighted workmen's café nearby came music, the sound of voices loud in argument, and the smell of new bread.

The last lamp drowned its golden moon in the road ahead. The last house vanished and we were running between hedgeless fields. To the right a pale sky still showed clear under the western rim of the rain clouds, and against it the bare trees that staked the road stood out black and sheer. The leaves of an ilex cut the half-light like knives. A willow streamed in the wind like a woman's hair. The road lifted itself ahead, mackerel silver under its bending poplars. The blue hour, the lovely hour . . .

Then the hills were around us, and it was dark.

Raoul was driving fast and did not speak.

I said at last, a little shyly, "You're back soon. You haven't been to Bellevigne, then?"

"No. I had business in Paris."

I wondered what kettles of fish he'd (in Mrs. Seddon's unlikely idiom) been frying. "Did you have a good time?"

He said, "Yes," but in so absent a tone that I hesitated to speak again. I leaned back in silence and gave myself up to the pleasure of being driven home.

It was not for some time that I—absorbed in my dreaming—noticed how he was driving. He always traveled fast and there was a slickness about the way the big car sliced through the dark and up the twisting valley that demonstrated how well he knew the road; but there was something in his way of handling her tonight that was different.

I stole a glance at his silent profile as we whipped around and over a narrow bridge that warped the road at right angles. He had done nothing that was actively dangerous; in the dark we would have had ample warning of an approaching car, but we were skirting danger so closely that it now occurred to me a little sickeningly to wonder if he were drunk. But as our headlights brushed a brilliant arc against the wall of rock, reflected light swirled through the car and in it I saw his face. He was sober enough; but that something was the matter was quite evident. He was frowning at the road ahead, his eyes narrowed on the flying dark. He had forgotten I was there. It seemed quite simply as if something had put him into a bad temper and he was taking it out on the car.

"What were you doing down in Thonon?" The question was no more than a *quid pro quo,* but he spoke so abruptly out of the silence that it sounded like an accusation, and I jumped and answered almost at random.

"What? Oh, it's my afternoon off."

"What do you usually do on your afternoon off?"

"Nothing very much. Shopping . . . a cinema, anything."

"You go out to friends sometimes?"

"No," I said, surprised. "I don't know anyone. I told you when we . . . I told you on Tuesday."

"Oh. Yes. So you did."

We had run into another shower, and big drops splashed and starred the windshield. The car slewed overfast around a sharp bend in the road, and rubber whined on the wet tarmac. He hadn't once so much as glanced at me. He was probably hardly aware of who it was he had in the car. So much for Cinderella.

I sat quietly beside him and nibbled the bitter crusts of common sense.

We had gone two-thirds of the way to Valmy before he spoke again. The question was sufficiently irrelevant and surprising.

"Who was that chap?"

I was startled and momentarily at a loss. I said stupidly, "What chap?"

"The man you were with in Thonon. You left the café with him."

"Oh, him."

"Who else?" The phrase, brief to the point of curtness, made me glance at him in surprise.

I said shortly, "A friend of mine."

"You told me you didn't know anyone hereabouts."

"Well," I said childishly, "I know him."

This provoked a glance, quick and unsmiling. But he only said, "How is Philippe?"

"All right, thank you."

"And you? No more mishaps?"

"No."

My voice must have sounded subdued and even sulky, but I was having a fight to keep it level and unbetraying. Pride had joined forces with

common sense, and the two were flaying me. The phantoms of those idiotic dreams wavered, mockingly, in the dark. . . . I don't know quite
what I had expected, but . . . that man, and this: the change was too
great; it was unnerving.

I was also making a grim little discovery that frightened me. The
dreams might be moonshine, but the fact remained. I was in love with
him. It hadn't been the wine and the starlight and all the trappings of
romance. It hadn't even been the charm that he'd been so lavish with
that night. Now I was undoubtedly sober and it was raining and the
charm wasn't turned on . . . and I was still in love with this cold-voiced
stranger who was making futile and slightly irritated conversation at me.
At least I'd had the sense all along to try and laugh at my own folly, but
it was no longer even remotely amusing.

I bit my lip hard, swallowed another choking morsel of that bitter
bread, and wished he would stop asking questions that needed answering. But he was persisting, still in that abrupt tone that made his queries
—harmless enough in themselves—sound like an inquisition.

It seemed he was still curious about William Blake, which, in view of
my promise to say nothing, was awkward.

"Who is he? English?"

"Yes."

"He took the Annecy bus, didn't he? A climber?"

"He's climbing from Annecy this week end."

"Staying there?"

"Yes."

"Did you know him in England?"

"No."

"Oh. Then he's been to Valmy?"

"Not that I'm aware of."

"Is he staying hereabouts for long?"

"Look," I said, cornered, "does it matter? What's the inquisition for?"

A pause. He said, sounding both stiff and disconcerted, "I'm sorry. I
wasn't aware I was trespassing on your private affairs."

"They're not private. It's just—I—I didn't mean . . . I didn't want to
tell you . . ." I floundered hopelessly.

He threw me an odd look. "Didn't want to tell me what?"

"Oh—nothing. Look," I said desperately, "I don't want to talk. D'you
mind?"

And now there was no doubt whatever about his mood. I heard him
say, "God damn it," very angrily under his breath. He wrenched the
Cadillac around at the Valmy bridge and hurled her up the zigzag about
twice as fast as he should have done. The car snarled up the ramp like a

bad-tempered cat and was hauled around the first bend. "You mistake me." Still that note of barely-controlled exasperation. "I wasn't intending to pry into what doesn't concern me. But—"

"I know. I'm sorry." I must have sounded nearly as edgy as he did, shaken as I was, not only by his anger and my failure to understand it, but by a humiliation that he couldn't guess at. "I expect I'm tired. I trailed about Thonon for a couple of hours looking for some dress material—oh!" My hands flew to my cheeks. "I must have left it—yes, I left it in the café. I put it on the ledge under the table and then William had to run for the bus and—oh dear, how stupid of me! I suppose if I telephone—oh!"

His hand had moved sharply. The horn blared. I said, startled, "What was that?"

"Some creature. A weasel, perhaps."

The trees lurched and peeled off into darkness. The next corner, steeply embanked, swooped at us.

I said, "Do you have to go so fast? It scares me."

The car slowed, steadied, and took the bend with no more than a splutter of gravel.

"Did you tell him about the shooting down in the beechwood?"

"What? Who?"

"This—William."

I drew a sharp little breath. I said clearly, "Yes, I did. He thinks that probably you did it yourself."

The car whispered up the slope and nosed quietly out above the trees. He was driving like a careful insult. He didn't speak. The devil rode me, spurred me to add, out of my abyss of stupid self-torment, "And I didn't know that I was supposed to account to my employer for everything I said and did on my afternoon off!"

That got him, as it was meant to. He said, between his teeth, "*I am not your employer.*"

"No?" I said it very nastily because I was afraid I was going to cry. "Then what's it to do with you what I do or who I see?"

We were on the last slope of the zigzag. The Cadillac jerked to a stop as the brakes were jammed on. Raoul de Valmy swung around on me.

"This," he said, in a breathless, goaded undertone. He pulled me roughly toward him, and his mouth came down on mine.

For a first kiss it was, I suppose, a fairly shattering experience. And certainly not such stuff as dreams are made on. . . . If Cinderella was out, so decidedly was Prince Charming. . . . Raoul de Valmy was simply an experienced man shaken momentarily out of self-control by anger and other emotions that were fairly easily recognizable even to me. I say "even to me" because I discovered dismayingly soon that my own poise was a fairly eggshell affair. For all my semisophistication I emerged from Raoul's embrace in a thoroughly shaken state which I assured myself was icy rage. And certainly his next move was hardly calculated to appease. Instead of whatever passionate or apologetic words should have followed, he merely let me go, restarted the car, opened the throttle with a roar, and shot her up the slope and onto the gravel sweep without a word. He cut the engine and opened his door as if to come around. I didn't wait. I whipped out of the car, slammed the door behind me and in a silence to match his own I stalked (there is no other word) across the gravel and up the steps.

He caught up with me and opened the big door for me. He said something—I think it was my name—in an undervoice sounding as if it were shaken by a laugh. I didn't look at him. I walked past him as if he didn't exist, straight into a blaze of light, and Léon de Valmy, who was crossing the hall.

He checked his chair in its smooth progress as I came in, and turned his head as if to greet me. Then his eyes flicked from my face to Raoul's and back again, and the Satanic eyebrows lifted, ever so slightly. I turned abruptly and ran upstairs.

If it had needed anything else to shake me out of my daydreams, that glance of Léon de Valmy's would have done it. I leaned back against the door in my darkened bedroom and put the back of my hand to a hot cheek. There was blood bittersweet on my tongue from a cut lip. . . . Léon de Valmy would have seen that too. The whip flicked me again. Not only my face, my whole body burned.

I jerked myself away from the door's support, snapped on the light, and began to tug savagely at my gloves. Damn Raoul; how dared he? How *dared* he? And Léon de Valmy—here the second glove catapulted down beside the first—damn Léon de Valmy, too. Damn all the Valmys. I hated the lot of them. I never wanted to see any of them again.

On the thought I stopped, halfway out of my coat.

It was more than possible that I wouldn't have the chance. The Demon King didn't have to be *en rapport* with me to guess what had happened tonight, and it was quite probable that he would take steps to dismiss me.

It didn't occur to me at once that, if there were any hint of trouble, Raoul would certainly tell his father the truth, that I had been kissed against my will, and that since for the greater part of the year Raoul was not at Valmy to trouble the waters I would probably be kept on.

I only know that as I hung my coat with care in the pretty paneled

wardrobe I felt depressed—more, desolate—at the prospect of never seeing any of the hated Valmys again.

My lip had stopped bleeding. I put on fresh lipstick carefully, and
did my hair. Then I walked sedately out and across my sitting room to
the schoolroom door.

I opened it and went in. The light was on, but no one was there. The
fire had burned low and the room had an oddly forlorn look. One of the
French windows was ajar and the undrawn curtains stirred in a little
breeze. On the rug lay an open book, its pages faintly vibrant to the
same draft.

Puzzled, I glanced at the clock. It was long past time for Philippe's
return from the salon. Madame de Valmy would be upstairs, dressing.
Well, I reflected, it wasn't my affair. On this night of all nights I wasn't
going to see why he was being kept late below stairs. No doubt he would
come up when his supper did.

I was stooping for a log to throw on the fire when I heard the sound. It
whispered across the quiet room, no more loudly than the tick of the
little French clock or the settling of the wood ash in the grate.

A very slight sound, but it lifted the hair on my skin as if that, too,
felt the cold breath from the open window. It was no more than a voiced
sigh, but, horribly, it sounded like a word . . . "Mademoiselle . . ."

I was across the schoolroom in one leap. I ran out onto the dark
balcony and turned to peer along the leads. To right and left the windows were shut and dark. From behind me the lighted schoolroom thrust
a bright wedge across the balcony, making my shadow, gigantic and
grotesque, leap and posture before me over the narrow leads.

"Philippe?"

The ends of the balcony were in deep darkness, invisible. I plunged
out of my patch of light and ran along past the windows. The balcony
floor was slippery with rain.

"Philippe? Philippe?"

That terrible little whisper answered me from the darkest corner. I was
beside it, kneeling on the damp leads. He was crouched in a tiny huddle
up against the balustrade.

Or rather, where the balustrade had been. It was no longer there. In its
place was merely the step-ladder which I had taken from the broom
closet that very afternoon to wedge across the unsteady coping. Beyond
this frail barrier was merely a gap of darkness and a thirty-foot drop to
the gravel and that terrible line of iron spikes. . . .

My hands were on him, my voice hoarse and shaking.

"Philippe? What happened? You didn't fall. Oh, God, you didn't fall
. . . oh my little Philippe, are you all right?"

Small cold hands came up and clung. "Mademoiselle . . ."

I had him in my arms, my face against his wet cheek. "Are you all
right, Philippe? Are you hurt?" I felt his head shake. "Sure? Quite sure?"
A nod. I stood up with him in my arms. I am not big myself, but he
seemed a featherweight, a bundle of birds' bones. I carried him into the
schoolroom, over to the fireplace, and sat down in a wing chair, cuddling
him close to me. His arms came up around my neck and clung tightly. I
don't know what I was saying to him; I just hugged and crooned rubbish
over the round dark head that was buried in my neck.

Presently he relaxed his strangle hold and stopped shivering. But
when I tried to stoop for a log to put on the fire he clutched me again.

"It's all right," I said quickly, "I'm only going to build the fire up. We
must get you warm, you know."

He suffered me to lean forward, throw some faggots onto the sullen
fire, and stir it until some little tongues of flame crept up around the new
wood and began to lick brightly at it. Then I sat back in the chair again.
It seemed to me that the reassurance of my arms was of more importance at that moment than bed or hot drinks or any of the remedies that
would follow shortly. I said gently, "Was it the car, Philippe?"

That little nod again.

"But I warned you the stone was loose. I told you not to go galloping
along there, didn't I?"

He said in a voice that sounded thinner and more childish than ever,
"I heard the horn. I thought . . . Papa always used to . . . on the drive
. . . to tell me he was coming. . . ."

I bit my lip, then winced. Of course, the horn. I remembered that
arrogant blare on the zigzag. I had seen nothing on the road. It had
merely been part, no doubt, of the flare of temper and excitement that
had driven Raoul to kiss me . . . and driven Philippe out into the darkness, running in a stubborn, passionate hope to fling himself against the
rotten stone.

I said, as much to myself as him, "I'd no idea the coping was as dangerous. It only seemed to move such a little. I thought it would hold.
Thank God I put the ladder across. Why I did . . . oh, thank God I
did!" Then a thought struck me. "Philippe, where was Berthe? I thought
she was with you."

"Bernard came for her. Something she'd forgotten to do."

"I see." I waited for a moment, holding him. "Look, Philippe, we've
got a lovely fire now. What about warming those frozen paws?"

This time he unclasped himself without demur, and slipped down onto the rug beside me, holding out his hands obediently to the now bright blaze of the fire. I ruffled his hair. "This is wet, too. What a beastly night to go running out in! You are a little ass, aren't you?"

He said, his voice still too tight and sharp, "I hit the stone and then it wasn't there. It went over with a bang. I bumped into something. I couldn't see it. I fell down. I couldn't see anything."

"It was the ladder you bumped into, Philippe. You couldn't have fallen over, you know. There wasn't really a gap. You couldn't see the ladder, but it's a very solid one. It was really quite safe. Quite safe."

"It was awful. I was frightened."

"I don't blame you," I said, "I'd have been scared stiff. It was awfully sensible of you not to move."

"I didn't dare. I knew you'd come." The plain, pale little face turned to me. "So I waited."

Something twisted inside me. I said lightly, "And I came. What a good thing I came up in your cousin Raoul's car instead of waiting for the bus!" I got up and bent over him, slipping my hands under his arms. "Now, come and get these things off. Up with you." I swung him to his feet. "Goodness, child, you've been lying in a puddle! What about a hot bath and then supper in bed with a fire in your bedroom as a treat?"

"Will you be there?"

"Yes."

"Have your supper in my room?"

"I'll sit on your bed, I promise."

The black eyes glinted up at me. "And play Peggitty?"

"Oho!" I said. "So you're beginning to make capital out of this, are you? What's more, you're getting too dashed good at Peggitty. All right, if you'll promise not to beat me." I swung him around and gave him a little shove toward the door. "Now go and get those things off while I run the bath."

He went off obediently. I rang the bell for Berthe, and then went to turn on the bath. As I watched the steam billowing up to cloud the tiles I reflected a little grimly that now I should have to face Léon de Valmy again tonight.

Above the noise of the taps I heard a knock on the door that led from my sitting room. I called, "Come in." Berthe had been very quick.

I turned then in surprise, as I saw that it wasn't Berthe, but Madame de Valmy. She never came to these rooms at this hour, and as I caught sight of her expression my heart sank. This, then, was it. And I hadn't had time to think out what to say.

I twisted the taps a little to lessen the gush of water, and straightened up to meet whatever was coming.

"Miss Martin, forgive me for interrupting you while you're changing—" Hardly a frightening opening, that; her voice was apologetic, hurrying, almost nervous. "I wondered—did you remember to get me my tablets in Thonon this afternoon?"

I felt myself flushing with relief. "Why, yes, madame. I was going to give them to Berthe to put in your room. I'm sorry, I didn't realize you'd want them straight away."

"I'm out of them, or I wouldn't trouble you."

"I'll get them now," I said. "No, really, it's no trouble, madame. You're not interrupting me; this bath isn't for me. Philippe!"

I bent to test the water, then turned off the taps. "Oh, there you are, Philippe. Hop in, and don't by-pass yours ears this time . . . I'll get your tablets straight away, madame. My bag's through in my sitting room."

As I came out of the bathroom and shut the door behind me I was wondering how to tell her about the recent near-tragedy. But as I looked at her all idea of this melted into a different consternation. She looked ill. The expression that I had thought forbidding was revealed now as the pallor, set lips, and strained eyes of someone on the verge of collapse.

I said anxiously, "Are you all right? You don't look well at all. Won't you sit down for a few minutes? Shall I get you some water?"

"No." She had paused by the fireplace, near a high-backed chair. She managed to smile at me; I could see the effort it took. "Don't worry, my dear. I—I didn't sleep well last night, that's all. I don't manage very well nowadays without my medicine."

"I'll get it straight away." Throwing her another doubtful look I ran toward my sitting room, only to remember that the tablets were after all still in the pocket of my coat. I turned swiftly.

"Madame!" The horrified anxiety of the cry was wrenched out of me by what I saw.

She had put a hand on the chair back, and was leaning heavily on it. Her face was turned away from me, as if she were listening to Philippe splashing in the bathroom, but her eyes were shut, and her cheeks were a crumpled gray. No beauty there. She looked old.

At my exclamation she started, and her eyes flew open. She seemed to make an effort, and moved away from the chair.

I ran back to her. "Madame, you *are* ill. Shall I call someone? Albertine?"

"No, no. I shall be all right. My tablets?"

"In my coat pocket in the wardrobe. Yes, here they are. . . ."

She almost grabbed the box I held out to her. She managed another smile. "Thank you. I'm sorry if I alarmed you . . . these things pass. Don't look so worried, Miss Martin." In the bathroom Philippe had set up a shrill tuneless whistling that came spasmodically between splashes. Héloïse glanced toward the noise and then turned to go. She said, with an obvious attempt at normality, "Philippe sounds . . . very gay."

"Oh, yes," I said cheerfully, "he's fine."

I opened the door for her, straight onto Berthe who had paused outside, one hand lifted to knock. . . .

"Oh, miss, you startled me! I was just coming." Her eyes went past me and I saw them widen. I said quickly, "Madame isn't too well. Madame de Valmy, let Berthe see you to your room. I only rang for her to light Philippe's bedroom fire, but I'll do that myself. Berthe," I turned to the girl, who was still looking curiously at Héloïse de Valmy's drawn face, "take Madame to her room, ring for Albertine and wait till she comes. Then come back here, please."

"Yes, miss."

As I knelt to light Philippe's bedroom fire my mind was fretting at a new problem—a minor one, which I suppose I had seized on almost as a relief from the other worries that beat dark wings in my brain. What were those tablets that were apparently the breath of life to Madame? Did she take drugs? The ugly thought swirled up through a welter of ignorant conjectures, but I refused to take it up. The things were only sleeping tablets, I was sure; and presumably some people couldn't live without sleeping tablets. But—the flames spread merrily from paper to sticks and took hold with a fine bright crackling—but why did she want the tablets now? She had looked as if she were suffering from some sort of attack, heart or nerves, that needed a restorative or stimulant. The sleeping tablets could hardly be the sort of lifesavers that her anxiety had implied.

I shrugged the thoughts away, leaning forward to place a careful piece of coal on the burning sticks. I was ignorant of such matters, after all. She had certainly seemed ill, and just as certainly old Doctor Fauré must know what he was about. . . .

Another burst of whistling and a messy-sounding splash came from the bathroom, and presently Philippe emerged, his hair in damp spikes, and his usually pale cheeks flushed and scrubbed-looking. He had on his nightshirt, and trailed a dressing gown on the floor behind him.

Something absurd and tender took me by the throat. I looked austerely at him. "Ears?"

He naturally took no notice of this poor-spirited remark, but came over to the hearthrug beside which the fire now burned brightly. He said, with palpable pride, "I escaped death by inches, didn't I?"

"You did indeed."

"Most people would have fallen over, wouldn't they?"

"Decidedly."

"*Most* people wouldn't have had the presence of mind to stay quite still, would they?"

I sat back on my heels, put an arm around his waist, and hugged him to me, laughing. "You odious child, don't be so conceited! And look, Philippe, we won't tell Berthe when she comes back, please."

"Why?"

"Because your aunt isn't well, and I don't want any alarming rumors getting to her to upset her."

"All right. But you'll—*you'll* tell my uncle Léon, won't you?"

"Of course. It's a marvel to me that he didn't hear the coping fall himself. He was in the hall when I got in, and that was only a few moments after—ah, Berthe. How is Madame?"

"Better, miss. She's lying down. Albertine's with her and she knows what to do. She says Madame will be well enough to go down to dinner."

"I'm glad to hear it. She . . . she took her tablets, Berthe?"

"Tablets, miss? No, it was her drops. She keeps them in the cabinet by her bed. Albertine gave her them."

"I . . . see. By the way, Berthe, weren't you supposed to be around the schoolroom wing while I was out?"

"Yes, miss, but Bernard came for me." She shot me a sidelong glance. "There was some linen I'd been sewing. Bernard wanted it for the master, and couldn't find it, though I'd told him where it was."

"I see. Well, that shouldn't have kept you very long."

"No, miss. But it wasn't where I'd put it. Somebody'd moved it. Took me quite a while to find." She was eying me as she answered, obviously wondering why I questioned her so sharply.

I said, "Well, Master Philippe went outside to play on the balcony and got wet, so he's had a bath and is to have supper in bed. Do you mind bringing it in here, Berthe, and mine as well, please?"

"Not a bit, miss. I'm sorry, miss, but you see Bernard was in a hurry and—" She broke off. She was very pink now and looked flustered.

I thought, but in no hurry to let you go, that's obvious. And I don't suppose you insisted. I said aloud, "It's all right, Berthe, it doesn't matter. Master Philippe's not a baby, after all. It was his own fault he got a wetting, and now he gets the reward, and you and I have the extra work. That's life, isn't it?"

I got up, briskly propelling Philippe toward the bed. "Now in you get, brat, and don't stand about any longer in that nightshirt."

I had supper with Philippe as I promised, and played a game with him and read him a story. He was still in good spirits, and I was glad to see that his own part in the accident was assuming more and more heroic proportions in his imagination. At least nightmares didn't lie that way.

But when I got up to go out to the pantry to make his late-night drink he insisted a little breathlessly on coming with me. I thought it better to let him, so he padded along in dressing gown and slippers and was set to watch the milk on the electric ring while I measured the chocolate and glucose into the blue beaker he always used. We bore it back to the bedroom together and I stayed with him while he drank it. And then, when I would have said good night, he clung to me for a moment too long, so that I abandoned my intention of seeing Léon de Valmy that night, and spent the rest of the evening in my own room with the communicating doors open so that the child could see my light.

When finally I was free to sit down beside my own fire I felt so tired that the flesh seemed to drag at my bones. I slumped down in the armchair and shut my eyes. But my mind was a cage gnawed by formless creatures that jostled and fretted, worries—some real, some half recognized, some unidentified and purely instinctive—that wouldn't let me rest. And when, very late, I heard a car coming up the zigzag I jumped to my feet, nerves instantly astretch, and slid quietly through the shadows to the door of Philippe's room.

He was asleep. I went wearily back into my bedroom and began to undress. I was almost ready for bed when someone knocked softly on the door.

I said in some surprise, "Who is it?"

"Berthe, miss."

"Oh, Berthe. Come in."

She was carrying a parcel, across which she looked at me a little oddly. "This is for you, miss. I thought you might be in bed, but I was told to bring it straight up."

"No, I wasn't in bed. Thank you, Berthe. Good night."

"Good night, miss."

She went. I sat down on the bed and opened the parcel in some mystification.

I sat there for some time, looking down at the silver-webbed folds of Italian stuff that glimmered against the coverlet. Then I saw the note. It read:

> *"For the kiss I can't honestly say I'm sorry, but for the rest I do. I was worried about something, but that's no excuse for taking it out on you. Will you count the fetching of your parcel as penance, and forgive me, please?"*
>
> R.

P.S. Darling don't be so Sabine about it. It was only a kiss, after all.

Before I got to sleep that night, I'd have given a lot, drugs or no, for some of Madame de Valmy's tablets.

CHAPTER X

I told my love, I told my love,
I told him all my heart . . .
WILLIAM BLAKE: *Poem from MSS.*

NEXT MORNING it might all have been illusion. Raoul left Valmy early, this time for the south and Bellevigne. I didn't see him go. Whether or not he and Léon had spoken of last night's incident I never discovered; certainly nothing was said or even hinted to me. When I braved my employer in the library to tell him about Philippe's second escape, he received me pleasantly, to darken as he listened into a frowning abstraction that could have nothing to do with my personal affairs.

He was sitting behind the big table in the library. When I had finished speaking he sat for a minute or two in silence, the fingers of one hand tapping the papers in front of him, his eyes hooded and brooding. I had the feeling that he had forgotten I was there.

When he spoke it was to say, rather oddly, "Again."

I said, surprised, "Monsieur?"

He glanced up quickly under his black brows. I thought he spoke a little wearily. "This is the second time in a very few days, Miss Martin, that we have had cause to be indebted to you for the same rather terrible reason."

"Oh. I see," I said, and added awkwardly, "it was nothing. Anyone—"

"Anyone would have done the same?" His smile was a brief flash that failed to light his eyes. "So you said earlier, Miss Martin, but I must insist as I did before that we are lucky to have so . . ." a little pause . . . "so foresighted a young woman to look after Philippe. When did you put the ladder there?"

"Only yesterday."

"Really? What made you do it?"

I hesitated, choosing my words. "The other day I went out myself along the balcony to—to wait for a car coming. I remembered the coping had felt a bit loose before, and tried it. It was loose, but I'd have sworn not dangerously. I intended to mention it to you, but honestly I'd no idea it was as bad. Then the car came, and . . . I forgot about it."

I didn't add that the day had been Tuesday and the car Raoul's. I went on, "Then yesterday, just before I was due to leave for Thonon I went out again, to see if it was going to rain. I remembered then about the coping, but I was in a tearing hurry for the bus, so I thought I'd just shove something across temporarily to make it safe, and see you when I got in. I'd seen a step-ladder in the schoolroom pantry, so I ran and got that. It seemed secure enough. I—I vowed I'd remember to tell you as soon as I got back. I—I'm terribly sorry." I finished lamely.

"You needn't be. You were not to know that the stone was as rotten as that. I did have a report on the stonework of that balcony some time ago, but there was no suggestion that the repair was urgent. There'll be trouble about this, you may be sure. But meanwhile let us just be thankful for whatever inspired you to put the ladder across."

I laughed, still slightly embarrassed. "Perhaps it was Philippe's guardian angel."

He said dryly, "Perhaps. He seems to need one."

I said, "There's a phrase for it, isn't there? 'Accident prone.'"

"It seems appropriate." The smooth voice held a note that, incongruously, sounded like amusement. I looked sharply at him. He met my look. "Well? Well, Miss Martin?"

"Nothing," I said confusedly. "I . . . it's just that . . . you take it so calmly. I'd have expected you to be angry."

"But I am," he said, "very angry." And meeting his eyes squarely for the first time during the interview I realized with a shock that he spoke a little less than the truth. He smiled again, and quite without amusement. "But being a rational man, I keep my anger for those who are to blame. It would ill become me, mademoiselle, to vent it on you. And I cannot spend it in protests, because that is . . . not my way."

He swung the wheel chair around so that he was turned a little away from me, looking out of the window across the rose garden. I waited, watching the drawn, handsome face with its fine eyes and mobile mouth, and wondering why talking with Léon de Valmy always made me feel as if I were acting in a play where all the cues were marked. I knew what was coming next, and it came.

He said, with that wry calmness that was somehow all wrong, "When one is a cripple one learns a certain . . . economy of effort, Miss Martin.

What would be the point of raging at you here and now? You're not to blame. How's Philippe?"

The question cut across my thoughts—which were simply that I'd have liked him better indulging in some of that profitless rage—so abruptly that I jumped.

"Philippe? Oh, he's all right, thank you. He was frightened and upset, but I doubt if there'll be any ill effects. I imagine it'll soon be forgotten—though at the moment he's inclined to be rather proud of the adventure."

He was still looking away from me across the garden. "Yes? Ah well, children are unpredictable creatures, aren't they? *Le pauvre petit,* let's hope he's at the end of his 'adventures,' as you call them."

"Don't worry, Monsieur de Valmy. He's having a bad spell, but it'll get over." I added, inconsequentially, "When does Monsieur Hippolyte get home?"

He turned his head quickly. The chair moved at the same moment so suddenly that the arm struck the edge of the desk. His exclamation was lost in my cry.

"You've knocked your hand!"

"It's nothing."

"The knuckle's bleeding. Can I get you—"

"It's nothing, I tell you. What were you saying?"

"I forget. Oh yes, I wondered if you knew just when Philippe's Uncle Hippolyte gets home?"

"I have no idea. Why?"

My eyes had been on his grazed hand. I looked up now to see him watching me, his face as usual calmly shuttered, but with something in that quiet gaze that held me staring without reply.

Then the brilliant eyes dropped. He moved a paper knife an inch or two and repeated casually, "Why do you ask?"

"Just that Philippe keeps asking me, and I wondered if you'd heard from Monsieur Hippolyte."

"Ah. Yes. Well, I don't know exactly, I'm afraid. My brother has always been slightly unpredictable. But he'll be away for another three months at least. I thought Philippe knew that. I believe his scheduled lecture tour finishes just before Easter, but he plans to stay for some time after that to assist the excavations at—as far as I remember—Delphi." He smiled. "My brother is a remarkably poor correspondent. . . . I imagine that Philippe knows just about as much as I do." He lifted the paper knife, placed it exactly where it had been before, looked up at me and smiled again, charmingly. "Well, Miss Martin, I won't keep you. I still have to divert some of that anger into its proper channels."

He was reaching for the house telephone as I escaped.

It occurred to me with wry surprise that "escape" was exactly the right word for my relieved exit from the library. The discovery annoyed me considerably. Damn it, the tiger played velvet paws with me, didn't he?

But, unreasonable as it was, I couldn't rid myself of the impression that some of that much-discussed anger had been—whatever he said, whatever the probabilities—directed straight at me.

It was only a fortnight now to the Easter Ball, and I had to work fast. The weather was bad, so walks with Philippe were not obligatory, and though I took him several times to the stables to play on wet afternoons, we had a good deal of spare time indoors when I cut and sewed. Philippe and Berthe, the maid, both appeared fascinated by the idea of making a dance dress, and hung over me, fingering the stuff and exclaiming over every stage in its manufacture. Berthe was of rather more practical help than Philippe, as she gave me the use of her machine, and—since she was of my height and build—let me fit the pattern on her, never tiring of standing swathed in the glinting folds while I pinned and pulled and experimented.

As the days went by the château hummed with activity and pleased expectation. If there was indeed any shortage of money here, it could not have been guessed at. I did gather, from odd snippets of gossip to which I was careful to pay no attention, that much of the cost for the ball must be borne by Monsieur de Valmy himself. Monsieur Hippolyte, it was whispered, didn't care for such things, and whereas in past years Philippe's father had willingly financed the affair and had invariably, with his wife, come from Paris to attend it, now that Monsieur Hippolyte was Philippe's co-trustee he was, I gathered, inclined to sit down rather tightly on the moneybags. Whatever the case, it seemed that Monsieur de Valmy was determined to recall at least some of the splendors of "the old Comte's" time. To my unaccustomed eye the preparations seemed lavish in the extreme. Rarely-used bedrooms were opened and aired—for there were to be guests over Easter week end—the great ballroom and the big drawing room were thrown open, chandeliers were washed, luster by luster, mirrors were polished, furniture and rugs spirited from one place to another, all, it seemed, under the eagle eye of Monsieur de Valmy. His chair was everywhere; if a servant dropped a piece of silver he was cleaning, the Master heard it; if a table was pushed along a parquet floor instead of being lifted, the Master spoke angrily from a corner of the room; he was even to be seen constantly on the upper corridors, swiftly propelling himself in and out of bedrooms and along corridors not commonly used by the family.

And so, bit by bit, corner by corner, the great house was prepared for the event of the year, and excitement seemed to thicken in the air as Easter drew nearer. Then came the final touches; flowers were carried in from the hot houses, camellias and lilies and gorgeous blooms I didn't recognize, with tub after tub of bluebells and narcissuses and tulips looking cool and virginal among the heavy-scented exotics. In one of the galleries there was even a miniature grove of willows over a shallow basin where goldfish glided, with cyclamens clustering like butterflies at the water's edge. Outside, floodlights had been fitted up, and a fountain like a firework shot its sparkling trails thirty feet toward Saturday's big yellow moon. For on Easter Eve the weather cleared, and Easter itself came in bright and beautiful, with a soft wind blowing that set the wild daffodils dancing in the woods, and put the seal on the success of the affair.

The Château Valmy was *en fête*.

On Sunday night after Philippe had gone to bed I put the finishing touches to my frock. Berthe had stayed to help me, and now paraded it delightedly before me, while I sat on the floor among a scatter of pins and watched her with critical eyes.

"Ye—es," I said. "Turn round again, will you? Thanks. It'll do, I think, Berthe."

Berthe twirled a curtsy in it, gay and graceful. It was amazing how she had shed her prim servant-maid attitude along with her uniform. In the shimmering dress she looked what she was, a pretty country girl, slim and young and—just now—flushed with excitement.

"It's *lovely*, miss, it's really lovely." She spun around so that the full skirt swirled and sank. She lifted a fold and fingered it almost wistfully. "You'll look beautiful in it."

"I've an awful feeling it'll look pretty home-made alongside the collection downstairs."

"Don't you believe it," said Berthe stoutly. "I've seen most of them; Mariette and me did most of the unpacking. The prettiest frock I think belongs to the Marquise in the yellow guestroom, and she's no oil painting herself by a long chalk."

"Hush, Berthe," I protested, laughing, "you mustn't say things like that to me!"

She began to waltz around the room, humming a tune. "Of course Madame's always nice. She looks lovely in *grande toilette*—like a queen. And that Madame Verlaine gets herself up very smart, doesn't she? Hers is black."

"Is Monsieur Florimond here?"

"Oh, he always comes. He says he wouldn't miss it for worlds. He dresses half the ladies, anyway."

I began to pick up the scattered pins, asking casually: "And Monsieur Raoul? Does he come to this affair as a rule?"

There was a tiny pause. At the edge of my vision I saw Berthe's circling form check and turn. I looked up to catch a sidelong glance before her eyes slid from mine. She plucked at a fold of the skirt. "He hasn't been for years. But they're expecting him—this time."

I said nothing, and picked up pins.

She came over to where I sat, her voice warming into naturalness again. "Why don't you try it on now, miss? Don't bother with those, I'll pick them up after."

"It's done," I said. "There, that's the lot, I think."

"Don't you believe it," she said darkly. "We'll be finding them for weeks. Go on, miss, put it on, do. I want to see you in it, with the silver shoes and all."

I laughed and got up. "All right."

"It's a shame you haven't got a decent mirror. That one in the wardrobe door's no good at all, not for a long frock."

"It's all right. I told Madame I was making a frock and she said I might use the glass in her room. I'll just go along now and give it the final check-up. Tomorrow night I'll have to make do in here."

She followed me into my bedroom, speaking a little shyly. "May I help you to dress tomorrow?"

"Why, Berthe, how nice of you! But you'll have so much to do! And I could manage quite well, really. I'm not used to luxuries, you know."

"I'd like to. I would really."

"Then thank you very much. I'd be awfully glad to have you."

Back in her uniform, she helped me pleasedly with the dress. At last I stood surveying myself in the narrow wardrobe mirror.

"Oh, miss, it's lovely!"

"We put a lot of work into it, Berthe. I'm terribly grateful to you for helping. I couldn't have managed without you."

I turned this way and that, eying the line and fall of the material, and wondering just how amateurish it was going to look against the other gowns downstairs. Then I saw Berthe's eyes in the glass. They were brilliant with uncomplicated excitement and pleasure. Her delight, it was obvious, wasn't fretted by the shades of Balenciaga and Florimond. "Oh, miss, it's lovely! There won't be one prettier! You'll look a picture! Wait, I'll get the shoes!"

She was scurrying toward a cupboard but I stopped her impulsively. "Berthe. . . ."

She turned.

"Berthe, would *you* like to wear it too, for your own dance on Tuesday? You've probably got another just as pretty, but if you'd like it—"

"Oh, *miss!*" Her eyes grew enormous and she gripped her hands together. "Me? Oh, but I *couldn't.* . . . *Could* I?"

"Why not? You look lovely in it, and it was practically made on you, after all. If you'd really like it, Berthe, I'd be terribly pleased for you to take it. I don't suppose anyone'll recognize it."

"No, they won't," she said ingenuously. "It'll be hired waiters here tomorrow, and Ber—the servants won't be about. If—if you really mean it—" She began to thank me again, but I said quickly,

"Then that's settled. Fine. Now I'd better fly if I'm to get to that looking glass before Madame comes upstairs."

Berthe dived once more for the cupboard.

"Your shoes! Put on your new shoes with it!"

"No, no, don't bother," I said hastily, making for the door, "I must run. Thanks again, Berthe! Good night!"

Madame de Valmy's bedroom adjoined a small sitting room which she used in the mornings. I went through, leaving the connecting door ajar.

Her bedroom was a beautiful room, all soft lights and brocade and elegant Louis Seize, with a positively fabulous glitter of silver and crystal on the toilet table. An enormous Venetian mirror flanked the bathroom door, apparently held to the silk paneling by the efforts of the whole cherub choir.

I stood in front of this. The long window curtains mirrored behind me were of rose-colored brocade. The lighting was lovely. As I moved I saw the gleam of the cobwebbed silver thread shift and glimmer through the white cloud of the skirt the way sunlight flies along blown gossamer.

I remember that the thought that surfaced first in my mind was that now Cinderella had no excuse to stay away from the ball. And—at midnight?

Impatiently I shook my thoughts free, angry that I could still fool around even for a moment with the myth that I knew was nonsense. I'd burned myself badly enough on that star already.

Someone was at the sitting-room door. Berthe must have come along with the silver sandals. I called, "Come in. I'm through here," and made a face at myself in the glass. Here were the glass slippers. Damn it, I didn't stand a chance. . . .

A quick tread across the sitting room. Raoul's voice said, "Héloïse, did you want me?"

Then he saw me. He stopped dead in the doorway.

"Why—hullo," he said. He sounded a little breathless, as though he'd been hurrying.

I opened my mouth to answer him, then swallowed and shut it again. I couldn't have spoken if I'd tried. I must just have gaped at him like a schoolgirl caught out in some escapade. I know I went scarlet.

Then I gathered up my skirts in clumsy hands and moved toward the doorway which he still blocked.

He didn't give way. He merely leaned his shoulders back against the jamb of the door and waited, as if prepared to settle there for the evening.

I took two more hesitating steps toward him, and then stopped.

"Don't run away. Let me look at you."

"I must. I mean, I'd better—"

He said, "Sabine," very softly, and the laugh in the word brought hotter color to my face and my eyes up to his.

I'm not sure what happened next. I think he moved a little and said, "All right. So you really want to run away?" And I think I said, somehow, "No," and then "Raoul," as his shoulders came away from the doorpost in a kind of lunge, and then he was across the room and had me in his arms and was kissing me with a violence that was terrifying and yet, somehow, the summit of all my tenderest dreams.

I pushed away from him at last, both hands against his chest. "But Raoul, *why?*"

"What d'you mean why?"

"Why me? Your father called me 'Jane Eyre,' and he wasn't far wrong. And *you*—you could have anyone. So . . . why?"

"Do you want to know why?" His hands turned me around to face the mirror again, holding me back against him. I could feel his heart hammering against my shoulder blade. His eyes met mine in the glass. "You don't have to be humble, *ma belle*. That's why."

An odd sensation took me, part triumphant and part forlorn. I said nothing. The cherubs peered at us blind-eyed. Behind us the rose and gold and crystal of the lovely room glowed like the Bower of Bliss. Raoul was watching my face.

He opened his mouth as if to say something, but before he could speak there came a slight sound from the other room. He turned his head sharply, and for a moment his hands tightened on my shoulders. Then he let me go and turned, saying coolly, "Ah, Héloïse. I was looking for you. I believe you wanted me."

I jumped and spun around. I felt the quick heat wash and ebb in my cheeks, leaving me cold and pale. We had been standing in full view of anyone entering the sitting room. Héloïse de Valmy was there now, just inside the door, with Albertine beside her. She was speaking over her shoulder to someone—presumably one of the guests—behind her in the corridor, beyond my range of vision.

A woman's voice returned a soft reply and I heard skirts rustle away. It was impossible to tell if Madame de Valmy had seen Raoul holding me, but I knew Albertine had. Avoiding her dark malicious eyes I came quickly out of the bedroom with Raoul behind me.

I said, stammering, "Madame . . . I was using your glass to–to try my frock. You said I might. . . ."

It was still impossible to tell whether she had seen. Her light-gray eyes looked me up and down without expression. As usual, they were un-smiling, but I could detect no hint of displeasure in her face.

She said, in her cold composed voice, "Of course. Is that the dress you have made, Miss Martin? It's very pretty. You must be an accomplished needlewoman. Perhaps one day you might do some work for me?"

So she had seen. I felt Raoul, beside me, make a little movement. The burning color washed back into my face. I said quickly, "It would be a pleasure, madame. Good night, madame. Good night, monsieur."

I didn't look at him. I slipped past Héloïse de Valmy into the wel-come dimness of the corridor, and ran back to my room.

The next day passed in a whirl. I spent all my time with Philippe, who, alone of all the people in the house, seemed untouched by the general excitement, and was, indeed, indulging in a bout of the sulks at being left out of the Easter revels.

Luckily I didn't have to face Madame de Valmy. Just after lunch Albertine—was there a spark of malice in the smooth voice and face as she said it?—brought me a message which asked if we could please direct our afternoon's walk to the village to make some small purchases, as none of the servants (had she or had she not hesitated on the phrase "other servants"?) could be spared?

I agreed politely, and chided myself, as I took a reluctant, foot-trailing Philippe down to Soubirous, for being oversensitive. Madame de Valmy would surely not put me so brutally in my place a second time, and as for Albertine, a servant's malice couldn't affect me.

But I began to wonder, a few minutes later, if this last was true. As I paused in the sunshine outside Monsieur Garcin's shop to fish in my bag for Albertine's note, the bead curtains over the chemist's doorway rat-tled aside, and Albertine herself came out. Albertine, who "could not be spared" today; for whom I was playing errand boy. She must have set out for Soubirous almost immediately after briefing me.

I stared at her in amazement. She showed no sign of confusion, but slipped by me with one of her dark sidelong looks and small-lipped Mona Lisa smiles. She went into the *confiserie* just beyond the café.

When I pushed through the swinging beads myself into the spicy dimness of the shop, I was tense and nervous and very ready to discover in Monsieur Garcin's voice and attitude that same sidelong malice that I had now certainly seen in Albertine.

I told myself firmly that this was only fancy. But as I emerged from the pharmacy I came face to face with Madame Rocher, the curé's housekeeper, and this time there was no doubt about the chilliness of the greeting. If the good Madame could have passed by on the other side she would undoubtedly have done so. As it was she simply stared, nodded once, and gave me *bon-jour* in a tone nicely calculated (as from virtuous matron to viper-in-the-bosom) to keep me in my place, while at the same time allowing just the faintest loophole for a possibly legitimate future. Philippe she greeted, quite simply, with pity.

And later, when I bought some chocolate in the *confiserie,* I thought Madame Decorzent's fat smile was a little stiff today, and her prune-black eyes were curious, almost avid, as she said, glancing from Philippe to me, "And when are you leaving us, mademoiselle?"

I said coolly, through the sudden hammering of my heart, "We don't go to Thonon for a good while yet, madame. Monsieur Hippolyte doesn't get back for three more months, you know."

And I almost swept Philippe out through the tinkling curtain of beads into the hot sunlight. Albertine had done her work all right. The news, with its attendant rumors, was all over Soubirous.

I ran the gauntlet of sundry other stares and whispers before I reached the bridge and faced—with poor Philippe maddeningly awhine beside me—the long trudge up through the water-meadows.

I hadn't realized before what hard going it must have been for Cinderella.

After tea I went to look for Mrs. Seddon, to talk to her about whatever rumors were being put about below stairs, only to be told that the fuss and overwork occasioned by the ball had brought on "one of her attacks," and that she had gone to bed, unfit to speak to anyone. So I stayed with Philippe, my mind hovering miserably between remembered —and surely disastrous?—ecstasy, and my apparently imminent dismissal from Valmy. I am glad to remember that some of my worry was on behalf of Philippe. . . .

By the time Berthe came up that evening to serve Philippe's supper, I was in a fairly lamentable state of nerves, and more than half inclined to shirk facing my host and hostess downstairs. Then Philippe chose to throw a tantrum, and refused with tears to go to bed at all unless I would come up later "in the middle of the night" and take him to peep at the dancing from the gallery. I promised, and, satisfied, he disappeared quietly enough with Berthe.

I shut the door on them, and went to run my bath.

Dressing for my first dance . . . and Raoul somewhere among the throng of dancers . . . I should have been happy, eager, excited. But my fingers shook as I opened a fresh bar of scented soap, and later on when I was sitting in my petticoat brushing my hair, and a knock sounded on the door, I turned to face it as if it were a firing squad.

"I'll go," said Berthe, who had disposed of Philippe and was helping me. She opened the door a little way, had a short muffled colloquy with whoever was outside, then shut the door and came back into the room holding a box.

I was still sitting at the dressing table, hair brush suspended. Berthe came over to me. She looked a little flushed as she handed me the box, and she avoided my eye.

"This is for you." Her tone—like her whole bearing that evening— was subdued and a little formal.

For a moment I thought of asking her what was being whispered, then I held my tongue. I didn't want to meet him—and Monsieur and Madame —fresh from Albertine's brand of backstairs gossip. The woman's glance had been smirch enough.

Et tu, Berthe, I thought, and took the box from her.

It was light and flat, with a cellophane lid glassing the dark heart-shaped leaves and fragile blossoms of white violets; milk-white blooms, moth-white, delicate in dark-green leaves. There was the faintest veining of cream on throat and wing.

A card was tucked among the leaves. Without opening the lid I could see the single letter in an arrogant black scrawl:—*R.*

I finished dressing in silence.

Then I pinned the violets on, said quietly, "Thank you, Berthe," and went toward the music and the laughter.

CHAPTER XI

I am two fools, I know,
For loving, and for saying so.
JOHN DONNE: *The Triple Fool.*

THE BALL was well underway, and I was thankful to see that Monsieur
and Madame de Valmy had finished receiving. Their place near the
banked flowers at the foot of the great staircase was empty. Now the hall
was brilliant with a shifting mass of people. I hesitated on the gallery,
having no mind to make an entrance alone down that impressive flight
of steps; then three young women came chattering past me from some
room along the corridor, and I followed as inconspicuously as I could in
their wake.

It was easy enough to slip unremarked through the throng and into the
ballroom itself, where I found a corner sheltered by a pillar and a bank
of azaleas, and settled down quietly to watch the dancers.

I couldn't see Léon de Valmy's chair anywhere, but Héloïse, looking
wonderful in a gown the color of sea-lavender, was dancing with an elderly bearded man on whose breast the blue ribbon of an Order showed.
I saw Florimond over by one of the windows talking, or rather listening,
to a terrifying-looking old woman with a beak of a nose and improbable
blue hair. He was leaning forward slightly, that flattering air of his assuring her that she was the most amusing and intelligent woman in the
room. For all I knew she may have been. But had she been the dreariest
hag on earth I am sure that Florimond would have looked exactly the
same.

I turned to look for Raoul. On a swirl of music the dancers near me
swung and parted and I saw him. He was dancing with a blonde girl with
slanting eyes and a beautiful mouth. She was in black, with a high neck
and a straight-cut skirt that spoke of Madame Fath and made her look
incredibly slender and fragile. She was dancing very close to him and
talking rapidly, with flickering upward glances through her long lashes.
I didn't see him speak, but he was smiling. They were a striking couple,
and danced so beautifully that more than one glance was thrown in their
direction and—I had nothing else to do but see it—more than one significant eyebrow lifted in their wake. It would seem that Mrs. Seddon had

been right: where Raoul went, rumor walked. I wondered who the girl was. When—if—he danced with me, what would the eyebrows do then? *Who's the new girl? My dear, nobody, obviously. And my dear, the dress. . . . The governess? . . . Oh. . . . Oh, I see. . . .*

The music stopped, and people drifted to the sides of the ballroom. I was hidden by the crowd. Nobody had noticed me. I sat still, glad of the sheltering pillar and the massed azaleas. Beside me a trickle of water ran down a little scale, soulless as the music of a spinet. There was a tank of fish here, too, and the water dripped into it from a bank of moss. The azaleas threw patterns on the water, and gold and silver fish moved warily underneath.

The music started again, obliterating talk, laughter, and the tiny tinkle of water. The glittering dresses took the floor. This time he led out an elderly woman with a dreadful gown of royal blue and magnificent diamonds. And then a dark hawk of a woman with a clever hungry face and hands like yellow claws. And then the lovely blonde girl again. And then a well-corseted woman with dyed hair who wore dramatic black with emeralds. And then a white-haired woman with a gentle face. And then the blonde again.

The fish hung suspended in water green as serpentine, fins moving rhythmically. A petal, loosed from a pink azalea, floated down to lie upon the surface. I remembered my promise to Philippe. I got up, shaking out the folds of my skirt. The fish, startled, shuttled about the tank under the hanging moss.

When a voice said: "Mademoiselle," just behind me, I started like a guilty thing upon a fearful summons, and dropped my handbag, missing the tank by millimeters.

The owner of the voice stooped a little ponderously to pick it up for me. I might have known he would come sooner or later to comfort the wallflower.

"Monsieur Florimond!" I said. "You startled me."

"I'm sorry." He handed me the bag with a smile. "But you must not fly away now, mademoiselle. I'm depending on you for an alibi."

"An alibi?"

He made one of his wide gestures. "My dear, I don't dance, and I've talked myself to a standstill. I thought perhaps if I cornered you quickly we could resume our flirtation, which is something I can do at any time without effort."

"And," I said, watching how his hand hovered already over his pocket, "have a quiet smoke at the same time? All right, Monsieur Florimond, I'll be your chimney corner."

"A sympathetic woman," said Florimond, unabashed, taking out his case, "is above rubies."

"Don't you believe it. No woman is above rubies," I said, sitting down again. "No thank you, I don't smoke."

"Above diamonds, pearls, and rubies," said Florimond, lowering himself into the chair beside me with a sigh, and proceeding, as to an elaborate ritual, to light a cigarette. He beamed at me through the resultant cloud of smoke. "That's a very pretty gown, my dear."

I laughed at him. "Shakespeare," I said, "congratulating Minou Drouet on a neat phrase? Thank you, monsieur."

His eyes puckered at the corners. "I meant it. But you're rather hiding your light under a bushel, aren't you? I've been watching for you, but I haven't seen you dancing."

"I don't know anyone."

"Oh, là-là! And didn't Héloïse introduce any young men?"

"I haven't seen her to speak to. I came down late."

"And now she is—ah, yes, there she is, dancing with Monsieur de St. Hubert." He scanned the floor. "Then where's Raoul? He knows everybody. Perhaps he—"

"Oh, no, please!" The exclamation burst out quite involuntarily. I met Florimond's eye of mild inquiry and finished lamely: "I—I was just going upstairs. I promised Philippe to go and see him. I—don't bother Monsieur Raoul, please."

"Upstairs? And not to come down again, is that it?" The kind eyes surveyed me. "And is that also why you came down so late and then hid among the flowers?"

"I don't—what d'you mean?"

His gaze fixed itself on the violets. He didn't answer. My hand moved in spite of me to cup the flowers, a curiously defensive gesture and quite futile. I said, "How did you know?" and touched the violets with a finger tip. "These?"

He shook his head. "My dear," he said gently, "haven't you learned yet that every breath the Valmys take is news in the valley?"

I said bitterly, "I'm learning." I looked away from him. A fish was nosing at the azalea petal, butting it gently from underneath. I watched it absorbedly. The dance music seemed to come from a great way off. Here among the flowers was a little walled garden of silence broken only by the liquid arpeggios of the dripping mosses.

At length he spoke. "You're very young."

"Twenty-three." My voice tried hard not to sound defensive.

"Mademoiselle—" he seemed to be choosing his words—"if you ever thought of leaving Valmy, where would you go?"

I stared at him through a moment of whirling silence. Here, too. It was true. It hadn't been imagination to see those dragon's teeth of scandal springing up in Albertine's malicious wake. Madame de Valmy or (something caught at my breathing) Monsieur himself had said something, hinted something about dismissing me. And Florimond the kind had sought me out to talk to me about it. Everybody, it seemed, was making my connection with Raoul their business.

I don't quite know what I was thinking about it myself. I couldn't see beyond the fact that I loved him; that he had kissed me; that he was here tonight. I wanted to see him; dreaded seeing him. About Raoul's feelings and purpose—his "intentions"—I didn't think at all. He was here, and I loved him. That was all.

I pulled myself together to hear Florimond saying, kindly, "Have you friends in France, or are you on your own over here, mademoiselle?"

I said in a tight little voice, "I don't know anyone in France, no. But I am not on my own, monsieur."

"What do you mean?"

"Monsieur Florimond, you are being very kind, and don't think I don't appreciate it. But let's be frank, now that we've gone so far. You are concerned about me because I was seen kissing Raoul de Valmy, and I'm to be dismissed. Is that it?"

"Not quite."

I said, surprised, "Then what?"

He said gently, "Because you are also in love with Raoul de Valmy, child."

I said, rather breathlessly, "So—what?"

"What I said. You are too young. You have nobody here to run to. You are too much alone."

"No. I told you. I'm not alone."

He looked a query.

I said very evenly, "Is it so very impossible that I should be able to run—as you put it—to Raoul?"

There was a pause. The words seemed to repeat themselves into the silence. The clasp of my bag was hurting my fingers when I gripped it. I looked at him. "Yes, monsieur. We are being frank, you and I. Is it so very impossible that Raoul should—care for me?"

"My dear—" said Florimond, and stopped.

"Yes, monsieur?"

He took a deep breath. "You and Raoul . . . ? No, mademoiselle. No and no and no."

I said, after a little pause, "Just how well do you know him, monsieur?"

"Raoul? Well enough. Not intimately, perhaps, but—" he stopped again and one large hand tugged at his collar. He didn't meet my eyes. He said, *"Hell!"* unexpectedly and explosively, and began to grind out his cigarette in the earth of the azalea tub.

I was too angry to let him off. "Then since you don't know him so very well, perhaps you'll explain what you meant."

He looked at me then. "My dear, I can't. I should never have said it. I've already done the unforgivable. I mustn't go further."

"Monsieur de Valmy being your host?"

He almost jumped. "You're a little too quick for me, my dear. Yes, that and other reasons."

Our eyes met, in a curious half-ashamed comprehension. But I was still angry. I said, "Since we're talking in riddles, monsieur, what makes you think that all tigers breed true?"

"Mademoiselle—"

"All right," I said, "we'll leave it. You've warned me. You've eased your conscience and it was very kind of you to bother. Shall we just wait and see?"

He breathed a great, gusty sigh. "I was wrong," he said. "You're not as young as I thought." He was groping for another cigarette, grinning amiably at me. "Well, I've said my piece—unwarranted cheek, and you've been very nice about it. And don't forget, when you do do that running, you've got at least one other person in France to run to."

My anger died. "Monsieur Florimond—"

"There," he said, "and now we'll drop the subject. What about that flirtation we were in the middle of? Do you remember just where we'd got to? Or would you rather have a quick game of chess?"

I gave a shaken little laugh. "It would certainly be quick. Compared with me, Philippe's a master. You'd mop me up in three minutes."

"A pity. There's nothing like chess and tobacco, judiciously mixed, for taking the mind off the advice of a doddering old fool who ought to know better." A large hand patted mine paternally, and was withdrawn. "Forgive me, child. I couldn't help it, could I, if the advice came too late?"

I smiled at him. "Monsieur Florimond, even if this isn't the right moment in our flirtation to say so, you are a darling. But yes . . . much too late."

Raoul's voice said, above me, "So here you are! Carlo, what the devil d'you mean by hiding her away in this corner? Damn it, I've been watching the doors for a couple of hours! I'd no idea she was finding you and the goldfish such fascinating company. What was the somber discussion, *mon vieux?* What's much too late?"

"You, for one thing," said Florimond, calmly. "Now take Miss Martin away and dance with her and try and atone for leaving her to the goldfish."

Raoul grinned. "I'll do that. Linda, come here."

I went.

Florimond's eyes followed me, still with that pucker of trouble about them. Then I forgot them as the music took us.

His voice said at my ear, "It's been an age. Had you been there long?"

"Not really."

"Why were you so late?"

"I was scared to come down."

"Scared? My God, why? Oh, of course, Héloïse."

"She saw us; you know that."

"Yes." He laughed. "D'you mind?"

"Of course."

"You'll have to learn not to."

My heart was beating anyhow up in my throat. "What d'you mean?"

But he only laughed again without replying and swept me around with the music in a quick turn. A pillar swirled past, a group of men, a wheel chair. . . .

Léon de Valmy.

He was watching us, of course. A shadow at the center of the kaleidoscope: a spider at the knot of the bright web . . . the stupid fancies rose from nowhere in a stinging cloud. I shook my head a little, angrily, as if that would dispel them. Damn the man, I wasn't afraid of him . . . was I?

As, momentarily, the dance took me around to face him again, I looked straight at him and gave him a brilliant smile.

He was taken aback: there was no doubt about that. I saw the black brows lift sharply, then his mouth twitched and he smiled back.

The other dancers came between us and cut him off from view. I was left with the sharp impression that my employer's smile had been one of quite genuine amusement, but that it was amusement at some joke I couldn't see. It was an impression that was quite particularly unpleasant.

"Raoul," I said suddenly, urgently.

"Yes?"

"Oh . . . nothing."

"Just Raoul?"

"Yes."

He slanted a look down at me and smiled. *"Soit,"* was all he said, but I had the odd feeling that he understood.

When the dance finished we were at the opposite end of the room from Léon de Valmy, and beside one of the long windows. Raoul showed no sign of leaving me. He waited beside me in silence. He seemed to be oblivious of the crowd surrounding us, though the eyebrows were certainly at work. I caught a few curious looks cast at us, but I wasn't worrying about them. I was busy trying to locate Madame de Valmy in the crowd, and to see her without actually catching her eye. But she wasn't there.

The music started again. Raoul turned back to me.

I said feebly, "Now look, you don't really have to bother about me. I'm—"

"Don't be idiotic," said he crisply, taking hold of me.

This lover-like speech naturally reassured me completely. I laughed. I forgot Héloïse de Valmy, the raised eyebrows, even Léon and his amusement. I said meekly, "No, monsieur," and was swept out onto the floor again.

"I've done more than my share tonight, by God," said Raoul with feeling. "I've danced with every dowager in the place. Don't try and thwart me now, my girl. . . . It's just as well I couldn't find you before or I might have neglected my duty."

We were dancing at the edge of the room, near the French windows which stood open to the mild night.

"As," he finished, "I am about to neglect it now. . . ."

And before I knew quite what he was about we were out of the ballroom and on the loggia, slipping as easily and unnoticeably out of the throng as a floating twig slides into a backwater. The music followed us through the long windows; and there was the Easter moon and the ghosts of jonquils dancing in the dark garden. My skirt brushed the narcissuses on the terrace's edge. Raoul's shoulder touched jasmine and loosed a shower of tiny stars. We didn't speak. The spell held. We danced along the moonlit arcade of the loggia, then in through the dark windows of the salon, where firelight warmed the deserted shadows, and the music came muted as if from a great way off.

We were in the shadows. He stopped and his arms tightened around me. "And now . . ." he said.

Later, when I could speak, I said shakily, "I love you. I love you. I love you." And, of course, after that singularly ill-advised remark it was impossible to speak or even breathe for a very long time indeed.

When at length he let me go and spoke, I hardly recognized his voice. But, slurred and unsteady as it was, it still held that little undertone of laughter that was unmistakably his. "Well, aren't you going to ask it?"

"Ask what?"

"What every woman in the world asks straight away. The vow returned. *'Do you love me?'*"

I said, "I'll settle for whatever you want to give."

"I told you before not to be humble, Linda."

"I can't help it. It's the way you make me feel."

He said, *"Oh God!"* in that queer wrenched voice and pulled me to him again. He didn't kiss me but held me tightly and spoke over my head into the darkness. "Linda . . . Linda, listen."

"I'm listening."

"This love thing. I don't know. This is honest. I don't know."

Something twisted at my heart that might—if it were not absurd—have been pity. "It doesn't matter, Raoul. Don't."

"It does. You have to know. There've been other women—you know that. Quite a few."

"Yes."

"This is different." A silence. The ghost of a laugh. "I'd say that anyway, wouldn't I? But it is. It is." His cheek moved against my hair. "Linda. That's the hell of a name for a Frenchwoman, isn't it? So now you know. I want you. I need you, by God I do. If you call that love—"

"It'll do," I said. "Believe me, it'll do."

Another silence. The fire burned steadily, filling the room with shadows. In one of the logs I could hear the whine and bubble of resin.

He gave a queer little sigh and then loosed me, holding me at arm's length. His voice was his own again, cool, casual, a little hard. "What were you and Carlo talking about?"

The question was so unexpected that I started. "I—why, I hardly remember. Things. And—oh, yes, my frock. Yes, we talked about my frock."

I saw him smile. "Come now, confess. You talked about me."

"How did you know?"

"Second sight."

"Oh, murder," I said. "Don't tell me you've got it as well."

"As well?"

"Your father's a warlock; didn't you know?"

"Oh? Then shall we just say that I've got excellent hearing. Did Carlo warn you that my intentions were sure to be dishonorable?"

"Of course."

"Did he, by God?"

"More or less. It was done by implications and with the nicest possible motives."

"I'm sure of it. What did he say?"

I laughed at him and quoted: " 'You and Raoul, no and no and no.' And you are not to be angry. I adore Monsieur Florimond and he was only talking to me for my own good."

He was looking down at me soberly. "I'm not likely to be angry. He was too damned near right. I don't mean about my motives, but that probably you and I—" He stopped. "I've told you how I feel. But you; you say you love me."

I said: "Yes and yes and yes."

I saw him smile. "Again thrice? You're very generous."

"I was canceling Carlo out. Besides, we have a poem in English which says, 'What I tell you three times is true.' "

Another pause. Then he said, still holding me, "Then you will take a chance on marrying me?"

I began to tremble. I said huskily: "But your father—"

His hands moved so sharply that they hurt me. "My father? What's it to him?"

"He'll be so angry. Perhaps he'll do something about it—make you leave Bellevigne, or—"

"So what? I'm not tied to him or to Bellevigne." He gave a short, half-angry laugh. "Are you afraid of harming my position? My prospects? By God, that's rich!"

I said falteringly, "But you love Bellevigne, don't you? You told me you did, and Mrs. Seddon said—"

"So she's been talking about me, too, has she?"

"Everybody does," I said simply.

"Then did she tell you I hadn't any future except Bellevigne, and that only until Philippe gets Valmy?"

"Yes."

"Well, she's right." He added more gently: "Does that three-times-true love allow you to take a chance on a barren future?"

"I said I'd settle for what you had to give, didn't I?"

Another of those little silences. "So you did. Then you'll marry me?"

"Yes."

"In the teeth of the warnings?"

"Yes."

"And without prospects?"

"Yes."

He laughed then, still on that curious note of triumph. "You needn't worry about that," he said cryptically. "Fair means or foul, I'll always have prospects."

"An adventurer, that's what you are," I said.

He was looking down, and the black eyes were veiled again. "Aren't you?"

I said slowly, "Yes, I believe I am."

"I know you are," said Raoul. "Diamond cuts diamond, my darling. Kiss me and seal the bargain."

Afterward he let me go. I said uncertainly, "Do we have to—tell them?"

"Of course. Why not? I'd like to shout it from the housetops now, but if you like we'll wait till tomorrow."

"Oh yes, *please.*"

I saw his teeth gleam. "Does it need so much hardihood, *ma mie?* Are you afraid of my father?"

"Yes."

He gave me a quick, surprised look. "Are you? You've no need. But I'll tell them myself if you'd rather. You can just keep out of the way until it's done."

I said, "They'll be—so very angry."

"Angry? You undervalue yourself, my dear."

"You don't understand. I'm—I was due to be sacked anyway. That doesn't make it any easier to tell them."

"Due to be *sacked?* What on earth do you mean?"

"What I say. I was rather expecting to be told tomorrow. That's why I didn't want to come down to the dance."

"But—why? What's the crime?"

I looked up at him and gave a little smile. "You."

It took him a moment to assimilate this. "Do you mean because Héloïse saw me kissing you? You were to be sacked for that? Rubbish," he said curtly.

"It's true. At least I think so. You—well, you heard how Madame spoke to me just afterward, and when I went into Soubirous today it was quite obvious that the story had got around." I told him about the reception I had had in the village. "Albertine—the maid—may just have been scandalmongering because she doesn't like me, but I think she probably knows what Madame intends to do."

He lifted a shoulder indifferently. "Well, it doesn't matter, does it? You needn't let it worry you now. In any case I'm sure you're wrong. Héloïse would never want to let you go."

I said rather shyly, "I thought that myself. I did think it . . . odd, because of Philippe."

He said quickly, "Philippe?"

"Yes. I—don't get me wrong; I don't think I did anything very great for Philippe. The shooting business in the wood was nothing. I just didn't lose my head and fuss him too much, but I—well, I did save him the time he nearly fell off the balcony, and your father said—"

Raoul said, "What time? What are you talking about?"

"Didn't you know?" I said, surprised. I told him about the grim little incident that had crowned my shopping trip to Thonon. He listened, his face turned away from me toward the fire. In the flickering light I couldn't read his expression. He reached abstractedly for a cigarette and lit it. Over the flare of the match I could see he was frowning. I finished: "And your father knew that night that you'd kissed me. I'm sure he did. You remember?"

A glint through the frown. "I remember."

"There wasn't any talk then about sending me away. But there is now, really."

He laughed. "Well, my love, we've given them more cause, haven't we? Let that be a comfort to you. It's very probable that everybody in the ballroom knows by this time that you've gone out with me, and is speculating wildly on the whys and wherefores."

I said tartly, "I don't suppose they have any doubt at all about the whys and wherefores. It's all very well you carrying off your love affairs *en grand seigneur,* Monsieur de Valmy, but I'm only the governess. No, don't laugh at me. I've got to face them tomorrow."

"With me, *chérie,* remember. And now let's forget tomorrow. This is tonight, and we are betrothed." He took my hands. "If we can't shout it from the housetops at least we can celebrate it to ourselves. Let's go and get some champagne."

"And some food," I said.

"You poor child! Haven't you fed?"

"Not a bite. I sat in my corner while you danced and drank and enjoyed yourself—"

"More fool you," said Raoul unsympathetically. "You had only to show yourself to be trampled to death by partners avid to let you dance and drink and enjoy yourself with them. Come on, then. Food."

The great dining room was brilliant with people and gay with chatter and the popping of corks. Raoul made his way through the crowd with me in his wake. Several people hailed him, and I saw a few curious glances cast at me, but he didn't stop. As we reached the big table all agleam with silver I remembered something and touched his sleeve.

"Raoul, I'd forgotten. I promised to go up and see Philippe halfway through the dance. I must go."

He turned quickly, almost as if I had startled him. "Philippe? What on earth for?"

"I think he felt left out of things. At any rate I did promise to go up at 'dead of night.' I can't disappoint him."

"You . . . do look after him a little beyond the line of duty, don't you?"

"I don't think so. Anyway I think I ought to go straight away, in case he goes to sleep and thinks I've forgotten."

"But I thought you were starving?"

"I am." I looked wistfully at the laden table. There was a silver dish of crab patties just beside me, creaming over pinkly under their crimped fronds of parsley. "But a vow's a vow."

"And you always keep your vows?"

"Always."

"I'll remember that."

I laughed. "They're only valid if you'll let me keep the one I made to Philippe. His came first."

"Then I suppose I must. But I insist on coming too, and I'm not letting you faint with hunger by the wayside." He glanced at his wrist. "It's close on midnight—that's 'dead of night,' isn't it? Why don't we break a few more rules and take some food upstairs? Then Philippe will get his excitement and we our celebration."

"Oh, Raoul, that's a wonderful idea! Let's do that!"

"All right. I'll fix some food and drink. What d'you like?"

I looked again at the table. "Everything," I said simply.

He looked startled. "You must be hungry!"

"I am. Even if I weren't—" I sighed—"I couldn't by-pass that. I never saw anything so wonderful in my life."

He was looking at me with a curious expression. "Do you mean to say you've never been to a dance before?"

"This sort of thing? Never."

"One forgets," he said.

"I try to," I said lightly, "at any rate the dreary past never produced anything remotely like this. May I have one of those meringues?"

"If you must. And I suppose you've never had champagne either? That's a thought. . . . Well, you shall have it tonight. Meringues and champagne, may God forgive me. Well, you go along up to Philippe and I'll follow as soon as I've organized the food. I'll bring a bit of everything."

"That's a vow," I told him, and made my way out through the crowd.

My main fear was of coming across Léon de Valmy. I turned away from the hall and main staircase and ran down a corridor toward the secondary stair that Philippe and I commonly used.

But I needn't have worried. I reached the stairs unnoticed and mounted them hurriedly, holding up my filmy skirts. The staircase gave onto the upper corridor almost opposite Madame de Valmy's bedroom door. I was nearly at the top when I half tripped as the catch of my sandal came loose. The sandal came off. I had to stop to pick it up.

As I straightened up, sandal in hand, two women came out of Madame de Valmy's sitting room. My heart seemed to catch in mid-beat, then I saw that neither was Héloïse. They were elderly women who had not been dancing. I recognized one of them as an inveterate eyebrow-raiser —first at the blonde, then at me. I wondered how high her overworked brows would go if she knew I had an assignation with Raoul upstairs, however closely chaperoned by Philippe.

The sandal was my alibi. I waited politely for them to pass me before I proceeded to my own room for the ostensibly-needed repairs. I smiled at them, receiving in return two courteous and beautifully-calculated inclinations as they sailed by me, making for the main staircase.

The corridor emptied itself of the last rustle. With a wary eye on Héloïse's door I picked up my skirts again and turned toward Philippe's room.

Somewhere a clock whirred to strike. Midnight. I smiled. Dead of night exactly. I hoped Philippe was still awake.

The clock was beating twelve as I moved quietly along the corridor. Then a thought touched me out of nowhere and I stopped short, staring down at the sandal in my hand. Midnight. The dropped slipper. The escape from the ball.

I realized that I was frowning. The thing was so absurd as to be obscurely disquieting. Then I laughed and shrugged.

"Bring on your pumpkins," I whispered cheerfully, and laid a hand on Philippe's door.

CHAPTER XII

These delicates he heap'd with glowing hand
On golden dishes and in baskets bright
Of wreathèd silver: sumptuous they stand
In the retired quiet of the night . . .
KEATS: *Eve of St. Agnes.*

Drink to heavy Ignorance!
Hob-and-nob with brother Death!
TENNYSON: *The Vision of Sin.*

PHILIPPE was awake. When I let myself quietly into his bedroom I found him sitting bolt upright in bed in his dressing gown, with his eyes on the door. The fire, which should have been out hours ago, was burning merrily. The curtains over the long balcony windows were drawn back, so that the moonlight flowed in bright dramatic slant across the head of the bed.

Full in its path sat the little boy, his skin blanched to a waxy pallor by the white light, the black eyes huge and brilliant. He looked very frail.

But he seemed animated enough. He said immediately, "You've been ages."

"You said 'dead of night,' remember. It's just midnight now."

"Midnight? Is it really?" He looked pleased. "I kept the fire on. I knew you'd come."

"Of course I came. How d'you manage to be so wide awake at this hour?" I saw the untouched tumbler of chocolate on the bedside table, and laughed. "Oh, I see. Cunning, aren't you? Didn't you feel sleepy at all?"

"I did a bit," he confessed, "but it kept me awake looking after the fire."

"Is that why you kept it on?"

The big eyes slid sideways from mine and he plucked at the coverlet. "I sort of hoped—I wondered if you'd stay for a bit now you've come."

I sat down on the bed. "Why, Philippe? Is anything the matter?"

A vigorous shake of the head was followed by one of those little sidelong looks that contradicted it. I reached out and laid a hand over his. "What is it, brat?"

He said in a sort of furious mutter, "Nightmares."

"Oh dear, I didn't know. How beastly! What sort of nightmares?"

"People coming in," said Philippe, "and touching me."

This, oddly enough, was more shocking than any more usual horror of pursuit and desperately hindered flight could be. I shifted my shoulders a little, as if with cold, and said rather too heartily, "Oh well, it's only dreams, after all. It's not real—unless you mean me. I come in sometimes after you're asleep."

"No," said Philippe rather wanly, "not you. I wouldn't mind you."

"Do you have the same dream often?"

He nodded.

"It doesn't wake you up? If it does, you should call. I'd come."

"I do call, but there's no noise."

I patted the hand. It seemed very small and cold. "That means you're still asleep. It's a horrid feeling, but it *is* only a dream. And it might easily be me, Philippe; I usually do look in last thing at night. You're always sound asleep."

"Am I?"

"Like a top. Snoring."

"I bet I'm not."

"I bet you are. Now listen, I've a treat for you, Monsieur le Comte de Valmy. Since your honor wouldn't deign to come down for supper on the night of the ball, would you like supper to come up to you?"

"Supper? But I've had supper!"

"That was hours ago," I said, "and I haven't had mine. Wouldn't you like to entertain your cousin Raoul and me at a midnight feast?"

"A midnight feast? Oh, Miss *Martin*." The big eyes sparkled in the moonlight, then looked uncertain. "Did you say my cousin Raoul?"

I nodded. "He said he'd bring the food, and—oh, here he is."

The door had opened quietly and now Raoul came in, delectably laden with bottles, and followed by one of the hired waiters with a tray. Raoul lifted a gold-necked aristocrat of a bottle in mock salute. *"Bonsoir, Monsieur le Comte.* Put the tray down there, will you? Thanks. Do you suppose you could collect the debris later on? Secretly, of course."

Not a muscle of the man's face moved. "Of course, sir."

Something passed from Raoul's hand to his. "Excellent. That's all, then. Thank you."

"Thank you, sir. M'sieur, 'dame." The man sketched a bow, aimed between the bed and me, and went out, shutting the door.

"Then it really is a midnight feast?" said Philippe, eying his cousin a little shyly.

"Undoubtedly." Raoul was dealing competently with the gold-topped bottle. "As clandestine and—ah, that's it! A grand sound, eh, Philippe?—cozy as one could wish it. That's an excellent fire. Are you warm enough, Linda?"

"Yes, thank you."

He was pouring champagne. Philippe, his doubts forgotten, came out of bed with a bounce. "Is that lemonade?"

"The very king of lemonades."

"It's jolly fizzy, isn't it? It went off like a gun."

"Gun or no, I doubt if it's your tipple, *mon cousin*. I brought some real lemonade for you. Here."

"That's more like it," said Philippe, accepting a tall yellow drink that hissed gently. "Mademoiselle, wouldn't you like some of mine?"

"It looks wonderful," I said, "but I daren't hurt your cousin's feelings."

Raoul grinned and handed me a glass of champagne. "I doubt if this is your tipple either, my little one, but I refuse to pledge you in anything less."

"Pledge?" said Philippe. "What's that?"

"A promise," I said. "A vow."

"And there's our toast," said Raoul, lifting his glass so that the firelight spun and spangled up through its million bubbles. "Stand up, Philippe; click your glass with mine . . . now Miss Martin's . . . so. Now drink to our vows, and long may we keep them!"

Philippe, puzzled but game, drank some lemonade, then, hesitating, looked from Raoul to me and finally down at the tray which the servant had set on a low table before the fire. "When do we start?"

"This minute," I said firmly, and sat down.

Even without the influence of the king of lemonades it would have been a wonderful feast. My betrothal supper, held between firelight and moonlight in a little boy's bedroom—to me a feast every bit as magical as the banquet Porphyro spread for his Madeleine on that 'ages long ago' St. Agnes' Eve. And the food was a lot better. I don't remember that St. Agnes' lovers—perhaps wisely—ate anything at all, but Philippe and I demolished an alarming number of the delicates that Raoul's glowing hand had heaped upon the tray.

He had made a very creditable attempt to bring "everything." I remember thin curls of brown bread with cool, butter-dripping asparagus; scallop-shells filled with some delicious concoction of creamed crab; crisp pastries bulging with mushroom and chicken and lobster; *petits fours* bland with almonds; small glasses misty with frost and full of some creamy stuff tangy with strawberries and wine; peaches furry and glowing in a nest of glossy leaves; grapes frosted with sugar that sparkled in the firelight like a crust of diamonds. . . .

Philippe and I ate and exclaimed, and chatted in conspiratorial whispers, while Raoul lounged beside the fire and smoked and drank champagne and watched us indulgently for all the world as if I and Philippe were of an age, and he a benevolent uncle watching us enjoy ourselves.

"Or an overfed genie," I said accusingly, having told him this, "bringing a feast to Aladdin starving in his garret, or was it cellar?"

"As far as I recollect he was still," said Raoul lazily, "in his mother's washhouse. Romance is running away with you tonight, Miss Martin, is it not?"

"Remind me to resent that another time when I feel more . . . more earthly."

He laughed. "More champagne?"

"No, thank you. That was wonderful. Wonderful champagne, wonderful supper. Philippe, if you get a nightmare after this, let it comfort you to know that you've asked for it!"

"I rather think," said Raoul, "that Monsieur le Comte is all but asleep already."

Philippe, curled up on the rug with his head against my knee, had indeed been rather silent for some time. I bent over him. The long lashes were fanned over the childish cheeks, and he was breathing softly and evenly. I looked up again at Raoul and nodded. He rose, stretched, and pitched his cigarette into the dying fire.

"We'd better put him to bed." He stood for a moment looking down at the child. He looked very tall in the firelight with Philippe curled at his feet. "Does he have nightmares?"

"He says so. People come in in the night and touch him. Rather horrid."

His eyes rested on me for a moment, but I had the odd impression that he didn't see me.

"As you say." He stooped then and picked the child up, holding him easily in his arms. He carried him toward the bed.

The side of the room where we had been sitting was in deep shadow, lit warmly by the now-fading fire. Behind us the white shaft from the moonlit windows had slowly wheeled nearer. The bed lay now full in the sharp diagonal of light.

Raoul carried the sleeping child across the room. He was just about to step into the patch of light—a step as definite as a chessman's from black to white—when a new shadow stabbed across the carpet, cutting the light in two. Someone had come to the window and stopped dead in the path of the moon.

The shadow, jumping across his feet, had startled Raoul. He swung around. Philippe's face, blanched by the moon, lolled against his shoulder. Héloïse de Valmy's voice said, on a sharp note of hysteria: *"Raoul! What are you doing here? What's wrong?"*

She was backed against the light, so I couldn't see her face, but the hand gripping the curtain was tight as a hawk's claw. The other hand went to her heart in a gesture I had seen before.

He said slowly, his eyes on her, "Nothing. What should be wrong?"

She said hoarsely, "What's the matter with Philippe?"

"My dear Héloïse. Nothing at all. He's asleep."

I thought it better not to wait for discovery. I got to my feet.

The movement of my white dress in the shadows caught her eye and she jerked around. *"Oh!"* It was a little choked scream.

"Easy," said Raoul. "You'll wake him up."

I came forward into the moonlight. "I'm sorry I startled you, madame."

"You here? What's going on? *Is* there something wrong?"

Raoul grinned at her. "A carouse, that's all. An illicit night out *à trois*. Philippe was feeling a bit left out of the festivities, so Miss Martin and I tried to include him in, that's all. He's just gone to sleep. Turn the bed down, Linda, and help me get his dressing gown off."

Héloïse de Valmy gave a rather dazed look about her. "Then I did hear voices. I thought I heard someone talking. I wondered. . . ." Her eye fell on the tray at the fireside, with its bottles and empty glasses and denuded silver dishes. She said blankly, "A carouse? You really *did* mean a carouse?"

Raoul pulled the bedclothes up under Philippe's chin and gave them a final pat before he turned around. "Certainly. He may suffer for those lobster patties in the morning, but I expect he'll vote it worth while." He looked across the bed at me. "Let me take you down again now."

His eyes were confident and amused, but I looked nervously at Madame de Valmy. "Were you looking for me, madame?"

"I? No." She still sounded rather at a loss. "I came to see if Philippe was asleep."

"You . . . don't mind our coming up here . . . bringing him some of the supper?"

"Not at all." She wasn't even looking at me. She was watching Raoul.

He said again, rather abruptly, "Let me take you downstairs," and came around the bed toward me.

Downstairs? Léon de Valmy, Monsieur Florimond, the eyebrows? I shook my head. "No, thank you. I—it's late. I'll not go down again. I'll go to bed."

"As you wish." He glanced at Madame. "Héloïse?"

She bent her head and moved toward the door. I opened it and held it for her. As she passed me I said hesitantly, "Good night, madame. And thank you for . . . the dance. It was—I enjoyed it very much."

She paused. In the dim light her face looked pale, the eyes shadowy. She had never looked so remote, so unreachable. "Good night, Miss Martin." There was no inflection whatever in the formal words.

I said quickly, almost imploringly, "Madame . . ."

She turned and went. The rich rustle of her dress was as loud in the silence as running water. She didn't look back.

Raoul was beside me. I touched his sleeve. "It was true after all. You see?"

He was looking away from me, after Héloïse. He didn't answer.

I said urgently, under my breath, "Raoul . . . don't tell them. I can't face it. Not yet. I . . . just can't."

I thought he hesitated. "We'll talk about it tomorrow."

I said quickly, "Let them send me away. I'll go to Paris. I can stay there a little while. Perhaps then we can—"

His hands on my shoulders turned me swiftly toward him, interrupting me. "My dear, if I'm not to tell Héloïse tonight, I'd better leave you now. Don't worry, it'll be all right. I'll say nothing until we've talked it over." He bent and kissed me, a brief, hard kiss. "Good night, *ma mie.* Sleep well. . . ."

The door shut behind him. I heard him walk quickly down the corridor after Héloïse, as if he were in a hurry.

CHAPTER XIII

"Yes," I answered you last night;
"No," this morning, sir, I say.
Colours seen by candlelight
Will not look the same by day.
    ELIZABETH BARRETT BROWNING: *The Lady's Yes.*

NEXT MORNING a note was brought up to the schoolroom at breakfast-time by Bernard, Léon de Valmy's man.

It looked as if it had been written in a tearing hurry, and it read:

My dear,

I can't stay today as I'd hoped. I find I must go back to Paris—a damnable "must." Forgive me, and try not to worry about anything. I'll be back on Thursday morning without fail, and we can get things worked out then.

Héloïse said nothing to me, and (as I'd promised you I wouldn't) I didn't talk to her. I don't think you need worry too much about that side of it, *m'amie;* if they have anything to say they'll undoubtedly say it to me, not you. Till Thursday, then, pretend, if you can—if you dare!—that nothing has happened. I doubt if you'll see much of Héloïse anyway. She overdid things, and I imagine she'll keep to her bed.

Yours,

R.

As a first love letter, there was nothing in it to make my hands as unsteady as they were when I folded it and looked up at the waiting Bernard. He was watching me; the black eyes in that impassively surly face were shrewd and somehow wary. I thought I saw a gleam of speculation there, and reflected wryly that it was very like Raoul to send his messages by the hand of the man who hadn't been out of Léon de Valmy's call for twenty years. I said coolly, "Did Monsieur Raoul give you this himself?"

"Yes, mademoiselle."

"Has he left already?"

"Oh yes, mademoiselle. He drove down to catch the early flight to Paris."

"I see. Thank you. And how is Mrs. Seddon today, Bernard?"

"Better, mademoiselle, but the doctor says she must stay quiet in her bed for a day or two."

"Well, I hope she'll soon be fit again," I said. "Have someone let her know I was asking after her, will you please?"

"Yes, mademoiselle."

"Bernard," said Philippe, putting down his cup, "you have a dance tonight, don't you?"

"Yes, monsieur."

"Down in the village?"

"Yes, monsieur."

"Do you have supper there as well?"

"Yes, monsieur."

"What sort of things do you have for supper?"

The man's dark face remained wooden, his eyes guarded—unfriendly, even. "That I really couldn't say, monsieur."

"All right, Bernard," I said. "Thank you."

As he went I wondered, yet again, what pretty little Berthe could see in him.

It was a very unpleasant and also a very long day.

I felt curiously bereft. Raoul had gone. Florimond left soon after breakfast. Mrs. Seddon did as Bernard had prophesied and kept to her room, and Berthe went about her tasks all day with that withdrawn and rather shamefaced expression which seemed—if it were possible—faintly to image Bernard's sullen mask.

Small wonder, then, that when Philippe and I were out for our afternoon walk, and a jeep roared past us carrying several men and driven by William Blake, I responded to his cheerful wave with such fervor that Philippe looked curiously up at me and remarked, "He is a great friend of yours, that one, *hein?*"

"He's English," I said simply, then smiled at myself. "Do you know what irony is, Philippe? *L'ironie?*"

"No, what?"

I looked at him doubtfully, but I had let myself in for a definition now and plunged a little wildly at it. *"L'ironie . . .* I suppose it's Chance, or Fate (*le destin*), or something, that follows you around and spies on what you do and say, and then uses it against you at the worst possible time. No, that's not a very good way of putting it. Skip it, *mon lapin;* I'm not at my best this afternoon."

"But I am reading about that this morning," said Philippe. "It has a special name. It followed you *comme vous dîtes* and when you do something silly it—how do you say it?—came against you. It was called Nemesis."

I stopped short and looked at him. I said, "Philippe, my love, I somehow feel it only wanted that . . . And it's practically the Ides of March and there are ravens flying upside down on our left and I walked the wrong way around Sainte-Marie-des-Points last Thursday afternoon, and—"

"You didn't," said Philippe. "It was raining."

"Was it?"

"You know it was." He chuckled and gave a ghost of a skip. "You do say silly things sometimes, don't you?"

"All too often."

"But I like it. Go on. About the ravens flying upside down. Do they really? Why? Go *on,* mademoiselle."

"I don't think I can," I said. "Words fail me."

On our way in from the walk we met Monsieur de Valmy.

Instead of coming up the zigzag itself we took the short cut which ran steeply upward, here and there touching the northerly loops of the road. We crossed the gravel sweep at the top. As we went through the stable-yard archway, making for the side door, the wheel chair came quietly out of some outbuilding and Léon de Valmy's voice said, in French, "Ah, Philippe. Good afternoon, Miss Martin. Are you just back from your walk?"

The quick color burned my face as I turned to answer. "Good afternoon, monsieur. Yes. We've just been along the valley road, and we came back up the short cut."

He smiled. I could see no trace of disapproval or coolness in his face. Surely if I were privately under sentence of dismissal, he wouldn't act quite so normally—more, go out of his way to greet us in this unruffled friendly fashion? He said, including Philippe in the warmth of his smile, "You've taken to by-passing the woods now, have you?"

"Well, we have rather." I added, "I'm nervous, so we keep near the road."

He laughed. "I don't blame you." He turned to Philippe with a pleasant twinkle. "And how are you this morning, after your excesses of last night?"

"Excesses?" said Philippe nervously.

"I'm told you had a midnight feast last night . . . an 'illicit night out à trois' was the phrase, I believe. No nightmares afterward?"

Philippe said, "No, *mon oncle.*" The amused dark gaze turned to me.

I said, almost as nervously as Philippe, "You don't mind? Perhaps it was a little unorthodox, but—"

"My dear Miss Martin, why should I? We leave Philippe very completely to your care and judgment, and so far we've been amply proved right. Please don't imagine that my wife and myself are waiting to criticize every move that's out of pattern. We know very little about the care of children. That's up to you. And a 'special treat' now and again is an essential, I believe? It was kind of you to spare time and thought to the child in the middle of your own pleasure. . . . I hope you enjoyed the dance?"

"Yes, oh yes, I did! I didn't see you last night to thank you for inviting me, but may I thank you now, monsieur? It was wonderful. I enjoyed it very much."

"I'm glad to hear it. I was afraid you might feel rather too much a stranger among us, but I gather that Raoul looked after you."

Nothing but polite inquiry. No glint of amusement. No overtone to the pleasant voice.

"Yes, monsieur, thank you, he did. . . . And how is Madame de Valmy this afternoon? She's not ill, is she?"

"Oh no, only tired. She'll be making an appearance at the dance in the village tonight, so she's resting today."

"Then she won't expect us—Philippe and me—in the salon tonight?"

"No. I think you must miss that." The smile at Philippe was slightly mischievous now. "Unless you'd like to visit me instead?"

Philippe stiffened, but I said, "As you wish, monsieur. In the library?"

He laughed. "No, no. We'll spare Philippe that. Well, don't let me keep you." The wheel chair swiveled away, then slewed back to us. "Oh, by the way . . ."

"Monsieur?"

"Don't let Philippe use the swing in the big coachhouse, Miss Martin. I see that one of the rivets is working loose. Keep off it until it's mended. We mustn't have another accident, must we?"

"No indeed. Thank you, monsieur, we'll keep out of there."

He nodded and swung the chair away again. It moved off with that disconcertingly smooth speed toward the gate to the kitchen garden. Philippe ran ahead of me toward the side door with the air of one reprieved from a terrible fate.

He wasn't the only one. I was reflecting that once again my imagination had betrayed me. That smile of Monsieur de Valmy's last night . . . Madame's coldness . . . my interpretation of them had been wildly wide of the mark. A guilty conscience, and a too-ready ear for gossip had given me a few bad hours. It served me right. There was obviously no idea of dismissing me; if there had been Monsieur de Valmy would never have spoken to me as he had. All was well . . . and even if there were snags in the future, Raoul would be here beside me.

"Mademoiselle," said Philippe, "you look quite different *Qu'est-ce que c'est?*"

"I think I've seen a raven," I said, "flying the right way up."

The rest of the day limped through without incident. I put Philippe to bed a little earlier than usual, and later on, as soon as I had taken him his late-night chocolate, I went thankfully to bed myself and slept almost straight away.

I don't remember waking. Straight out of deep sleep, it seemed, I turned my head on the pillow and looked with wide-open eyes toward the door. The room was dark and I could see nothing, but then there came the stealthy click of the door closing, and soft footsteps moved across the carpet toward the bed. I think that for a moment or two I didn't realize I was awake, but lay still listening to the ghostly approach in a sort of bemused half-slumber.

Something touched the bed. I heard breathing. I was awake and this was real. My heart jerked once, in a painful spasm of fear, and I shot up in the bed, saying on a sharply rising note, "Who's that?"

As I grabbed for the bedside switch a voice that was no more than a terrified breath said, "Don't put the light on. Don't!"

My hand fell from the switch. The intruder's terror seemed to quiver in the air between us, and in the face of it I felt myself growing calm. I said quietly, "Who is it?"

The whisper said, "It's Berthe, miss."

"Berthe?"

There was a terrified sound that might have been a sob. "Oh, *hush,* miss, they'll hear!"

I said softly, "What's the matter, Berthe? What's up?" Then a thought touched me icily and I put a hand to the bedclothes.

"Philippe? Is there something the matter with Philippe?"

"No, no, nothing like that! But it's—it's—I thought I ought to come and tell you . . ."

But here the distressful whispering was broken unmistakably by gulping sobs, and Berthe sat down heavily on the end of the bed.

I slipped from under the covers and padded across the room to lock the door. Then I went back to the bed and switched on the bedside lamp.

Berthe was still crouched on the bottom of my bed, her face in her hands. She was wearing the silver-netted frock, with a coat of some cheap dark material thrown around shoulders which still shook with sobs.

I said gently, "Take your time, Berthe. Shall I make you some coffee?"

She shook her head, and lifted it from her hands. Her face, usually so pretty, was pinched and white. Her cheeks were streaked with tears and her eyes looked dreadful.

I sat down beside her on the bed and put an arm around her. "Don't, my dear. What is it? Can I help? Did something happen at the dance?" I felt the shoulders move. I said on a thought, "Is it Bernard?"

She nodded, still gulping. Then I felt her square her shoulders. I withdrew my arm but stayed beside her. Presently she managed to say, with rather ragged-edged composure, "You'd better get back into bed, miss. You'll get cold like that."

"Very well." I slipped back into bed, pulled the covers around me, and looked at her. "Now tell me. What is it? Can I help?"

She didn't answer for a moment. Nor did she look at me. Her eyes went around the room as if to probe the shadows, and I saw terror flick its whiplash across her face again. She licked her lips.

I waited. She sat for a moment, twisting her hands together. Then she said fairly calmly, but in a low, hurried voice, "It is Bernard . . . in a way. You know I'm—I'm going to marry Bernard? Well, he took me to the dance tonight, and I wore your frock and he said I looked a princess and he started—oh, he was drinking, miss, and he got . . . you know—"

"I know."

"He was drunk," said Berthe, "I've never seen him that way before. I knew he'd taken a good bit, of course, he often does, but he never shows it. I—we went outside together." Her eyes were on her fingers, plaited whitely in her lap. Her voice thinned to a thread. "We went to my sister's house. She and her man were at the dance. It—I know it was wrong of me, but—" She stopped.

I said, feeling rather helpless and inadequate, "All right, Berthe. Skip that part. What's frightened you?"

"He was drunk," she said again, in that thin little voice. "I didn't realize at first . . . he seemed all right, until . . . he seemed all right. Then . . . afterward . . . he started talking." She licked her lips again. "He was boasting kind of wildlike about when we were married. I'd be a princess, he said, and we'd have money, a lot of money. I'd—I'd have to marry him soon, now, he said, and we'd buy a farm and be rich, and we'd have . . . oh, he talked so wild and silly that I got frightened and told him not to be a fool and where would the likes of him get money to buy a farm. And he said . . ."

Her voice faltered and stopped.

I said, wondering where all this was leading, "Yes? He said?"

Her hands wrung whitely together in the little glow of the lamp. "He said there'd be plenty of money later on . . . when Philippe—when Philippe—"

"Yes?"

"—was dead," said Berthe on a shivering rush of breath.

My heart had begun to beat in sharp slamming little strokes that I could feel even in my finger tips. Berthe's eyes were on me now, filled with a sort of shrinking dread that was horrible. There was sweat along her upper lip.

I said harshly, "Go on."

"I—I'm only saying what he said. He was drunk . . . half-asleep. He was—"

"Yes. Go on."

"He said Monsieur de Valmy had promised him the money—"

"Yes?"

"—when Philippe died."

"*Berthe!*"

"Yes, miss," said Berthe simply.

Silence. I could see sweat on her forehead now. My hands were dry and ice cold. I felt the nails scrape on the sheets as I clutched at them. The pulse knocked in my finger tips.

This was nonsense. It was nightmare. It wasn't happening. But something inside me, some part of brain or instinct listened unsurprised. This nightmare was true, I knew it already. On some hidden level I had known it for long enough. I only wondered at my own stupidity that had not recognized it before. I heard myself saying quietly, "You must finish now, Berthe. Philippe . . . so Philippe is going to die later on, is he? How much later on?"

"B—Bernard said soon. He said it would have to be soon because Monsieur Hippolyte cabled early today that he was coming home. They don't know why—he must be ill or something; anyway he's canceling his trip and he'll be here by tomorrow night, so they'll have to do it soon, Bernard says. They've tried already, he says, but—"

I said, "They?"

"The Valmys. Monsieur and Madame and Monsieur—"

"No," I said. "No."

"Yes, miss. Monsieur Raoul," said Berthe.

Of course I said, "I don't believe it."

She watched me dumbly.

"*I don't believe it!*" My voice blazed with the words into fury. But she didn't speak. If she had broken into protestation perhaps I could have gone on fighting, but she said nothing, giving only that devastating shrug of the shoulders with which the French disclaim all knowledge and responsibility.

"Berthe. Are you sure?"

Another lift of the shoulders.

"He said so? Bernard said so?"

"Yes." Then something in my face pricked her to add: "He was drunk. He was talking—"

"I know. Kind of wild. That means nothing. But this can't be true! It can't! I know that! Berthe, do you hear me? *It—simply—isn't—true.*"

She said nothing, but looked away.

I opened my lips, then shut them again, and in my turn was silent.

I don't intend—even if I could—to describe the next few minutes. To feel something inside oneself break and die is not an experience to be relived at whatever merciful distance. After a while I managed, more or less coherently, to think, spurred to it by the savage reminder that Philippe was what mattered. All the rest could be sorted out, pondered, mourned over, later; now the urgent need was to think about Philippe.

I pushed back the bedclothes. Berthe said sharply, "Where are you going?"

I didn't answer. I slipped out of bed and flew to the bathroom door. Through the bathroom . . . across the child's darkened bedroom. . . . Bending over the bed, I heard his breathing, light and even. It was only then, as I straightened up on a shaking wave of relief, that I knew how completely I had accepted Berthe's statement. What was it, after all? A frightened girl's version of the drunken and amorous babbling of a servant? And yet it rang so true and chimed in with so many facts that without even half a hearing it seemed I was ready to jettison the employers who had shown me kindness and the man with whom an hour ago I had been in love.

Stiffly, blindly, like a sleepwalker, I went back to my own room, leaving the connecting doors ajar. I climbed back into bed.

"Is he all right?" Berthe's whisper met me, sharp and thin.

I nodded.

"Oh, miss, oh, miss. . . ." She was wringing her hands again. I remember thinking with a queer detached portion of my mind that here was someone wringing her hands. One reads about it and one never sees it, and now here it was. When at length I spoke it was in a dead flat voice I didn't recognize as my own. "We'd better get this clear, I think. I don't say that I accept what Bernard says, but—well, I want to hear it . . . all. He says there's a plot on hand to murder Philippe. If that's so, there's no need to ask why; the gains to Monsieur and Madame and— the gains are obvious."

The words came easily. It was like a play. I was acting in a play. I didn't feel a thing—no anger or fear or unhappiness. I just spoke my lines in that dead and uninflected voice and Berthe listened and stared at me and twisted her hands together.

I said, "You say 'they've tried already.' I suppose you mean the shot in the woods and the balcony rail?"

"Y—yes."

"So." I remembered then the white expectancy on Madame de Valmy's face as Philippe and I came up from the woods that day. And the night of the balcony rail: she hadn't come upstairs that night to get any tablets; she had come because she couldn't stand the suspense any longer. Léon de Valmy, stationed in the hall, must have heard the crash from the forecourt. My mind leaped on from this to recollect those two interviews with my employer in the library. I said harshly, "This could be true. Oh, my dear God, Berthe, it could be true. Well, let's have it. Who fired the shot? Bernard himself?"

"No. That was Monsieur Raoul. Bernard dug the bullet out."

I forgot about its being a play. *"I don't believe it!"*

"Miss—"

"Did Bernard say so?"

"Yes."

"In so many words?"

"Yes."

"Then he's lying. He probably did the shooting himself and—" But here I saw her face and stopped. After a while I said fairly calmly, "I'm sorry. I did ask you to tell me just what he said, after all. And I—I'm pretty sure that what he said is true in the main. It's just that I can't quite bring myself to—to believe—"

"Yes, miss. I know."

I looked at her. "Oh, Berthe, you make me ashamed. I was so wrapped up in my own feelings that I forgot the way you'd be feeling, too. I'm sorry. We're both in the same boat, aren't we?"

She nodded wordlessly.

Somehow the knowledge steadied me. I said, "Well, look, Berthe. We've got to be tough about this for Philippe's sake, and because there isn't much time. Later on we can work it out and—and decide who's guilty and who isn't. At present I suppose we must assume they're all in it, whether or not we can believe it in our heart of hearts. And I'm pretty sure that Monsieur and Madame are guilty—in fact I know they are. I'm very much to blame for not seeing it before, but who on earth goes about suspecting an impossible outlandish thing like *murder?* That's something that happens in books, not among people you *know.* I suppose I ought to have seen it straight away, when Philippe was shot at in the woods. And Raoul . . . Raoul was out there; he admitted it himself, and Bernard was sent straight out, and I suppose he removed the bullet then and went back later with someone else to 'discover' it. Yes, and I was right in thinking that Monsieur de Valmy knew I spoke French; I'd shouted it at—at the murderer in the beechwood, and talked it to Philippe all the way home. Then the affair of the balcony rail, Berthe—I suppose that and the swing in the barn were extras? Off-chances? Booby-traps that might work sooner or later?"

"Yes."

"And then the Cadillac's horn blasting at—perhaps at nothing— brought Philippe out to his death?" I added shakily, "Do I have to believe that, too?"

"I don't know what you're talking about, miss. What horn? Bernard never said anything about any horn."

"Oh? Well, skip it. It's over, thank God, without harm. Now we have to think what to do."

I looked down at my hands while I tried to marshal my thoughts. And the pattern was forming in a way I didn't want to examine too closely. It was all there. I tried to make myself look at it all quite coldly and in order, from the time when Philippe had been sent up to Valmy and so delivered by the unsuspecting Hippolyte straight into the hands of murder. . . .

The first step—and it was taken immediately—had been to get rid of the only person close to Philippe and trusted by Hippolyte—the child's nurse. Someone must replace her, and it was judged better to find a young woman without family or guardian who, in the event of an 'accident' to her pupil, wouldn't be able to call upon friends and relatives to exonerate her from possible charges of carelessness (or worse) should there be a mistake and doubts arise. So Madame de Valmy had made inquiries of a friend in London who was known to supply her friends with domestic help from an orphanage. Who better than an orphan, and a foreigner at that—someone who, in the accumulated bewilderments of a new job, a new country, and a foreign language, would hardly be in a position to observe too much or defend herself too readily. . . . There had in sober fact been that slight overemphasis on my Englishness . . . my instinct to hide my Continental origin had, absurd though it had seemed, been right.

So the scapegoat had been found and brought to France. They waited. There was plenty of time. I had been allowed to settle in; my life with Philippe formed its own quiet pattern, an ordinary day-to-day pattern which appeared pleasantly normal except that Monsieur de Valmy couldn't quite keep his bitter tongue off the child who stood between him and so much. So it had gone on. I had stayed there three weeks, settled and happy, though still not quite at ease with my employers. Then the attempt was made and, by the purest chance, it failed. The second was a longer chance, but quite safe for them—the rotten coping had already been reported, so Bernard had made sure of the stone's collapse and then waited for an accident to happen when none of the interested parties was anywhere near. And the second "accident" failed too, because of me. If the first, or even the second, had come off, "accident" would almost certainly have been the verdict . . . and no doubt an entirely baffling series of alibis was in any case available. Certainly the one person who couldn't be found guilty was the interested party, Léon de Valmy. It would have been a tragedy, and it would have blown over, whispers and all, and Léon would have had Valmy. It was even possible that there'd have been no whispers at all. . . . Léon was highly thought of, and a first-rate landlord: the country folk would for many years past have regarded him as the *seigneur,* and they might have been only too pleased when the custody of Valmy passed unequivocally into his hands.

Berthe was still crouching at the foot of my bed, watching me dumbly. I said, "And now, Berthe, what's next?"

"I don't know. I don't know."

"You must. This is what matters. Think. Bernard let so much out; he must have told you that."

"No. I don't think he knew himself. I think it wasn't to be him. That's all." She floundered, gulped, and began to sob again.

Out of nowhere, unbidden, unwanted, a picture flashed onto the dark screen of my mind. Philippe's sleeping head lolling back against Raoul's shoulder, and Héloïse's voice saying hoarsely: *"What's the matter with Philippe?"* And Raoul giving her that hard quelling look. *"Nothing at all. He's asleep."*

I said shakily, "And Bernard said nothing to indicate when? Or how?"

"No, honestly he didn't. But it was to be soon because of Monsieur Hippolyte coming back. The cable came early this morning and it really put the Master out, Bernard said."

"And Hippolyte's coming back tomorrow?" I caught my breath. *"Today,* Berthe. It's today, d'you realize that? *Today?"*

"Why . . . yes, I reckon it is. It's nearly one o'clock, isn't it? But I don't rightly know when Monsieur Hippolyte'll get here. I think it won't be till night, and then he mayn't get up to Valmy till Thursday."

I said quietly, "Monsieur Raoul has gone to Paris till Thursday, Berthe. If the cable came 'early' this morning he would probably know about it, but he still went to Paris. So he can't be in it, can he? Bernard was wrong."

She said in that dull voice that was stupid with shock and succeeded in sounding stubborn, "Bernard said he was in it. Bernard said he fired the shot."

It was useless—and cruel—to spend myself in protests. I said, "All right. The point is that if we're to decide how to protect Philippe we must have some idea where the danger's coming from. I mean, nobody's going to listen to us unless we have some sort of a case which, God knows, we haven't got yet. Let's begin with the things we know. You say it's not to be Bernard."

She gulped and nodded. She was steadier now, I saw, and her breathing was less ragged. Her hands had stopped wrenching at each other. She was listening with some sort of attention.

I said, "I think we can count out the idea that there are any more
booby-traps waiting about. They've got to make quite certain this time;
they can't wait for chance to act for them. And in any case, too many
'accidents' of the same kind might make people begin to think. That
was why Monsieur de Valmy warned me about the swing in the barn
. . . yes, he did that this afternoon, *after* he'd heard that Hippolyte was
coming back. He was as nice as ninepence, though I'd been quite sure
that he and Madame—oh, well, that doesn't matter. Well, Bernard's out,
and booby-traps are out. There are limits to what Monsieur de Valmy
can do himself, and from the way things have gone up to now I have a
feeling he'll keep well out of it, since he's the person who stands most
obviously to gain. And Raoul isn't here, so it can't be Raoul." In spite of
myself my voice lightened on the words. I said almost joyously, "That
leaves Madame, doesn't it?"

"Are you sure?" said Berthe.

"That it's Madame? Of course I'm not. But—"

"That he's gone," said Berthe.

I stared at her. "What *do* you mean?"

She gave a little boneless shrug. "It's a big place."

Something crept over my skin like a cold draft. "You mean . . . he
may still be here somewhere . . . hiding?"

She didn't speak. She nodded. Her eyes, watching me painfully, were
once more alive and intelligent.

I said almost angrily, "But he went. People must have seen him go.
Bernard said—oh, that's not evidence, is it? But his car's gone. I noticed
that when we came through the stableyard this afternoon."

"Yes, he left. I saw him. But he could have come back. There's such
things," added Berthe surprisingly, "as alibis."

I said slowly, "Yes, I suppose there are. But that he should be here
. . . hiding . . . no, it's too farfetched and absurd."

"Well," said Berthe, "but it's absurd to think Madame would do it,
isn't it?"

"Oh God," I said explosively, "it's absurd to think anyone would do
it! But I can't believe the thing hinges on Raoul. No—" as she was about
to speak—"not only for the reason you think, but because if he is in it, I
can't see where I come in at all. *That's* fantastic if you like."

"How d'you mean?"

"If he was involved in this murder thing, why get involved with me?
You know he was, of course?"

"Everybody knew."

I said bitterly, "They did, didn't they? Well, why did he? Surely it
was a dangerous and unnecessary thing to do?"

"Perhaps," she said disconcertingly, "he just can't help it. You're awfully pretty, aren't you, and Albertine says that when they were in Paris she heard—"

"Ah, yes," I said. "Albertine hears an awful lot, doesn't she? You mean that he automatically turns the power on for every young female he meets? His father's like that, have you noticed? He's got a technique all his own of disarming you with his affliction and then switching on charm like an arc light. Well, it could be, but I don't think so. Raoul's not like his father; he's got no need to waste himself where it doesn't matter. And in this case it might have been actually dangerous to get involved with me if he *was* . . . Third Murderer."

"If he is in it with them, and he started to—well, to—"

"To make love to me?"

"Yes, miss. If he did that, and, like you said, it wasn't safe, mightn't that be why Monsieur and Madame were so annoyed about it?"

"I thought they were at first, but they weren't. I told you. Monsieur was awfully nice to me this afternoon."

"Oh, but they were, miss. Albertine said you were to be sent away. Everyone knew. They were all talking about it. And why should they bother to send you away, unless Monsieur Raoul was in with them, and it wasn't safe, like you said? Otherwise you'd hardly think they'd trouble their heads about his goings-on, because—oh, I'm sorry, miss, I do beg your pardon, I'm sure."

"It's all right. 'Goings-on' will do. Well, they might be annoyed even so, because Philippe was in their charge and I—no that won't do. If they're all set to murder the child they won't give a damn about the moral code of his governess. But no, Berthe, it won't fit. It doesn't make sense. I still can't throw Monsieur Raoul in, you know. And not just because of the way I feel, either. It went too far, our affair—beyond all the bounds of reason if he *was* involved in his father's game. He asked me to marry him."

"Yes, I know."

"*You know?*"

"Yes, miss. Everybody does."

I don't think I spoke for a full five seconds. "Do they? Second sight or just more gossip?"

"I don't know what you mean. Bernard told Albertine and she told the rest of us."

"When was this?"

She looked uncomfortable. "Well, she'd been saying things about you for quite a time. She'd been saying you were, well—"

"Yes?"

"She said you were out to get him, miss, and that Monsieur and Madame were furious and you were going to be sent away. And then yesterday she was saying it had happened, like."

"Yesterday? You mean after the ball?"

"That's right."

"Did she say she knew for certain?"

"I don't know. She was sounding sure enough about it. She said—oh, well, never mind. She's a nasty one sometimes, that one."

"Yes. Let it pass. I've had my fill of Albertine. But let's think," I said a little desperately, "if she and everyone else were talking about our engagement, then, even if they hadn't been actually told, you'd think Monsieur and Madame would know too?"

"That's right, you would."

"But you said they were genuinely furious before that—when it was known that he and I were, well, interested in each other."

"Oh yes. I'm sure of that."

"But I tell you it doesn't make sense. I told you, I saw Monsieur de Valmy yesterday—when presumably he knew as much about it as everyone else—and he was extremely nice to me. And neither of them sent for me to ask me about it or—or anything. I—I can't work it out, Berthe. My head's spinning and it feels as if it's going to burst. If they *knew,* and didn't mind, then Raoul can't be in it, can he? When I saw him, Monsieur Léon must have already laid his plans because he'd already had Hippolyte's cable. . . ."

My voice trailed away into nothing. I swallowed hard. I repeated, unrecognizably: *"He'd already had Hippolyte's cable."*

In the silence that followed she stirred and the bed creaked.

I said slowly, "He and Madame *were* angry with me before; I know they were. I believe they *were* planning to send me away. But Hippolyte's cable changed all that. They had to make a plan in a hurry and that plan included me. How does *that* fit?"

"Well—"

"It does, you know. But how? *How? Are* you sure Bernard said nothing?"

"I'm sure," she said desperately. "Don't you fret, miss. I'd go bail you'll be in no danger."

"What makes you think I'm worrying about that?" I said, almost sharply. "But we must get this straight, don't you see? It's the only way we'll be able to do anything to help Philippe. What can they be planning to do that includes me? What the sweet hell can they be planning?"

She said, "Maybe you've nothing to do with it at all. Maybe they just think it'd look funny if something happened to Philippe the day you were sent off, so they've decided they'll have to keep you."

"Yes, but marriage is a bit—"

"Maybe they want to make sure you'll hold your tongue if you suspect anything," said Berthe.

"Oh, dear God," I said wearily, "they surely can't imagine that I'd suspect a child was murdered and do nothing about it?"

"But if you were going to marry him, and everyone knew—"

"What difference would that make? They'd never be idiot enough to think I'd *help* them? No, it's nonsense. They'd never use marriage as a bait to make me hold my tongue. Why, good heavens—"

"I wasn't going to say that." There was some new quality in Berthe's voice that stopped me short. She was still speaking softly, but there was some curious vibrancy in the tones that held me. She said, "Everybody knows you're engaged to Monsieur Raoul. If Philippe died, you'd be Madame la Comtesse de Valmy one day."

"What do you mean?" Then I saw. I finished in a voice that wasn't a voice at all, "You mean that when the cable came and they made their plan, it *did* include me? That they've given me a motive for murder? That they can't risk another 'accident' without a scapegoat ready to hand in case things go wrong and people ask questions? Is that what you mean?"

Berthe said simply, "Why else should he ask you to marry him?"

"Why else indeed?" I said.

I had checked up again on Philippe. He still slept peacefully. The house was quiet. I tiptoed back into my bedroom and reached for my dressing gown.

Berthe said, "Is he all right?"

I was putting the dressing gown on with hands that shook and were clumsy. "Yes. You realize, I suppose, that the likeliest time for anything to happen is tonight, now, and everybody's out at the dance except Mrs. Seddon?"

"Mr. Seddon didn't go. He stayed with her."

"Oh? Well, I'd trust them all right, but she's ill and I doubt if he'd be much use—even if they'd believe us, which isn't likely." I found my slippers and thrust my feet hastily into them. "Will you stay with Philippe and mount guard over him? Lock his door and window now."

"What are you going to do?"

"The only possible thing. What's the time?"

"Going on quarter past one. I—we came away early."

"Did Bernard come up with you?"

"Yes." She didn't look at me. "I persuaded him to bring me up in the brake. It wasn't difficult. He—he's asleep now in my room." She finished in a thin little voice: "It was awful, driving up that zigzag with him so drunk still. . . ."

I was hardly listening. I was reflecting that, apart from the Seddons, we were alone in the house with Léon de Valmy and Bernard. Thank God the latter still had to sleep it off. I said, "Was Madame de Valmy at the dance?"

"Yes, but she'll have left by now. She never stays long."

"I see. Now can I get to the telephone in Seddon's pantry without being heard or seen? Does he lock it?"

"No, miss. But he goes to bed at midnight and he always switches it through to the Master's room then."

Something fluttered deep in my stomach. I ignored it. "Then I'll switch it back again. How d'you do it?"

"There's a red tab on the left. Press it down. But—he might hear it. Miss—what are you going to do?"

"There's only one thing I can do. We must have help. D'you mean that if I use the telephone it'll ting in the Master's room or something? Because if so I can't use it. And I can't go out and leave Philippe. You may have to go for the police yourself if you can—"

"*The police?*"

I was across at the door that gave on the corridor, listening. I turned and looked back at her in surprise.

"Who else? I must tell the police all this. They may not believe me, but at least I can get them up here and if there's a fuss it'll make it impossible for another attempt on Philippe to be made. And tonight or tomorrow Monsieur Hippolyte gets back and he can take care of Philippe when the row's over and I've been sent—home."

"*No!*" said Berthe so violently that the syllable rang, and she clapped a hand to her mouth.

"What d'you mean?"

"You're not to go to the police! You're not to tell anyone!"

"But my dear girl—"

"I came to tell you because you'd been kind to me, because I liked you and Philippe. You've been so good to me—always so nice, and there was the dress and—and all. I thought you might have got mixed up in it somehow, with Monsieur Raoul and all that. . . . But you mustn't let on I told you! You mustn't!"

The new fear had sharpened her voice, so that I said urgently, "Be quiet, will you! And don't be a fool! How can you expect me to say nothing—"

"You are not to tell them about Bernard! You can go away if you're afraid!"

I must have looked at her blankly. "Go away?"

"If it's true what we said, and you're likely to be blamed for a murder! You can make an excuse in the morning and leave straight away! It's easy! You can say you don't want to marry him after all, and that you know you can't stay as governess after what's happened. It's likely enough. They can't make you stay anyway, and they won't suspect."

"But, Berthe, stop! That's only guesswork! And even if it's true you can't seriously suggest that I should *run away* and leave Philippe to them?"

"I'll look after him! I'll watch him till Monsieur Hippolyte gets back! It's only one day! You can trust me, you know that. If you upset their plans and they've nobody to blame, maybe they won't do anything!"

"Maybe they will," I rejoined grimly, "and blame you instead, Berthe."

"They wouldn't dare. Bernard wouldn't stand for it."

"You're probably right. But I'm not risking Philippe's life on any 'maybes.' And you don't understand, Berthe. The thing to be stopped isn't *my* being involved, but Philippe's murder! I know you came to warn me, and I'm grateful, but there's simply no question of my leaving. I'm going to ring the police this very minute."

Her face, paper-white, had flattened, featureless; starched linen with two dark holes torn for eyes. "No! No! No!" Hysteria shook her voice. "Bernard will know I've told you! And Monsieur de Valmy! I daren't! You can't!"

"I must. Can't you see that none of these things *matter?* Only the child."

"I'll deny it. I'll deny everything. I'll swear he never said a word or that I spoke to you. I'll say it's lies. I will! I will!"

There was a little silence. I came away from the door.

"You'd do—that?"

"Yes. I swear I would."

I said nothing for a bit. After a few seconds her eyes fell away from mine, but there was a look in her face that told me she meant what she said. I fought my anger down, reminding myself that she had lived all her life in Valmy's shadow, and that now there was the best of reasons why Bernard should still be willing—and free—to marry her. Poor Berthe; she had done a good deal: more I could hardly expect. . . .

"Very well," I said, "I'll leave you out of it and I won't mention Bernard. We'll let the past die and just deal with the future. I'll put it to the police as simply my own suspicions. I'll think of something. And then

I'll go straight along to Léon de Valmy and tell him that I've spoken to them. That should finish the matter quite as effectively."

She was staring at me as if I were mad. "You'd—*dare?*"

I had a sudden inner vision of Philippe in Raoul's arms. "Oh yes," I said, "I'd dare."

She was shivering now, and her teeth were clenched as if she was cold. "But you mustn't. He'd guess about Bernard—and me. Someone'd tell him Bernard was drunk tonight. He'd know. You can't do it."

"I must and will. Don't be a fool, Berthe. You know as well as I do that I've got to. . . ."

"No, no, no! We can look after him! With two of us he'll be all right. It's only for one day. We can watch Bernard—"

"And Madame? And Léon de Valmy? And God knows who else?"

She said blindly, hysterically, "You are not to tell! If you don't swear not to go to the police I shall go to Bernard now! He'll be sober enough to stop you!"

I took three strides to the bedside and gripped her by the shoulders. "You won't do that, Berthe! You know you won't! You can't!"

Under my hands her shoulders were rigid. Her face, still pinched and white, was near my own. My touch seemed to have shaken the hysteria out of her, for she spoke quietly, and with a conviction that no scream could have carried, "If you tell the police, and they come to see the Master, he'll guess how you found out. And there'll be a fuss, and he'll just deny everything, and laugh at it. They'll say that you—yes! They'll say you tried to marry Monsieur Raoul and were slighted and you're doing it out of spite, and then the police will laugh too and shrug and have a drink with the Master and go away. . . ."

"Very likely. But it'll save Philippe and a bit more slander won't hurt me."

"But what do you suppose will happen to me when it's all over?" asked Berthe. "And Bernard? And my mother and my family? My father and my brothers have worked at Valmy all their lives. They're poor. They've got nothing. Where can they go when they're dismissed? What can we do?" She shook her head. "You must please—*please*—do as I say. Between us we can keep him safe all right. It's best, miss, honestly it's best."

I let my hands drop from her shoulders.

"Very well. Have it your own way. I'll keep my mouth shut." I looked at her. "But I swear to you that if anything happens to Philippe—or if any attempt is made—I'll smear this story, and the Valmys across every newspaper in France until they—and Bernard—get what they deserve."

"Nothing will happen to Philippe."

"I pray God you're right. Now go, Berthe. Thank you for coming as you did."

She slid off the bed, hesitating. "The frock?"

I said wearily, "Keep it. I'll have no use for it where I'll be going. Good night."

"Miss—"

"Good night, Berthe."

The door clicked shut behind her, and left me alone with the shadows.

CHAPTER XIV

Fill the cup, Philip,
And let us drink a dram.
Anonymous Early English Lyric.

THERE WAS only one possible plan that would make certain of Philippe's safety. He had to be removed from Léon de Valmy's reach and hidden till help came.

There wasn't a minute to lose. Léon de Valmy might well assume that one-thirty would be a dead hour in the schoolroom wing. And the servants would be coming back from the dance between three and four. If anything was to be done tonight it would be done soon.

I was back at my bedside, tearing off my dressing gown with those wretchedly shaky hands, while my mind raced on out of control. I couldn't think; I didn't want to think; there were things I didn't want to face. Not yet. But Philippe had to be got away. That was all that mattered. I had decided that I didn't dare use the telephone; it might somehow betray me to Léon de Valmy, and besides, it was possible that Berthe would wait to see if I approached the pantry—and in her present shaken and terrified mood I couldn't answer for her reactions. And there was no help in Valmy. Mrs. Seddon was ill; Seddon himself was elderly, conventional and, I suspected, none too bright. Berthe and I between us might have guarded Philippe if we had only known from what danger, but as it was . . . no, he had to be got away to the nearest certain help, and then, as soon as possible, to the police. I didn't let the promise Berthe had blackmailed from me weigh with me for a second; being a woman, I put common sense in front of an illusory "honor," and I'd have

broken a thousand promises without a qualm if by doing so I could save
Philippe.

I had flung my dressing gown down and was reaching for my clothes
when I heard the sound from the corridor.

Even though I had been listening for it I didn't at first know what it
was. It came as the thinnest of humming whispers through the turmoil
of my brain. But at some level it must have blared a warning, for my
hand flashed to the bedside light and switched it off just as Philippe's
door opened very quietly, and I knew what the whisper had been. The
wheel chair.

I stayed where I was, frozen, one hand still on the light switch. I don't
think I was even breathing. If there had been the slightest sound from
the other room I think I'd have been through there like a bullet from a
gun, but the wheel chair never moved, so I stayed still, waiting.

Nothing. No movement. After a while Philippe's door shut once more,
very softly. The whisper was in the corridor again.

I don't know what instinct thrust me back into my bed and pulled the
clothes up around me, but when my bedroom door opened I was lying
quite quietly with my back to it.

He didn't come in. He simply waited there in silence. The seconds
stretched out like years. I thought, I wonder what he'd do if I turned
over, saw him, and screamed? The employer caught creeping into the
governess's bedroom, the lights, the questions, the scurrying feet in the
corridor . . . could you laugh that one off, Monsieur de Valmy? Tiny
bubbles of hysteria prickled in my throat at the thought of Léon de
Valmy pilloried in the role of vile seducer—then I remembered how
pitifully he was insured against the risk, and lay still, all my perilous
amusement gone. In its stead came a kind of shame and a pity that, rather
horribly, did nothing to mitigate my fear. There was something curiously
vile about the mixture of emotions. My muscles tensed themselves against
it and I started to tremble.

He had gone. The door had closed noiselessly behind him. I heard
the whisper of the wheels fade along the corridor, toward his room.

I slipped out of bed and padded across to the door, where I stood listening until, far down the corridor, I thought I heard another door shut
softly. Seconds later, I heard the faint whine of the lift. He had been
checking up, that was all. But he had also told me all I wanted to know.
The story was true. And I had to get Philippe out of it, and fast. Somehow I was calm again. I shut and locked my door, then with steady hands
drew the curtains close and turned on the bedside light. I dressed quickly,
picked up my coat and strong shoes, and went through the bathroom into
Philippe's room.

This was going to be the hardest part of the job. I put the coat and shoes down on the chair where I had sat for last night's midnight feast, then, with a glance at the sleeping child, I crossed to the door and locked it. Deliberately, I refused to hurry. If this was to succeed at all it must be taken calmly.

The room was light enough. The long curtains hung slightly apart, and between them a shaft of light fell, as it had done last night, to paint a bright line across the carpet. Something struck my foot as I crossed the floor, and rolled a little way, glittering. A frosted grape. Berthe had scamped the cleaning today, it seemed.

I pushed aside the heavy curtain, and latched the window. Behind me Philippe moved and sighed, and I paused and looked over my shoulder toward the bed, with one hand still on the window catch, and the other holding back the curtain.

The shadow falling across me brought me around again like a jerked puppet to face the window. Someone had come along the balcony, and was staring at me through the gap in the curtains. I stood there, held rigid in the noose of light that showed me up so pitilessly. I couldn't move. My hand tightened on the window catch as if an electric current held it there. I looked straight into Héloïse de Valmy's eyes, a foot from my own.

She showed no surprise at my presence, nor even at the fact that I was dressed to go out. She merely put a hand to the window fastening, as if expecting to find it open. She shook it, and then her hands slid over the glass as if trying to push a way in. Then she took hold of the latch once more, rattling it almost impatiently.

I could hardly refuse to let her in. I noticed that there were no pockets to her long ivory-colored robe, and that her hands were empty. Besides, if she was here to harm Philippe she would hardly demand entry from me in this unruffled fashion. Wondering confusedly how I was going to explain the fact that I was up and dressed at one-thirty in the morning, I opened the window. I said, as coolly as I could, "Good evening, madame."

She took no notice, but walked calmly past me into the room. Her robe whispered across the carpet. She stopped near the head of the bed. In the dim room her shadow threw a yet deeper darkness over the sleeping child. She put out a hand slowly, almost tentatively, to touch his face. It was a gentle touch, a meaningless gesture, but I recognized it. This was Philippe's nightmare. This had happened before.

If she had had some weapon, if her approach had been at all stealthy —anything but this apparently calm and routine visit—no doubt I would have moved more quickly. As it was, her hand was still hovering over

the boy's face when I flew after her. I reached Philippe just as her fingers
touched him. He didn't move. She drew her hand back, and straightened
up. I went around the bed and reached a protective hand to draw the
sheet up to the child's face. I faced her across the bed. Whatever my
feelings toward the Demon King, I was not afraid of his wife. I said,
"What is it, madame? What do you want?"

She didn't answer. She hadn't even acknowledged my presence. This
was carrying ostracism a bit too far. I began to say something angry,
then stopped, bewildered, to watch her.

She had turned to the little table that stood beside the bed. Her hands
moved now over the clutter of objects on the table—a lamp, a book, a
little clock, the tumbler that had held Philippe's chocolate, a couple of
soldiers, a biscuit. . . . I thought she was going to switch the light on,
and made a half-movement of protest. But her hands, groping in a
curious blind fashion, passed the lamp, moved softly over the clock and
the tin soldiers, and hovered over the tumbler. She picked this up.

I said, "Madame de Valmy—"

She turned at that. She had lifted the tumbler as if to drink from it, and
across the rim her eyes met mine again. With her back to the moonlight,
her face was a pale blur, her eyes dark and expressionless, but as I looked
at her, bewildered and beginning once more to be frightened, I understood. The goose-pimple cold slid, ghost-handed, over my skin.

The open eyes, no less than the smooth stealthy hands, were indeed
blind. . . . I stared into the woman's expressionless face for one eerie
moment longer, while the child breathed gently between us, then, very
quietly, I moved to one side, down to the foot of the bed.

She stood still, with the tumbler held to her face, staring at the place
where I had been. . . . *You see, her eyes are open: Ay, but their sense
is shut.* . . . I stood and watched her as if she were a ghost on a moonlit stage. The verses marched on through my brain as if someone had
switched on a tape recorder and forgotten it. I remember feeling a sort
of numb surprise at their aptness. *Lo you, here she comes! This is her
very guise, and upon my life, fast asleep.* . . .

So Héloïse de Valmy, like Lady Macbeth, had that weighing on her
heart which sent her sleepwalking through the night to Philippe's room.
And would she, like that other murderess, give away what she had seen
and known? I knew nothing about sleepwalkers except what I remembered of that scene in *Macbeth*. And Lady Macbeth had talked. Was it
possible that I could get Héloïse de Valmy to do the same? *Observe her,
stand close.*

I was gripping the rail at the foot of Philippe's bed. Without it, I think
I would have fallen.

I said hoarsely, "Madame."

She took no notice. She put the tumbler down surely and quietly, and turned to go. The moonlight rippled along the lovely folds of her robe; it caught her face, gleaming back from eyes wide and glossy as a doll's.

I said, "Héloïse de Valmy, answer me. How will you kill Philippe?"

She was on her way to the window. I walked with her. She went smoothly, and at the right moment her hand went up to the curtain. For one fearful moment I thought I had been mistaken and she was awake, but then I saw her fumble the curtains and hesitate as a fold tangled in her robe. The fixed eyes never moved, but she fetched a sigh and faltered. *Heaven knows what she has known.* The obsessive question burst from me. "Is Raoul helping you to kill Philippe?"

She paused. Her head inclined toward me. I repeated it urgently in her ear, *"Is Raoul helping you?"*

She turned away. It wouldn't work. She was going, and her secrets with her, still locked in sleep. I reached an unsteady hand and drew the curtain aside for her.

She walked composedly past me and out of sight along the balcony.

But she had told me one thing. I saw it as soon as I turned.

God, God forgive us all. I stood over Philippe in the moon-dappled darkness, with the tumbler in my hand.

I woke him quietly. I used a trick I had read about somewhere in John Buchan—a gentle pressure below the left ear. It seemed to work; he opened his eyes quite naturally and lay for a moment before they focused on me in the moonlight. Then he said, as if we were resuming a conversation, "I had another nightmare."

"I know. That's why I came in."

He lifted his head, and then pushed himself into a sitting position. "What's the time?"

"Half-past one."

"Haven't you been to bed yet? Have you been to the dance in the village? You didn't tell me."

"No, I haven't been out. I got dressed again because—"

"You're not going out now?" The whisper sharpened so abruptly that my finger flew to my lips.

"Quiet, Philippe. No—that is, yes, but I'm not leaving you alone, if that's what you're afraid of. You're coming, too."

"I am?"

I nodded, and sat down on the edge of the bed. The big eyes watched me. He was sitting very still. I couldn't tell what he was thinking. God knows what my voice sounded like. I know my lips were stiff. I said, "Philippe."

"Yes, mademoiselle?"

"Do you . . . feel all right? Not—not sleepy or anything?"

"Not really."

"Quite fit and wide awake?"

"Yes."

I said hoarsely, "Did you drink your chocolate?"

His eyes slid around in that narrow sidelong look toward the tumbler, then back to me. He hesitated. "I poured it away."

"You *what?* Why?"

"Well . . ." he said uncertainly, eying me, then stopped.

"Look, Philippe, I don't mind. I just want to know. Was it nasty or something?"

"Oh no. At least I don't know." Again that look. Then a sudden burst of candor, "They left the bottle last night and I found it and kept it. I didn't tell you."

I said blankly, "Bottle?"

"Yes," said Philippe, "that smashing lemonade. I had that instead. It wasn't fizzy any more but it was fine."

"You . . . never said anything when I went to make your chocolate."

"Well," said Philippe, "I didn't want to hurt your feelings. You always made the chocolate and—what's the matter?"

"Nothing. Nothing. Oh, Philippe."

"What *is* it, Miss Martin?"

"I guess I'm tired," I said. "I had a late night last night and I haven't slept tonight."

"You don't mind?"

"No, I don't mind."

"Why haven't you slept tonight?"

I said, "Now listen, *mon p'tit*. Did you know your Uncle Hippolyte is coming home tomorrow—today?"

I saw the joy blow across his face the way a gleam runs over water and felt, suddenly, a deep and calm thankfulness. There was port in this storm, it seemed.

Philippe was saying in a quick, excited whisper, "When is he coming? Why is he coming back? Who told you? When can we go to see him?"

"That's what I came to wake you for," I said, as if it was the most reasonable thing in the world. "I thought that we might go straight away. The—the sooner the better," I finished lamely, all my half-thought-out excuses dying on my lips under that steady wide stare.

"Do you mean we are going to the Villa Mireille *now?* To meet my Uncle Hippolyte?"

"Yes. He won't be there yet, but I thought—"

Philippe said, devastatingly, "Does my Uncle Léon know?"

I swallowed. "Philippe, my dear, I don't expect you to understand all this, but I want you to trust me, and come with me now as quickly and quietly as you can. Your Uncle Léon—"

"You are taking me away from him." It was a statement, not a question. His face was expressionless, but his eyes were intent, and he was breathing a little faster.

"Yes," I said, and nerved myself for the inevitable "Why?" But it didn't come. The child supplied the terrible answer for himself.

He said in that somber, unsurprised little voice, "My Uncle Léon hates me. I know that. He wishes I was dead. Doesn't he?"

I said gently, "Philippe, *mon lapin,* I'm afraid he might wish you harm. I don't like your Uncle Léon very much either. I think we'll both be better away from here, if you'll only trust me and come with me."

He pushed back the bedclothes without a second's hesitation, and grabbed at the back of his nightshirt, ready to haul it over his head. In the act he stopped. "The time I was shot at in the wood, that was not an accident?"

The question, coming grotesquely out of the folds of the nightshirt, made me gasp. There was no need, it appeared, to pretend, even about this. I said, "No, it wasn't an accident. Here's your vest."

"He tried to kill me?"

"Yes." The word sounded so flat that I added quickly, "Don't be afraid, Philippe."

"I'm not afraid." He was fighting his way into his shirt now. As he emerged from the neck of it I saw that he spoke the truth. He was taut as a wire, and the long-lashed black eyes—Valmy eyes—were beginning to blaze. "I've been afraid for a long time, ever since I came to Valmy, but I didn't know why. I've been unhappy and I've hated my Uncle Léon, but I didn't know why I was afraid all the time. Now I know, and I'm not frightened any more." He sat down at my feet and began to pull his socks on. "We'll go to my Uncle Hippolyte and tell him all this, and then my Uncle Léon will be guillotined."

"*Philippe!*"

He glanced up at me. "What would you? Murderers go to the guillotine. He's a murderer."

Tigers breed true, I thought wildly, *tigers breed true.* He had even, for a flash, had a look of Léon de Valmy himself. But he was only a child; he couldn't know the implications of what he was saying. I said,

"He's not, you know. You're still alive, and going to stay that way. Only we must hurry, and be terribly quiet. Look, your shoes are here. No, don't put them on. Carry them till we get out."

He picked them up and got up, turning toward me, then, with a sudden duck back into childhood, he reached for my hand. "Where are we going?"

"I told you. To your Uncle Hippolyte."

"But we can't go to the Villa Mireille till he's there," he said uncertainly. "That's where they'll look for us straight away in the morning."

"I know." His hand quivered in mine, and I pulled him against my knees and put an arm around him. "But we'll be quite safe. We'll follow our star, Philippe. It'll not let us down. D'you remember Monsieur Blake, the Englishman?"

He nodded.

"Well, he has a cabin up in Dieudonné woods where he spends the night sometimes. I know he's there tonight, because I saw his light shining like a star before I went to bed. We'll go up there straight away, and he'll look after us and take us to your uncle's house tomorrow. It'll be all right, you'll see. I promise you it will."

"All right. Shall I take this scarf?"

"Yes. Was that your warm jersey you put on? Good. We'll lock the balcony window, I think. . . . Okay now? Be terribly quiet."

I paused by the door, my hand on the key, and listened. Philippe drifted to my elbow like a ghost. His eyes looked enormous in a pale face. I could hear nothing. Beyond the door the great house stretched dark and almost untenanted. And Madame de Valmy was certainly asleep, and Bernard was drunk, and the tiger himself—waiting down there for death to be discovered—the tiger himself was crippled. . . .

With a hand that slipped a little on the doorknob I eased the door open, then took Philippe's hand and tiptoed with him out into the dark corridor. Past the clock that had sounded midnight for us, down the stairs where I had lost my slipper, along the dim stretches of corridor walled with blind doors and the sidelong painted eyes of portraits . . . the great house slid past us in the darkness as insubstantial as scenery in a Cocteau fantasy, until our breathless and ghostly flight was blocked by the heavy door that gave onto the stableyard and freedom.

It was locked. There must be some other way left for the servants to come in, but I didn't dare turn aside to explore. The heavy key turned easily and quietly, but still the door wouldn't move. My hands slid over the studded wood in the darkness, searching for a bolt. Beside me I heard Philippe take a little breath and begin to shiver. Standing on tiptoe, groping above my head, I found the bolt, and pulled. It moved with a scream like a mandrake torn up in a midnight wood. The sound seemed to go on and on, winding back along the corridor in a creeping echo. I pulled at the door with shaking hands, listening all the time for the whine of the wheel chair. The door wouldn't budge. Still it wouldn't budge. I tried to feel if it had a spring lock beside the key, but couldn't find one. He would be coming any minute now, to find us cornered in this dark passageway. It didn't need the shrieking bolts to tell him where we were and what we were doing. I could almost hear my panic-stricken thoughts pouring down the corridor to shout it at him. He would know. Oh yes, he would know. We were *en rapport,* the Demon King and I. . . .

"It's all right," whispered Philippe, "I brought my torch. Look."

He stooped down to the other bolt, drew it quietly, and the door opened.

We went out into the night air.

CHAPTER XV

Enter these enchanted woods,
You who dare.
GEORGE MEREDITH: *The Woods of Westermain.*

I HAD no idea how to find William Blake's forest hut, but from my window at Valmy I had noticed that the light seemed to be very near a broad, straight ride that slashed up through the pines from somewhere near the Valmy bridge. Philippe and I had only to cross the bridge and climb up from the road, bearing slightly right, and we were bound to strike the open ride. Once in this we must follow it up toward the first ridge, and no doubt sooner or later the light itself would guide us to the hut.

It sounded easy, but in practice it was a long and exhausting climb. I dared not use Philippe's torch so near the road, nor later in the ride, open as this was to every window on Valmy's west front.

In the forest it was very dark. My eyes had by now adjusted themselves, and we were able to pick our way between the trees without actual mishap, but very slowly, and with many stumbles and grazes, as the thick carpet of pine needles was crisscrossed, and in places piled with

dead and spiky branches left when the woods were thinned. Once
Philippe tripped and was only saved from falling by my hand, and once
I had to bite back a cry of pain as I stumbled against some fallen snag
of wood that stabbed at my leg for all the world like a sword. But
Philippe made no complaint and, crazy though it may sound, I myself,
with every yard of midnight wood put between me and Valmy, felt safer
and happier. This wild mountainside, tingling with the smell of the thick
pines, was for all its secret and murmurous life no place of fear; that was
Valmy with its lights and luxury. I realized that once again the word in
my mind was "escape"; it was as if the brilliance and comfort of life at
Valmy had been closing in, subtle, stifling, oversophisticated. Now I
was free. . . . The darkness took us. The air was cool and the silence
was thick with peace.

My guess had been right. After perhaps twenty minutes of our steep,
stumbling progress we came at a climbing angle upon the open ride. This
was some fifteen yards wide, and ran in a dead-straight slash from top
to bottom of the hillside. I supposed it was a fire-break, or a road left
open for tractors—whatever its purpose, it would be easier going for
Philippe and myself.

It was, we found, very little better underfoot, as here, too, the dead
boughs were thickly strewn. But at least we could see to pick our way.
Clutching at my hand, and panting, Philippe climbed gamely beside
me. We turned once to look at Valmy. On the far side of the valley the
château, catching the moon, swam pale above its own woods, its side
stabbed with a single light. Léon de Valmy still waited.

With a little shiver I turned my face back toward the sweet-smelling
wild mountain of Dieudonné, and we plodded on up the moonlit can-
yon between the pines.

"All right, Philippe?"

"Yes, mademoiselle."

If any other creature moved in the forest that night, we never saw it.
The only eyes that glittered at us were the stars, and the million drops
of stardew that shivered on the fallen boughs. The breeze was failing,
and in its pauses the breaking of the dead stuff under our feet sounded
like thunder. I found myself, absurdly, with a quick over-the-shoulder
glance at Léon de Valmy's remote little light, trying to tread more
softly, and eying in some dread the gaunt black shadows that the moon
flung streaming behind us down the open ride.

But no new terror waited under the swimming moon, and, when we
stopped to rest, no sound came to us except the labored sound of our
own breathing, and the age-old singing of the pines, and the rustle of
wind-made showers as the dew shook down from the boughs.

It was Philippe who saw the hut. I had been straining my eyes upward through the trees on our left for a glimpse of William's light, and as we neared the summit of the hill, had begun to worry to myself in case we had already passed it hidden from us by the thick pines.

Then, as we stopped for one of our now frequent breathers, Philippe tugged at my hand.

"There," he said breathlessly, and nodded toward a break in the southern wall of trees.

I turned thankfully, only to pause and stare, while a little chill slid over me.

It was certainly a hut—*the* hut, as it was placed pretty well where I had expected to find it. It was small and square, beautifully made, chalet-fashion, of hewn pine logs, with a railed veranda around it, a steep-pitched overhanging roof, and slatted wooden shutters. At back and sides the pines crowded so closely up to the eaves that you would have thought a lamp would be burning even by day.

But now the windows showed no light at all. At one there was a tiny glow, as of firelight, but the welcoming lamp—the star—was out. I stood clutching the boy's hand, and staring at those blank windows.

I noticed all at once how black the trees were and how they crouched and crowded over the hut. I saw how our shadows streamed back from us grotesque and ink-black down the open ride. I moved, and a giant gesture mocked me. The night was full of whispering.

"He'll be fast asleep," said Philippe cheerfully, and not whispering at all.

I almost jumped, then looked down at him. I had to control an impulse to hug him. "Why, of course," I said, not too steadily. "Of course. I—I was forgetting it'll soon be daylight. I hope he doesn't mind being awakened again! Come along, Monsieur le Comte!"

He set off sturdily, ahead of me this time, for the hut. I followed him thankfully. We were here, safe, at our star. It was Valmy now whose alien glimmer showed a crow's mile away. I spared a last quick glance for that cold point of light. Already it seemed remote, distance drowned. I would never go there again.

I found my eyes were full of tears. Not one, but a swarm of stars swam in the liquid distance. Angrily, I put up a hand to brush the tears away, and looked again.

Not one, but a swarm of stars.

Three lights now glared from the white bulk that was Valmy. And even as I stared, with the quick hot thrill twisting belly-deep inside me, another window sprang to life, and another. My bedroom, my sitting room, the schoolroom . . . and then I saw two tiny lights break from the shadows below and slide away as a car came out of the courtyard. The alarm had been given. Dear God, the alarm had been given. He hadn't waited till morning. He'd checked on us again, and now Valmy was up. I could almost hear the quick footsteps, the whispering, the whine of the wheel chair, the humming telephone wires. The bright windows stared with their five eyes across the valley. Then, even as I wondered through my sick panic why he should have roused the place, the lights went out quickly, one by one, and Valmy sank back into quiet. Only the single point of brilliance still showed, and below, the car's lamps dropped down two quick flickering curves of the zigzag and then vanished as they were switched off.

I'd been wrong. There had been no alarm. He'd found us gone, made sure, and then gone back to wait by his telephone. He had the rest of the night, and his hound was out after us. Bernard, drastically sobered? Raoul?

I turned and ran in under the darkness of the pines, as Philippe's soft rapping sounded on the door of the hut.

Half a minute went by; three-quarters. I stood beside Philippe, trying to still that little twist of terror deep inside me. In a moment now it would be over; the Englishman's feet would tread comfortably toward the door; the hinges would creak open; the firelit warmth would push a wedge into the cool night across the veranda floor.

The forest was still. The air breathed cold at my back. A minute; a minute and a half. No sound. He would be still asleep.

"Shall I knock again?"

"Yes, Philippe. Harder."

My nerves jumped and tingled to the sharp rap of knuckles on wood. The sound went through the stillness like the bang of a drum. It seemed to me that it must startle the whole forest awake.

In the backwash of the silence that followed I heard, away below us on the road, the snarl of a car going fast.

There was no sound from the hut.

"There's no one in." The quiver in the child's voice—he must be very tired after all—made me pull myself together.

"He's sound asleep," I said calmly. "Let's see if we can get in. He won't mind if we wake him."

Philippe lifted the latch and pushed. A little to my surprise the door opened immediately. He took a step forward, hesitating, but I propelled him gently in front of me straight into the room. The sound of that engine reiterated from the valley was making my skin crawl.

"Mr. Blake!" I called softly as I shut the door. "Mr. Blake! Are you there?"

Silence met us, the unmistakably hollow silence of an empty house.

I knew from what William had told me that the hut only had one room, with a penthouse scullery at the back. The door which presumably led to this was shut. The room in which we now stood was the living, eating, and sleeping room of the place.

He could not have been gone long. It didn't need the memory of the lighted window to prove that he had been there and until quite late. The wood stove still glowed faintly, and the smell of food hung in the air. He must have been working up here, made himself a meal, and then decided, late as it was, to go down to the Coq Hardi. The blankets on the bed in the corner were neatly folded in a pile.

It was a bare little room, its walls, floor, and ceiling all of pine, still, in the heat from the stove, smelling faintly of the forest. There were a sturdy, handmade table, a couple of wooden chairs, and a hard-looking bed with a box underneath. A small cupboard hung in one corner, and a shelf over the bed held a few books. On pegs near the stove was a miscellany of things—ropes, a rucksack, an old khaki coat. Some spare tools lay beneath on a pile of clean sacking. In the far corner an upright ladder led to a small square trap door.

"Can't we stay here?" There was the faintest suspicion of a whine in Philippe's voice; he must be very nearly exhausted, and indeed, the thought of going further appalled me. And where could we go? This must be what the mired fox felt like when it found its way to earth with the last calculated ounce of strength. I glanced at the shut door, at the glowing stove, at Philippe.

"Yes, of course." The car would be raking the road to the Villa Mireille. They would never look for us here. I said, "D'you think you could climb that ladder?"

"That? Yes. What's up there? Why do we have to go up there?"

"Well," I said, "there's only one bed down here, and that's Mr. Blake's. He may come back and need it. Besides, we'd be better hidden away up there, don't you think? Can you keep as still as a mouse if anybody comes in?"

He looked up at me, big eyes in a pinched little face. He was biting his lip. He nodded. I think if Léon de Valmy had come in at that moment I could have killed him with my bare hands. As it was I said briskly, "Well, we mustn't leave any sign we've been here, just in case somebody else comes looking for us before Mr. Blake gets home. Are your shoes wet? Ah, yes, they are a bit, aren't they? So are mine. We'll take them off—no, stay on the mat, *petit*—that's fine. Now, you carry them and perch here by the stove while I reconnoiter the loft."

Luckily the trap door was light, and, it seemed, in frequent use. At any rate it opened easily and quietly, and, standing on the ladder with my head and shoulders through the opening, I raked the loft with the beam of Philippe's torch. I had been praying fervently as I climbed that the place would be not too bad. Now I gave a sigh of relief. The loft was almost as clean as the living room, and quite dry. It was used as a storeroom, and I could see some boxes and canisters, some more rope, a drum of wire, and—what was more to the purpose—a pile of tarpaulins and sacking on the chimney side of the steep-roofed little chamber.

I went quickly down again and reported this to Philippe. "It's beautifully warm," I said cheerfully, "right over the stove. Can you shove your shoes in your pockets and swarm away up while I collect some blankets? I'll pass them up to you. I can't spare the torch for a moment, so don't explore too far."

As I had hoped, there were extra blankets in the box under the bed. I dragged these out with wary flashes of the torch, and with some little trouble got them one by one up the ladder and into Philippe's waiting grasp. At last I pulled myself up beside him, and sent a final beam raking the little room. . . . Nothing betrayed us; the floor was dry, the bed undisturbed, the door shut but not locked. . . .

We shut the trap door quietly and crawled—only in the center of the loft could one stand—to make our bed. The warmth from the chimney was pleasant, the blankets thick and comforting; the little dark loft with its steep-pitched roof gave an illusion of safety.

So presently, having shared a stick of chocolate and said our prayers, from both of which exercises we derived immense comfort, we settled down for what remained of the night.

Philippe went to sleep almost immediately, curled in his usual small huddle up against me. I tucked the blankets thankfully around him, and then lay listening to his light breathing, and to the million tiny noises of the large silence that wrapped us in.

The breeze seemed finally to have dropped, for the forest—so close to us lying up under the shingles—was still. Only a faint intermittent murmur, like a long sigh, came from the pines. Inside the cottage came, from time to time, the tiny noises of a building stirring in its sleep; the creak of a settling board, the fall of charred wood in the stove, the tiny scratching of a mouse in the wall. I lay there, trying to empty my mind of worry and speculation about the coming day. It was Wednesday; only the one day to go and then I could deliver my charge, either at the Villa Mireille itself, or, if that proved difficult, by any telephone. The thing was easy. Easy.

And if, as seemed likely, William Blake called at the mountain hut in the morning, then it became easier still. Once we had him as escort the last shred of danger vanished. All I had to do now was relax and try to sleep. Neither Léon de Valmy nor Bernard would think of looking for us here. I had once spoken of "William" to Raoul (the thought brought me momentarily awake again) and he might connect the name—but of course Raoul wasn't in it. Raoul was in Paris. He had nothing to do with it. We were safe here, quite safe. . . . I could sleep. . . .

The lifting of the door latch sounded, in that sleepy silence, like a pistol shot.

Even as one part of my mind stampeded in panic like the mice now scurrying from the sound, the other rose light and dizzy with relief. It was William Blake, of course. It couldn't be anyone else. I must have slept longer than I'd thought, and now it was early morning, and he had come back.

I lifted my head to listen, but made no other movement. Something else which had nothing whatever to do with my mind and its conclusions kept me clamped down like a hare in her form.

I waited. Philippe slept.

Below us the door shut very softly. The newcomer took two or three steps, then stopped. I could hear him breathing hard, as if he'd been hurrying. He stood perfectly still for a long time. I waited for the homely sounds of a log in the stove, the rasp of a match, the opening of the scullery door, but there was nothing except the stillness, and the rapid breathing. And then there was a pause of complete silence, as even the breathing stopped.

I think mine did too. I knew now it wasn't William Blake. I knew why he had paused with held breath, standing with ears at the stretch and, probably a torch-beam raking the darkness. He had been listening for sounds of the quarry. It couldn't be true, but it was. The hound was here already.

Then his breath came out again with a gasp, and he moved across the floor.

Now came the quiet *chunk* of closing shutters, the chink of the lamp globe, the scrape of a match; but the sounds were about as homely as the click of a cocked gun.

I heard the slight clatter of the globe sliding into its socket, then a muttered curse as, I suppose, the wick went out again. Seconds later came the scrape of another match.

It couldn't be morning yet, and it certainly wasn't William Blake. The curse had been in French, and in a voice I thought I recognized. Bernard's. The hunt was up with a vengeance.

The lamp was burning now. I could see, here and there, tiny threads of light between the ceiling boards. He was moving about, with a slow deliberation that was far more terrifying than haste. Only his breathing still hurried, and that, surely, should have been under control by now. . . .

I found that I was shaking, crouched together in my form of blankets. It wasn't the climb up the mountainside that had hurried Bernard's breathing and made his big hands clumsy on the lamp. It was excitement, the tongue-lolling excitement of the hound as it closes in. He knew we were here.

He crossed the floor to the base of the ladder.

But he was only making for the scullery. I heard the door open, then more sounds of that deliberate exploration. A bolt scraped: he was barring the back exit. He was coming back.

My bitten lips tasted salt; my hands were clenched so tightly on a fold of blankets that my nails scored the stuff. I hadn't told Philippe about Bernard, had I? If he should wake, he might not be frightened . . . but let him sleep, dear Lord, let him sleep. . . . Perhaps Bernard doesn't know about the loft; perhaps he won't notice the ladder . . . if only Philippe doesn't wake up and give us away. . . .

He came out of the scullery and shut the door. This time he didn't pause to look around. He took two unhurried strides across to the ladder. I heard the wood creak as he laid hold of it.

Someone trod rapidly across the veranda outside. I heard Bernard jerk out an oath under his breath. The door opened again. A strange voice said, "*Que diable?* Oh, Bernard, it's you. What the devil are you doing up here?"

The ladder creaked again as Bernard released it. "*Holà,* Jules." He sounded sober enough, but his voice was thick and not too steady. He seemed disconcerted, almost shaken. "I might ask you the same, mightn't I? What brings you up here at this hour?"

The other shut the door and came across the room. "Night patrols, a curse on it. Ever since we had that fire up in Bois-Roussel we've had them. The boss is convinced it's willful damage and he won't listen to anything else. So I have to tramp up and down between Bois-Roussel and Soubirous the whole bloody night, and me only a fortnight wed. Dawn's a lousy time to be out in anyway, and when I think where I might be—"

Bernard laughed and moved away from the ladder. "Hard luck, friend. I expect you make out, *tout de même.*"

"As to that," said Jules frankly, "I can go to bed the whole bloody day, can't I? Here, let's make this stove up . . . aha, that's better! Now, tell me what brings you up here at this hour? It's gone five, surely? If you're wanting the Englishman he's down at the Coq Hardi for the night. What's he done?"

Bernard said, so slowly that I could almost hear the calculation clicking behind the words, "No, it's not the Englishman."

"No? What then? Don't tell me you're my fire-raiser, Bernard?" Jules laughed. "Come now, what's up? Come clean or I'll have to take you in for trespass. It's bound to be either duty or a woman, and I'm damned if I can see why either should bring you up here."

"As it happens, it's both," said Bernard. "There's queer doings at the Château Valmy tonight. You've heard of young Philippe's governess; Martin's her name?"

"The pretty little thing that's been dangling after Monsieur Raoul? Who hasn't? What's she done?"

"She's disappeared, that's what she's done and—"

"Well, what if she has? And what the devil would she be doing up here anyway? There's an obvious place to look for her, my friend, and that's in Monsieur Raoul's bed, not the Englishman's."

"For God's sake can't you keep your mind out of bed for two minutes?"

"No," said Jules simply.

"Well, try. And let me finish what I was telling you. Here. Have a cigarette."

A match snapped and flared. The sharp smell of the Gauloise came up through the boards to where I lay. I could see the two men as plainly as if the ceiling were of glass, their dark faces lit by the crackling stove, the blue smoke of the cigarettes drifting up through the warm air to hang between them. Bernard said, still in that queer note of overmeasured thoughtfulness, "The boy's gone, too."

"The boy?"

"Young Philippe."

A pause, and a long soft whistle. "Great God! Are you sure?"

"Damn it, of course we're sure! They've both vanished. Madame went along a bit ago to have a look at the boy—he's not strong, you know, and it seems she's been worried about him. She's not sleeping very well . . . anyway, she went along, and he wasn't in his room. She went to rouse the governess and found her gone, too. No word, no note, no nothing. We've searched the château from cellar to roof, the Master and I. No sign. They've gone."

"But what in the world for? It doesn't make sense. Unless the girl and Monsieur Raoul—"

"You can leave him out of it," said Bernard sourly. "I've told you she's not snug in *his* bed. For one thing, what would she want with the boy if that's where she's bound? He'd not be a help, would he?"

"No, indeed," said Jules, much struck. "But—well, the thing's crazy! Where would they go, and why?"

"God knows." Bernard sounded almost indifferent. "And they'll probably turn up very soon anyway. The Master didn't seem very worried, though Madame was properly upset. It's made her ill—she has a bad heart, you know—so the Master told me to get out and scout around the place for them. I've been down to Thonon, but there's no sign. . . . He paused, and then I heard him yawn.

Beside me Philippe moved a little and stretched in his sleep. His shoes must have been lying near him, and through the blankets his knee touched one of them and pushed it with a small scraping sound over the boards. It was the slightest of noises, but it seemed to fill the pause like thunder.

But Bernard had heard nothing. He was saying, indifferently, "Ten to one it's all nonsense anyway. I probably shouldn't have told you about it, but since you've caught me on your land—" He laughed.

"But why should they be up here?"

"The Master's idea. It seems the girl was seen in Thonon with the Englishman. I tell you, the whole thing's crazy. It stands to reason it's only one of two things; either they're both off together on some silly frolic, or the boy's gone out adventuring on his own and the girl's found him gone and set off to fetch him back."

Jules sounded dubious. "It doesn't seem very likely."

Bernard yawned again. "No, it doesn't, but boys are queer cattle—almost as queer as women, friend Jules. And he and the Martin girl are very thick. The two of them had a midnight feast the other night, so I'm told. They'll not have gone far . . . the boy hasn't got his papers. Depend on it, it'll be some silly lark or other. What else could it be?"

"Well, as long as Monsieur isn't worried," said Jules doubtfully. There was a little silence, through which I heard the hiss of the stove and the shifting of a man's feet. Then Bernard said briskly, "Well, I think I'd better be off. Coming?"

Jules didn't answer directly. He said, in a voice which had a tentative, sidelong sound, "That girl Martin . . . There was talk. A lot of talk."

"Oh?" Bernard didn't sound interested. As if you didn't know, I thought, lying in my form not four feet from his head.

"People were saying," said Jules hesitantly, "that she and Monsieur Raoul were fiancés."

"Oh, that," said Bernard. A pause. "Well, it's true."

"*Diable!* Is it really? So she got him?"

"If you put it that way."

"Don't you?"

"Well," said Bernard, sounding amused, "I imagine Monsieur Raoul may have had something to say in the matter. You can't tell me that any girl, however pretty, could lead that one up the garden path unless he very much wanted to go."

"There's ways and ways," said Jules sagely. "He knows what he's about, of course, but damn it, there comes a time. . . ." He laughed. "And she's nothing like his usual. That gets us every time, doesn't it? Fools."

"He was never a fool," said Bernard. "And if he wants to marry her—well, that's what he wants."

"You don't persuade me he's really fallen, do you? For the little English girl? Be your age, man. He wants to sleep with her and she won't let him."

"Maybe. But it's quite a step from that to marriage . . . for such as him."

"You're telling me. Well, perhaps the reason's more pressing still. Perhaps she has slept with him and now there's a little something to force his hand. It has been done," said Jules largely. "I should know."

"Oh? Congratulations." Bernard's voice sounded almost absent. "But I doubt if that's it."

That's big of you, I thought, biting my knuckles above him while Jules' words crawled like lice along my skin. The stove top clanked as someone lifted it to drop a cigarette butt on the logs. Bernard said again, "Look, I must go. Are you coming?"

"Bernard . . ." Jules had dropped his voice for all the world as if he knew I was listening. He sounded urgent and slightly ashamed. The effect was so queer, so horrible almost, that my skin prickled again.

"Well?" said Bernard, impatiently.

"The girl—"

"Well?" said Bernard again.

"Are you so sure . . . that she—" Jules paused and I heard him swallow—"that she means well by the boy?"

"What the devil d'you mean?"

"Well . . . I told you there'd been talk. People have been saying that she . . . well, has ambitions."

"Ambitions? Who hasn't? Very likely she has, but why should that make her 'not mean well' by the brat? What d'you—" Bernard's voice trailed off and I heard him draw in his breath. He said on a very odd note, "You can't mean what I think you mean, friend Jules."

Jules sounded defiant. "Why not? Why should her ambitions stop at marrying Monsieur Raoul? What does anyone know about her after all? Who is she?"

"An English orphan—I think of good family. That's all I know." A pause. "She's fond of the boy."

Jules said, "The boy will not make her Madame la Comtesse de Valmy."

A longer pause. Bernard's laugh, breaking it, sounded a little strained. "The sooner you get back to that bed of yours the better, *mon ami*. The night air's giving you fancies. And I must get back. Ten to one the thing's over and they're both safely back in bed. I hope Monsieur gives them hell in the morning for all the trouble they've caused. Come now—"

Jules said stubbornly, "You may laugh. But I tell you that Monsieur Garcin said—"

"That old woman of a chemist? You should have better things to do than listen to village clack."

"All the same—"

Bernard said irritably, "For God's sake, Jules! You can't make every pretty girl a criminal because she makes a play for her betters. Now look, I've got to go. Which way are you bound?"

Jules sounded sulky. "Down toward Soubirous. It's wearing on for morning."

"And your trick's over? Right. I'll go down that way with you. I brought the brake up to the end of the track, so I'll run you down. You go on now while I turn the lamp down and close up."

"Okay." The stove top clanked again as the second cigarette butt followed the first. I heard Jules tread heavily toward the door. Beside me Philippe stirred again and muttered something in his sleep. The footsteps stopped. Jules said sharply, "What was that?"

"What?"

"I heard something. Through there, perhaps, or—"

Bernard said softly, "Open the door. Quickly." Jules obeyed. The fresh gray-morning smell pierced the blue scent of cigarettes and woodsmoke. "Nothing there." Jules' voice came as if from a distance. I imagined him out on the veranda peering around the wall.

Bernard, just below us still, laughed his short hard laugh. "A mouse, friend Jules. You're seeing a tiger in every tree tonight, aren't you?" He stretched noisily and yawned. "Well I'm for bed as well, though mine'll not be as warm as yours, I'm afraid. What time does the Englishman get up here as a rule?"

"Pretty early—that is, if he's coming up here this morning. I wouldn't know."

"Ah. Well, let's be going. I hope to God the excitement's over down at Valmy. Why the hell the Master should send me up here anyway I can't imagine. Go on, *mon ami*. I'll turn the lamp down and close up. I'll follow you."

"I'll wait for you."

"Eh? Oh, very well . . . there, that's it. I suppose the stove's safe? Yes, well . . . I'd have thought that bed of yours would have put a bit of hurry into you, friend Jules." He was going. His voice dwindled toward the door. Beside me Philippe moved his head and his breath touched my cheek softly.

Jules' voice said, with the good temper back in it, "Ah, that bed of mine. Let me tell you, *copain* . . ."

The door shut quietly, lopping off Jules' embroidery of his favorite motif. I heard his voice faintly, fading off into the dawn-hush that held the forest. I hadn't realized how quiet it was outside. Not a bough moved; not a twig brushed the shingles. Philippe breathed softly beside me. From somewhere a wood pigeon began its hoarse cooing.

Soon the sun would be up. It would be a lovely day. I lay back beside Philippe, shaking as if I had the fever.

The reprieve from terror had been so sudden that it had thrown me out of gear. All through that conversation I had crouched, straining every sense to interpret the two men's intentions, but with my mind spinning in a useless, formless confusion. At one moment it seemed to me that I ought to call out and disclose our presence to Jules, who was not a Valmy employee, and who would at any rate save us from any harm that Bernard might intend. At the next moment I found myself dazedly listening to Jules accusing, Bernard defending me. And what he'd had to say was odd enough: Léon de Valmy was not perturbed; it was known that I was fond of the boy; and Monsieur Raoul "could be left out of it. . . ." Bernard, in fact, had taken some pains to suppress the very gossip that I had imagined he and Albertine had engineered. No wonder I was shaken and confused. Had I been wrong? Could I possibly have been wrong? Surely Léon de Valmy, if he were guilty, must know from my flight with Philippe that I suspected him. If he were guilty, he couldn't be unperturbed; and if he were guilty, why should Bernard defend me to Jules? *And Raoul was out of it.* Dear Lord, had I been wrong?

But something fretted at me still. The whole conversation had had about it a curious air of inversion, something off-key that had sounded in Bernard's defense of me and in that slow, deliberative tone he had used.

I lay there quietly, savoring our safety and the stillness of Dieudonné, while the pigeon cooed peacefully in the pine-tops outside, and the racing blood in my body slowed down to normal. Philippe stirred again and said, "Mademoiselle?" and relaxed once more into sleep. I smiled a little, thinking with another quick uprush of relief that, had he spoken so clearly before, Bernard must surely have heard him. After all, he had been standing just below us, while Jules was almost at the door. . . .

On the thought I came upright in the darkness, dry-lipped, my heart going wild again in my breast.

Bernard must surely have heard him. Of course Bernard had heard him.

Bernard had known we were there.

So that was it. No other explanation would fit the facts and explain the curious overtones to that conversation. No wonder it had seemed off-key. No wonder I had been bogged down between friend and enemy.

Bernard had known. And it hadn't suited him to find us while Jules was there. That was why, though he'd been interrupted on his way up to the loft, he hadn't finished the search. That was why he had refused to "hear" what Jules had heard; why he had tried to get Jules to go on ahead while he stayed behind to "close up."

It also explained very effectively his playing down of the effect of our flight at Valmy. Whatever was discovered in the morning, it was obvious that Bernard's presence in the forest would have to be explained. The simplest and safest thing to do was obviously to tell some version of the truth. With me crouched not four feet above his head he'd had to play a very careful game. I was listening, and he didn't want to flush the quarry . . . not before he had a chance to come back alone.

Because of course he would come back. I was out of my blankets almost before the thought touched me, and creeping soundlessly across the floor to the trap door. For all I had heard Jules talking away down the forest path I was taking no risks of a door that closed to leave the enemy inside and waiting. I lay flat beside the trap and slowly, slowly, eased it up till the tiniest crack showed between it and the floor. I peered through as best I could. Some light through the badly-fitting shutters showed an empty room.

I flew back to Philippe's side, but as I put out a hand to shake him awake I checked myself. I knelt beside him, my hands clutched tightly together, and shut my eyes. I could not waken the child on this wave of shaking terror. I must take control again. I must. I gave myself twenty seconds, counting them steadily.

He would come back. He would take Jules home in the shooting brake, let himself be seen starting for Valmy, and then he would come back. He would be as quick as he could, because the night was wearing on for morning, and the night and the day were all they had.

I didn't take the thought further; I didn't want it put into words. I left it formless, a beat of fear through my body. How they would get away with it I couldn't—wouldn't—imagine, but in my present state of mind and in that dark hole at the top of the lonely forest anything seemed possible. I knelt there and made myself count steadily on through perhaps the worst twenty seconds of my life, while the terror, pressing closer, blew itself up into fantasy . . . the Demon King watching us from behind that bright window a mile away, hunting us down from his wheel chair by some ghastly kind of radar that tracked us through the forest. . . . I whipped the mad thought aside but the image persisted; Léon de Valmy, like a deformed and giant shadow, reaching out for us wherever we happened to be. Why had I thought I could get the better of him? Nobody ever had, except one.

The silly tears were running down my face. I bent to rouse Philippe.

CHAPTER XVI

Seventh Coach

Oh Sammy, Sammy, vy worn't there a alleybi!
DICKENS: *Pickwick Papers.*

HE CAME AWAKE instantly. "Mademoiselle? Is it morning?"

"Yes. Get up, chicken. We've got to go."

"All right. Are you crying, mademoiselle?"

"Good heavens, no! What makes you think that?"

"Something fell on me. Wet."

"Dew, *mon p'tit*. The roof leaks. Now come along."

He jumped up straight away, and in a very short space of time we

were down that ladder, and Philippe was lacing his shoes while I made
a lightning raid on William Blake's cupboards.

"Biscuits," I said cheerfully, "and butter and—yes, a tin of sardines.
And I brought cake and chocolate. Here's riches! Trust a man to look
after himself. He's all stocked up like a squirrel."

Philippe smiled. His face looked a little less pinched this morning,
though the gray light filtering through the shutters still showed him pale.
God knows how it showed me. I felt like a walking ghost.

"Can we make up the stove, mademoiselle?"

"Afraid not. We'd better not wait here for Monsieur Blake. There are
too many people about in the wood. We'll go on."

"Where to? Soubirous? Is that where he is?"

"Yes, but we're not going toward Soubirous. I think we'll make
straight for Thonon."

"Now?"

"Yes."

"Without breakfast?" His mouth drooped and I'm sure mine did too.
There had been a tin of coffee in the cupboard and the stove was hot; I'd
have given almost anything to have taken time to make some. Almost
anything.

I said, "We'll find a place when the sun's up and have breakfast outside. Here, put these in your pockets." I threw a quick glance around the
hut. "All right, let's go. We'll make sure no one's about first, shall we?
You take that window . . . carefully now."

We reconnoitered as cautiously as we could from the windows, but
anyone could have been hidden in the trees, watching and waiting. If
Bernard had taken Jules down to Soubirous he wouldn't be back yet, but
even so I found myself scanning the dim ranks of the trees with anxious
fear. Nothing stirred there. We would have to chance it.

The moment of leaving the hut was as bad as any we had yet had. My
hand on the latch, I looked down at Philippe.

"You remember the open space, the ride, that we came up? It's just
through the first belt of trees. We mustn't go across it while we're in
sight of Valmy. We must go up this side of it, in the trees, till we've got
over the top of the ridge. It's not far. Understand?"

He nodded.

"When I open this door, you are to go out. Don't wait for me. Don't
look back. Turn left—that way—uphill, and run as fast as you can. Don't
stop for anything or anyone."

"What about you?"

"I'll be running with you. But if—anything—should happen, *you are
not to wait for me.* You are to go on, across the hill, down to the nearest

house, and ask them to take you to the police station in Thonon. Tell them who you are and what has happened. Okay?"

His eyes were too big and bright, but he nodded silently.

On an impulse, I bent and kissed him.

"Now, little squirrel," I said, as I opened the door, *"run!"*

Nothing happened, after all. We slipped out of the hut unchallenged, and still unchallenged reached the summit of the ridge. There we paused. We had broken out of our hiding place with more regard for speed than silence, but now we recollected ourselves and moved quietly but still quickly for a hundred yards more of gentle downhill before we halted on the edge of the ride.

Peering through a convenient hazel bush we looked uphill and down. The ride was straight and empty. On the far side the trees promised thick cover.

We ran across. Pigeons came batting out of the pine tops like rockets, but that was all. We scurried deep into the young forest of larch and spruce, still so thickly set that we had to brush a way between the boughs with hands constantly up to protect our eyes.

The wood held the wet chill of early morning, and the boughs dripped moisture. We were soon soaked. But we held on doggedly on a long northward slant that I hoped would eventually bring us to a track or country road heading toward Thonon.

It was Philippe who found the cave. I was ahead of him, forging a way through the thick branches and holding them back for his passage, when I pushed through a wet wall of spruce, to find myself on the edge of an outcrop of rock. It was a miniature cliff that stuck out of the half-grown trees like the prow of a ship. The forest parted like a river and flowed down to either side, leaving the little crag with its mossy green apron open to the sky. I could hear the drip of a spring.

I said, "Watch your step, Philippe. There's a drop here. Make your way down the side. That way."

He slithered obediently down. I followed him.

"Miss Martin, there's a cave!"

I said thankfully, "And a spring. I think we might have a drink and a rest, don't you?"

Philippe said wistfully, "And breakfast?"

"Good heavens. Yes, of course." I had forgotten all about food in the haste that was driving me away from Bernard, but now I realized how hungry I was. "We'll have it straight away."

It wasn't really a cave, just a dry corner under an overhang, but it provided some shelter from the gray forest chill, and—more—gave us an illusion of safety. We ate without speaking, Philippe seemingly intent on his food, I with my ears straining for sounds that were not of the forest. But I heard nothing. The screech of a jay, the spattering of waterdrops off the trees, the clap of a pigeon's wing and the trickle of the spring beside us . . . these made up the silence that held us in its safety.

And presently the sun came up and took the tops of the springtime larches like fire.

It may sound a silly thing to say, but I almost enjoyed that morning. The spell of the sun was potent. It poured down, hot and bright, while in front of it the wet grayness steamed off the woods in veils of mist, leaving the spruces gleaming darkly brilliant and lighting the tiny larch flowers to a red flush along the boughs. The smell was intoxicating. We didn't hurry; we were both tired, and, since we had followed no paths, it would only be the purest chance that would put Bernard onto our trail. And on this lovely morning it was impossible to imagine that such an evil chance existed. The nightmare was as good as over. We were free, we were on our way to Thonon, and Monsieur Hippolyte arrived tonight. . . . And meantime the sun and the woods between them lent to our desperate adventure, not the glamour of romance, but the everyday charm of a picnic.

We held hands and walked sedately. In the older belts of the forest the going was easy. Here the trees were big and widely spaced, and between them shafts of brilliant sunlight slanted down onto drifts of last-year's cones and vivid pools of moss. Ever and again the wood echoed to the clap and flurry of wings as the ringdoves rocketed off their roosting places up into the high blue.

Presently ahead of us we saw brighter sunlight at the edge of the mature forest. This ended sharply, like a cliff, for its whole steep length washed by a river of very young firs—babies, in all the beauty of rosy stems and a green as soft as wood sorrel. They split the older forest with a belt of open sunshine seventy yards wide. Between them the grass was thick and springing emerald already through the yellow of winter. On their baby stems the buds showed fat and pink.

We halted again at the edge of the tall trees before braving the open space. The young green flowed down the mountainside between its dark borders, plunging into the shadow that still lay blue at the bottom of Dieudonné valley. Looking that way I could see the flat fields where cattle grazed; the line of willows that marked a stream; a scatter of houses; a farm where someone—tiny in the distance—stood among swarming white dots that must be hens.

No one was on the hillside. The inevitable wood pigeon played high above the treetops, riding the blue space like surf in ecstatic curved swoops and swallow dives, wings raked back and breast rounded to the thrust of the air.

Nothing else moved. We plunged—Philippe was chest-high—across the river of lovely young trees. The grass-green tufts brushed hands and knees softly, like feathers; they smelled of warm resin. Halfway across Philippe stopped short and cried, "Look!" and there was a fox slipping like a leaf-brown shadow into the far woods. He paused as he reached them and looked back, one paw up and ears mildly inquiring. The sun was red on his fur. Along his back the fine hairs shone like gold. Then he slid quietly out of sight and the forest was ours again.

All morning the enchantment held, our luck spinning out fine and strong, like the filigree plot of a fairy tale. Almost, at times, we forgot the dark and urgent reason for our journey. Almost.

Some time before noon we came, after a slowish journey of frequent stops, and one or two forced diversions, on the road I had hoped to find. This was a narrow road between steep banks, that wound stonily the way we wanted to go, high above the valley which carried the main traffic route to the south. Our last stage had taken us through a rough tract of thorns and dead bracken, so it was with some thankfulness that we clambered through the wire fence and negotiated the dead brambles that masked the ditch.

Our luck had made us a little careless. As I landed on the gravel surface of the road, and turned to reach a hand to Philippe, the clang of metal and the swish of a car's tires close behind me brought me around like a bayed deer.

A battered Renault coasted around the bend in a quiet whiffle of dust that sounded a good deal more expensive than it looked. She slithered—with a few bangs and rattles that belied that expensively silent engine—to a stop beside us. The driver, a stout gray-stubbled character in filthy blue denims, regarded us benevolently and without the least curiosity from under the brim of a horrible hat.

He was a man of few words. He jerked a thumb toward the north. I said, "S'il vous plaît, monsieur." He jerked the thumb south. I said, "Merci, monsieur," and Philippe and I clambered into the back seat to join the other passengers already there. These were a collie dog, a pig in what looked like a green string bag, and a rather nasty collection of white hens in a slatted box. A large sack of potatoes rode de luxe beside the farmer in the front seat. As I began, through the embraces of the collie, to say rather awkwardly, "This is very kind of you, monsieur," the Renault lurched forward and took a sharp bend at a fairly high

speed and still without benefit of engine, but now with such a succession
of clanks and groans and other body noises that conversation—I realized
thankfully—was an impossibility.

He took us nearly two miles, then stopped to put us down where a
farm track joined the road.

To my thanks he returned a nod, jerked his thumb in explanation
down toward the farm, and the Renault after it. The track down which
he vanished was a dirt road of about one in four. We watched, fascinated, until the Renault skated to a precarious standstill some two
inches from the wall of a Dutch barn, and then turned to go on our way,
much heartened by an encounter with someone who quite obviously had
never heard of the errant Comte de Valmy, and who was apparently
content to take life very much as it came. He might also, I thought
cheerfully, be deaf and dumb. Our luck seemed to be running strongly
enough even for that.

Our road ran fairly openly now along the hillside, so we kept to its
easier walking. The lift had done something to cheer Philippe's flagging
spirits; he walked gamely and without complaint, but I could see that he
was tiring, and we still had some way to go . . . and I had no idea
what we might yet have to face.

He set off now cheerfully enough, chatting away about the collie and
the pig. I listened absently, my eyes on the dusty length of road curling
ahead of us, and my ears intent on sounds coming from behind. Here
the road wound between high banks topped with whins. I found myself watching them for cover as we passed.

Half a mile; three-quarters; Philippe got a stone in his shoe and we
stopped to take it out. We went on more slowly after that. A mile; a mile
and a quarter; he wasn't talking now, and had begun to drag a bit; I
thought apprehensively of blisters, and slackened the pace still further.

I was just going to suggest leaving the road to find a place for lunch
when I heard another car. An engine, this time, coming from the north.
She was climbing, and climbing fast, but for all that, making very little
more noise than the old Renault coasting. A big car: a powerful car
. . . I don't pretend I recognized the silken snarl of that engine, but I
knew who it was. The sound raked up my backbone like a cruel little
claw.

I breathed, "Here's a car. Hide, Philippe!"

I had told him what to do. He swarmed up the bank as quick and
neat as a shrew mouse, with me after him. At the top of the bank was a
thicket of whins, dense walls of green three or four feet high with little
gaps and clearings of sunlit grass where one could lie invisibly. We
flung ourselves down in one of these small citadels as the Cadillac took

a bend three hundred yards away. The road leveled and ran straight below us. He went by with a spatter of dust and the *hush* of a gust of wind. The top was down and I saw his face. The little claw closed on the base of my spine.

There was no sound in the golden noon except the ripple of a skylark's song. Philippe whispered beside me, "That was my cousin Raoul, mademoiselle."

"Yes."

"I thought he was in Paris?"

"So did I."

"Is he—couldn't we have—wouldn't he have helped us?"

"I don't know, Philippe."

He said, on a note of childish wonder, "But . . . he was so nice at the midnight feast."

A pause.

"Wasn't he, mademoiselle?"

"I—yes. Yes, Philippe, he was."

Another pause. Then, still on that terrible little note of wonder, "My cousin Raoul? My cousin Raoul, too? Don't you trust him, mademoiselle?"

"Yes," I said, and then, desperately, *"No."*

"But why—"

"Don't Philippe, please. I can't—" I looked away from him and said tightly, "Don't you see, we can't take risks of any kind. However sure we are we've got to be—we've got to be sure." I finished a bit raggedly. "Don't you see?"

If he saw anything odd in this remarkably silly speech he didn't show it. With a shy but a curiously unchildlike gesture he put out a hand and touched mine. "Mademoiselle—"

"I'm not crying, Philippe. Not really. Don't worry. It's only that I'm tired and I didn't get much sleep last night and it's long past time for food." Somehow I smiled at him and dabbed at my face while he watched me with troubled eyes. "Sorry, *mon p'tit.* You're standing this trek of ours like a Trojan and I'm behaving like a fool of a woman. I'm all right now."

"We'll have lunch," said Philippe, taking a firm hold of the situation.

"Okay, Napoleon," I said, putting away my handkerchief, "but we'd better stay where we are for a little while longer, just to make sure."

"That he's really gone?"

"Yes," I said, "that he's really gone."

Philippe relaxed obediently into the shelter of the whins, and lay chin on hand, watching the road below him through a gap in the thick green.

I turned on my back so that the sun was on my face, and closed my eyes. Even then I didn't want to face it. I wanted to go on, blind, cowardly, instinct-driven . . . but as I lay there listening for the engine of his car the thing that I had been trying to keep back, dammed out of mind, broke over me. And before I had thought further than simply his name I knew how very far I was—still was—from jettisoning him along with the others. Instinct might make me shrink from Léon de Valmy, and keep me a chilly mile away from Héloïse, but—it seemed—whatever evidence, whatever "proof" I was offered, I still sprang without thought straight to his defense.

Because you want it that way. Haven't you been enough of a fool, Cinderella? I stirred on the warm grass with sharp discomfort, but still somewhere inside me hammered the insistent advocate for the defense. . . .

Everything that had happened since Raoul had entered the affair, everything he had said and done, could bear an innocent interpretation as well as a guilty one . . . or so I told myself, groping wearily, confusedly, back through the fogs of memory. A word here, a look there— never did frailer witnesses plead more desperately. He had not known of the attempts to get a non-French-speaking governess; he hadn't been worried, only amused, at the thought that I might have eavesdropped on his father's conversation; he had seemed as shocked as I was over the shooting in the wood; his sharp questions about William Blake, and that curiously touchy temper he had shown, might have been due to jealousy or some other preoccupation, and not to the realization that the "friendless" orphan was in touch with a tough-looking Englishman in the neighborhood; and that blast of the horn that brought Philippe out onto the balcony—that might have been fortuitous. Bernard hadn't spoken of it. As for Bernard's flat statement to Berthe that it had been Raoul who had shot at Philippe in the wood, I didn't regard that as evidence at all. Even in his drunken mood, and however sure he had made himself of Berthe, Bernard might well hesitate to admit that kind of guilt to her. Then at the dance . . .

But here the pleading memories whirled up into a ragged and flying confusion, a blizzard so blinding that, like Alice among the cards, I came to myself trying to beat them off. And I was asked to believe that these, too, were dead and painted like a pack of cards? Something to put away now in a drawer, and take out again, years hence, dusty, to thumb over in a dreary game of solitaire? Yes, there it was. For Philippe's sake I had to assume Raoul's guilt. I couldn't afford to do anything else. The child had only one life to lose, and I couldn't stake it. Raoul was guilty till he could be proved innocent. In that, if in no other part of my crazy fear-driven plans, I had been right. He was here but we couldn't run to him.

Close to my ear Philippe whispered, "Mademoiselle."

I opened my eyes. His face was close to mine. It was scared. He breathed, "There's someone on the hilltop behind. He's just come through the wood. I think it's Bernard. D'you suppose he's in it too?"

I nodded and put a swift finger to my lips, then lifted my head cautiously and peered through the screening whins toward the hill behind us. At first I saw nothing but the trees and the tangling banks of scrub, but presently I picked him out. It was Bernard. He was above us, about two hundred yards away, standing beside a big spruce. There was no need to tell Philippe to keep close; we both lay as still as rabbits in our thickets of green. Bernard was standing motionless, scanning the slope below him. The moments dragged. He was looking our way. His gaze seemed to catch on us, to linger, to pass on, to return . . .

He was coming quickly down the hill in our direction.

I suppose a rabbit stays still while death stalks it just because it is hoping against hope that this is not death. We stayed still.

He had covered half the distance, not hurrying, when I heard the Cadillac coming back.

My hand pressed hard over Philippe's on the short turf. I turned my head and craned to stare up the road. My muscles tensed themselves as if they would carry me without my willing it straight down into his path.

I don't know to this day whether I really would have run to him then or not, but before I could move I heard the brakes go on. The tires bit at the soft gravel of the road and the car pulled up short some fifty yards away from us. I could see him through my screen of whins. He was looking uphill toward Bernard. The horn blared twice. Bernard had stopped. I saw Raoul lift his hand. Bernard changed course and walked quickly down the hill toward the car. He jumped the ditch and hurried up to the door. Raoul said something to him, and I saw Bernard shake his head, then turn with a wide gesture that included all the hill from where we lay back to Dieudonné. Then Raoul gave a sideways jerk of the head and Bernard went around the hood and got in beside him.

The Cadillac went slowly by below us. Raoul was lighting a cigarette and his head was bent. Bernard was talking earnestly to him.

I turned to meet Philippe's eyes.

After a while I got up slowly and reached a hand down to him.

"Come along," I said, "let's get back from the road and find somewhere to have lunch."

After we had eaten we took to the woods again without seeing another soul, and some time in the middle of the afternoon our path led us out of a wild tangle of hornbeam and honeysuckle onto a little green plateau; and there, not so very far to the north of us we saw at last, through the tops of the still-bare trees, the blue levels of Lac Léman.

CHAPTER XVII

Upon thy side, against myself I'll fight,
And prove thee virtuous. . . .
Shakespeare: *Sonnet 88.*

"This," I said, "is where we stop for a while."

Philippe was surveying the little dell. It was sheltered and sun-drenched, a green shelf in the middle of the wood. Behind us the trees and bushes of the wild forest crowded up the hill, dark holly and the bone-pale boughs of ash gleaming sharp through a mist of birch as purple as bloom on a grape. Below the open shelf the tangle of boughs fell steeply toward Thonon. Those bright roofs and colored walls were, I judged, little more than a mile away. I saw the gleam of a spire, and the smooth sweep of some open square with brilliant flowerbeds and a white coping above the lake. Even in the town there were trees; willows in precise Chinese shapes, cypresses spearing up Italian-fashion against the blue water, and here and there against some painted wall a burst of pale blossom like a cloud.

At my feet a small stream ran, and a little way off, under the flank of a fallen birch, there were primroses.

Philippe slipped a hand into mine. "I know this place."

"Do you? How?"

"I've been here for a picnic. There were foxgloves and we had *pâtisseries belges.*"

"Do you remember the way down into Thonon? Where does it land us?"

He pointed to the left. "The path goes down there, like steps. There's a fence at the bottom and a sort of lane. It takes you to a road and you come out by a garage and a shop where they keep a ginger cat with no tail."

"Is it a main street?"

He wrinkled his forehead at me. "We—ell . . ."

"Is it full of shops and people and traffic?"

"Oh, no. It has trees and high walls. People *live* there."

A residential area. So much the better. I said, "Could you find your way from there to the Villa Mireille?"

"Of *course*. There's a path between two garden walls that takes you to the road above the lake and then you go down and down and *down* till you get to the bottom road where the gate is. We always went by the funicular."

"I'm afraid we can't. Well, that's wonderful, Philippe. We're practically there! And with you as guide—" I smiled at him—"we can't go far wrong, can we? Later we'll see how much I can remember of what you told me about the Villa Mireille, but just for the moment I think we'll stop and rest."

"Here?"

"Right here."

He sat thankfully down on the fallen birch. "My legs are *aching*."

"I'm not surprised."

"Are yours?"

"Well, no. But I did miss my sleep last night and if I don't have a rest this minute I shall go to sleep on my feet."

"Like a horse," said Philippe, and giggled, albeit a little thinly.

I flicked his cheek. "Exactly like a horse. Now, you get tea ready while I make the bed."

"English tea?"

"Of course."

The grass was quite dry, and the sun stood hot overhead in the calm air. I knelt down beside the birch log and carefully removed two dead boughs, a thistle, and some sharp stones from our "bed," then spread out my coat. Philippe, solemn-eyed, was dividing the last of William's biscuits into equal parts. He handed me mine, together with half a stick of chocolate. We ate slowly and in silence.

Presently I said, "Philippe."

"Yes, mademoiselle?"

"We'll be down in Thonon pretty soon now. We really ought to go straight to the police."

The big eyes stared. He said nothing.

I said, "I don't know where the nearest British Consul is, or we'd go to him. I don't suppose there's one in Évian, and we can't get to Geneva because you've no passport. So it should be the police."

Still he said nothing. I waited. I think he knew as well as I did that the first thing the police would do would be to face us both with Léon de Valmy. After a while he asked, "What time will my Uncle Hippolyte get home?"

"I've no idea. He may be here already, but I think we may have to wait till late . . . after dark."

A pause. "Where is this Monsieur Blake?"

"I don't know. He may be out somewhere in Dieudonné, or he may have gone back up to the hut. But we—we couldn't very well wait for him there." He gave me a quick look and I added hastily, "We might telephone the Coq Hardi from Thonon. They might be able to give him a message. Yes, that's a good idea. We can try that."

Still he said nothing. I looked at him a little desperately. "You want to go and look for your uncle first? Is that it?"

A nod.

"Philippe, you'd be quite safe if we went to the police, you know. We—we should do that. They'd be frightfully nice to you, and they'd look after you till your Uncle Hippolyte came—better than I can. We really should."

"No. Please. Please, Miss Martin."

I knew I ought to insist. It wasn't only the eloquence of Philippe's silences, and the clutch of the small cold hand that decided me. Nor was it only that I was afraid of facing Léon de Valmy . . . though, with the anger spilled out of me and dissolved in weariness, my very bones turned coward at the thought of confronting him in the presence of the police.

There was another reason. I admitted it out of a cold gray self-contempt. I might have braved Léon de Valmy and the police, but I didn't want to face Raoul. I was a fool; moreover, if I allowed any more risk to the child I was a criminal fool . . . but I would not go to the police while there was any chance that Raoul might be involved. I wasn't ready, yet, to test the theories of that advocate for the defense who pleaded still so desperately through today's tears. I couldn't bring the police in . . . not yet. If they had to be told, I didn't even want to be there. I was going to wait for Monsieur Hippolyte and, like a craven, hand the whole thing to him. Let the *deus ex machina* fly in out of the clouds and do the dirty work. I was only a woman, and a coward, and not ready, even, to face my own thoughts.

I gave a little sigh. "All right. We'll go to the Villa Mireille first. In any case they've already searched it."

"How d'you know?"

"Eh? Oh, well, I imagine they have, don't you? But your uncle won't be there yet, *petit,* of that I'm sure. We'll stay here a little while and rest.

I don't feel fit for very much more just yet. Here, you may as well finish the last of the chocolate."

"Thank you." He gave me a watery smile. "I'm sleepy."

"Well, curl up there and sleep. I'm going to."

"I'm thirsty, too."

"I imagine the stream's all right. It comes straight down the hillside. Let's risk it anyway."

We drank, and then lay down in the sun, curled close together on my coat, and soon we slept.

I needn't have been afraid that any restless ecstasy of the mind would keep me awake. Sleep fell from nowhere like a black cloud and blotted me out. I never stirred or blinked until the sun had his chin on the hilltop beyond Dieudonné valley, and the shadows of the naked trees stretched long-fingered across the glade to touch us with the first tiny chill of evening.

Philippe was awake already, sitting with knees drawn up and chin on them, gazing a little somberly at the distant housetops, purpling in the fading light. The lake was pale now as an opal, swimming under the faint beginnings of mist. In the distance on the further shore we could see, touched in with rose and apricot, the snows of Switzerland.

Brightness falls from the air. . . . I gave a little shiver, then got to my feet and pulled the silent Philippe to his. "Now," I said briskly, "you show me that path of yours, *petit,* and we'll be on our way."

His memory proved accurate enough. The path was there, and the narrow country road, and the corner with the garage and the shop, past which we hurried in case anyone should recognize him from his previous visits. He never spoke, and his hand in mine had become perceptibly more of a drag. I watched him worriedly. His frail energy was running out visibly now, sand from the brittle glass. I thought of the long wait that probably still lay ahead of us, and bit my lip in a prolonged pain of indecision.

The dusk had fairly dropped now over the town. We walked along a high-walled street where the pavements were bordered with lopped willows. The lamps had come on, and festoons of gleaming telegraph wires pinned back the blue dusk. Few people were about. A truck started up from the garage and drove off with a clatter, its yellow lights like lion's eyes in the half-light. A big car purred by on its own hasty business. Two workmen on bicycles pedaled purposefully home. From a side street came the raucous voice of a radio and the smell of frying.

Philippe stopped. His face, lifted to mine, looked small and pale. He said, "That's the way, mademoiselle."

I looked to my right where a vennel led off the street between two high ivy-covered walls. It was narrow and unlighted, vanishing into shadow within twenty yards. A loose spray of ivy tapped the wall; its leaves were sharp and black and clicked like metal.

From the opposite side of the road came a burst of laughter, and a woman's voice called something shrill and good-natured. The café door clashed, and with the gush of light came once again the heavenly hot smell of food.

The child's hand clutched mine. He said nothing.

Well, what was luck for if it was never to be tempted?

I turned my back on the black little alley. Two minutes later we were sitting at a red-topped table near the stove while a long thin man with a soiled apron and a face like a sad heron waited to be told what we would have to eat.

To this day I vividly remember the smell and taste of everything we had. Soup first, the first delicious hot mouthful for almost twenty-four hours. . . . It was *crème d'asperge,* and it came smoking-hot in brown earthenware bowls with handles like gnomes' ears, and asparagus tips bobbed and steamed on the creamy surface. With the soup came butter with the dew on it, and crusty rolls so new that where they lay on the plastic tabletop there was a tiny dull patch of steam.

Philippe revived to that soup as a fern revives to water. When his omelette arrived, a fluffy roll, crisped at the edges, from which mushrooms burst and spilled in their own rich gravy, he tackled it with an almost normal small boy's appetite. My own brand of weariness demanded something more solid and I had a steak. It came in a lordly dish with the butter still sizzling on its surface and the juices oozing pinky-brown through the mushrooms and tomatoes and tiny kidneys and the small mountain of crisply-fried onions . . . if *filet mignon* can be translated as *darling steak* this was the very sweetheart of its kind. By the time that adorable steak and I had become one flesh I could have taken on the whole Valmy clan singlehanded. I complimented the waiter when he came to clear, and his lugubrious face lightened a little.

"And what to follow, mademoiselle? Cheese? A little fruit?"

I glanced at Philippe, who shook his head sleepily. I laughed, "My little brother's nearly asleep. No, no cheese for me, thank you, monsieur. A *café filtre,* if you please, and a *café au lait.* I fingered the purse in my pocket. "And a Bénédictine, please."

"Un filtre, un café au lait, une Bénédictine."

He swept the last crumb from the table, gave the shiny red top a final polish with his cloth, and turned away. I said, "Could monsieur perhaps get me some *jetons?"*

"Assuredly." He took the money I held out and in a short time the cups were on the table and I had a little pile of *jetons* in front of me.

Philippe roused himself to blink at them. "What are those?"

I gaped at him. Then it came to me that Monsieur le Comte de Valmy had, of course, never had to use a public telephone. I explained softly that one had to buy these little metal plaques to put in the slot of the telephone.

"I should like to do it," said Monsieur le Comte decidedly, showing a spark of animation.

"So you shall, *mon gars,* but not tonight. Better leave it to me." And I rose.

"Where are you going?" He didn't move, but his voice clutched at me.

"Only to the corner behind the bar. See? There's the telephone. I'll be back before my coffee's filtered. You stay here and drink your own— and Philippe, don't look quite so interested in those men over there. Pretend you've been in this sort of place dozens of times, will you?"

"They're not taking any notice."

Nor were they—yet. The only other occupants of the little café besides ourselves were a gang of burly workmen absorbed in some card game, and a slim youth with hair cut *en brosse* whispering sweet somethings into the ear of a pretty little gipsy in a tight black sweater and skirt. Nobody after the first casual glance had paid the slightest attention to us. The *stout patronne* who sat over some parrot-colored knitting behind the bar merely smiled at me and nodded as I picked my way between the tables toward her and asked if I might telephone. Nobody here, at any rate, was on the lookout for a young woman with brown hair and gray eyes, on the run with the kidnaped Comte de Valmy.

It wasn't only luck that protected us, I thought, as I fumbled with the half-forgotten intricacies of the telephone; it was common sense to suppose that the chances of our being seen and recognized now, here, were very small. One had read dozens of "pursuit" books, from the classic *Thirty-nine Steps* onward, and in all of them the chief and terrible miracle had been the unceasing and intelligent vigilance of every member of the population. In sober fact, nobody was much interested. . . .

Here one of the card players raised his eyes from the game to look at me; then he nudged his neighbor and said something. The latter looked up too, and his stare raked me. My heart, in spite of the soothing logic of my thoughts, gave a painful jerk, as with an effort I forced my gaze to slide indifferently past them. I turned a shoulder and leaned against the wall, waiting, bored, for my connection. From the corner of an eye I saw the second man say something and grin. I realized with a rush of amused relief that any pursuit that those two might offer would have

other and quite natural motives that had nothing whatever to do with
the errant Comte de Valmy.

"*Ici le Coq Hardi,*" quacked a voice in my ear.

I jerked my attention back to it, and my imagination back to the
teeming little inn at Soubirous.

"I want to speak to Monsieur Blake, please."

"Who?"

"Monsieur Blake. The Englishman from Dieudonné." I was speaking
softly, and mercifully the radio was loud enough to prevent my being
overheard. "I understand he stays with you. Is he there now?"

There was some altercation, aside, that I couldn't make out. Then it
stopped abruptly, as if cut off by a hand over the mouthpiece. To my
fury I found that my own hand was damp on the receiver.

Then the voice said into my ear, "No, he's not here. Who's that wanting him?"

"Is he likely to be in tonight?"

"Perhaps." Was I being jumpy, or was it suspicion that put the edge on
that unfriendly voice? "He didn't say. If you ring back in half an hour.
. . . Who is that speaking, please?"

I said, "Thanks very much. I'll do that. I'm sorry to have—"

The voice said, harsh and sharp, "Where are you speaking from?"

Suspicion. It bit like an adder. And the Coq Hardi was on Valmy land
and presumably the news would reach the château just as quickly as
wires could carry it. If I could put them off—let them think I was safe
for another half-hour . . .

I said pleasantly, with no perceptible hesitation, "From Évian. The
Cent Fleurs. Don't trouble Monsieur Blake. I'll ring him up later on.
Thank you so much."

And right in the teeth of another question I rang off.

I stood for a moment looking unseeingly at the telephone, biting my
lip. Needless to say I had no intention of waiting to ring up again, but in
putting off pursuit I had also put off William Blake. If he got my message
at all, and if he was aware of the story that must by now be rife in Soubirous, he might realize I needed help and set straight off for Évian
and the huge crowded floor of the Cent Fleurs, which certainly wouldn't
remember if a young woman accompanied by a small boy had used the
telephone at some time during the evening.

Somehow I was very sure of William Blake's desire—and solid capac-
ity—to help. Now I had had to cut myself off from that, and only now
did I realize how much I had depended on the comfort of his company
when the inevitable showdown came. I was well aware that even the
interview with Hippolyte wouldn't be altogether plain sailing. Never

before had I felt so miserably in need of a friend—someone who, even if they could do nothing, would simply be there. I gave myself a mental shake. I mustn't start this. Just because, for a few short hours, I had laid flesh and spirit in other hands, I didn't have to feel so forsaken now. I'd hoed my own row for long enough—well, it seemed I must go on doing just that. What one has never really had, one never misses. Or so they say.

I went back to my table, unwrapped three lumps of sugar, and drank my coffee black and far too sweet. The Bénédictine I drank with appreciation but, I'm afraid, a lack of respect. It was the effect, and not the drink I craved. I took it much too quickly, with half a wary eye on the card players in the other corner.

Then, just as they were nicely involved in a new round of betting, I quietly paid the waiter, nodded a good night to Madame and went—unfollowed except by Philippe—out of the café.

CHAPTER XVIII

If thou wilt leave me, do not leave me last,
When other petty griefs have done their spite,
But in the onset come. . . .
                    SHAKESPEARE: *Sonnet 90.*

THE VILLA MIREILLE stood right on the shore of Lac Léman. It was one of a row of large wealthy houses—châteaux, almost—which bordered the lakeside, being served to landward by a narrow pretty road some two hundred feet below the town's main boulevards. Most of the houses stood in large gardens plentifully treed and guarded from the road by high walls and heavy gates.

It was dark when we reached the Villa Mireille. The gate was shut and as our steps paused outside there was the rattle of a heavy chain within, and a dog set up a deep barking.

"That's Beppo," whispered Philippe.

"Does he know you?"

"No—I don't know. I'm frightened of him."

Here the door of the concierge's lodge opened, and the light from it rushed up the trees that made a crowded darkness beyond the gate. A woman's voice called something, shrilly. The barking subsided into a whining growl. The door shut and the trees retreated into murky shadow.

I said, "Is there another way in?"

"You can get in from the lake-shore. The garden runs right down, and there's a boathouse. But I don't know the way down along the lake."

"We'll find it."

"Are we going further?" His voice was alarmed and querulous; tears of pure fatigue were not far away.

"Only to find a way down to the lake. We can't go in past Beppo and Madame—what did you say her name was?"

"Vuathoux."

"Well, unless you'd like to go straight to her—"

"*No.*"

I said, "You'd be safe, Philippe."

"She would telephone my Uncle Léon, wouldn't she?"

"Almost certainly."

"And my cousin Raoul would come?"

"It's possible."

He looked at me. "I would rather wait for my Uncle Hippolyte. You said we could."

"All right. We'll wait."

"Would you rather wait for my Uncle Hippolyte?"

"Yes."

"Then," said Philippe, swallowing, "perhaps we will find the way quickly?"

We did—three houses along from the Villa Mireille. A small wicket, swinging loose, gave onto a dim shrubbery, and as we slipped cautiously inside we could see the dim bulk of a house looming unlighted among its misty trees. No dog barked. We crept unchallenged down a long winding path, along beside a high paling bordering an open stretch of grass, and eventually once again between big trees toward the murmur of the lake.

Neither moon nor stars showed tonight.

Over the water mist lay patchily, here thick and pale against the dark distances, here no more than a haze veiling the lake's surface as breath mists a dark glass, here as faint as the sheen that follows a finger stroking dark velvet. Long transparent drifts of vapor wreathed up from the water and reached slow fingers across the narrow shore toward the trees. The water lapped hollowly on the shingle beside us as we crunched our way back toward the villa's garden. The night was not cold, but the water breathed a chill into the air, and the slowly-curling veils of mist brushed us with a damp that made me shiver.

"That's the boathouse," whispered Philippe. "I know where the key's kept. Are we going to go in?"

The boathouse was a small square two-storied building set, of course, over the water, at the head of an artificial bay made by two curving stone jetties. The shore was very narrow here, and from the yard-wide strip of shingle rose the steep bank crowded with trees that edged the grounds of the Villa Mireille. The rear wall of the boathouse was almost built up against this bank, and the beeches hung their branches right over the roof. Mist and darkness blurred the details, but the general effect of desertion, looming trees, and lapping water was not just exactly what the moment demanded for Philippe and me.

I said briskly, "I want to go up through the garden and take a look at the house. For all we know he's already here. Would you like to stay in the boathouse? You could lock yourself in, and we'd have a secret signal—"

"*No,*" said Philippe again.

"All right. You can scout up the garden with me. Very carefully, mind."

"Madame Vuathoux is deaf," said Philippe.

"Maybe. But Beppo isn't. Come on, *petit.*"

The bank was steep and slippery with clay and wet leaves that lay in drifts between the roots of the beeches. Above it was the rough grass of a small parkland studded with more of the great trees. We crept softly from one huge trunk to the next; the spring grass was soft and damp underfoot, and there was, incongruously, the smell of violets. Elms now, and horse chestnuts. I could feel the rough bark of the one, and the sticky buds of the other licked at my hand. The hanging fronds of willow brushed us wetly, clung, hindered us. We pushed through into a grove of willows as thick as a tent, and paused. We were almost at the house now. The willows curtained the edges of a formal lawn; the terrace of the house lay beyond this, thirty yards away. Near us was the metallic gleam of a small pool and I could see something that looked like a statue leaning over it.

I took Philippe's hand and we crept softly up behind the plinth of the statue, where the willows hung like an arras down to the water's surface. I pulled the trailing stems aside and scanned the façade of the house. None of the windows showed light, but there appeared to be a lamp over the front door, illuminating the drive. The door itself was out of our range of vision, but the glow of the lamp showed part of a circular gravel sweep, and banks of rhododendrons. Up here the mist was still only a blurring of the air, a thickening of the lamplight that lay like hoar-frost on the wet leaves.

I said softly, "The windows on the terrace. What room's that?"

"The salon. It's never used. My uncle Hippolyte has his study up-stairs. The end window. There's no light in it."

I looked up at it. "Then I'm afraid he's not home yet."

"Are we going in?"

I thought for a moment. "Where's the back door?"

"Round the other side, near the lodge."

"And near Beppo? Then that's out. And I doubt if there are any windows open. And there's that light over the front door. . . . No, Philippe, I think we'll wait. What do you think?"

"Yes. I—*there's a car!*"

His hand gripped mine almost painfully. The road was not more than twenty yards away on our right. A car was coming along it, slowing down rapidly through its gears. Brakes squealed. A door slammed. Footsteps. A bell clanged. Seconds later through the clamor of the dog we heard the chink of iron and the squeak of a hinge, as Madame Vuathoux hastened to open the gates.

Philippe's grip tightened. *"My uncle Hippolyte!"*

A man's voice said something indistinguishable beyond the banked shrubs.

"No," I said on a caught breath. "Raoul."

The cold hand jerked in mine. I heard the concierge say, in the loud toneless voice of the very deaf, "No, monsieur. Nothing, monsieur. And has there been no trace of them found?"

He said curtly, "None. Are you sure they couldn't have got in here? This is where they'll make for, that's certain. Is the back door locked?"

"No, monsieur, but I can see it from my window. Nobody has been there. Or to the front. Of that I am sure."

"The windows?"

"Locked, monsieur."

"No telephone call? Nothing?"

"Nothing, monsieur."

There was a pause. In it I could hear my own heart hammering.

"All the same," he said, "I'll have a look around. Leave the gates open, please. I'm expecting Bernard here any minute."

Another heart-hammering pause. Then the car started up and the lights turned in slowly off the road, slithering metallically across the sharp leaves of the rhododendrons. He parked it in front of the door, and got out. I heard him run up the steps, and then the door shut behind him. The dog still whimpered and growled a little. Back at the lodge, the concierge called something to it, and after a few moments it fell silent.

I felt the cold hand twitch in mine. I looked down. The child's face

was a blur with great dark pools for eyes. I whispered, "Keep close behind the statue. He may put some lights on."

I had hardly spoken before the salon windows blazed to brilliant
oblongs, and the light leaped out across the terrace to touch the lawn.
We were still in shadow. We waited, tense behind the statue. It was the
figure of a boy, naked, leaning over to look at himself in the pool; a
poised, exquisite Narcissus, self-absorbed, self-complete. . . .

Room after room leaped into light, was quenched. We followed his
progress through the house; light and then black darkness. The windows
on the terrace facing us remained lit. Finally they were the only ones.
He came to one of the long windows, opened it, and stepped out onto
the terrace. His shadow leaped across the lawn to the edge of the water.
He stood there for a minute or two, very still, staring at the night. I put
a gentle hand on Philippe's head, pushing it down so that no faint probe
of light would touch his face. We were crouching now. My cheek was
against the stone of the plinth. It was cold and smooth and smelt of
lichen. I didn't dare lift my head to look at Raoul. I watched the tip of
his shadow.

Suddenly it was gone. In the same moment I heard another car come
fast along the road. Lights swept in at the gate. The salon windows went
black, blank. I lifted my head and waited, straining my ears.

Steps on the gravel. Raoul's voice, still on the terrace, saying, "Bernard?"

"Monsieur?" The newcomer came quickly around the corner of the
house. I heard Raoul descending the terrace steps. He said in that quick
hard voice he had used to Madame Vuathoux, "Any sign?"

"None, monsieur, but—"

I heard Raoul curse under his breath. "Did you go back to the hut?"

"Yes. They weren't there. But they'd been, I swear they—"

"Of course they had. The Englishman was up there last night till midnight. I know that. They'd go to find him. Have you found out where he
is?"

"He's not back yet. He went out with a party up to the plantation beyond Bois-Rousel early this morning and they're not back yet. But,
monsieur, I was trying to tell you. I rang up just now, and they told me
she'd telephoned him at the Coq Hardi. She—"

"She telephoned him?" The words flashed. "When?"

"Thirty to forty minutes ago."

"*Sacré dieu.*" I heard his breath go out. "Where was she speaking
from? Did the fools think to ask?"

"Yes, indeed, m'sieur. They had heard the scandal from Jules, you
understand, and—"

"Where was she speaking from?"

"The Cent Fleurs, in Évian. They said—"

"Half an hour ago?"

"Or three-quarters. No more."

"Then the Englishman can't have heard anything. He must be still away with the party. She's not with him yet."

He turned away abruptly and Bernard with him. Their voices faded but I heard him say roughly, "Get over to Évian immediately with that car. I'm going myself. We have to find them, and quickly. Do you hear me? Find them."

Bernard said something that sounded surly and defensive, and I heard Raoul curse him again. Then the voices faded around the corner of the house. Seconds later the Cadillac's engine started, and her lights swept their circle out of the driveway. The dog was barking once more. Madame Vuathoux must have come out of her cottage at the sound of the second car, for I heard Bernard speak to her, and she answered him in that high, overpitched voice, "He said he'd be here at twelve. Twelve at the latest."

Then Bernard, too, was gone. I lifted my head from the cold plinth and slid an arm around Philippe. I waited for a moment.

Philippe said, with excitement coloring the thin whisper, "He's coming at twelve. Did you hear?"

"Yes. I don't suppose it's far off nine now. Only three more hours to wait, *mon gars*. And they've gone chasing off to Évian."

"He came down the terrace steps. He must have left a window open. Shall we go in?"

I hesitated, then said dully, "No. Only three more hours. Let's play it quite safe and go back and lock ourselves in the boathouse."

The boathouse looked, if possible, rather more dismal than before. Philippe vanished around the back of it and after a minute reappeared with a key which he displayed with a rather wan air of triumph.

"Good for you," I said. "Lead the way, *mon lapin*."

He went cautiously up the steep outside stair to the loft over the boats. The treads were slippery with moss and none too safe. He bent over the door, and I heard the key grate around in the lock. The door yawned, creaking a little, on a black interior from which came the chill breath of dust and desertion.

"Refuge," I said, with a spurious cheerfulness that probably didn't deceive Philippe at all, and switched on the torch with caution.

The loft, thank heaven, was dry. But that was its only attraction. It was a cheerless little black box of a place, a dusty junk hole crowded with the abandoned playthings of forgotten summers. I found later that one of the concrete piers of the harbor had a flat platform in its shelter which in happier days made a small private lido. Here in the loft had been carelessly thrust some of the trappings that in July's sunshine were so amusingly gay; striped canvas chairs, a huge folded umbrella of scarlet and dusty orange, various grubby objects which looked as if, well beaten and then inflated, they might be air cushions, a comical duck, a sausage-like horse with indigo spots. . . . Seen by flashlight in the chilly April dark, with a vigil ahead of us and fear at our elbow, they looked indescribably dreary and grotesque.

There was a small square window low down in the shoreward wall. I propped a canvas chair across it to conceal the flashlight from a possible prowler, then turned to lock the door.

Philippe said dolefully behind me, "What are we going to do till twelve o'clock?"

"Failing Peggitty and chess," I said cheerfully, "sleep. I really don't see why you shouldn't. You must be worn out, and there's nothing now to worry you and keep you awake."

"No," he said a little doubtfully, then his voice lightened. "I shall sleep in the boat."

"Little cabbage, the boat isn't there. Besides, how wet. Now up here," I said falsely, gesturing with the light toward the dreary pile, "it's much nicer. Perhaps we can find—"

"Here it is." And Philippe had darted past me and was pulling out from under three croquet mallets a half-deflated beachball and a broken oar, a flat yellowish affair that looked like a cyclist's mackintosh.

"What in the wide world—" I said.

"The boat."

"Oh. Oh, I see. Is it a rubber dinghy? I've never seen one."

He nodded and spread his unappetizing treasure out on the unoccupied half of the floor. "You blow it up. Here's the tube. You blow into that and the sides come up and it's a boat. I want to sleep in it."

I was too thankful that he had found something to occupy him to object to this harmless whim.

"Why not?" I said. "It's a good solid damp-proof ground sheet anyway. And after all, who minds a little dust?"

"It's not a ground sheet. It's a *boat*." He was already rootling purposefully behind some dirty canvas in a corner.

"*Ça se voit,*" I said untruthfully, eying it.

"You blow it *up,*" explained Philippe patiently, emerging with an unwonted spot of color in his face, from between an oil drum and the unspeakable spotted horse.

"Darling, if you think either of us has got enough blow left in them—"

"With *this*." He was struggling with some heavy-seeming object. I took it from him.

"What is it?"

"A pump. It's *easy*. I'll *show* you." He was already down on the floor beside the dismal yellow mass, fitting the nozzle of the pump to the mouth of the tube. I hadn't the heart to dissuade him. Besides . . . I had been uneasily aware for some minutes now of the bitter little draft that crept under the door and meandered along the boards, cutting at my ankles. Philippe was busy with the footpump, which seemed remarkably easy to work. If the blessed boat really would inflate . . .

It would. Presently Philippe lifted a face flushed with pride and effort and liberally festooned with cobwebs from a business-like rubber dinghy whose fat sausage-like sides would certainly stem any wandering drafts. I praised him lavishly, managed to parry offers to blow up the horse, the duck, and the beachball as well ("just to *show* you") and finally got us both disposed in our draft-proof but decidedly cramped bed, curled up for warmth together in our coats and preparing to sit out the last three hours or so of our ordeal.

The ghastly minutes crawled by. The night was still, held in its pall of mist. I could hear the occasional soft drip of moisture from the boughs that hung over us, and once some stray current of air must have stirred the trees, for the budded twigs pawed at the roof. Below in the boat-house the hollow slap and suck of water told of darkness and emptiness and a world of nothing. . . . Compared with this burial in the outer dark last night's lodging had had a snug homely quality that I found myself remembering—Bernard or no Bernard—with longing.

And it was cold. Philippe seemed warm enough, curled in a ball with his back tucked into the curve of my body and my arms over him; at any rate, he slept almost straight away. But as the minutes halted by I could feel the deadly insidious cold creeping through me, bone by bone. It struck first at my exposed back, then, slowly, slithered through my whole body, as if the blood were literally running cold through the veins and arteries that held me in a chilled and stiffening network. Cramped as I was, I dared not move for fear of waking the child. He had had, I judged, just about as much as he could take. Let him sleep out the chilly minutes before the final rescue.

So I lay and watched the darkness beyond my canvas barrier for a glimpse of light from the villa, and tried not to think, not to think about anything at all.

It was the beachball that put an end to the beastly vigil. Disturbed

from its winter's rest and moved, I suppose, by some erratic draft, it
finally left its place on a pile of boxes and rolled, squashily elliptical in
its half-deflated state, off its perch and down onto the floor. It fell on me
out of nowhere with a silent, soggy bounce, and jerked me with a yelp
out of my stiff, half-dozing vigil. I sat up furiously. Philippe's voice said,
sounding scared, "What was that?"

I reached clumsily for the flashlight. "The beachball, confound it, I'm
sorry, Philippe. Don't be frightened. Let's have a look at the time. . . .
Quarter to twelve." I looked at him. "Are you cold?"

He nodded.

I said, "Let's get out of here, shall we? There's no light up at the villa
yet, so I vote we try that terrace window. Only a few minutes more
now. . . ."

The mist was thicker now. Our little light beam beat white against it.
It lay heavy as a cloudbank among the trees, but over the lawn near the
house it showed only a pale haze that thinned and shifted in the moving
light.

The lamp still glowed over the front door. Its circle of light seemed to
have shrunk as the trees crowded and loomed closer in the mist. No
other light showed.

We slipped quietly across the lawn and up the terrace steps. The long
window stood ajar, and we went in.

The salon was a big room, and in the light of a cautious torch it looked
even bigger. The little glow caught the ghostly shapes of shrouded furniture, the gleam of a mirror, the sudden glitter of the chandelier that
moved with a spectral tinkle in the draft from the window. The meager
light seemed only to thicken the shadows and make the room retreat
further into dusk. It smelled of disuse, melancholy, dry as dust.

We hesitated just inside the window.

I whispered, "We'll go to your Uncle Hippolyte's room. That'll have
been prepared, surely? There'll be a fire or a stove. And is there a telephone in it?"

He nodded and led the way quickly across the salon. If he was scared
he didn't show it. He moved almost numbly, as if in a bad dream. He
pushed open a massive door that gave onto the hall and slipped through
it without a look to right or left into the shadowed corners. I followed.

The hall was a high dim square where I could just make out a graceful
branching staircase. Tiles echoed our quick footsteps hollowly. No other
sound. We fled upstairs. Philippe turned left along a wide gallery and
finally stopped before a door.

"It's Uncle Hippolyte's study," he whispered, and put a hand to the knob.

The room, sure enough, was warm. Like pins to a magnet we flew across the carpet to the big stove and hugged it as closely as we could with our chilled bodies. I said, sending the flashlight raking around the room, "Where does that door lead?"

"There's another salon. Bigger. It's never used now."

I went across and pushed the door open. The flashlight once more probed its way over the ghosts of furniture. Like the room downstairs, this was still shrouded in its winter covers. It smelled musty, and the silk-paneled walls, as I put up a gentle finger, felt dusty and brittle, like a dead moth's wing. From the empty darkness above came the now familiar phantom tinkling of a chandelier.

I crossed the carpet softly and paused by a shrouded shape that seemed to be a sofa. I lifted the dust cover and felt underneath it . . . damask cushions fraying a little, silk that caught on the skin and set the teeth on edge. "Philippe," I called softly.

He appeared beside me like a smaller, frailer ghost. He was shivering a little. I said very matter-of-factly: "I don't suppose it'll be needed, but every fighter has to have a possible line of retreat worked out. If for any reason we still want to hide, I'd say this is as good a place as any. Under the dust cover. It makes a tent, see? And you'd be pretty snug underneath and quite invisible."

He saw. He nodded without speaking. I cast him a look as I covered the sofa again and followed him back into the study. I pulled the salon door almost, but not quite, shut behind me.

I glanced at my wrist. Five minutes to twelve. The window looked out over the drive. No sign of a car. I turned to Hippolyte's desk and picked up the telephone.

CHAPTER XIX

So, uncle, there you are.
SHAKESPEARE: *Hamlet.*

A MAN's voice said, "Coq Hardi."

At least it was not the same unpleasant and suspicious voice, but there was no harm in trying to disarm it further. It was five minutes to twelve, but just in case. . . .

I said quickly, eagerly, "Guillaume? Is that you, *chéri?* It's Clothilde."

He said blankly, "Clothilde?"

"Yes, yes. From Annecy. You haven't forgotten? You told me to—"

The voice was amused. "Mademoiselle, a moment. Who is it you want?"

"I—isn't that Guillaume? Oh *mon dieu,* how silly of me!" I gave a nervous giggle. "I am sorry, monsieur. Perhaps—if he isn't in bed?—if you will have the goodness to fetch him. . . ."

He was patience itself. "But of course. With the greatest of pleasure. But Guillaume who, Mademoiselle Clothilde? Guillaume Rouvier?"

"No, no. I told you. Monsieur Blake, the Englishman. Is he there? He did tell me—"

"Yes, he's here. Content yourself, Mademoiselle Clothilde. He's not gone to bed. I'll fetch him." I heard him laugh as he moved away from the telephone. No doubt William's stock would soar at the Coq Hardi. . . .

Philippe had moved up close to me. In the faint glow that the front door light cast up through the uncurtained window his face looked small and pale, the eyes enormous. I winked and made a face at him and he smiled.

William said in my ear, sounding bewildered and suspicious, "Blake here. Who is that, please?"

"I'm sorry if I've embarrassed you," I said, "but I had to get you somehow, and that seemed the best way. Linda Martin."

"Oh, it's *you.* The barman said it was a *petite amie.* I couldn't think—what's been going on? Where are you? Are you all right? And the boy—"

"For heaven's sake! Can anyone hear you, William?"

"What? Oh yes, I suppose they can. But I don't think they know English."

"Never mind, don't risk it. I daren't call you for long because it mayn't be safe, but I . . . I need help, and I thought—"

He said quietly, "Of course. I heard the local version of what's happened, and I've been hop—expecting you'd get in touch with me. I—I've been terribly worried—I mean, you being on your own, and all that. What is it? What can I do?"

I said gratefully, "Oh, William . . . Listen, I can't explain now, it would take too long. Don't worry any more; we're safe, both of us, and I think the whole thing will be over in a few minutes, but . . . I'd be awfully grateful if you'd come along. There's no danger now, but there'll be . . . scenes, and I don't somehow feel like facing them alone. I know it's a lot to ask of someone you hardly know, and it's a shocking time of night, but I wondered—"

"Tell me where you are," said William simply, "and I'll come. I've got the jeep. *Is* it the Cent Fleurs?"

"No, no. So they told you I'd rung up before?"

"Yes. I've just got back from Évian."

"Oh, William, no!"

"Well," he said reasonably, "I thought you were there. I didn't know anything about this business till we got in tonight, you know. I was up at the hut till late last night, working, but I was due today to go with a couple of men over to the south plantations and we had to make an early start, so I slept at the pub. We were out all day and got back lateish, and then I was told you'd rung up from the Cent Fleurs, and of course I heard all the stories that were going around. I rang up the Cent Fleurs and they didn't remember you, so I skated down to Évian in the jeep—"

"Did you see Raoul de Valmy there?"

"Don't know him from Adam," said William simply. "Is he looking for you, too?"

"Yes."

"Oh. I thought you might have—I mean, someone said—" he stopped, floundering a little.

I said, "Whichever of the stories you heard, it isn't true. We're on our own."

"Oh. Ah. Yes. Well," said William cheerfully, "tell me where you are now and I'll be straight over."

"We're in Thonon, at the Villa Mireille. That's Hippolyte de Valmy's place; he's the brother—"

"I know. Have you seen him?"

"He's not back yet. Expected any minute. We're waiting for him. I—I'll explain when I see you why we didn't go straight to the police. Just for the time being, will you not say anything? Just—come?"

"Sure. I'm halfway there already. Repeat the name of the place, please."

"The Villa Mireille. Anyone'll tell you. It's on the lakeside. Take the lower road. M-I-R-E-I-L-L-E. Got it?"

"Yes, thank you . . . sherry."

"What? Oh, I see. Is the barman listening?"

"Yes."

"Then you'll have to say good-by nicely, I'm afraid."

"I don't know how."

"Say '*à bientôt, cherie.*'"

"Ah biang toe sherry," said William grimly, and then laughed. "I'm glad you're in such good spirits, anyway," he added.

"Yes," I said drearily. "See you soon. And thank you, William. Thank you a lot. It's nice not to be . . . quite on one's own."

"Think nothing of it," said William, and rang off.

The handset was hardly back in its cradle when the car came down the road. We stood together, just back from the dark window, and watched the lights. It slowed and changed gear for the gate. Its lights swung around in the mist and slid across the study ceiling.

Philippe's hand slid into mind, and gripped. My own was shaking. He said inadequately, "Here he is."

"Yes. Oh, Philippe."

He said wonderingly, "You have been afraid too, all the time?"

"Yes. Terribly."

"I didn't know."

"I'm glad of that."

The car had stopped. Lights were cut, then the engine. Feet crunched on the gravel and the car door slammed. Steps, quick and assured, mounted to the front door. We heard the rattle of the handle. Then the sounds weren't outside the house any longer, but inside; the slight sound of the big door opening, a step on the tiled floor. . . .

He had come. It was over.

I said shakily, "*Dieu soit béni,*" and made for the study door.

I hadn't even considered what I was going to say to Hippolyte. It was possible that in some fashion he had already been greeted with the news. It was also possible that he had never even heard of me. I didn't care. He was here. I could hand over.

I flew along the carpeted gallery and down the lovely curve of the stairs.

The hall lights were not on. The front door was ajar, and the lamp that hung outside it over the steps cast a long panel of gold across the tiles. Outside I saw the car gleaming in the mist. The newcomer stood just inside the door, one hand raised as if in the act of switching on the lights. He was silhouetted against the lamplit haze beyond, a tall, power-fully-built man, standing stock-still, as a man does when he is listening.

On the thick carpet my feet made little more noise than a ghost's. I reached the center stair and hesitated, one hand on the balustrade. I started slowly down the last flight toward him.

Then he saw me, and raised his head.

"So you are here," he said.

That was all, but it stopped me as if he had shot me. I stood clutching the banister till I thought the wood would crack. For one crazy moment I wanted to turn and run, but I couldn't move.

I said, in an unrecognizable voice that broke on the word, "Raoul?"

"*Lui-même.*" There was a click as the lights came on—a great chande-lier that poured and flashed light from a thousand glittering crystals. They struck at my eyes and I flinched and put up a hand, then dropped it and looked at him across the empty hall. I had forgotten all about Phi-lippe, about Hippolyte, about William Blake even now tearing down from Soubirous; I could see nothing but the man who stood there with his hand on the light switch, looking up at me. There was nothing except the thing that lay between us.

He dropped his hand, and shut the door behind him. He was quite white, and his eyes were hard as stones. There were lines in his face I hadn't seen before. He looked very like Léon de Valmy.

He said, "He's here? Philippe?" His voice was very even and quiet, but I thought I could hear the blaze of anger licking through it that he didn't trouble to suppress.

The question was answered by Philippe himself. He had followed me as far as the gallery, and there had stopped, prompted by a better in-stinct than my own. At his cousin's question he must have moved, for the stir in the shadows above him made Raoul lift his head sharply. I followed his look just in time to see Philippe, a small silent wraith, melt back into the darkness of the gallery.

Then Raoul moved, and fast. He took the hall in four strides and was coming upstairs two at a time. His leap out of immobility had been so sudden that I reacted without reason, a blind thing in a panic. I don't re-member moving, but as I let go the banister I fled—was swept—up the stairway in front of him, only to check desperately on the landing and whirl to face him.

I shrieked, *"Run, Philippe!"* and put up frantic, futile hands to break the tempest.

They never touched him. He stopped dead. His arms dropped to his sides. I moved slowly back till I came up against the curve of the banister rail and leaned there. I don't think I could have stood unsupported. He wasn't looking after Philippe. He was looking at me. I turned my head away.

Behind me, along the gallery, I heard the study door shut, very softly. Raoul heard it too. He lifted his head. Then he looked back at me. "I see," he said.

So did I. I had seen even while shock reacting on weariness had driven me stupidly and headlong from him up the stairs. And now I saw the look that came down over his face, bleak bitter pride shutting down over anger, and I knew that I had turned my world back to cinders, sunk my lovely ship with my own stupid, wicked hands. I couldn't speak, but I began to cry—not desperately or tragically, but silently and without hope, the tears spilling anyhow down my cheeks, and my face ugly with crying.

He didn't move. He said, very evenly, "When I reached the Château Valmy this morning and my father told me that you had gone, he seemed to think you would have come to me for help. I told him no, you thought I was in Paris till Thursday, but I'd left my apartment there on Tuesday evening, and you couldn't know where I was. It was only later that I found you hadn't tried to get in touch with me there at all." His voice was quite expressionless. "There was only one reason I could think of why you hadn't telephoned me. When I . . . put this to my father he denied that any harm had come to you. I didn't believe him."

He paused. I couldn't look at him. I put up a hand to wipe away the tears that streaked my face. But they kept falling.

"I told him then that I intended to make you my wife, and that if anything happened to you, or to the boy and through him to you, I would kill him—my father—with my own hands."

I looked at him then. "Raoul . . ." But my voice died away. I couldn't speak.

He said slowly, answering my look, "Yes. I believe I did mean it," and added one word, one knell of a word, "then."

We had neither of us heard the other car. When the hall door swung open to admit two people—a man and a woman—we both jumped and turned. The woman was Héloïse de Valmy; the man was a stranger to me, but even if I had not expected him I would have known that this was Hippolyte. In him, too, the Valmy likeness was strong; he was a younger, gentler edition of Léon de Valmy—Lucifer before the fall. He looked kind, and his voice as he addressed some remark to Héloïse sounded pleasant. But for all the gentleness and the marks of anxiety and fatigue, I thought I could see in him the same hard force as in the other men— cooler, perhaps, and slower, but in the circumstances none the worse for that. My *deus ex machina* would be capable enough, thank God.

Neither he nor Madame de Valmy had seen us above them on the landing, because at that moment Madame Vuathoux, who must this time have seen the lights of the car, came bustling into the hall from the back regions, vociferous with welcome.

"Monsieur—but you are welcome! I was so afraid that, with this mist —oh!" She stopped and her hands went up as if in horror. *"Tiens,* madame—she is ill? What is the matter? Of course, of course! What horror! Has there still been no word?"

I hadn't noticed till she mentioned it, but Héloïse de Valmy was indeed clinging to Hippolyte's arm as if she needed its support. In the merciless light from the chandelier her face looked ghastly, gray and haggard like the face of an old woman. The concierge surged forward with cries of commiseration.

The little boy—nothing was heard yet, no? And of course Madame was distracted. *La pauvre* . . . Madame must come upstairs . . . there was a stove lit . . . a drink . . . some bouillon, perhaps?

Hippolyte de Valmy interrupted her "Monsieur Raoul is here?"

"Not yet, monsieur. He came this evening, and then left for Évian. He said he would be back at midnight to see you. It is after—"

"His car's outside."

Raoul moved at that, almost idly. He said, "Good evening, *mon oncle.*"

Madame Vuathoux gaped up at him, at last stricken dumb. Hippolyte turned, eyebrows raised. Héloïse said, "Raoul!" just as I had done, and with no less horror in her voice. New lines etched themselves in her face and she swayed on her feet, so that Hippolyte tightened his grip on her arm. Then she saw me shrinking behind Raoul against the banister and she cried my name, almost on a shriek, "Miss Martin!"

Madame Vuathoux found her voice again at that. She echoed the cry. *"La voilà!"* There she is! In this very house! Monsieur Raoul—"

Hippolyte said curtly, "That will do. Leave us, please."

There was silence until the door had shut behind her. Then he turned again to look up at us. He surveyed me without expression, then he gave a formal little nod and looked at Raoul. "You found them?"

"Yes, I found them."

"Philippe?"

"He's here."

Héloïse said hoarsely, "Safe?"

Raoul's voice was very dry. "Yes, Héloïse. Safe. He was with Miss Martin."

Her eyes fell before his and she gave a little moaning sigh. Hippolyte said, "I think we had better talk this thing out quietly. Come up to the study. Héloïse, can you manage the stairs, my dear?"

No one looked at me, or spoke. I was a shade, a ghost, a dead leaf dropped by the storm into some corner. My story was over. Nothing would happen to me now. I would not even be called upon to explain to Hippolyte. I was safe, and I wished I was dead.

Héloïse and Hippolyte were coming slowly up the stairs. Raoul turned past me as if I didn't exist and began to mount the flight to the gallery. I went after him quietly. I had stopped crying, but my face still stung with tears, and I felt tired, so tired. I found I was pulling myself up by the banisters as if I were an old woman.

Raoul had opened the study door and switched on the light. He was waiting. I didn't look at him. I passed him with my head bent, and went straight across the study to the door that gave onto the salon.

I pushed it open.

I said wearily, "Philippe? It's all right, Philippe, you can come out." I hesitated, conscious that Raoul, too, had crossed the room and was standing just behind me. Then I said, "You're quite safe now. Your Uncle Hippolyte's here."

For some reason—no reason at all—the others had followed us into the salon, ignoring the comfort of the study stove.

Hippolyte had taken the cover from the sofa, and now sat there, with Philippe in the crook of his arm. On the other side of the empty grate Héloïse sat huddled in a small chair of golden brocade. Someone had twitched the dust sheet off that and it lay in a bundle at her feet.

With its light on, the salon seemed more ghostly than ever. The light of the big chandelier dripped icily from its hundred glittering prisms. It fell coldly on the white shrouds that covered the furniture, and struck back from the pale marble of the fireplace where Raoul stood, one elbow on the mantelpiece, as I had seen him stand in the library at Valmy.

I sat as far away from them as possible. At the end of the long room was a piano, a concert-sized grand encased in green baize; to this I retreated in silence, and sat down on the long piano bench with my back to the instrument. My hands clutched at the edge of the bench. I felt numb and unutterably weary. There was talking to be done—well, let them do it, the Valmys, and get it over and let me go. It was no longer anything to do with me. I raised my head and looked at them down the

length of that beautiful dead room. They might have been a million
miles away.

Hippolyte had been talking to Philippe in an undertone, but now he
looked up at Raoul and said in his quiet voice, "As you may have
guessed, Héloïse drove into Geneva to meet my plane. She has told me a
rather . . . odd story."

Raoul was selecting a cigarette. He said without raising his eyes,
"You'd better tell me what it was. I've heard several versions of this odd
story lately, and I confess I'm a little confused. I'd like to know which
one Héloïse is trying to sell now."

She made a little sound, and Hippolyte's lips tightened. "My dear
Raoul—"

"Look," said Raoul, "this thing has gone a long way beyond politeness
or the conventions of—filial duty. We'll get on a lot better if we simply
tell the truth." His eyes rested indifferently on Héloïse. "You know, you
may as well cut your losses, Héloïse. You must know my father was
pretty frank with me this morning. I suppose he may intend to deny it all
now, but I confess I can't see where that'll get him—or you. I don't know
what he sent you down to Geneva to say, but the thing's over, Héloïse.
You can abandon your—attitudes. There are no witnesses here that matter, and you'll certainly need my Uncle Hippolyte to help you if the hell
of a scandal is to be avoided. Why not give it up and come clean?"

She made no reply, but sat there in a boneless huddle, not looking at
him.

He watched her for a moment without expression. Then his shoulders
lifted a fraction and he turned back to Hippolyte. "Well," he said, "since
it appears that Héloïse isn't playing, you'd better let me start."

Hippolyte's face, as he glanced from one to the other looked suddenly
very tired. "Very well," he said. "Go ahead. You rang me up in Athens
in the small hours of Tuesday morning to ask me to come home as you
were anxious about Philippe. You spoke of accidents, and insisted that
Philippe might be in some danger. You also said something not very
clear about Philippe's governess. Héloïse, too, spoke of her tonight—also
not very clearly. I take it that this is the young woman in question, and
that there have been recent and alarming developments which Héloïse
has been attempting to explain to me. I must confess to some confusion.
I am also tired. I hope you will be very brief and very lucid."

Raoul said, "You can forget Philippe's governess." (That was me—
"Philippe's governess." He hadn't even glanced at me. He was a million
miles away.) He went on, "She never was in it, except incidentally. The
story begins and ends with my father. That was why I said this thing had
gone beyond convention. Because your starting point, *mon oncle,* is this:

your brother—my father—with the help or at any rate the connivance of his wife—has been trying for some time past to murder Philippe."

I heard Héloïse give a faint sound like a moan, and I saw the child turn his head to look at her from the shelter of Hippolyte's arm. I said in a hard little voice I didn't recognize as my own, "Philippe is only nine years old. Also he has just been through a considerable ordeal and is very tired and probably hungry. I suggest that you allow me to take him downstairs to some reliable person in the kitchen."

They all jumped as if one of the shrouded chairs had spoken. Then Hippolyte said, "Certainly he should go downstairs. But I should like you to remain here, if you will. Ring the bell, please, Raoul."

Raoul glanced at me, a look I couldn't read, and obeyed.

We waited in silence, and presently the door opened. It wasn't Madame Vuathoux who stood there, but an elderly manservant with a pleasant face.

"Gaston," said Hippolyte, "will you please take Master Philippe downstairs and see he gets something to eat? Have Madame Vuathoux or Jeanne get a room ready for him . . . the little dressing room off my own, I think. Philippe, go with Gaston now. He'll look after you."

Philippe had jumped up. He was smiling. The gray-haired servant returned the smile. "Come along," he said, and put out a hand. Philippe ran to him without a backward look. The door shut behind them.

Hippolyte turned back to Raoul. I could see, I'm not sure how, the rigid control he was exerting over face and hands. His voice was not quite steady, but it was as pleasant and gentle as ever. He said, "Well, Raoul, you'd better go on with your story. And I advise you to be sure of your facts. You . . . he's my brother, remember."

"And my father," said Raoul harshly. He knocked the ash off his cigarette into the empty fireplace with an abrupt movement. "As for my facts, I haven't a great many, but you can have them. I only really came into the story myself"—here his eyes lifted and met mine; they were like slate —"this morning."

He paused for a moment. Then he began to talk.

He said, "I don't have to tell you the background to the story; that my father, if Philippe had never been born, would have succeeded to Valmy, where he has lived all his life and which he loved with what (particularly since his accident) is an obsessive love. When his elder brother didn't marry he assumed that Valmy would be some day his, and he never hesitated to divert the income from his own estate, Bellevigne, into Valmy. I have run Bellevigne for him since I was nineteen, and I know just how steadily, during those early years, the place was milked of everything that might have made it prosperous. My father and I have fought

over it time and again . . . after all, it is my heritage as well, and I wasn't
as sure as he that Étienne wouldn't get himself a son one day."

Hippolyte said, "I know. Léon would never listen."

"Well," said Raoul, "Étienne did marry, and got Philippe. I don't intend to distress you with my father's reactions to that fact; mercifully
he had the sense to keep them from Étienne . . . possibly so that
Étienne would let him go on living at Valmy. But the immediate result
was that Bellevigne's income was put back where it belonged, and I had
the job to build up what had been steadily ruined for years." Something
like a smile touched the hard mouth. "I may say I enjoyed the fight. . . .
But last year, Étienne was killed."

He looked down at Hippolyte. "And immediately Valmy started to
take the money out of Bellevigne again."

The older man made a little movement. "As soon as that?"

Raoul smiled again. It wasn't a nice smile. "I'm glad you're so quick
in the uptake. Yes. He must have decided then and there that something
had to be done about Philippe. There were six years before the child in-
herited. The chance would come."

Hippolyte said, hard and sharp, "Be sure of your facts."

"I am. It'll save time and heart-searching if you know here and now
that my father has admitted his intention of murdering Philippe."

A pause. Hippolyte said, "Very well. I'll accept that. To whom did he
admit this?"

Raoul's mouth twisted. "To me. Content yourself, *mon oncle,* it's still
only a family affair."

"I—see." Hippolyte stirred in his chair. "And so I went off to Greece
and handed Philippe over."

"Yes. Somewhat naturally I hadn't tumbled to the significance of what
had happened over Bellevigne. One doesn't," said Raoul evenly, "readily
assume one's father is a murderer. I was merely puzzled and furious—
so furious at being thrown back to the foot of the cliff I'd been climbing
that I didn't stop to think out the whys and the wherefores. I just spent all
my energy on one blazing row after another. When I went up to Valmy
at the beginning of April I thought I'd find out how Philippe was getting
on there. I don't pretend for a moment that I thought there was anything wrong; I told you, one doesn't think in that sort of way of one's
own family and the people one knows. But . . . anyway, I went up to
Valmy to 'sound' things, as it were. And things seemed all right. I'd
heard Philippe had a new governess, and I wondered . . ." Here his
glance crossed mine momentarily and he paused. He added, "Valmy
was never a house for children, but this time it seemed all right. Then,
next day, there was an accident that might have been fatal."

He went on, in that cold even voice, to tell Hippolyte about the shooting in the woods, while Hippolyte exclaimed, and Héloïse stirred in her chair and watched the floor. She made no sound, but I saw that the fragile gold silk of the chair arm had ripped under her nails. Raoul was watching her now. There was no expression whatever on his face.

"Even then," he said, "I didn't suspect what was really going on. Why should I? I blamed myself bitterly for that later, but I tell you, one doesn't think that way." He dropped his cigarette stub onto the hearth, and turned away to crush it out with his heel. He said a little wearily, as if to himself, "Perhaps I did suspect; I don't know. I think I may have fought against suspecting." He looked at his uncle. "Can you understand that?"

"Yes," said Hippolyte heavily. "Yes."

"I thought you would," said Raoul. "A damnable exercise isn't it?" He was already lighting another cigarette.

Hippolyte said, "But you suspected enough to make you go back pretty soon? And again at Easter?"

Raoul's attention was riveted on lighting the cigarette. "It wasn't altogether suspicion that drove me back. Nor did I see anything to rouse me into active worry until the Easter Ball—the night I rang you up. But that night two things happened. Miss Martin told me that there'd been another accident—a coping of the west balcony was suddenly dangerously loose overnight, and only the fact that she noticed it and shoved something across the broken bit saved Philippe from a particularly nasty end on some spiked railings underneath."

This had the effect of making Hippolyte turn and look at me. The expression in his face made me wonder, for the first time, what Héloïse had been telling him about me on the way from Geneva. From the look on his face it had been nothing to my credit. As Raoul went on to speak of the midnight feast with Philippe I saw the expression deepen—as if Hippolyte were being given a very different picture of me from the one he had got from Héloïse. "And there was something so odd about Héloïse that night," said Raoul. "She seemed frightened, if that were possible, and then there was Miss Martin's talk of nightmares. . . . But it was really the second accident that shook me. I went straight to the telephone in the small hours, and eventually got hold of you. It seemed the best thing to do, for us to tackle him together and find out what was going on and force him to . . . see reason. I thought you might also hand the child over to my care if you had to leave again. I've no authority at all where Philippe's concerned, and for obvious reasons I preferred not to enlist official help at that point. Hence the SOS to you." He gave his uncle that fleeting, joyless smile. "In any case, as far as the police were concerned, my father still held the winning card, which was that nothing had happened. He had, and has, committed no provable crime. But I thought that if you cabled you were coming home it would put paid to whatever he might be planning. If even then," he finished very wearily, "he really was planning anything."

There was another of those silences. Hippolyte looked across at Héloïse. Raoul went on, "It seems odd, now, that I should ever have been so slow to believe him capable of murder. I should have known . . . but there it is. I tell you it's not the sort of thing one readily accepts. It certainly wasn't the sort of thing I felt I could tax him with . . . and I doubt if that would have done much good anyway. If the interview I had with him this morning is anything to go by—" He broke off, and then gave a little shrug. "Well, I had sent for you. I'd done what I could to silence my own uneasiness, and I knew Miss Martin was dependable. I told myself I was being a fool. I didn't want to leave Valmy next morning, but I got an early call from Paris, and had to go. It was to do with some money I'd been trying to raise on Bellevigne, and the chap I wanted was passing through Paris that afternoon. I had to catch him. So I went. I'd intended to stay in Paris till Wednesday afternoon, then to come over here and meet you when you got in from Athens, and go up to Valmy with you on Thursday. But once I got away from Valmy I found I was worrying more and more; it was as if, once I got out of his range, I could see him more clearly. Anyway, I think I saw for the first time that this impossible thing might be true, and there might really be danger —immediate danger. I did ring up Valmy in the afternoon and got my— got him. I made some excuse—I forget now what it was—and asked a few questions. He told me about your cable, and I'll swear he even sounded pleased at the prospect of seeing you. Everything seemed to be normal, and when I rang off I was convinced yet again that the whole thing was a bag of moonshine." He drew on his cigarette and the smoke came out like a sigh. "But . . . well, by the evening I couldn't stand it any longer. I rang up the airport and was lucky. There was a seat on a night flight. I'd left my car at Geneva, and I drove straight up to Valmy. I got there early this morning, to find that Miss Martin and Philippe had disappeared."

He flicked ash from his cigarette. "Just as a matter of interest, Héloïse, how did you account for that to my uncle when you met his plane?"

Still she didn't speak. She had turned away her head so that her cheek was pressed against the wing of the chair. She looked as if she were hardly listening. Her face was gray and dead. Only her fingers moved, shredding, shredding the gold silk under them.

Hippolyte began, looking so uncomfortable that I had a rough idea what the story had involved: "It wasn't very coherent. I did gather—"

I said, "It doesn't matter. I'll tell you what did happen. I found out on Tuesday night what Monsieur de Valmy was planning. Bernard got drunk at the dance and told Berthe, one of the maids. She told me. I had to get Philippe away. I—I didn't know where to go. We hid, and then came here to wait for you. That's all."

I could feel Raoul's eyes on me. Between us stretched the empty ghost-filled spaces of that alien room. I said no more. If I never told him the rest, I couldn't do it here.

Hippolyte turned back to Raoul. "Go on. You got back and found them gone. I assume that at this point you did tackle Léon?"

"I did." Something new had come into the even voice, something that made me stir on my bench and look away. I didn't want to watch his face, though heaven knew, there was nothing there to read. He said, "There were various—theories as to why the two had run away, but to me it only meant one thing; that Miss Martin had had some proof that Philippe was in danger, and had removed him from harm's way. I blamed myself bitterly for not having let my own suspicions take root. So I attacked my father."

"Yes?"

Raoul said, "It wasn't a pleasant interview. I'll cut it very short. He started by denying everything, and—you know him—he denied it so well that he made me look a fool. But the fact remained that Lin—Miss Martin had bolted. I kept at him and eventually he changed his ground. He suggested then that as far as Philippe's fate was concerned Miss Martin mightn't be entirely disinterested." He flicked ash off his cigarette, not looking at me.

Hippolyte said, "What do you mean?"

Raoul didn't answer. I said briefly, "Monsieur de Valmy had reason to believe I was in love with Monsieur Raoul."

I saw Hippolyte raise his brows. In his own way he was as quick as Léon. He said, "So you might have had an interest in disposing of Philippe? A very longsighted young lady. And what was your reaction to this—suggestion, Raoul."

"It was so absurd that I wasn't even angry. I laughed. I then told him that he had got the facts right only so far. The interest was on both sides and it was serious—in other words that I intended to make Miss Martin my wife, and if any harm came to her or to Philippe he'd have me to answer to as well as the police."

Hippolyte flashed a look from Raoul to me, and back again, then his eyes dropped to his hands. There was a long pause. Something in the way the interview was going must have prompted him to ignore the information in Raoul's last speech, for all he said was, "And then?"

Raoul said, in a very hard, dry voice, "I'll cut this short. It's pretty unspeakable. He changed his ground again, and suggested cutting me in. Yes. Quite. He pointed out the advantages that I and my wife would get from Philippe's death. He—didn't seem to understand that I might be able to resist them. And he was convinced I would be able to persuade her too, as my wife, to acquiesce in his plans. Between us we could pacify you when you arrived, see you back to Greece, and then take our time over Philippe. We could cook up some story of Linda's having run away to me—everyone was saying that anyway—and get through the bigger scandal by making it a purely sex affair. He then suggested that I find Linda and allow people to believe she had run off to meet me."

"Yes?"

It was, perhaps, the most horrible thing about the interview that neither Léon's son nor his brother showed surprise. Distress, yes; horror, perhaps; but not surprise. Not even at a wickedness that couldn't conceive of disinterested good.

Raoul said, "I didn't say much. I—couldn't, or I'd have laid hands on him. I merely said that neither of us would ever connive at harming Philippe, and we had better stop talking nonsense and find the pair of them, or there might be a scandal he'd find it hard to get out of. I thought that Linda might have tried to get in touch with me in Paris, and rang up there and then in front of him, but there hadn't been a call. I left a message with the concierge in case Linda rang up later, but I'd been so sure she'd ring me up that I thought my father had lied about their escape from Valmy, and that something had happened to them, so—oh well, never mind that now. I knew I was wrong almost straight away, because Bernard—you know his man?—came in. Apparently he'd been out looking for them. He got a bit of a surprise to see me, and I lost no time in making it very plain that it was in his best interest to find Linda and Philippe quickly. I thought they might have gone for help to the Englishman who works over on Dieudonné—I'd discovered that Linda knew him, and was glad she had at least one friend in the district. I rang up the Coq Hardi at Soubirous, where he sleeps sometimes, but he'd already gone out, and he wasn't expected back till dinnertime. I told Bernard to go up to the hut where the Englishman keeps his things, but he said he'd been already and they weren't there. He told me where else he'd been. I sent him out again with instructions to report to me, and some sort of plan of search, the best I could devise with the little I knew . . . well, none of this matters now. He knew very well he'd better play in with me, and play safe. When he'd gone I told my father again, quite plainly, that if any harm came to those two even if it looked like the most obvious accident in the world, I would kill him. Then I went out with the car." His voice was suddenly flat and very tired. "That's all."

I sat still, looking down at my feet. That was all. Only another fifteen hours or so spent combing the valleys, ringing up Paris, making carefully casual inquiries (I found later) of the Consulate, the hospitals, the police. . . .

One or two things became plain: first, that Léon de Valmy had had no idea that the convenient rumor of my engagement was, in fact, true; second, that Raoul knew nothing of the final hurried poison plot, and was unaware that Léon de Valmy had ever had any positive intention of harming me; Bernard, coming in on the interview, must have realized immediately that his master's guns were spiked; somehow, Léon de Valmy had tipped him the wink that the hunt must be called off, and from then on the man had, perforce, co-operated with Raoul in his search. Whether or not I had been right about our danger last night in the woods, we had been safe since early this morning . . . since Raoul had come home. Because of Raoul, the dogs had been called off. We had been quite safe all day, because of Raoul. I sat very still, watching my feet.

The silence was drawing out. I heard the lusters quiver like the music of a ghostly spinet. I looked down the length of the lovely dead room toward the group by the fireplace.

Both men were watching the woman in the chair.

She was sitting very still, but her stillness wasn't even a travesty of the poise I knew. The delicate flower had wilted to pulp. She lay back in her chair as if she had no bones, and her hands were motionless at last on the shredded silk of the chair arms. Her pale eyes were fully open now; they moved from Raoul's face to Hippolyte's painfully. There was no need for her to speak. It was all written in her face, even, I thought, a dreadful kind of relief that now it had all been said.

The door opened and Philippe came in. He was carrying a steaming cup of bouillon very carefully between his hands. He brought it to me and held it out. "This is for you. You had an ordeal too."

I said, "Oh, Philippe . . ." and then my voice broke shamefully. But he didn't appear to notice this. He was looking at Héloïse, silent and slack in her chair. He said doubtfully, "Aunt Héloïse, would you like some too?"

That did it. She began to cry, on a thin dry note that was quite horrible to listen to.

I leaned forward, kissed Philippe's cheek, and said quickly, "Thank you, *p'tit,* but Aunt Héloïse isn't well. Better just run along. Good night now. Sleep well."

He gave one wondering look, and went obediently.

Héloïse didn't put her hands to her face. She lay back in her chair and sobbed tearlessly on that dreadful, jerky note. Hippolyte de Valmy, now as gray-faced as she, watched her helplessly, touching a handkerchief to his lips with an unsteady hand. Then, after a few moments' hesitation, he moved to a chair beside her, took one of her unresisting hands and began, rather feebly, to pat it. He was murmuring something through her sobs, but the uncertain comfort had no effect.

Raoul stood apart from the two of them, silent, and with the shutters still down over his face. He didn't look at me.

I believe I opened my lips to say something to him, but at that moment Héloïse began at last to speak. Her voice was terrible, thin and shaken and breathless.

She said, "It's true, yes, it's true what he says, Hippolyte. He made Léon tell him . . . there was a scene . . . dreadful things . . . he had no right. . . ." She turned suddenly toward him and her free hand closed over his, clutching at him. "But I'm glad you know, Hippolyte. You'll get us out of it, won't you? You'll see there's nothing said? You won't take it further? It's not a police matter! You heard what Raoul told you—it's only in the family! That's it, it's only in the family! Bernard won't dare speak, and Raoul can't say anything; how can he? Léon's his father, isn't he? Surely that means something?" She shook his arm, leaning nearer, her voice hurrying and breathless: "You can't let it all come out, you know that! You can't do that to Léon, you and Raoul! There's no harm done . . . the boy's safe and the girl's all right. Don't look like that, Raoul. You know you can put it right between you if you want to! The Martin girl's in love with you; she'll keep her mouth shut, and—"

"Héloïse, please!" This, sharply, from Hippolyte. He had freed himself and moved slightly away from her. He was looking at her almost as if he'd never seen her before. "You say it's all true? You did know of it? You?"

She had sunk back in her chair. She swallowed another of those sharp convulsive sobs and moved her head to and fro against the chair-back. "Yes, yes, yes. Everything he told you. I'll admit everything, if only you'll help." Something in his tone and look must have got through to her here, for her voice changed. "I—I'm not wicked, Hippolyte, you know that. I didn't want to hurt Philippe, but . . . well, it was for Léon's sake. I did it for Léon." She met his stony look and added sharply, "You know as well as I do that Valmy should be his. Surely he has the best right to it? It's his home. You know that. Why, you've said so yourself! And he's not like other men. You know that, too; you should realize he's not like other people. He should have had Valmy. He should! He'd had enough to bear without being turned out of his home!"

Her brother-in-law moved uncomfortably. "I cannot see that Léon would be grateful for this special pleading, Héloïse. And at the moment it's beside the point. What we're discussing is a good deal more serious. Attempted murder. Of a child."

"Yes, yes, I know. It was wrong. It was wrong. I admit that. But it didn't happen, did it? There's no harm done, Raoul said that himself! *That* doesn't have to be taken any further! Oh, you'll have to talk to Léon about it, I can see that, but you'll see he stays on at Valmy, won't you? There's no reason why he shouldn't! People are talking, but it'll soon be forgotten if you stand by us and don't bring things into the open. And I know you won't! You know how Léon feels! You'll see he keeps Valmy, won't you? He should have talked to you before—I wanted him to, instead of trying to arrange things this way. I was sure you'd see his point of view, and you do, don't you? I'm sure there's some way things can be fixed! You can come to some arrangement, can't you? Can't you?"

He started to say something, then bit it back, saying instead, calmly enough, "It's no use discussing it any more here. This is getting us nowhere. Héloïse—"

"Only promise me you won't take it to the police!"

"I can't promise anything. All I can say is that we'll try and compromise between what's right and what's best."

She seemed not to be listening. Something had broken in her, and now she couldn't stop. She was out of control; her hands and lips were shaking. The pleading voice poured on, admitting with every desperate syllable what must never—even in her mind—have been in words before.

"It'll kill him to go to Bellevigne! And all our money's in Valmy! We looked after Valmy, you can't say that we didn't! Every penny went into the estate! You can't say he was a bad trustee!"

"No," said Hippolyte.

She didn't even notice the irony. The dreadful single-mindedness she showed was ample explanation of how Léon had persuaded her to help him against what better instincts she must have possessed. She wept on, "It was for Léon's sake! Why shouldn't he get something—just this thing —out of life? Valmy was his! You know it was! Étienne had no right to do this to him, no right at all! That child should never have been born!"

Raoul said suddenly, as if the words were shaken out of him, "God pity you, Héloïse, you've begun to think like him."

This stopped her. She turned her head quickly toward him. I couldn't see her eyes, but her hands clenched themselves on the arms of the chair. Her voice went low and breathless, "You," she said, "you. You always hated him, didn't you?"

He didn't answer. He had taken out another cigarette and was making rather a business of lighting it.

"He's your father," she said. "Doesn't that make any difference? Can you stand by and see him ruined? Doesn't it mean anything to you that he's your father?"

Raoul didn't speak. For all the expression on his face he mightn't even have been listening. But I saw his brows twitch together as the match burned him.

Suddenly her hands hammered the chair arms. She shouted at him, "Damn you, are you condemning your own father?" Even the vestiges of common self-control had gone; her voice rose to the edge of hysteria. *"You* to stand there and call him a murderer! *You* who have everything, everything, and he a cripple with nothing to call his own but that ruined relic of a place in the south! You condemn him, you talk fine and large of right and wrong and murder and police, and who's to say what you'd have done if you'd been in his place? How do you know what *you'd* have been if you'd smashed your car up one fine day on the zig-zag and cracked your spine and two lives along with it? Yes, two! Would she have looked at you then? Ah yes, it only takes one look from you now, doesn't it, but would she? Would she have stayed with you and loved you the way I've loved him all these years and done for you what I've done for him—and glad to, mind that, *glad to?* Oh, no, not you!" She stopped and drew a long shivering breath. "Oh, God, he's a better man with half a body than you'll ever be, Raoul de Valmy! You don't know . . . oh dear God, how can you know . . . ?"

Then she put her hands to her face and began to weep.

Quite suddenly, the scene was unbearable. And I didn't belong in this anywhere any more. I stood up abruptly.

It was at this moment that the door went back with a slam against the silk-paneled wall, and William Blake came in with a rush like an angry bear.

CHAPTER XX

Eighth Coach

Death has done all death can.
BROWNING: *After.*

"WHO THE DEVIL are you?" said Raoul.

Since he said it in French, William Blake took not the slightest notice. He stopped just inside the door, breathing hard. He looked, as ever, enormous; very English, with the untidy blonde hair, and very safe. He looked down the room at me, ignoring everyone else.

"Linda? What's going on here? Are you all right?"

I said, between a laugh and a sob, "Oh, William!" and ran to him down the length of the room, bouillon and all.

He didn't exactly fold me in his arms, but he did catch me, and, with some presence of mind, hold me away from him, so that the bouillon didn't spill all over his ancient jacket, but only on the priceless Savonnerie carpet.

"Here, steady on," he said. "Are you sure you're all right?"

"Yes, quite all right."

Hippolyte had turned and risen in surprise at the interruption, but Héloïse was past caring for the presence of a stranger. She was weeping freely now, the sobs tearing at the atmosphere of the beautiful over-civilized room. Hippolyte paused, looking helplessly from the newcomer back to her. Raoul said, without moving, "It's the Englishman. I told you about him."

I saw William wince from the sound of sobbing, but he stood his ground, his jaw jutting dangerously. "Did they hurt you?"

"No, oh no. It's not them, William, it's all finished, honestly."

"Anything I can do?"

"Not a thing, except . . . take me out of here."

Behind me I heard Hippolyte say with a kind of controlled desperation, "Héloïse, please. My dear, you must try and pull yourself together. This is doing no good, no good at all. You'll make yourself ill. Héloïse!"

William said, "Okay. We'll get you out of this. And fast." He put
an arm around my shoulders, and turned me toward the door. "Let's
go."

I saw Hippolyte take half a step toward us. "Miss Martin—"

But here Héloïse sobbed something incoherently and caught at his
sleeve, a desperate little gesture that broke something inside me.

I said, "I can't stand this, William. Wait."

I thrust the half-empty pot of bouillon into his hands, and went back
to Madame de Valmy. Hippolyte stood aside and I went down on my
knees in front of the little gold chair. I was kneeling at Raoul's feet. I
didn't look up at him, and he never moved. Her hands were still over her
face. The sobs were less violent now. I took her wrists gently and pulled
them down and held her hands.

I said, "Madame, don't. Don't cry any more. We can talk this thing
over quietly when you're feeling better. It won't do any good to make
yourself ill." Then to Hippolyte, "Can't you see she's beside herself?
There's no point in letting this go on. She doesn't know what she's saying. She must be got to bed. . . . Madame, there'll be some way to arrange everything, you'll see. Don't cry any more. Please."

The sobbing caught in her throat. She looked at me with those pale,
drowned eyes. The beauty had all gone. The delicately rouged cheeks
sagged slack and gray, and her mouth was loose and blurred with crying.
I said, "There've been enough tears over this, madame. Don't distress
yourself any more. Nothing's going to happen to you. It's all over now.
Here, take my handkerchief. . . . Why, you're cold! I don't know why
you're sitting here when there's a stove in the study; and you haven't
been well lately, have you? Shall we go in there, and perhaps we can get
Gaston to bring some coffee? Can you get up? Let me help you. . . ."

She got to her feet slowly, stiffly, and I led her across to the study
door. She came obediently, as if she were sleepwalking. The others followed. Nobody spoke. She was weeping still, but quietly, into my handkerchief. I put her into a chair near the stove, and knelt again beside her
on the rug.

I don't know quite what else I said to her, but the sobbing stopped,
and presently she lay back in the chair quietly, and looked at me. She
looked exhausted, dazed almost. She said abruptly, in a flat, sleepwalker's tone, "I liked you, Miss Martin. I liked you from the first."

I said soothingly, "I know you did. It's all right. Don't worry now.
We'll get you home, and—"

"You wouldn't really have been blamed for the accidents, you know.
We didn't mean to blame you. We never meant at the beginning to make
you responsible."

NINE COACHES WAITING

"No."

"Léon liked you too. He said you were gallant. That was the word. He said, 'She's a gallant little devil and it'd be a pity if we had to bring her down.' "

Raoul said very quietly, from behind me, "And just what did he mean by that?"

Madame de Valmy took no notice. She seemed oblivious of anyone but herself and me. She held my hands and looked at me with those pale dazed eyes, and talked in that tired monotone that she didn't seem to be able to stop. "He said that just a day or so ago. Of course, after the second accident on the balcony we were going to have to dismiss you, you know. He said you were too wide-awake and now you'd begin to suspect us if anything else happened. We were pleased when you gave us the excuse to send you away. You thought I was angry, didn't you?"

"Yes, madame."

"Then we got the cable. We had to do something in a hurry. There were the rumors in the village about you and Raoul, and about your being dismissed, but Léon said it might come in useful later anyway, if the village had been linking your names."

Behind me I heard Raoul take in his breath as if to speak. I said quickly, to divert her, "Yes, madame, I know. Albertine started to talk, didn't she? Well, don't think about that now."

"She never knew what we were trying to do," said Madame de Valmy. "But she didn't like you. She never liked you. It was she who told me about the muddle you'd made with the prescriptions that time. She only told me to show you up. She thought I'd think you careless and silly. It was only spite. But that's what made us think of the poison, you see. That was the only reason we thought of using those pills. We weren't trying to fix it on you, Miss Martin. It was to have looked like an accident. It was in the glucose, you understand. The poison was in the glucose that you used every night to make his chocolate with."

"Madame—"

"Luckily there wasn't much left in the tin, so we soaked the blue color off the tablets and powdered them up and made a strong mixture. Too strong perhaps. It may have been bitter. He didn't take it, did he?"

"No. But that wasn't why." I turned desperately to Hippolyte, who was standing silently over by the desk. "May I ring and ask for some coffee, Monsieur de Valmy? I really think—"

"We hadn't time to think of anything better," said Héloïse. "It was to look like an accident. If he had taken it and died they might not have thought of murder. Those antihistamine pills are blue. The doctor might have thought he'd taken them as sweets. Children do. We meant to empty out the rest of the glucose and leave one or two pills by his bed. There were some in a jar on your mantelpiece, where he might have found them and eaten them. You mightn't have been blamed. They would have thought you'd forgotten to give them to Mrs. Seddon. Léon said you might not be blamed even then."

Behind me Raoul said, "Just what are you talking about, Héloïse?"

She looked up at him with that dead, sleepwalker's look. She seemed to have forgotten her outburst. She answered him mechanically, "The poison. It wasn't a very good plan, but we had to be sure and it was all we could think of that might look like an accident. But he didn't take it. It's all right. She said so. I was just explaining to her that we didn't mean her any harm. I like her. I always did."

I said quickly, "Madame, you're upset. You don't know what you're saying. Now we're going to have some coffee, and we'll see you home."

Across me Raoul said, "And if Miss Martin *had* been blamed? If murder *had* been suspected? You had made it common knowledge, hadn't you, that she and I—that there might be an interested reason to get rid of Philippe?"

She said nothing. She stared up at him.

"Was that what my father meant when he said that the gossip 'might have been useful later'?"

I heard Hippolyte begin to say something, but Raoul cut across it. "On Tuesday night, Héloïse . . . who was it found Philippe had gone?"

"Léon did. He stayed awake. We were going to empty out the rest of the glucose and—"

"So you said. He found Philippe gone. And then?"

"He thought he must have felt ill and gone for Miss Martin. But there was no light there. She'd gone too."

"And when he couldn't find them, what then?"

"He sent Bernard out to look for them."

Raoul said, "With what instructions?"

She said nothing. Under the hammering of his questions she seemed to have come partly to life again. Her eyes were conscious now, blinking nervously up at him.

"With what instructions, Héloïse?"

Still she didn't answer. She didn't need to. Her features seemed to flatten out and melt like candle grease. Hippolyte said, harshly, "That's enough, Raoul."

"Yes," said Raoul. "I think it is."

He walked out of the room and shut the door behind him.

For a moment nobody moved. Then Héloïse came to her feet, thrusting me aside so that I fell over on the rug.

She stood there with her hands slack at her sides. She said, almost conversationally, "Léon. He's gone to kill Léon." Then she crumpled beside me on the rug in a dead faint.

I left her there. I remember leaping to my feet, to stand like a fool on the rug beside her, gaping at the shut door. I remember Hippolyte starting forward and shouting, *"Raoul! Come back, you fool!"* He was answered by the slam of the front door. He turned with a sound like a groan and jumped for the telephone. I remember that, as he touched it, it began to ring.

Before it had threshed once I was out on the gallery and racing for the head of the stairs. There were steps behind me and William's hand caught at my arm. "Linda, Linda. Where are you going? Keep out of this. You can't do a thing."

Outside, an engine roared to violent life. A door slammed. The Cadillac gained the road, paused, whined up through her gears, and snarled away into the silence.

I shook off William's hand and fled down the curving stairs. Across the hall, and struggling with the heavy door . . . William reached over my shoulder and yanked it open. The lamp over the door showed the dark circular drive walled in with misty trees . . . a big black car . . . a battered jeep . . . the scored grooves in the gravel where the Cadillac's tires had torn their circle. The smell of her exhaust hung in the air.

I ran out.

William caught at my arm. "For God's sake, Linda—"

"We've got to stop him! We've got to stop him!"

"But—"

"Didn't you understand? He's gone to kill Léon. He said he would, and they'll have to kill him for it. Don't you understand?"

He still held me. "But what can you do? You've been mixed up in enough of their dirty game as it is. Let me take you away. There's nothing you can do. You said yourself it was finished. What's it to you if they murder each other?"

"Oh, dear God, what's it to me? William—" I was clinging to him now—"William, you have to help. I—I can't drive a car. Please, William, please, *please*—"

The night, the misty trees, the solitary lamp in its yellow nimbus, were all part of the roaring horror that enveloped me, that was only my own blood pounding in my ears. . . .

He said quietly, "Very well, let's go," and his hand closed over mine for a moment. As the world steadied around me I saw that he was opening the door of the jeep.

I said shakily, "No. The other." I ran to the big Daimler and pulled

the door open. It was the Valmy car. Héloïse must have had it down to
the airport to meet Hippolyte.

William followed me. His voice was doubtful. "Ought we to?"

"It's faster. The key's in. Oh, William, hurry!"

"Okay."

And then we were away. Our wheels whined around in the same
circle, skidding on the gravel. Our lights raked the trees, the lodge, the
willows fronded with weeping mist. . . . We took the gate cautiously,
gained the road, and swung right.

Along the narrow, fog-dimmed road with its soaring dark trees; a
sharp turn left, a steep little climb between echoing walls; right again,
then a series of dizzy, whipping turns through the steep streets that
climbed up to the town. Now we had reached the upper level, and were
clear of the mist. We swept along a wide curved boulevard where lamps
flickered by among the pollard willows. . . . A sharp swing right, and
we scudded across the empty market place where cobbles gleamed
damply and a few flattened cabbage leaves lay in a gutter like a drift of
giant leaves. William had got the feel of the car now. We swirled right-
handed into a badly-lighted avenue and gathered speed. The lopped
chestnuts flicked past us one by one, faster, faster, faster. . . .

We were out of the little town. Our headlights leaped out ahead of us,
and the engine's note rose powerfully, and held steady.

Ahead of us the road forked. A signboard flashed up in the white
light and tore toward us.

We took the left for Valmy.

William was, I thought, as good a driver as Raoul, but Raoul had not
only a start, but a faster car which was, moreover, the one he was accustomed to drive. But after a while I began to hope that even these
advantages might not help him too much, for very soon after leaving
Thonon we met the mist again. Not the tree-haunting gray mist that had
risen from the lake to moat the Villa Mireille, but little clouds and clots
of white brume, breathed up from the river to lie in all the hollows of a
road that was never far from the water. Each time the car's nose dipped
a dazzling cumulus of white struck back the light at us, swept over us,
blinded, engulfed us, then even as the engine slowed and hesitated we
roared up out of cloud again into the calm black air. At first the experience was unnerving; the moment of blindness was like a great white
hand thrust against your face, so that you flinched backward against the
upholstery, and were conscious of your eyes' catlike dilation. But with
each succeeding dive into the cloud the car's hesitation became less apparent and after a while I realized that William was losing very little

speed. He seemed to know unerringly just how the road lifted and curved, where the mist would lie for fifty yards and where for five, and he sliced through the fog patches with the confidence of the man who—literally—knows his road blindfold. He must have driven up and down it scores of times in the course of his job; it was even probable that he knew it better than Raoul, who for some time had lived most of his year between Bellevigne and Paris. We might catch him yet. . . .

So at any rate I told myself, huddled down in the seat beside William and staring with eyes that winced through the marching clouds of mist to catch a glimpse of a vanishing tail-light around some curve ahead.

William said, "What was all that about, Linda?"

"What d'you mean? Oh—I keep forgetting you don't speak French." I gave a shaky little laugh. "I'm sorry, William. I—I'm not thinking very clearly tonight. I haven't even said thank you for coming. I've just rushed you into my affairs and used you like this. I—I'm terribly grateful. I really am."

"Think nothing of it. But you'd better put me in the picture, hadn't you?"

So I told him the story from the beginning—not very clearly, I'm afraid, and with halts and pauses due to weariness and the fear that clawed at me, while the car roared on up that wicked valley road and the night went by us smoothly as a dream. The dark road fell away, streamed, poured away behind us; the thin gray trees reeled past us into nothingness; the mist clouds marched, fled, broke and streamed away from us in mackerel flakes like rack in the wind.

The red tail-light struck at my eyes like a dagger.

I said hoarsely, "There. William. Look, there."

He didn't answer, but I knew he'd seen it. Then it vanished and a moment later the blinding white swamped us again. Out into a patch of clear darkness, and then another cloud was on us, but this time thin, so that our yellow-dimmed lights made rainbows in it that wisped away along our wings, and we were through.

The car gathered speed up a steady straight rise. And the fleeing red light was there, not three hundred yards ahead.

He didn't seem to be traveling so very fast. We were gaining, gaining rapidly. Two hundred yards, a hundred and fifty . . . the gap dwindled. We were coming up fast. Too fast.

"It's only a truck," said William, and lifted his foot.

We ran up close behind it and asked to be let by.

It was one of those appalling monsters so common in France, far too high and wide for any road, and far too fast for their size. And it became obvious very soon that this one had no intention of allowing us the road. Ignoring the flickering of our lights it roared along, rocking a little on the bends, but never yielding an inch of the crown of the road.

I don't know how long we were behind it. It seemed a year. I sat with my nails driving holes into the palms of my hands, and my teeth savaging my lip while I stared with hatred at the dirty blackboard of the truck held in our lights. It was carrying gravel, which dripped through the cracks onto the road. Someone had chalked a face like a gremlin on the left-hand panel. To this day I can see the license plate with the chip off the corner and read the number. 920-DE75. . . . I stared at it without consciously seeing it at all, and thought of the Cadillac roaring on ahead, of Raoul and Léon and the terrible little scene that, unbelievably, was so soon to be acted out in the Valmy library.

I said again, "William. . . ."

"If the Caddy passed him," said William calmly, "we can. Hold on." There wasn't even a trace of impatience in his voice. He drew out to the left, flickered his lights again, and waited. The truck lumbered on. We were on an upgrade now, and the truck was slowing. It held the road, and once again we drew patiently in behind it.

So we went in procession up the hill. A sob rose and burst in my throat and I put the back of my hand hard against my teeth in an effort for self-control.

The truck slowed, slowed again, and checked as it was rammed into bottom gear. We crawled toward the head of the rise.

The trees that crowned the hilltop swelled into light that soared toward us. Lights were coming up the other side of the hill, and coming fast. Their gray aurora spread, splayed brighter, lifted into gold. The truck topped the crest of the road, black against the approaching glare, and swung sharply over to its right to make way for the oncoming car.

Our own lights flashed once, and dimmed. Something hit me in the small of the back as the Daimler shot forward like a torpedo into the gap.

Lights met lights with a clash that could be felt. Then we whipped to the right almost under the truck's front bumper. I heard the yell of a horn and something that might have been a shout, but we were through with a little to spare and dropping downhill with the rush of a lift.

"Oh, you honey," said William affectionately to the car, and then sent me a grin. I had bitten the back of my hand but his breathing wasn't even ruffled. "It's nice," he said mildly, "to have the horses. . . ."

The road lifted once more, to shake itself clear of mist. William's foot went down and those horses took hold. My eyes strained through the darkness ahead for that telltale light among the trees.

But no light showed till we rounded the curve where the road begins the long drop to the Valmy bridge, and saw the lurch and sway of lights that cut their way up the zigzag nearly half-a-mile ahead.

I must have made some small sound, for William gave me a glance and said, "Don't fret, my dear. They'll talk it over, surely?" But he didn't sound convinced, and neither was I. We'd both seen Raoul's face. And the way those distant headlights now slashed their way up the zigzag was some indication that the mood still held.

I saw them vanish at the top under the château's bright windows. William accelerated, and we shot down the last hill, met a wall of mist hood-high, slowed, sang down to second for the turn onto the bridge— and then stopped short, with brakes squealing.

I said breathlessly, "What is it?"

"Can two cars pass on that road?"

"The zigzag? No. But—"

He nodded toward it. I followed his gaze and said, "Oh, dear Lord," on a dreary little sob. A car had nosed its way down off the driveway and was taking the first hairpin with some caution. It got around, and came on its decorous way down. . . .

"Where are you going?" asked William sharply.

I was fumbling with the door. "There's a path straight up from the bridge through the wood . . . steps . . . I think I could—"

He reached across and his hand closed over mine. "Don't be silly. You'd break your heart and I'd still be there before you. Sit still."

"But William—"

"My dear girl, I know. But there's nothing else to do." His voice was calm. "Look, he's nearly down. Sit still."

I was shaking uncontrollably. "Of course. It—it doesn't matter to you, does it?"

His eyes were grave and gentle. "And it does to you? It really does?"

I said nothing. The descending car swung around the last bend, and her lights sank toward the bridge. There was mist lying as it had lain that night.

William said gently, "I'm sorry, Linda."

The car was crossing the bridge, nosing through the mist. It paused, and moved out into the road with a lamentable crash of gears. William's hand shifted and the Daimler leaped for the gap and went over the bridge with the mist flying out from the headlamps like spray in the teeth of a destroyer.

For a fleeting second before the cliff cut it off from view I lifted my eyes and saw the Château Valmy, brightly lighted against the night sky. That was what William meant; I knew it. The castle in the air, the

Cinderella dream—nonsense for a night. *Banquets abroad by torchlight, music, sports, nine coaches waiting!*

Not for you, Linda my girl. You get yourself back to North London.

The Daimler lurched up and around the final curve, and skidded wildly as her wheels met the gravel of the drive. She came to a rocking halt just behind the parked Cadillac.

There was another car in the drive and a van of sorts, but I hardly noticed them. I had my door open before our wheels had shrieked to a stop, and was out and stumbling up the steps to the great door.

Seddon was in the hall. He started forward when he saw me and I heard him say, "Oh, Miss Martin—" but I fled past him as if he didn't exist, and down the long corridor that led to the library.

The door was slightly ajar and a light showed. As I reached it my panic courage spilled out of me like wine from a smashed glass and I stopped dead with my hands actually on the panels ready to push.

Inside the room there was no sound.

I pushed the door open softly, took three steps into the room, and stopped short.

There were several men in the room, but I only saw two of them.

Raoul de Valmy was standing with his back to the door, staring down at his father.

For once Léon de Valmy was not in his wheel chair. He had fallen forward and out of it onto the floor. His body lay clumsily, pulled a little crooked by whatever harness he wore under his clothes. His head was turned to one side, his cheek against the carpet. His face was smooth, wiped clean of every line and shadow; beauty and evil had emptied themselves from it together. Now there was nothing there at all.

From where I was you could hardly see the blackened hole in the temple.

I would have fallen where I stood but that William's arms came around me from behind and swept me up and out of the silent room.

CHAPTER XXI

Ninth Coach

Look you, the stars shine still.
JOHN WEBSTER: *The Duchess of Malfi.*

. . . WARMTH, and the sound of liquid, and the smell of azaleas . . .
And someone was patting my hand. But there was no music, and the
voice that said my name was not Florimond's. Nor was Raoul there waiting to sweep me out onto the terrace and under the moon. . . .

William said, "Here, Linda, drink this."

The liquid burned sourly on my tongue and made me gasp. I opened
my eyes.

I was in the small salon, lying on the sofa before the fire. Someone had
made this up recently. Tongues of pale flame licked around the new logs.
I stared at them dazedly. I had never fainted before, and the memory of
the roaring dizziness frightened me and I put an unsteady hand up to
my eyes. The salon still swam around me, too bright and a little out of
focus.

"Finish it," urged William.

I obeyed him meekly. It was detestable stuff, whatever it was, but it
ran into my body warm and potent, so that in a few moments more my
eyes and fingers and even my brain were mine again. And my memory.

"How d'you feel now?" asked William.

I said drearily, "Oh, fine. Just fine. I'm sorry, William. That wasn't a
very useful thing to do."

He took the glass from my hand and put it on the mantelpiece. Then
he sat down on the sofa beside me. "Nothing we've done tonight has
been so terribly useful, has it?"

I found myself staring at him in a kind of daze. Of course. It was
nothing to him. I said, dragging the words up from the depths, "Have
they . . . taken him away yet?"

"Not yet."

"William. I've got to . . . see him. Just for a moment. I've got to."

I heard stupefaction in his voice. "But, my dear Linda—"

"When will he go?"

"I've no idea, the police are still busy. The ambulance is waiting."

I gave a little gasp and turned my head sharply. "Ambulance? Is he hurt? What's happened?" I sat up and gripped his arm. The bright roaring mist was there again. Dimly through it I saw William's eyes, puzzled and a little shocked. Dimly I heard him say, "But Linda. Didn't you realize? I thought you knew. He's dead."

My grip must have been savaging his sleeve. His hand came up to cover mine, quietly. "He shot himself," said William, "some time before Raoul and you and I got here."

"Oh," I said, in a silly high voice, "Léon. Léon shot himself. The ambulance is for Léon."

"Why—who else?"

I heard myself give a cracked breathless little laugh. "Who indeed?" I said, and burst into tears.

It was hard luck on William. And for a shy British amateur, he was certainly doing very well. He produced some more of that filthy drink, and patted my hand some more too, and put a large comforting arm around me.

"I thought you'd grasped the situation," he was saying. "I thought it was just the shock of seeing, er, Monsieur Léon that made you faint. . . . The butler chap was telling me all about it just now when he brought the drink for you. I thought you heard. I'd no idea you were right out."

"I—I wasn't really. I heard you talking. But I didn't take it in. It was like voices in a dream . . . coming and going."

The arm tightened momentarily. "You poor kid. Better now?"

I nodded. "Go on, tell me. What did Seddon say?"

"Is that his name? Thank God he's English! Well, he told me he'd gone in to look at the library fire soon after eleven, and found him dead on the floor, the way you saw him. Nobody heard the shot. He called the police and the doctor straight away, and then the Villa Mireille, but got no answer there."

"That would be before Philippe and I got into the house."

"Oh? They tried again later, twice. I suppose the first time was while you were telephoning me, and then they finally got Monsieur Hippolyte. That would be the call that came through as we left the house. Hippolyte's on his way up. He'll be here before long."

"If he knows how to drive the jeep."

"Oh, murder," said William. "I never thought of that."

I said, "Are they sure it was suicide?"

"Oh, quite. The gun was in his hand, and there's a letter."

"A letter. Léon de Valmy left a letter?"

"Yes. The police have it. Seddon didn't read it, but from what the police asked him he pretty well gathered what it said. It admitted the first two attempts to murder Philippe, involving Bernard, but nobody else. He states categorically that neither Raoul nor Madame de Valmy knew anything about them. He never mentions this last affair of the poison—I suppose that would almost certainly involve his wife. He simply says that Bernard must have let something out to you about the two early attempts, and you got in a panic and bolted with Philippe. I think that's about the lot. You've certainly nothing to worry about."

"No." I was silent for a moment. "Well, I shan't volunteer anything else unless they ask me. I don't somehow want to pile anything more onto Madame de Valmy, whatever she did. *He's* dead, you see. She's got that to go on living with. Funny, one somehow imagines her snuffing quietly out now, the way the moon would if the sun vanished. Somehow it's like Léon to let her out, and me, and yet to turn the wretched Bernard in . . . though I suppose it was impossible to hide his part in it. And Bernard failed, after all."

"That's not why," said William. "When Bernard found you both gone and Raoul on the trail he must have realized that Léon de Valmy's bolt was shot and that there'd never be a future and a fortune for him the way he'd been promised. He moved onto the winning side, probably with an eye to the future, and played in with Raoul all day, looking for you and Philippe. Then last night—three or four hours ago—he came and tried to retrieve the lost fortune by putting the black on Monsieur Léon."

"Blackmail?"

"Yes. It's in the letter. He threatened to turn informer. If you ask me, that's what tipped Léon de Valmy's scales toward suicide in the end. I mean, there's no end to blackmail, is there?"

I said slowly, "You're probably right. I was wondering what had made him kill himself instead of waiting to see what Raoul and Hippolyte would do. After all, it was still all in the family. But when one thinks about it . . . Even if Raoul and Hippolyte and I had agreed to hush the whole thing up for Philippe's sake and the sake of the family—what was there left for Léon de Valmy? Hippolyte would be able to put any sort of pressure on that he liked, and he might have insisted on Léon's leaving Valmy. Even if Léon was allowed to stay, Hippolyte would start sitting down tight on the moneybags, and presumably Raoul would be in a position to stop Léon milking Bellevigne any more. . . . And in any case Léon would have had to get out in six years' time. And we all—

even Philippe—knew what he'd done and what he was. . . . And then, finally, the wretched fool Bernard started to blackmail him. Yes, one can see a desperate moment for Léon, and no future. Certainly he wasn't the kind of man to submit to blackmail; he'd literally die sooner, I'm sure of it. It only surprises me that he didn't kill Bernard first, but I suppose Bernard would be on guard against that, and he did have certain physical advantages. What did happen to Bernard anyway? *Did* Léon kill him?"

"No, he's disappeared. There'll be a hue and cry, but I suppose it's to be hoped that he gets away, and the rest of the story with him."

I said, "Yes. Poor little Berthe."

"Who's that?"

"Oh, nobody. Just one of the nobodies who get hurt the most when wicked men start to carve life up to suit themselves. You know, William, I doubt if I was altogether right about why Léon de Valmy killed himself. . . . I imagine all those things would be there, part of it, in his mind, but it would be something else that tipped him over. I think I knew him rather well. He'd been beaten. He'd been shown up. And I don't think he could have taken that, whatever happened later. He was— I think the word's a megalomaniac. He had to see himself as larger than life . . . everything that happened was seen only in relation to him. . . . He sort of focused your attention on himself all the time, and he could do it, William. I believed he liked to think he could play with people just as he wanted to. He *couldn't* ever have taken second place to anyone. To shoot himself, making that magnanimous gesture with the letter . . . yes, that was Léon de Valmy all right." I leaned back wearily. "Well, whatever his reasons, it made the best end, didn't it? Oh, God, William, I'm so tired."

He said anxiously, "Are you all right? What about some more brandy?"

"No, thanks. It's all right. This is just the anticlimax hitting me."

"D'you want to go now? Perhaps we could—"

"Go. Where to?"

He pushed his fingers through his hair. "I—yes, I hadn't thought of that. They didn't exactly get the red carpets out at the Villa Mireille, did they? Though if you ask me they owe you a ruddy great vote of thanks, and I'll tell them so myself if nobody else does!"

"They know, for what it's worth," I said.

"But you don't want to stay here, do you?"

"What else can I do? When Monsieur Hippolyte gets around to it, he'll see that I get my passage paid back to England."

"You'll go home?"

"Yes." I looked at him and gave a smile of a sort. "You see, when you're in my position you can't afford to make the grand gesture, William. I can't just sweep out. I'm afraid I must wait here till the police have asked all their questions. I think I'll go along and see Berthe now, and then come back here and wait for them."

"Hang on, here's someone coming," said William. "Yes, here they are."

I must still have been in a semidazed condition, because, although I remember quite well exactly what the police inspector looked like, I can't recall our interview with any accuracy. I did gather that after Léon de Valmy's death the frightened servants had poured out the story of Philippe's and my disappearance and all the accompanying rumors, but that the suicide's letter, together with what Hippolyte de Valmy had said over the telephone and—finally—an interview with Raoul, had strangled stillborn any doubts about myself. This much I understood soon enough: the inspector's manner with me was gentle and even respectful, and I found myself answering his questions readily and without any anxiety other than the dreadful obsessional one—the fox under my cloak that kept my eyes on the open door all through the half-hour or so of question and answer, and made my heart jump and jerk every time anyone passed along the corridor.

The inspector left us eventually when Hippolyte arrived. I saw them pass the door together on the way to the library. Hippolyte was still pale and tired looking, but very composed. It was easy to suppose that, once the shock was over, the news would prove a relief.

I wondered fleetingly about Héloïse, and then again, sharply, about Berthe. But as I got to my feet to go in search of her Seddon came in with coffee, and in response to my inquiries told me that the police had dealt with her very kindly, and had (when the interview was over) sent her in one of their cars down to her mother's house in the village. I supposed this was the car that had held us up at the zigzag. There was nothing more to be done for Berthe except to hope that Bernard could be forgotten, so I sat wearily down again while Seddon poured me some coffee. He lingered for a while, asking me about Philippe, to vanish at length in the direction of the hall when Hippolyte came into the room.

William got to his feet a little awkwardly. I put my coffee cup down on the floor and made to follow suit, but Hippolyte said quickly, "No, please," and then, in English, to William, "Don't go."

I began to say, "Monsieur de Valmy, I—we're awfully sorry—"

But he stopped me with a gesture, and coming over to the sofa he bent over me and took both my hands in his. Then, before I knew what he was about, he kissed them.

"That is for Philippe," he said. "We owe you a very great deal, it seems, Miss Martin, and I have come belatedly to thank you and to ask you to forgive me for my rather cavalier treatment of you at the Villa Mireille."

I said rather feebly, "You had other things on your mind, monsieur." I wanted to tell him not to bother about me but to go back to his own worries and his own personal tragedy, but I couldn't, so I sat and let him thank me again with his grave courteous charm, and tried not to watch the door while he talked, or to think how like Raoul's his voice was.

I realized suddenly that he had left the past and was talking about the future.

". . . He will stay with me at the Villa Mireille for the time being. Miss Martin—dare I hope that after your very terrible experience you will stay with him?"

I stared at him for some time, stupidly, before I realized what he was asking me. He must, in his own tragic preoccupation, have forgotten Raoul's confession concerning me. I said, "I—I don't know. Just at the moment—"

"I quite see. I had no right to put it to you now. You look exhausted, child, and no wonder. Later, perhaps, you can think it over."

There was a queer sound from the corridor, a kind of slow, heavy shuffling. Then I knew what it was, Léon, leaving the Château Valmy. I looked down at my hands.

Hippolyte was saying steadily, "If under the circumstances you prefer not to spend the night here, there's a place for you as long as you choose to stay at the Villa Mireille."

"Why, thank you. Yes, I—I would like that. Thank you very much."

"Then if we can find someone to take you down—"

He had glanced at William, who said immediately, "Of course." Then he stammered and added awkwardly, "I say, sir, I'm terribly sorry about taking the car. We thought—that is, we were in a hurry. I really am awfully sorry."

"It's nothing." Hippolyte dismissed the theft with a gesture. "I believe you thought you might prevent a tragedy—a worse one than what actually happened." His eyes moved somberly to the door. "I'm sure you will understand me when I say that . . . this . . . was not altogether a tragedy." Another glance at William, this time with the faintest glimmer of a smile underlying the somber look. "You'll find your own—extraordinary vehicle—outside. And now good night."

He went. I picked up my coffee cup absently, but the stuff was cold and skinning over. I set it down again. A log fell in with a soft crash of sparks. No movement now outside in the corridor. I looked at the clock. It had stopped. *The world-without-end hour. . . . Nor dare I chide the world-without-end hour, whilst I (my sovereign) watch the clock for you. . . .*

"Linda," said William. He came and sat beside me on the sofa. He reached out and took both my cold hands in his. Safe, gentle hands; steady, sensible hands. "Linda," he said again, and cleared his throat.

I woke to the present as to a cold touch on the shoulder. I sat up straighter. I said, "William, I want to thank you most awfully for what you've done. I don't know what I'd have done without you tonight, honestly I don't. I'd no business to call you in the way I did, but I was so terribly on my own, and you were my only friend."

"It's a friend's privilege to be used," said William. He loosed my hands. There was a pause. He said, "If you are going to stay with Philippe, I might see you now and again, mightn't I?"

"I don't suppose I'll be staying."

"No?"

"No."

"I see." He got to his feet and smiled down at me. "Shall I run you down to the Villa Mireille now in the jeep?"

"No, thanks, William. I—think I'll wait."

"Okay. I'll say good night, then. You'll look me up before you leave, won't you?"

"Of course. Good night. And . . . thanks a lot, William. Thank you for everything."

I forgot him almost as soon as the front door shut behind him. Someone had come out of the library. I could hear Hippolyte's voice, and Raoul's, talking quietly. They were coming along the corridor together.

My heart was hurting me. I got up quickly and moved toward the door. Hippolyte was talking, saying something about Héloïse. I shrank against the wall to the side of the door so that they wouldn't see me as they passed.

". . . A nursing home," said Hippolyte. "I left her with Doctor Fauré. He'll look after her." There was something more—something about a small allowance, a pension, and "somewhere away from Valmy, Paris or Cannes," and finally the words, dimly heard as they moved away along the corridor, "her heart," and "not very long, perhaps. . . ."

They had reached the hall. Hippolyte was saying good night. I went softly out into the corridor and hesitated there, waiting for Hippolyte to leave him. I was shaking with panic. Léon and Héloïse might have faded already into the past, poor ghosts with no more power to terrify, but I had a ghost of my own to lay.

Raoul's voice, now, asking a question. Seddon's answer, almost indistinguishable. It sounded like *"Gone."* A sharp query from Raoul, and, clearly, from Seddon, "Yes, sir. A few minutes ago."

I heard Raoul say, grimly, "I see. Thank you. Good night, Seddon."

Then I realized what he had been asking. I forgot Hippolyte's presence and Seddon's. I began to run down the corridor. I called, "Raoul!"

My voice was drowned in the slam of the front door.

I had reached the hall when I heard the engine start. Seddon's voice said, surprised, "Why, Miss Martin, I thought you'd gone with Mr. Blake!" I didn't answer. I flew across the hall, tore open the great door, and ran out into the darkness.

The Cadillac was already moving. As I reached the bottom of the steps she was wheeling away from the house. I called again, but he didn't hear—or at least the car still moved, gathering speed. Futilely, I began to run.

I was still twenty yards behind it when it slid gently into the first curve of the zigzag, and out of sight.

If I had stopped to think I should never have done what I did. But I was past thinking. I only knew that I had something to say that must be said if I was ever to sleep again. And I wasn't the only one that had to be healed. I turned without hesitation and plunged into the path that short-circuited the zigzag.

This was a footway, no more, that dived steeply down the hillside toward the Valmy bridge. I had taken it with Philippe many a time. It was well kept, and the steps, where they occurred, were wide and safe, but it could be slippery, and in the dark it could probably be suicide.

I didn't care. Some kind freak of chance had made me keep Philippe's torch in my pocket, and now by its halfhearted light I went down that dizzy little track as if all my ghosts hunted me at heel.

Off to the left the Cadillac's lights still bore away from me on the first long arm of the zigzag. The engine made very little sound. I hurtled, careless of sprains and bruises, down through the wood.

It couldn't be done, of course. He was still below me when he took the first bend and the headlights bore back to the north, making the shadows of the trees where I ran reel and flicker so that they seemed to catch at my feet like a net.

The path twisted down like a snake. The whole wood marched and shifted in his lights like trees in a nightmare. Just before he wheeled away again I saw the next segment of my path doubling back ten feet below me. I didn't wait to negotiate the corner with its steps and its handrail. I slithered over, half on my back, to the lower level, and gained seven

precious seconds before the dark pounced again in the wake of the retreating car.

The third arm of the zigzag was the longest. It took him away
smoothly to the left without much of a drop. I flung myself down a steep
smooth drop, caught at a handrail to steady myself, and then went three
at a time down a straight flight of steps. The rail had driven a splinter
into my hand, but I hardly felt it. A twig whipped my face, half blinding
me, but I just blinked and ran on. Down the steps, around, along over a
little gorge bridged with a flagstone . . . and the great headlights had
swung north and the shadows were once more madly wheeling around
me. They blurred and wavered, caught at me like the ropes of a great
web. My breath was sobbing; my heartbeats hammered above the sound
of the oncoming car, and there was a silly little prayer on my lips.
"Please, please, please," it was, and it spun in my brain like a prayer
wheel to the exclusion of any kind of sense or thought.

I didn't stop. Two more sweeps of the zigzag, and the Valmy bridge,
and—he was away. I left the path and simply went down the shortest
way between the trees, a steep slope ending in a rocky drop below which
was the bridge itself. I fetched up hard against the trunk of a beech at
the very edge of the drop. The mist lying over the river swirled up into
silver as the Cadillac wheeled and then dived smoothly for the last
bend.

I went over the drop. The stone was glowing queerly in the light that
came off the mist. I suppose I got scratches and knocks, I don't know. I
do know that I slipped once and gripped at a holly bush to save myself
and even as I bit the cry off I heard the shriek of the Cadillac's brakes.

I found out later that something had run across the road. I like to
think it was the same anonymous little creature that had been there the
first time Raoul kissed me. At any rate it stopped the car for those few
precious seconds—just those few seconds.

I dropped into the road just as his lights swept around the last curve.

I ran onto the bridge. The mist swirled up waist-high. It was gray, it
was white, it was blinding gold as the glare took it.

I shut my eyes and put both hands out and stayed exactly where I
was.

Brakes and tires shrieked to a stop. I opened my eyes. The mist was
curling and frothing from the car's hood not three yards from me. Then
the headlights went out and the grateful dark swept down. In the small
glow of the car's sidelights the mist tossed like smoke. I took three fal-
tering, trembling steps forward and put a hand on her wing. I leaned
against it, fighting for breath. The little prayer wheel still spun, and the

prayer sounded the same: *"Please, please, please. . . ."* But it was different.

He got out of the car and walked forward. He was on the other side of the hood. In the uncertain, fog-distorted light he looked taller than ever.

I managed to say, "I was . . . waiting. I've got to . . . see you."

He said, "They told me you'd gone." He added unemotionally, "You little fool, I might have killed you."

My breathing was coming under control, but my legs still felt as if they weren't my own. I leaned heavily on the wing of the car. I said, "I had to tell you I was sorry, Raoul. It's not exactly—adequate—to tell a man you're sorry you suspected him of murder . . . but I am. I'm sorry I even let it cross my mind. And that was all it did. I swear it."

He had his driving gloves in his hand and he was jerking them through and through his fingers. He didn't speak.

I went on miserably, "I'm not trying to excuse myself. I know you'll not forgive me. It would have been bad enough without what—was between us, but as it is . . . Raoul, I just want you to understand a little. Only I don't somehow know how to start explaining."

"You don't have to. I understand."

"I don't think you do. I was *told,* you see, told flatly that you were in it, along with your—with the others. Bernard had said so to Berthe. He told her that you had done the shooting in the wood. I imagine he realized, even when he'd gone so far, that he'd better not own to *that.* And he may have thought you *would* condone the murder once you saw the advantages of it. I didn't believe it, even when she told me flatly. I couldn't. But the rest was so obvious, once I knew, about . . . them, I mean, and there was nothing to prove you weren't in it with them. Nothing except the—the way I felt about you."

I paused, straining my eyes to see his expression. He seemed a very long way away.

I said, "I don't expect you to believe it, Raoul, but I was fighting on your side. All the time. I've been through a very private special little hell since Tuesday night. You called it a 'damnable exercise,' remember? Everything conspired to accuse you, and I was half silly with unhappiness and . . . yes, and doubt, till I couldn't even trust my own senses any more. . . . Oh, I won't drag you through it all now; you've had enough, and you want to be done with this and with me, but I—I had to tell you before you go. It was simply that I couldn't take the chance, Raoul! You do see that, don't you? Say you see that!"

He jerked the gloves in his fingers. His voice was quite flat, dull, almost. "You were prepared to take chances—once."

"Myself, yes. But this was Philippe. I had no right to take a chance on Philippe. I didn't dare. He was my charge—my duty." The miserable words sounded priggish and unutterably absurd. "I—was all he had. Beside *that*, it couldn't be allowed to matter."

"What couldn't?"

"That you were all I had," I said.

Another silence. He was standing very still now. Was it a trick of the mist or was he really a very long way away from me, a lonely figure in the queerly-lighted darkness? It came to me suddenly that this was how I would always remember him, someone standing alone, apart from the others even of his own family. And, I think for the first time, I began to see him as he really was—not any more as a projection of my young romantic longings, not any more as Prince Charming, the handsome sophisticate, the tiger I thought I preferred. . . . This was Raoul, who had been a quiet lonely little boy in a house that was "not a house for children," an unhappy adolescent brought up in the shadow of a megalomaniac father, a young man fighting bitterly to save his small inheritance from ruin . . . wild, perhaps, hard, perhaps, plunging off the beaten track more than once . . . but always alone. Wrapped up in my loneliness and danger I hadn't even seen that his need was the same as my own. He and I hoed the same row, and he for a more bitter harvest.

I said gently, "Raoul, I'm sorry. I shouldn't have bothered you with this just now. I think you've had about all you can take. What can I say to you about your father, except that I'm sorry?"

He said, "Do you really think I would have shot him?"

"No, Raoul."

A pause. He said in a very queer voice, "I believe you do understand."

"I believe I do." I swallowed. "Even the last twenty-four hours—with the world gone mad and values shot to smithereens—I must have known, deep down, that you were you, and that was enough. Raoul, I want you to know it, then I'll go. I loved you all the time, without stopping, and I love you now."

Still he hadn't moved. I turned back toward the château. I said, "I'll leave you now. Good night."

"Where are you going?"

"Someone'll take me to the Villa Mireille. Your Uncle Hippolyte asked me to go there. I—I don't want to stay at Valmy."

"Get into the car. I'll take you down." Then, as I hesitated, "Go on, get in. Where did you think I was going?"

"I didn't think. Away."

"I was going down to the Villa Mireille to look for you."

I didn't speak; didn't move. My heart began to slam again in slow painful strokes.

"Linda." Under the quiet voice was a note I knew.

"Yes?"

"Get in."

I got in. The mist swirled and broke as the door slammed. Swirled again as he got in and slid into the seat beside me. It was dark in the car. He seemed enormous, and very near.

I was trembling. He didn't move to touch me. I cleared my throat and said the first thing that came into my head. "Where *did* you get this car? Roulette?"

"Écarté. Linda, do you intend to stay at Villa Mireille for a while with Philippe?"

"I don't know. I haven't thought things out yet. I'm awfully fond of him, but—"

Raoul said, "He'll be lonely, even with Hippolyte. Shall we have him with us at Bellevigne?"

I said breathlessly, "Raoul. Raoul. I didn't think—" I stopped. I put shaking hands up to my face.

"What is it, sweetheart?"

I said, very humbly, into my hands, "You mean you'll still . . . have me?"

I heard him take a quick breath. He didn't answer. He turned suddenly toward me and pulled me to him, not gently. What we said then is only for ourselves to remember. We talked for a long time.

Later, when we could admit between us the commonplace of laughter, he said, with the smile back in his voice, "And you've still not made me own it, my lovely. Don't you think it's time I did?"

"What are you talking about? Own what?"

"That I love you, I love you, I love you."

"Oh, *that*."

"Yes, damn it, *that*."

"I'll take a chance on it," I said. And those were the last words I spoke for a very long time.

And presently the car edged forward through the mist and turned north off the Valmy bridge.

My Brother Michael

FOR KIM IN LOVING MEMORY

AUTHOR'S NOTE

The quotations from Professor Gilbert Murray's translation of the *Electra* of Euripides appear by kind permission of Messrs. Allen & Unwin. I am also indebted to the editors of the Penguin Classics for permission to use extracts from Sophocles and Euripides in translations by E. F. Watling and Philip Vellacott; to Messrs. Faber and Faber for their leave to use the lines from Dudley Fitts' translation of *The Frogs* of Aristophanes; and to the Clarenden Press, Oxford, for the lines from Ingram Bywater's translation of Aristotle *On the Art of Poetry*.

If it were possible to do so adequately, I should like here to thank my friends in Greece—especially Electra and her family—for their very great kindness to me during my visits to their country; and I must add a particular note of thanks to those people in Delphi itself who helped me to gather information for this book: Mr. George Vouzas, of the Apollon Hotel; Mario, who showed me round; "Pete" Gerousis, who patiently answered all my questions; and the caretaker of the studio, who assured me that "things like that could never happen in Delphi." I believe him. At any rate, they never did.

M. S.

MY BROTHER MICHAEL

*If you do not love the Greeks, you
cannot love anything.*

REX WARNER

CHAPTER I

Why, woman,
What are you waiting for?
SOPHOCLES: *Electra*
(tr. E. F. Watling).

"NOTHING EVER HAPPENS to me."

I wrote the words slowly, looked at them for a moment with a little sigh, then put my ballpoint pen down on the café table and rummaged in my handbag for a cigarette.

As I breathed the smoke in I looked about me. It occurred to me, thinking of that last depressed sentence in my letter to Elizabeth, that enough was happening at the moment to satisfy all but the most adventure-hungry. That is the impression that Athens gives you. Everyone is moving, talking, gesticulating—but particularly talking. The sound one remembers in Athens is not the clamour of the impatiently congested traffic, or the perpetual hammer of pneumatic drills, or even the age-old sound of chisels chipping away at the Pentelic marble which is still the cheapest stone for building . . . what one remembers about Athens is the roar of talking. Up to your high hotel window, above the smell of dust and the blare of traffic it comes, surging like the sea below the temple at Sunium—the sound of Athenian voices arguing, laughing, talk-talk-talking, as once they talked the world into shape in the busy colonnades of the Agora, not so very far from where I sat.

It was a popular and crowded café. I had found a table at the back of the room near the bar. All along the outer wall big glass doors gave on to the pavement, standing open to the dust and din of Omonia Square, which is, in effect, the commercial centre of Athens. It is certainly the centre of all the noise and bustle of the city. The traffic crawled or surged past in a ceaseless confusion. Crowds—as jammed as the traffic—eddied on the wide pavements. Knots of men, most of them impeccably dressed in dark city clothes, discussed whatever men do discuss at mid-morning in Athens; their faces were lively and intent, their hands fidgeting unceasingly with the little loops of amber "nervous beads" that the men of the Eastern Mediterranean carry. Women, some fashionably dressed, others with the wide black skirt and black head-covering of the peasant, went about their shopping. A donkey, so laden with massed flowers that it looked like a moving garden, passed slowly by, its owner shouting his wares in vain against the hurly-burly of the hot morning streets.

I pushed my coffee cup aside, drew again at my cigarette, and picked up my letter. I began to read over what I had written.

"You'll have had my other letters by now, about Mykonos and Delos, and the one I wrote a couple of days ago from Crete. It's difficult to know just how to write—I want so much to tell you what a wonderful country this is, and yet I feel I mustn't pile it on too thick or you'll find that wretched broken leg that prevented your coming even more of a tragedy than before! Well, I won't go on about *that,* either. . . . I'm sitting in a café on Omonia Square—it's about the busiest place in this eternally busy city—and calculating what to do next. I've just come off the boat from Crete. I can't believe that there's any place on earth more beautiful than the Greek islands, and Crete's in a class by itself, magnificent and exciting and a bit grim as well—but I told you about it in my last letter. Now there's Delphi still to come, and everyone, solo and chorus, has assured me that it'll be the crown of the trip. I hope they're right; some of the places, like Eleusis and Argos and even Corinth, are a bit disappointing . . . one leaves oneself open to the ghosts, as it were, but the myths and magic are all gone. However, I'm told that Delphi really is *something.* So I've left it till last. The only trouble is, I'm getting a bit worried about the cash. I suppose I'm a bit of a fool where money is concerned. Philip ran all that, and how right he was. . . ."

Here a passing customer, pushing his way between the tables towards the bar-counter, jogged my chair, and I looked up, jerked momentarily out of my thoughts.

A crowd of customers—all male—seemed to be gathering at the bar for what looked like a very substantial mid-morning snack. It appeared that the Athenian businessman had to bridge the gap between breakfast and luncheon with something rather more sustaining than coffee. I saw one plate piled high with Russian salad and thick dressing, another full of savoury meatballs and green beans swimming in oil, and innumerable smaller dishes heaped with fried potatoes and small onions and fish and pimentos and half a dozen things I didn't recognize. Behind the counter was a row of earthenware jars, and in the shadow of their narrow necks I saw olives, fresh from the cool farm-sheds in Aegina and Salamis. The wine bottles on the shelf above bore names like Samos and Nemea and Chios and Mavrodaphne.

I smiled, and looked down again at the page.

". . . but in a way I'm finding it wonderful to be here alone. Don't misunderstand me, I don't mean *you!* I wish like anything you were here, for your own sake as well as mine. But you know what I do mean, don't you? This is the first time for years I've been away on my own—I was almost going to say 'off the leash'—and I'm really enjoying myself in a way I hadn't thought possible before. You know, I don't suppose he'd ever have come here at all; I just can't see Philip prowling round Mycenae or Cnossos or Delos, can you? Or letting me prowl either? He'd have been all set to dash off to Istanbul or Beirut or even Cyprus—anywhere, in short, where things are *happening*, not centuries ago in the past, but *now*—and even if they weren't happening, he'd make them.

"Fun—yes, it was always fun, but—oh, I'm not going to write about that either, Elizabeth, but I was right, absolutely right. I'm sure of it now. It wouldn't have worked, not in a million years. This trip on my own has shown me that, more clearly than ever. There's no regret, only relief that perhaps, now, I'll have time to be myself. There, now I've admitted it, and we'll drop the subject. Even if I am quite shatteringly incompetent when I am being myself, it's fun, and I muddle along somehow. But I do admit . . ."

I turned the page, reaching forward absently with my left hand to tap ash from my cigarette. There was a paler circle showing still against the tan at the base of the third finger, where Philip's ring had been. In ten days of Aegean sunshine, it had begun to fade . . . six long years fading now without regret, leaving behind them a store of gay memories that would fade too, and a sneaking curiosity to know if the beggar maid had been really happy once she was married to King Cophetua. . . .

"But I do admit there's another side to this Great Emancipation. Things do seem a trifle dull occasionally, after so many years spent being swept along in Philip's—you must admit—magnificent wake! I feel just a little bit high and dry. You'd have thought that something—some sniff of an adventure—would have happened to a young woman (is one still young at twenty-five?) marooned on her own in the wilds of Hellas, but no! I go tamely from temple to temple, guidebook in hand, and spend the rather long evenings writing up notes for that wonderful book I was always going to write, and persuading myself I'm enjoying the peace and quiet. . . . I suppose it's the other side of the picture, and I'll adjust myself in time. And if something exciting did happen, I wonder just what sort of a showing I'd make—surely I've got *some* talent for living, even if it looked feeble beside *his* overplus? But life never does seem to deliver itself into the hands of females, does it? I'll just finish up as usual in the hotel bedroom, making notes for that book that'll never get written. Nothing ever happens to me."

I put down the cigarette, and picked up my pen again. I had better finish the letter, and on a slightly different note, or Elizabeth was going to wonder if I wasn't, after all, regretting the so-called emancipation of that broken engagement.

I wrote cheerfully, "On the whole, I'm doing fine. The language wasn't a difficulty after all. Most people seem to speak a bit of French or English, and I have managed to acquire about six words of Greek—though there have been difficult moments! I haven't managed the money quite so well. I won't pretend I'm exactly broke yet, but I rather let myself go in Crete—it was worth it, ye gods, but if it means passing up Delphi I shall regret it. Not that I *can* miss Delphi. That's unthinkable. I must get there somehow, but I'm afraid I may have to scamp it in a one-day tour, which is all I can afford. There's a tour bus on Thursday, and I think I'll have to be content with that. If only I could afford a car! Do you suppose that if I prayed to all the gods at once—?"

Someone cleared his throat just above me. A shadow crept half-apologetically across the page.

I looked up.

It wasn't the waiter, trying to winkle me out of my corner table. It was a little dark man with patched and shabby dungarees, a greasy blue shirt, and a hesitant smirk behind the inevitable moustache. His trousers were held up with string, which it appeared he didn't trust, because he held on to them firmly with one grimy hand.

I must have looked at him with a chilly surprise, because the apologetic look deepened, but instead of going away he spoke in very bad French.

He said, "It is about the car for Delphi."

I said stupidly, looking down at the letter under my hand, "The car for Delphi?"

"You wanted a car for Delphi, *non?*"

The sun had probed even into this corner of the café. I peered at him against it. "Why, yes, I did. But I really don't see how—"

"I bring it." One grimy hand—the one that wasn't holding up his trousers—waved towards the blazing doorway.

My eyes followed the gesture, bemusedly. There was indeed a car, a large shabby-looking black affair, parked at the pavement's edge.

"Look here," I said, "I don't understand—"

"*Voilà!*" With a grin, he fished what was patently a car key from his pocket, and dangled it above the table. "This is it. It is a matter of life and death, I understand that—oh, perfectly. So I come as quick as I can—"

I said with some exasperation, "I haven't the remotest idea what you're talking about."

The grin vanished, to be replaced by a look of vivid anxiety. "I am late. This I know. I am sorry. Mademoiselle will forgive me? She will be in time. The car—she does not look much but she is good, oh, a very good car. If mademoiselle—"

"Look," I said patiently, "I don't want a car. I'm sorry if I misled you, but I can't hire one. You see—"

"But mademoiselle said she desired a car."

"I know I did. I'm sorry. But the fact is—"

"And mademoiselle said it was a matter of life and death."

"Madem— I didn't. You said that. I'm afraid I don't want your car, monsieur. I regret. But I don't want it."

"But mademoiselle—"

I said flatly, "I can't afford it."

His face lighted at once with a very white-toothed and singularly attractive grin. "Money!" The word was contemptuous. "We do not speak of money! Besides," he added with great simplicity, "the deposit is already paid."

I said blankly, "Deposit? Paid?"

"But yes. Mademoiselle paid it earlier."

I drew a breath that was three parts relief. It wasn't witchcraft after all, nor was it an intervention of the ironic gods of Greece. It was a simple case of mistaken identity.

I said firmly, "I'm sorry. There has been a mistake. That is not my car. I didn't hire it at all."

The dangling key stilled for a moment, then swung in front of me with unimpaired vigour. "It is not the car mademoiselle saw, no, but that one was bad, bad. It had a—how do you say?—a crack in it that the water came out."

"A leak. But—"

"A leak. That is why I am late, you see, but we get this car, oh so good, since mademoiselle say it is so urgent a matter that Monsieur Simon have the car at Delphi straightaway. You leave straightaway you are in Delphi in three hours—four hours"—his look lingered on me momentarily, summing me up—"five hours maybe? And then perhaps all is well with Monsieur Simon and this matter of life and—"

"Death," I said. "Yes, I know. But the fact remains, monsieur, that I don't know what you're talking about! There is some mistake, and I'm sorry. It was not I who asked for the car. I gather that this, er, Monsieur Simon's girl was to have been in this café waiting for the car? . . . Well, I can't see anybody here at present who might fill the bill. . . ."

He spoke quickly, so quickly that I realized afterwards that he must have followed my rapid French only sketchily, and was pouncing on a phrase that made sense—the sense he wanted to hear. The key still swung on his fingertip as if it were hot and he wanted to drop it. He said, "That is it. This café. A young lady sitting alone. Half past ten. But I am late. You are Simon's girl, yes?"

He looked, with that bright brown uncomprehending gaze, so like an anxious monkey that my near-exasperation vanished, and I smiled at him, shaking my head, and summoned up one of my six hard-learned words of Greek. *"Ne,"* I said, as forcefully as I could. *"Ne, ne, ne."* I laughed and held out my cigarette case. "I'm sorry there's been a muddle. Have a cigarette."

The cigarette seemed to be an amazing cure-all for worry. The lines vanished magically from his face. The vivid smile flashed. The key dropped with a jingle in front of me while the hand that wasn't holding up his pants reached for my cigarette case. "Thank you, mademoiselle. It is a good car, mademoiselle. Have a good journey."

I was feeling in my bag for matches, and not until I raised my head did I really take in what he'd said. And by then it was too late. He had gone. I caught a glimpse of him sliding through the crowd at the café door like a whippet let off a string, then he vanished. Three of my cigarettes had gone too. But the car key lay on the table in front of me, and the black car still stood outside in the violent sunlight.

It was only then, as I sat gaping like an idiot at the key, the car, and the sunlight on the cloth where a moment ago the little man had cast a shadow, that I realized that my momentary piece of showing-off was likely to cost me pretty dear. I remembered a little sickly that in Greek, *"ne"* means "yes."

Of course I ran after him. But the crowd surged and swayed on the pavement, regardless, and there was no sign in any direction of the shabby messenger of the gods. My waiter followed me anxiously onto the pavement, ready to grab, I suppose, if I showed signs of taking off without paying him for my coffee. I ignored him and peered earnestly in all directions. But when he showed signs of retreating to bring up reinforcements to escort me personally back to my table and the bill, I judged it time to give up the search. I went back to my corner, picked up the key, threw a quick, worried smile at the still-pursuing waiter, who didn't speak English, and pushed my way towards the bar-counter to seek out the proprietor, who did.

I elbowed my way through the crowd of men, with a nervously reiterated *"Parakalo,"* which, apparently, was the right word for "Please." At any rate the men gave way, and I leaned anxiously over the counter. *"Parakalo, kyrie—"*

The proprietor threw me a harassed sweating glance over a pile of fried potatoes, and placed me unerringly. "Miss?"

"*Kyrie,* I am in difficulty. A queer thing has just happened. A man has brought that car over there—you see it, beyond the blue tables—to deliver it to someone in the café. By a mistake he appears to think I'm the person who hired it. He thinks I'm driving it up to Delphi for someone. But I know nothing about it, *kyrie;* it's all a mistake, and I don't know what to do!"

He threw a dollop of dressing over some tomatoes, pushed them towards a large man perched on a small stool at the counter, and wiped a hand over his brow. "Do you wish me to explain to him? Where is he?"

"That's the trouble, *kyrie.* He's gone. He just left me the key—here it is—and then went. I tried to catch him but he's vanished. I wondered if you knew who was supposed to be here to collect the car?"

"No. I know nothing." He picked up a large ladle, stirred something under the counter, and threw another look at the car outside. "Nothing. Who was the car for?"

"Monsieur, I told you, I don't know who—"

"You said it was to be driven somewhere—to Delphi, was it? Did this man not say who it was for?"

"Oh. Yes. A—a Mr. Simon."

He spooned some of the mixture—it seemed to be a sort of bouillabaisse—into a plate, handed it to a hovering waiter, and then said, with a shrug, "At Delphi? I have not heard of such a one. It is possible somebody here saw the man, or knows the car. If you wait a moment I will ask."

He said something then, in Greek, to the men at the counter, and became on the instant the centre of an animated, even passionate discussion which lasted some four or five minutes and involved in the end every male customer in the café, and which eventually produced, with all the goodwill in the world, the information that nobody had noticed the little man with the key, nobody knew the car, nobody had ever heard of a Monsieur Simon at Delphi (this though one of the men was a native of Crissa, only a few kilometres distant from Delphi), nobody thought it in the least likely that anyone from Delphi would hire a car in Athens, and (finally) nobody in their senses would drive it up there anyway.

"Though," said the man from Crissa, who was talking with his mouth full, "it is possible that this Simon is an English tourist staying at Delphi. That would explain everything." He didn't say why, merely smiling with the great kindness and charm through a mouthful of prawns, but I got his meaning.

I said apologetically, "I know it seems mad, *kyrie,* but I can't help feeling one ought to do something about it. The man who brought the key said it was"—I hesitated—"well, a matter of life and death."

The Greek raised his eyebrows; then he shrugged. I got the impression that matters of life and death were everyday affairs in Athens. He said, with another charming smile, "Quite an adventure, mademoiselle," and turned back to his plate.

I looked at him thoughtfully for a moment. "Yes," I said slowly, "yes." I turned back to the proprietor, who was struggling to scoop olives out of one of the beautiful jars. It was apparent that the rush hour and the heat were beginning to overset even his Athenian good manners and patience so I merely smiled at him and said, "Thank you for your goodness, *kyrie.* I'm sorry to have troubled you. It seems to me that if the matter really is urgent, then the person who wants the car will certainly come and get it as arranged."

"You wish to leave the key with me? I will take it, and then you need have no more worry. No, it will be a pleasure, I assure you."

"I won't trouble you yet, thanks. I must confess"—I laughed—"to a little curiosity. I'll wait here for a bit, and if this girl comes, I'll give her the key myself."

And to the poor man's relief, I wriggled back out of the press and returned to my table. I sat down and ordered another coffee, then lit another cigarette, and settled down to a pretence of finishing my letter, but in reality to keep one watchful eye on the door, and the other on the shabby black car that should—surely—by now have been hurtling along the Delphi road on that matter of life and death. . . .

I waited an hour. The waiter had begun to look askance again, so I pushed aside my untouched letter and gave an order, then sat playing with a plateful of beans and some small pink fish while I watched, in an expectancy that gradually gave way to uneasiness, the constant coming-and-going at the café door.

My motive in waiting hadn't been quite as straightforward as I had suggested to the proprietor of the café. It had occurred to me that, since I had become involved in the affair through no fault of my own, be able to turn it to advantage. When "Simon's girl" arrived to car, it might surely be possible to suggest—or even ask outright—that I might be her passenger as far as Delphi. And the possibility of getting a lift up to Delphi was not the only one which had occurred to me. . . .

So the minutes dragged by, and still no one came, and somehow, the longer I waited, the less possible it seemed to walk out of the café and leave everything to settle itself without me, and the more insidiously did that other possibility begin to present itself. Dry-mouthed, I pushed it aside, but there it was, a challenge, a gift, a dare from the gods. . . .

At twelve o'clock, when nobody had appeared to claim the car, I thrust my plate aside, and set myself to consider that other possibility as coolly as I could.

It was, simply, to drive the car up to Delphi myself.

It was apparent that, for whatever reason, the girl wasn't coming. Something must have prevented her, for otherwise she would simply have telephoned the garage to cancel the order. But the car—the urgently wanted car—was still there, already an hour and a half late in starting. I, on the other hand, wanted very badly to go to Delphi, and could start straightaway. I had come straight up from Piraeus off the Crete steamer, and had everything with me that I needed for a short stay in Delphi. I could go up today, deliver the car, have two days there with the money saved on the bus fare, and come back with the tourist bus on Thursday. The thing was simple, obvious, and a direct intervention of providence.

I picked up the key with fingers that felt as if they didn't belong to me, and reached slowly for my only luggage—the big brightly coloured hold-all of Mykonos weaving—that hung on the back of a chair.

I hesitated with my hand touching it. Then I let the hand drop, and sat, twisting the key over and over, watching with unseeing eyes the way the sun glinted on it as it turned.

It couldn't be done. It was just one of those things that couldn't be done. I must have been mad even to consider doing it. All that had happened was that Simon's girl had forgotten to cancel the order for the car and claim the deposit. It was nothing to do with me. No one would thank me for intervening in an affair that, in spite of my silly mistake, had nothing whatever to do with me. That phrase "a matter of life and death," so glib a chorus, so persuasive an excuse to interfere—it was only a phrase, after all, a phrase from which I had built up this feeling of urgency which gave me (I pretended) the excuse to act. *In any case, it had nothing to do with me.* The obvious—the only—thing to do was to leave the car standing there, hand over the key, and go away.

The decision brought with it a sense of relief so vivid, so physical almost, at it startled me. On the wave of it I stood up, picked up the car key, a swung my hold-all up to my shoulder. The unfinished letter to Elizabeth lay on the table. I reached for it, and as I folded it over to thrust it into my bag, the sentence caught my eye again. "Nothing ever happens to me."

The paper crackled suddenly as my fingers tightened. I suppose moments of self-knowledge come at all sorts of odd times. I have often wondered if they are ever pleasant. I had one such moment now.

It didn't last long. I didn't let it. It was with a sort of resigned surprise that I found myself once more at the counter, handing a slip of paper across it to the proprietor.

"My name and address," I said rather breathlessly, "just in case someone does come for the car later on. Miss Camilla Haven, the Olympias Hotel, Rue Marnis. . . . Tell them I—I'll take care of the car. Tell them I did it for the best."

I was out in the street and getting into the car before it occurred to me that my last words had sounded uncommonly like an epitaph.

CHAPTER II

It's a long way to Delphi.
EURIPIDES: *Ion*
(*tr. Philip Vellacott*).

EVEN IF it wasn't Hermes himself who had brought me the key, the hand of every god in Hellas must have been over me that day, because I got out of Athens alive. More, unscathed.

There were some sticky moments. There was the shoeblack who was so urgent to clean my shoes that he followed me to the car and clung to the side and would certainly have been hurt when I started off, if only I'd remembered to put the car into gear. There was the moment when I turned—at a cautious ten miles per hour and hugging the left-hand pavement—out of Omonia Square into St. Constantine Street, and met a taxi almost head-on on what I thought was his wrong side, till the volume and fervour of his abuse shocked me back onto my own right. Then there was the encounter in the narrow alley with two furious pedestrians who stepped off the pavement without a single glance in my direction. How was I to know it was a one-way street? I was lucky with my brakes that time. I wasn't so lucky with the flower-donkey, but it was only the flowers I touched, and the driver was charming about it. He refused the note I hastily held out to him and he actually gave me the flowers I'd knocked out of the donkey's pannier.

All things considered, people were very forgiving. The only really unpleasant person was the man who spat on the hood as I came hesitatingly out from behind a stationary bus. There was no need for such a display of temper. I'd hardly touched him.

By the time I got to the main road that leads out of Athens along the Sacred Way I'd found out two things. One was that a few weeks spent in punting around the English country roads in Elizabeth's old Hillman (Philip, understandably, had never let me touch his car) was not really an adequate preparation for driving through Athens in a strange car with a left-hand drive. The other was that the shabby black car had an unexpectedly powerful engine. If it had been less shabby and ancient-looking—if it had been one of the sleek winged transatlantic monsters commonly used as taxis in Athens—I should never have dared myself to drive it, but its shabby façade had reassured me. Almost it could have been the old Hillman I'd learned on. Almost. I hadn't been in it three minutes before I discovered that it had an acceleration like the kick of a jet, and by the time I'd assessed its possibilities as a lethal weapon—which were limitless—it was too late. I was out in the traffic and it seemed safer to stay there. So I hung on grimly to the wheel, changing hands now and again as I remembered that the gear levers were on the right, and prayed to the whole Olympian hierarchy as we jerked and nudged our terrified and apologetic way out through the city suburbs, turning at length into the great double road that runs along the coast towards Eleusis and Corinth.

After the packed and flashing streets, the road seemed open and comparatively empty. This was the Sacred Way; down this wide sea-bordered road the ancient pilgrims had gone with songs and torches to celebrate the Mysteries at Eleusis. This lake now lying to the right was the holy lake of Demeter. Across that bay on the left, the island of Salamis lay like a drowned dragon, and there—*there*—Themistocles had smashed the Persian fleet. . . .

But I looked neither to right nor left as I drove. I had been this way before, and had got the first sharp disillusion over. There was no need, here, to leave oneself open to the ghosts; they had long since gone. Now, the Sacred Way ran straight and wide (the tar sweating a little in the sun) between the cement factories and the ironworks; the holy lake was silted up with weeds and slag; in the bay of Salamis lay the rusty hulks of tankers, and the wine-dark water reflected the aluminium towers of the refinery. At the other side of the bay belched the chimneys of Megara, and above them a trio of Vampire jets wheeled, screaming, against the ineffable Greek sky. And this was Eleusis itself, this dirty village almost hidden in the choking clouds of ochreous smoke from the cement works.

I kept my eyes on the road, my attention on the car, and drove as fast as I dared. Soon the industrial country was behind us, and the road, narrower now and whitening with dust under the pitiless September sun, lifted itself away from the shore and wound up between fields of red earth set with olives, where small box-like houses squatted, haphazardly it seemed, among the trees. Children, ragged and brown and thin, stood in the dust to stare as I went by. A woman, black-clad, and veiled like a Moslem, bent to lift bread from the white beehive oven that stood under an olive tree. Scrawny hens scratched about, and a dog hurled itself yelling after the car. Donkeys plodded along in the deep dust at the road's edge, half hidden under their top-heavy loads of brushwood. A high cart swayed along a track towards the road; it was piled with grapes, gleaming waxily, cloudy green. The flanks of the mule were glossy, and bloomy as dark grapes. The air smelt of heat and dung and dust and the lees of the grape harvest.

The sun beat down. Wherever the trees stood near the road the shade fell like a blessing. It was not long past noon, and the heat was terrific. The only relief was the breeze of the car's movement, and the cloudy heads of the great olives sailing between the road and the great brazen bowl of the sky.

There was very little traffic out in the heat of the day, and I was determined to take full advantage of the afternoon lull, so I drove on through the hot bright minutes, feeling confident now, and even secure. I had got the feel of the car, and I was still steadfastly refusing to think about what I had done. I had taken a "dare" from the gods, and the results would wait till I got—if I got—to Delphi.

If I got to Delphi.

My confidence in myself had been steadily growing as I drove on through an empty landscape, through country that grew wilder and more beautiful as the road shook itself clear of the olive groves and climbed the hills that lie to the north of Attica. It even survived the series of frightening hairpin bends that sink from the summit of these hills towards the flat fields of the Boeotian plain. But it didn't survive the bus.

This was the service bus from Athens and I caught up with it halfway along the dead-straight road that bisects the plain. It was small, evil-looking, and smelly. It also seemed to be packed to the doors with people, boxes, and various livestock, including hens and at least one small goat. It was roaring along in a fifty-yard trail of dust. I drew carefully out to the left, and pressed forward to pass.

The bus, which was already in the middle of the road, swung over promptly to the left and accelerated slightly. I moved back, swallowing dust. The bus went back to the crown of the road and settled back to its rackety thirty miles an hour.

I waited half a minute, and tried again. I crept cautiously up to its rear wheel and hoped the driver would see me.

He did. Accelerating madly, he surged once again into my path, got me well and truly behind him, then settled back complacently into the centre of the road. I went back once more into the choking dust-train. I was trying not to mind, to tell myself that when he had had his joke, he would let me safely by, but I could feel my hands beginning to tighten on the wheel, and a nerve was jumping somewhere in my throat. If Philip had been driving . . . but then I told myself, if Philip had been driving, it wouldn't have happened. Women drivers are fair game on the roads of Greece.

Here we passed a board which said, in Greek and English letters: THEBES 4 km.; DELPHI 77 km. If I had to stay behind the bus all the way to Delphi. . . .

I tried again. This time as I pulled out to approach him I sounded the horn decisively. To my surprise and gratitude, he drew over promptly to the right, and slowed down. I made for the gap. There was just room, no more, between the bus and the verge, which was of deep, crumbling dry soil. Taut with nervous concentration, I pressed forward and accelerated.

I wasn't getting past. The bus rocked and roared alongside, travelling faster, keeping pace with me. My car had the speed of it, but the gap was narrowing and I wasn't sure enough of my judgment to force the big car past. The driver of the bus closed in more sharply. I don't know if he would actually have forced me off the road, but as the swaying dirty-green enamel rocked nearer, I lost my nerve, as he had known I would. I stood on the brakes. The bus roared on. I was left once more in the dust.

Ahead of us I could see the first scattered houses of Thebes, the legendary city that, I knew, was gone even more irrecoverably than Eleusis. Where Antigone led the blind Oedipus out into exile, the old men of Thebes sit on the concrete pavements in the sun, beside the gas pumps. The game of *tric-trac* that they sit over, hour after hour, is probably the oldest thing in Thebes. There is a fountain somewhere, beloved of the nymphs. That's all. But I had no time then to mourn the passing of the legends. I wasn't thinking about Oedipus or Antigone, or even about Philip or Simon or my own miserable prelude to adventure. I just drove on towards Thebes with my eyes fixed in hatred ahead of me. There was nothing left in life at that moment but the desire to pass that filthy bus.

Presently the chance came. A knot of women, waiting by the roadside, signalled him to stop, and he slowed down. I closed up behind, my eyes on the strip to the left of him, my hands slippery on the wheel, and that nerve beginning to jump again.

He stopped, right in the centre of the road. There was no possible space to pass. I stopped behind him and waited, then, as he drew away from me again, and I let in the clutch, I stalled the engine. My hand shook on the ignition. The engine wouldn't start. At the edge of my vision I caught sight of a face at the rear window of the withdrawing bus, a dark young face, split in a wide grin. As I started the car and followed I saw the youth turn as if to nudge someone on the back seat beside him. Another face turned to stare and grin. And another.

Then, close behind me—so close that it nearly sent me into the ditch with fright—I heard a horn. As I swerved automatically to the right a jeep, driven fast on its wrong side, roared up from behind, overtook me rather too wide, with the nearside wheels churning dust, and charged straight, at the same headlong pace, for the rear of the bus, with its horn still blasting like a siren. I caught a fleeting glimpse of a girl driving, a young, dark face, with lashes drooping over her eyes and a bored, sulky mouth. She was lounging back in her seat, handling the jeep with casual, almost insolent, expertise. And, woman driver or no, the bus made way for her, whipping smartly over to the right and staying there respectfully while she tore by. I didn't consciously decide to follow her; in fact I'm not sure yet whether I trod on the accelerator deliberately, or whether I was feeling for the brake, but something hit me in the small of the back, and the big black car shot forward, missed the bus by inches, and stormed past in the wake of the jeep, with two wheels on the crown of the road and the other two churning up enough dust to have guided the children of Israel straight into Thebes. Where the bus had its offside wheels I neither knew nor cared. I didn't even look in the mirror.

I swept into Thebes and dived smartly down the wrong side of the dual carriageway which is the road through to Levadia and Delphi.

The hand of Hermes, god of wayfarers, was over me still. There was a horse fair at Levadia, which, with its accompanying trappings of fiesta, jammed the streets; but after that I met nothing, except slow little caravans of country people on their way by mule and donkey-back to the fair; and once a train of gypsies—real Egyptians—on the move with mules and ponies covered in bright blankets.

Soon after I had passed Levadia the country began to change. The grim banalities of Attica, the heavy Technicolour prosperity of the plains, sank back and were forgotten as the hills crowded in. The road reared and twisted between great ribs of brown hill that thrust the landscape up into folded ranges. At the foot of the steep waterless valleys dead streams curled white along their single beds, like the sloughed skins of snakes. The sides of the valley were dry with the yellowish growth of burned grass, and drifts of stones and crumbling soil.

Bigger and bigger grew the circling hills, barer the land, drawn in with great sweeps of colour that ran from red to ochre, from ochre to burnt umber to lion-tawny, with, above all, the burning, the limitless, the lovely light. And beyond all, at length, a grey ghost of a mountain massif; not purple, not faintly blue with distance like the mountains of a softer country, but spectre-white, magnificent, a lion silvered. Parnassus, home of the ghosts of the old gods.

I stopped only once to rest, some way beyond Levadia. The road, which wound high along the hillside, was in shadow, and the air, at that height, was cool. I sat for about fifteen minutes on the parapet that edged the road. Below me, deep in a forked valley, was a place where three tracks met; the ghost of an ancient crossroads where once a young man, coming from Delphi to Thebes, struck an old man down out of his chariot, and killed him. . . .

But no ghosts moved today. No sound, no breath, not even the shadow of a hanging hawk. Only the bare lion-coloured hills, and the illimitable, merciless light.

I got back into the car. As I started the engine I reflected that the god of wayfarers, who had done very well by me so far, had only some twenty miles' more duty to do, and then he could abandon me to my fate.

In fact, he abandoned me just ten kilometres short of Delphi, in the middle of the village of Arachova.

CHAPTER III

> But if I don't get out from under pretty damned soon, there'll be a disaster in the rear.
>
> ARISTOPHANES: *The Frogs*
> (*tr. Dudley Fitts*).

ARACHOVA IS a showplace. It is not self-consciously so, but its setting is picturesque in the extreme, and the Greek style of building does the rest.

The village is perched on a precipitous hillside, and the houses are built in tiers, one up behind the other, the floor of one level with the roof of the next. The whole village looks as if it were just about to slide into the depths of the valley below. The walls are white and the roofs are rose-red, and over every wall hang flowering plants, and vines rich with

grapes, and great dollops of wool dyed the colours of amber and hya-
cinth and blood. Along the short main street are places selling rugs which
hang out in the sunlight, brilliant against the blinding white walls. The
street itself has some corners, and is about eight feet wide. On one of
these corners I ran into a truck.

Not quite literally. I managed to stop with the hood of my car about
nine inches away from his, and there I stayed, paralyzed, unable even
to think. The two vehicles stood headlamp to headlamp, like a pair of
cats staring one another out, one of them preserving a mysterious silence. I had, of course, stalled the engine. . . .

It became apparent all too soon that it was I, and not the truck driver,
who would have to back. The whole village—the male portion of it—
turned out to tell me so, with gestures. They were charming and delightful and terribly helpful. They did everything except reverse the car for
me. And they obviously couldn't understand why anyone who was in
charge of such a car shouldn't be able to reverse it just like *that*.

Eventually I reversed it into somebody's shop doorway.

The whole village helped to pick up the trestle table, rehang the rugs,
and assure me that it didn't matter a scrap.

I straightened up the car and reversed again, into a donkey. The whole
village assured me that the donkey wasn't hurt and it would stop in a
kilometre or so and come home.

I straightened up the car. This time I churned out a reasonably straight
course for ten yards while the village held its breath. Then came a bend
in the road. I stopped. I definitely was not prepared to chance reversing
over the two-foot parapet into somebody's garden twenty feet down the
hillside. I sat there breathing hard, smiling ferociously back at the villagers, and wishing I had never been born and that Simon hadn't either.
My bolt was shot.

I had stopped in a patch of sunlight and the glare from the white
walls was blinding. The men crowded closer, grinning delightedly and
making gallant and—no doubt fortunately—incomprehensible remarks.
The truck driver, also grinning, hung out of his cab with the air of a man
prepared to spend the whole afternoon enjoying the show.

In desperation, I leaned over the door of the car and addressed the
most forward of my helpers, a stout, florid-looking man with small
twinkling eyes, who was obviously vastly delighted with the whole business. He spoke a fluent if decidedly odd mixture of French and English.

"Monsieur," I said, "I do not think I can manage this. You see, it's
not my car; it belongs to a Monsieur Simon, of Delphi, who requires it
urgently, for business. I—I'm not very used to it yet, and since it's not
mine I don't like to take risks. . . . I wonder, could you or one of these

gentlemen back it for me? Or perhaps the driver of the truck would help, if you would ask him? You see, it's not my car. . . ."

Some rag of pride led me to insist on this, until I saw he wasn't listening. The smile had gone from the cheerful sweating face. He said, "Who did you say the car was for?"

"A Monsieur Simon, of Delphi. He hired it from Athens, urgently." I regarded him hopefully. "Do you know him?"

"No," he said, and shook his head. But he spoke a little too quickly, and as he spoke his eyes flickered away from mine. The man at his elbow looked at me sharply, and then asked a question in rapid Greek, where I thought I caught the word "Simon." My friend nodded once, with that swift flicker of a sidelong look back at me, and said something under his breath. The men near him stared, and muttered, and I thought I saw a new kind of curiosity, furtive, and perhaps even avid, replacing the naïve amusement of a moment ago.

But this was only the most fleeting of impressions. Before I could decide whether to pursue the inquiry or not, I realized that none of the men were looking at me any more. There was some more of that swift and semi-furtive muttering; the last of the cheery grins had disappeared, and the men who had been crowding most closely round the car were moving away, unobtrusively yet swiftly, bunching as sheep bunch at the approach of the dog. One and all, they were looking in the same direction.

At my elbow came the fluttering click of "nervous beads," and the stout man's voice said softly, "He will help you."

I said "Who?" before I realized he was no longer beside me.

I turned my head and looked where they all were looking.

A man was coming slowly down a steep-stepped alley that led uphill between the houses on my right.

He was about thirty years old, dark-haired and tanned like all the others in the group near the car, but his clothes, no less than his air and bearing, made him look unmistakably English.

He was not tall, an inch or two under six feet, perhaps, but he was broad in the shoulder, and held himself well, with a sort of easy, well-knit movement that spoke of training and perfect physical fitness. I thought him good-looking; a thinnish sun-browned face, black brows, straight nose, and a hard mouth; but just at the moment his expression was what Jane Austen would have called repulsive—meaning that, whatever thoughts held him in that slightly frowning abstraction, it was obvious that he didn't intend them to be disturbed.

He seemed to be hardly aware of where he was, or what he was doing. A child scampered up the steps and pushed by him, apparently unnoticed. A couple of hens flapped across under his feet without making him pause. A hanging plant splashed petals in a scarlet shower over the white sleeve of his shirt, but he made no move to brush them away.

When he reached the foot of the alleyway, he paused. He seemed to come abruptly out of his preoccupation, whatever it was, and stood there, hands thrust into the pockets of his flannels, surveying the scene in the street. His eyes went straight to the group of men. I saw the slight frown disappear, and the brown face became a mask, remote, cold, reflecting oddly the wariness that I had seen in the villagers. Then he looked straight at me, and it was with something of a shock that I met his eyes. They weren't dark, as I had expected. They were grey, very clear and light, and violently alive.

He came down the last step and crossed to the door of the car. The group melted away from us. He took no more notice of them than he had of the hens, or the falling geranium petals.

He looked down at me. "You seem to be in trouble. Is there anything I can do?"

"I'd be terribly grateful if you *could* help me," I said. "I—I've been trying to back the car."

"I see." I thought I heard amusement behind the pleasant voice, but his face still expressed nothing. I said bleakly, "I was trying to get it to go *there*." "There" was a space beyond the curve of the road which, about fifty yards back, looked as remote as the moon.

"And she won't go?"

"No," I said shortly.

"Is there something wrong with her?"

"Just," I said, "that I can't drive."

"Oh." It was amusement. I said quickly, "It's not my car."

Here the truck driver leaned out of his cabin and shouted something in Greek, and the Englishman laughed. The laugh transformed his face. The mask of rather careful indifference broke up, and he looked all at once younger and quite approachable, even attractive. He shouted something back in what sounded to me like excellent Greek. At any rate the driver understood, because he nodded and withdrew into his cab, and I heard the truck's engine begin to roar.

The newcomer laid a hand on the door.

"If you'll allow me, perhaps I can persuade her to go."

"I shouldn't be surprised," I said bitterly, as I moved over. "I was told this was a man's country. It's true. Go ahead."

He got into the car. I found myself hoping that he would miss the gears, forget to start the engine, leave the handbrake on—do even a single one of the damned silly things I'd been doing all day, but he didn't.

To my fury the car moved quietly backwards, slid into the cobbled
space beyond the corner, paused about two inches away from a house
wall, and waited there politely for the truck to pass.

It approached with an appalling noise and a cloud of black smoke. As
it drew level, its driver, leaning out of his cab, yelled something at my
companion and sent a grinning black-eyed salutation to me that somehow, without a word being intelligible, made me understand that,
though incompetent, I was female and therefore delightful, and that was
just how it should be.

The truck roared on its way. I saw its driver glance back and lift a
hand to the men who still stood in a little group near the café door.
One or two of them responded, but most were still watching, not the
car, but my companion.

I glanced at him. I knew then that I was right. He was aware of it
too. His eyes, narrowed against the sun, showed none of that vivid
aliveness that I had surprised in them. He sent the group a look, slow,
appraising, utterly without expression. I thought he hesitated. A hand
went to the car door, as if he were going to get out, then it dropped back
onto the wheel, and he turned to me in inquiry.

I answered his look before he spoke. "Don't give a thought to my
amour-propre, will you? Of course I should love you to drive the beastly
thing through the village for me. I haven't a rag of pride left, and as
long as I get this car to Delphi in one piece, my self-respect can be sal-
vaged later. Believe me, I'm terribly grateful."

He smiled. "You must be tired, and it's dreadfully hot. Have you come
far?"

"From Athens."

His brows shot up, but he said nothing. The car was moving with the
minimum of noise and fuss through the narrow street. The little group
of men had disappeared, melting chin-on-shoulder into the café as the
car approached them. He didn't glance aside after them.

I said defiantly, "Yes, all the way. And not a scratch."

"Congratulations. . . . And here we are. Clear of the houses and all
set for Delphi. You did say Delphi?"

"I did." I regarded him thoughtfully. "I suppose you wouldn't by any
chance be going that way yourself?"

"As it happens, yes."

"Would you—?" I hesitated, then took the plunge. "Would you like a
lift? In a manner of speaking, that is?"

"I should be delighted. And if the manner of speaking means will I
drive—with pleasure, ma'am."

"That's wonderful." I relaxed with a little sigh. The car purred round

the last corner and gathered speed up a long curling hill. "I've really
quite enjoyed myself, but you know, I've missed half the scenery."

"Never mind. You brought some of it with you."

"What d'you mean?"

He said coolly, "The feathers on the hood. Very original they look, and
quite striking."

"The—oh!" My hand flew to my mouth. "*Feathers?* Honestly?"

"Indeed yes. Lots of them."

I said guiltily, "That must be the hen just outside Levadia. At least, it
was a cockerel. White ones?"

"Yes."

"Well, it was asking for it. I even hooted the horn, and if you'd heard
this horn you'd know that cockerel was bent on death. I didn't kill him,
though, really I didn't. I saw him come out the other side and dash away.
It *is* only feathers, truly it is."

He laughed. He, too, seemed in some indefinable way to have relaxed.
It was as if he had left his preoccupations behind him in Arachova,
and with them that impression he had given of a rather formidable reserve. He might have been any pleasant, casually met stranger on holiday.

"No hen'll look at that chap till he's grown a new tail," he said cheerfully, "and you don't have to make excuses to me. It wasn't my cockerel."

"No," I said, "but I've a feeling this is your—" I stopped.

"This is what?"

"Oh, nothing. Merciful heavens, what a view!"

We were running along a high white road that hugged the side of
Parnassus. Below us to the left the steep hillside fell away to the valley of
the Pleistus, the river that winds down between Parnassus' great flanks
and the rounded ridges of Mount Cirphis, towards the plain of Crissa
and the sea. All along the Pleistus—at this season a dry white serpent of
shingle beds that glittered in the sun—all along its course, filling the valley
bottom with the tumbling, whispering green-silver of water, flowed the
olive woods; themselves a river, a green-and-silver flood of plumy
branches as soft as sea spray, over which the ever-present breezes slid,
not as they do over corn, in flying shadows, but in whitening breaths,
little gasps that lift and toss the olive crests for all the world like breaking spray. Long pale ripples followed one another down the valley.
Where, at the valley's end, Parnassus thrust a sudden buttress of gaunt
rock into the flood, the sea of grey trees seemed to break round it, flowing on, flooding out to fill the flat plain beyond, still rippling, still moving with the ceaseless sheen and shadow of flowing water, till in the west

the motion was stilled against the flanks of the distant hills, and to the south against the sudden sharp bright gleam of the sea.

I said, after a while, "Are you staying in Delphi?"

"Yes. I've been there a few days. Have you come for long?"

I laughed. "Till the money gives out, and I'm afraid that won't be long enough. I only hope there'll be a room for me somewhere. I came up unexpectedly and haven't booked. Someone told me the Apollon was good."

"It's very nice. Delphi's fairly full just now, but you'll get a room somewhere, I'm sure. Perhaps we can persuade the Apollon to throw someone out for you." A pause. "Hadn't we better introduce ourselves? My name's Lester."

"I'm Camilla Haven." I hesitated. Could I possibly be right in my guess about him? I thought over it again: the villagers' reaction to the name Simon in Arachova; their demeanor when this man appeared; the voice at my elbow murmuring, "He will help you. . . ." Together, they seemed to add up to the solution of my problem. I said slowly, watching him, "I've got a sort of alias today, though. You might say I'm . . . 'Simon's girl.'"

The dark brows shot up. One of those quick, light, electrifying glances, then he was watching the road again. He said evenly, "How very gratifying. But why? Because I rescued you in Arachova?"

I felt the blood coming into my cheeks. I hadn't thought of that one. I said quickly, "No. I only meant I'd been deputizing for her—the other girl—since Athens. With the car."

"The car?" he said blankly.

"Yes." I swallowed and shot a glance at him. This was going to sound even sillier than I had imagined. "This is—oh, dear, I've begun at the wrong end but . . . well, this is your car. The one from Athens."

I could see nothing in his glance this time except puzzlement, with possibly a dash of doubt about my sanity.

"I'm afraid I don't follow. My car? From Athens? And what 'other girl'? Forgive me, but—just what are you talking about?"

"I'm sorry. I shouldn't have jumped it on you like that. I'd better begin at the beginning. I—I've done a rather silly thing, and I hope you're not going to be too angry with me, Mr. Lester. I'll explain exactly how it happened in a moment, if you'll let me, but the important thing is that this is the car you're expecting. The girl you sent to hire it didn't turn up to claim it, and I was handed the key by mistake, so—well, I brought it up here for you. I—I hope it's all right. It was the most marvellous luck to find you—"

"Just a moment. Forgive me for interrupting, but—well, I still haven't the remotest idea what you're talking about. You say someone hired this car in Athens and you were given the key, and drove it up here?"

"Yes." This time it was my voice that sounded flat and blank. "It wasn't—it wasn't you?"

"Decidedly not. I know nothing about a car from Athens or anywhere else."

"But back there in Arachova—" I hesitated, feeling more than ever confused and foolish.

"Yes?" The car slowed, dipped onto a little bridge set at an angle over a narrow gorge, then accelerated up the curling hill beyond. His tone was casual, but somehow I got the impression of sharp interest. "Just what made you think I ought to know about it?"

I said quickly, "Was I wrong? I thought . . . look, you *are* called Simon, aren't you?"

"That is my name. They told you in Arachova? Those men?"

"No. That is, yes, in a way. But . . . never mind that now. You did say you were staying in Delphi?"

"Yes."

I said flatly, stupidly, "Then it *must* be you! It must be!"

"I do assure you it isn't." The quick appraising glance he gave me must have shown him the distress in my face, because he smiled then, and said gently, "But I'm afraid I still don't quite see where the mystery comes in. Surely the garage also gave you the hirer's name and address? Have you lost it, or forgotten to write it down, or something?"

I said in a very small voice, "That's just it. I never knew it."

He looked startled, and then, I thought, amused. "I see. You never knew it. Except, I take it, that his name was Simon?"

"Yes. I told you I'd done something silly. It seemed all right at the time, and I thought in Arachova that it had turned out beautifully, like a story, but now . . ." My voice trailed away. I looked away from him across the blue depths of the valley, and spoke my thoughts with artless and quite unguarded emphasis. "Oh dear, and it would have been so *wonderful* if it *had* been you!"

The words were hardly out before I realized what they sounded like. For the second time in a few minutes I felt the heat wash scarlet into my cheeks. I opened my lips to say something, anything, but before I could speak he said pleasantly, "I wish it had. But look, don't worry so about it. It can't be as bad as you think, and perhaps, if you'll let me, I can help you. Would you care to tell me just what's happened?"

I told him. I kept to a bare recital of the facts, from the moment when the little man approached me with the key, to the fateful second of decision which had landed me—so neatly, as I had thought—at Simon

Lester's feet in Arachova. Only the facts: nothing of the miserable tangle of motive; the fear and self-questioning and uneasy bravado . . . but somehow, as I finished the story, I had a feeling that I had told him rather more than I intended. Oddly, I didn't mind. I had told him. He had said he would help. It was over to him. It was a familiar feeling, and yet not quite familiar. . . .

I sat back, relaxed and at ease for the first time since eleven that morning, while below us the breeze ran with white feet over the billowing olives, and beside us, along the high hot road, the sun beat the smell of dust out of the red earth, and the rock glowed and sent the heat back like a blast.

He had made no comment on the silly story as I told it. Now he merely said, "I see. So it really only amounts to this: that you've brought up an unknown car for an unknown man who wants it for something unspecified, and you don't know where to find him."

"That's not a very kind way of putting it, but—yes. I told you it was silly."

"Maybe. But in your place I'd have done exactly the same."

"*Would* you?"

He laughed. "Of course. What right-minded person could resist a challenge like that?"

"Honestly?"

"Honestly."

I let out a long breath. "You've no idea how much better you've made me feel! But at least you'd have managed the adventure properly! It seems to me that it's not enough to be bold; one has to be competent as well. *You'd* never have got stuck in Arachova—and if you had, you'd have been able to back the car!"

"Ah, yes," he said, "Arachova." The shutters were up once more. He added, half under his breath, "Simon, of Delphi. . . ."

I said quickly, "It does seem odd, doesn't it? That there should be two? I told you that the man from Crissa didn't know anyone of that name hereabouts. Delphi's small, isn't it?"

"Lord, yes."

"Then he'd know, wouldn't he? That was why I was so sure it must be you."

He didn't answer. There was that look again, smooth, blank; the unclimbable wall with spikes at the top. I gave him a doubtful glance he didn't see, and said, tentatively, "Could there have been some kind of mistake? I mean, suppose it *is* you; suppose someone got a message wrong, and the whole thing is just a mix-up? Do you know anyone in Athens, perhaps, who might have—?"

"No." The syllable was definite to the point of curtness. "It's quite impossible. I've had no communication with Athens during the last week at all, so it's hard to see how any message can have gone astray. And you say it was a girl who did the hiring. I've no idea who that could be. No, I'm afraid it's nothing whatever to do with me." A pause, then he added in a different voice, as if he felt he had been too abrupt, "But please don't worry about it any more. We'll soon get it straightened out, and then you can settle down and enjoy Delphi. I think you'll vote it's been worth it."

"It'll have to be pretty good."

"It is." He nodded, almost idly, ahead of the car. "You can't see the village from here, but the ruins are this side of the bluff, in the curve of the mountain under those high cliffs. There—that's Apollo's temple, below the cliffs they call the Shining Ones. You see?"

I saw. Ahead of us the mountain thrust that great buttress out into the valley, the river of olive trees swirling round it as the water swirls round the prow of a ship, to spread out beyond into a great flat lake that filled the plain. High up, in the angle where the bluff joined the mountain, I saw it, Apollo's temple, six columns of apricot stone, glowing against the climbing darkness of the trees behind. Above them soared the sunburned cliffs; below was a tumble, as yet unrecognizable, of what must be monument and treasury and shrine. From where we were the pillars seemed hardly real; not stone that had ever felt hand or chisel, but insubstantial, the music-built columns of legend: Olympian building, left floating— warm from the god's hand—between sky and earth. Above, the indescribable sky of Hellas; below, the silver tide of the olives everlastingly rippling down to the sea. No house, no man, no beast. As it was in the beginning.

I realized then that Simon Lester had stopped the car. We must have stood there for some minutes, at the edge of the road, in the shadow of a stone pine. He didn't speak, and neither did I.

But I noticed that it wasn't Apollo's shining columns that held him. His gaze was on something nearer at hand, away up the side of Parnassus above the road. I followed his look, but could see nothing; only the bare rock shifting and flowing upwards with the liquid shimmer of the heat.

After a bit I said merely, "And the village is just the other side of the bluff?"

"Yes. The road runs through those trees below the ruins and then round that shoulder into Delphi. Beyond the village it drops rather steeply to the plain. Crissa—where your friend in the café comes from— is about halfway down. At the bottom the road forks for Amphissa and Itea."

"Itea? That's the fishing port, isn't it? Where the pilgrims used to land in the old days when they were making for the shrine?"

"Yes. You can just see the houses away over there at the edge of the sea." He turned the subject abruptly, but so smoothly that I realized that he was following his own thoughts, and that these had not been about the view, or the road to Itea. "I'm still rather curious to know how you knew my name. I understand it was from those men in Arachova. Was . . . something said?"

"Not really. I'd been trying to explain to the men why I really didn't dare try and reverse the car there—I'd never reversed it before, of course, and it *is* such a length. I told them it wasn't mine, but that it was for someone called Simon, at Delphi. I thought they looked as if that meant something. . . . Then one of them said something to the others, and they all turned and stared at you. It was just the way they looked, somehow. I don't know if you noticed?"

"I noticed."

"Well, that was all. I suppose, when you arrived, they assumed that you were the person to deal with the car. Then, when you told me you came from Delphi, I guessed you might be Simon—my 'Simon.' They . . ."—I hesitated—"they seemed to assume you were the right one, too."

There was an infinitesimal pause before his hand went to the ignition. "Ah, well," he said smoothly, "the sooner we get to Delphi and find your man, the better, don't you think?"

"I do indeed." I laughed. "After all this, we'll probably find him watching beside the road and dancing with impatience; that is, if the little man was right and it really is a matter—" I stopped. Until I repeated the words, half-automatically, I'd forgotten them myself.

"It is what?"

I said slowly, looking at him, "A matter of life and death. . . ."

We were moving again, quickly now. Below us the sea of olives flowed and rippled like smoke. Above, the pitiless sun beat down on the rock with a heat like the clang of brass.

He said, "Is that all he told you?"

"Yes. But he repeated it."

" 'A matter of life and death'?"

"Just that. Only of course we were speaking in French. The phrase was *'il y va de la vie.'* "

"And you got the impression he meant it seriously?"

I said slowly, "Yes. I believe I did. I don't know if I took it in really urgently at the time, but you know, I think that's really why I did this silly thing with the car."

"You took the car, and the risks with it, because of some subconscious feeling of urgency about the affair?"

I said, "That makes it sound more definite than it was, and there were —other reasons. . . . But yes. Yes."

The car roared up a long incline, swept round and down a curling hill. I leaned back against the hot leather, folded my hands in my lap, and said, not looking at him, "If the little man was right, it's just as well you're not 'Simon,' isn't it?"

He said, quite without expression, "Just as well. And here we are. What comes first? Simon, or the hotel?"

"Both. I imagine the hotel people are as likely to know of him as anyone, and at least I expect they speak English. My six words of Greek won't get me very far alone."

"On the other hand," said Simon gravely, "they might get you a good deal further than you intended."

CHAPTER IV

"And thou camest to Crissa under snow-clad Parnassus, to its foot that faces west, and rocks overhang the spot, and a hollow, stony, wood-clad vale stretches beneath it."

Homeric *Hymn to Apollo.*

To MY RELIEF the hotel had a room to offer.

"But only for tonight, I'm afraid," said the proprietor, who spoke, after all, excellent English. "I deeply regret, but I cannot be certain about tomorrow. I have had a—what do you call it? A provisional booking. Perhaps I can take you, perhaps not. If not, there is the Kastalia further along the street, or the Tourist Pavilion at the other end of Delphi. It has a magnificent view, but," he smiled charmingly, "it is very expensive."

"It couldn't have a better view than this," I said.

This was true. The village consists only of two or three rows of flat-topped houses, washed ochre and pink and dazzling white, set in their tiers along the steep side of the hill. At the beginning of the village the road divides into a Y that makes the two main streets, and at the junction stands the Apollon Hotel, facing over the valley towards the distant gleam of the Corinthian Gulf.

Outside the hotel, on the edge of the road which was used as a terrace, two big plane trees made a deep island of shade for some wooden tables and chairs. Simon Lester had parked the car just beyond these, and was waiting there. When I had completed the formalities of booking I went out to speak to him.

"It's all right. They can take me for tonight, and just at the moment that's all I care about." I held out my hand. "I have to thank you very much, Mr. Lester. I don't quite know where I'd have been without your help. I've a feeling it might have been somewhere at the bottom of the valley, with the eagles of Zeus picking my bones!"

"It was a pleasure." He was looking down at me, measuringly. "And now what are you planning to do? Rest and have some tea first, or is that"—a gesture indicated the car—"worrying you too much?"

I said uncertainly, "It is, rather. I think I'd better go right ahead and do what I can."

"Look," he said, "if you'll forgive my saying so, you look as if you'd better have that rest. Won't you please leave this to me, at any rate for the time being? Why don't you go and lie down, and have tea brought to your room—they make excellent tea here, by the way—while I make a few inquiries for you?"

"Why, I—you mustn't—I mean, it's absurd that you should be landed with my difficulties," I said, a little confusedly, and conscious only of a strong desire that he should, in fact, be landed with them all. I finished feebly, "I couldn't let you."

"Why not? It would be too cruel if you turned on me now and told me to mind my own business."

"I didn't mean it like that. You know I didn't. It's only—"

"That it's your affair and you want to see it through? Of course. But I must confess I'm seething with curiosity myself by now, and after all it's partly my affair too, since my alter ego has managed to involve me. I really would be very grateful if you'd let me help. Besides," he added, "wouldn't you honestly much rather go and have a rest and some tea now, while I do the detecting for you in my fluent but no doubt peculiar Greek?"

"I—" I hesitated again, then said truthfully, "I should adore to."

"Then that's settled." He glanced at his wrist. "It's about twenty past four now. Shall we say an hour? I'll report back at five-thirty. Right?"

"Right." I looked at him a little helplessly. "But if you do find him, and he's angry—"

"Well?"

"I don't want you made responsible for what's happened. It wouldn't be fair, and I'd much rather face my own music."

"You'd be surprised," he said cryptically, "how reponsible I feel already. All right, then. See you later."

With a quick wave of the hand he was gone down the steps to the lower road.

My room overlooked the valley, and had a long window with a balcony. The shutters were closed against the sun, but even so the room seemed full of light, globed in light, incandescent with it. As the door shut behind the maid who had shown me upstairs, I went across to the window and pulled back the shutters. Like a blast the heat met me. The sun was wheeling over now towards the west, full across the valley from my window, and valley and plain were heavy with sleepy heat. The tide of olives had stilled itself, and even the illusion of coolness created by those rippling grey leaves was gone. In the distance the wedge of shining water that showed at the edge of the plain struck at the eyes like the flash from a burning-glass.

I closed my eyes against it, pulling the shutters to again. Then I slipped off my dress, and had a long, cool wash. I sat on the edge of the bed for some minutes after that, brushing my hair, till I heard the maid coming back with the tea. I had my tea—Simon Lester had been right about its excellence—propped against pillows, and with my feet up on the bed. I don't think I thought any more about Simon—either of the Simons—or about the car, or about anything except the shadowed quiet of the little white room.

Presently I put the tray off my knees onto the table by the bed, and lay back to relax. Before I knew it was even near, sleep had overtaken me. . . .

I woke to a feeling of freshness and the incongruous sound of rain. But the light still drove white against the shutters, and when I opened them a crack I saw that the sun still blazed, deeper now and lower, but at full power. Half my window was in shadow now, where the plane trees put a bough or two between it and the falling sun. The sound of rain, I realized, was the sound of their leaves, pattering and rustling in the breeze that had got up to cool the evening.

I glanced down at the terrace below the balcony. He was there, sitting under one of the plane trees, smoking. His chair was pulled up to the railing that edged the terrace, and one arm lay along this. He sat there, relaxed, looking at nothing, completely at ease. The car was standing where he had parked it before. If—as appeared to be the case—he had not located another "Simon" to deliver it to, the fact didn't appear to worry him unduly.

I reflected, as I looked down at him thoughtfully, that it would probably take a good deal to worry Simon Lester. That quiet manner, that air of being casually and good-temperedly on terms with life . . . with it all went something that is particularly hard to describe. To say that he knew what he wanted and took it, would be to give the wrong impression; it was rather that whatever decisions he had to make, were made, and then dismissed—this with an ease that argued an almost frightening brand of self-confidence.

I don't know how much of this I saw in him on that first day; it may be that I simply recognized straightaway the presence of qualities I myself so conspicuously lacked; but I do remember the immediate and vivid impression I got of a self-sufficiency harder and more complete than anything conveyed in years of Philip's *grand-seigneur* gasconading, and at the same time quite different in quality. I didn't see yet where the difference lay. I only know that I felt obscurely grateful to Simon for not having made me feel too much of a fool, and, less obscurely, for having so calmly undertaken to help me in the matter of the "other Simon. . . ."

I wondered, as I closed the shutters again, if he had even bothered to make the gesture of looking for him.

On the whole, I imagined not.

In this, it seemed, I had done him less than justice.

When I went downstairs I found him, hands thrust deep in trouser pockets, in earnest contemplation of the car, together with a Greek to whose bright blue shirt was pinned the insignia of a guide.

Simon looked up and smiled at me. "Rested?"

"Perfectly, thank you. And the tea *was* good."

"I'm glad to hear it. Perhaps you're strong enough, then, to bear the blow?" He jerked his head towards the car.

"I thought as much. You've not found him?"

"Not a sign. I've been to the other hotels, but there's no visitor of that name. Then I went along to the Museum to meet George here. He tells me that he doesn't know anyone called Simon in Delphi, either."

The Greek said, "Only yourself, *Kyrie* Lester."

"Only myself," agreed Simon.

I said, rather helplessly, "What shall we do?"

"*Kyrie* Lester," said the Greek, watching him rather curiously, "could it not be, perhaps, that there *is* no other Simon? And that it is not a mistake? That someone is—how do you put it?—using your name?"

"Taking my name in vain?" Simon laughed, but I knew that this had already occurred to him. It had occurred to me, too. "It doesn't seem likely. For one thing, who would? And for another, if they did, and it was urgent, they'd surely have appeared by now to claim the damned thing."

"That is probably true."

"You can bet it's true. But I'm going to get to the bottom of this very odd little affair—and not only for the sake of Miss Haven here, who's worried about it. Look, George, you are sure about it? No Simons at all, however unlikely? A grandfather with a wooden leg, or a mule-boy aged seven and a half, or one of the men working up on the excavations?"

"About the last I do not know, of course, though assuredly you are right and they would have come to look for it. In Delphi, nobody. Nobody at all."

"Then the places nearby? You're a native, aren't you? You'll know a fair number of people all around here. Crissa, for instance. It might be Crissa . . . that's only a few kilometres away. What about that?"

George shook his head. "No. I am sure. I would have remembered. And in Arachova . . ."

Simon ran a finger along the wing of the car, then contemplated the tip of it for a moment. "Yes?"

George said, regretfully, "No. I do not remember anyone in Arachova, either."

Simon took out a handkerchief and wiped his fingertip clean again. "In any case I can find out. I'm going back there tonight."

The Greek gave him a quick bright glance that held, I thought, curiosity. But he only said, "Ah. Well, I regret, but that is all I can tell you, except—oh, but that is not the same; it is of no use to you."

"We'll have it, though, please. You've thought of someone?"

George said slowly, "There is a Simonides at Itea. I do not think this is the man, but he is the only one I know of. But perhaps, *kyrie,* you would like to ask someone else? I do not know everybody, me. Elias Sarantopoulou, my cousin, he is also in the Tourist Police. He is at the office now, or perhaps he is at the café . . . if you like to come with me I will show you the place; it is opposite the Post Office."

"I know it," said Simon. "Thanks, but I really doubt if your cousin will know any more than you. This is an irritating little problem, isn't it? It'll probably solve itself very soon, but meanwhile I suppose we must do something. We'll try your Simonides at Itea. Who is Simonides, what is he?"

George, of course, took him literally. "He has a little baker's shop near the cinema in the middle of the main street, facing the sea. Giannakis Simonides." He glanced at his wrist. "The bus goes in ten minutes. The shop is not far from the place where the bus stops."

Simon said, "We have a car," then grinned as he caught my eye. My answering smile was a rather brittle one. The car stood there like a mockery. I hated the sight of it.

Simon nodded to George, said something in Greek, then pulled open the car door for me.

I said doubtfully, "Ought we to?"

"Why not? This is a quite legitimate attempt at delivery. Come along, the sooner we get down to Itea the better. It'll be dark in an hour. Are you tired?"

"Not now. But—you'll drive, won't you, Mr. Lester?"

"You bet I will. You haven't seen the Itea road. And please call me Simon. It's more euphonious than 'Mr. Lester,' and besides . . ." his grin, as he slid into his seat beside me, was malicious ". . . it'll give you an illusion of comfort."

I didn't answer that one, except with a look, but as we drove off I said suddenly, and almost to my own surprise, "I'm beginning to feel frightened."

The glance he gave me held surprise but, oddly enough, no amusement. "That's a strong word."

"I suppose so. Perhaps it isn't, either, from me. I'm the world's most complete coward. I—I wish I'd had the sense to let well enough alone. The beastly thing should still be standing there in Omonia Square, and—"

"And you'd still be wishing madly you were in Delphi?"

"There is that," I acknowledged. "But you do see, don't you?"

"Of course I do."

The car had crept carefully through Delphi's narrow upper street, topped the rise opposite the presbytery, and then dived down to meet the lower road out of the village.

I said abruptly, "Do you suppose for a moment that this Simonides is the man we're looking for?"

"It doesn't seem very probable." Perhaps he felt this to be a little brusque, for he added, "We might as well try it, all the same."

"Something to make me feel progress is being made?" No answer to this. I said, "You know, it really would be carrying coincidence a bit too far to suppose there are two Simons in Delphi."

"It's not," he said evenly, "a very common name."

I waited, but he didn't speak again. We had left the village behind, dropping in a gradual descent between dykes of red earth and stones where the road had been recently widened. The ditches and mounds showed raw as wounds in the sunburnt earth. The rich rays of the now-setting sun flooded it with strong amber light against which the dry thistles that grew everywhere stood up delicate and sharp, like intricate filigree of copper wire. Above the road the new hotel, the Tourist Pavilion, showed as raw and new and wounding as the torn ditches alongside us. The curved windows flashed as we passed beneath and wheeled into the first hairpin of the descent to the plain of olives.

I said casually, "Are you just holidaying here in Delphi?"

I had meant it as a non sequitur, a conversational make-weight, the normal casual query with which you might greet anyone you met in such a place; but even as I said it I could hear how it pointed back to my last remark. I started to say something else, but he was already answering without any indication that he saw my question as other than innocent.

"In a way. I'm a schoolmaster. I have a house at Wintringham. Classics is my subject."

Whatever I had expected it wasn't this; this seal and parchment of respectability. I said feebly, "Then of course you're interested in the classical sites. Like me."

"Don't tell me you're a colleague? Another beggarly usher?"

"Afraid so."

"Classics?"

"Yes. Only in a girls' school that just means Latin, to my sorrow and shame."

"You don't know Ancient Greek?"

"A little. A very little. Enough sometimes to catch a word and follow what's being said. Enough to know my alphabet and make a wild guess at what some of the notices mean, and to have had a queer feeling at the pit of the stomach when I went to see *Antigone* in the Herodes Atticus Theatre in Athens and heard the chorus calling on Zeus against that deep black sky that had heard the same call for three thousand years." I added, feeling slightly ashamed of what I'd let him see, "What a ghastly road."

The car heeled yet again round a hairpin curve and plunged on down the great shoulder of Parnassus that sticks out into the Crissa Plain. Below us was a village, and below it again the flood of olives, flowing mile-wide now down to the sea.

Simon said cheerfully, "The buses all have icons stuck up in front of the driver, *and* with a little red light in front, run off the battery. On this road the icon swings madly from side to side at the bends and everybody crosses themselves."

I laughed. "Including the driver?"

"This is true. Yes, including the driver. I have a feeling that sometimes," said Simon, "he also shuts his eyes." He pulled the big car round an even sharper bend, missed an upcoming truck by inches, and added, "You can open yours now. This is Crissa."

I felt the colour come into my cheeks. "I'm sorry. I must be losing my nerve."

"You're still tired, that's all. We'll have something to drink in Itea before we seek out this Simonides."

"No, please," I protested, almost too quickly.

He eyed me for a moment. "You really are scared, aren't you?"

"I—yes, I am."

"I shouldn't worry; I really shouldn't. It can't matter, or it'd have been settled long before this."

"I know. I know it's nonsense. It's silly and it's trivial and it doesn't mean a thing, but I told you I'm the world's worst coward. It's true. I've been persuading myself for years that I'd be as competent and self-sufficient as anyone else, given the chance, but now I know. . . . Why, I can't even bear *scenes,* so why I ever thought I could get away with this sort of mayhem I have no idea." I stopped. It occurred to me with a queer little shock that I would never have said anything like that to Philip, not in a hundred years.

Simon was saying calmly, "Never mind. I'm here, aren't I? Whatever we get into, I'll talk you out of it, so sit back and relax."

"If," I said, "we find Simon."

"If," said Simon, "we do."

I was glad enough, when we got to Itea, to leave everything to him.

Itea is the port which in ancient times saw the landing of the pilgrims bound for the shrine of Apollo at Delphi. The shrine was a religious centre for the whole ancient world for many hundreds of years, and to us nowadays, used to modern transport, it is astonishing to contemplate the distances that men travelled on foot and on horseback or in small ships, to worship the God of light and peace and healing, or to ask the advice of the famous Oracle enshrined below the temple. The easy way was by Itea. The sea journey, for all its hazards, was less exhausting and dangerous than the journey by road through the mountains, and here into the little port of Itea the pilgrims crowded, to see from the harbour the winding river valley of the Pleistus and, beyond the shoulder of Parnassus where modern Delphi stands, the bright cliffs of the Shining Ones that guard the holy spring.

Today Itea is a grubby little fishing village, with one long street of shops and *tavernas* facing the sea and separated from it by the road and then perhaps fifty yards of dusty boulevard where pepper trees give shade and the men of the village gather for the usual drinks and ices and sticky honey-cakes.

Simon stopped the car under the trees and led me to a rickety iron table which seemed to have fewer attendant wasps than the others. I would have liked tea again, but felt so ashamed of this insular craving—and so doubtful of getting anything approaching what I wanted—that I asked for fresh lemonade, and got it, delicious and cold and tangy with the real fruit, and with it a *pasta* something like shredded wheat, but frantically oversweet with honey and chopped nuts. It was wonderful. The wasps loved it too. When we had finished it, I defiantly asked for another, and stayed to eat it while Simon went off to look for the baker's shop of Simonides.

I watched him go, thoughtfully beating off an extra-large and persistent wasp.

Somehow I didn't think Giannakis Simonides was our man. "Monsieur Simon, at Delphi . . ." And there was only one Monsieur Simon at Delphi.

There was that queer reserve, too, in Simon's manner; there was Arachova; and the way he had shelved my question as to what he was doing in Delphi. The thing had ceased to be a slightly awkward puzzle. It was fast becoming a mystery, with Simon Lester at its centre. And Simon's girl . . .

I finished my cake now and got up. Simon had paid the waiter before he had left me. I could see him standing in a doorway some distance up the street. The place was apparently a restaurant, for outside it stood the big charcoal stove, and over this a whole lamb revolved slowly on the spit, which was being turned by a stout woman in a blue apron. Simon appeared to be questioning her; she was nodding vigorously, and then, with a wave of her free hand, seemed to be directing him further up the street.

He looked back, saw me standing under the pepper trees, and raised a hand in salute. Then he made a vague gesture towards the other end of the street, and set off that way, walking fast.

Taking his gesture to mean that he had some information, but that he didn't expect me to follow him, I stayed where I was and watched him. He went perhaps a hundred yards, hesitated, then glanced up at a billboard and plunged into the darkness of a deserted cinema. As he vanished, I turned in the opposite direction and began to walk along the boulevard. I was only too thankful to leave the enquiry to him. If he really was in the centre of the mystery, he could keep it to himself, and welcome. . . .

Meanwhile I would do what I had come to Delphi for. Since chance had brought me down to Itea, the start of the ancient pilgrimage, I would try and see the shrine as the old pilgrims had seen it on their first landing from the Corinthian Gulf.

I walked quickly along the harbour's edge. On my right the sea paled towards sunset, and across the opal shimmer of the bay came a fishing boat, turquoise and white, with her prow raked in a proud pure curve above its liquid image. Under a sail of that same scarlet had the worshippers come into harbour when the God was still at Delphi.

I left the sea's edge and walked rapidly across the street. I wanted to get behind the ugly row of houses, back into the old olive woods, where I could look straight up towards the Pleistus valley with nothing but immemorial rock and tree and sky between me and the shrine.

Behind the main street were a few sorry alleys of concrete, with houses, as usual, scattered seemingly at random in the dust patches between the trees. I passed the last house, skirted a building that looked like a ruined warehouse, and followed a cracked stretch of concrete which appeared to lead straight into the outskirts of the forest of olives. The concrete was criss-crossed with cracks, like crazy paving, and thistles grew in the fissures. I startled a browsing donkey, and it plunged off under the trees in a smother of dust, to be lost in the shadows. Soon the concrete came to an end, and I found myself walking through soft earth in the deeper twilight of the trees. The breeze had strengthened with the approach of evening, and overhead the olives had resumed their liquid rippling.

I hurried on towards a space ahead where stronger light promised a clearing. I was lucky. There was a slight rise in the ground, and to the north of it the great olives thinned. From the top of the little ridge, across the ruffling crests of the trees, I could see the old Pilgrims' Way, unscarred by my own century. I stood for a few minutes, gazing up towards the shrine in the now rapidly fading light.

The temple columns were invisible behind the curve of the Crissa bluff, but there was the black cleft of Castalia, and above it the great cliffs whose names are Flamboyant and Roseate, the Shining Ones. . . . The dying sun ran up the Flamboyant cliff like fire.

This was, I thought, the way to come to Delphi . . . not straight up into the ruins in the wake of a guide, but to land from a small boat in a bay of pearl, and see it as they would have seen it, flaming in the distance like a beacon, the journey's end.

Something like a fleck of darkness went by my cheek. A bat. It was deep twilight now, the swift-falling Aegean dusk. I turned to see lights pricking out in the houses behind me. I could just see the streetlamps, faint and far between, along the sea front. They looked a long way away. Where I stood the shadow of a huge olive brooded like a cloud. I turned to go back to the village.

Instead of returning the way I had come, I took what I judged to be the direction of the car, and, plunging down from the ridge into the depths of the wood, I set off quickly through the twisted and shadowy trunks.

I had gone perhaps a hundred yards before the trees began to thin. Some way off to my left I saw the lights of the first house, an outpost of the village, and was hurrying towards it through the soft dust when a sudden flash of light quite near me, and to my right, brought me up short, startled. It was the flash of an electric torch, deep in the trees. Perhaps my adventures of the day had worked on my imagination rather too well, or perhaps it was the ancient mystery that I had been attempting to call up, but the fact remains that I felt suddenly frightened, and stood very still, with the trunk of an enormous olive between me and the torch-light.

Then I realized what it was. There was a house set by itself deep in the grove, the usual two-windowed box of a place with its woodpile and its lean-to shed and its scrawny chickens gone to roost in the vine. The flash I had seen showed me a man bending over a motor vehicle of some sort which was parked close to the side of the house. It looked like a jeep. As I watched he jerked the hood open, shone the light into the engine, and leaned over it. I saw his face highlighted by the queerly refracted light, a very Greek face, dark, with hair crisping down the wide cheek-bones in the manner of the heroes, and a roundish head covered with close curls like a statue's.

Then somebody in the cottage must have kindled the lamp, for a soft oblong of light slanted out of one of the windows, showing the dusty clutter outside—a woodman's block with the axe still sunk in it and gleaming as the light caught it, a couple of old gasoline cans, and a chipped enamel bowl for the hens' food. My causeless fear vanished and I turned quickly to go.

The man by the jeep must have seen the movement of my skirt in the darkness, because he looked up. I caught a glimpse of his face before the torch went out. He was smiling. I turned and hurried away. As I went, I thought the torch-beam flicked out to touch me momentarily, but the Greek made no move to follow.

Simon was sitting in the car, smoking. He got out when he saw me and came round to open my door. He answered my look with a shake of the head.

"No go. I've asked all the questions I could and it's a dead end." He got into the driver's seat and started the engine. "I really think we'll have to call it a day—go back to Delphi and have dinner and leave it to sort itself out in its own good time."

"But will it?"

He turned the car and started back towards Delphi. "I think so."

Bearing in mind what I had been thinking before about the "mystery," I didn't argue. I said simply, "Then we'll leave it. As you wish."

I saw him glance at me sideways, but he made no comment. The lights of the village were behind us, and we gathered speed up the narrow road. He dropped something into my lap, a leafy twig that smelt delicious when my fingers touched it.

"What is it?"

"Basil. The herb of kings."

I brushed it to and fro across my lips. The smell was sweet and minty, pungent above the smell of dust. "The pot of basil? Was it under this stuff that poor Isabella buried Lorenzo's head?"

"That's it."

There was a pause. We passed a crossroads where our lights showed a sign, AMPHISSA 9. We turned right for Crissa.

"Did you go to look for the Pilgrims' Way back there in Itea?" asked Simon.

"Yes. I got a wonderful view just before the light went. The Shining Ones were terrific."

"You found the ridge, then?"

I must have sounded surprised. "You know it? You've been here before?"

"I was down here yesterday."

"In Itea?"

"Yes." The road was climbing now. After a short silence he said, with no perceptible change of expression, "You know, I really don't know any more about it than you do."

The basil leaves were cool and still against my mouth. At length I said, "I'm sorry. Did I make it so obvious? But what was I to think?"

"Probably just what you did think. The thing's slightly crazy anyway, and I doubt if it'll prove to matter at all." I saw him smile. "Thank you for not pretending you didn't know what I meant."

"But I did. I'd been thinking about very little else myself."

"I know that. But nine women out of ten would have said 'What d'you mean?' and there we'd have been, submerged in a lovely welter of personalities and explanations."

"There wasn't any need of either."

Simon said, "'O rare for Antony.'"

I said involuntarily, "What d'you mean?"

He laughed then. "Skip it. Will you have dinner with me tonight?"

"Why, thank you, Mr. Lester—"

"Simon."

"Simon, then, but perhaps I should—I mean—"

"That's wonderful then. At your hotel?"

"Look, I didn't say—"

"You owe it to me," said Simon coolly.

"I owe it to you? I do not! How d'you work that out?"

"As reparation for suspecting me of—whatever you did suspect me of." We were climbing through the twisting street of Crissa, and as we passed a lighted shop he glanced at his wrist. "It's nearly seven now. Could you bear to dine in half an hour's time—say at half past seven?"

I gave up. "Whenever it suits you. But isn't that fearfully early for Greece? Are you so very hungry?"

"Reasonably. But it's not that. I—well, I've things to do and I want to get them done tonight."

"I see. Well, it won't be too early for me. I only had a snack for lunch, and I was too frightened to enjoy that. So thank you. I'd like that. At the Apollon, you said? You're not staying there yourself?"

"No. When I got there the place was full up so I got permission to sleep in the studio up the hill. You won't have seen it yet. It's a big ugly square building a couple of hundred feet up behind the village."

"A studio? An artist's studio, do you mean?"

"Yes. I don't know what it was used for originally, but now it has a caretaker, and is let out to visiting artists and bona fide students who can't afford to pay for a hotel. I suppose I'm up there under slightly false pretences, but I wanted to be in Delphi for some days and I couldn't find a room. Now that I'm settled into the studio I find it'll do me admirably. There's only one other tenant at present, an English boy, who's a genuine artist . . . and good, too, though he won't let you say so."

"But surely you've a perfectly good claim on the studio, too?" I said. "After all, you count as a student. And as a classicist you've a bona fide claim on any concession. It's not a question of 'false pretences' at all."

He sent me a sideways look that I couldn't read in the darkness. He said rather shortly, "I'm not here to pursue my classical studies."

"Oh." It sounded lame, and I hoped it hadn't sounded like a question. But the syllable hung there between us like a dominant awaiting resolution.

Simon said suddenly, into the darkness straight ahead, "My brother Michael was here during the war."

Crissa was below us now. Far down to our left as we climbed along the face of the bluff the lights of Itea were strung along like beads under the thin moon.

He said, still in that expressionless way, "He was in the Peloponnese for some time, as B.L.O.—that's British Liaison Officer—between our chaps and the *andartes,* the Greek guerillas under Zervas. Later he moved over into the Pindus region with ELAS, the main resistance group. He was in this part of the country in nineteen forty-four. He stayed with some people in Arachova; a shepherd called Stephanos and his son Nikolaos. Nikolaos is dead, but Stephanos still lives in Arachova. I went over to try and see him today, but he's away in Levadia, and not expected back till this evening—so the woman of his house told me."

"The woman of his house?"

He laughed. "His wife. You'll find everyone has to belong, hereabouts. Every man belongs to a place, and I'm afraid that every woman belongs to a man."

"I believe you," I said, without rancour. "I suppose it gives meaning to her life, poor thing?"

"But of course. . . . Anyway I'm going down to Arachova again tonight to see Stephanos."

"I see. Then this is a—a sort of pilgrimage for you? A genuine pilgrimage to Delphi?"

"You could call it that. I've come to appease his shade."

I caught my breath. "Oh. How stupid of me. I'm sorry. I didn't realize."

"That he died? Yes."

"Here?"

"Yes, in nineteen forty-four. Somewhere on Parnassus."

We had wheeled up onto the last stretch of the road before Delphi. To our left blazed the lighted windows of the luxurious Tourist Pavilion. Far down now on the right the thin moon was already dying out in a welter of stars. The sea was faintly luminous beneath them, like a black satin ribbon.

Something made me say suddenly, into the dark, "Simon."

"Yes?"

"Why did you say 'appease'?"

A little silence. Then he spoke quite lightly. "I'll tell you about that, if I may. But not just at this moment. Here's Delphi. I'll leave you and the car at your hotel, and I'll meet you on the terrace here in half an hour. Right?"

"Right." The car drew up where it had stood before. He came round and opened my door for me. I got out, and when I would have turned to repeat some words of thanks for his help in my afternoon's quest he shook his head, laughed, raised a hand in farewell and vanished up the steep lane beside the hotel.

With a feeling that things were moving altogether too fast for me, I turned and went indoors.

CHAPTER V

*"But enough of tales—I have wept for these
things once already."*
EURIPIDES: *Helen*
(*tr. Philip Vellacott*).

ANY FEARS I might have had that Simon's melancholy pilgrimage would be allowed to cloud my first visit to Delphi were dispelled when I came down at length to dinner, and walked out to the hotel terrace to find a table.

Seven-thirty was certainly an outrageously early hour for dining in Greece, and only one other of the tables under the plane trees was occupied, and that, too, by English people. Simon Lester wasn't there yet, so I sat down under one of the trees from whose dark boughs hung lights, which swung gently in the warm evening air. I saw Simon then below the terrace railing, making one of an extremely gay and noisy group of Greeks which surrounded a fair boy in the garb of a hiker, and a very small donkey almost hidden under its awkwardly loaded panniers.

The fair young man looked very much as if he had just completed some arduous trek in the wilds. His face, hands, and clothes were filthy; he had a generous stubble on his chin, and his eyes—I could see it even from where I sat—were bloodshot with fatigue. The donkey was in rather better case, and stood smugly beside him, under its load of what appeared to be the paraphernalia of an artist—boxes, roughly wrapped canvases, and a small collapsible easel, as well as a sleeping bag and the rather unappetizing end of a large black loaf.

Half the youth of Delphi seemed to have rallied to the stranger's welcome, like the wasps to my honey-cake. There was a great deal of loud laughter, atrocious English, and back-slapping—the last an attention which the stranger could well have done without. He was reeling with tiredness, but a white grin split the dirty bearded face as he responded to the welcome. Simon was laughing too, pulling the donkey's ears and exchanging what appeared to be the most uproarious of jokes with the young Greeks. Frequent cries of "Avanti! Avanti!" puzzled me, till I realized that they coincided with the jolly slaps under which the donkey, too, was reeling. At each slap a cloud of dust rose from Avanti's fur.

Eventually Simon looked up and saw me. He said something to the fair boy, exchanged some laughing password with the Greeks, and came swiftly up to the terrace.

"I'm sorry, have you been waiting long?"

"No, I've just come down. What's going on down there? A modern Stevenson?"

"Just that. He's a Dutch painter who's been making his way through the mountains with a donkey, and sleeping rough. He's done pretty well. He's just here from Jannina now, and that's a long way through rough country."

"He certainly got a welcome," I said, laughing. "It looked as if all Delphi had turned out."

"Even the tourist traffic hasn't quite spoiled the Greek *philoxenia*—the 'welcome' that literally means 'love of a stranger,'" said Simon, "though goodness knows Delphi ought to be getting a bit blasé by now. At least he'll get the traditional night's lodging free."

"Up at the studio?"

"Yes. This is the end of his trek. Tomorrow, he says, he'll sell Modestine—the donkey Avanti—and get the bus for Athens."

I said, "I thought when I saw the easel and what-not that he must be your English painter friend from the studio."

"Nigel? No. I doubt if a venture like that would ever occur to Nigel. He hasn't the self-confidence."

"You said he was a good painter, though?"

"I think he's good," said Simon, picking up the menu and absently handing it to me. It was in Greek, so I handed it back again. "But he's convinced himself—or else some fool has told him—that his own particular style is no good any more. I admit it's not the fashion, but the boy can draw like an angel when he likes, and I should have thought that was a gift rare enough to command attention even among some of to-day's more strident talents." He handed me the menu. "He doesn't use colour much—what will you have to start with?—but the drawing's very sure and delicate, and exciting at the same time."

I gave the menu back to him. He scrutinized the scrawled columns. "Hm. Yes. Well, some fool's told Nigel that his style's *vieux jeu,* or something. 'Emasculate' was one of the words, I believe. It's got him on the raw, so he's hard at work trying to form a style that he thinks will 'take,' but I'm terribly afraid it won't work. Oh, he's clever, and it's arresting enough, and it may catch on and find him a market of a sort—but it's not his own, and that never works fully. Another pity is that he's been here in Delphi a bit too long and got tied up with a girl who wasn't very good for him. She's gone, but the melancholy remains." He smiled. "As you see, it's with me, rather. I'm all the company Nigel's had up at the studio for the last three days, and I've been playing confidant."

"Or housemaster?"

He laughed. "If you like. He's very young in many ways, and habit dies hard. One takes it for granted one is there to help, though I'm not just sure how much anyone can do for an artist at the best of times. And at the worst they go into a kind of wilderness of the spirit where the best-intentioned listener can't even follow them."

"As bad as that?"

"I think so. I told you he was good. I believe the agony is in proportion to the talent. . . . Look, what are you going to eat? Why don't you choose something?" He handed me the menu.

I gave it patiently back. "I shall die of hunger in a minute," I told him. "Have you *looked* at this dashed menu? The only things I recognize are *patates, tomates,* and *melon,* and I refuse to be a vegetarian in a land which produces those heavenly little chunks of lamb on sticks with mushrooms between."

"I'm sorry," said Simon penitently, "here they are, see? *Souvlaka.* Well, so be it." He ordered the meal, then finally cocked an eyebrow at me. "What shall we drink? How's the palate coming on?"

"If that means can I swallow retsina yet," I said, "the answer is yes, though what it has to do with a palate I cannot see." Retsina is a mild wine strongly flavoured with resin. It can be pleasant; it can also be rough enough to fur the tongue with a sort of antiseptic gooseflesh. It comes in beautiful little copper tankards, and smells like turpentine. To acquire—or to pretend to acquire—a taste for retsina is the right thing to do when in Greece. As a tourist, I'm as much of a snob as anyone. "Retsina, certainly," I said. "What else, with *souvlaka?*"

I thought I saw the faintest shade of irony in Simon's eye. "Well, if you'd rather have wine—"

I said firmly, "They say that once you've got used to retsina it's the finest drink in the world and you won't ever take anything else. Burgundies and clarets and—well, other drinks, lose their flavour. Don't interrupt the process. The palate is faint yet pursuing and I expect I'll like it soon. Unless, of course, *you'd* like a nice sweet Samian wine?"

"Heaven forfend," said Simon basely, and, to the waiter, "Retsina, please."

When it came, it was good, as retsina goes—and the dinner along with it was excellent. I'm not a person whom the sight of olive oil repels, and I love Greek cooking. We had onion soup with grated cheese on top; then the *souvlaka,* which comes spiced with lemon and herbs, and flanked with chips and green beans in oil and a big dish of tomato salad. The cheese, and *halvas,* which is a sort of loaf made of grated nuts and honey, and is delicious. And finally the wonderful grapes of Greece, bloomed over like misted agates and cooled with water from the spring above the temple of Apollo.

Simon talked entertainingly through the meal without once mentioning Michael Lester or his purpose in visiting Delphi, and I myself forgot completely the cloud that was still hanging over my day, and only recollected it when a truck, chugging up past the terrace, slowed down to pass the car which stood parked at the edge of the narrow road.

Simon followed my look. He set down his little cup of Greek coffee, and then looked across the table at me.

"Conscience still active?"

"Not so active as it was. There's not so much room. That was a heavenly meal, and thank you very much."

"I wondered—" said Simon thoughtfully, and then stopped.

I said just as thoughtfully, "It's a long walk to Arachova. Is that it?"

He grinned. "That's it. Well? It's your car."

I said fervently, "It's not, you know. I never want to touch it again. I—I've renounced it."

"That's a pity, because—with your permission which I take it I have— I'm going to drive down to Arachova in a few minutes' time, and I was rather hoping you'd come too."

I said, in very real amazement, "Me? But you don't want me!"

"Please," said Simon.

For some reason I felt the colour coming hot into my cheeks. "But you don't. It's your own—your private affair, and you can't possibly want a stranger tagging along with you. This may be Greece, but that's carrying *philoxenia* a bit too far! After all—"

"I promise not to let anything upset you." He smiled. "It's a long time ago, and it's not a present tragedy any more. It's just—well, you can call it curiosity, if you like."

"I wasn't worrying about its upsetting me. I was thinking only that— well, dash it, you hardly know me, and it *is* a private matter. You said it could be called a 'pilgrimage,' remember?"

He said slowly, "If I said what I really want to say you'd think I was crazy. But let me say this—and it's true—I'd be terribly grateful if you'd give me your company this evening."

There was a little pause. The group of Greeks had long since dispersed. Both artist and donkey had vanished. The other English diners had finished and gone into the hotel. Away over the invisible sea the thin

moon hung, apricot now among the white scatter of stars. Above us the
breeze in the plane trees sounded like rain.

I said, "Of course I'll come," and got to my feet. As he stubbed out
his cigarette and rose I smiled at him with a touch of malice. "After all,
you did tell me I owed you something."

He said quickly, "Look, I never meant—" and he caught my look and
grinned. "All right, ma'am, you win. I won't try and bully you again."
And he opened the car door for me.

"Michael was ten years older than me," said Simon. "There were just
the two of us, and our mother died when I was fifteen. My father
thought the sun rose and set in Michael—and so did I, I suppose. I remember how dead the house seemed when he was drafted off to the
Med. . . . and Father just sat every day with the papers and the radio,
trying to learn what he could." A little smile touched his lips. "It wasn't
easy. I told you Michael came over here with the S.A.S.—the Special
Air Service—when Germany occupied Greece. He was doing undercover
work with the resistance in the mountains for eighteen months before he
was killed, and of course news came very thinly and not always accurately. Occasionally men managed to get letters out. . . . If you knew
someone was going to be picked up at night and taken off you did your
damnedest to get a letter to him in the hope that he in his turn would get
through, and the letter might eventually be mailed home from Cairo
. . . but it was chancy, and no one in those days carried any more papers
on him than he could help. So news was sparse and not very satisfactory.
We only ever got three letters from Michael in all that time. All he told
us in the first two was that he was well, and things were going according
to plan—and all the usual formulae that you don't believe, but that just
tell you he was alive when he wrote the letter four months before you got
it."

He paused while he negotiated a sharp bend made more hair-raising
than ever by the dark.

"We did eventually find out a certain amount about his work in
Greece from chaps who'd been with him here in Force One Thirty-
three, and had been in touch with him off and on through the fighting. I
told you he was a B.L.O. attached to guerrillas. Perhaps I'd better tell
you the set-up in Greece after the German invasion—or do you know all
about it?"

"Not a great deal. Only that ELAS was the main guerrilla organization, and was more concerned in feathering its own Commie nest than
in fighting Germans."

"So you do know that? You'd be surprised how many people never grasped it, even in nineteen forty-four when the Germans got out of Greece and ELAS turned on its own country—tried to stage a Communist *coup d'état*—and started murdering Greeks with the arms and cash we'd smuggled to them, and which they'd hidden safely away in the mountains till they could use them for the Party."

"But there were other guerillas who did an honest job, surely?"

"Oh, yes. To begin with there were quite a few groups, and it was Michael's job among other things to try and bring them together in a more or less coherent plan of campaign. But it broke his heart as it broke the heart of every B.L.O. in Greece. ELAS set to work and smashed every other guerrilla organization it could get its filthy hands on."

"You mean actually fought its own people *during* the German occupation?"

"Indeed, yes. Smashed some groups and assimilated others until eventually there was only one other important resistance group, EDES, under a leader called Zervas, an honest man and a fine soldier."

"I remember. You said he was in the Peloponnese."

"That's it. ELAS tried hard to liquidate him too, of course. Don't mistake me, there were some brave and good men with ELAS too, and they did some damned good work, but there was rather a load of . . ." he paused fractionally, "infamy . . . to counteract the better things. It doesn't make good reading, the story of the resistance in Greece. Village after village, raped and burned by the Germans, was thereafter raped and burned by ELAS—their own people—for whatever pathetic supplies they could produce. And the final abomination was the famous battle of Mount Tzoumerka where Zervas with EDES was facing the Germans, and ELAS under Ares—of all the damned arrogant pseudonyms for one of the most filthy sadistic devils that ever walked—ELAS waited till Zervas was heavily engaged, and then attacked him on the flank."

"Attacked *Zervas?* While he was fighting the Germans?"

"Yes. Zervas fought a double-sided battle for several hours, and managed to beat off the Germans, but he still lost some of his valuable supplies to ELAS, who stashed them away, no doubt, against the end of the German war and the day of the New Dawn."

There was a silence, underlined by the humming of the engine. I could smell dust, and dead verbena. The autumn stars were milky-white and as large as asters. Against their mild radiance the young cypresses stood like spears.

"And that brings me to the reason for my visit to Delphi," said Simon.

I said, "Michael's third letter?"

"You're quick, aren't you? Yes, indeed, Michael's third letter."

He changed gear, and the car slowed and turned carefully onto a narrow bridge set at right angles to the road. He went on in his pleasant, unemotional voice, "It came after we had had news of his death. I didn't read it then. In fact, I never knew Father had had it. I suppose he thought it would bring the thing alive again for me, when I'd just got over the worst. I was seventeen. And later, Father never talked about Michael. I didn't know of the letter's existence till six months ago, when Father died, and I, as his executor, had to go through his papers. The letter . . ."

He paused again, and I felt a curious little thrill go through me—the inevitable response (conditioned by tales told through how many centuries?) to the age-old device of fable: the dead man . . . the mysterious paper . . . the frayed and faded clue leading through the hills of a strange land. . . .

"The letter didn't say much," said Simon. "But it was—I don't know quite how to describe it—it was excited. Even the writing. I knew Michael pretty well, for all the difference in our ages, and I tell you he was as excited as all-get-out when he wrote that letter. And I think it was something he'd found, somewhere on Parnassus."

Again that queer little thrill. The night swooped by, full of stars. On our left the mountain loomed like the lost world of the gods. All of a sudden it didn't seem possible that I was here, and that this—this ground where our tyres whispered through the dust—was Parnassus. The name was a shiver up the spine.

I said, "Yes?" in a very queer voice.

"You must understand," he said, "that when I read that letter in the end, I read it against a background of information picked up after the war. We'd found out, my father and I, just where and how Michael had been working, and we'd talked to some of the fellows he'd met here. We were told that he'd been sent up into this area in the spring of nineteen forty-three and for over a year before he was killed he was working with one of the ELAS bands whose leader was a man called Angelos Dragoumis. I couldn't learn very much about this Angelos—that was the name he was generally known by, and I gather that it was desperately inappropriate; only one of the other Force One Thirty-three chaps had actually met him, and the few enquiries I've made here in the last day or so have been quietly stone-walled. The Greeks aren't proud of men like Angelos. I don't mean that his group didn't do one or two brilliant things: they were with Ares and Zervas when the Gorgopotamos viaduct was destroyed in the teeth of the Germans, and there was the affair of the bridge at Lidorikion, where they—oh, well, that doesn't matter just now. The thing is that this man Angelos seems to have rather modelled himself on the ELAS Commander, Ares, and he made himself felt in the country hereabouts just as Ares did."

"You mean he plundered his own side?"

"That and worse. The usual beastly record of burning and rape and torture and smashed houses, and people—where they weren't murdered —left to starve. The extra unpleasant touch is that Angelos came from this district himself . . . yes, I know. It's hard to take, isn't it? He's dead, anyway . . . at least, that's the assumption. He vanished across the Yugoslav border when the Communist *putsch* failed in December, nineteen forty-four and he hasn't been heard of since."

"I imagine that in any case he'd not dare reappear in these parts," I said.

"True enough. Well, anyway, that was the man Michael was working with, and, as I say, they did get some pretty good results in the military line—but then the Germans arrived here in force, and Angelos' band scattered and went into hiding in the hills. Michael, I gather, was on his own. He evaded capture for some weeks, hiding somewhere up here on Parnassus. Then one day a patrol spotted him. He got away, but one of their bullets hit him—not a bad wound, but enough to disable him, and with no attention it might have proved serious. One of his contacts was Stephanos, the shepherd from Arachova that we're going to see tonight. Stephanos took Michael in, and he and his wife nursed and hid him and would, I think, have got him out of the country if the Germans hadn't descended on Arachova while Michael was still here."

Along the road the young cypresses stood like swords. They had come along this very road. I said, "And they found him."

"No. But they'd been told he was here, and so they took Stephanos' son Nikolaos out and shot him, because his parents wouldn't give Michael away."

"Simon!"

He said gently, "It was a commonplace. You don't know these people yet. They stood and let their families be murdered in front of them rather than betray an ally who'd eaten their salt."

"The other side of the picture," I said, thinking of ELAS, and Angelos.

"As you say. And when you think harshly of ELAS, remember two things. One is that the Greek is born a fighting animal. Doesn't their magnificent and pathetic history show you that? If a Greek can't find anyone else to fight, he'll fight his neighbour. The other is the poverty of

Greece, and to the very poor, any creed that brings promise has a quick way to the heart."

I said, "I'll remember."

"Perhaps we've forgotten," he said, "what poverty means. When one sees . . . ah, well, never mind now. But I think that most things can be forgiven to the poor."

I was silent. I was remembering Philip again, and a beggar under the ramparts at Carcassonne; Philip saying "Good God!" in a shocked voice, dropping five hundred francs into the scrofulous hand, and then forgetting it. And now here was this quiet, easy voice, talking in the dark of past infamies, expressing as a matter of course the sort of enormous and tolerant compassion that I had never met—in the flesh—before. . . .

> "Poor naked wretches, wheresoe'er you are,
> That bide the pelting of this pitiless storm,
> How shall your houseless heads and unfed sides,
> Your looped and windowed raggedness, defend you . . . ?"

It came to me with a shock like an arrow out of the dark that—mystery or no mystery—I liked Simon Lester very much indeed.

He said, "What is it?"

"Nothing. Go on. The Germans shot Nikolaos and Michael left."

"Yes. Apparently he moved out again into the mountains. After this point I know very little about what happened. So far I've pieced together the bare facts from what we were told after the war by one of the other B.L.O.'s who was over here, and from the priest at Delphi, who wrote to my father some time back, when he was making his first enquiries."

"Didn't Stephanos write?"

"Stephanos can't write," said Simon. "What happened next we can only guess at. Michael went off back into the hills after the tragedy of Nikolaos' death. His shoulder wasn't fully healed, but he was all right. Stephanos and his wife wanted him to stay, but Nikolaos had left a small son and a daughter, and . . . well, Michael said he wasn't risking any more lives. He went. And that's all we know. He went up there"—a gesture towards the shadow-haunted mountain—"and he was caught and killed there, somewhere on Parnassus."

I said after a minute or two, "And you want to talk to Stephanos and find out where he is?"

"I know where he is. He's buried at Delphi, in a little graveyard not far from the studio, above the shrine of Apollo. I've been to the grave already. No, that's not what I want from Stephanos. I want to know just where Michael died on Parnassus."

"Stephanos knows?"

"He found the body. It was he who sent Michael's last letter off, together with the other things he found on the body. He got them smuggled somehow to this other B.L.O. and we got them eventually. We didn't know who'd sent them until later we were officially told that Michael was buried at Delphi. We wrote to the *papa*—the priest. He told us the simple facts, so of course my father wrote to Stephanos, and got a reply through the priest again, and—well, that seemed to be that."

"Until you saw Michael's letter."

"Until I saw Michael's letter."

We had rounded a shadowy bluff and there ahead, pouring down the mountainside like a cascade, were the steep lights of Arachova.

The car drew gently in to the side of the road and stopped. Simon switched the engine off and reached into an inner pocket for a wallet. From this he took a piece of paper and handed it to me.

"Wait a moment till I get my lighter to work. Would you like a cigarette?"

"Thank you."

After we had lighted our cigarettes he held the little flame for me while I unfolded the flimsy paper. It was a scrawl on a single sheet of cheap paper, smudged as if with rain, a bit dirty, torn here and there along the old folds, and dog-eared from being read and re-read. I opened it gently. I had the queerest feeling that I shouldn't have been touching it.

It was fairly short. "Dear Daddy," it began . . . why should there by something so very endearing about the thought of Michael Lester, a tough twenty-seven, using the childhood's diminutive? . . .

"Dear Daddy, God knows when you'll get this, as I see no chance of its getting taken off in the near future, but I've got to write. We've been having a bit of a party, but that's over now and I'm quite all right, so don't worry. I wonder, do you find this code of army-slang clichés as bloodily maddening as I do? At the best of times I suppose it has its uses, but just now—tonight—there is something I really want to say to you; to record, somehow, on paper—nothing to do with the war or my job here or anything like that, but still impossible to commit to paper and how *the hell* can I get it across to you? You know as well as I do that anything might happen before I see anyone I can send a private message by. If my memory were a little better—and if I'd paid a bit more attention to those classical studies (oh God, a world ago!) I might send you to the right bit in Callimachus. I think it's Callimachus. But I've forgotten where it comes. I'll have to leave it at that. However, I'm seeing a man I can trust tomorrow, and I'll tell him, come what may. And all being well, this'll be over some day soon, and we'll come back here together to the bright citadel, and I can show you then—and little brother Simon too. How is he? Give him my love. Till the day—and what a day it'll be!

"Your loving son,
"Michael."

The signature was a scrawl, running down almost off the page. I folded the paper carefully, and gave it back to Simon. He snapped the lighter out, and put the letter carefully away. He said, "You see what I mean?"

"Well, I don't know your brother, but I take it that wasn't his usual style."

"Far from it. This reads very oddly to me. Queer, rapid, allusive; almost—if I didn't know Michael so well—hysterical. A feminine type of letter."

"I see what you mean."

He laughed, and started the engine. "Sorry. But it's my guess he really was under some strong emotion when he wrote that letter."

"I think I'd agree. Of course he was in a tough spot, and—"

"He'd been in dozens before. And then all that about a private message, and 'getting it across.' He really had something to say."

"Yes. I take it you've had a look through your Callimachus, whoever he may be?"

"I have. He wrote a deuce of a lot. No, there's no clue there."

"And the 'bright citadel'?"

"That's a translation of a phrase the Delphic Oracle once used to Julian the Apostate. I think that must be the one he means. It refers to Apollo's shrine at Delphi."

"I see. That doesn't get us much further."

We were moving again towards the lights of Arachova. I said, "You used the word 'clue.' Just what are you hoping to find, Simon?"

"What Michael found."

After a little pause I said slowly, "Yes, I see. You mean the bit about 'we'll come back here together to the bright citadel and I'll show you'?"

"Yes. He'd found something and he was excited about it and he wanted to 'record' it—he uses that word, too, remember?"

"Yes. But don't you think that perhaps—?" I stopped.

"Well?"

I said, with some difficulty, "Might you not be seeing something that isn't there? I do agree it's an odd letter, but there's another way of reading it, isn't there? A quite simple way. It's the way that I'd have taken it myself . . . except of course that I didn't know your brother Michael."

"And that way?"

"Well, say it *was* excitement, or rather emotion, of a sort, wouldn't there be a reason for it? Might he not quite naturally have things he wanted to say to your father and to you? I mean . . ." I stopped again, embarrassed.

He said simply, "You mean it was plain and simple affection? That Michael may have had a premonition he'd not get out of the jam he was in, and wanted to say something to my father . . . a sort of farewell? No . . . no, Camilla, not Michael. If he felt very deeply about people he kept it to himself. Nor do I think he'd dabble in 'premonitions.' He knew the risks and he didn't fuss. Besides he does say he wants to 'show' Father something, and me . . . here, in Greece."

"Perhaps the country itself. Heaven knows it's exciting enough. Would your father have been interested?"

Simon laughed. "He was a classicist too. He'd been here half a score of times before."

"Oh. Oh, I see. Yes, that does make a difference."

"I think so. No, I'm right. He'd found something, Camilla." A tiny pause, and that electric thrill again, which quivered to nothing as Simon added flatly, "I'm pretty certain I know what it was, too, but I could bear to make sure. And for a start, I'd like to know just where Michael died, and how. . . ."

Another pause. He must have been thinking back to my remarks about the letter, for he said thoughtfully, "No, all things taken together, I know I'm right. Though it does seem a little odd. . . . You may be right about the 'emotion'—though it wouldn't be like Mick. He was the most casual-seeming devil to talk to that you ever knew. It took quite some time before you guessed that he was probably the toughest too, and the most self-sufficient."

Like little brother Simon. . . . The thought came so pat and so clearly that for one terrible moment I was afraid I had said it aloud. And I had an uncomfortable feeling that he knew just what I was thinking.

I said quickly and idiotically, "Here's Arachova."

It was one of the rather less necessary remarks. Already we were hemmed in by the crowding walls, and the coloured rugs—still hanging outside the vividly lit shops—almost brushed the sides of the car. There were two or three donkeys, freed from rope and saddle, wandering loose in the street. I saw a goat on someone's garden wall. It gave us an evil, gleaming glance before it leaped away into shadow and vanished. There was the familiar smell of dust and dung and gasoline fumes and the lees of wine.

Simon parked the car in the place where it had been that afternoon. He stopped the engine and we got out. We walked back towards the steep alleyway, where I had first seen him. Opposite the foot of it was one of the village cafés, a dozen tables in a whitewashed room open to the road. Most of the tables were full. The men watched us . . . or rather, they didn't look at me. They all watched Simon.

He paused at the foot of the alley and put a hand under my elbow. I saw that light, wary look touch the groups of dark-faced men, linger, leave them. He smiled down at me.

"Up here," he said, "and watch where you go. The steps are tricky and the donkeys have provided a few extra natural hazards. Stephanos, naturally, lives at the very top."

I looked up. The alley was about four feet wide and had a gradient of one in three. The steps were just too far apart and were made of sharp chunks of Parnassus with the minimum of dressing. The donkeys—a herd of healthy donkeys—had been that way many times. There was one dim light halfway up.

For some reason it occurred to me at that moment to wonder just what I had got myself into. ELAS, Stephanos, a man called Michael dying on Parnassus and lying bleaching to earth again above Delphi . . . all this, out of nowhere, and now a steep dark little alley and the pressure of Simon's hand on my arm. I wondered sharply just what we were going to learn from Stephanos.

And suddenly, I knew that I didn't want to hear it.

"*Avanti,*" said Simon beside me, sounding amused.

I pushed the coward impulse aside, and started up the alleyway.

CHAPTER VI

. . . Seek
Thy brother with a tale that must be heard
Howe'er it sicken.

EURIPIDES: *Electra*
(*tr. Gilbert Murray*).

STEPHANOS' HOUSE was a small two-storied building, set at the top of the stairway. Its bottom storey opened straight on the alley, and housed the beasts—a donkey and two goats and a gaggle of skinny hens—while stone stairs led up the outer wall of the house to the top storey where the family lived. At the head of the steps a wide concrete platform served as porch and garden in one. Its low parapet was crowded with pots full of greenery, and roofed with a trellis of rough branches which formed a pergola for the vine. I saw Simon stoop to avoid a loaded bough, and a hanging bunch of grapes brushed my cheek with a cold gentle touch. The top half of the door was open, and the light streamed out to gild the vine tendrils. There was a hot oily smell from the family's supper, mixed with goat, and donkey, and the furry musk-smell of geraniums where I had brushed a hand against one of the flowerpots.

We had been heard coming up the steps. As we crossed the platform the lower half of the door opened, and an old man stood there, large against the weak light from within.

I paused. Simon was behind me, still in shadow. I moved aside to let him pass me, and he came forward, hand outstretched, with some greeting in Greek. I saw the old man stiffen as he peered out. His mouth opened as if to make some involuntary exclamation, then he seemed to draw back a little. He said formally, "Brother of Michael, you are welcome. The woman of the house said you would come tonight."

Simon withdrew the hand which the old man hadn't appeared to notice, and said, with equal formality, "My name is Simon. I'm glad to meet you, *Kyrie* Stephanos. This is *Kyria* Haven, a friend who has brought me down in her car."

The old man's look touched me, no more. He inclined his head, saying slowly, "You are both welcome. Be pleased to come in."

He turned, then, and went into the room.

I should perhaps make it clear here that this and most of the subsequent conversation was in Greek, and that therefore I didn't understand it. But afterwards Simon gave me as exact a translation as he could, and at the time I was able to follow what I may perhaps call the emotional movements of the conversation. So I shall set the interview down as it occurred.

It seemed apparent to me, from the first short exchange on the balcony, that our welcome wasn't exactly a glowing one, and this surprised me. I had seen during my stay in Greece so much of the miracle of Greek hospitality, that I was both disconcerted and repelled. It didn't worry me that Stephanos hadn't spoken to me—I was only a woman, after all, and as such had pretty low social rating—but his rejection of Simon's outstretched hand had been quite deliberate, and his gesture now, as he invited us to follow him in, was heavy and (it seemed) reluctant.

I hesitated, glancing at Simon doubtfully.

He didn't appear to be in the least put out. He merely lifted an eyebrow at me, and waited for me to precede him into the house.

The single living and sleeping room of the house was high and square. The floor was of scrubbed boards, the walls whitewashed and hung with vivid holy pictures in appalling colours. Light came from a single naked electric bulb. In one corner stood an old-fashioned oil stove, and above it shelves for pans and a blue curtain that no doubt concealed food and crockery. Against one wall was an immense bed, covered now with a brown blanket and obviously used during the day as a sofa. Above the bed hung a small icon of the Virgin and Child, with a red electric bulb glowing in front of it. A victorian-looking cupboard, a scrubbed table, a couple of kitchen chairs and a bench covered with cheap oil cloth made up the rest of the furniture. A note of vivid colour was supplied by the one rug on the boarded floor. It was locally woven, in brilliant scarlet and parrot green. The room had the air of great poverty and an almost fierce cleanliness.

There was an old woman sitting over near the stove on one of the hard chairs. I took her to be Stephanos' wife—the woman of the house. She was dressed in black, and even in the house wore the Moslem-looking headscarf, which veils mouth and chin, and which gives the field workers of Greece such an Eastern look. It was pulled down now below her chin, and I could see her face. She looked very old, as the peasant women of the hot countries do. Her face had lovely bones, fine and regular, but the skin had dried into a thousand wrinkles, and her teeth had decayed. She smiled at me and made a gesture of shy welcome, to which I responded with a sort of bow and an embarrassed "Good evening" in Greek, as I took the chair she indicated. She made no further move to greet us, and I noticed that her look in reply to Simon's greeting was uneasy, almost scared. Her gnarled hands moved in her lap, and then she dropped her eyes to them and kept them there.

Simon had taken the other chair near the door, and the old man sat down on the bench. I found myself staring at him. So much a part of the land of myth was he that he might have come straight out of Homer. His face was brown, wrinkled like the woman's, and in expression patriarchal and benevolent. The white hair and beard were curled like those of the great Zeus in the Athens Museum. He was dressed in a sort of long tunic of faded blue, buttoned close down the front and reaching to his thighs; beneath it he wore what looked like white cotton jodhpurs bound at the knee with black bands. On his head was a small soft black cap. The knotted, powerful hands looked as if they were uneasy without a crook to grasp.

He looked at Simon under thick white brows, ignoring me. The look was grave and—I thought—measuring. In the corner beside me, the old woman sat silent. I could hear the animals moving about below us, and the quick tread of someone coming up the alley from the street.

Stephanos had just opened his mouth to speak, when there was an interruption. The quick steps outside mounted the stone stairs at a run. A youth came across the balcony with a rush and paused in the doorway, one hand on the jamb of the door, the other thrust into his waistband. It was a very dramatic pose, and he was a very dramatic young man. He was about eighteen, lean and brown and beautiful, with thick black curls and a vivid, excited face. He wore ancient striped flannels, and the loudest and most awful shirt I have ever seen.

He said, "Grandfather? He's come?"

Then he saw Simon. He didn't appear to notice me at all, but I was getting used to that, and merely sat quiet, like the woman of the house. The boy flashed a delighted smile at Simon, and a flood of rapid Greek, which was interrupted by his grandfather's saying repressively, "Who told you to come, Niko?"

Niko whirled back to him. All his movements were swift like those of a graceful but restless young cat. "They told me at Lefteris' that he had come again. I wanted to see him."

"And now you see him. Sit down and be silent, Niko. We have much to say."

I saw Niko throw a quick appraising glance at Simon. "Have you told him?"

"I have told him nothing. Sit down and be silent."

Niko turned to obey, but his look lingered on Simon. The dark eyes glinted with something that could have been excitement mixed with amusement—or even malice. Simon met it with that masked indifferent look that I was beginning to know. He had taken out his cigarette case and now he glanced at me. I shook my head. "Niko?" The boy put out a hand, then stopped, drew it back, and sent Simon another of his vivid smiles. "No, thank you, *kyrie*." A glance at his grandfather, then he crossed to the big bed and threw himself on it. Simon found his lighter, lit a cigarette with a certain deliberation, then put his lighter carefully back in his pocket before he turned to Stephanos.

The latter was sitting motionless. He still didn't speak. The silence came back, heavy, charged, and the boy stirred restlessly on the bed. His eyes never left Simon's face. Beside me the woman hadn't moved, but as I glanced at her I saw her eyes slide sideways to meet mine, only to drop swiftly to the hands in her lap as if in an ecstasy of shyness. I realized then that she had been covertly studying my frock, and the knowledge came to me suddenly, warmingly, that Stephanos, too, was shy.

Perhaps Simon had divined this too, for he didn't wait for Stephanos, but spoke easily, bridging the moment.

"*Kyrie* Stephanos, I'm very glad to meet you at last, and the woman of your house. My father and I wrote to you to thank you for what you did for my brother, but—well, letters can't say it all. My father is dead now, but I'm speaking for him too when I say thank you again. You'll understand it isn't always possible to put into words all that one feels—all one would like to say, but I think you will understand what I feel, and what my father felt." He turned his head to smile at the woman. She didn't smile back. I thought she made a little sound as if of pain, and she moved in her chair. Her narrow lips worked in and out, and her fingers gripped each other painfully.

Stephanos said, almost roughly, "There is nothing for you to say, *kyrie*. We did no more than we should."

"It was a very great deal," said Simon gently. "You couldn't have done more if he, too, had been your son." A quick glance at the old woman. "I shan't say much about that, *kyria,* because there are memories that you won't want to revive; and I shall try not to ask any questions that might distress you. But I had to come and thank you, for my father, and for myself . . . and to see the house where my brother Michael found friends in the last days of his life."

He paused, and looked round him slowly. There was silence again. Below us the animals shuffled and one of them sneezed. There was nothing in Simon's face to read, but I saw the boy's speculative glance on him again before it turned as if in impatience to his grandfather. But Stephanos said nothing.

At length Simon said, "So it was here."

"It was here, *kyrie*. Below, behind the manger, there is a gap in the wall. He hid there. The dirty Germans did not think to look behind the sacks of straw, and the dung. Would you like me to show you?"

Simon shook his head. "No. I told you I don't want to remind you of that day. And I don't think I need ask you anything much about it, as you told us most of it in the letter that the *papa* wrote for you. You told me how Michael had been wounded in the shoulder and had come here for shelter, and how, after . . . later on, he went back into the mountains."

"It was just before dawn," said the old man, "on the second of October. We begged him to stay with us, because he was not yet well, and the wet weather comes early in the mountains. But he would not. He helped us to bury my son Nikolaos, and then he went." He nodded towards the intent youth on the bed. "There was that one, you understand, and his sister Maria, who is since married to Georgios who has a shop in the village. When the Germans came the children were out in the fields with their mother, or who knows? They too might have been killed. *Kyrie* Michael"—he pronounced it as a trisyllable, Mi-ha-eel— "would not stay, because of them. He went up into the mountains."

"Yes. A few days later he was killed. You found his body somewhere over between here and Delphi, and you took it down to be buried."

"That is so. What I found on his body I gave after three weeks to Perikles Grivas, and he took it to an Englishman who was going by night from Galaxeidion. But this you know."

"This I know. I want you to show me where he was killed, Stephanos."

There was a short silence. The boy Niko watched Simon unwinkingly. I noticed that he had taken out a cigarette of his own and was smoking it.

The old man said heavily, "I will do that, of course. Tomorrow?"

"If it's convenient."

"For you, it is convenient."

"You're very good."

"You are the brother of Michael."

Simon said gently, "He was here a long time, wasn't he?"

Beside me the woman moved suddenly and said in a clear soft voice, "He was my son." I saw with a wrench of discomfort that there were tears on her cheeks. "He should have stayed," she said, and then repeated it almost desperately, "He should have stayed."

Simon said, "But he had to go. How could he stay and put you and your family in that danger again? When the Germans came back—"

"They didn't come back." It was Niko who spoke, clearly, from the bed.

"No." Simon turned his head. "Because they caught Michael in the mountains. But if they hadn't caught him—if he had still been hiding here—they might have come back to the village, and then—"

"They did not catch him," said the old man.

Simon turned back sharply. Stephanos was sitting still on the bench, knees apart, hands clasped between them, his heavy body bent slightly forward. His eyes looked fathoms dark under the white brows. The two men stared at one another. I found myself stirring on my hard chair. It was as if the scene were taking place in slow motion, silent and incomprehensible, yet powered with emotions that plucked uncomfortably at the nerves.

Simon said slowly, "What are you trying to tell me?"

"Only," said Stephanos, "that Michael was not killed by the Germans. He was killed by a Greek."

"By a Greek?" Simon echoed it almost blankly.

The old man made a gesture that might have come straight from *Oedipus Rex*. To me, still not understanding anything except that the men's talk had an overtone of tragedy, it conveyed a curiously powerful impression of resignation and shame.

"By a man from Arachova," he said.

It was at this moment that the light chose to go out.

The Greeks were obviously accustomed to the whims of the electric system. With scarcely a moment's delay the old woman had found and lit an oil lamp, and placed it on the table in the middle of the room. It was a frightful-looking lamp of some cheap bright metal, but it burned with a soft apricot light and the sweet smell of olive oil. With the heavy shadows cast on his face, Stephanos looked more than ever like a tragic actor. Niko had rolled over on his stomach and was watching the two other men bright-eyed, as if it were indeed a play. I supposed that, for him, his father's death and Michael's seemed so remote that this talk of them was no more than a breath from an exciting past.

Simon was saying, "I . . . see. That makes a lot of things a lot plainer. And of course you don't know who it was."

"Indeed we do."

Simon's brows shot up. The old man smiled sourly. "You are wondering why we have not killed him, *kyrie,* when we called Michael our son?"

From the bed Niko said in a smooth voice that was certainly malicious, "That is not the way the English work, grandfather."

Simon flicked him a look but said, mildly, to Stephanos, "Not exactly. I was wondering what had happened to him. I gather he's alive."

"I'll explain. I should tell you first of all that the man's name was Dragoumis. Angelos Dragoumis."

"*Angelos?*"

The old man nodded. "Yes. You know of him, of course. I told you in the letter the *papa* wrote for me that Michael had worked with him. But I should never have told you this of Angelos, if you had not come. Now that you are here, these things cannot be hidden. It is your right to know."

Simon was carefully extinguishing his cigarette in the lid of a match-box. His face was still and shuttered, his eyes hidden. I saw the boy Niko roll over again on the bed and grin to himself.

"You know that Angelos was the leader of the ELAS troop that Michael was working with," said Stephanos. "When Michael left here he went up, I think, with the intention of rejoining them. They had scattered when the big German search operation started in the hills, and most of them had moved north, Angelos with them. What brought Angelos back in this direction I don't know, but certain it is that he fetched up against Michael over on Parnassus and murdered him there."

"Why?"

"I do not know. Except that such murders were not rare in those days. It may be that Michael and Angelos had had some quarrel over the action of Angelos' troops. Perhaps Michael was putting too much pressure on him; we know now that Angelos was anxious to save his men and his supplies for a different battle later—after the Germans had gone."

I saw Simon look up sharply, those light-grey eyes vividly intent. "Angelos was one of them? Are you sure?"

"Certain. He played for high stakes, did Angelos Dragoumis. He was in Athens soon after the Germans had left Greece, and we knew he was active in the massacre at Kalamai. Oh yes, you may be sure that he was betraying the Allies all the time."

He smiled thinly. "I do not think that Michael can have known. No, this was some other quarrel. It may simply have been that two such men could never come together, and agree. Angelos was bad, bad from the heart, and Michael . . . he did not like having to work with such a one. They had quarrelled before. He told me so. Angelos was an arrogant man, and a bully, and Michael—well, Michael could not be driven either."

"True enough." Simon was selecting another cigarette. "But you said he was 'murdered.' If two men quarrel and there's a fight, that isn't murder, Stephanos."

"It was murder. It was a fight, but not a fair one. Michael had been wounded, remember."

"Even so—"

"He was struck from behind first, with a stone or with the butt of a gun. There was a great mark there, and the skin was broken. It is a miracle that the blow didn't kill him, or stun him, at least. But he must have heard Angelos behind him, and turned, because in spite of the traitor's blow from behind, and Michael's wounded shoulder, there was a fight. Michael was—a good deal marked."

"I see." Simon was lighting his cigarette. "How did Angelos kill him? I take it he wasn't using a gun. A knife?"

"His neck was broken."

The match paused, an inch from Simon's cigarette. The grey eyes lifted to the old man's. I couldn't see their expression from where I sat, but I saw Stephanos nod, once, as Zeus might have nodded. Niko's eyes narrowed suddenly and glinted between their long lashes. The match made contact. "It must have been quite a scrap," said Simon.

"He wouldn't be easy to kill," said the old man. "But with the wounded shoulder, and the blow on the head . . ."

His voice trailed off. He wasn't looking at Simon now; he seemed to be seeing something beyond the lamplit walls of the room, something remote in place and time.

There was a pause. Then Simon blew out a long cloud of tobacco smoke. "Yes," he said. "Well. And the man Angelos . . . what happened to him?"

"That I can't tell you. He has not been back to Arachova, naturally. It was said that he went with many of his kind into Yugoslavia, when their bid for power failed. In fourteen years, nobody has heard of him, and it is probable that he is dead. He had only one relative, a cousin, Dimitrios Dragoumis, who has had no news of him."

"A cousin? Here?"

"Dragoumis lives now at Itea. He also fought in Angelos' troop, but he was not a leader, and—well, some things are best forgotten." The old man's voice roughened. "But the things that Angelos did to his own people, these are not forgotten. He was at Kalamai; it is said he was also at Pyrgos, where many hundred Greeks died, and among them my own cousin Panos, an old man." The gnarled hands moved convulsively on his knees. "No matter of that. . . . But I do not speak merely of his politics, *Kyrie* Simon, or even of what such as he do in war. He was evil, *kyrie,* he was a man who delighted in evil. He liked the sight of pain.

He liked best to hurt children and old women, and he boasted like Ares of how many he himself had killed. He would put a man's eyes out— or a woman's—and smile while he did it. Always that smile. He was an evil man, and he betrayed Michael and murdered him."

"And if he has not been seen here since my brother died, how can you be sure he murdered him?"

"I saw him," said the old man simply.

"You saw him?"

"Yes. It was he beyond doubt. When I came on them he turned and ran. But I couldn't follow him." He paused again, one of those heavy terrible little pauses. "You see, Michael was still alive."

I saw Simon's eyes jerk up again to meet his. The old man nodded. "Yes. He lived only a minute or so. But it was enough to hold me there beside him and let Angelos get away."

"Angelos made no attempt to attack you?"

"None. He, too, had been badly mauled." There was satisfaction in the old shepherd's eyes. "Michael died hard, even with that traitor's bash on the back of the head. Angelos might have shot at me, but later I found his revolver lying under a boulder, as if it had been flung there in the struggle. The countryside was full of Germans, you see, and he must have counted on killing Michael quietly, after he'd stunned him, but he wasn't quick or clever enough, and Michael managed to turn on him. When I came to the head of the cliff and saw them below me, Angelos was just getting to his feet. He turned to look for his gun then, but my dog attacked him, and it was all he could do to get clear away. Without his gun, he could have done nothing." He wiped his mouth with the back of a knotted brown hand. "I took Michael down to Delphi. It was the nearest. That's all."

"He didn't speak?"

Stephanos hesitated, and Simon's glance sharpened. Stephanos shook his head. "It was nothing, *kyrie*. If there had been anything I would have put it in the letter."

"But he did speak?"

"Two words. He said, 'The Charioteer.'"

The words were *"O Eniochos,"* and they were classical, not modern, Greek. They were also familiar to me, as to many visitors to Delphi, because they refer to the famous bronze statue that stands in the Delphi Museum. It is the statue of a youth, the Charioteer, robed in a stiffly pleated robe, still holding in his hands the reins of his vanished horses. I glanced at Simon, wondering where, in an exchange bristling with the names "Angelos," and "Michael," the Charioteer could have a place.

Simon was looking as puzzled as I. "'The Charioteer'? Are you sure?"

"I am not quite sure. I had run hard down the path to the foot of the cliff, and I was out of breath and much distressed. He lived only a matter of seconds after I got to him. But he knew me, and I thought that was what he said. It is a classical word, but of course it is familiar because it is used of the statue in the Delphi Museum. But why Michael should have tried to tell me about that, I do not know. If indeed that was what he whispered." He straightened his back a little. "I repeat, I would have told you if I had been sure, or if it had meant anything."

"Why did you not tell us about Angelos?"

"It was over then, and he had gone, and it was better to let Michael's father think he had died in battle and not at the hand of a traitor. Besides," said Stephanos simply, "we were ashamed."

"It was so much over," said Simon, "that when Michael's brother comes to Arachova to find out just how his brother died, the men in Arachova avoid him, and his host won't shake his hand."

The old man smiled. "Very well, then. It is not over. The shame remains."

"The shame isn't yours."

"It is that of Greece."

"My country's done a thing or two lately to balance it, Stephanos."

"Politics!" The old man made a gesture highly expressive of what he would wish to see done to all politicians, and Simon laughed. As if at a signal, the old woman got to her feet, pulled back the blue curtain, and brought out a big stone jar. She put glasses on the table and began to pour out the dark sweet wine. Stephanos said, "You will drink with us, then?"

"With the greatest of pleasure," said Simon. The old woman handed him a glass, then Stephanos, Niko, and finally me. She didn't take one herself, but remained standing, watching me with a sort of shy pleasure. I sipped the wine. It was as dark as mavrodaphne and tasted of cherries. I smiled at her over the glass and said tentatively, in Greek, "It's very good."

Her face split into a wide smile. She bobbed her head and repeated delightedly, "Very good, very good," and Niko turned over on the bed and said in American-accented English, "You speak Greek, miss?"

"No. Only a few words."

He turned to Simon. "How come you speak such good Greek, eh?"

"My brother Michael taught me when I was younger than you. I went on learning and reading it afterwards. I knew I would come here one day."

"Why you not come before?"

"It costs too much, Niko."

"And now you are rich, eh?"

"I get by."

"*Oriste?*"

"I mean, I have enough."

"I see." The dark eyes widened in a limpid look. "And now you have come. You know about Angelos and your brother. What would you say if I told you something else, *kyrie?*"

"What?"

"That Angelos is still alive?"

Simon said slowly, "Are you telling me that, Niko?"

"He has been seen near Delphi, on the mountain."

"What? Recently?" said Simon sharply.

"Oh, yes." Niko flashed that beautiful mischievous smile up at him. "But perhaps it is only a ghost. There are ghosts on Parnassus, *kyrie,* lights that move and voices that carry across the rocks. There are those who see these things. Myself, no. It is the old gods, not?"

"Possibly," said Simon. "Is this the truth, Niko? That Angelos was seen?"

Niko shrugged. "How can I tell? It was Janis who saw him, and Janis is—" he made a significant gesture towards his forehead. "Angelos killed his mother when the *andartes* burned his father's farm, and ever since then Janis has been queer in the head, and has 'seen' Angelos—oh, many times. If ghosts are true, then he still walks on Parnassus. But Dimitrios Dragoumis—that is true enough. He has asked many questions about your coming. All the men here in Arachova know that you are coming, and they talk about it and wonder—but Dragoumis, he has been to Delphi and to Arachova and has asked questions—oh, many questions."

"What is he like?"

"He is a little like his cousin. Not in the face, but in the—what do you say?—the build. But not in the spirit either." His look was innocent. "It may be that you will meet Dragoumis. But do not be afraid of him. And do not worry yourself about Angelos, *Kyrie* Simon."

Simon grinned. "Do I look as if I was worrying?"

"No," said Niko frankly, "but then, he is dead."

"And if Janis is right, and he is not dead?"

"I think," said Niko almost insolently, "that you are only an Englishman, *Kyrie* Simon. Not?"

"So what?"

Niko gave a charming little crack of laughter and rolled over on the bed. Stephanos said suddenly and angrily, in Greek, "Niko, behave yourself. What does he say, *Kyrie* Simon?"

"He thinks I couldn't deal with Angelos," said Simon idly. "Here, Niko, catch." He threw the boy a cigarette. Niko fielded it with a graceful clawed gesture. He was still laughing. Simon turned to Stephanos. "Do you think it's true that Angelos has been seen hereabouts?"

The old shepherd slanted a fierce look at his grandson under his white brows. "So he has told you that tale, has he? Some rumour started by an idiot who has seen Angelos at least a dozen times since the end of the war. Aye, and Germans too, a score of times. Don't pay any attention to *that* moonshine."

Simon laughed. "Or to the lights and voices on Parnassus?"

Stephanos said, "If a man goes up into Parnassus after sunset, why should he not see strange things? The gods still walk there, and a man who would not go carefully in the country of the gods is a fool." Another of those glowering looks at his grandson. "You, Niko, have learned a lot of folly in Athens. And that is a terrible shirt."

Niko sat up straight. "It is not!" he protested, stung. "It is American!"

Stephanos snorted and Simon grinned. "Aid to Greece?"

The old man gave a gruff bark of laughter. "He is not a bad boy, *kyrie,* even if Athens has spoiled him. But now he comes home to work, and I will make a man of him. Give *Kyrie* Simon some more wine." This to his wife, who hurried to refill Simon's glass.

"Thank you." Simon added, in a different tone, "Is it true that this man Dragoumis has been asking questions about me?"

"Quite true. After it was known that you were coming, he asked many questions—when you came, for how long, what you meant to do, and all that." He smiled sourly. "I don't speak much to that one, me."

"But why? Why should he be interested? Do you suppose he had anything to do with Michael's death?"

"He had nothing to do with it. That much we found out after the war, before he came back here. Otherwise he would not," said Stephanos simply, "have dared come back. No, he knew nothing about it. Once before, a year—more—eighteen months ago—he spoke to me and asked me what had happened, and where it was that Michael was killed. He showed a decent shame and he spoke well of Michael; but I do not talk of my sons to every man. I refused to speak of it. And no one else knew the whole truth except the priest at Delphi who is since dead, and my own brother Alkis who was killed in the war."

"And now me."

"And now you. I will take you there tomorrow and show you the place. It is your right."

He looked up under the white brows at Simon for another considering moment. Then he said slowly, irrelevantly, "I think, *Kyrie* Simon, that you are very like Michael. And Niko—Niko is even more of a fool than I had thought. . . ."

CHAPTER VII

The Oracles are dumm,
No voice or hideous humm
  Runs through the arched roof in words deceiving
Apollo from his shrine
Can no more divine . . .
MILTON: Nativity Hymn.

SIMON DIDN'T SPEAK on the way back to Delphi, so I sat quietly beside him, wondering what had been said in that sombre and somehow very foreign-seeming interview. Nothing that Stephanos—exotically Homeric —had said could have been ordinary, while about Niko's racy intelligent beauty there was something essentially Greek—a quicksilver quality that is as evident today under the cheaply Americanized trappings of his kind as it was in the black and red of the classical vase paintings.

When at length, as we neared Delphi, trees crowded in above the road blocking out the starlight, Simon slowed the car, drove into a wide bay, and stopped. He switched the engine off. Immediately the sound of running water filled the air. He turned out the lights, and the dark trees crowded closer. I could smell the pines, cool and pungent. They loomed thick in the starlight, rank on rank of scented stone pines crowding up towards the cleft where the water sprang. Beyond the trees reared the immense darkness of rock, the Shining Ones no longer shining, but pinnacles and towers of imminent blackness.

Simon took out cigarettes and offered one to me. "How much of that did you understand?"

"Nothing whatever, except that you were talking about Michael and the ELAS leader Angelos." I smiled. "I see now why you didn't mind my sitting in on your private affairs."

He said abruptly, "They've taken a very queer turn."

I waited.

"I'd like to tell you, if I may."

"Of course."

So we sat there in the car and smoked, while he told me, fully and accurately, what had passed in the shepherd's cottage. So vivid were my own visual impressions of the recent scene that I was able without difficulty to impose my picture, so to speak, over his, and see where movement and gesture had fitted in with the words.

When he had finished I didn't speak, for the sufficient reason that I could find nothing to say. The instinct that had halted me at the foot of the alley steps had been a true one: these waters were too deep for me. If I had felt myself inadequate before—I, who had been afraid of a mild skirmish over a hired car—what was I to feel now? Who was I, to offer comfort or even comment on a brother's murder? The murder might be fourteen years old, but there's a kind of shock in the very word, let alone the knowledge of the deed, however many years lie between it and the discovery. I didn't know Simon well enough to say the right thing, so I said nothing.

He himself made no comment, beyond telling me the story of the interview in that give-nothing-away voice of his that I was beginning to know. I did wonder fleetingly if he would say anything more about Michael's letter, or about the "find" which he, Simon, had said he knew of. . . . But he said nothing. He threw his finished cigarette over the side of the car into the dust, and it appeared that he threw the story with it, because he said, with a complete change of tone and subject:

"Shall we walk up through the ruins? You haven't seen them yet, and starlight's not a bad start. Unless, of course, you'd rather wait and see them for the first time alone?"

"No. I'd like to go."

We went up the steep path through the pines. Now that my eyes were used to the darkness it was just possible to see the way. We crossed the narrow rush of water and were on a track soft with pine needles.

After a while we came out from under the trees into an open space where fallen blocks made treacherous walking, and dimly in the starlight I could see the shape of ruined walls.

"The Roman market place," said Simon. "Those were shops and so on over there. By Delphi's standards this is modern stuff, so we by-pass it quickly. . . . Here we are. This is the gate of the temple precinct. The step's steep, but there's a wide smooth way up through the buildings to the temple itself. Can you see?"

"Fairly well. It's rather . . . stupendous by starlight, isn't it?"

Dimly I could make out the paved road that zigzagged up between the ruined walls of treasuries and shrines. The precinct seemed in this light enormous. Everywhere ahead of us, along the hillside, below among the pines that edged the road, above as far as the eye could reach in the starlight, loomed the broken walls, the spectral pillars, the steps and pedestals and altars of the ancient sanctuary. We walked slowly up the Sacred Way. I could make out the little Doric building that once housed the Athenian treasure, the grim stone where the Sybil sat to foretell the Trojan War, the slender pillars of the Portico of the Athenians, the shape of a great altar . . . then we had reached the temple itself, a naked and broken floor, half up the mountainside, held there in space by its massive retaining walls, and bordered with the six great columns that even in the darkness stood emphatic against the star-crowded sky.

I took a little breath.

Beside me, Simon quoted softly, " 'The gods still walk there, and a man who would not go carefully in the country of the gods is a fool.' "

"They *are* still here," I said. "Is it silly of me? But they are."

"Three thousand years," he said. "Wars, treachery, earthquake, slavery, oblivion. And men still recognize them here. No, it's not silly of you. It happens to everyone with intelligence and imagination. This is Delphi . . . and, well, we're not the first to hear the chariot wheels. Not by a long way."

"It's the only place in Greece I've really heard them. I've tried to imagine things—oh, you know how one does. But no, nothing, really, even on Delos. There are ghosts at Mycenae, but it's not the same. . . ."

"Poor human ghosts," he said. "But here . . . I suppose that if a place was, like Delphi, a centre of worship for—how many?—about two thousand years, something remains. Something inheres in stone, I'll swear, and here it's in the very air. The effect's helped by the landscape; I suppose it must be one of the most magnificent in the world. And of course this is just the setting for the holy place. Come up into the temple."

A ramp led up to the temple floor, which was paved with great stone blocks, some broken and dangerous. We picked our way carefully across this until we stood at the edge of the floor, between the columns. Below us was the sheer drop of the retaining wall: below that the steep mountainside and the ghosts of the scattered shrines. The far valley was an immensity of darkness, filled with the small movements of the night wind, and the sound of pine and olive.

Simon's cigarette beside me glowed and faded. I saw that he had turned his back on the spaces of the starlit valley. He was leaning against a column, gazing up the hill behind the temple. I could see nothing there but the thick shadows of trees, and against them more pale shapes of stone.

"What's up there?"

"That's where they found the Charioteer."

The word brought me back to the present with the tingle of a small electric shock. I had forgotten, in the overpowering discovery of Delphi, that Simon would have other preoccupations.

I hesitated; it was he, after all, who had sheered away from the story onto the neutral ground of Delphi. I said a little awkwardly, "Do you suppose Stephanos was right? Does it make any kind of sense to you?"

"None at all," he said cheerfully. His shoulder came away from the pillar. "Why don't you come up to the studio now, and meet Nigel, and have some coffee or a drink?"

"I'd like to, of course, but isn't it awfully late?"

"Not for this country. As far as I can make out nobody goes to bed at all, except in the afternoons. When in Greece, you know. . . . Are you tired?"

"Not a bit. I keep feeling I ought to be, but I'm not."

He laughed. "It's the air, or the light, or the simple intoxication of being alive in Hellas. It lasts, too. Then you will come?"

"I should love to."

As I picked my way across the temple floor with his hand under my arm I had time to feel surprise at myself, and a sort of resignation. Here I went again, I reflected. . . . Just in this way I had drifted along at Philip's bidding, in Philip's wake. But this was different. Just what the difference was I didn't stop to analyze.

I said, "Aren't we going down to the road? Why this way?"

"We don't need to go down. The studio's away up above the temple, just over the mountain's shoulder towards Delphi. It's easier to go up through the rest of the shrine."

"But the car?"

"I'll go and get it later when I've seen you down to your hotel. It's no distance from there by the road. This way, and watch your step. It's easier here. . . . These steps lead up towards the little theatre. That thing on the right was put up by Alexander the Great after a narrow escape in a lion hunt. . . . Here's the theatre. It's tiny compared with Athens or Epidaurus, but isn't it a gem?"

In the starlight the broken floor looked smooth. The semicircular tiers of seats rose, seemingly new and unbroken, towards their backdrop of holly and cypress; it lay, a little broken marble cup of a theatre, silent except for the tiny scuffling of a dry twig that the breeze was patting idly along the empty flags.

I said on an impulse, "I suppose you wouldn't—no, I'm sorry. Of course not."

"What do you suppose I wouldn't do?"

"Nothing. It was silly, under the circumstances."

"The circumstances? Oh, that. Don't let that worry you. I suppose you want to hear something recited here in Greek, even if it's only *thalassa! thalassa!* Is that it? . . . What's the matter?"

"Nothing. Only that if you go on reading my thoughts like that you're going to be a very uncomfortable companion."

"You ought to practise too."

"I haven't the talent."

"Perhaps that's just as well."

"What d'you mean?"

He laughed. "Never mind. Was I right?"

"Yes. And not just *thalassa,* please. Some lines of verse, if you can think of anything. I heard someone reciting in the theatre at Epidaurus and it was like a miracle. Even a whisper carried right up to the topmost tier."

"It does the same here," he said, "only it's not so stupendous. All right, if you'd like it." He was feeling in his pockets as he spoke. "Half a minute; I'll have to find my lighter. . . . If you want to get your voice properly carried you have to locate the centre of the stage . . . it's marked by a cross on the flagstones. . . ."

As he pulled the lighter from his pocket I heard the small musical chink of metal on stone. I stooped quickly after the sound. "Something fell; some money, I think. Here . . . not far away, anyway. Shine the light down, will you?"

The lighter flicked into flame and he bent with it near the ground. Almost immediately I saw the sharp gleam of a coin. I picked it up and held it towards him. The orange-coloured flame slid alive and sparkling across the little disc in my palm. I said, "That's surely—*gold?*"

"Yes. Thank you." He took it and dropped it into his pocket. He might have been discussing a lost halfpenny, or at most a threepenny stamp. "That was one of the souvenirs that Stephanos sent us. I told you he sent what was on Michael's body when he died. There were three of these gold sovereigns." He moved away from me, holding the lighter low over the flags, searching for the central mark. You'd have thought there was nothing in his mind except the pleasant task of showing a girl over the Delphic ruins.

"Simon . . ."

"Here it is." He straightened up, the lighter still burning in his hand. He must have seen my look, because he smiled at me, that sudden, very attractive smile. "You know, I did tell you it was no longer a present tragedy, didn't I? I told you not to worry. Now, come here to the centre, and hear how your voice is picked up and carried high over those tiers of seats."

I moved forward to the spot. "I know you did. But when you told me that, you didn't know that your brother Michael had been murdered. Doesn't that make a difference?"

"Perhaps. There, do you hear the echo?"

"Glory, yes. It's weird, isn't it? As if the sound were coming back at you from those crags up there, and swirling all round you. It's like something tangible; like—yes, like sound made solid. . . . Are you really going to recite something, or would you rather not?"

I thought he misunderstood me deliberately. "With this lack of audience, I think I might. What'll you have?"

"You're the classicist. I leave it to you. But wait a moment. I'm going up into the back stalls."

I climbed the narrow aisle and found a seat two thirds of the way up the amphitheatre. The shaped marble of the seat was surprisingly comfortable, and the stone was still warm from the day's sun. The circular stage looked small below me. I could just make out its shape. Simon was nothing but a bodiless shadow. Then his voice came up out of the well of darkness, and the great rolling Greek lines rose and broke and echoed, rounding like a wind among the high crags. A phrase, a name, swam up from the flood of sound, giving directions to the music, like flights to an arrow. "Hades, Persephone, Hermes. . . ." I shut my eyes and listened.

He stopped. There was a pause. The echo went up the cliff, hung like the murmur of a gong, and died. Then his voice came clearly and softly, speaking in English; music translating music.

> ". . . Hades, Persephone,
> Hermes, steward of death,
> Eternal Wrath and Furies,
> Children of gods,
> Who see all murderers
> And all adulterous thieves, come soon!
> Be near me, and avenge
> My father's death, and bring
> My brother home!"

He had stopped speaking again. The words died into silence high above me, and in the wake of the echo, it seemed, the night wind moved. I heard the hollies rustle behind me, and then, further up the hill, a scatter of dust and pebbles under the foot of some wandering beast, a goat, perhaps, or a donkey; I thought I heard the clink of metal. Then the night was still again. I got up and started down the steep aisle.

Simon's voice came, pitched quietly and perfectly clear. "That do?"

"Beautifully." I reached the bottom and crossed the stage. "Thank you very much; but—I thought you said the tragedy was over?"

For the first time since I had known him (some seven hours? Could it possibly be only half a day?) he sounded disconcerted. "What d'you mean?" He left the centre of the stage and came to meet me.

"That speech was a bit—immediate, wasn't it?"

"You recognized it?"

"Yes. It's from Sophocles' *Electra,* isn't it?"

"Yes." There was a pause. He had a hand in his pocket, and now as he withdrew it I heard the chink of coins. He jingled them absently up and down. Then he said, "I was wrong, then. It's not over . . . at least not until Stephanos shows us the place tomorrow, and—"

He stopped. I reflected that Simon Lester seemed to have a remarkably royal habit of using the first person plural. I should have liked to say " 'Show *us?*' " but didn't. I said merely, "And?"

He said abruptly, "And I find what Michael found—what he was killed for. The gold."

"The gold?"

"Yes. I told you I'd an idea what it was that Michael might have found. I thought that, as soon as I read his letters, and remembered the sovereigns he was carrying. And after what Stephanos told us, I'm sure. It was gold he found, Angelos' little hoard of British gold, stashed away against the day of the Red Dawn."

"Yes, but Simon . . ." I began, then stopped. He knew Michael better than I did, after all.

The sovereigns clinked together as he thrust them back into his pocket. He turned away towards the side of the amphitheatre.

"This is the way up to the path. I'd better go first, perhaps; the steps are badly broken in places."

He reached a hand back to me, and together we mounted the steep flight. At the top he paused and seemed to reach up into the darkness. I heard the rustle of leaves. He turned back to me and put something round and polished and cool into my hand. "There you are. It's pomegranate. There's a little tree growing behind the topmost seats, and I've been longing for an excuse to pick one. Eat it soon, Persephone; then you'll have to stay in Delphi."

The path led us out at last above the trees, where we could see our way more clearly. It was wide enough now to walk side by side. Simon went on, speaking softly, "I think I'm right, Camilla; I think that's what Michael found. I'd suspected it before, but now I know he was murdered by his man Angelos, I'd bet on it for a certainty."

I said rather stupidly, still following my own thoughts, "But Stephanos said he was killed in a quarrel. Angelos and he—"

"If Michael had been quarrelling with a type like that he wouldn't be very likely to turn his back on him," said Simon. "I'm surprised Stephanos didn't think that one out for himself."

"But if it was an old quarrel, and Michael thought it was forgotten, but Angelos—"

"The same applies. I just don't see Michael trustfully turning his back on a man who'd once had—or thought he had—the sort of grudge that leads to murder."

"I suppose not."

"But take all the bits of the picture and put them together," said Simon, "and what d'you get? I told you that we—the British—were flying in arms and gold during the Occupation, for the use of the *andartes*. Angelos, as we now learn from Stephanos, was working for the Communist *putsch* at the end of the German Occupation of Greece; therefore, we can assume that he had an interest in holding back arms and supplies for later use. That's an assumption; but what facts have we? Angelos, when his men scatter northwards to avoid the Germans, comes south—alone. He meets Michael and kills him. He is interrupted before he can search the body, and on Michael are found gold sovereigns, and a hastily scribbled letter indicating that he has found something."

"Yes," I said, "but—"

"If Angelos had such a cache of guns and gold, and Michael, the B.L.O., had found it, would it not be the complete motive for Michael's murder?"

"Yes, of course it would. You mean that Michael, when he met him, tackled him about it and—oh, no, that won't do, will it? There's the same objection—that Angelos wouldn't have had the chance to hit him over the head."

"I can't help thinking," said Simon softly, "that Angelos saw something that told him Michael had found the cache. It's probably in some cave or other—Parnassus is honeycombed with them; and supposing that Michael, after he left Stephanos' house, had taken shelter in the one where the stuff was hidden? He'd stay there a few days till the Germans left the area, and then Angelos, doubling back to his treasure chest, would see the British officer coming out of the cave, his cave. . . . It could be, you know. And if Michael didn't see Angelos, as seems obvious, the Greek waited and took his chance and tried to wipe him out then and there. Which means—"

"Which means that, if you're right, the cache was very near the place where Michael was murdered," I said.

"Exactly. Well, we shall see."

"If there was anything, it'll have been taken long since."

"Probably."

"Angelos would come back and take it. If not immediately, then later."

"If he lived to come back. Three months after Mick's death he was out of the country for good."

I said, as casually as I could, "Was he? And what if Niko was possibly —just possibly—right? If he *were* still alive? Now, I mean?"

Simon laughed. "It's on the lap of the gods, isn't it?" One of the coins spun in his hand as he tossed and caught it. "What do you say? Shall we offer gold to Apollo if he'll bring Angelos back to Delphi now?"

"Aegisthus to Orestes' knife?" I tried to speak equally lightly, but in spite of myself the words sounded harsh and hollow.

"Why not?" The coin dropped into his hand again and his fingers closed on it. He was a shadow in the starlight, watching me. "You know, I told you the truth when I said the tragedy was over. I don't feel chewed up or dramatic about Mick's death, even after what I've learned tonight. But, damn it all, he was murdered, in a filthy way, and—if I'm right—for the filthiest of motives. And the murderer got away with it, and possibly with a fortune into the bargain. I've no particular desire to find the fortune, but I want to know, Camilla. That's all."

"Yes, I see."

"I came here to talk to Stephanos and see Michael's grave, and to leave it at that. But I can't leave it now, not till it's really over, and I know why it happened. I don't suppose there'll be anything left to tell me, after all this time, but I have to look. And as for Orestes"—I heard the smile in his voice—"I've no particular ambition for revenge, either, but if I did meet the murderer . . . don't you see that I'd quite like a word with him?" He laughed again. "Or do you share Niko's opinion of my abilities?"

"No. No, of course not. But this man Angelos . . . well, he's—" I floundered and stopped.

"Dangerous? So you don't think that—if I do meet him—I ought to have it out with him?"

"An eye for an eye?" I said. "I thought we didn't believe in that any more."

"Don't you believe it. We do. But in England there's a fine, impersonal, and expensive machinery to get your eye for you, and no personal guilt except your signature on a cheque to the Inland Revenue. Here, it's different. Nobody's going to do the dirty work for you. You do it yourself and nobody knows but the vultures. And Apollo."

"Simon, it's immoral."

"So is all natural law. Morals are social phenomena. Didn't you know?"

"I don't agree."

"No? You stick to that, Camilla. This is the loveliest country in the world, and the hardest. Much of it, and you're apt to find yourself thinking in its terms instead of your own. There are times, I'd say, when you have to. . . . But you stand by your guns." He laughed down at me. "And for a start, don't believe a word I say. I'm a normal law-abiding citizen, and a most upright and solemn schoolmaster. . . . Now, enough of this Orestean tragedy. Michael's dead these fourteen years, and Delphi's been here three thousand, so we'll let Delphi bury its dead. It does it just here, incidentally; that's the graveyard just beside the path, under the trees. And now, if you're to get any sleep at all tonight, what about chasing up that drink? That's the studio there."

Without another glance in the direction of the graveyard, he led the way at a quickened pace over level ground towards the lights of the studio.

CHAPTER VIII

Whom the gods love . . .
Menander
(*tr. Lord Byron*).

THE STUDIO was a big rectangular building situated on top of the bluff behind the village of Delphi. Later, in daylight, I was to see it as a big ugly box of a place, set down on a flat plateau quarried out of the living rock, so that, while its front windows commanded a magnificent view of the valley, its back looked out onto a wall of rock as high as its second storey. On this, the north side, were the big "front" doors, impressive affairs of plate glass which were never used. The tenants got in and out by a small door in the east end, which gave on the corridor running the length of the ground floor.

Inside, the place was as bare and functional as possible. Corridors and stairs were of marble, and spotlessly clean. On the lower floor, and to the left of the corridor, were the artists' bedrooms, facing south over the valley. These were simple in the extreme, each bedroom holding nothing but an iron bedstead with blankets and pillows, a washbasin with h. and c. both perpetually c., a small and inevitably unsteady table, and hooks for hanging clothes. Opening off each bedroom was a marble-floored shower stall—also, presumably, c. Opposite the bedrooms were other doors which I never saw opened, but which I imagined might be some sort of kitchen premises, or rooms for the caretaker. The resident artists worked on the upper floor where the light was better; here a row of rooms on the north side of the corridor served as studios and store-rooms for their work.

But all this I was to discover later. Tonight the building was merely an ugly oblong box of a place planted down in a small quarry, with the light from a bare electric bulb showing us the door.

We had hardly got into the echoing corridor, when a door a short way along it opened, and a young man came out like a bullet from a gun. He caught at the jamb of the door as he catapulted out and hung on, almost as if he felt the need of the door's support. He said in a high excited voice, "Oh, Simon, I was just—" Then he saw me and stopped, disconcerted, still theatrically posed in the stream of light that came from the door.

There was something about this method of appearance that was very like Niko's, but there the resemblance ended. The young man—who I supposed was Nigel—had none of Niko's beauty or promise of strength, and very little, in consequence, of Niko's assurance. There was no conscious drama in his actions, and indeed now he was looking miserably embarrassed, almost as if he would have liked to retreat into his room and lock the door. He was tallish, and thin, and fair. His skin had taken the sun badly, and his eyes, which were that puckered blue that you see in sailors and airmen and men who habitually gaze into the distances, looked as if they had had too much sun. He had a straggling little beard that made him look young and rather vulnerable, and his hair was bleached to the colour and texture of dry hay. He had a weakly sensual mouth and the strong ugly hands of the artist.

Simon said, "Hullo, Nigel. This is Camilla Haven, who's staying at the Apollon. I've brought her up for a drink, and she wants to see your drawings. Do you mind?"

"Oh. No. Not at all. Delighted," said Nigel, stammering a little. "C-come into my room, then. We'll have a drink here." As he stood aside for me to pass him, slightly more flushed than before, I found myself wondering if he had been drinking alone in his room. There was that queer look about his eyes, a sort of sense that he was clutching at himself as really, as physically, as he had clutched at the door jamb, and in the same effort to control.

His room, basically as bare as the rest of the building, was frantically but rather pleasantly untidy. It was as if the artist's personality, far richer than it appeared from the look of him, had spilled over without his knowing it into the monastic-looking little cell. At the foot of the bed a rucksack stood on the floor, its contents bursting out in confusion. I saw two shirts, as brightly but rather more respectably coloured than Niko's, a tangle of rope, some dirty handkerchiefs which had obviously been pressed into use as paint rags, three oranges, and a copy of the *Collected Poems of Dylan Thomas*. The towel which was flung over the edge of the washbasin was as brightly yellow as a dandelion. Nigel's pyjamas, in a huddle on the bed, were striped in wine and turquoise. And everywhere on the cracked white walls there were sketches, drawing-pinned haphazardly; they were in a variety of styles, so that, looking from the bold to the delicate, from the pencil sketches to the watercolours curling up at the edges as they dried, I remembered what Simon had told me.

But I had no time to do more than glance, because our host had dived past me, and was dragging forward the room's best chair, a canvas affair of grubby orange.

"W-won't you sit down, Miss—Er? It's the best there is. It's quite clean really."

I thanked him and sat down. Simon had wandered over to the window, and hitched himself up onto the wide sill, where he sat, one leg swinging. Nigel, still with that air of disconcerted fussiness, was rummaging rather wildly among bottles on the floor of the shower stall. In a moment he emerged clutching two tumblers and a large bottle of ouzo.

"Do you like this stuff?" he asked me anxiously. "It's all there is."

There was something about Nigel that disarmed me into a deliberate lie. "I love it," I said, and waited resignedly while he poured a generous dollop into one of the tumblers, and handed it to me. "Would you like water with it?"

Now, ouzo is the Greek absinthe. It is made from aniseed, and tastes fairly mild and (to my mind) incredibly unpleasant. I find it quite undrinkable neat. On the other hand, if you add sufficient water to make it swallowable, there is a lot more to swallow.

I said bravely, "Yes, please."

Nigel grabbed a carafe from above the washbasin. Again it struck me sharply that his movements were a parody of Niko's. They were swift and abrupt and angular, but where Niko's had the grace of a striking cat, Nigel's were clumsy and almost uncoordinated. It was odd for an artist to be clumsy, I thought, then as I watched Nigel pour water into my glass, I saw that his hand was shaking. That was still odder.

The liquid misted, clouded, and went entirely beastly like quinine. I said, "When. Thanks," and smiled at Nigel, who was watching me with an anxious-puppy expression that made him look younger than ever. He was, I judged, about twenty-three, but the beard made him look nineteen. I smiled bravely and lifted the glass.

"*Gia sou, Kyrie* Nigel," I said. "I'm sorry, but I don't know your other name."

"Make it Nigel," he said unhelpfully, but with apparent pleasure.

As I drank carefully, I caught Simon's eye, to see that he knew quite well what I felt about ouzo. I scowled at him and took another drink, reflecting yet again that *Kyrie* Simon Lester saw a damned sight too much. I controlled the shudder that shook me as the liquor went down, and then watched fascinated as Nigel filled Simon's tumbler two thirds full, grabbed a glass for himself and filled that, and then raised it to his lips, said "*Gia sou*" quickly, and drank half of it at one fell gulp, neat.

"Cheers, comrade," said Simon. "Have you had a good day?"

Nigel, choking a little over the liquor, managed to say, "Yes. Oh, yes, thanks. Very."

"Where did you go?"

The young man waved a vague hand, which almost knocked the ouzo bottle off the table, but unfortunately didn't quite. "Up there."

"You mean up in the precinct?"

"No. Up the hill."

"Onto Parnassus again? Did you go up over the old track to hunt up some shepherds after all?" He turned to me. "Nigel's got a contract for a series of drawings of 'Hellenic types'—heads of peasants and old women and shepherd boys and so forth. He's done some quite striking ones in a sort of heavy ink line-and-wash."

Nigel said suddenly, "It's exciting. You can't know how exciting. You see a grubby little boy watching the goats, and when you really start to draw him you realize you've seen him a dozen times already in the museums. And I found a girl last week in Amphissa who was pure Minoan, crimped hair and all. It makes it difficult, too, of course, because try as you will, it looks as if you're copying the original Grecian Urn."

I laughed. "I know. I've met one Zeus and one rather wicked Eros and a couple of dozen assorted satyrs today already."

"Stephanos and Niko?" said Simon.

I nodded. "Nigel ought to meet them."

Nigel said, "Who are they?"

"Stephanos is a shepherd from Arachova and he's straight out of

Homer. Niko's his grandson and he's—well, simply a beauty, American-Greek style. But if it's only the head you want, you could hardly do better." I reflected, as I spoke, that Simon had apparently told Nigel nothing about Michael or his mission that evening.

Nor did he tell him now. He said, "You may meet them yet. Stephanos is usually somewhere up between Delphi and Arachova—near that track I took you over yesterday. Is that the way you went again today? How far?"

"Quite a long way." Nigel looked round him vaguely, as if embarrassment had descended on him again, and added quickly, "I was sick of sitting about in the precinct and the valley. I wanted a walk. I got up above the Shining Ones and onto the track and then—well, I just went on walking. It was hot, but up there, there was a breeze."

"No work today?"

Simon's question was no more than idle, but a flush had crept up under Nigel's raw sunburn. It made him look cagey, but I guessed it was only shyness. He said, "No," very shortly, and buried his nose in his glass.

I said, "No shepherds playing pan-pipes to their flocks? On Parnassus? You shake me, Nigel."

He grinned at that. "No, more's the pity."

"And no gods?" I said, thinking of the starlit temple.

But his shyness asserted itself here completely. He said, almost snappily, "No! I tell you I did hardly anything! I was just walking. Anyway those heads are a bore. They're only bread and butter. You wouldn't like them."

"I'd love to see some of your work, though, if you could be bothered to show it. Simon's been telling me how awfully good your drawings are—"

He interrupted in a voice so quick and hoarse that it gave the effect of a small outburst of temper. "Good? Simon's talking bilge. They're not good. They please me, but that's all."

"Some of them are, very good," said Simon quietly.

Nigel sneered at him. "The niminy-piminy ones. The sweet little Ruskin-and-water ones. Can't you just hear the Sunday-paper critics turned loose over them? They're useless and you know it."

"They're first class and *you* know it. If you could—"

"Oh God, if, if, if," said Nigel rudely. He set his glass down on the table with a sharp click. "You know damn well they're useless."

"But they're what you want to do, and they show the way you want to go, and that's the point, isn't it? They are 'Nigel Barlow,' and what's more, they're uncommon."

"They're useless." The repetition was emphatic.

"If you mean they're not easy to make a living out of here and now, I agree. But I still think—"

" 'To thine own self be true'?" said Nigel, on a high-edged note that might have been excitement but sounded like bitterness. "Oh God, don't be a prosy old bore! And anyway it doesn't matter a damn. Not a damn, do you hear me?"

Simon smiled at him. I think it was then that I first really saw what lay behind that good-tempered and apparently unruffled self-command of Simon's; what made it so very different from the more flamboyant self-confidence I had envied. Simon cared. He really did care what happened to this casually-met, troubled, and not very attractive boy who was being so wretchedly rude. And that was why he had come back after fourteen years to find out what had happened to Michael. It was not a present tragedy, and he was not, after all, an Orestes. But he cared—for his father's sake, for Stephanos', for the woman's. "Any man's death diminishes me, because I am involved in Mankind." That was it. He was involved in mankind, and, just at this moment, that meant Nigel. "One takes it for granted," he had said, "that one is there to help." I suppose one gets to know men quickest by the things they take for granted.

He had set his glass down and now laced his fingers round one knee. "All right. Exit Polonius. Well, d'you want us to find you a selling line, Nigel?"

Nigel said, not rudely now, but still with a touch of that hot and slightly sulky impatience, "You mean a gimmick to make people come and look at them? A bloody little quick-sales trick to crowd a one-man show somewhere in the wilds of Sheffield or something? Two pretty drawings sold and my name in the local press? Is that what you mean?"

Simon said mildly, "One has to start somewhere. Couldn't you count it as part of the fight? And at least it might mean you hadn't to fall back on the ultimate degradation."

"What's that?" I asked.

He grinned. "Teaching."

"Oh. Well, I do see what you mean," I said.

"I thought you would."

Nigel said sulkily, "It's all very well to laugh, but I wouldn't be any good at it and I should loathe it, and that would be dreadful."

"The final hell," agreed Simon cheerfully. "Well, we must find you a gimmick, Nigel. Make them come to mock and remain to pay. You must make your pictures out of sequins, or do all your painting under water, or get yourself into the popular press as the Man who Always Paints to the Strains of Mozart."

Nigel gave him a reluctant and slightly shamefaced grin. "Count Basie, more likely. All right, what shall it be? *Art trouvé,* or bits of rusty iron twisted any old way and called 'Woman in Love,' or 'Dog eat Dog,' or something?"

"You could always," I said, "travel through Greece with a donkey, and then write a book, illustrated."

Nigel turned to me at that, but with the look of someone who has hardly been listening. I wondered again if he had been drinking too much. "What? A donkey?"

"Yes. There was a Dutch boy in Delphi this evening who'd just got in from Jannina. He'd been walking over the hills like Stevenson, with a donkey, and painting on the way. I gathered that he'd done a lot of sketching in the villages and more or less paid his way with them."

"Oh, that chap. Yes, I've met him. He's here now."

"Of course, I forgot. Simon told me he'd come up here to sleep tonight. Did you see his work?"

"No. He was too tired to bother. He went to bed at about nine, and I think it'd take an atom bomb to wake him." His look lingered on me as if he were with difficulty bringing me into focus and himself back into the conversation. He said slowly, "Being true to oneself . . . knowing that one can do a thing if only the world will give one the chance . . . but having to fight for it every step of the way. . . ." The blurred blue gaze sharpened and fixed itself on Simon. "Simon . . ."

"Yes?"

"You say a gimmick would be 'part of the fight,' because, in the first place, it would make people stop and look? If my stuff's not really good, no gimmick will get it anywhere beyond the first hurdle. You know that. But if it *is* good, then once people have stopped and paid attention, the *work itself* is what'll count. That's true, isn't it?"

"It could be. In your case I imagine a lot might depend on the gimmick." Simon smiled. "I have a feeling that quite a few good artists have been driven along a path they never intended in the first place as anything but an odd deviation—a wallop in the public's eye. Naming no names, but you know who."

Nigel didn't smile. He seemed still hardly to be listening, but very busy following his own thoughts. He hesitated, then said suddenly, "Well, and that's being true to oneself, isn't it? And don't you think *that* means, come what may, one should take what one wants and needs? Go straight ahead the way you know you have to go, and the devil take the hindmost? Artists—great artists—work that way, don't they? And doesn't the end justify them?" As Simon seemed to hesitate, he whipped round on me. "What do *you* think?"

I said, "I don't know specially about great artists, but I've always imagined that the secret of personality—I won't say 'success'—was one-track-mindedness. Great men *do* know where they're going, and they never turn aside. Socrates and the 'beautiful and good.' Alexander and the Hellenizing of the world. On a different level, if I may—Christ."

Nigel looked at Simon. "Well?" His voice was sharp, like a challenge. *"Well?"*

I thought, There *is* something going on here that I don't understand. And I don't think Simon understands it either, and it worries him.

Simon said slowly, those cool eyes vividly alive now, watching the younger man, "You're partly right. The great men know where they're going; yes, and they get there, but surely it's a case of driving themselves without pause, rather than juggernauting over all the opposition? You think Polonius was a prosy old bore—you brought him in, remember, not me. I don't agree with him, but do him the justice of looking at the end of the quotation. 'To thine own self be true, . . . Thou canst not then be false to any man.' If being true to oneself means ignoring the claims of other people then it simply doesn't work, does it? No, your really great man—your Socrates—doesn't drive along a straight path of his own cutting. He knows what the end is, yes, and he doesn't turn aside from it, but all the way there he's reckoning with whatever—and whoever—else is in his way. He sees the whole thing as a pattern, and his own place in it."

I quoted, thinking back, " 'I am involved in Mankind'?"

"Exactly."

"What's that?" said Nigel.

"A quotation from John Donne, a poet who became Dean of St. Paul's. This comes in one of his Devotions . . . 'No man is an island, entire of itself.' He's right. In the end it's our place in the pattern that matters."

"Yes, but the artist?" said Nigel almost fiercely. "He's different, you know he is. He's driven by some compulsion: if he can't do what he knows he *has* to do with his life he might as well be dead. He's got to break through the world's indifference, or else break himself against it. He can't help it. Wouldn't he be justified in doing almost anything to fulfil himself, if his art were worth it in the end?"

"The end justifying the means? As a working principle, never," said Simon. "Never, never, never."

Nigel sat forward in his chair. "Look, I don't mean anything dreadful like—like murder or crime or something! But if there was no other way—"

I said, "What are you planning to do, for goodness' sake? Steal the donkey?"

516 MY BROTHER MICHAEL

He swung round on me so sharply that I thought he was going to fall off his chair. Then he gave a sudden laugh that sounded very much to me like the edge of hysteria. "Me? Walk to Jannina and write a book about it? Me? Never! I'd be scared of the wolves!"

"There aren't any wolves," Simon's voice was light, but he was watching Nigel rather closely, and I saw the shadow of trouble in his face.

"The tortoises then!" He grabbed the bottle again and turned back to me. "Have some more ouzo? No? Simon? Here, hold your glass. Did you know, Miss Camilla I've-forgotten-your-other-name, that there were tortoises running about on the hills here? Wild ones? Imagine meeting one of those when you were all alone and miles from anywhere."

"I'd run a mile," I said.

"What *is* it, Nigel?" asked Simon from the windowsill.

For a moment I wondered just what was going to happen. Nigel stopped in mid-movement, with the bottle in one hand. He was rigid. His face went redder, then white, under the peeling sunburn. His ugly spatulate fingers clenched round the bottle as if he were going to throw it. His eyes looked suffused. Then they fell away from Simon's, and he turned to set the bottle down. He said in a curiously muffled voice, "I'm sorry. I'm behaving badly. I was a bit high before you came in, that's all."

Then he turned back to me with one of his quick angular movements that were like those of an awkward small boy. "I don't know what you must think of me. You must think I'm a pretty good heel, but things were getting me down a bit. I—I'm temperamental, that's what it is. Great artists are." He grinned shamefacedly at me, and I smiled back.

"It's all right," I said. "And all great artists have had a horrid struggle for recognition. As long as it doesn't come after you're dead, it's all the sweeter when you get it, and I'm sure you will."

He was down on his knees, lugging a battered portfolio from under the bed. "Here," he said, "I'll show you my drawings. You can tell me if you think they're worth anything. You can tell me." He was dragging a sheaf of papers out of the portfolio.

I said feebly, "But my opinion's no use. I really don't know anything about it."

"Here." He thrust a drawing into my hand. "That's one of the ones Simon talks about. And this." He sat back on his heels on the floor, and sent Simon a look that might almost have been hatred. "I'll be true to myself, Polonius. You can be bloody sure I will. Even if it means being true to nobody else. I'm not involved with mankind, as your old parson friend puts it. I'm myself. Nigel Barlow. And some day you'll know it, you and all the rest. Do you hear?"

"I hear," said Simon peaceably. "Let's see what you've done, shall we?"

Nigel pushed a drawing towards him, and then a handful at me. "This. And this. And this and this and this. They may never set the Thames on fire, but given a push and a bit of luck they're good enough to make me. . . . Aren't they?"

As I looked down at the drawings on my knee I was conscious of Nigel's fixed stare. For all the wild and whirling words the vulnerable look was there again, and on that final question the overemphatic voice had broken into naïve and anxious query. I found myself hoping with ridiculous fervour that the drawings might be good.

They were. His touch was sure and strong, yet delicate. Each line was clean and definite and almost frighteningly effective; he had managed to suggest not only shape, but bulk and texture, by pure drawing with the minimum of fuss. Somehow the technique suggested the faded elegance of a French flower-print combined with the sharp, delicate, and yet virile impact of a Dürer drawing. Some were mere sketches, but over others he had taken greater pains. There were rapid studies of the ruined buildings—part of a broken arch with the sharp exclamatory cypresses behind it; Apollo's columns standing very clear and clean; a delightful drawing of three pomegranates on a twig with shiny drooping leaves. There were several of olive trees, lovely twisted shapes with heads of blown silver cloud. In the plant and flower studies he used colour, in faint washes of an almost Chinese subtlety.

I looked up to see him watching me with that anxious-puppy stare from which all trace of belligerence had gone. "But Nigel, they're wonderful! I told you I didn't know much about it, but I haven't seen anything I liked as much in years!"

I got up from my chair and sat down on the bed, spreading the drawings round me, studying them. I picked one of them up; it was the drawing of a clump of cyclamen springing from a small cleft in a bare rock. The textural differences of petal, leaf and stone were beautifully indicated. Below the flowers, in the same cleft, grew the remains of some rock plant that I remember having seen everywhere in Greece; it was dead and dry-dusty, crumbling away against the rock. Above it the cyclamen's winged flowers looked pure and delicate and strong.

Over my shoulder Simon said, "Nigel, that's terrific. I haven't seen it before."

"Of course you haven't. I only did it today," said Nigel rudely, making a quick movement as if to snatch it back. Then he appeared to remember, as I had, that he'd told Simon he had done no work that day, for he dropped his hand and sat back on his heels, looking uncomfortable.

As usual, Simon took no notice. He lifted the drawing and studied it. "Did you mean to use colour in it? What made you change your mind?"

"Simply that there wasn't any water handy." And Nigel took the paper from him and put it back in the portfolio on the floor.

I said, rather quickly, "May I see the portraits?"

"Of course. Here they are—my bread-and-butter drawings." There was a curious note in his voice, and I saw Simon glance again at him, sharply.

There was a whole sheaf of portraits, done in an entirely different style. This was effective in its way, the beautiful economy of his drawing telling even in the thick, dramatic, and overemphatic line. His brilliance of execution had here become a slickness, the clever blending of a few stock statements into a formula. In a way, too, the originals of the portraits might have come from stock. What Nigel had been doing was, of course, to find "types" and to set these down; but, while some of these were discernibly living people, others could have been abstractions of well-known "Hellenic types" taken from statues or vase paintings or even from the imagination. There was one fine-looking head that might have been Stephanos, but it had a formal and over-typed air like an illustration to a set of Greek myths. A girl's face, all eyes, and deep shadows thrown by a veil, could have been captioned, "Greece: the Gate to the East." Another portrait—more familiar in type to me and so possibly more alive—was that of a young woman with the Juliette Gréco face, large lost eyes and a sulky mouth. Beneath it was the drawing of a man's head that, again, seemed purely formal, but was oddly arresting. The head was round, set on a powerful neck, and covered with close curls that grew low on the brow, like a bull's. The hair grew down thickly past the ears, almost to the jawline, as one sees it in the heroic vase paintings, and these sidepieces were drawn in formally, like the hard curls on a sculptured cheek. The upper lip was short, the lips thick, and drawn tightly up at the corners in the fixed half-moon smile that shows always on the statues of the archaic gods of Greece.

I said, "Simon, look at that. That's the real 'archaic smile.' When you see it on crumbly old statues of Hermes and Apollo you think it's unreal and crude. But I've actually seen it on men's faces here and there in Greece."

"Is that new too?" asked Simon.

"Which? Oh, that. Yes." Nigel gave him a quick upward glance, hesitated, then appeared to abandon his pretences, whatever they were. "I did it today." He took the drawing from me and studied it for a moment. "Perhaps you're right; it's too formal. I did it half from memory, and it's gone a bit too much like a vase painting. However."

"It's the Phormis head to the life," said Simon.

Nigel looked up. "Yes, so it is! That's it. I wondered what he reminded me of. I suppose I drew it in. Still, it makes a 'type' for the collection, and as Camilla says, it does exist. She's seen that queer fixed grin here and there, and so've I. Interesting, I thought."

"What's the Phormis head?" I asked.

Simon said, "It's a head found, as far as I remember, at Olympia, and is supposed to be that of Phormis, who was a playwright. That head is bearded, and this isn't, but it's got the same heavy wide cheeks and tight curls, and that typical smile."

I laughed. "Oh dear, and it's still walking these mountains. It makes me feel raw and new and very, very Western. That face, now—"

My hand was hovering over the Juliette Gréco girl.

Simon laughed. "That's real enough, and very Western indeed," he said. "That's our one and only Danielle, isn't it, Nigel? You're surely not going to put her in among the 'Hellenic types'?"

"Danielle?" I said. "Oh, she *is* French, then? Somehow I thought she looked it."

Nigel had taken the drawing from Simon, and was stuffing that, too, away. He said in a muffled voice, "She was here as secretary to a chap attached to the French School."

"French School?"

"Of archaeology," said Simon. "It's the French School which has the 'right' or whatever they call it to excavate here at Delphi. They've been working here again recently on the site—there was some talk of a hunt for a lost treasury fairly high up the hill. You'll see a lot of exploratory pits dug on both sides of the road, too, but all they found there was Roman."

"Ah, yes. Modern stuff."

He grinned. "That's it. Well, they've had to pack up, because I believe funds gave out. Some of their workmen are still here tidying up—there are trucks and tools and what-have-you to be removed. But the archaeologists have gone, more's the pity."

I saw Nigel throw him a sidelong glance, and remembered suddenly something that Simon had said to me earlier. "He's been here in Delphi too long, and got tied up with a girl who wasn't very good for him."

I said, "Yes. I'd rather have liked to watch them at it. And think of the excitement if anything did turn up!"

He laughed. "*That* sort of excitement, I believe, is the rarest kind! Most of the long years are spent shifting tons of earth a couple of yards, and then putting them back again. But I agree. It would be terrific. And what a country! Did you see that glorious thing of the Negro and the horse that the workmen dug up when they were mending the drains in

Omonia Square a few years ago? Imagine wondering what you might find every time you set out to dig your garden or put a plough to the hillside! After all, even the Charioteer—" He stopped, and turned his cigarette over in his fingers as if he were admiring the twist of blue smoke that curled and frothed from it.

Nigel looked up. "The Charioteer?" He was still kneeling on the floor, shuffling the drawings in the folder into some sort of order. "The Charioteer?" he repeated mechanically, as if his mind was on something else.

Simon drew on the cigarette. "Uh-huh. He wasn't dug up till eighteen ninety-six, long after the main shrines and treasuries had been excavated. Not long ago I read Murray's *History of Greek Sculpture,* and wondered why the author was so sketchy about Delphi, till I realized that, when he wrote his book in eighteen ninety, the half was not told him. Who knows what else is still up there in the odd corners under the trees?"

Nigel had sat back on his heels, his hands moving vaguely and clumsily among the drawings. If they were indeed his bread and butter he was, it occurred to me, remarkably careless of them.

He looked up now, the drawings spilling again from his hands.

"Simon." It was that strung-up voice again.

"Well?"

"I think I—" Then he stopped abruptly and turned his head. The studio's outer door had opened and shut with a bang. Rapid footsteps approached along the corridor.

To my surprise Nigel went as white as a sheet. He swung round towards me, swept the rest of the drawings off the bed into an unceremonious heap, then hastily gathered them all together to shove back into the folder on the floor.

As unceremoniously, the door burst open.

A girl stood there, surveying the untidy and crowded little room with an expression of weary distaste. It was the girl of the portrait, Gréco-look and all. It was also, I thought with a lightly quickened interest, the girl whose jeep, outside Thebes, had bullied the bus into submission in such a masterly way. She looked as she had then, completely in control of the situation, and rather bored with it.

She drawled, without removing the cigarette from the corner of her mouth, "Hullo, Simon, my love. Hullo, Nigel. On your knees praying over my picture? Well, the prayer's answered. I've come back."

CHAPTER IX

A girl—
No virgin either, I should guess—a baggage
Thrust on me like a cargo on a ship
To wreck my peace of mind!
                    SOPHOCLES: *Women of Trachis*
                    (*tr. E. P. Watling*).

DANIELLE WAS slightly built, of medium height, and had made the most (or the worst, according to the point of view) of her figure by encasing it in drainpipe jeans and a very tight sweater of thin wool, which left nothing to wonder at except how in the world did she get her breasts that shape and into that position. They were very high and very pointed and the first thing that one noticed about her. The second was her expression, which was very much the weary-waif look of Nigel's picture. Her face was oval, and palely sallow. Her eyes were very big and very black, carefully shadowed with a blend of brown and green that made them look huge and tired. She had long curling lashes that caught the smoke wisping up blue from the cigarette that appeared fixed to her lower lip. She wore pale lipstick, which looked odd and striking with the sallow face and huge dark eyes. Her hair was black and straight and deliberately untidy, cut in that madly smart way that looks as if it had been hacked off in the dark with a pair of curved nail-scissors. Her expression was one of world-weary disdain. Her age might have been anything from seventeen to twenty-five. She looked as if she hoped you would put it at something over thirty.

I should perhaps say here that her eyelashes were very long, quite real, and quite beautiful. This is in case it should be thought that my description of Danielle smacks of prejudice. The only reason that I had then for prejudice was the expression on Nigel's face, stuck there on his knees on the floor with his ungainly hands full of the delicate drawings, turning to face the door, and saying *"Danielle!"* in a cracked young voice that gave him away immediately and very cruelly.

He shoved the drawings clumsily into the folder and got to his feet.

After that first greeting she had ignored him. Nor, after one cool glance, had she looked at me. Her eyes were all over Simon.

She said again, "Hullo." I don't quite know how she made the simple dissyllable sound sexy, but she did.

"Hullo," said Simon, not sounding sexy at all. He was looking ever so slightly amused, and also wary, which annoyed me. Why it should, I'm not prepared to say, and didn't try at the time.

Nigel said hoarsely, "What are you doing here? I thought you'd left Delphi."

"I had. But I came back. Aren't you going to ask me in, Nigel dear?"

"Of course. Come in. It's wonderful—I mean I didn't expect you back. Come in. Sit down." He darted forward and dragged out the best chair —the one I had vacated—for her. But she walked past it towards Simon, who was standing by the window. She went very close to him. "I'm sleeping in the studio, Simon. I got tired of the Tourist Hotel, and anyway I can't afford it now. You don't mind me coming here, do you . . . Simon?"

"Not in the very least." He looked across her at me. "You'd better be introduced. Camilla, this, as you'll have guessed, is Danielle. Camilla Haven; Danielle Lascaux. I told you that Danielle was here for some time with the French School. She was Hervé Clément's secretary. You probably know the name. He wrote *Later Discoveries at Delphi*."

"I read it not long before I came here. How d'you do?" I said to Danielle.

She gave me a brief stare, and a barely civil nod. Then she turned, and with what looked like very conscious grace, sat down at the opposite end of the bed from me, curled her slim legs up under her, and leaned back against the bed-head. She tilted her head and sent Simon a long look between narrowed lids.

"So you've been talking about me?"

Nigel said eagerly, "It was your portrait—the one I did of you." With one of his ungraceful gestures he indicated the untidily stuffed portfolio lying on the bed beside me.

"Oh, that."

"It's very good, don't you think?" I said. "I recognized you as soon as you came in."

"Uh-huh. Nigel's quite a clever boy, we know that." She sent him a smile that was a shadow of the one she'd given Simon, then reached out an idle hand and pulled two or three sheets out of the folder. I saw Nigel make a small sharp movement, as if of involuntary protest, then he sat down in the orange canvas chair, his hands dangling between his bony knees.

"Yes, I suppose it's a good enough portrait. Are my eyes really as big as that, Nigel?" She was leafing through the drawings: her own portrait;

the one we had called the "Phormis head," with the close curls and tight smile; the cyclamen; and a drawing I hadn't yet seen, of a man's head and shoulders. "Flowers?" said Danielle. "Are they *paying* you to do things like that, Nigel? . . . *Who's this?*"

Her voice had changed on the query, so abruptly that I was startled. I saw Simon turn his head, and Nigel almost jumped. "Who? Oh, that. That's a chap I saw today on Parnassus. We were just saying before you came in that he was like—"

"No, no!" She had been holding the Phormis head and another drawing. She dropped the former abruptly, and thrust the other forward. "Not that one. This."

Something in her voice suggested an effort for self-command, and to my surprise her hand was unsteady. But when I said, "May I?" and leaned forward to take the drawing gently from her, she let it go without protest. I looked at it with interest, and then more sharply. It showed the head and bared throat of a young man. The face was beautiful, but not with Niko's vital and very Greek beauty; this was remote, stern, perhaps a little sad. He was not, I thought, a "Hellenic type" at all, though something about him was oddly familiar. But it appeared that he was not intended to form part of Nigel's gallery. This was the only portrait I had seen where Nigel had used what I might call his "flower technique." It was in his own style; the work was delicate, sure and arrestingly beautiful.

"Why, *Nigel* . . ." I said. "Simon, look at this!" Danielle let the others fall to the coverlet. She appeared abruptly to have lost interest, only asking, "Did you do these today?"

"Yes." And Nigel, before Simon had time to do more than glance at the drawing, had finally and this time effectively swept every drawing back into the folder and shoved it under the bed. He looked flustered, and every bit as resentful as he had earlier. But Danielle didn't pursue the subject. She leaned back again and said in her usual slightly bored tone, "For God's sake, Nigel, *are* you going to offer me a drink?"

"Of course." Nigel dived for the bottle of ouzo, put it down again so that it rocked and nearly spilt, then dashed to rinse a tumbler out in the basin.

I put my own glass down and made as if to get to my feet. But at that moment I caught Simon's eye, and I thought he shook his head very slightly. I sat back.

He looked down at the girl. "I thought you'd gone, Danielle. Hasn't the 'dig' packed up?"

"Oh, that. Yes. We got to Athens last night, and really I thought it would be rather a *thing* to be back in civilization again, but I had the most dreary scene with Hervé, and then I thought to myself I really might as well be back in Delphi with . . ." she smiled suddenly, showing very white teeth . . . "back in Delphi. So here I am."

Nigel said, "You mean you've got the sack?"

"You could call it that." She watched him for a moment through the cigarette smoke, then she turned to me. "Simon told you the polite fiction," she said. "Actually, of course, I was Hervé Clément's mistress."

"Danielle!"

"For God's sake, Nigel!" She hunched an impatient shoulder. "Don't pretend you didn't know." Then to me, "But he was getting to be a bit of a bore."

"Really?" I said politely.

I thought her look was calculating under the long lashes. "Yes, really. They all do, sooner or later, don't you think? Do you find men bore you, Camilla Haven?"

"Occasionally," I said. "But then so—occasionally—do women."

That one went straight past her. "I hate women anyway," she said simply. "But Hervé, he was honestly getting to be the utter *end*. Even if he hadn't quit the 'dig' here and gone back to Athens, I'd have had to leave him." She blew out a long cloud of smoke, and turned her head to look up at Simon. "So back I came. But I'll have to sleep here, at the studio. I'm on my own now, so I haven't got the cash for the Tourist Pavilion, or anywhere else for that matter. . . ." She smiled slowly, still looking at Simon. "So I'll have to sleep rough."

What it was in her intonation I do not know, but somehow she managed to say the last simple sentence as if it meant sharing a bed with a sadist, and that meant Simon. I felt another spasm of intense irritation. I knew I should have wanted to feel sorry for Danielle, or even amused, but somehow it wasn't possible. I was beginning to suspect that she was not trying to ape a pathetic maturity; the *weltschmerz* wasn't a pose, it was real, and rather dreadful. So was the weariness in the big lost eyes. But the pity I should have owed her I felt for Nigel, now feverishly drying the tumbler and saying rapidly:

"It's wonderful to have you back. You know that. And of course you must stay in the studio. We'd love to have you, and you'll be quite all right here. There's only me and Simon and a Dutch painter—"

"A Dutch painter?"

Simon said smoothly, "A boy of about twenty who has walked from Jannina and is very, very tired."

She shot him a look up under the fabulous lashes. "Oh." She threw the half-smoked cigarette into the washbasin where it lay smouldering. "Give me another cigarette, Simon."

He obeyed. "Camilla?"

"Thank you," I said.

Nigel pushed past me with a tumbler three parts full of neat ouzo. "Here's your drink, Danielle." His face was anxious, concentrated. He might have been carrying the Holy Grail. She took it from him and gave him a brilliant smile. I saw him blink, and the flush on the burnt cheekbones deepened. She lifted the glass towards him.

"*Gia sou,* Nigel darling. I'm glad I came back. . . . But you're not drinking with me."

It should have been corny, but it wasn't. The expression on the boy's face was naked. He turned and grabbed the bottle and poured an inch or two of liquor into his empty glass. But even as he turned back, the girl yawned, stretched, tilted her head back on its long neck, and put out a hand towards Simon. Her fingernails were very long and very red. Her fingers ran caressingly down his sleeve. "Actually," she said, still in that bored, velvet voice, "actually, you know, I'm Simon's girl. Aren't I, Simon?"

I must have jumped about a foot. Simon looked down through the smoke of his cigarette, and said lazily, "Are you? Delighted, of course. But perhaps in that case you'll tell me why you hired a car for me in Athens this morning?"

The hand froze, then withdrew quickly. The thin body twisted on the bed in the first movement she had made unconsciously since she came in. It wasn't sexy in the least. It was plain startled. "What are you talking about?"

"The car you hired in my name this morning. The car you were to have picked up at the Alexandros restaurant."

The black eyes held his for a moment, then dropped. "Oh, that." Her voice was calm and husky as usual. "How did you find out?"

"My dear Danielle, you hired it for me, didn't you? And you failed to pick it up. Naturally the people at the Alexandros got in touch with me."

"But that's impossible! How did they know?" She was scowling up at him now.

"Never mind how. Tell me why."

She shrugged and drank ouzo. "I wanted to come back to Delphi. I told you that I hired a car. They never take any notice in Greece of a woman, so I gave your name."

"And said it was a matter of life and death?"

"What? Don't be silly. Of course I never said that." She laughed. "You're very dramatic, Simon."

"Perhaps. A dramatic place, this. It gets into the blood. But you did hire the car."

"Yes."

"And came without it."

"Yes."

"Why?"

I thought unhappily, Because a fool of a girl called Camilla Haven had already taken it. Why couldn't Simon let well enough alone? Somehow I didn't particularly want to tangle with Danielle Lascaux. And she had every right to be mad with me if she had hired the beastly car—in whatever name—and had then presumably had to hunt up other transport for herself when she found it gone. All the same, she would have to be told sooner or later. . . .

"Why?" asked Simon.

She said sulkily, "Because I got the offer of the jeep from Hervé. It was more convenient."

I said, "I was right, then. I thought I recognized you. You were the girl in the jeep that overtook me just before Thebes. I remember you particularly. You were driving on the wrong side of the road."

She yawned, showing her tongue between her teeth. She didn't even look at me. "Probably. I find it more exciting that way."

Simon said, "Then you got up here well before Camilla did. Where've you been?"

She said, almost bad-temperedly, "What's it matter? Around."

I said, "In Itea?"

Danielle shot upright on the bed. Some ouzo spilled. "What are you talking about?" I saw a look of surprise touch Simon's face, then the familiar expressionless mask shut down. With the faintest quickening of the blood, I thought, He's interested. This means something.

I said, "I saw the jeep in Itea this evening. It was parked beside a house that stands right away from the village in the olive woods. I hadn't realized till this minute that it was the same one, but now I remember. It had a little tinsel doll hanging in the windscreen—where they usually have the icons. I remember noticing that when you passed me near Thebes."

She wasn't drinking. The smoke from that eternal cigarette crept up in a veil hiding the expression of her eyes. "This evening? How can you be so sure? Wasn't it dark?"

"Oh, yes. But there was a man with a torch tinkering with the engine, and the light caught the tinsel. Then the lights went on in the house."

"Oh." She drank a gulp of neat ouzo. It didn't appear to affect her. "Well, I expect it was the same jeep. I was down there, with . . . someone I know." Again that intonation, that glance up towards Simon. Nigel was watching her like a lost dog. I thought it was some—surprising—impulse of mercy that made her add, "I always go down to Itea in the afternoons. I've done it for weeks. I go to swim. Nigel knows that."

Nigel responded instantly, almost as if the last sentence had been a plea of proof. "Of course I know. But—did you really go there today before you even came up here?"

"Uh-huh." She gave him a narrow, glinting smile. "You were out, weren't you?"

"Yes."

"I thought you might be. And I'd brought Elena a present from Athens, so—"

"Elena?" said Nigel quickly.

"My friend in Itea. She often bathes from the same place as me, so I went back to her house with her."

"Oh!" said Nigel.

I thought she watched him for a second before she turned back to me. "And you, Camilla Haven? *You* went down to Itea first, before you came up here?"

"I only came up here an hour ago. I'm only visiting. I'm staying at the Apollon."

"But you went straight to Itea." The words were sharp, almost, and sounded so much like an accusation that I said quickly, "I called at the hotel first." Then I added, "I went down to Itea to find the hirer of the car."

There was a little silence. "The . . . hirer of the car?" repeated Danielle.

"Yes. I—it was I who brought the car up from the Alexandros in Omonia Square. I—I was looking for the 'Monsieur Simon' who was alleged to be wanting it."

She blew out a small cloud of smoke and leaned back against the head of the bed, regarding me through it. "I . . . see. You brought my car up here? You?"

"Yes," I said unhappily. "I was in the Alexandros restaurant when the man from the garage came, and he mistook me for you. He gave me the keys and told me it was urgent, and that 'Monsieur Simon' wanted the car at Delphi as soon as possible. I—we got in a muddle of cross-purposes, and he vanished, leaving me with the key, and no idea of the address of the garage. I didn't know what to do, but I wanted to come here myself, and—well, he'd been so insistent that it was a 'matter of life and death' that—"

"That stuff again," said Danielle.

"That stuff again." I added, "I'm glad I don't seem to have incon-

venienced you after all. You must have got here well before me. I told
you you passed me before Thebes."

She said quite sharply, "And why did you have to go to Itea to find
Simon?"

"Oh, I didn't. I—well, he found me quite easily. But of course as he
didn't know anything about the car, that didn't help. We went to look
for another 'Simon,' actually a Simonides who keeps a baker's shop
near the cinema."

"That's not," said Danielle, "in the olive woods."

"No. I went to see the Pilgrims' Way."

"The Pilgrims' Way?" she said blankly.

Simon said, "Yes. You ought to know all about that, Danielle."

She said quickly, "Why?"

"My dear girl. Because you've worked here as an archaeologist's
secretary."

"Mistress," said Danielle automatically.

Nigel said suddenly from behind me, "I wish you wouldn't talk like
that."

She opened her mouth as if to say something blistering, but shut it
again, and gave him one of her slow smiles. I didn't look at him. I said
quickly, "Look, Danielle, I really am terribly sorry about this car. I suppose I—yes, I did think I might be doing the right thing, but it seems I
was a bit hasty. I do hope it isn't going to cause any inconvenience *now,*
because—"

"You brought it up here." She turned her head to give me a narrow
look through the curling smoke. "You keep it."

I looked at her for a moment. Then I said slowly, "I suppose that is
fair enough."

"You weren't asked to bring it here. I don't want it. You're stuck with
it, and I hope you can afford to pay for it." She turned away to flick ash
towards the washbasin. It missed and fell to the floor.

There was a short silence. I said carefully, "Whom do I pay?"

Her head came quickly back to me. "What d'you mean?"

"What I said."

"Well, me, of course. Didn't they tell you the deposit had been paid?"

"Oh, yes, they told me that."

"So what?" said Danielle.

I stood up and picked up my handbag. "Only that it surprises me a
bit that you didn't call in on the garage after you'd got the jeep, and cancel the car. If you're as short of money as you've been telling us, I'd have
imagined the deposit would have come in very handy. In fact, I can't

see why you should have hired a car at all. The bus is cheaper. Perhaps you'll let me have the receipt, with the address of the garage?"

She sounded sulky. "Tomorrow. I have it somewhere."

"Very well." I turned to smile at Nigel. "I really must go, Nigel, or it'll be dawn before I get to bed. Thank you very much for the drink, and for letting me see the drawings. I think they're wonderful—I honestly do; and that last one is . . . well, a masterpiece. That isn't trite; it's true. Good night."

Simon was on his feet. As I turned to go, he made as if to move forward, but Danielle came off the bed in one quick wriggle. It brought her very close to him.

"Simon"—the claws were on his arm again—"my room's the one at the end, and the shower's stuck, or something. The damned thing drips and I'll never get to sleep. D'you suppose you could fix it for me?"

"I doubt if I'd be much good with it. In any case I'm seeing Camilla home now, and then I—"

I said stiffly, "There's not the slightest need to see me home. I can find my way quite easily."

"—and then I've got to go back and pick the car up. We left it below the shrine."

Nigel had opened the door for me. I looked back at Simon, with Danielle clinging to his arm. "You really needn't trouble. The car is my responsibility . . . as Danielle has pointed out."

His eyes, amused, met mine. I bit my lip, and said, "All right. I—it's very kind of you."

"Not at all. After all, if the car was hired in my name I've a sort of responsibility myself, wouldn't you say, Danielle?"

She flashed me one look of pure venom, under her lashes, then lifted them again to him. Her voice was all honey. "Not really. But if that's how you feel. . . . You'll come and fix that shower later, won't you? It really is a bore."

"Not tonight," said Simon. "Good night. Good night, Nigel, and thanks a lot. See you later."

On the way down to the hotel—which took about twelve minutes and was very steep and rough—we concentrated on not breaking our ankles and on not talking about Danielle. For me, the first was the easier task of the two.

At the hotel Simon said, "Camilla."

"Yes?"

"Come off it."

I laughed. "Very well."

"I grant you every right to the highest horse, or deepest dudgeon, or whatever it is, in Christendom. All right?"

"Perfectly."

"Don't worry about the damned car. I didn't pursue it in front of— well, back there, but I'll be very glad of it myself now that it's here, so don't give it another thought."

"I will not," I said clearly, "allow you to pay for my—my folly."

"We will not," said Simon calmly, "argue about it now. You should be in bed. You've had a long day, and tomorrow will probably be longer."

"I shall probably have to go tomorrow."

"Tomorrow? My God, the dudgeon isn't as deep as that, is it?"

"Dudgeons are high. No, it's not that. But there may not be a room at the hotel."

"Oh, I forgot. Well, look here, why not come up to the studio? You've seen it. It's plain, but clean, and very convenient. And now it seems"— the grey eyes crinkled at the corners—"that you'll be chaperoned."

"I'll think about it," I said, without much enthusiasm.

He hesitated, then said, "I hope you will. I—please don't go tomorrow. I was hoping you'd come with me."

I stared at him. "But—I thought you were going up Parnassus with Stephanos?"

"I am. I want you to come. Will you?"

"But Simon—"

"Will you?"

I said huskily, "This is absurd."

"I know. But there it is."

"It's your own very private business. Just because I—I bulldozed you into my affairs it doesn't mean you have to ask me to tag along in yours."

The amusement was there again. "No. Will you?"

"Yes. Of course."

"It'll be a long trek. An all-day job. If the hotel says they can't keep you you'll let me ring up Athens for you and get you into the studio?"

"Ring up Athens?"

"It's the property of the University Fine Arts Department, and you're not an accredited artist any more than I am. You'll have to come in as a student."

"Oh, of course. And Danielle?"

He grinned. "Maybe archaeologists count. If she gives my name to hire a car, she may give Hervé's when she wants a room in the studio."

"I suppose so. Well, please ring up Athens for me and I'll move in tomorrow night. What time do we start?"

"I'll call for you at half past eight." He gave me his sudden smile. "Good night, Camilla. And thank you."

"Good night."

As he turned to go, I said, before I could prevent myself, "Don't forget to go and fix the taps, will you?"

"Taps," said Simon gently, "bore me. Good night."

CHAPTER X

What a personage says or does reveals a certain moral purpose; and a good element of character, if the purpose so revealed is good. Such goodness is possible in every type of personage, even in a woman.

ARISTOTLE: *The Art of Poetry*
(*tr. Ingram Bywater*).

NEXT MORNING I awoke early, so early that, when I found I couldn't easily go to sleep again, I decided to get up and see the ruins on my own before the day's adventures started. The thought made me, with a wry little smile, remember that I hadn't yet posted my letter to Elizabeth. When I was ready to leave my room I fished it out of my bag, opened it, and added a hasty postscript.

"Did I say nothing ever happened to me? It's started as from yesterday. If I live I'll write and let you know what you're missing.
"Love, Camilla."

The sun was already hot and bright, though it was only just a little past seven o'clock. I walked along the village street to post my letter, then turned into the steep way that climbs between terraced streets to the mountainside above.

This was a flight of wide steps, bounded by whitewashed walls from which the sun beat back. The already blinding white was muted everywhere by greenery; from every wall and roof spilled vines and hanging ferns, the vivid pinks and scarlets of geraniums, and brilliant cascades of marigolds and black-eyed Susans. At my feet hens pecked and scratched about. Now and then I stood aside as a donkey or a mule picked its dainty accurate way down the steps, while a black-veiled peasant woman, following it, smiled and gave me a soft "Good morning."

The steps took me eventually clear of the village, on to the hillside where piles of rubble and kerbstones indicated that a new road was being built. I made my way carefully along this, watched by the friendly and curious stares of the workmen, and, before I was aware that I had come so far, found myself clear of the last house, and out on the open hillside above the studio.

The climb had been steep, and the sun was hot. The path led along the foot of a low cliff-wall, which cast, at this early hour, a narrow shade. I found a flat rock in a recess of shadow, and sat down to recover from the climb.

The path that I was on seemed to be a continuation of the one that Simon and I had taken last night. It passed above the studio, then slanted down into the knot of pines that I remembered, and vanished thence more steeply towards the ruined temple precincts. Not far from where I sat, below me now and to the right of the path, I could see the studio, dumped down raw and square and ugly in its quarried plateau. Beyond it the valley of the olives swam and shimmered in the immense liquid distance of light, and beyond that again mountain after mountain, and the sea.

Then my attention was taken by a movement near the studio.

Someone was as early abroad as I. I heard the scuffle of footsteps mounting the rough path that led up from the plateau. Then I saw him, a thin, fair-haired figure carrying a rucksack, and clambering at a fair speed but with very little noise towards the path where I sat in the shadow. He hadn't looked in my direction; he was making for the knot of pines above the shrine, and moving away from me rapidly.

He reached the path. He was about seventy yards away from me, near the fence that marked the graveyard. He stopped, and turned, as if to pause for breath and survey the view.

I was just about to get to my feet and hail him, when something about the way he was acting caught my attention, and I stayed still. He had taken a couple of quick steps back and sideways, into the shadow of a pine tree. The dappled shade netted and hid him, maculate, invisible. He stayed there, stock-still, and he wasn't looking at any view; his head was bent as if he studied the ground at his feet, but I knew, suddenly, that he was listening. He didn't move. There was no sound in the lovely bright morning but the chime of a goat bell from the other side of the valley, and the crowing of a cock down in the village. No sound from the studio; no movement.

Nigel lifted his head, and was looking about him, still with those wary, abruptly stealthy movements. It was quite obvious that, wherever he was going, he didn't want to be followed and, remembering Danielle, I thought

I saw his point. And I wouldn't interrupt his getaway either. Smiling to myself, I stayed where I was. I didn't think he would see me unless I moved, nor did he. He turned suddenly, and, leaving the path, plunged uphill through the pines towards the higher levels where the ancient stadium stood, and, beyond it, the track that led above the Shining Ones and away into the upper reaches of Parnassus.

I gave him a minute or two, and then I got up and went on. Soon I, too, was under the shadow of the pines, and to my right was the tumbledown fence, and the thicket of dried weeds that edged the graveyard.

I don't quite know what made me do it, except that somehow, already, Michael Lester's affair was my own. I pushed open the creaking gate and went in among the stones. When I found it I had to spell it out very slowly to be sure it was the one.

ΜΙΧΑΕΛ ΛΗΣΤΗΡ

This alien cross, an alien epitaph . . . and in my ear Simon's voice, claiming him still. " 'My brother Michael.' " And behind that again I could hear the ghosts of other voices, other claims: " 'The woman of my house, the cousin of Angelos, the brother of Michael' " . . . " 'No man is an Island, entire of itself.' "

I stood there in the hot early-morning silence and thought about Simon. Today, I was committed to Simon's quest. I, too, had answered a claim. He was going to see the place where Michael had died, and he had wanted me to go too.

And I? Why had I said that I would go? I had said last night that it was absurd, and so it was. . . . But I had a queer feeling that, quite apart from Simon's need of me, I had a need of my own. I, too, had something to find.

A bird, small and bright as a blown leaf, flew across the hot stillness. I turned away and made my way between the dusty mounds towards the gate.

I was thinking now, not of Simon, but of myself. Not of the self, the identity I had felt it so necessary to assert when I had sent back Phil's ring, but of the identity I had assumed so lightly yesterday and which, it seemed, I could not yet put off. Not Camilla Haven, but just "Simon's girl."

I let myself quickly through the gate and hurried down the path till it brought me out above the ruins of the great shrine.

I've already written enough of Delphi, and indeed it's not easy to write about. The place takes the heart and the senses and wrings them dry. Eyes and ears and the instinct of worship are all that is needed there.

I walked slowly downhill in the sunlight. Here was the little pomegranate tree, clinging to a cleft in the marble of the theatre. Its leaves hung now without a rustle, dark green and still. The fruit was flame-coloured and as glossy as witchballs. Here were the breakneck steps . . . and here the stage of the theatre, where Simon had spoken last night; I could see the mark at the centre, where one's voice was taken and flung high up the mountainside. And now the steps to the precinct . . . that must be the monument of Alexander . . . and this the temple floor of Apollo.

The six great columns stood up like fire against the immense depths of the valley.

No one was about. I crossed the temple floor and sat down at the edge with my back to one of the columns. The stone was hot. Above my head the crumbling capitals were alive with the wings of martins. Far below me the olives shimmered along the valley. In the distance Helicon was blue, was silver, was grey as Aphrodite's doves. Everywhere were the voices of songbirds, because Delphi is sanctuary. Somewhere in the morning distance sheep bells were ringing. . . .

It was still only eight o'clock when I left my seat and walked down the Sacred Way from the temple to the edge of the precinct, where a thick rank of pines keeps it from the road below. I went along the path under the pines, then down to the museum which sits in a curve of the road. I already seemed to have been up and about for so long that it was a surprise to find the doors still shut. There was a man in guide's uniform sitting under the trees on the other side of the road, so I crossed over to speak to him.

"The Museum?" he said in answer to my query. "I am afraid it doesn't open till half past nine. But would you like a guide now for the ruins, no?"

"Not this morning, thank you," I said. "I've just been up there. But possibly tomorrow, if I'm still in Delphi. . . . Will you be about here?"

"Always, at this time." He had a dark square face, and, surprisingly, blue eyes. His look was sophisticated, and he spoke very good English.

I said, "I wanted to see the Charioteer."

"Of course." He grinned, showing very white teeth. "But there are other things too, here in Delphi."

"Oh, yes, I know, but isn't he the first thing everyone looks for in the Museum?"

"Of course," he said again. "If you come with me tomorrow I will take you also round the Museum myself."

"I should like that very much." I hesitated. "Do you—I wonder if you know the young English artist who is staying up at the studio? Thin and fair, with a little beard?"

"Yes. I know him. He has been here in Delphi for quite a time, no?"

"I believe so. Does he—has he been to the Museum much?"

"Indeed, yes. He comes very often to draw. Have you seen any of his drawings, *kyria*? They are very good, very good indeed."

"He showed me some of them last night, but not, I think, any of the statues and antiquities. I imagine he would do those well. Did he do any of the Charioteer?"

"Of course. Did you not say yourself that he is the first thing one looks for? And certainly in our small Museum he is the *pièce de résistance.*"

"Was he—did you notice if the artist was here yesterday?"

The guide didn't seem to be at all surprised at the odd catechism. His experience of tourists must have bred in him a vast tolerance. He shook his head. "I do not think so. I was here all day, but he may have been down here while I was up in the ruins. The tour takes nearly an hour. If you wish to see him, he sleeps up at the studio above the site, where they are building the new road."

"Perhaps I'll see him later." I judged it time to drop that particular catechism. "What new road are they making away up there above the village? Where can it possibly go?"

"To the stadium. Have you seen that yet?"

"Not yet."

"It is high above the shrine. Many tourists who come to Delphi never see it at all, because the climb is too steep. It is very beautiful—just the old oval race-track with the tiers of seats, exactly as it was in ancient times, and with the view . . . always that view of the olives and the valley and the sea. So now they make a road to let the cars and buses take the tourists up."

I stifled a pang at the thought of yet another wild and lovely sanctuary invaded by cars and buses, and said, "Ah, yes. I suppose anything that will bring money into Greece is a good thing. You are a native of Delphi, *kyrie?*"

"No. I am a man of Tinos."

"Oh. Then . . . I suppose you weren't here during the war?"

He smiled. "No. I was busy—very busy—on my island."

My island. There it was again. *A man of Tinos.*

Then he would not remember Michael Lester. It was possible that he had never heard of him. In any case—I caught at myself—I must not let myself go beyond even Simon's claim on my interest. I said merely, "Of course."

He was rolling a cigarette with neat, quick movements.

"There was certainly no need *then* for guides in Delphi, *kyria*. No one was troubling then about the shrine and the sanctuary and the Charioteer! We may say, if you like, that it is a pity—if men had had the time to come, as they came here in the days of the Oracle, when Delphi was the centre of the world, no doubt they would have found their quarrels healed." That quick sophisticated look, and the sudden grin again. "That, you understand, is what I always say when I show my tourists round. It is a very effective bit of patter. The Amphictyonic League of Delphi. The League of Nations. The U.N. Very effective."

"I'm sure it is. Do you add the bits about the fights between Delphi and her neighbours, and the laying waste of Crissa, and the monuments for Athenian victories over the Spartans, and Spartan victories over the Athenians, and the Argive monument stuck down just where it would annoy the Spartans most, and—"

"Sometimes." He was laughing. "I shall have to—what do you say?— watch my step when I show you round tomorrow, shall I not?"

"Not really. I read up an awful lot specially before I came. It makes it more exciting to *know* what happened here. I looked at a lot of photographs too." I hesitated again. "The Charioteer . . ." I said slowly.

"What of him?"

I was carrying a guide-book in my hand; *A Concise Guide of Delphi*, it was called, and on the cover there was a photographic reproduction of the head of the famous statue. I held it out. "This. I've heard so much about him, but I can't help wondering if I'll really like him. Those eyes; they're inlaid with onyx and white enamel, aren't they? And there are long metal eyelashes? They do look alive, I admit, but—look, you see what I mean?" I indicated the print. "That narrow forehead and the heavy jaw; it's not strictly a beautiful face, is it? And yet everyone says he's so wonderful."

"And so will you. No picture gives the true impression. It's the same with the great Hermes at Olympia. In photographs he is effeminate, the marble too smooth, and shining like soap. But the statue itself takes away the breath."

"I know. I've seen it."

"Then prepare yourself to see the Charioteer. It is one of the great statues of Greece. Do you know the thing that comes to me first when- ever I see him again—which is every day?"

"What?"

"He is so very young. All that gravity, that grace, and so young with it. It used to be thought that he was the owner of the team—the winner of the race—but now they say that he was probably the driver for some lord who owned the chariot."

I said hesitantly, "There's a bit in Pausanias' account of Delphi, isn't there, about a chariot of bronze with a naked 'lord of the car' who might have had a driver, a youth of good family?"

"I believe there is, yes. But it could hardly apply to our Charioteer, *kyria;* the evidence is that he was probably buried in a great landslip during an earthquake in three seventy-three B.C., and, without being uncovered again, was built into the—what do you call it?—the supporting wall—the 'earth-holder' is the Greek word—that was erected to stop the rocks and earth from engulfing the temple again."

"Retaining wall," I said.

"Ah, thank you. The retaining wall. Well, you see, our Charioteer had vanished a few centuries before Pausanias came to Delphi."

"I see. I didn't know that."

He had finished rolling the cigarette. He put it between his lips and lit it with a spluttering of loose tobacco.

He said, "They say now that the Charioteer was part of a victory group erected by one Gelon, the winner of a chariot race, but anything may be true. So much was lost or destroyed or stolen over the centuries that the truth about our discoveries is only guesswork. And Delphi suffered much, because she was so rich. I think it is reckoned that there were six thousand monuments here—at any rate that is the number of inscriptions that have been uncovered." He smiled. "The landslide that broke and hid the Charioteer was an act of the gods, because it kept him out of the hands of the robbers. The Phocians laid the sanctuary waste barely twenty years after he was buried, and of course in later times countless treasures were destroyed or stolen."

"I know. Sulla and Nero and the rest. How many bronzes do they reckon Nero took to Rome?"

"Five hundred." He laughed again. "I *shall* have to watch my patter tomorrow, I can see!"

"I told you I only read it up just before I came. And there's so much—"

A sudden clatter and a volley of shouts from somewhere behind the Museum startled me, and I stopped and glanced over my shoulder. "What on earth's that?"

"Nothing. A little disagreement among the workmen."

"A little disagreement? It sounds like a major war!"

"We are always a fighting race, I am afraid. There is trouble today among the workmen. There are still men here from the 'dig' of the French archaeologists—the 'dig' is finished, but workmen have remained to clear up, and to remove the rails that the trucks ran on, the things of that kind. A mule strayed during the night, and now they have discovered that some tools are missing, and they are accusing the men who work on the stadium road of theft, and so—well, you hear that there is a little disagreement."

"Some tools and a mule?" I listened to the uproar for a moment or two. It sounded like the battle of El Alamein in stereophonic sound. I said drily, "Perhaps they haven't heard of the Amphictyonic League and the peace of Delphi."

He smiled. "Perhaps not."

"And now I really must go. I'll let you know if I can come with you tomorrow. You say you'll be here at this time?"

"Always."

I had a sharp inner vision of a life where one would be—always—serenely on the Delphi road in the early morning sun. "I'll try and be here by eight if I'm coming. If I can't—"

"It does not matter. If you come, I will take you with the greatest of pleasure. If not, it does not matter. Are you staying at the Apollon?"

"Yes."

"It is very nice, yes?"

"Delightful." I lingered for a moment, looking at the closed door of the Museum. He was watching me through the smoke of his cigarette with that shrewd, incurious blue gaze. I said, "Kyrie . . . you weren't here during the war, of course, but you'll know what happened to the statues and things from the Museum? The Charioteer, for instance? Where was he? Hidden?"

"Only in a manner of speaking. He was in Athens."

"Oh. Yes. I see."

Behind me a shabby black car slid to a halt. Simon grinned at me over the door and said, "Good morning."

"Oh, Simon! Am I late? Have you had to hunt for me?"

"The answer to both those is no. I was early and they told me you'd come down here. Have you had breakfast?"

"Hours ago."

"Why people should adopt that disgustingly self-righteous tone whenever they manage to achieve breakfast before eight o'clock I do not know," said Simon. He leaned across the car and opened the door for me. "Come along, then, let's go. Unless of course you'd like to drive?"

I didn't bother to answer that one, but slipped quickly into the passenger's seat beside him.

As the car turned the corner and gathered speed along the straight stretch below the temple I said, without preliminary, "The Charioteer was in Athens during the war. Presumably in hiding."

He gave me a quick glance. "Oh. Yes, it would be, wouldn't it?" I saw him smile.

I said, almost defensively, "Well, you did get me into it, after all."

"I did, didn't I?" A little pause. "Did you come down through the temple this morning?"

"Yes."

"I thought you might do that. I've been up there myself most mornings by about six."

"Not today?"

He smiled. "No. I thought you'd like it to yourself."

"You're very—" I began, and stopped. He didn't ask me what I'd been going to say. I said, not quite irrelevantly, "Do you ever lose your temper, Simon?"

"What in the world makes you ask that?"

"Oh, come, I thought you were a thought-reader!"

"Oh. Well, let me see. . . . Last night?"

"That didn't take much guessing. Yes, of course. Nigel was abominably rude to you. Didn't you mind?"

"Mind? No."

"Why not?"

"I don't think I'd have minded from Nigel anyway, because he's not very happy. Life isn't easy for him, and on top of everything he has to fall for that girl, and she's led him the hell of a dance. But last night—" He paused, and I saw again that pucker of worry round his eyes. "Last night there was something wrong. Really wrong, I mean; not just Nigel's too-usual brand of nerves and temperament and frustrated talent, and that little she-witch playing him on a very barbed hook. There was something more."

"Are you sure he wasn't just a bit drunk? He said he was."

"Possibly. But that's part of the trouble—he doesn't drink much as a rule, and last night he was fairly putting it away, though he's like you—he doesn't like ouzo. No, there was definitely something very wrong, and I'd give quite a lot to know what it was."

"I take it he didn't tell you anything after you got back to the studio? I got the impression he was going to come out with something just as Danielle interrupted."

"Yes, so did I. But I didn't see him again. His room was empty when I went back. I waited a bit, but eventually went to bed. I didn't hear him come in."

"Perhaps," I said a little drily, "he was fixing the taps."

"That did occur to me. But no. Danielle's door was standing open. She wasn't there either. I think they'd gone for a walk, or down to the village for another drink, or something. And Nigel had gone when I got up this morning."

I said. "He went up the mountain. I saw him."

"You saw him?"

"Yes, at about seven o'clock. He went up past the graveyard through those pines, as if he were going farther up the hill."

"Alone?"

"Yes. In fact, he looked rather as if he wanted to be left very much alone. I didn't speak to him, and I don't think he saw me."

Simon said, "Well, let's hope he does some work today, and draws it out of himself, whatever it is. I expect I'll see him tonight." He glanced at me, smiling. "Did you make any more discoveries this morning?"

"Only one," I said, before I thought.

"And that?"

I found myself telling him, quite simply. "It was just my own discovery. We talked about it last night, with Nigel. It's something we're taught from childhood, but I'd never really had it brought home to me till now."

"What is it?"

"That saying of 'your parson friend,' as Nigel called him."

"Ah, yes, that." He was silent for a moment, then he quoted it softly, as if half to himself, " 'No man is an Island, entire of itself; every man is a piece of the Continent, a part of the main; if a Clod be washed away by the Sea, Europe is the less, as well as if a Promontory were, as well as if a Manor of thy friends or of thine own were; any man's death diminishes me, because I am involved in Mankind; And therefore never send to know for whom the bell tolls; It tolls for thee.' . . . Terrific piece of writing, isn't it? One should remember it more often."

The car slowed down and drew out to pass a little group of three donkeys pattering along in the dust at the edge of the road. On the foremost an old woman sat sideways; she had a distaff in her left hand, the spindle in her right, and as she rode she spun the white wool ceaselessly, without looking at it. She ducked a smiling salute to us as we went by.

Simon said, "What brought that home to you this morning?"

I hesitated, then said flatly, "Michael's grave."

"I see." And I thought he did.

I said, "It's this confounded country. It does things to one—mentally and physically and, I suppose morally. The past is so living and the present so intense and the future so blooming imminent. The light seems to burn life into you twice as intensely as anywhere else I've known. I suppose that's why the Greeks did what they did so miraculously, and why they could stay themselves through twenty generations of slavery that would have crushed any other race on earth. You come here thinking you're going to look at a lot of myth-haunted ruins and picturesque peasants and you find that . . ." I stopped.

"That what?"

"No. I'm talking piffle."

"It's good piffle. Go on. What do you find?"

"You find that the grave of Michael Lester is as moving and as important as the 'tomb of Agamemnon' at Mycenae, or Byron or Venizelos or Alexander. He, and the men like him, are a part of the same picture." I stopped, and then said helplessly, "Greece. Damn it, what is it that it does to one?"

He was silent a moment, then he said, "I think the secret is that it belongs to all of us—to us of the West. We've learned to think in its terms, and to live in its laws. It's given us almost everything that our world has that is worth while. Truth, straight thinking, freedom, beauty. It's our second language, our second line of thought, our second country. We all have our own country—and Greece."

We sailed round a bend of the road and ahead of us the deep valley opened to show a great rounded beauty of a mountain, silver-green, blue-veined, cloud-grey.

"Why, damn it all," said Simon. "That hill in front of us. That's Helicon. *Helicon.* And then you wonder why this country gets you in the wind?"

"Not any more," I said.

And we didn't speak again till we came to Arachova and found Stephanos and Niko waiting for us in the café on the corner.

"Do you like my socks?" asked Niko.

"They're wonderful," I said truthfully. They were, indeed, in that landscape, something to be wondered at. They were luminous, and of a startling shade of shocking pink. They shone among the bleached hot stones of the mountain track like neon signs against a clear sky.

"They light up," explained Niko.

"I can see that. Where did you get them?"

"In Athens. They are the latest thing from New York."

"Do you go to Athens often?"

"No. I went to work there when I was fourteen. I was a page boy at the Acropole Palace Hotel."

"I see. Is that where you learned your English?"

"Some of it. I also learn it here in the school. Is good, huh?"

"Very good. Why didn't you stay in Athens?"

"Is better here." Niko looked back along the track we were climbing. Away below us Arachova had dwindled to a toy waterfall of coloured roofs. Niko turned back to me almost as if he were puzzled. "Here there is nothing. Is no money. But is better here. Arachova is my village." Again that look. "You think I am crazy? *You* come from London where there is plenty money. All Greeks are a little crazy, huh? But you think I am stupid to leave Athens?"

"There is a sort of divine madness about all the Greeks I've met," I said, laughing. "But you're not crazy, Niko. It's better here, certainly, money or no money. Don't ever live in a town unless you have to! And I don't live in London. I live miles away from it, in a country village, just like you."

"Like Arachova?" He was vastly surprised. I had long since discovered that to all Greeks England meant London and nothing else. London, the huge, the golden-pavemented, the jacinth-gated.

"Not quite like Arachova."

"And that is your village, as Arachova is mine."

I said, "Not quite, Niko. We've lost that way of feeling, I'm afraid. How far is this place that we're making for?"

"Making? *Oriste?*"

"Going to. The place where Michael died." I said it softly, with my eye on Simon's back where he walked with Stephanos a few yards ahead of us.

"About an hour from here. More, perhaps. It is nearer to Delphi than Arachova. It is in a . . . I do not know the word: a hollow place, a—" he stopped and made a scooping gesture.

"A corrie? Like this?"

"Yes. That is it. A corrie, where the rocks have fallen near the foot of a cliff. My grandfather know the way. He tell me it looks to the northwest—that is, away from Delphi and Arachova, towards Amphissa. This track goes along the face of the mountains and then we leave it and climb up towards these cliffs where the corrie is. I think that many, many years ago there was a road for beasts, but not now. I do not know how far. I have never been, me. My grandfather, he know the way. You are tired?"

"No. It's rather hot, but I'm not tired."

"In Greece," said Niko reflectively, eyeing me, "the women are very strong."

I thought of the village cafés, with their day-long complement of cheerfully idle men. "I imagine they have to be," I said.

"Oh, yes." Niko misunderstood me, probably deliberately. "In Greece the men are tough. Oh, very tough."

Somehow, at that moment, Niko's racy beauty managed to look very tough indeed. His swagger, and the look he gave me, were the plainest possible invitation to the kind of suggestive verbal sparring that the Mediterranean men seem to love. But two could play at the game of misunderstanding. I said cheerfully, "Then if we do meet the shade of Angelos on the hill, I shall feel quite, quite safe with you, Niko."

"How?" He was momentarily thrown off his stride. "Oh, yes! But of course you will be safe with me! I should kill him, you understand. He helped to kill my great-grandfather's brother's son Panos, so of course I should kill him. And"—the swagger gave way again to Niko's own brand of youthful and artless high spirits—"it would be easy, because he is old and I am young."

"I suppose he's all of forty," I agreed. "And just how old are you, Niko?"

"I am seventeen."

I said mendaciously, "Really? I'd have thought you were much older than that."

He flashed me his delighted smile. "Would you? Would you really? And how old are you, beautiful miss?"

"Niko! Don't you know the rules better than that? I'm twenty-five."

"So old? But you do not look like twenty-five," he said generously. "It is a good age to be, not? See, this bit is rough. Take my hand, miss."

I laughed. "I'm not as old as all that, Niko. And I'm truly not a bit tired. Just hot."

It was indeed very hot. As we climbed steadily northwest, the sun beat down on the right, throwing shadows sharp and hard as graphite along the white rock. The track where we walked was only by courtesy a track. It was not steep, cutting at a slant along the great flank of the mountain, but it was very rough, and some of the stones were sharp. We had long since left any trees behind, and the mountainside, unpunctuated now by pine or cypress, stretched one great wing of burning white from the high hard blue sky down to the dry watercourse deep on our left. Beyond the tortured path of this dead stream, the rock rose again, this time violently blocked in with cobalt shadow. High above, so that to glance at them hurt the eyes, three birds hung, circling slowly and with moveless wings, like some mobile toy on invisible threads. I thought I could hear their faint, sweet mewing. Nothing else broke the silence except the scrape and clink of our feet, and the sound of our breathing.

The track ran straight up to what looked like a wall of fallen rocks and rubble, and there stopped, obliterated. Stephanos, in front, had halted, and turned to speak to Simon, who was just behind him. He said something, gesturing towards the barricade of rock.

It looked like a landslip, a great torrent of red and ochreous earth frozen even as it poured down the steep wing of the mountain. It was spiked with broken rock and great white slabs of fallen limestone. Further down the mountainside it fanned out like the delta of a red river. Enormous blocks of stone had hurtled down with it, flung carelessly, as by the hand of an angry god, to dam the narrow gash of the watercourse.

Stephanos had turned aside to climb rather painfully up the steep hillface beside the landslide.

"Is this where we leave the track?" I asked.

Simon turned. "No. That's still with us. This stuff's just lying across it. If we follow Stephanos up a little there's a place where it's safer to cross."

"It must have been quite a storm," I said, surveying the torrent of rocks in front, and the gigantic flung boulders far below us.

"Not storm. Earthquake," said Simon, then laughed at my expression. "Yes, one forgets, doesn't one? I told you this was a savage country. And this, I believe, is a baddish area. They've had quite a history of tremors hereabouts. The miracle is that any of the shrines and temples have a single pillar left standing. Can you manage?"

"Yes, thanks. Don't help me, Simon. I've got to keep my end up with Niko."

"Of course—and mine too, I think. . . . That's it. We cross here. It seems stable enough, but watch yourself."

We made our way slowly across the detritus of the earthquake. From higher up I could see where a whole slice of the mountain cliff above us had been torn away and thrown down. It had splintered into great white spearheads, against which the smaller fragments were piled in the drift of dark-red earth. We scrambled down this uncomfortable ramp towards the path which had shaken itself clear of the debris.

"I suppose the Earth-Shaker turned over in his sleep," I said, "and not so very long ago, either, by the look of it. The cracks look fairly fresh, don't they?"

Stephanos must have understood the drift of what I was saying. He had turned to wait for us on the track, and now spoke to Simon. "What does he say?" I asked.

"He says that there were two or three small shocks—this, by the way, is a small shock—about twelve years ago. A little further on, the mountain has been shifted about much more drastically. He says that only someone who was out on this part of Parnassus almost daily would still know his way about, once he had left the track. He also says that the place we are making for is almost completely changed since he found Michael there. It was just an open space at the foot of a low cliff, and now it's closed in by fallen rock into a kind of corrie, or hollow."

Stephanos nodded as he finished. He gave me a look from under his magnificent white brows. He asked Simon a question.

"Are you tired?" asked Simon.

"No, thanks."

Simon smiled. "Don't exhaust yourself keeping Britain's end up, will you?"

"I'm not. It's only the heat."

There was a flash of shocking-pink socks beside me as Niko dropped off the rubble to land as neatly as a goat. He dragged a water bottle out of a large pocket and unscrewed the top. "Have a drink, miss."

I drank thankfully. The bottle smelt ammoniac, like a nice donkey, but the water was good and still reasonably cool.

"Greek peasant women," said Niko, watching me with that limpid look of his, "can go for hours over the roughest country without food or drink."

"So," I said, stoppering the bottle and handing it back to him, "can camels. Thank you, Niko, that was wonderful."

"It was a pleasure, beautiful miss." Niko turned to Simon and held out the bottle. His look and gesture expressed, somehow, the most tender solicitude.

Simon, smiling, shook his head.

"Good," said Stephanos, and turned to go on. He and Simon forged ahead once more, and Niko and I took up our positions in the rear.

It must have been getting on for noon when we neared the corrie.

We left the track some way beyond the fall of rock and turned, in Stephanos' unfaltering wake, up into a markless desert of rock and dry earth. Sometimes we trudged upwards through sienna-coloured dust strewn cruelly with small boulders, and sometimes we walked more easily across great serrated flanges of the white and living rock. The sun was at its height and the heat was intense. The air wavered with it till the whole vast sweep of rock seemed to pulsate. If it hadn't been for the cool breeze that blew steadily at that height, it would have been insupportable.

By the time we were two-thirds of the way to the corrie, and had done most of the climbing, I had got my second wind, and was walking fairly easily. I was, I felt, upholding British Womanhood not too badly.

"The Greek peasant women," said Niko, beside me, "used to carry great loads of wood and grapes and things across here. Regularly."

"If you tell me one more thing about Greek peasant women," I said, "I shall scream and lie down and refuse to move another step. Besides, I don't believe you."

He grinned. "It is not true," he conceded. "I think that you are very wonderful."

"Why, Niko, that's nice of you!"

"And very beautiful too," said Niko. "Would you like an apple?"

And he fished an apple out of his pocket and handed it to me with very much the air of a Paris presenting the prize to Aphrodite. His look of intense and dazzled admiration was, one felt, one that had been tried before and found to work.

It still worked. My morale soared. I laughed and took the apple and thanked him, and then a diversion was created because neither he nor Stephanos would allow me to eat it without peeling it, and Niko wanted to peel it for me and Stephanos had the knife, so, being Greeks, they plunged into a passionate discussion about this while Simon peeled the apple and then handed it to me.

"For the fairest," he said.

"There's not," I said, "a lot of competition. But thank you all the same."

Soon after that we reached our destination.

CHAPTER XI

That ground will take no footprint. All of it
Is bitter stone. . . .

EURIPIDES: *Electra*
(*tr. Gilbert Murray*).

THE CORRIE did not lie at any great height. Arachova itself is almost three thousand feet above sea level, and we had climbed no more than eight or nine hundred feet in all since we had left the village. We were still only in the foothills of the vast highland of Parnassus, but we might have been lost, a million miles from anywhere. Since the village had dwindled out of sight we had seen no living creature except the lizards, and the vultures that circled and cried so sweetly, high in the dazzling air.

The place wasn't, properly speaking, a corrie. It was a hollow scooped out of a line of low cliffs that topped a steep, mile-long ridge like the crest along a horse's neck. From a distance the cliff looked fairly uniform, but on approach it could be seen that it had been split and torn into ragged bays and promontories where half a hundred winter torrents had gouged their headlong way down the mountainside.

Here and there lay evidence of a swifter and more wholesale violence. Earthquakes had wrested great chunks from the crag, quarrying back into the limestone face, throwing the enormous debris down, so that for hundreds of feet below the jagged cliffs, a loose and sometimes dangerous scree valanced the sloping hillside.

As we neared the edge of this, Stephanos turned aside, into a short steep detour that took us out above the level of the cliff top, and we approached the line of crags at a long slant that brought us eventually to the edge.

The old man stopped then, leaning on his crook, and waited for us to come up with him.

Simon stood beside him, looking down.

"This is the place?"

"This is the place."

It could have been a quarry hacked out of the cliff face during countless patient years. It had probably taken five seconds of earthquake for the Earth-Shaker to tear that semicircular scar back into the cliff and fling the wreckage down before it in still formidable walls of jagged rock. The result of the earthquake's action was to make a roughly circular hollow, a sort of irregular crater some seventy yards across, which was walled to the north by the living cliff on which we stood, and shut in almost completely for the rest of its diameter by the vast sections of tumbled rock.

The centre of the crater floor was clear, but the encircling walls were piled in the now familiar way with red dust and rock debris. In spring, I thought, it would probably be beautiful, for it was sheltered, and I could see the dead remains of some scrubby plants and bushes where the melting snows and then the rain must have fed some alpine vegetation. Below us clung the lovely green of a little juniper, and just beside my feet the rock held two thick bushes that looked like holly, but which bore, incongruously, acorns with enormous cups as prickly as sea urchins.

To the right, on the west side of the corrie, was what appeared to be the only way out. This was a break in the wall of rock, towards which the smooth crater floor lifted in a rocky ramp. From the height where we stood I thought I could see, beyond and below this "gate," the ghost of an old track, leading westwards to vanish round a spur of the mountain.

Stephanos caught the direction of my glance. "That is the way he went."

He spoke in Greek, of course, and Simon translated for me, at the time in snatches, and more fully later; but once again I shall put the old man's words down directly, as they came.

"That is the way he went, down the old track towards Amphissa. It comes out above a disused quarry near the Amphissa road, behind the olive groves." He fell silent for a moment or two, looking down at the hollow beneath our feet. No one spoke. The sun beat on the back of our necks, and I felt, suddenly, very tired.

Then the old man spoke again, slowly, reminiscently. "I came to the head of the cliff just at this point. It was different then, you understand . . . here, where we stand, there was a pinnacle of rock, like a cat's tooth. It disappeared in the earthquake, but then it was a landmark that even an Athenian could not have missed. And below the cliff, then, there was no hollow, as you see it now, walled and gated like a fortress. There was only the cliff, and below us some big rocks lying, and a space of clean stone. It was there that I saw them, Michael and Angelos. And the place is not covered. I marked it, and I know. It was there." The crook pointed. Almost in the centre of the dazzling floor of smooth stone, a little pile of stones, a cairn, threw a small triangular shadow. "I put those there later," said Stephanos, "after the earthquake had moved the cliff and the place was altered beyond recognition." There was another pause of silence, then he glanced sideways at me. "We will go down now. . . . Will you tell the lady to be very careful, *Kyrie* Simon? The path is steep, and made only for goats, but it is the quickest way."

As Simon transmitted the warning, I saw that there was indeed a path down into the corrie. It left the cliff top just beside us, between the two bushes of holly oak, and wound steeply down past more mats of holly and the dusty ghosts of thistles, into the bottom of the hollow. It was down this way that the dog must have raced to attack Angelos, and then Stephanos himself, to run to Michael's side as he lay dying in the sun. . . .

The sun was so high that almost the whole of the corrie bottom was shadowless. But where the cliff path debouched onto the level, a wing of rock cast a comforting angle of blue shade. I stopped there, and sat down with my back against the warm stone. Stephanos moved forward without pausing, and Simon followed him. Niko flung himself down beside me on the dusty ground. I hoped he wouldn't speak, and he didn't. He broke off a piece of a dead thistle and began scratching patterns in the dust. He wasn't paying much attention to his drawing; his intent gaze never left the other men.

Stephanos led Simon across the floor of the corrie, and stopped beside the little cairn. He was pointing down at it and talking, rapidly now. His hand moved and gestured, then came back to the same spot. Almost I could see the dying man lying there in the baking sun, the shepherd coming to the cliff top where a fang of rock stuck up like a cat's tooth, the dog dashing down that snaking path, the murderer turning to bolt out of the "gate" and down the track towards Amphissa and the sea. . . .

Then Stephanos turned heavily and trudged back to where we sat. He lowered himself down beside me with a sigh, then said something short to Niko, who got out a battered packet of cigarettes and handed him one. He gave his grandfather a light, then turned, with his brilliant smile, to offer a cigarette to me. We lit up in silence.

Simon was still standing in the centre of the corrie, but he wasn't looking down at the cairn where his brother had died. He had turned, and that cool appraising stare of his was slowly raking the sides of the corrie . . . the tumbled wall of rock that hemmed us in . . . the great sections that had fallen outward from the crag, and now made the two side wings of the corrie, piled high in vast slabs and wedges against the old solid rock of the cliff . . . the hollow curve of a shallow cave exposed in the scooped segment of broken crag, a cave that had been deep before the front of the cliff had fallen away and left its recesses naked to the air. . . .

My cigarette was mild and loosely packed and tasted slightly of goat; there was something about the beautiful Niko, I reflected, that harked back fairly consistently to the lower animals. I had half-smoked it, and Niko's was gone entirely, when Simon's shadow fell beside us.

"What about lunch?" he asked.

The slight tension—of Stephanos' making, not Simon's—was broken, and we chatted over lunch as if it had been a normal picnic. My tiredness was rapidly dissolving, with the rest in the pleasant shade, and the solid excellence of the food we had bought in Arachova. We had rolls—a little dry after their progress in Niko's rucksack—with generous pieces of cold lamb sandwiched in; cheese in thick juicy slices; a paper full of olives that felt as if they were warm from the tree but were really warm from Niko; a hard-boiled egg; a very solid and very sweet chunk of some sort of cake made with fresh cherries; and a large handful of grapes, also warm and slightly tired-looking, but tasting ambrosially of the sun.

I noticed that Simon, as he ate, still looked about him, his eyes returning time after time, thoughtfully, to the recently torn cliff behind us. "This was done in the earthquake you spoke of, soon after the war?"

Stephanos said, through a mouthful of cake, "That is so. There were three or four shocks that year. It was nineteen forty-six. The villages were not affected, but a lot of rock was moved up here." He jerked his head towards the cliff. "This is not the only place of its kind. All along this ridge there are places where the tremors, and then the weather, have taken bites out of the hill. What the earthquake starts, the ice and snow don't take many winters to finish. There are three, four, five hollows, much like this one, where very little trace of the original cliff face remains. Only the goat track that we came down on . . . see? . . . there the cliff itself has not been moved, but you see the rocks piled against it as high as a ruined church. Oh, yes, I told you, *Kyrie* Simon, that a man who was not always out on the hill would soon miss his landmarks."

"The pinnacle, for instance, that used to stand above the cliff?"

"I told you about that? Yes, I did, I remember. It was not so very high, but it served as a landmark for kilometres around. It was what guided me to Michael on that day. He knew of a cave here, he said, near the Cat's Tooth, and he meant to lie up in it until the German drive was over. I came up bringing him food, and to try and make him come back to Arachova where his wound might be cared for. But this I have spoken of already."

Simon's eyes were on the shallow apse of the exposed cave. They were narrowed slightly, as if against the sun, and his face gave nothing away. "A cave? That one? It would be deep enough before half of it fell in."

Stephanos lifted his heavy shoulders. "I do not know if that was the one or not. Possibly. But you must understand that the cliff is full of caves . . . some parts of Parnassus are a honeycomb of such places where an army could hide in safety."

Simon had taken out cigarettes. "Camilla? I think I'd like to take a quick look around, all the same. Cigarette? Catch, Niko. . . ." He got slowly to his feet, and stood looking down at the old man sitting heavily in the shade. "And you carried Michael from here to Delphi?"

Stephanos smiled. "It was fourteen years ago, and I was younger. And the way to Delphi is much shorter than the way we came . . . but steep, you understand, because Arachova lies nearly four hundred metres higher than Delphi. That is a big start on a climb like this, so we came by Arachova today."

"I still think it was . . . well, quite a feat. And now I'm going to poke around for a bit. I want a good look at that cave. It looks as if there's another small opening at the back of it. Will you come, or are you resting?"

"I will come."

"Niko?"

One swift graceful wriggle, and Niko was on his feet and brushing dust from his trousers. "I come. I have very good eyesight, me. If there is anything to be seen, I will see it. I can see in the dark, as well as any cat, so if there is an inner cave, I shall guide you, *Kyrie* Simon."

"We'll follow your socks," said Simon drily, and Niko grinned. The socks flashed across the corrie at a run, and were dimmed in the shadow of the cave's recess. Stephanos was getting slowly to his feet. Simon looked down at me and raised his eyebrows.

I shook my head, so he and Stephanos left me, and went more slowly in the wake of the luminous socks. A buttress of shadow swallowed them.

I finished the cigarette and stubbed it out, then sat relaxed and still, enjoying the shade and the silence and the bright dazzle of heat beyond my shadowed corner. The men were out of sight, either in the cave or somewhere beyond the piles of massive debris that buttressed the far side of the corrie. I couldn't hear them now. The silence was intense, thick as the heat. I was part of it, sitting as still as a lizard on my stone.

Some movement, real or imagined, at the head of the cliff path, caught my eye, and I turned to look, wondering half idly if Niko had found some way back to the cliff's head while I had been sitting there half-asleep. But there was nothing there, only the sun hammering on the white rock. The shadows, purple and anthracite and red, seemed themselves to flicker with movement. Against the violent patterns of light and shade, the green of the holly oaks and the cool curve of the juniper arching out from the face of the cliff were as refreshing as the sound of a spring. I remembered, suddenly, that as I had clambered down past them, there had been other green things below us, hardly noticed in the hazards of that steep exhausted scramble down the cliff.

Where there was green, there must certainly, in September, be water . . . cold water, not Niko's tepid bottle that smelled of goat. The thought brought me eagerly to my feet. A shadow at the cliff top flickered again, but I hardly noticed. My eyes were on the corner below the slim bow of the juniper, where, like a mirage, showed a glimpse of vivid emerald. . . .

I got up, skirting the corrie's edge, picking my way between the enormous fallen blocks. I slid between two rough rocks that caught at my clothes, bent my head to pass under a wing of limestone that shored up the cliff like a flying buttress—and there was the grass. The colour was so startling, and so beautiful after the dazzling changes rung by sun and stone that I must have stood quite still, gazing at it, for a full minute. It flowed in a deep and vivid ribbon of green between two boulders streaked liberally with the red of water-borne iron. But there was no water now. There might be some spring, I thought, that was dependent on intermittent showers high on the peaks; perhaps, like snow on the desert's face, the grass sprang up in the wake of a shower and faded with the next day's sunset. . . . It lay there, itself like a small pool of cool water, a green thought in a green shade, moist to the touch, and lending the corner of the corrie a freshness that the shadowed rock had not had.

I sat gratefully down, with my hands spread on the ground and the soft grass springing up between my fingers. Among the green were tiny flowers, bells of pale blue, like pygmy harebells. Some of these grew on the face of the cliff itself, and their seeds had, in the last decade, flown and rooted everywhere in the fallen debris of earthquake. Only here in this moist corner were they still in flower, but I could see fading clumps of seeding stems on all sides among the boulders. Other alpines had grown here too; there was something with a pale furry leaf and a thin dry flower-stem left sticking out like a hummingbird's tongue; a tuft of tendrils dried into hexagonal shapes till they looked like bunches of brown chicken-wire; a tiny plant of the acorned holly, rooting purposefully in a thin crack. Then with another shock of pleasure I saw one more flower that had not yet died of drought. In a cleft just above eye level there was a plant of cyclamen. The leaves, blue-green and veined palely, were held out in stiff formal curves on their red stems. The flowers were soft rose-pink, a dozen of them, and clung like a flight of moths to the dry cliff. Below the flowers, in the same cleft, grew the remains of another rock plant, dead, fraying away to dust in the drought. Above it the cyclamen's flowers looked pure and delicate and strong. . . .

Something was fretting at the edge of my mind. I stared at the cyclamen, and found I was thinking of the Dutch painter and his donkey surrounded by the laughing village lads, and I wondered, without knowing why, what Nigel was doing now.

We went back by the shorter route.

It appeared that the search of the cave had yielded nothing, and apparently Simon didn't want to delay Stephanos and Niko by making a more prolonged investigation. We left the corrie by the gap in the west side, and scrambled down the steep slope below the scree.

We had nearly reached the bottom of the dry valley that lay below the ridge, when we came on the barely visible track that I had glimpsed from the top of the crags. Even this was appallingly rough going. We made our careful way along it for some hundred yards or so, and then it forked. The right branch fell steeply away, curling out of sight almost at once round a spur of cliff. The left-hand branch turned downhill for Delphi. We took this, and in just over half the time the outward journey had taken, we saw ahead of us the edge of the high land, and, beyond it, the gap where the Pleistus valley cuts its way down to the sea.

Stephanos paused and spoke to Simon. The latter turned to me.

"Stephanos has come back this way because he thinks you may be tired. This path will lead you straight down to Delphi. It comes out above the temple, and you can get down behind the Shining Ones, and then through the stadium. The drop down to the cliff top is steep, but there's no danger if you take care. I'll come down with you if you like, but you can't possibly miss the way."

I must have looked slightly surprised, because he added, "The car's at Arachova—remember? I thought I'd go back along the top with Stephanos now, and collect it. But there's no need to drag you the whole way."

I said gratefully, "Oh, Simon—that car! I'd forgotten all about it. I don't really see why you should have to shoulder all the responsibility for my bit of nonsense, but I must confess I'll be awfully glad if you will! Don't tell Niko, but I really am beginning to feel I'd like to be home."

"Well, it won't take you long from here, and it's all downhill. No—look, dash it, I'll come with you."

"I wouldn't dream of letting you, if it means your trailing back later on to Arachova for the car. I can't possibly get lost between here and Delphi, and I promise to be careful on the cliff path." I turned to hold out a hand to Stephanos and thank him, then did the same to Niko. It was like Stephanos, I thought, virtually to ignore me all the time, and yet to lead the whole party some hour or so out of its way to show me the quick way home. The old man nodded gravely over my hand and turned away. Niko took it with a melting look from those beautiful eyes and said, "I will see you again, miss? You come to Arachova often?"

"I hope so."

"And you will come to see the rugs in my sister's shop? Is very good rugs, all colours. Local. Is also brooches and pots of the very best Greek style. For you they are cheap. I tell my sister you are my friend, yes?"

I laughed. "If I buy any rugs and pots I'll come to your sister's shop, Niko. That's a promise. And now good-bye, and thank you."

"Good-bye, miss. Thank you, beautiful miss."

The luminous socks plunged away along the path after Stephanos.

Simon grinned. "His grandfather'd have the hide off him if he could understand half he says. Is there such a thing as innocent depravity? Niko's it if there is. A little of Athens superimposed on Arachova. It's a fascinating mixture, isn't it?"

"When it's as beautiful as Niko, yes. . . . Simon, was it true that you didn't find anything in the cave? Or was there something that you didn't want to talk about in front of the others? You didn't see anything at all?"

"Nothing. There was a small inner cave, but it was as blank as a

scoured pot. . . . I'll tell you about it later on; I'd better be off after
them now. I'll be in to the Apollon for dinner and I'll see you then.
Afterwards we'll get you installed at the studio. You'll dine with me, of
course?"

"Why, thank you. I—"

"Take care of yourself, then. See you at dinner." And with a lift of the
hand he was gone in the wake of the shocking pink socks.

I stared after him for a few seconds, but he didn't look back.

It occurred to me, with a slight sense of surprise, that this time yesterday I hadn't even met him.

I turned and began to make my careful way down towards Delphi.

CHAPTER XII

*Seize her! Throw her from Parnassus, send her bounding down the cliff-ledges, let
the crags comb out her dainty hair!*

EURIPIDES: *Ion*
(*tr. Philip Vellacott*).

IT WAS late afternoon, and the sun was straight ahead of me when at
length I came out on top of one of the great cliffs that stand above the
Shrine at Delphi. Far below me and to the right lay the temple precinct,
its monuments and porticos and its Sacred Way looking small and very
clean cut in the sun, like the plaster models that you see in museums. The
pillars of Apollo were foreshortened, and tiny as toys. Directly beneath
me was the cleft of the Castalian Spring. The tangle of trees filled it like
a dark waterfall. Already, beyond the tree-filled cleft, the Flamboyant
cliff was taking the late afternoon sun like flame.

I moved back a few feet from the edge, and sat down on a stone. To
one side of me grew a thicket of tallish juniper. Beyond and all around
this was the usual dusty expanse of hot stone. The path to the stadium led
off to the right past the bushes, but I was tired, and here at the cliff top a
a cool breeze from the sea allayed the still-hot blaze of afternoon.

I sat quietly, chin on hand, looking down at the dreaming marbles of
the shrine below, at the blue-and-silver depths of the valley where hawks
circled below eye level, at the great cliff beside me burning in the sun.
. . . No, I thought, I could not leave Delphi yet. Even if it meant sleep-

ing in the studio near the intolerable Danielle, in order to save what I must owe on the car, I couldn't leave. There must be tomorrow—and the day after, and the day after . . . how long a succession of days would it take before I had begun to learn and see and taste what Delphi had to show? I must stay. And my decision (I told myself quickly) had nothing to do with Simon Lester and his affairs. Nothing. Nothing whatever. On the thought I found myself wondering just what Simon would have decided that we should do tomorrow. . . .

"What are you doing up here?"

The question came from close behind me. I turned sharply. Danielle had come out from behind the thicket of juniper. Today she had on a wide bell of scarlet skirt and a turquoise-coloured blouse that was open at the neck. Very open. The inevitable cigarette clung to her bottom lip. Her mouth was rouged a pale pink against her sallow skin. Today her fingernails were pale pink too. On the thin brown hands it looked odd and slightly improper.

"Why, hullo," I said pleasantly. If I was to be the girl's neighbour tonight in the studio, it didn't do to let last night's irritation with her bad manners reappear.

But Danielle had no such scruples. It was quite obvious that manners, bad or good, had no place in her scheme of things. She simply was, and if others didn't like it, they had to endure it. She repeated in that sharp voice that sounded as if she really wanted to know, "What are you doing up here?"

I said, letting a note of mild surprise creep in, "Sitting looking at the view. And you?"

She came towards me. She moved like a model, hips thrown forward and knees close. She stood between me and the edge of the cliff in one of the attitudes you see in fashion drawings—one hip out, toes at twenty past seven, one thin hand gesturing with the cigarette. Any minute now she would open her mouth and let the tip of her tongue appear.

She said, "It's a long climb from the shrine on a hot afternoon."

"Isn't it? Has it tired you very much, or did you just come round the top from the studio?"

She gave me a glittering glance. I couldn't see for the life of me why she should care what I was doing up here, but she obviously did. And I certainly wasn't going to tell her where we had been. That was Simon's pilgrimage, and no one else's. If he chose to take me along, well, that was his affair. But I wasn't going to tell Danielle.

She said, "Where's Simon?"

"I don't know," I said truthfully. "Were you looking for him?"

"Oh, not really." To my surprise she came forward and sat down not two yards from my feet. She swore once, viciously, in French, as her hip met a thistle, then she settled herself gracefully on the dusty ground and smiled at me. "A cigarette?"

"Why, thanks very much," I said, before I thought.

She regarded me for a while in silence, while I smoked and tried not to feel annoyed that now I could hardly get up and leave her, which I very much wanted to do. Really, I reflected, when faced with this sort of person why do we hold madly on to our own tabus; why could my careful manners not allow me to get up—as Danielle certainly would have done in my place—say, "I'm bored and you are a mannerless little trollop and I don't like you," and then walk away down the hill? But there I sat and looked pleasantly noncommittal and smoked her cigarette. I must admit that it was a good one, and—after Niko's—nectar and ambrosia. I wondered why she had offered the olive branch, and eyed her warily. "I fear the Greeks, even when bringing gifts. . . ."

"You weren't in to lunch at the Apollon."

"No," I agreed. "Were you?"

"Where did you have lunch?"

"I had a picnic. Out."

"With Simon?"

I raised my eyebrows and tried to register cold surprise at the inquisition. It had no effect whatever. "With Simon?" she repeated.

"Yes."

"I saw him go out in the car."

"Did you?"

"He picked you up somewhere?"

"Yes."

"Where did you go?"

"South."

This set her back for half a minute. Then she said, "Why don't you want to tell me where you went and what you've been doing?"

I looked at her rather helplessly. "Why should I?"

"Why shouldn't you?"

"Because," I said, "I don't like being catechized."

She digested this. "Oh?" She turned those big tired eyes up to me, and asked, "Why? Have you and Simon been up to something?"

Said by Danielle, the harmless question could only mean one thing. I said explosively, "My God!" Then I began to laugh. I said, "No, Danielle. We have not. We took the car down to Arachova and left it there, then we walked back over the hill towards Delphi. We had a picnic at a place where there is a lovely view of Parnassus. Then I came on towards home and Simon went back for the car. If you sit here long enough you'll see him drive past below you. In case you don't know it by sight, the car you hired is a big black one. I don't know the make. I know very little about cars. Will that do? And thank you for the cigarette. I must be going." And I stubbed out the two-thirds-smoked cigarette and got to my feet.

She made a little movement without getting up, a sinuous little wriggle in the dust, like a snake. She smiled up at me. The cigarette had dropped from her lip and was smouldering on the ground beside her. She made no attempt to retrieve it. She was smiling and showing pretty white teeth with her tongue between them. The tongue was pale like her lips and nails. "You're annoyed with me," she said.

I felt suddenly very old with all the adult weight of my twenty-five years. "My dear girl," I said, "what could possibly lead you to imagine that?"

"You see, it's only," said Danielle from the dust, "that I'm jealous about Simon."

I wanted passionately to turn and run, but this gambit hardly provided me with a good exit line. I merely shed most of those adult years at one go and said feebly and childishly, "Oh?"

"Men," said the voice of the dust snake, "are all the same, mostly. But there really is something about Simon. I expect even you feel it, don't you? On the whole my lovers bore me, but I want Simon. I genuinely do."

"Really."

"Yes. Really." The flat little voice held no inflection. "And I can tell you just what it is about Simon. It's—"

I said sharply, "No, really, Danielle!"

She shot me a look. "You're in love with him yourself, aren't you?"

"Don't be absurd!" To my horror I sounded almost too emphatic. "I hardly know him! And besides, this is not the—"

"What difference does that make? It takes me two seconds to know whether I want a man or not."

I turned away. "Look," I said. "I must go. I expect I'll be seeing you later. Good-bye."

"Are you seeing him again tomorrow?"

The question was said idly, in that same flat voice; but it was not quite idle. Something made me pause and turn back to her.

She didn't meet my look. She was tracing a line in the dust with a pink-tipped forefinger. "What's he doing tomorrow?"

Definitely not quite idle. I said, "How do I know?" as coldly as I could, before it occurred to me that I did know, quite well. He would certainly go straight back to the corrie, to look for Michael's hypothetical cave. And he just as certainly wouldn't want Danielle tagging after him. The whole of this embarrassing interview seemed to indicate that she was prepared to do just that.

I said, in the tone of one conceding a point to a stubborn adversary, "All right. I'll tell you. I am seeing him. We're going to Levadia for the day. There's a horse fair, and gipsies, and he wants to take photographs."

"Oh." She was looking away over the valley with eyes narrowed against the sun. Then she sent another of those glinting looks up at me. "But what a bloody waste," she said.

Though I was used to her by now, I didn't quite manage to control the little flicker of anger that ran through me. I said, "So he didn't come to repair the taps last night?"

The beautiful eyelashes fluttered, and her eyes narrowed over a look of the most intense venom. "You're very outspoken, aren't you?" said Danielle.

"My bad manners," I said. "I'm sorry. And now I must go if I'm to get a bath before dinner. See you later. Did you know I was to come and stay at the studio from tonight?"

Her eyes opened wide. The dislike was still there, and now annoyance, and then both were suddenly, curiously, overlaid by what looked like calculation. "That'll be convenient, won't it?" said Danielle, meaning what only Danielle could mean. Then I saw her look change again. It slid over my shoulder and I saw surprise in her face, and something else.

I turned quickly.

A man had come out from behind the clump of juniper. He was obviously a Greek, dark, broad-cheekboned, with crisp curled hair that showed a hint of grey, and a smudge of a moustache over a mouth at once thin-lipped and sensual. He was of medium height, and stockily built. I guessed his age to be around forty. He was dressed in a grey striped suit, rather shabby, and a dark crimson shirt with a vermilion tie that would have clashed if the colours had not been harmlessly faded.

He spoke in French. "Why, hullo, Danielle."

It was as if he had told her quite plainly, *"It's all right."* I could see the look of surprise fade. She relaxed. "Hullo. How did you know I was here?"

I thought, Because you've just been together behind the juniper bushes and I interrupted you. Then I shook the thought away with the wry reflection that this was what contact with Danielle did. Five minutes with her, and a full half-pound of civet would hardly sweeten the imagination.

Danielle said idly—too idly—from the dust, "This is Camilla Haven. She's been out with Simon this afternoon and she's sleeping at the studio tonight." Then to me, "Dimitrios is a guide."

The man bowed and sent me a smile. *"Enchanté."*

"He doesn't speak English," said Danielle. "Do you know French?"

"Yes," I said, and murmured something polite.

Dimitrios said, "Mademoiselle has been to see the shrine this afternoon?"

"No. I went this morning early."

"Ah. And now you come up to the top of the Shining Ones to see the last of the sun."

I said, "It'll be some time still till dark, surely?"

"Perhaps not so long," said Dimitrios. I saw Danielle turn her head to look at him. Her head was on a level with my thigh, and I couldn't see her eyes for the curtaining lashes. Something crept along my spine like a cold-footed insect. The man, no less than the girl, gave me the creeps.

I gave myself another of those hearty mental shakes. "I must be going. If I'm to have a bath before dinner and arrange about—"

"These rocks," said Dimitrios, "are called the Phaedriades, the Shining Ones. Always I tell my tourists the story of the Shining Ones. Between them flows the Castalian Spring, whose water is the best in Greece. Have you tried the water of the spring, mademoiselle?"

"No, not yet. I—"

He came a step nearer. I was between him and the edge of the cliff. "They stand over the shrine like guardians, do they not? Because that is what they are. They were not only the protectors of the holy place, but they were themselves the place of execution. There were people executed on these cliffs—for sacrilege, mademoiselle. Did you know that?"

"No. But—"

Another step. He was smiling, a smile of great charm. He had a pleasant voice. Beside me in the dust I saw Danielle lift her head. I saw that her eyes now watched me, not the man. She was smiling at me with the utmost friendliness, her eyes for once bright, not tired at all. I moved back from him a step or two. It brought me within four feet of the edge.

Dimitrios said suddenly, "Be careful." I jumped and his hand came out to my arm. It was gentle on the flesh. "You are not here for execution as a traitor to the god, mademoiselle." He laughed, and Danielle smiled, and I thought suddenly, wildly, Why the hell can't I just pull my arm away and run? I hate the pair of them and they frighten me, and here I stand because it isn't polite to go while the damned man's talking.

"I always tell my tourists," he was saying, "one particular story. There was a certain traitor who was brought up here for execution. Two of them came with him to the edge . . . just there . . . to throw him

over. He looked over . . . yes, mademoiselle, it is a long way down, is
it not? . . . and then he said to them, Please will you not send me over
face first, please will you let me fall with my back to the drop? One understands how he felt, mademoiselle, does one not?"

His hand was still on my arm. I pulled back against it. It slid gently
up the flesh to the inside of my elbow. I noticed that his nails were
bitten to the quick and that his thumb was badly cut and crusted with
dried blood. I started to turn from him and to pull my arm away, but his
fingers tightened. His voice quickened a little in my ear, "So they threw
him over, mademoiselle, and as he fell, he—"

I said breathlessly, "Let me go. I don't like heights. Let me go, please."

He smiled. "Why, mademoiselle—"

Danielle's voice said, dry and thin, "Are these your tourists, Dimitrios?"

He gave an exclamation under his breath. His hand dropped from
my arm. He turned sharply.

Three people, a man and two women, were coming slowly along the
path from the direction of Arachova. The women were plain, dumpy,
middle-aged; the man was stoutish, and wore khaki shorts and had an
enormous camera slung over one perspiring shoulder. They looked at
us with incurious red faces as they plodded past like beef cattle in a
row, like angels of heaven.

I shot away from the brink of the cliff the way a cork leaves the
very best champagne. I didn't bother to say anything polite to Dimitrios,
and I didn't even fling a good-bye at Danielle.

I hurried down the path in the wake of the three tourists. Neither the
Greek nor the girl made any move to follow me, and after a while I
slackened my pace and walked more slowly, trying to control my
thoughts. If Danielle and her damned lover—for that the Greek was her
lover I had no doubt at all—had tried for some silly reason to frighten
me, they had succeeded. I had felt both frightened, and a fool, and it
was a beastly mixture. But there had surely been nothing more than that
. . . a spiteful trick and a distorted sense of humour? It was absurd to
imagine anything more. I had only done so because I had spent an ex-
acting and physically tiring day. I disliked Danielle and I had shown it,
and she had wanted to frighten and humiliate me because I had interrupted her sordid meeting with the Greek behind the junipers. And
even, perhaps, because of Simon. . . .

I had reached the stadium. The flat racetrack lay empty and silent in
the sun, cupped in its tiers of marble seats. I almost ran across the bare
dust, hurried between the columns of the starting gate, and down into the
path that led to the shrine. I found that my heart was still hammering

in my breast, and my throat was tight. The path dipped, dropped, twisted past a well where water trickled, and came precipitously down onto the smooth track above the theatre. There were my three tourists, still comfortably trudging along, talking something incomprehensible that might have been Dutch. There were people, too, in the theatre just below me, people on the steps, people everywhere on the floor of Apollo's temple. It was quite safe to stand here under the trees and wait for my heart to slow down. Quite safe. . . .

The slanting sun was golden on the quiet stones, was apricot, was amber, was a lovely liquid wash of light and peace. A bee went past my cheek.

Beside me was the pomegranate tree. The fruit glowed in the rich light. I remembered the cool feel of it in my hand last night, and Simon's voice saying: "Eat it soon, Persephone, then you'll have to stay in Delphi. . . ."

Well, I was going to stay. I was still going to stay.

My breathing was back to normal. Apollo the healer had done his work.

I went composedly down the steps, across the sunbaked circle of the theatre, down through the scented pines that rim the shrine, and along the main road to the hotel.

Even when, washing for dinner, I saw on my bare arm a streak of dried blood—Dimitrios' blood from that cut thumb—I felt only a brief moment of disgust. I had been stupid and imaginative and had had a fright; that was all.

But I felt a curious reluctance to go down to dinner before Simon appeared, and I wished with a quite startling fervour that I was not committed to sleeping in the studio that night.

CHAPTER XIII

. . . With hollow shriek the steep of Delphos *leaving.*
MILTON: *Nativity Hymn.*

IT MUST have been close on three o'clock in the morning when something woke me. My room was second from the end of the long corridor, next to Danielle's, and at the opposite end from the outer door, near which were the rooms of the two men. The Dutch painter had gone that day, so we four were the only occupants of the studio.

For some time I lay in that heavy state between sleep and waking where it is hard to disentangle reality from the trailing clouds of dream. Something had woken me, but whether I had heard a noise, or whether it was the dream itself that had startled me awake, I couldn't tell. There was no sound outside. The quiet air of Delphi wrapped us round. I moved my cheek against the hard pillow—pillows in Greece are always made like bricks—and prepared to drift back into sleep again.

From the next room came the sound of a movement, and then the creak of the bed—two sounds so completely normal and expected that they should never have roused me further. But with them came a third sound that brought my eyes wide open in the dark and my cheek up off the pillow, and made nonsense of the normality of the night. Someone was talking, very softly: a man.

My first thought was embarrassment of having heard, my next irritation succeeded by disgust. If Danielle had to have her lover in her room I didn't want to be pilloried, sleepless, on the other side of a too-thin partition. I turned over with as much fuss of bedclothes and creak of bedsprings as I could, to let them know how thin the wall was, then I pulled the sheet—it was too hot for blankets—over my head, and tried to stop my ears to the sounds that succeeded the whispering.

Sleep had gone for good. I lay rigid under the sheet with my eyes wide open in the darkness and my hands as hard as I could bear to hold them over my ears. It wasn't that I'm particularly a prude; but being forced to listen in on anyone's more private moments isn't pleasant, and I didn't want any part or parcel or hint of the more private moments of Danielle. Her public moments were quite embarrassing enough.

I wondered how the unpleasant Dimitrios had got into the place. Even though he was only here to visit Danielle, I didn't one bit like the idea of his being free to come and go. I supposed that he might have climbed in by her window, and if so, sooner or later he would go out the same way. I would no doubt hear him scramble out and drop the twelve feet or so to the floor of the rocky platform where the studio was built. I waited, furious with Danielle for subjecting me to this, furious with myself for minding, furious with Dimitrios for pandering to her monstrous egotism. It was a beastly experience.

How long it was before there was quiet from the next room I don't know. It seemed an age. But after a while all was silent, except for the whispering again, and then I heard someone moving furtively across the floor. I waited for the sounds of the window, and the cat-foot drop to the ground outside. But they didn't come. I heard the door to the corridor open, and steps went stealthily past my door.

That brought me upright in bed with a quick nervous jerk of the heart. If Danielle wanted to let a man in and out of her room, very well. But she had no damned right to let a man like Dimitrios loose inside the place. Had she—*had she?*—given him a key?

Then, out of the dark, came another thought that kicked through those nerves again.

Perhaps it wasn't Dimitrios at all.

Perhaps it was Nigel.

I was out of bed and had thrust my feet into my slippers, and was shrugging my way into the light summer coat that also served me for a dressing gown, before I quite realized myself what I was going to do. Then I had fled across the little room and had, very softly, opened my door and was peering out into the corridor.

I suppose this bit isn't pretty. It wasn't any business of mine if Nigel had gone to Danielle's room and got what had been so patently his heart's desire. But when I had thought of him I had had a memory, sudden and bright and clean, of the young eagerness of Nigel's face; the vulnerable eyes and the weak mouth and the silly boy's beard. And I had seen his drawings, the visions of tree and flower and stone that he had translated with such impeccable and yet impassioned skill. If this, too, was Nigel . . . I had to know. Call it sheer, vulgar, woman's curiosity if you like, but I had to know if the impossible Danielle could really annex him like that—if she was really prepared to make Nigel, whom she despised, squander himself in worship at her shoddy little shrine.

I believe I was thinking, incoherently, that something must be done to stop her ruining Nigel, and then, even more incoherently, of Simon. Simon must be told tomorrow. Simon would know what to do. . . .

I slipped softly out of my room. The outer door at the end of the corridor had its upper half of glass, and outside it the dark was slackening off into dawn. The pane was grey. Against it I saw him.

He was almost at the end of the corridor, standing outside a door—Nigel's door—as if he had paused there waiting for something. I shrank against the wall, but even if he had looked back he could not have seen me against the darkness at my end of the passage. I stayed still, pressed against the cold marble, and felt humiliated and angry and ashamed all at once, wishing I hadn't known, wishing I was still fathoms deep in sleep, wishing I could remember Nigel by his work and not, as now, through the smudgy little whispers of Danielle. . . . "Men are all the

same anyway . . . it bores me . . . I want Simon . . . I genuinely
do. . . ."

The silhouette at the corridor's end moved at last. He took a step forward and put his hand to the knob of the door Then he paused again,
momentarily, with his head bent, as if listening.

I thought I must have made some sound and that he had heard me,
because I could see, now, that it wasn't the Greek: it was too tall. It
wasn't Nigel either. It was Simon.

If I had been in a condition to think, the swift and complete rebellion
of every nerve and muscle in my body, and of every drop of blood in
my brain, would have told me finally about myself and Simon. But I
had hardly realized what I had seen, when the night broke open rather
more really, and very much more noisily.

Simon pushed open Nigel's door. I saw him reach up as if for the
light switch, but even as he moved the beam of a powerful torch speared
out of the darkness of the room to catch him full on the face and chest.
I saw his fractional check and recoil, as if the light were a physical
blow in the eyes, but the pause was less than momentary, no more than
the tensing before the spring. Before he had even blinked once he had
launched himself forward along the beam of light, with the speed of a
bullet. I heard an impact, a curse, the swift stamp and flurry of feet on
the stone floor, and then all hell seemed to break loose inside the room.

I ran down the corridor and paused in the doorway. The little room
seemed to be a pandemonium of violently struggling bodies. In the
weaving, flashing beam of the torch the two men looked enormous, and
their shadows towered and waved grotesquely over ceiling and walls.
Simon was the taller, and seemed to have a momentary advantage. He
had the other's wrist in one hand and seemed to be struggling to twist
the man's arm so that the torch would light his features. The beam swung
wildly, erratically, as the other fought to resist him, the light sweeping in
violent, broken arcs through the darkness. It caught me, standing in the
doorway, and raked a brilliant curve across my feet and the skirt of the
nightdress below my coat. Someone snarled something incomprehensible
in Greek, and then the man had wrenched his arm free from Simon's grip
and, with a grunt of effort, brought the heavy torch down in a vicious
blow aimed for Simon's head. Even as the blow whistled down, Simon
jerked aside, so that the torch came down with a sickening sound on the
side of his neck. It must have struck a muscle, for his grip seemed to
loosen, and the Greek tore free.

It must, after all, have been Dimitrios. I saw the stocky body and
broad shoulders in the erratic light before Simon was on him again, and

the torch flew wide, to strike the wall beside me and fall to roll somewhere near the foot of the bed. Darkness stamped down. I had no time to wonder about Dimitrios—why he had come to Nigel's room, why Simon had followed him, or even—strangest of all—why Nigel himself didn't appear to be here, when the two men, at grips again, hurtled past me to come violently up against the door of the shower stall. There was a crack as a wooden panel gave way; somewhere on the floor was the sharp explosion of breaking glass; one of the flimsy chairs went over with a splintering sound; then the bedsprings crashed and whined as the two bodies went down on the bed together.

I flung myself to my knees not two feet from the heaving bed, groping wildly for the torch. Somewhere here I had heard it roll . . . not far, surely? . . . these things rolled in semicircles . . . ah! . . . there it was. I clutched it, groping at the metal to find the catch, wondering if the fall had broken the bulb. . . .

It was a heavy torch and the catch was stiff. The bed, rocking like a ship in a storm, shot away a foot from the wall on screaming castors, hurtled back again with a crash that should have brought the plaster off the walls. The springs creaked, strained, gave again with an appalling noise as the men slithered to the edge and then fell to the floor.

A moment of gasping stillness, and then they were on their feet again. A pause, filled with the sound of heavy breathing. I jumped to my feet, still wrestling with the torch, and suddenly the thing flashed on in my hand. For the second time that night it caught Simon full in the eyes. And this time the Greek, seizing the advantage like lightning, charged down the beam, out of the blinding light. Simon went down with a crash that shook the room. I saw him catch the edge of the bed with his shoulder as he fell. The blow must have momentarily crippled him, but, surprisingly, the Greek didn't follow it up. Nor did he turn to deal with me. He had his back to me, and the light waveringly pinned for a moment the heavy bull-like shoulders, the dark curled hair. . . . He didn't even look round. I heard a gasping snarl in French, *"Put the bloody thing out, will you?"*

I hit him as hard as I could over the head.

I missed him. Just as the blow fell, something warned him. He didn't turn into the light. He lashed backwards with a crooked elbow that caught the torch, knocking it flying, then swept on to strike me full across the breast in a heavy blow that sent me staggering to fall at the foot of the bed. The torch hurtled wide a second time and went out for good. As I went down I saw, in one swift flash of the flying light, the Greek turn and leap for the doorway, with Simon after him in a lunge. And in the doorway stood Danielle, fully dressed, with wide brilliant eyes and parted lips.

She whipped back to let the man pass. Then, with a languid-seeming movement that was nevertheless as swift as a snake's, she stepped into the path of Simon's rush. I heard the other man running up the corridor towards her room and the open window, as Simon came violently up against her body. I heard her gasp as his weight jammed her hard against the doorpost. He stopped short.

I couldn't see more than the dim outlines of movement against the grey light of the corridor, but she must have been clinging to him, for he said, harsh and breathless, *"Let me go!"* and she laughed in her throat. Along the corridor a door slammed. Simon moved sharply and I heard him say, very softly, "Do you hear me? Take your hands away, or you'll get hurt."

I hadn't heard him even sound ruffled before; now I realized with something like a sharp little shock that he was angry. Danielle must not have set much store by it, for I heard her murmur, with the breath hurrying through the husky voice, "Go on doing that. I like it. . . ."

There was a second of frozen silence, then in the near-darkness the group by the door exploded into movement. The girl was flung aside against the other door jamb with a violence that sent the breath out of her in a sharp cry that held more surprise than anything else. Before she could recover herself Simon was back in the room, hurling himself across it towards the window, tearing at the catch.

The casement was rusty, and it must have been stiff. As it screeched wider I heard, like an echo at the other end of the building, the shriek of rusty hinges, and the thud as a heavy body dropped to the ground. Steps clattered and slithered away into the darkness.

Simon was up on the sill, a dark bulk against the greying sky. But before he could swing himself out and after the quarry Danielle flew after him like an arrow and clung to his arm.

"Simon . . . Simon, let him go, Simon dear, what a fuss. . . ." In spite of his recent violence she clung to him still, pleading in that voice which under its overtones of sexiness might have held a touch of fear. "Simon, no! He was with me. Don't you understand? *With me.*"

I saw his hand fall from the window catch. He turned. "What? What d'you mean?"

"What I say. He was in my room. He only came to see me."

I said from the floor beside the bed where I was still sitting, "It's true. I heard them."

I heard her laugh again, but the sound didn't hold its usual assurance. Simon shook her off as if she didn't exist and dropped lightly back into the room. "I—see. He's gone, anyway . . . Camilla? Are you all right?"

"Perfectly. Is there any light?"

"I think the bulb's out. Half a minute." He seemed to be feeling in his pockets. "What are you doing down there? Did that brute hit you?"

"Yes, but I'm all right. I was just—I was keeping out of the way." I got up a bit unsteadily and sat on the bed, just as Simon found matches and struck one. He surveyed me by its light. I smiled rather waveringly up at him. I saw then that he was dressed only in a pair of grey flannels. In the light of the match I could see the gleam of sweat on his chest and a shining dark trickle of blood from a cut at the base of the neck, where a deep V of sunburn showed. He was breathing a little faster than usual—not much, but perceptibly a bit faster—and his eyes for once didn't look cool and amused at all. But the match burned steadily in a tremorless hand. I asked anxiously, "What about you?"

"Don't give it a thought. Honours were about even . . . more's the pity."

Danielle said petulantly, "What did you have to fight for?"

He said crisply, "My dear girl, he attacked me. What would you expect me to do?" He had lit another match and was looking round the room for the light bulb.

I said, "That was Dimitrios, wasn't it?"

Simon gave me a fleeting look of surprise as he picked the light bulb up from the washbasin. Danielle turned her head as if startled, then smiled that cat-and-cream smile of hers. "You recognized him? Of course."

Simon had dragged one of the wooden chairs forward, and now mounted it to fit the light bulb into its socket. The light flashed on, harsh on the disorder of the bare little room. He got off the chair, looking at me.

"Are you sure you're all right?"

"Quite. But, Simon—where's Nigel?"

"I've no idea. He hasn't been to bed; that much is apparent." In spite of the tossed state of the bed, the sheet still lay tucked flatly in. No one had slept there. Simon hesitated, then turned to Danielle. She was standing near the door, leaning against the wall in a pose of lazy grace. Her eyes looked long and sleepy again under the thick lashes. She had taken a cigarette out of a pocket and was lighting it. She dropped the burnt-out match on the floor. All through the operation the narrow glinting gaze had been on Simon . . . all over him.

He said flatly, "You say that man was with you? How did he get in?"

"I let him in."

"By the door?"

"No. By my window."

"Come off it, Danielle. Your window's twelve feet from the ground. Don't tell me you plaited sheets or let down your hair for him. Did you unlock the door for him, or has he got a key?"

She said sulkily, under the coldness of his voice, "I don't see what the hell it's got to do with you, but yes, I did unlock it."

"It's got everything to do with me that your visitor was apparently prowling round where he's no damned right to be. And there's the little detail that he went for me with apparent intent to do damage, if not worse. What was he doing in Nigel's room?"

"How do I know?"

"He jumped out of your window in the end. He could have gone that way in the first place. Why didn't he?"

"It was easier to get out through the door, and quieter. The key's in the lock."

"Then why did he come in here?"

She shrugged. "He must have heard you moving and dodged in so that you wouldn't see him. I don't know."

"He couldn't have known there was no one in the room."

"I'd told him they were nearly all empty. I expect he took a chance. And now I'm tired of this, and tired of the inquisition, and I'm going to bed." She straightened, yawning deliberately and daintily, like a cat, showing all her pretty teeth and that pale pink tongue. Then she turned her head and let the big sleepy eyes move insolently over me. Simon had found the end of a battered pack of cigarettes in his trouser pocket and had given me one. He bent over me to light it. His breathing was quite even again now. If it hadn't been for the cut where the torch had hit him, and that thin glaze of sweat drying on his skin, you would never have guessed that a few minutes ago he had been fighting for his life in the dark.

Danielle said, sounding suddenly waspish, "What are you doing here anyway, Camilla?"

"I heard a noise and I came along."

She smiled. "And got knocked down. Did he hurt you?"

"I hope not as much as I hurt him."

She looked momentarily startled, and this gave me a quite absurd prick of satisfaction. "You hurt him? How?"

"I hit him over the back of the neck with the torch. Hard."

She stared at me for a moment longer, a very queer look.

"You hit him?" Her voice sounded quite shaken. "I can't see—you

have no business. . . . He is my lover, and if I wish to let him come here—"

I said sharply, "He was doing his best to kill Simon. And besides, I owed him something."

She looked at me almost stupidly. "You—owed him something?"

"Yes. And don't play the innocent, Danielle. You didn't look so innocent on the Shining Ones this afternoon."

"I . . . see."

She let out a breath. Simon said sharply, "What are you talking about? What happened?"

"Nothing. It was Camilla's imagination. She thinks Dimitrios—oh, it's so silly that I won't speak of it. It was a joke. And now I'm sick of this. I'm going." She dropped the half-smoked cigarette on the floor and turned quickly. I got to my feet.

"Just a minute," said Simon pleasantly. "No, please don't go yet, Camilla. We're forgetting Nigel. Danielle, have you any idea where he might be? Did he say anything last night to—?"

She said viciously, "Why should I know where the fool went? I don't know and I don't care. He could be dead as far as I'm concerned."

I said, "I think I know where he went."

Simon was dabbing at his cut neck with a handkerchief. I saw his brows shoot up. "You seem to know an awful lot tonight."

"Doesn't she?" Danielle had stopped in the doorway, and turned her head sharply. Her voice was not, like his, amused. "All right, you tell us."

I said, "It's only a guess. But . . . well, Simon, d'you remember our talk in here the other night, about Nigel and his work, and needing a gimmick, and the Dutch boy walking from Jannina and all that?"

"Yes. You're not suggesting that Nigel has taken a leaf out of that boy's book, are you?"

I said, "There's been a mule stolen from the excavations above the shrine. I know because the guide told me this morning . . . yesterday morning, I suppose I should say. And I saw Nigel early the same morning, and he was trying not to be seen—"

"Where?" asked Danielle.

"Just outside the studio here."

"Which way was he going?"

"I didn't see. He seemed to be making farther up Parnassus—towards the stadium."

"Ah well," said Simon, "you may be right. I suppose what Nigel does is very much his own affair, and he was certainly feeling thoroughly unsettled. He may easily have cut loose for a few days." He turned to rinse his bloodstained handkerchief out under the tap. "I think we'd better just tidy his room up and get out of it. There's blood on the washbasin here, and I'm afraid the floor isn't all it should be. We'd better have a look at the damage and do what we can."

I said, "Leave that. I'll clean the basin up. But let me have a look at that cut, will you? Danielle, perhaps you'll be good enough to clear the floor and pick up that broken glass?"

She sent me one of those looks of glittering dislike, which was, this time, quite justified. "It won't take you long. I'm tired. You forget, I haven't been to sleep yet tonight, and oh, how I need that sleep. . . ." She yawned, sent another narrow-eyed look at me, and went out rather quickly, shutting the door behind her.

Seconds later, from the other end of the corridor, came like an echo the slam of her bedroom door.

CHAPTER XIV

Courage is a thing
All men admire. Think what it will mean
For your good name and mine, if you do this.
SOPHOCLES: *Ajax*
(*tr. E. F. Watling*).

IN NIGEL'S ROOM there was the sort of silence that is usually called pregnant. But at least, I reflected, there was no longer any need to suppress the urge to discuss Danielle. . . .

My eyes met Simon's in the mirror. "You wanted to get rid of her, didn't you?"

"You're coming on with that thought-reading, aren't you? I did indeed."

"Why?" I added, carefully, "Apart, that is, from the obvious reasons."

The brief amusement in his eyes vanished as he turned and looked down at me. His look was grave, sombre even. "Because I don't like the feel of this thing, Camilla."

"The feel of it?"

"Yes. Too much is happening. Some of it may be irrelevant, or it may matter the hell of a lot. Danielle and this man, for instance. . . . And Danielle and Nigel. I've begun to wonder."

"Then I was right. Turn round towards the light and let me have a look at that cut . . . you didn't want me to go on talking about Nigel in front of her?"

"No."

"It's not deep, but you're going to have a bruise and a stiff shoulder, I think. Have you any antiseptic in your room? You don't think he's gone off with a Modestine into the mountains?"

"Yes. No, I mean. No, I don't believe he's off on a trip, but yes, I have some antiseptic."

"Then don't forget to put it on. The wound's quite clean and it's stopped bleeding." I stood back and looked at him inquiringly. "Then what have Danielle and Nigel and this Greek of hers got to do with us—with you, I mean?"

He said slowly, "This Greek—this lover of Danielle's . . . you said his name was Dimitrios?"

"Yes. I met him yesterday on the way back from the corrie. He was with her above the Shining Ones."

"Ah, yes. The Shining Ones. What happened there, incidentally? What did you 'owe' Dimitrios?"

"Oh, it was nothing, really. He was unpleasant in a greasy sort of way, and talked a lot about people being thrown off the cliff and so on. We were awfully near the edge and he could see I didn't like it, and it amused him . . . and Danielle too. It was just a nasty little trick to make me look a fool—which I did, I may say. I bolted."

There was a frown between his eyes. "I see. Camilla, has nothing occurred to you about this—Dimitrios?"

"Occurred to me? What sort of thing? I don't like him, and I think—" I stopped short. I said, on a long breath, *"Dimitrios!"*

"Exactly. You remember? Angelos had a cousin called Dimitrios Dragoumis, who had gone to live at Itea. At Itea, mark you."

"And I saw the jeep down at Itea . . . Danielle had driven it straight down there when she got in from Athens! If it's the same Dimitrios . . . then Dimitrios Dragoumis is Danielle's lover, and that was his house I saw. She wasn't visiting any friend called 'Elena,' she was visiting him, and I'll bet, if the jeep's anything to go by, that she was there when I passed the house!"

"You're certain it was the same jeep?"

"Quite. I told you I recognized the doll hanging in the windscreen. There was someone tinkering with the engine, and that wasn't Dimitrios, but all the same, I've a feeling we're right. It's the same Dimitrios. That would explain why Danielle's so darned interested in you." I added, "Or partly."

He passed that one.

"Well, then, say we're right, and let's look at what we have . . . Dimitrios Dragoumis is Danielle's lover. Whether there actually is anyone called Elena or not, it's quite true that Danielle has been in the habit of spending her afternoons down near Itea, swimming. She told me once she'd found a secluded little cove where the water was clean (it's filthy in Itea itself) but she wouldn't tell me where it was. My guess is that she met, not 'Elena,' but Dimitrios, on these swimming expeditions, and took up with him. He may have been there to fish—he's a fisherman, did I tell you, and owns a caique?"

"He told me he was a guide."

"There's no guide in Delphi of that name, that I do know; and if he took the trouble to lie . . ." He didn't finish the sentence. He was frowning down at his cigarette. "Well, let's go on. Dimitrios, the cousin of Angelos, sends Danielle into Athens to hire him a car—on a matter of life and death. In other words, in a hell of a hurry."

"Well?"

His eyes lifted. "An expensive need. And he's a sailor. Why would he want a car?"

I sat down again on the bed. "I don't know. Go on."

Absently, he flicked a gout of ash into the washbasin.

"Danielle hired a car for him, but then got the better offer of a jeep from her French friend Hervé Clément, and came up in that. She didn't revisit the garage to let them know . . . and she hadn't given them Dragoumis' name—hence all the nonsense about 'Monsieur Simon,' and the interfering but well-meant efforts of Miss Camilla Haven. But Danielle's actions do spell something, don't they?"

"Urgency," I said slowly, "yes. And secrecy?"

"Exactly. And I could bear to know what's urgent and secret about Danielle, and Dimitrios the cousin of Angelos," said Simon.

A pause. A beetle blundered in through the open casement, hit the wall with a crack like a pistol shot, and zoomed out again into the dark.

"But—the car?" I said, seizing on what was still my own piece of the mystery. "Why the car? You said Dimitrios Dragoumis was a fisherman. What would he need a car for, from Athens, with all that hush-hush nonsense about it?"

"That's just it," said Simon. "He is a fisherman, and he owns a boat. And now he has a jeep . . . got from Athens and kept very quiet locally. To me, that adds up to one thing. Transport."

I said, in a voice that sounded queer, "Urgent, secret transport . . ." Then, sitting up briskly, "But—*no,* Simon. It's absurd."

"Why?"

"I can see what you're getting at . . . the reason why Angelos' cousin might need this urgent and secret transport. You mean that you think Dimitrios has found Angelos' cache—whatever it was that Michael found on Parnassus? And the jeep and the caique are to carry—oh!"

"Well?"

"*The mule!* Simon—the mule!"

He nodded. "You can't take a jeep up Parnassus, can you? The mule was stolen the night I saw Stephanos. Danielle brought the jeep up the same day. I'll bet you anything you like that Dimitrios' caique will shortly be lying carefully invisible in one of the tiny inlets beyond Amphissa."

I said, "Look, hold on, Simon. You're only guessing. It *could* have been Nigel who took the mule. He's gone off somewhere, and we were talking about the Dutch boy to him, and—"

"And it would have been very much simpler for Nigel to have bought the donkey—which went dirt cheap—off the Dutch boy," said Simon, "than to have stolen a mule from the excavations. He wasn't all that hard up, and there really wasn't all that need of secrecy for *him.* In fact, if he was off on a trek of that sort, you'd even have thought publicity was necessary."

"Yes, I suppose so. All the same, he looked pretty secretive when I saw him sloping off yesterday morning."

"Oh? But I still don't think he took the mule. It vanished on Monday night, and that night Nigel was up here. Of course he did go out later for a walk with Danielle, but I hardly think—"

I said tautly, "You're right. It wasn't Nigel. I've just remembered something. When we were in the theatre, and you were reciting, I was up near the top row of seats, and I heard something moving up the hillside above me. You know how you hear something without really taking it in consciously, until, later, something reminds you? Well, it was like that. I thought nothing of it—if I heard it at all, I thought it was just the breeze, or a stray goat or donkey or something. But I remember now that I heard metal—a small chinking of metal, like a shod hoof, or the nails of a boot."

Simon smiled slightly. "The beasts here aren't shod. Hadn't you noticed? And the locals wear rope-soled espadrilles on the hill. If you heard movement and the chink of metal, Camilla, then you heard a beast's bridle. It sounds to me as if you really might have heard the mule being stolen. Friend Dimitrios, taking the mule off up the hill. Well, well."

I said sharply, "Simon, if he was above the theatre when you were reciting, he'd hear us, wouldn't he?"

"Almost certainly." He laughed. "Though I'm afraid he'd hardly appreciate *Electra*. He's not likely to know any classical Greek."

"Not only that," I said uneasily, trying to remember. "We talked about Michael, and—"

"In English, though. It's very probable he doesn't understand that well enough, either. Let's hope not."

I cried, "He doesn't! Danielle told me so yesterday—and there'd be no reason for her to lie to me then. . . . But look, Simon, you can't be right; about the reason for all this, I mean. It really is absurd. Maybe Dimitrios is up to no good, and maybe Danielle is in it, and maybe they did steal the mule and hire the car to transport something, but it can't, it just can't, be Michael's 'treasure'!"

"Why not?"

"Because it's too much to swallow that Dimitrios should have spent fourteen years or so looking for the stuff, and just have found it now. Oh, I grant you he could have searched a thousand years and never found it, especially if he didn't have precise information from Angelos— and he probably didn't, because you can be sure Angelos meant to come back when things had simmered down enough for him to leave Yugoslavia and come home. He may not have told Dimitrios at all. Dimitrios may merely have guessed that Angelos had hidden something, and not have known where to start looking. But what I can't swallow is the assumption that he should have found Angelos' cache *now,* this week, the very week you're in Delphi. That's too much of a coincidence, and I don't believe it."

"But is it?"

"How d'you mean?"

He said slowly, "You've got it the wrong way round. Supposing those two things *have* happened at the same time: I am here in Delphi, and Dimitrios finds Angelos' cache on Parnassus. You call it coincidence. I call it cause and effect."

"You mean—?"

"That the two incidents are certainly related, but not by chance. Dimitrios found the hiding place, not just while I happen to be here— but simply *because* I'm here."

I stared up at him. I passed my tongue over my lips. "You mean— that he followed us up to the corrie yesterday?"

"Precisely that. He could have found out when we were going and he could have come to spy."

I said hoarsely, "He did. When I was sitting there in the corrie and you were in the cave with the other two men, I thought I saw something move at the top of the cliff. It could have been someone watching."

His gaze sharpened. "Are you sure of that?"

"Not really. But I thought there was movement, and looked up, but couldn't see anything. The sun was in my eyes."

"I see. Well, it might have been Dimitrios. And then he followed us down, intending to meet Danielle on top of the Shining Ones. Could be."

I said, "I did her an injustice. I thought they'd been together, and I'd interrupted them."

"He'd hardly have had time to get down there before you. Most of the way it's pretty open, and we might have seen him." He thought for a few moments. "Well, let's look at the sequence of events, shall we? Dimitrios, you'll remember, did try to find out from Stephanos—the only man who knew anything definite about the place where Michael died—anything he could about Michael's death. He didn't get anything out of Stephanos. Perhaps he did try to find the place himself. Perhaps he did gather a slender clue or two from his cousin before he left the country. But even with definite instructions from Angelos he still could have been raking the mountain all this time and found nothing. All the marks, like the Cat's Tooth pinnacle, have gone, and anything could lie buried under that earthquake rubble for fourteen years—or fourteen hundred—undiscovered. Angelos himself, if he were still alive, and if he came back to look, would be in exactly the same case."

I said, rather breathlessly, "Niko said there were ghosts on the hill . . . lights . . . d'you remember?"

"Niko talked a lot of rubbish, but he may well have told the truth there. Dimitrios may have been seen searching. But, to go on with the story—supposing he *had* searched all that time, and had had no luck in locating the cache, then, after years, he heard that I, Michael Lester's brother, was coming to Delphi. This might prove to be his chance. What is more likely than that Stephanos would show me, Michael's brother, the place? When I arrived, Stephanos was away in Levadia, but Dimitrios could easily find out when he was coming back. It's quite some time since I planned this visit; Dimitrios could have known, and taken time over his preparations. Supposing we were right, and he had noticed Danielle driving down almost daily to Itea with the jeep to bathe? Here was transport of the kind he would need. He wouldn't dare buy or hire transport locally; he's well known, and people would ask questions. But it would be easy enough to scrape acquaintance with Danielle, and buy her silence—and her help—with a promise to cut her in on the final haul. It would only remain to collect a mule or a donkey, and there again Danielle was the answer. I'll bet you she took the mule; she'd worked with the archaeologists for weeks, and she knew just where everything was kept and how to get at it. . . . What is it?"

"I've just remembered. It wasn't only a mule. I remember. The guide said 'some tools and a mule.' "

"*Did* he?" His voice was still quiet, but the light-grey eyes blazed in his brown face. "Well, well, well. . . . Does it make sense, or not? Or am I jumping ahead too fast?"

"Pretty fast. They're rather scrappy bricks, and made with awfully little straw, but they could be solid. Go on."

"Where was I? Yes: Dimitrios has everything lined up for the day when Simon Lester should arrive and lead him straight to the spot where Michael died. But then he—Dimitrios—has a stroke of bad luck."

"Danielle's boss leaves Delphi, and she has to go too—with the jeep?"

"Exactly. She went on Sunday, perforce. She must have gone straight to the garage in Athens and arranged to pick up a car next day, as soon as she could get free of Monsieur Clément." He grinned. "We know what happened next. Her error. But luck came in again, as she persuaded Hervé to let her have the jeep. And she came back. She took the jeep down to Itea. Whether she brought Dimitrios up that night with her we can't know, but she probably did. She—or he—took the mule and a crowbar or so from the workmen's sheds above the shrine, *et voilà.*"

I said, "And then all Dimitrios had to do was to wait and follow us. Too easy."

"Much too easy. I should have thought of it after what Stephanos told me, but I admit it never seriously occurred to me—till I saw the earthquake damage up there—that anything that Mick found might still be hidden. However. There it is. You can bet your boots he was up there yesterday, and now all he has to do is to hunt that fairly small stretch of cliff, and then he and Danielle are made for life." He smiled down at me. "I admit it *is* a lot of bricks to make with very little straw, but where else is the straw to go? We have certain facts, and we must fit them in somewhere with the knowledge that friend Dimitrios is up to no sort of good."

"And he is the cousin of Angelos. . . . Yes, I see what you mean. But why did he come here tonight? Just to see Danielle again?"

He said soberly, "Ah, that . . . that's what I meant when I said I didn't like the feel of this affair. What we've discovered—or guessed, if you like—so far, is straightforward enough, but Nigel . . ." He paused, then turned to pitch the stub of his cigarette out of the open window. "Nigel. He's in this somewhere and I want to know where."

"You mean that Dimitrios came to see *him?*"

"No. Dimitrios came here looking for something. And I could bear to know what." He glanced round the room. "And I could also bear to know where Nigel is."

I said, "The drawings have gone."

"What? Oh, the ones on the wall. So they have. Well, the sooner we find out what else is gone the better. . . ." He began to move round the bare untidy little room as he spoke. "We'll soon see if he intended—no, don't you bother, Camilla. Sit still. There's not much searching to be done in a place this size, even if a couple of gorillas have turned everything upside down first. . . ."

"Dimitrios didn't take anything with him, anyway," I said.

"No, he didn't, did he? One might say he hardly had time. That's one satisfactory thing about tonight's affair."

"Perhaps Danielle was telling the truth. Perhaps he did only come in here to hide from you when he heard you move."

"Not on your life." He had opened the shower stall and was rummaging inside. "He didn't have time, after he'd heard me move, to take that light bulb out. He did that as soon as he got into the room, and to me that means he had some business in here that was going to take a minute or two, and he didn't want to risk being surprised and recognized. I must have heard him almost straightaway—I'd been lying awake wondering where the blazes Nigel was, and as soon as I heard the movements I got up. It didn't take me long to roll off the bed and grab my flannels and get into them, and then to get to the door. He hadn't quite shut the door—for quietness' sake, I suppose—and when I saw torchlight moving beyond it I knew it wasn't Nigel, and I went carefully. As I shoved the door open, I saw the light swinging round the room as if it was looking for something. That was all, because of course he turned on me."

I laughed. "Yes, and you told Danielle he attacked you—which, sir, was a lie. I was watching, and you went bald-headed for the poor chap before he even had time to say "Good evening!"

He grinned. "And for a very good reason. He whipped round when he heard me at the door, and he pulled a knife. I thought it best not to give him time to think about using it."

I drew a long breath. "I—see. You were right about the feel of this thing, weren't you? All I can say is, that for a member of our staid and slightly stuffy profession, your reactions are—well, fairly rapid, not to say decisive."

He was still smiling. "Two strenuous years' conscription in the tough end of the Artists' Rifles . . . besides what Michael taught me all unofficial-like. It bears fruit—besides, I'm rather afraid I enjoyed it. I like a good and dirty fight. . . . I say, Camilla."

"Yes?"

"His things *are* all gone."

"Everything? Not just his painting things?"

"Everything, I think. The rucksack—see, he used to hang it on this peg. I suppose he didn't carry a razor, but the towel's gone too, and the soap, and what clothes he had. And unlike me he was conventional even in this climate and wore pyjamas. Are they tucked down there under the sheet?"

"I don't think so. No, they're not."

He said, sounding at once puzzled and relieved, "Then he meant to go anyway. Damn the boy, he might have told me, and saved me a couple of sleepless hours. Well, at least he isn't sitting up on Parnassus somewhere with a sprained ankle, whatever else he's got himself into. I'll just make sure there's nothing down here. . . . Ah, there's the Greek's knife. I thought I heard it fly under the bed. And that hellish clanging noise we made was Nigel's apology for a wastepaper basket. . . . Lord, what a mess! Orange peel and pencil shavings and all the dud drawings he's thrown away. I really think we'll have to bribe our way out of this, Camilla my girl."

"For goodness' sake, let me help." I slipped from the bed to the floor and gathered up a handful of papers. I dropped them into the biscuit tin that served Nigel for a wastebasket. "I'll clear this stuff up. You see if that chair'll mend, and straighten the table. There's no damage except the broken glass, and we better leave that till morning and see if we can find a brush and—*Simon!*"

He was busy straightening the furniture. He swung round. "What is it?"

"These papers . . . they're not 'dud drawings' at all. They're—they're the finished things, his Hellenic types!" I shuffled them through my hands. "Yes, look, here they are! There's that head that's a bit like Stephanos, and the smiling one that looked like a statue, and that must be the Minoan girl he told us about—and here's a shepherd boy. And more . . . look." I began to leaf through them rapidly. My hand wasn't quite steady. I said, "I know he was doing them under protest, and he *was* feeling at odds with life, but surely, Simon, he can't afford to throw them away? What in the world—?" I stopped short.

Simon said sharply from above me, "What is it?"

I said shakily, "This one. This is the head, that lovely, lovely head. The young man with the strange face. And look, he's torn it up. Not the others, but this. It's torn right across." I looked down at the fragments on my lap and said sadly, "He needn't have torn it up. It was beautiful."

He stooped to take the pieces from me, and studied them for a few moments in silence.

At length he said, "What else is there? Not the flower studies, surely?"

"No. No. They're all the 'types,' except that lovely head."

I heard him take a breath, as if of relief, and when he spoke I knew he had had the same fleeting stab of fear as I myself. "Then—whatever made him go—I don't think we need worry overmuch. That fit of the blues hasn't made him plan anything foolish after all; he's taken the good stuff with him. Except this . . ." He opened his fingers, and let the fragments drift down onto my lap. The action was like a shrug; a sigh. "Ah, well, we can't guess what's biting the boy. But I'll be thankful when I know—"

I said abruptly, "*The cyclamen.*"

He said, suddenly sounding very weary, "Is that there as well, after all?"

"No. It's not here. That's not what I meant. But I've remembered something, Simon, and I think it's important. Yesterday, when we were up in the corrie—Michael's corrie—I saw a plant of cyclamen growing in the rock. I didn't realize it at the time—at least I think I must have subconsciously, because I know I was thinking about Nigel as I looked at it —but it was the same plant that was in the drawing. I tell you, I didn't connect it then; but now, when we were talking about his drawings, I somehow saw it again. And it was the same. I'm sure of it. And that means that Nigel's been up in that corrie too!" I drew a deep breath. "And perhaps, if *Nigel* had found Angelos' cave, that would explain some of the things he said on Monday night. Simon, Nigel was in that corrie, and, if you ask me, Nigel found the cave! And Angelos' hoard was still there!"

Simon said, hard and sharp, "Then if Nigel found anything in that corrie, he found it on Monday. He did that drawing on Monday."

"Yes, and he told you he'd done no work, till we found that he'd slipped up over the Phormis head and the cyclamen!"

He said slowly, "It could be. I went up some of the way over the track with him on Sunday. He might have gone back on his own and stumbled on the place. One of those weird freaks of chance, but they do happen. Oh, my God, suppose he did?"

We stared at each other. I said, "And yesterday morning I saw him setting off again . . . and looking secretive about it. Simon, perhaps it was *Nigel* who took the mule. Perhaps we're wrong about Danielle. Perhaps Nigel's trying to move the stuff, whatever it is, himself."

Simon said, in a harsh voice that was anything but casual, "And if he is? If he's got across that damned Greek in the process? Don't forget he's somewhere in this too."

"Perhaps he's working with that damned Greek," I said.

"Perhaps."

I said, "Simon, don't worry so. One thing's obvious; he did mean to go. He's cleared up here, and he's scrapped the stuff he didn't want. Whatever he's up to, and even if his affairs *have* tangled with Dimitrios', he's gone deliberately. He may have got himself into something illegal, or at most immoral, but he meant to, and—well, you can't really be his keeper to that extent, can you?"

He hesitated, then suddenly smiled. "I suppose not. At least, not till it's daylight."

I said, making a statement of it, "You're going up there, of course."

"Of course. I intended to anyway, and now it seems I shall have to."

"When do we start?"

He looked down at me for a moment. That unreadable mask had shut down again over his face. I don't know what I expected him to say. I know what nine men out of ten would have said—and Philip would have said it twice.

Simon didn't say it at all. He said merely, "I'll come and call you. And now you'd better go and sleep. We'll have to make an early start."

I got to my feet. "Will you take Stephanos and Niko?"

"No. For one thing it would take too long, and for another, if there's anything to be found that Nigel and/or Dimitrios haven't already found and moved, I don't want witnesses till I know where Nigel comes in, and whose property it is. If it is arms and gold, the ownership might be a rather delicate political question under present circumstances."

"Heavens, yes. I hadn't thought of that."

"And now let me see you back to your room. . . . By the way I haven't thanked you yet for bashing friend Dimitrios over the head for me."

"I'd never have got near him," I said truthfully, "if he hadn't thought I was Danielle. And I missed him anyway."

"All the same it was a stout effort."

He opened the door, and I went past him into the chilly corridor.

"They taught us a lot," I said sedately, "in the tough end of St. Trinian's."

CHAPTER XV

"Tell the Emperor that the bright citadel is fallen to the ground; Apollo has no longer any shelter, or oracular laurel tree, or speaking fountain. Even the vocal stream has ceased to flow."

The Delphic Oracle to the Emperor Julian.

IT CAN'T have been much after six when Simon woke me. I had sleepily answered "Come in" to his knock before I remembered that I was no longer in the hotel, and this was not likely to be a chambermaid with a cup of tea. As I turned my head, looking, still sleepy-eyed, towards the door, it opened. Simon didn't come in, but I heard his voice.

"Camilla."

"Mmm? Oh—Simon. Yes?"

"Could you bear to get up now, d'you suppose? I think we ought to move. I've got coffee on a Primus if you would like to come along and get it when you're dressed."

"All right."

"Good." The door shut. I shot, fully awake now, out of bed, and began to dress quickly. From my window I could see the morning sunlight sliding like apricot bloom over the rounded top of Mount Cirphis.

In my room it was still cool, for which I was grateful. I wasn't so grateful about the icy gush of water from the taps—both taps—but in any case washing at Delphi is a penance; the water is as hard as pumice stone, and just about as good for the skin . . . but it woke me up fully and finally, and it was with a tingling sense of new adventure that at length I went quickly along to Simon's door and tapped.

"Come in."

I noticed that he was making no attempt to keep his voice low this morning, and he must have seen a query in my face as I entered, because he looked up from the Primus he was tending and said briefly, "Danielle checked out an hour ago."

"Oh?"

"I followed her down as far as the upper road. I didn't see where she went in the village, but I did see a jeep drive off north."

"That means she's either making for Itea or further along towards Amphissa?"

"Yes. Coffee?"

"Lovely. Simon, this smells like heaven. Rolls too? You're very efficient."

"I went along to the baker's after I'd seen Danielle off the premises. Here's the sugar."

"Thank you. Where do you think she's gone?"

"God knows, and there's not much point in guessing. Probably to pick Dimitrios up in Itea—though if the jeep was in Delphi it seems odd he didn't take it last night when he got out of the studio. How d'you feel today?"

"I'm fine, thanks. And you? How's the shoulder? You're sure that was all the damage?"

"Certain. And it's really hardly stiff at all. I feel ready for anything." He was sitting on the edge of his bed, a cup of coffee in one hand and a roll in the other, looking, as ever, completely relaxed and at ease. "And you?" he said. "Ready for your adventure?"

I laughed. "I can hardly believe that two days ago I was writing to my friend that nothing ever happened to me. Is it Goethe who says somewhere that we ought to beware what we ask the gods for, because they might grant it? I asked for adventure, and it seems I got it."

He didn't smile. He appeared to consider what I'd been saying for a minute or two, then he said, quite seriously, "I ought not to let you come, you know."

I didn't ask why. I drank coffee and watched the sunlight wheel a fraction to touch the edge of the window frame. A butterfly hovered, then winnowed down to cling to the strip of sunlit stone. Its wings fanned gently, black velvet shot with gold.

Simon said, "Don't mistake me. I don't think we—you, are in any danger; but it'll be a hard day, especially following after yesterday and last night. The only possible danger is running unexpectedly into Dimitrios, who'll certainly be up there, but if we're reasonably careful, that can be avoided. I don't think he'll be expecting us. He probably thinks that, now I've seen the place, that closes the account for me."

"In any case I told Danielle we were going to the fair at Levadia."

"*Did* you? Good for you. Was she showing interest, then?"

I smiled. "Yes, she showed interest. She asked me flat out where you were going today. I—well, I'm afraid I just mistrusted her on principle, and told her a lie." I set down my coffee cup. "It seems it's just as well. Dimitrios certainly won't be looking out for us."

"Excellent," said Simon. "Of course, there's no reason anyway why he should have expected me to go up there again, is there? He doesn't know I know of the existence of any 'treasure.' If Michael had sent any information home, Dimitrios might well imagine I'd have come long ago. Cigarette?"

"Thank you."

He leaned forward to hold his lighter for me. "No," he said, "I think Dimitrios will see it as a pilgrimage for me; and that's over. All the better. But we'll be very careful, just the same. With any luck we'll see what's going on, and where Nigel comes in—and then we can think about possible reinforcements." He sent me a grin as he got up off the bed and reached for his haversack. "In any case, don't worry. All things being equal, I can deal with friend Dimitrios. And I refuse to be afraid of Nigel. Even if he has got himself mixed up in anything for the sake of the cash, he'd never in a million years do violence for gain. Or so I think."

"I agree."

"Apart from those two there's Danielle." That swift grin again. "Well, I wouldn't like to swear that I could precisely 'deal with' Danielle, but let's say I'm not afraid of her."

"We might be wrong about them," I said. "There may be nobody up there at all, except Nigel."

"It's possible"—he was packing the haversack as he talked: more of the fresh rolls, some fruit, chocolate, water: Spartan fare, but nonetheless appropriate for that—"it's quite possible that we are wrong about Dimitrios and Danielle, but in any case I'm not concerned at the moment with Michael's 'find' except as it touches Nigel." A look. "You're convinced about those flowers in the drawing, aren't you?"

"Absolutely."

"Well, that's one thing we're sure of in a maze of guesswork. We don't really know a damned thing about Dimitrios and Danielle, but we do know Nigel has been in that corrie, and we do know he was wildly excited about something that same night. And Dimitrios came here, for some purpose, to visit Nigel's room. We'll freeze on to those facts, and let the rest develop as it will. . . . Are you ready to start?"

"Yes."

"Then let's go."

Already the morning sun was warm overhead, but the rocks were still cool from the night. The path past the graveyard was wide enough for us to walk side by side.

Simon said, "All I'm hoping today is that—if you're right—we run across Nigel and see what he's up to, and knock some sense into his silly young head before he gets himself involved in something he can't get out of. And incidentally—this is the path off to the stadium—and incidentally, find the cave."

He had stopped where the narrow path left our track, and waited for me to precede him. I paused, and looked at him straightly. "Tell me one thing. Why *are* you letting me come?"

For the second time since I had known him, he seemed oddly at a loss. He hesitated, as if looking for the right words.

I said, "Granted that you don't want Stephanos and Niko along. But you'd get along much faster and do much better alone, *Kyrie* Lester, and you know it. You also know quite well that if we *do* run into Dimitrios it might develop into quite a sticky party. Why don't you leave me at home to get on with my knitting?"

A pine branch cast a bar of shade across his face, but I thought I saw a smile behind the light-grey eyes. "You know the reasons quite well, *Kyria* Haven."

"Reasons?"

"Yes."

"Well, I know the first. I wished a little too hard for an adventure, so I can darned well take what comes, and four eyes are better than two if we want to find Nigel and the cave?"

"Not quite. I had the idea that you were looking rather hard for something on your own account."

I turned abruptly and led the way up the narrow path between the pines. I said, after a bit, "Perhaps I was." Then, later still, "You—do see rather a lot, don't you?"

"And you know the second reason."

It was shady under the pines, but my cheeks felt hot. I said, "Oh?" and then felt furious with myself because the syllable seemed to be inviting an answer. I added hastily, "I can show you where the cyclamen is, of course."

"Of course," said Simon agreeably.

We had reached the stadium. We crossed the slanting shadows of the starting gate and left the trees. Behind us in the holly oaks and cypresses the birds flashed and sang. The singing echoed and rang up the limestone cliffs.

We crossed the stadium floor in silence and took the steep path that led to the rocky reaches of Parnassus.

We saw no one on our way to the corrie.

Most of the way from Delphi the track was easy to follow, and, apart from one open stretch soon after we had left the top of the Shining Ones, it wound along rocky valleys which would have offered plenty of cover in case of alarm. But the hot desert of broken rocks seemed as empty as yesterday. We travelled in short bursts, going fairly fast, but with frequent pauses in the shade to get our breath and to scan the surrounding country for signs of movement.

At length, as we made our way up a steep dry watercourse, I looked upwards to the right and saw the line of cliffs that held the corrie. Simon, who was ahead of me, stopped and turned.

"We'll wait here, I think, and eat. Look, here's a good place, in the shade between these two boulders. We can't be seen, and we can keep an eye on the valley and on those cliffs. I'd like to be quite sure no one else is about before we make our way up."

I sat down thankfully in the place he indicated, and he produced food from the haversack. The rolls didn't taste quite as good as they had in the cool of the morning, but as I ate I began to feel better. The tepid water was a benison, and the fruit was ambrosia itself. . . .

I let Simon do the watching. After I had eaten I relaxed against the rock with eyes half-shut against the light, and he lit a cigarette for me. He showed no sign of hurry or impatience, or even curiosity. We smoked in silence, and I saw his eyes move almost idly across the landscape, up to the corrie, along the cliff, down the scree, back to the corrie.

At the very edge of my vision there was a movement.

I turned my head sharply, eyes fully open now. I could see nothing. But there had been a movement; of that I was sure. I was just about to touch Simon's arm when I saw it again; it was as if one of the rocks of the scree had moved . . . a goat. It was only a goat. As it walked forward, taking shape against the void of tumbled rock, I saw others with it, two, three of them, moving purposefully along some age-old track of their own. I was wondering half-idly if there was a goatherd with them, and if perhaps they had strayed from the troop, when I thought I heard, far away over the cliff top, the sound of a pipe. Even as I heard it and strained my ears to catch the notes, it faded, and I dismissed it as fancy. The thin, broken stave had been purely pastoral, something from a myth of Arcady, nymphs and shepherds and pan-pipes and green valleys. But this was Parnassus, home of more terrible gods.

I relaxed again and watched the smoke from my cigarette wind up in the sunlight. I remember that I didn't think at all about the business of the day. I thought about Parnassus, and the gods who lived there, and Simon. . . .

I stole a look at him. He was looking almost dreamily up towards the cliffs. He looked about as tense and vigilant as in the fifth hour of the House Cricket Match. He caught my look and smiled, and moved his hand lazily to knock ash from his cigarette. I said, "A penny for them?"

"I was wondering if there was anyone with those goats. I don't think so."

"I thought I heard a pipe being played, away over there," I said, "but I expect I imagined it. Did you hear anything?"

"No. But it's possible. I don't think those three would be up here on their own. You must have very good hearing. I never heard a sound."

He crushed out his cigarette and got up, reaching a hand down to me. "Shall we go up now? I think we're unobserved, but I don't want to cross that big open stretch towards the corrie 'gateway.' If we skirt it, and go up that gully there, I think we can get round without the risk of being seen, and it'll bring us out above the cliff where we were yesterday. It'll be a bit of a stiff pull, I'm afraid. Are you tired?"

"Not a bit."

He laughed. "One up to British womanhood. Come along. And keep down. This is where the real stalk starts."

Simon lay flat at the corrie's lip, looking downwards. I crouched behind him, a little way back from the cliff edge. I waited, watching him for a signal.

It seemed an age before he moved. Then he turned his head and lifted a hand, with a slow cautious movement that carried its own warning.

In spite of myself, I could feel tension pull my nerves taut, like cold wires touching the skin. I inched forward until I lay beside Simon. I was screened by one of the low holly oaks. I lifted my head slowly till my eyes were above the level of the edge. I looked down into the corrie. There was no one there.

As I looked at him, with surprise in my face and a question, he put his lips to my ear. "Dimitrios is here."

Again that coward jerk of the heart. Every vein in my body was contracting, little thrilling wires tightening till my muscles wouldn't obey me. I found I had ducked my head down again behind the holly oak, and my cheek was on my hand in the hot dust. The hand was cold.

Simon breathed, just beside my ear, "He's just vanished somewhere underneath us. I saw him duck under that piece in the corner." He jerked his head slightly towards it. "Is that where you went exploring yesterday?"

I nodded. I swallowed, and managed to say quite evenly, "What was he doing?"

"I don't know. He just seemed to be hanging about. Waiting for someone or something. Nigel, perhaps, or—"

He broke off and seemed to go lower into the ground. I shrank down beside him. The holly oak hid me, and I peered down.

Then I saw Dimitrios. He came out from somewhere below us, ducking his head as he passed under the flying buttress that seemed to shore up the cliff. He was smoking, and his eyes were frowning and narrowed against the high blaze of the sun. He walked carefully over the rocky floor of the corrie towards the northern gap in the wall. Every now and again he stopped, and slanted his head as if to listen.

He reached the corrie entrance, and stopped there, looking down towards Amphissa. Once he turned his head and looked the other way, the way we had come, from Delphi. Then he came back into the corrie. He flung down the butt of his cigarette and lit another. I noticed sweat on his dark face and dust yellowish-white on his clothes. He wasn't in the dark suit today; he was wearing dungarees in dull faded blue, and a khaki shirt with a red kerchief knotted at the neck.

The cigarette was lit now. He dropped the match, then looked round him for a few moments as if undecided. He took a few steps into the corrie and I thought he was going back towards the corner where the cyclamen was, but he stopped suddenly, as if impatient of waiting, turned sharply on his heel, and walked, rapidly now, as if his mind was at last made up, out of the corrie.

Simon said in my ear, "Gone to meet Nigel, or Danielle, do you suppose? Give him a minute or two."

We gave him five. They seemed very long minutes. There was no other sound in the hot morning but our own breathing. The sun beat down on us as we lay on the bare earth. I was thankful when Simon moved at last.

We got quickly to our feet, and went down the twisting little path like a couple of mountain goats. We almost ran across the corrie floor and ducked under the fallen rock into the corner.

There it was, the patch of brilliant green, and the drifts of tiny blue bells, the lovely traces of the mountain rain. But today it was different.

Simon had checked. "Is this the place?"

"Yes, but—" I caught my breath and pushed past him, to stand staring at the cliff.

The cyclamen had gone. Where it had clung to its crack in the rock there was now a black fissure. The crack had widened, split, and gaped open, as pressure had been exerted on the weather-rotted rock. I could see the raw white marks where the crowbars had gained their leverage.

A slab, similarly marked, lay at our feet, newly fallen, and crushing the fresh grass. Yesterday it had been leaning against the rock face, masking what lay behind from my casual glance. Today there was a split in the face of the rock, some seven feet high by a foot and a half wide—a narrow fissure which angled sharply up to a point at the top. It opened onto darkness. The cave. Michael's cave.

My mouth was dry. I said hoarsely, "Yesterday that slab was leaning up against the cliff, at an angle. There was a crack behind it, very narrow. I remember now. It didn't look like an entrance to anything, but that must have been it."

He nodded, but he wasn't looking at me, or at the mouth of the cave. He looked past me, up at the cliff top, the corrie walls, all round us. No movement; no sound.

There was a pile of mule droppings on the grass, that hadn't been there yesterday. I pointed to them silently, and Simon nodded. He said softly, "We were right, then. . . . We'll go in. You wait here a moment. And keep those ears of yours open. I won't be long."

He disappeared into the darkness of the cleft. I waited. Once again, far away, I thought I heard that little thread of music, the ghostly echo of the pan-pipes. Heard now, in this hot cruel corrie, the sound spoke no longer of Arcadia, and the kindly god of flocks and herds. It was a panic prickle along the flesh.

It had gone. I had imagined it again. I stood with my hands tightly clasped together in front of me, and made myself wait without moving.

Simon showed in the darkness of the cleft, like a beckoning ghost. I almost ran towards him into the cool darkness of the cave.

After the glare of day the place was dead-dark. It was like running against a black velvet curtain. I stopped, blinded. I felt Simon's arm come round me, guiding me in out of the light, then he switched on a torch. The light seemed feeble and probing after the blaze of day, but we could see.

We were in a widish passage which sloped gently downwards for some five or six yards and then turned abruptly to the left. The original entrance must have been wide, but it had been blocked by successive falls of stone to leave only the narrow cleft through which we had come. The passage itself was clear enough, and smelt fresh and cool.

Simon said, "The slope gets steeper. There's another twist down to the right, and then the cave itself . . . Here. Quite a place, isn't it?"

It was indeed. The main cave was huge, a great natural cavern the size of a young cathedral, with a high curved ceiling that vanished into darkness, and clefts and recesses that swallowed the feebly-probing torch-light. Stalactites and stalagmites made strangely shaped, enormous pillars. Fallen rock lay here as well. In some of the dimly seen apses there were boulders and masses of rough stone showing, in the elusive light, like the massive tombs that lie between the columns of a cathedral. Somewhere I could hear the faint drip of water. The place was impressive, magnificent even, but it was a ruin. Dust and rubble lay everywhere, some of it recent-looking, some of it apparently undisturbed for centuries.

The torch-light moved, swept, checked. . . .

Simon said, "There."

He said it softly, almost idly, but I knew him now. My heart gave that painful little jerk of excitement. The light was holding something in its dim circle, a circle which seemed to have brightened, sharpened, focussed. . . . There was a pile of rubble by a column to the left of the cavern mouth. It looked at first like any of the other heaps of fallen debris, then I saw that among the shapes of the broken rock, more regular shapes showed . . . a cubed corner . . . the dusty outline of a box. . . . And beside them in the rubble the dull gleam of metal: a crowbar and a shovel.

The torch-light swept further. "See that? They've shifted some of it already. See where it's been dragged through the dust?" He sent the light skating quickly round the rest of the great cavern. Nothing. Another time I would have exclaimed over the ghostly icicles of rock, the arches, the chambered darknesses that the corners held, but now my whole interest, like the torch-light, was centred on that pile of rock debris and what it contained.

Simon paused for a moment, cocking his head. No sound except the drip of water somewhere, very faintly. He moved forward with me beside him, and bent over the exposed corner of the box.

He didn't disturb it. The torch worked for him. "There's the government stamp. This isn't gold, Camilla. It's guns."

"Guns?"

"Uh-huh. Small and useful Sten guns." He straightened up and switched the light out for a moment. In the thick darkness his voice was soft and grim. "There's an excellent market for this sort of thing at several points in the Med just now. Well, well."

I said, "I don't believe that Nigel would do that."

The torch flashed on again. "Come to think of it, neither do I. I wonder . . ." He moved off round the pile, exploring deeper into the darkness behind the big stalagmite.

"Simon," I said, "d'you mean these were flown in here during the war?"

"Yes. I told you. Gold and arms galore."

"But that was nineteen forty-two, wasn't it? They wouldn't keep, surely?"

I heard him laugh. "You talk as if they were fish. Of course they'll 'keep.' They're packed in grease. They'll come out as good as new. . . . Ah. . . ."

"What is it?" In spite of myself my voice sharpened.

"Ammo. Stacks of it. My God, this'd take a couple of days to shift, this stuff. No wonder . . ." His voice trailed away.

"Simon? What is it?"

He said without a trace of inflection, "The gold."

I moved forward so fast that I tripped over a root of the stalagmite and almost fell. *"Where?"*

"Steady there. So this is what treasure trove does to you. Here." The torch-light was steady on the pile of broken rock. Among the dust and splintered fragments the corners of two small boxes showed. They were of metal, but the corner of one had been smashed open, and under the dusty gaping metal was the living gleam of gold.

Simon was saying, "That's Michael's little find, Camilla. That's why Mick was murdered. But I still don't quite see. . . ." He paused, and I saw his brows draw together, but after a while he went on in his even voice, "Well, we were right, as far as it went. Two boxes, at least, and there may be more under the rubble."

"They're very small, aren't they?"

"One of them would be one man's work, all the same. Did you know that gold was almost twice as heavy as lead? They'll have quite a job shifting what they've got here."

I said, "They?"

He answered my look. "I'm afraid you were right about Nigel. I think he *was* on his way up here yesterday morning, and it's Nigel who's been working here while Dimitrios was in Delphi."

I said apprehensively, "But we still don't know they're working to-gether. If Dimitrios came up last night, or early today, and found Nigel here, and set about him the way he did with you—"

He shook his head. "No. Think it out. There must be two of them in it. Look at this stuff again; look how it's buried. Angelos probably did throw a bit of rubble and small stones over it to hide it, but he never put this pile of rock over it. This has come down in an earth tremor—proba-bly the one that shut the cave and broke the cliff above us. Shifting this kind of thing is sheer hard work, and Dimitrios just hasn't had time to do everything alone."

"You mean—?"

"Work it out. There must be two men on the job, Camilla. If Nigel found the cave, it still hadn't been opened up yesterday, enough to let those boxes be carried out. Whether Nigel showed it to Dimitrios, or whether Dimitrios found it himself as soon as we left the corrie yesterday, the man simply hasn't had time single-handed to do all this. Remember he followed us almost straight down to Delphi; he wouldn't have had time to get his tools from where they were hidden, and shift that slab. And even if he came back to do that later, he was down in Delphi again in the middle of the night."

"What about Danielle?"

"She couldn't have got up here and then back again between the time you saw her on the Shining Ones, and the time she went to bed last night. What's more she couldn't, physically, do this sort of job."

He paused for a moment, as if listening, and then went on. "And look at the situation just now. We know Danielle went north with the jeep. She won't have had time to get up here from the Amphissa road. Dimitrios is waiting for someone, but it's not Danielle. The mule's been here, hasn't it, and gone? At a guess, Dimitrios is waiting for whoever has taken the mule over, loaded, to meet the jeep. Nigel."

The torch flashed again, momentarily, over the gold. He said, "You remember Stephanos saying that the old track leads to a disused quarry near the Amphissa road? It sounds the sort of place where they might park the jeep out of sight while they ferry the stuff across the hill with the mule. They seem to have made a start on the guns. I imagine they'll stack the loot somewhere down near the road till they can get it all away together; and if they've any sense they'll leave the gold safely here till the last minute. . . . Did you hear anything?"

We stood very still with the light out. "No," I said. Then, slowly, "You know, I—I don't trust Dimitrios."

I heard the ghost of a laugh in the dark. "Today's great thought, Camilla, my darling? You surprise me."

He had surprised me too, but I hoped my voice didn't show it. I said, "I was thinking of Nigel. Even if they are working together now, it's only because Nigel found the stuff first, and Dimitrios wants help to shift it. Once the work's done—" I stopped, and licked dry lips.

"I know." No trace of amusement now. "Well, we're here now, so that should be taken care of."

"Yes. But Simon"—even to me the whisper sounded thin and miserably uncertain—"Simon, what are we going to do?"

"Wait. What else can we do? We don't know the score yet, but no doubt we soon will."

He switched on again, and the light flicked round the cavern. "There's plenty of cover here, and we'll hear them in good time—or at least you will. If Nigel comes up alone, all the better, but if it should be Dimitrios coming back . . ."

He grinned down at me, but some quality in the grin brought the reverse of comfort. I said suddenly, accusingly, "You *want* him to come back."

"And if I do?" The smile deepened at the expression on my face. "By God, Camilla, don't you see? I pray he does come back. There's your score to settle as well as mine, and now there's that idiotic boy to straighten out. . . . It would be better if Dimitrios came. Don't you see?"

"Oh, yes, I see."

His hand came out, momentarily, to touch my cheek, a moth-light touch. "Don't be scared, my dear. I'm not going to get myself killed and leave you alone with the wolves." He gave a little laugh. "I've not the slightest intention of fighting fair . . . and two can play at the game of attacking down a torch-beam."

I said, I hoped steadily, "He may be armed."

"I'm pretty sure he's not. There wasn't room for a gun in those dungarees."

"He's probably got himself another knife."

"Probably. And I've got his. Two can play at that game too."

"*Simon!*"

I heard him laugh again as he moved away. "Poor Camilla. . . . Now, half a minute. Stay where you are. I'll be back."

He slid, with wary flashes of the torch, out of the cave, and the small light dwindled and vanished into the curve of the passageway. He was gone perhaps two minutes. I stayed just where I was, with the gold at my feet, and one hand in my pocket nervously fingering the bulk of the Greek's torch, which I had picked up in Nigel's room last night, and found to be still serviceable. Then the will-o'-the-wisp light danced back along the passage wall, and Simon was beside me.

"Not a sign of either of them, so we'll have a closer look at this stuff, I think."

"Do you want any help?"

"No, thanks. Scout around and find a bolt hole to make for when he comes." He was already busy, crouching beside the pile of rubble, his hands moving gently over the dusty surfaces.

I left him to his task, his hands moving among the dust just as Michael's hands must have moved fourteen years ago when he made the same discovery. I flashed my torch back momentarily as I moved away. It showed his crouching body, the quiet intent face, the hands. . . . Michael Lester finding evidence of treachery to the Allies. For some reason I gave a little shiver. They said ghosts walked, didn't they? And the ghost of Angelos, who smiled as he killed? "If ghosts are true," Niko had said, "then he still walks on Parnassus. . . ."

The cave was even bigger than I had thought. I passed between pillars of stalagmites as massive as Apollo's columns at Delphi, and into an anteroom as deep as a private chapel. There was ample cover. Simon and I could lie hidden almost anywhere, when Dimitrios came. . . .

The light was uncertain in my hand. Its beam touched the walls, the fallen masses that blocked the antechamber, and diffused itself into nothingness among the dark recesses. But even as I turned back, the edge of the light shimmered momentarily with a sliding, liquid gleam. I paused. There was the drip of water again, more clearly now. I went forward, the torch exploring ahead of me. The floor lifted a little, and there was a streak of damp on it that caught the light. I could feel the freshness in the air, above the dead dust-smells of the cave, and there was the drip of water, closer now and clearer; there must be some spring in the cave—perhaps the same spring whose overflow fed the grass and flowers outside. I went forward quickly now, the light flicking over the rock in eager search. There was the now-familiar pile of broken rock against the rear wall of the cave; there the wall itself, streaked with damp and seamed with black fissures; there a wrecked stalagmite leaning drunkenly against a slab that lay at an angle to the wall. . . .

There was something very familiar about the slab. It only took me a couple of seconds to realize why. It was the same shape, and leaned in the same way, as the slab that yesterday had barred the cave mouth, and today lay tumbled in the grass outside.

I approached it slowly, knowing what I would find. As I paused beside it I could hear the drip of water plainly. Then I felt the skin prickle cold again along my arms and back.

With the drip of water came another sound, a sound that I had heard already twice that day and disbelieved, as I disbelieved it now. The sound of a pipe. Pan's pipe . . . it played a delicate little fall of notes; another; again. Silence, and the drip of water.

And the sound had come from behind the leaning slab.

With the hair lifting along my arms I bent to peer behind it. I was right. There was a gap, narrow, perhaps eight inches wide, but still a gap. And it didn't, like the other cave mouth, give onto darkness. Beyond it, the darkness slackened.

I think I had forgotten Dimitrios. I said softly, and even to me the echoes of my voice sounded queer, "There's a way through here. I'm going to see."

I don't know if Simon answered. I was squeezing through the narrow gap. The rock scraped me, caught at my clothes, then let me through. I was in a widish passage which led upwards in a gentle curve. The floor was smooth. Round me the darkness slackened further, and more clearly through the torch-light the walls of the gallery took shape. Ahead of me it curved more sharply to the right, and beyond the curve I could see that the light grew clearer. The drip of the water was clear and loud.

Then it came again, the sound I had been listening for above the trickle of water; a little stave of music, hauntingly off-key. . . .

I rounded the corner. Ahead was the light, the arch of the gallery framing a blaze muted by moving green. I caught a glimpse of grass, and the hanging boughs of some slender tree dappling the sunlight at the mouth of the tunnel.

I almost ran the rest of the way. I ducked under the arch and came suddenly, blindingly, into a little dell.

It wasn't a way out. It was a small enclosure, like a light-well. Centuries ago this had been a circular cave into which the gallery had run, but the roof had fallen in and let in the sun and the seeds of grass and wild vines, and the spring had fed them, so that now, in the heart of the mountain, was this little well of vivid light roofed with the moving green of some delicate tree.

The music had stopped. The only sound was the drip of the spring and the rustle of leaves.

But I had no thought to spare for Pan and his music. Apollo himself was here. He was standing not ten feet from me as I came out of the tunnel. He was naked, and in his hand was a bow. He stood looking over my head as he had stood for two thousand years.

I heard Simon coming along the tunnel behind me. I moved aside. He came quickly out of the dark archway into the dappled light. He was saying, "Camilla, I—" then he stopped as if he'd been struck in the throat. I heard him say, "Oh, God," under his breath. He stopped just behind me.

Some draught moved the curtain of leaves. Light flickered and burned from the bow, and shifted along the bronze of the throat and face. A broken arrow of gold lay in the grass at the statue's feet.

After a lifetime or so I heard myself saying shakily, "This . . . *this* is what Nigel found. He was here. Look."

I stooped and picked up the little water pot from where it lay in the damp moss at my feet.

CHAPTER XVI

*Apollo shows himself not to everyone, but only to him who is good. He who
sees him is great; he who sees him is not a small man. We will see thee, O far-
striker, and we will never become small!*

CALLIMACHUS: 2.9.

"YES." Simon turned the pot over in his hand. "That's out of Nigel's
sketching-box. He may have heard the water when he was drawing the
cyclamen outside, and that led him into the cave and then through here
. . . to this." His eyes, like mine, were fixed on the statue. The face was
god-like; remote, wise, serene, but young, and with a kind of eagerness
behind the level brows.

I said breathlessly, "It's the face in the drawing, isn't it?—the lovely
drawing he tore up. . . . I said it looked like a statue. D'you remember
how he snatched it back from us?"

Simon said slowly, "That was when Danielle was there. But before
that—d'you remember my saying that he seemed to be on the verge of
telling me something, and then when Danielle came in he stopped short
and shut up?"

"Of course. Then she *can't* have recognized it, can she? He'd only
found the cave that day, and it's obvious he wasn't going to tell her about
it!"

"And by God he was right," said Simon. "Guns and gold is one thing;
in a way that kind of treasure trove is legitimate prey for greasy thugs
like Dimitrios, and if the boy thought he could get something out of a
spot of gun-running, well, that's his affair. But *this* . . ." he went down
on one knee in the grass. Very gently he lifted the golden arrow. Where
it had lain the whitened grass roots showed a clear print. He put it down
again. "As I thought. Nothing's been touched. You can't tell me friend
Dimitrios could have kept his paws off a bit of loose gold." He got to his
feet with a breath of relief. "No, the boy's kept his mouth shut, and
there's quite enough in the outer cave to fix Dimitrios' interest there.
Thank God for the artist's conscience. But I think the sooner I get hold
of Nigel the better."

"You—you don't think Dimitrios'll come exploring, like I did, and
find it?"

He laughed under his breath. "I'd bet on it that he won't; he's far too busy, for one thing, and for another, now that I come to think of it, even if he was dying of thirst he'd never squeeze through the gap."

"I suppose not. But how in the world did *he* get in here? And why?" I put a hand to my head. "I—I can't seem to think straight about anything just at the moment. I feel knocked kind of sideways."

"I'm not surprised. No wonder Nigel was 'high' that night. He must have been half out of his mind with excitement. And no wonder Mick —well, never mind that now. I doubt if we'll ever know just how and why the Apollo got here, but we can make a pretty good guess, I think. You know that the sanctuary at Delphi, after it ceased to be able to protect itself and its vast wealth, was plundered again and again. We don't know where a fraction of the stolen statues went. It was the metal ones that were taken; gold went first, of course; and then bronze, to be melted down for weapons. . . . From the look of this one, with that gold on it, it would be one of the most precious, and it's certainly one of the most beautiful. Why shouldn't some priest, or some small band of devotees, have decided to save it; cart it out of Delphi and find sanctuary for it till the troubled times were over?"

"But—why here? And *how?*"

"There used to be a track this way—the natives refer to it as 'the old track,' and, in these parts, God knows how old it might be. We came along it part of the way. Even so, it must have been quite a trek. Myself, I'd have brought the thing up in a mule litter. I suppose the plan was to retrieve the statue later when things were safe, or even, if this happened at a very desperate time, to set up a sort of small secret sanctuary high on the mountain. If they'd just wanted to hide the statue, after all, they could have buried it, but they've *placed* it, haven't they? And with the Greek instinct for drama, they've put it at the end of a dark tunnel, in the blazing light, and all its trappings round it. . . . Did anything strike you about the cave, Camilla?"

"You mean that it was a bit like a cathedral—or a temple?"

He nodded. "It's a common enough quality in big vaulted places with stalactites and so on, but nonetheless impressive. The priests who were so fanatical to save this statue must have known of the cave for long enough. Not only that . . . there was this inner shrine, full of light, the perfect 'bright citadel' for the god—so here he is. Look at that vine, Camilla, and that tree."

I looked at him stupidly. "The vine? It's a wild vine, isn't it? And the tree—is that a sort of laurel?"

"A bay. Apollo's laurel," said Simon softly.

"But Simon, after two thousand years—"

"Trees live a long time, and when they die they leave seedlings. And vines run wild. Those were planted, Camilla. You notice how the Apollo is just under the lip of the overhang, and the vines and that spindly tree make a screen? I don't know if you *can* get to the top of this light-well and look down, but you'd see nothing. . . . And there is the spring. Yes, I think this was a sacred cave, with a sacred spring, and what more natural than that the priest who was so eager to save his god should house him here? And I'll bet that if we look closely we'll find that the entrances to both inner and outer caves were artificially blocked up—"

"They were. I noticed that. The slab that Dimitrios had moved was the same as the one that was across this inner tunnel."

"And then, after God knows how many years, the earthquakes opened the doors again . . . for Angelos. And Michael."

"*Michael!*" I looked at him almost guiltily. I had forgotten Michael. "Of course. The letter. The bright citadel. Oh, Simon."

He gave a little smile, and quoted softly: " 'Tell the Emperor that the bright citadel is fallen to the ground; Apollo has no longer any shelter, or oracular laurel tree, or speaking fountain. Even the vocal stream has ceased to flow.' Yes, Mick proved the Delphic Oracle wrong. That's what the letter meant."

I said, "You know, I didn't say anything, but I thought your brother wouldn't have written quite the way he did about a cache of arms, or even gold. All he'd have had to do, surely, was to divert them back to their proper uses?"

"I know. That's what got me too. But I never thought of anything like *this*." His voice didn't change, but suddenly I got the sharp impression of intense excitement. "My God," said Simon, "who could have imagined this?"

We stood side by side staring at the statue. I think it was the loveliest thing I have ever seen. The shadows played over the bloomed bronze of the body; the eyes dwelt on some remote distance beyond and above our heads, as the eyes of lions do. They were curiously alive, carefully inlaid with enamel and some black stone, so that the dark pupils seemed to flicker and glow with the movement of light and shade. I only knew of one other statue that had eyes like that.

Simon echoed my thoughts, softly, "The Charioteer."

I said, "You think so? You think he's by the same hand?"

"I don't know a darned thing about it, but that's what he makes me think of."

"That's what he made Michael think of," I said.

He nodded. "And Nigel too, if you remember. . . . It was when we were talking about the Charioteer that Nigel seemed suddenly to make up his mind to tell me about this. It may only have been because we were talking in general about discovering statues, but I don't think so. I seem to recollect some tension when the Charioteer was mentioned."

"It's not only the eyes," I said, "but the whole impression of strength going along with grace . . . a sort of liquid quality—no, that's the wrong word, it sounds too weak, whereas this is—well, terrific. Simon, why shouldn't he be not only by the same hand, but part of the same group? It's only so much guesswork, isn't it, that the Charioteer was part of a victory statue for some potentate or other? Heavens above, if there were six thousand statues there, you'd think there might have been a chariot statue of Apollo somewhere in Apollo's own sanctuary? And why shouldn't the Charioteer be the driver, and this—the god himself—the Lord of the Car?"

"Why not indeed?" said Simon.

"What are you smiling at? I can't help getting excited, can I? And why shouldn't I have a theory? It seems to me—"

"No reason at all. And it seems to *me* that one theory's as good as another. Yours at any rate is the most exciting one that comes to hand. . . . No, I was smiling at something quite different. Dimitrios."

"Oh!" It was like being jerked out of the sunlight into cold water. "I—I'd forgotten all about him."

"I should like to . . . now," said Simon. He had never taken his eyes off the statue. "But I'm afraid we must deal with that little matter before we come back to this."

"What do we do about it?" I asked, rather blankly.

He gave it one long look before he turned away. "We leave it here in its bright citadel, and we get back to the land of shadows, my dear. We know now what Michael found, and we also know what Michael was murdered for. That chapter's closed, I think, with the death of Angelos. But the one that's still open is what we've got to deal with now. Nigel found the bright citadel too, and I admit to feeling rather strongly that Dimitrios and Danielle shouldn't really be let in on . . . this."

I said almost violently, "They'll not touch it if I can stop them."

"Then we'd better get back into the cave and play watchdog. Camilla . . ."

"Yes?"

He stood for a moment looking down at me. The guarded look was there again, with some expression behind the cool eyes that made me wonder what was coming. But he only said, rather lamely, "I shouldn't have let you come."

I didn't answer.

He said, "You're frightened, aren't you?"

Still I said nothing. I wasn't looking at him. I wondered fleetingly why I didn't mind his knowing. All at once he was very close to me, and his hand came under my chin, gently lifting my face to meet his gaze. "You know why I brought you, don't you?"

"Yes."

"And I was right."

"Yes. I know."

"You underrate yourself so shockingly, Camilla. You're not to play second fiddle any more. Understand?"

"Yes."

He hesitated, and then said rather abruptly, "You made a discovery yesterday; remember? 'No man is an Island.' It's true in more ways than one. Don't go on hating yourself because there are some things you can't do and can't face on your own. None of us can. You seem to think you ought to be able to deal with anything that comes along, much as I might, or someone like me. That's absurd; and it's time you stopped despising yourself for not being something you were never meant to be. You'll do as you are, Camilla; believe me, you will."

I didn't quite trust myself to answer. After a second or so I said, lightly, "All I ask the gods is that one day I'll see you, too, shaken right out of that—that more-than-sufficient calmness of yours, onto the plane of mortals like me! The day that happens, I'll sacrifice to Apollo myself!"

He grinned. "I might have to hold you to that. But meanwhile you can be sure that it won't be friend Dimitrios that'll do it. I'm going back now to see if he's around—or Nigel. Would you rather stay here?"

"No. I'll come with you. I—I'd like to know what's going on."

His hand touched my cheek as it had once before, a moth's touch. "Then don't be scared, please. I'll not let Dimitrios get near you."

"All right. What do I do?"

"Nothing yet. Just keep out of sight, and do as you're told before you're told to do it."

"What could be simpler? Very well."

"And now we'll go back."

The Apollo looked serenely over our heads as we turned and left the sunlight.

The cave was still empty. We waited in the shelter of the cleft, listening, and then Simon squeezed his way through without using the torch. After a minute or two I heard his voice softly in the dark. "It's all right. You can come through."

I slid through the narrow opening. The beam of Simon's torch lit the way for me, and then played over the tilted slab. "See? Those are chisel

marks. You were right. The slab was hacked to fit across the opening.
And that crack above . . . that'll be where the rock shifted in the tremor
that opened up the cave again for you and me . . . and Michael."

I ran a slightly unsteady finger along one of the marks. "Two thousand
years. . . . Oh, Simon, I wish we could know—" I stopped abruptly.

"Mmm?" The torch was still moving over the old tool marks. He
seemed absorbed.

I managed to whisper calmly enough, "He's coming back. I can hear
him."

The torch snapped out. A moment's unbreathing silence. "Yes. You
get back through the cleft and wait till we see what he's up to. I hope to
God it's Nigel."

As the breathed sentence ended I felt his hand on my arm. I obeyed
him, slipping back through the narrow opening to wait, heart beating
jerkily again, against the rock on the other side of the slab. I felt him beside me, pressed close to the edge of the cleft.

The steps came closer, hesitated at the door of the cave, and then came
in. The sounds were at once dulled by the dust and made hollower by
the cave's echoes. They were succeeded by other sounds: the dull thud of
a spade hacking at the pile of rubble; the chink as it struck stone, and
then metal; the sounds of breathing and effort; a soft expletive in Greek
and then the splintering of wood and a thud; a dragging sound. . . .
He had uncovered a box and was dragging it nearer the mouth of the
cave in readiness for transportation.

I felt Simon's body, close to mine, tense like a runner's at the starting
tape. His arm was across me, holding me still against him. It was like a
steel bar. I wondered if he would attack Dimitrios now, out of the
dark. . . .

But he didn't move, except to shift his shoulders and head slightly
so that I thought he could see round the edge of the slab. He stayed like
that for what seemed an age, rock-still. I could feel the pulse beating in
the hollow of his elbow; it was unhurried. Mine, under it, was tumbling
along anyhow, like a faulty engine.

The arm relaxed. I felt him turn his head, and his breath was on my
temple. I heard the barest thread of a whisper, "He's gone out again. Did
you hear a mule?"

"I don't think so."

"Stay here. I'll come back."

A swift, compelling pressure of the arm round me, then it lifted. A
movement beside me, the scrape of cloth on stone, and he was gone.
The cleft felt cold and damp. I shifted my shoulders with the sudden

chill and hunched my arms close to my sides and waited, listening. The echo of my coward pulses seemed to fill the cave. . . .

I heard his steps in the dust just before he reached the cleft again and slid through. It was warmer with him there. He bent his head and said softly, "He's left the box just inside the entrance and gone out again. He seems uneasy; I think he's wondering if anything's happened to whoever's coming with the mule. I think I'd better go after him."

He wasn't touching me, so he didn't feel the jerk of my heart. He just heard me say, "Yes?" quite calmly.

"It's just on the cards something has happened to delay Nigel, and I'd like to know what. And I want to know the way they're taking. That track peters out very soon. I'll follow Dimitrios down till I see where he's bound, and then if a chance occurs I'll . . . well, deal with him."

"You mean you'll *kill* him?"

"Good God, no. But I'd like him put safely out of action while we get time to work this thing out our own way. . . . And now I must go, or I'll lose the blighter."

I hadn't realized that my hand had gone up to the breast of his shirt. His came up to cover it, warm and steadying. I said, and I couldn't quite keep the shake out of my voice, "Simon, take care."

"Be sure of that. Now, don't worry, my—don't worry. I'll be all right, and so will you. Stay here, under cover. You'll be as safe as a house in this part of the cave, and anyway I promise you I won't let Dimitrios out of my sight. Right?"

"R-right."

His other arm came round my shoulders, and momentarily he pulled me against him. It was a gesture of comfort and reassurance, no more. . . . But I thought his lips brushed my hair.

For the second time the arm dropped from my shoulders and he turned away as swiftly and lightly as a ghost. This time he switched on his torch, and I saw his shadow leap back, gigantic, along the wall of the cleft as he slipped through. I pressed forward till I could see into the cave. The little circle of light danced away through the faintly echoing spaces of darkness; the pillars and buttresses and masses of rock sent towering shadows reeling up the walls to stretch and lose themselves into the blackness of the vaulted roof. Simon, moving swiftly, himself like a shadow, dwindled across the empty darkness and was gone like a wraith into the outer tunnel. A shadow flickered back momentarily over the rock, then darkness swallowed it.

My hands were spread flat against the inner side of the slab. My eyes ached with the darkness. It was cold again. I had to exert all my self-control to stop myself running out and across the cave after him into the blessed sunlight.

At length I turned and made my way rather drearily back to the bright solitude of Apollo's sanctuary.

How long I waited there I don't know. At first I sat quietly enough in a corner where the sun fell unmasked by leaves, gazing at the statue of the god and trying to empty my mind of all worry about what was going on outside.

But after a while the very beauty and stillness of the place began to oppress me. I found I could sit still no longer, and, getting to my feet, I picked up Nigel's waterpot and carried it over to the spring. Under the thin trickle I rinsed it carefully, and drank. I rummaged in Simon's haversack and found what remained of our food, half of which I ate. After that I got myself another drink. Then I fidgeted about the little glade, examining the statue more closely, looking—but without touching them —at the broken pieces of gold in the grass, fingering the leaves and ferns. . . .

When I found myself stooping for a third time to drink at the spring, I realized that fear had given place to a sort of impatient irritation. Sunlight and peace had done their work too well: I was now thoroughly on the fidget. I found myself glancing almost second by second at the watch on my wrist—an automatic act which irritated my nerves still further, as I hadn't the remotest idea what time it had been when Simon left me. I hovered near the mouth of the tunnel, fingering my torch. . . .

After all, I told myself, I was perfectly safe. Simon was with Dimitrios, and I wasn't in the least afraid of Nigel. I wanted something to do; I wanted to know what was going on; I wanted Simon's presence. . . .

I went cautiously along the tunnel, back into darkness, hesitated in the shelter of the slab, then let myself through into the main cave.

I, too, used my torch this time. A last absurd jump of the nerves made me send the light skating once round the vaulted darkness, almost as if I expected to find that, after all, Dimitrios had not gone. But the place was empty. There really was nothing to be afraid of; if he came back I would hear him, and would have ample time to take sanctuary again. Moreover, Simon was on his tail, and if Dimitrios returned I could depend on Simon to come with him.

The torch-beam was steady now. I went softly across to the arch of the outer tunnel, and then turned off the light. I felt my way carefully along the wall of the curving passage, until, as I rounded the first bend, the darkness slackened, and I could see my way.

There was no box standing beside the entrance. Dimitrios must have set off carrying it. So much the better, I thought, vaguely. It meant he did intend to go right down to the jeep; and it would slow him down and make it easier for Simon to follow him.

I edged forward until I could see out into the corrie.

Here, too, that faint sense of surprise assailed me to see it unchanged; dazzlingly hot, still, deserted. . . .

The glare hit at the eyes. I could smell the dust and the mule dung and some dried aromatic plant that crumbled to powder under the hand I put up to the rock beside me. There was no sound at all. Nothing moved; even the hot air hung still.

I hesitated. The temptation to get out of the cave was strong, to climb the cliff path above me, and take refuge somewhere higher up the mountain where I could at once be free and yet hidden, and, more important, see any movement that there might chance to be near the corrie. But Simon must know where to find me, and he had told me to stay here. I must stay.

I went back into the cave.

I remember that I stood there for some minutes, looking round me almost idly. I was trying to picture the place before the earthquake that had first shaken down some of the stuff that blocked the aisles and recesses between the pillars. It was very possible that this had been a sacred cave. Here the Apollo had been carried by hasty, reverent hands; here, perhaps, sacrifices and other acts of worship had been made before the holy place had been finally sealed and hidden and left to its two thousand years of silence.

The beam of my torch suddenly dimmed, then brightened again. But the warning spurred me into movement. With only one brief glance back at the entrance, and a couple of seconds' pause to listen for sounds of Dimitrios' approach, I set myself to a careful exploration of the cave.

I don't quite know what I was looking for. I certainly wasn't consciously hoping to find further "treasure"—either of the kind in Angelos' hoard, or relics of Apollo's worship. But it wasn't very long before I did in fact come on evidence of another cache. In a deep bay between two pillars, at the edge of the cave not far from the stack of boxes, a pile of rubble—a shallow barrow of the stuff heaped away in a bay of rock— looked as if it had been recently disturbed.

I approached it and bent over, sending the now perceptibly dimming beam probing among the broken fragments.

I could see nothing that suggested boxes or articles concealed there, but, quite clear in the dust at my feet, was the print of a rope-soled shoe, and the marks beside it as of something being dragged.

I went closer and stooped to peer. The beam slid over the pile, caught on something, and halted. It jerked in my hand once, then fixed, still, and far too bright now, on what lay behind the pile of rock and dirt.

The murderer hadn't bothered to bury Nigel. His body had been dragged and then flung into this meagre hiding, and now lay, stiff and horrible and indescribably grotesque, between the heaped rubble and the wall of the cave.

In the paralyzed moment before I dropped the torch from a numbed hand, and let the merciful darkness loose again, I saw what had happened to Nigel. You can see an awful lot in a split second's acute terror and shock; the picture your brain registers then is complete, the stuff of a million lingering nightmares still to come. Nothing is missed; every bestial detail is there for the mind to come back to, turn over, re-picture without ceasing.

He had been tied. The rope had gone now—no doubt the murderer had need of it—but the boy's wrists were scored raw where he had struggled. He had been tied, and tortured. In that one glance I had seen the shabby green shirt ripped down off one thin shoulder, and, on the upper arm, shocking against the peeling skin, a series of marks whose sickening regularity could mean only one thing. He had been burned four or five times, deliberately. Other things I saw that, at the time, meant nothing, but which, in nightmare recapitulations of that second's horror, I have since seen and recognized a score of times. I don't intend to describe them. Let it remain that Nigel had died, in pain. His eyes were open. I remember how they gleamed in the light of the torch. And his teeth clenched, grinning, on some fragment that might have been skin . . . Dimitrios' bitten thumb . . . the filthy murderous hand that had slid down my arm yesterday at the Roseate Cliff.

It was on that flash of realization that the torch dropped and the dark stamped down. I don't know what happened then. I remember, one moment, the picture in the torch-light, vivid, terrible, complete, then the next moment it was dark, and the rock was cold; it was crushing me, tearing my clothes, tripping my running footsteps; it was soft to my falling, whimpering body. . . .

I was lying at Apollo's feet on the damp moss. My hair was wet, and my hands, and the breast of my frock. Something was hurting my right hand where it pressed deeply into the grass. It was the broken end of the gold arrow. I sat looking at it for a very long time before I even saw it.

Dimitrios, I was thinking stupidly, confusedly; Dimitrios . . . he had murdered Nigel yesterday. While we had been here in the corrie, in the bright sunlight, Nigel had been in the cave with his murderer, tied and hurt and—no, that wouldn't do; he hadn't been gagged, and we'd have heard him. He was dead before we got up here, and then Dimitrios had come down to Delphi to search his room. . . .

I stared down at the beautifully worked fragment of gold in my hand, and tried to think. . . . But all that would come to me was that Nigel, poor muddled, eager young Nigel, who was a good artist, had been murdered by Dimitrios. . . .

Dimitrios! This time the thought came anything but confusedly; it whipped into my brain with a point as sharp as the one that pricked my palm. I was on my feet, and the gold arrow spun, glittering, forgotten, to the grass. Dimitrios, whom Simon and I had casually dismissed as someone who could easily be "dealt with"—Dimitrios was out there on the hillside, and Simon was tailing him, waiting for a chance to attack him, unconscious of the fact that the Greek was a murderer as vile and ruthless as ever his cousin Angelos had been. . . .

Momentarily I had forgotten poor Nigel. I ran back into the tunnel with never a thought of what lay there in the cave.

The darkness came up against me like a tangling net. As I rounded the first bend in the tunnel I had to stop short, then feel my way forward slowly, my hands shaking and slipping on the cool rock.

I reached the slab. I pressed my body into the narrow cleft, craning to peer forward into the cave. But I couldn't see at all; the darkness boiled still against my wide-open eyes with shapes and spangles of a million fizzing colours. Without my torch, and blinded like this with my swift dive back out of the light, I would be helpless to cross the cave. I shut my eyes and waited there for the swarming dark to clear. The slab felt cold and damp under my flat-spread hands.

Then I heard him.

I thought at first it was the surge of the knocking pulses that nailed me to the rock, but then I knew it was the soft tread of rope-soled shoes in the dust.

I stayed where I was, frozen to the rock, and opened my eyes.

I could see now. Light was moving in the cave, a powerful light. Not Simon—Simon's torch, like mine, had begun to fail . . . and in any case, the steps had not been Simon's. But at least where Dimitrios was, Simon would be. And from the way the Greek came forward into the cave with unhurried confidence, he still didn't know of Simon's presence.

Even as the thought came, I heard a tiny sound outside the cave. My eyes flew in apprehension to the Greek. He was behind the light and I couldn't see him, but the moving beam never faltered. He hadn't heard. The sound came again, and now I knew it for what it was; the chink of metal was a bit jangled. Dimitrios had brought the mule.

The Greek passed out of my small range of vision. I waited till I heard the familiar scrape and shift of a box and the clatter of settling stones, and the grunts and short breathing of effort. Then I inched my way nearer the edge of the slab and peered round it, a centimetre at a time.

He had put the torch down in a little niche above him, so that the beam was directed onto the rock pile. His thick powerful body was stooping over this. His back was towards me; he had laid his jacket down beside him, and under the blue shirt I could see the bulge and play of his muscles as he heaved at one of the half-buried boxes. Then he dragged it out into his arms, and straightened up, holding it. I hadn't before realized how immensely strong he must be. He carried the box slowly over to the cave mouth and went out of sight with it up into the tunnel. I heard him dump it there. I heard him coming back. Still with that unhurried soft tread he came out of the tunnel mouth, into the steady beam that illumined the cave.

For the second time in those few minutes, I felt the kick of shock over the heart.

It wasn't Dimitrios. It wasn't anyone I had seen before.

But hard on the moment of shock and confusion, I knew that I was wrong. I had seen him before, and more than once. Now, faced in the queerly lit darkness with that heavy head, the thick dark curls tight like a bull's and crisping down the swarthy cheekbones towards the smiling thick-lipped mouth, I knew him. This was the Phormis head of Nigel's drawing: this was the face like an archaic statue's, with the wide fleshy cheekbones and the up-cornered, tight-lipped smile. More—this was the face I had seen, unnoticing and unremembering, bending over the engine of the jeep outside Dimitrios' cottage. And it must have been *this* face, not the Apollo (which it was certain she had never seen), that Danielle had recognized among Nigel's drawings. . . .

But before I could follow this further, two other memories flashed, sparks into the dry tinder of fear . . . Nigel saying to Danielle, "That's a chap I saw today on Parnassus," and Simon's voice in the dark, translating for me something Stephanos had told him, "He'd kill, and smile while he did it. Always that smile. . . ."

Angelos. Angelos himself. And Dimitrios was God knows where. And Simon was with him.

Angelos turned back to the pile of rubble. The torch-light slid over the thick skin, shiny with sweat. The smile never altered. No doubt he had smiled as he and Dimitrios killed Nigel between them. No doubt he would smile when Simon, having disposed of Dimitrios, came openly up to the cave to find me. . . .

Angelos straightened his thick body and stood still, as if listening. He turned his head. There were sounds outside, not metal-shod this time, but the sounds of someone hurrying towards the cave.

I remember thinking, with a kind of numbed calmness, that if I screamed, it would warn Simon—but it would warn Angelos too. He was expecting Dimitrios, and he could have no idea that Simon and I were here. He had made no move to douse the torch. But on the other hand, if Simon had dealt with Dimitrios, Simon too would be off his guard. . . .

The steps came closer; were in the tunnel. Angelos' hand went to his pocket. I took in my breath.

With a stumbling rush and a flurry of breathing, Danielle hurried into the cave.

CHAPTER XVII

> Ah there is Justice in heaven,
> And fire in the hand of God,
> The reckoning must be made in the end.
> SOPHOCLES: *Electra*
> (*tr. E. F. Watling*).

THE MAN RELAXED, but his voice, pitched low, was angry. "What the hell are you doing here?"

She had stopped at the edge of the torch-light. She looked at once younger and much prettier than I had seen her. She had on the turquoise blouse and scarlet cotton skirt, and her haste had flushed her face and hurried her breathing, making her seem more normal and less cynically in control of herself. She hadn't looked at Angelos. Her eyes were riveted on what remained of the cache of boxes.

"So that's it!" Like him, she spoke in French.

"That's it." He regarded her sourly. "I told you last night we'd located it, didn't I? So why the devil didn't you do as you were told and stay out of sight till I came for you?"

She walked forward slowly while he was speaking, her eyes still on the stuff at his feet. Now she looked up under her lashes with that provocative gamine grin. "I wanted to see for myself what was going on. Don't be angry . . . nobody saw me come."

"Did you see Dimitrios on your way up?"

She shook her head. She was stooping over the pile, prodding with a toe at the broken box that showed the gleam of gold. I saw her breasts rise and fall quickly, as if with excitement. He said sharply, "No sign of him?"

"No."

He swore and struck the spade almost savagely into the stones. "Then where the hell is he? I came by the high way—it's shorter if you know your road . . . and if you didn't see him either—"

"I came by the high way too." Again that smiling look up through the lovely lashes. "How did you think I found my way here? I waited where I thought you'd come, and then I followed you."

He grunted. "Clever, eh? Then that means he's gone down the other way to look for me. Blast the man; he's as jumpy as a bean on a griddle, and about as much use. And you—you should have stayed away till I came for you. I told you I didn't want you up here."

She laughed. "Maybe I didn't trust you, Angelos. Maybe you wouldn't have come for me."

He gave a short laugh. "Maybe."

"Well, I wanted to see *this,*" she said, almost childishly, "and besides, I didn't want to hang about down there all day. That damned jeep's dynamite anyway."

"Why? The stuff's not in it."

"No, but—"

"Did you park it where I told you?"

"Of course I did. Angelos, why d'you have to do this in daylight? You're crazy."

"I know what I'm doing. There's next to no moon just now, and this country's murder with a mule on a black night, and I daren't use a light. There'll be nobody about between here and the place where I'm stacking the stuff, and we can ferry the whole lot from there to the jeep in a couple of hours after dusk." He added, with a sort of heavy irony, "Always providing, of course, that you do as you're told, and that my cool-headed cousin gets back in time to give me a bit of help with the hard work!"

She laughed. She had recovered her breath now, and with it her own particular brand of throaty charm. She straightened up and gave him one of her long-lidded glinting looks. "Well, I can help instead, can't I? You won't send me back now? Don't you think, Angelos *mou,* that you might pretend to be a little bit pleased to see me?"

She moved up close to him as she spoke, and he pulled her to him and kissed her in a way that managed to be perfunctory and yet lustful. I saw her press her thin body against him, and her hands crept up to move among the thick curls on the back of his head.

I drew back a little in my crevice, shutting my eyes momentarily as if against this new discovery. *Angelos* her lover. *Angelos.* Through the whirl of fear and confusion the facts twisted and readjusted themselves into a different pattern.

It had been Angelos, not Dimitrios, who had scraped acquaintance with Danielle on those long afternoons at Itea; this deliberately, not only to while away the boredom of inaction, but because she had the use of the jeep, whereas to buy or hire other transport would involve inquiries later, and provoke the very gossip the cousins had to avoid.

And by the same token it had been Angelos, not Dimitrios, who had broken into the studio last night. I remembered now, quite clearly, that the hand which had reached back for the torch had not had a torn thumb. And I remembered Danielle's little smile when I had so swiftly identified her lover as Dimitrios. . . .

Angelos pushed her away, not too gently. "You know damned well you should have stayed away. There's no room in the games I play for anyone with baby-nerves."

She was lighting a cigarette. She said, almost snappishly, "It wasn't nerves; it was curiosity, and I've a right to know what's going on. Baby-nerves, indeed, after what I've done for you! You'd never have got the jeep but for me, and I got you the tools and the mule on Monday night, didn't I? And I've played spy on the Englishman and that wretched girl he's taken in tow—and all you do is walk in last night out of the blue, stay with me half an hour, and tell me damn all except that today's the day, and I'm to get the jeep to the quarry, and you expect that to be that! You might have landed me in a hell of a jam last night, but you never said a word to me!"

"What d'you mean?" He was working again, levering at a solid lump of rock that was wedging down a couple of boxes. The dislodged dirt and small stones hissed down to the floor. He seemed hardly to be listening to her.

She said sharply, "You know quite well what I mean. When you came to my room last night, you said you hadn't seen Nigel, and—"

"Nigel?"

"The English artist. I told you. He was throwing out hints on Monday night about getting rich and famous, and he was drunk. After the others had left I gave him another couple of ouzos and took him for a walk. . . . Did I tell you that?" She was watching the man through the wisping smoke of her cigarette, and her tone was provocative. He neither looked up nor took the slightest notice.

She tapped ash off with a sharply pettish movement. "Well? It was obvious he'd found something up here on the hill. You said you were going to wait for him yesterday and find out what it was, and where—"

"So what? We didn't need to, did we? Your English friends came and showed us the way."

"They showed you the cave too?"

He laughed shortly. "Hardly. If they'd found the cave yesterday we'd not have been able to get near it now for troops three deep round the door!"

She moved impatiently. "I didn't mean that way. Of course they didn't find it, or they wouldn't be trailing harmlessly off to Levadia today. But you *did* find it pretty quickly, didn't you? Dimitrios told me at the Shining Ones that you'd found the place, and that you were working on it then while he came down to do some final clearing-up."

He had laid aside the crowbar, and was using the spade to shift some of the smaller debris. The thud of digging echoed dully. He didn't look up. He said, "When Stephanos showed them the spot where I broke Michael's neck I knew where the cave lay. Everything was changed, but I knew the crack must open on the cave. I couldn't get through it the way it was, but after I'd sent Dimitrios down I got to work and opened it up."

"I know. You told me this last night." She wasn't, as usual, letting the cigarette hang from her lips as she talked. She was smoking in jerky movements that spoke of tightly strung nerves. She said, making it sound like an accusation, *"But you never mentioned Nigel."*

He straightened up from his work, eyeing her, his head thrust forward like a bull's, and his look at once formidable and wary. The fixed half-moon smile on the thick mouth was in its own way terrifying. He said roughly, "Come on. What is all this? Why the hell should I mention Nigel?"

She blew a long plume of smoke, then said flatly, "When you left me last night, you went to Nigel's room. Why?"

"That's simple enough, isn't it? You'd told me he'd done a drawing of me as like as a photograph. I wanted to destroy it."

"But he'd cleared out—packed up and gone. You knew that. I'd told you that. I'd been in myself that evening to try and find the drawing, and all his stuff was gone. He'd taken it with him."

"Oh, no," said Angelos, "he hadn't."

"What d'you mean? You never saw him. How d'you know what he had on him?"

She stopped. I saw her eyes widen as they met his look. Her lips parted so that the cigarette fell to the ground and lay there smouldering. She ignored it. She was staring at him. He was standing very still, leaning on the spade, watching her. I could see sweat on the heavy face and on his hairy forearms.

He said again, softly, "Well?"

Her voice was shaken clear of any of its carefully affected overtones. It came clear and thin, like a little girl's. "You did see him? Yesterday? He *did* tell you where the cave was?"

"Yes, we saw him. But he didn't tell us anything. I told you the truth about that."

"Then—then—why did you lie about seeing him?"

The smile deepened as the thick lips parted. "You know why. Don't you?"

There was a long pause. I saw the pink tongue come out to lick once, quick as a lizard's, across her rouged lips. "You—killed him? Nigel?"

No reply. He didn't stir. I saw her throat muscles move as she swallowed. There was no horror or regret or fear in her face; it was blank of expression, with parted lips, and wide eyes fixed on the man. But her breathing hurried. "I . . . see. You didn't tell me."

His voice was soft, almost amused. "No, I didn't tell you. I didn't want to scare you away."

"But—I still don't understand. Didn't he know about the cave? Wasn't I right?"

"He knew; you can be sure of that. But he didn't tell us. We tried, but he wouldn't come through with anything that made sense."

She swallowed again. She hadn't taken her eyes off him. She might have been a waxwork but for the eyes, and the convulsive muscles of the throat. "Did you—have to kill him?"

He shrugged his heavy shoulders. "We didn't, in a manner of speaking. The bloody little pansy died on us. A pity." His head sank lower. The smile seemed to thicken. "Well? Scared? Going to scream and run?"

She moved then. She came close to him again, and her hands came up to the breast of his shirt. "Do I look as if I wanted to run, Angelos *mou*? Would I be the sort you'd want along with you if I was that kind of baby-nerve?" The hands slid up his shoulders and over them to the back of his neck. She pressed closer. "I know all about you, Angelos Dragoumis. . . . Don't think that I don't. They still tell quite a few stories about you, here in Delphi. . . ."

A laugh shook him. "You surprise me."

She pulled his head down, and said, against his mouth, "Do I? Does it surprise you to know that that's why I'm here? That that's why I like you?"

He kissed her, lingeringly this time, then thrust her away from him with his free hand. "No. Why should it? I've met women like you before." He still held the spade in his other hand, and now he turned back to his task. Danielle said, eyeing the broad back a little sulkily, "Where is he?"

"Near enough."

I saw her eyes show white for a moment as she gave a quick over-the-shoulder look into the shadowed corners. Then she shrugged and reached in her pocket for another cigarette. "You may as well tell me what happened."

"All right. Only stand back out of the way. That's better. Well. . . . We waited beside the Delphi track for the boy, but he didn't come that way. He must have started early and gone some other way round, because the first we saw of him was when he was away beyond us and almost up to these cliffs. We got up as close as we could without his seeing us, but when we'd worked our way up that gully that lies east of here, he'd vanished. We got up above the line of cliff, and separated; then waited. After a bit we saw him, just appearing walking out of the corrie here, as cool as you please. So we came down the cliff and got hold of him."

"Why did you have to do that? The English couple were coming. Once you saw the place where Michael died—"

"A bird in the hand," said Angelos, and I saw the thick grin deepen again. "For all I knew, Stephanos wouldn't remember the exact spot, and it was certain that your artist friend had just come out of some hiding place. Besides, he'd done that drawing of me. He'd seen me."

She was lighting another cigarette. The flame of the match wasn't quite steady. Her eyes looked wide and brilliant above it. "What did you do?"

He sounded indifferent. "We tried to scare him into talking at first, but he wouldn't come through. To tell you the truth I began to think you were wrong and he hadn't found a thing, only then he began to babble something about a cave and 'something beyond price' and he was damned if he'd let us touch it. Then we really got going. . . ." He straightened up and got out a cigarette. He thrust it between his lips, and leaned forward to get a light from hers.

I thought, I shall see that smile in my dreams. . . .

"But he still wouldn't say anything that made sense," said Angelos. "Babbled about water, and some flowers. . . ." The contempt in the thick French made the words sound obscene. "My English is fair enough, but I couldn't get all the words. In the end there was something about gold, I'm pretty sure, but just as we were getting to that, he died on us. God knows we'd hardly started. It looked to me as if he had a groggy heart."

"What happened then?"

"We'd hardly finished with him when we saw Stephanos and the boy from Arachova bringing the English couple along. We threw the body behind some rocks and waited and watched till the old man took them to the corrie and showed them the place. It's altered completely; I might have looked for a thousand years, let alone the last two. As soon as they'd gone, I got down into the corrie and started looking round. It was dead easy. Your Nigel helped us after all with his crazy blathering; there was only one place where grass grew, and flowers, and it was much where I expected the cave to lie, if Stephanos had been accurate. We soon saw where the entrance was. Getting into it was another matter, but of course with the boy dead on our hands we had to be sure there'd be no inquiries until we'd got clear off and no traces left. So I got on with the job alone while I sent Dimitrios down to see you as arranged. I told him not to tell you about Nigel, but to get quietly into the studio and clear the stuff out of his room as if he'd packed up and gone. He did that. You'll find all the boy's stuff in the back of the jeep under the sacking. Dimitrios brought a big folder of drawings, but like a fool he was in too much of a hurry to check them, and he never saw that the picture of me wasn't there. . . . It mightn't have mattered, but that's the sort of detail that can sometimes matter the hell of a lot. I thought it worth attending to, anyway. I'm officially dead, and by God I'm staying that way, and no rumours!"

"Did you find it?"

"No. I didn't have time. There was a lot of paper with the rubbish in a tin on the floor in his room. That fool Dimitrios hadn't thought it worth bothering about. But in fact if that's where the drawings are, nobody's going to take any notice of them. They'll just think he's tidied up and left."

"They do. The English couple think he's gone on a trek over the hills —with the mule."

"Do they?" He sounded amused. "Then that's that, isn't it?"

He had cleared the boxes now of their covering of stones. He stooped to work one of them clear of the pile. She watched the play of the great muscles for a few moments in silence. Then she said again, "Where is he?"

"Who?"

"My God, Nigel of course! Did you just leave him out there for the vultures?"

"Not likely. They'd have given us away more quickly than anything else. He's here."

For the first time I saw some strong feeling move her. It was like a spring tensing. *"Here?"*

He jerked his head sideways. "Over there." He jerked the box free at last, straightened up, and carried it out of the cave. The torch still shone strongly enough from its niche on the pillar. Danielle stood still for a moment, staring towards the dark corner where Nigel's body lay, then, as if with an effort, she walked forward, took the torch down from its niche, and went over to the pile of rubble that hid the pathetic body. The light shone down on what lay, mercifully, beyond my range of vision.

It was at that moment that I remembered my own torch, dropped near Nigel's body. If she saw it . . . if the light from her torch picked up its glint in the dust. . . .

Angelos was coming back. He said irritably, "Still no sign. He seems to have taken one of the small boxes down himself by the lower track. Or else we'd have seen him." Then he looked across and saw where she was. She still had her back to him. The heavy face watching her didn't change its expression, but something in the look of the eyes made my blood thicken. "Well?"

She turned abruptly, "Are you going to leave him here?"

"Where else? Take him in the jeep to the bay at Galaxeidion?"

She ignored the irony. "Aren't you going to bury him?"

"My God, girl, there's no time. I've got enough to do shovelling half Parnassus off this stuff. You can throw some dirt down over him if you like, but it hardly matters. Something for you to do while I load up."

She came quickly back into the middle of the cave. "I'm not staying here."

He laughed. "As you wish. I thought you weren't squeamish, *ma poule?*"

"I'm not," she said pettishly, "but can't you see it won't do to leave him here, even if we do cover him? It's obvious already there's been someone at work here, and if anyone does come up they're bound to see—"

"Why should anyone come?"

She hesitated, eyeing him. "The Englishman, Simon—"

"What of him? You told me yourself he'd gone off to Levadia."

"I know, but—well, I was still thinking about what happened in the theatre, on Monday night."

In the theatre, on Monday night . . . I leaned back against the rock, trying, through the mists of tension and fear, to remember . . . the sounds I had heard as I sat there: the tiny jingling . . . it had after all been Danielle, taking the stolen mule off to meet the men. And Simon and

I had talked, down there in the theatre. . . . It wasn't only the speech from *Electra* that those wonderful acoustics had sent up to Danielle, above us in the dark. And Danielle understood English . . . What had we said? *What, in heaven's name, had we said?*

It appeared that, whatever it was, she had reported it to him before. He laughed. "Oh, that. It's no news. Of course he knows Michael was murdered. D'you think Stephanos wouldn't tell him that? What difference does it make? Nobody knows *why*."

"But if he suspected you were still alive—"

"Him?" The thick voice held nothing but amused contempt. "In any case, how should he? Nigel's dead, and no one's going to recognize that picture now."

"There was the gold," said Danielle.

The dark was boiling round me. As clearly as if he were just beside me, I heard Simon's voice again. *"It's not over . . . till I find what Michael found . . . the gold."*

"Gold, gold, gold—you see it everywhere, don't you, *ma poule?*" He laughed again. For some reason his spirits seemed to be rising. "You didn't *see* it was gold, now, did you? She picked something up and you saw it glitter, and your imagination did the rest."

"I tell you it was gold. I saw her staring at it."

The dark slowly cleared. Against it I saw a picture—not the one they were speaking of, but later; Simon, coming away from the centre-mark just before he spoke. . . . She hadn't heard. By the mercy of the gods of the place, she hadn't heard.

Angelos had turned away and was lugging another box clear of the pile. "There. That's as much as the poor bloody mule can take on one trip. . . . Now, forget that nonsense for five minutes, and you can give me a hand loading up. He found no gold yesterday, and that's a fact. He's got no reason to come back here. He's been, and seen all he can. Why should he come again? To bring a posy for Michael?" He laughed again, unpleasantly. "By God, I almost wish he would! . . . I owe him something, after all."

She said, with a sort of spite, "And her. She hit you."

"She did, didn't she?" he said cheerfully. "I think we'll wait till Dimitrios comes. He can't be much longer." He paused, looking round the cave. "It's queer to be back . . . and it looks just the same. Just the same. These pillars, and that bit of rock like a lion's head, and the drip of water somewhere. I never found the spring. . . . Can you hear it?"

She said impatiently, "But Nigel. You must do something about the body. Can't you see—?"

"You may be right." His voice was almost absent. It was clear that

Nigel had long since ceased to matter at all. "In fact he may do us a better turn dead than he did alive. . . . *He* can go over the cliff with the
jeep. Yes, there's the water. I thought so. It's over here somewhere. . . ."

Danielle's voice stopped him as he moved There was a note in it that
I hadn't heard before. "The jeep? Over the cliff? I didn't know you
planned to do that."

"You don't know all I plan to do, my fair lady," he said. He turned
back to her as he spoke, and I couldn't see his face. I saw hers. It looked
suddenly thinner, and sharp, like a frightened urchin's. He said, "What
is it now? We've got to get rid of the jeep somehow, haven't we? If the
boy's found in the sea with it that accounts for him as well."

She said, almost in a whisper, "It's mine. Everybody knows I brought
it up from Athens."

"So what? Everybody'll assume you were in it too, and that will be
that."

Still she didn't move, but stared up at him. She looked very childish
in the turquoise top, and scarlet bell of skirt. He went towards her till
she had to tilt back her head to look him in the eyes. He said on a note
of impatience, and something else, "What is it now? Scared?"

"No. No. But I was wondering—"

"What?"

She spoke still in that hurried whisper. "What you were going to do
with the jeep if you . . . if you hadn't had Nigel's body to send over the
cliffs with it?"

He said slowly, "The same, of course. They'd have thought you were in
it and had been—"

He stopped abruptly. Then I heard him laugh. His big hand went
slowly out and ran down her bare arm. It looked very dark against her
pale olive flesh. There were black hairs on the back of it. "Well, well,
well . . . My poor little pretty, did you really think I'd do a thing like
that to you?"

She didn't move. The thin arm hung slack by her side. Her head was
tilted back, the big eyes searching on his face. She said in that flat little
voice, "You said '*He* can go over the cliff in the jeep. . . .' as if you'd
planned it for someone else. As if—"

He had an arm round her now, and had pulled her close to him. She
went to him unresisting. His voice thickened. "And you thought I meant
you? *You?* My little Danielle . . ."

"Then who?"

He didn't answer, but I saw her eyes narrow and then flare wide again.
She whispered, *"Dimitrios?"*

His hand came quickly over her mouth and his body shook as if with a laugh. "Quietly, little fool, quietly! In Greece, the mountains have ears."

"But, Angelos *mou—*"

"Well? I thought you said you knew me, my girl? Don't you see? I had to have his help, and his boat, but when did *he* earn the half share of a fortune? The stuff's mine, and I've waited fourteen years for it, and now I've got it. D'you think I'm going to share it—with anyone?"

"And—what about me?"

He pulled her unresisting body closer to him. He laughed again, deep in his throat. "That's not sharing. You and I, *ma poule,* we count as one. . . ." His free hand slid up her throat, under her chin, and then forced her head up so that her mouth met his. "And I still need *you.* Do I still have to convince you of that?" His mouth closed on hers then, avidly, and I saw her stiffen for just a moment as if she was going to resist, then she relaxed against him and her arms went up to his neck. I heard him laugh against her lips, and then he said hoarsely, "Over there. Hurry."

I shut my eyes. I turned my head away so that my cheek, like my hands, pressed against the cool rock. It smelt fresh, like rain. I remember that under my left hand there was a little knob of stone the shape of a limpet shell. . . .

I don't want to write about what happened next, but in justice to myself I think I must. As I shut my eyes the man was kissing her, and I saw his hand beginning to fumble with her clothes. She was clinging to him, her body melting towards his, her hands pulling his head down fiercely to meet her kisses. Then when I couldn't see any more I heard him talking, little breathless sentences I couldn't catch—didn't try to catch—in a mixture of Greek and his thick fluent French. I heard him kick a stone out of the way as he pulled her down onto the dusty floor of the cave near the rubble pile . . . near Nigel's body. . . .

I only heard one sound from her, and it was a little half-sigh, half-whimper of pleasure. I'll swear it was of pleasure.

I was shaking, and covered with sweat, and hot as though the chilly cleft were an oven. Under the fingers of my left hand the stone limpet had broken away. I was holding a fragment of it in my curled fingers, and it was embedded in the flesh, hurting me.

I don't know how long it was before I realized that the cave was quiet, except for the heavy breathing.

Then I heard him getting to his feet. His breathing was deep and even. He didn't say anything, and I didn't hear him move away. There was no sound from Danielle.

I opened my eyes again, and the dimming torch-light met them. He was standing beside the pile of rubble, smiling down at Danielle. She lay there, still looking up at him. I could see the glint of her eyes. The sweat on his face made the wide fleshy cheeks gleam like soapstone. He stood quite still, smiling down at the girl who lay at his feet staring back at him, her bright skirt all tossed-looking in the dust.

I thought, with crazy inconsequence, How uncomfortable she looks. Then, suddenly, She looks dead.

Presently Angelos stooped, took her body by the shoulders, and dragged it across the cave to pitch it down in the rubble beside Nigel.

And that is how Danielle Lascaux was murdered within twenty yards of me, and I never lifted a finger to help her.

CHAPTER XVIII

Go while the going's good,
Is my advice. . . .
                    SOPHOCLES: *Philoctetes*
                        (*tr. E. F. Watling*).

BY THE MERCY of providence I didn't faint, or I'd have pitched straight out into the torch-light. But the narrow cleft held my body up, and my mind (numbed, I suppose, by the repetition of shock), seemed only very slowly to take in what had happened.

It was as if some sort of mental censor had dropped a curtain of gauze between me and the scene in the cave, so that it took on a kind of long-distance quality, the murderer moving about his dreadful business at a far remove from me, as a creature of fiction moves on a lighted stage. I was invisible, inaudible, powerless, the dreamer of the dream. With light would come sanity, and the nightmare vanish.

I watched him, still in that queer dead trance of calm. I think if he had turned in my direction I would hardly have had the wit to draw back, but he didn't. He dropped Danielle's body down in the dust beside Nigel's, and stood for a moment looking down at them, lightly dusting his hands together. I wondered for a moment if he was, after all, going to shovel the dirt over the bodies, then it occurred to me that Danielle's useless spark of instinct had been right; his plan for disposing of Nigel in the jeep had come a little too pat. It was Danielle who had brought the jeep; it was Danielle who was to be found with the wreck of it. . . . That had been his plan all along. I saw it now clearly. I didn't believe for a moment that he intended to kill his cousin Dimitrios—but even if that were true, he had certainly never intended to share anything with Danielle. What she had to offer was only too easily found elsewhere. What was equally certain was that he hadn't wanted to kill her here. He must have intended to save himself the transport of her body by killing her when the job was over, but her half-frightened queries had aimed just a little too near the mark for comfort. Better kill her now, and risk the extra load to be ferried down after dusk.

He had turned back now to the pillar where the torch was lodged. I watched him, still as if he were an actor in a play—a bad actor; there was no expression on his face, no horror or anxiety, or even interest. He reached up a hand, picked up the torch, and switched it off. The darkness came down like a lid on a stifling box. He seemed to be listening. I could hear his untroubled breathing, and the tiny rustle of settling dust under the girl's body. There was no sound from outside.

He switched on the light again and went out of the cave. A bridle jingled as the mule moved, but it appeared that he hadn't untied it. I heard him move off, his soft footsteps unaccompanied by the sharper ones of the beast. He must have decided to reconnoitre the corrie before daring to lead out the mule. . . .

The footsteps dwindled steadily. I couldn't hear them any more. I waited, straining my ears. Nothing but the soft movement of dust in the cave, and the restless shifting of the mule's hoofs in its corner. He must have left the corrie—perhaps to look for Dimitrios' approach.

One thing was certain: Angelos had no idea that Simon had any reason for further curiosity about the corrie. He felt as safe from discovery in this remote stretch of Parnassus as he would on the mountains of the moon.

And Simon? Simon, too. . . .

I was out of the cleft and flying across the dark cave. There was no light, but I don't remember that I needed it. My body was acting of itself, like a sleepwalker's, and like a sleepwalker's it must have dodged every obstacle by instinct. My brain, too . . . I had no conscious plan, not even any coherent thought, but at some queer submerged level I knew I had to get out of that cave, to Simon. . . . There was something about Dimitrios coming back, and Simon . . . something about warning Simon that here was not one shifty little crook to deal with, but two men who were murderers . . . something important to tell Simon . . . and more important than anything, I had to get out of the darkness, out of that stifling cage of rock, into the blessed light . . .

The sun struck down at me like a bright axe. I put a hand to my eyes, flinching as if at an actual blow. I was blinded, swimming in a sea of light. My other hand, groping out before me, touched something warm and soft, that moved. I jerked away with a little gasp of terror and in the same moment I realized that it was the mule, tethered in the narrow corner outside the cave. Its muzzle was deep in the grass, and it hardly paused to roll a white eye back at me before it resumed its eager cropping. The warm ammoniac smell of its coat brought a momentary, comfortless, memory of Niko. I thrust past it, ducked heedlessly under the buttress, and ran out into the corrie.

There was no sign of Angelos. I turned and ran for the foot of the cliff path.

The heat in the bottom of the corrie was palpable. I felt the sweat start out on my body as soon as I left the shade. The air weighed on me as I ran. My lungs laboured to drag it in, and dust was burning and rough in my throat. The corrie was a well of heat, in which nothing moved except me, and I thrust through it blindly, with the whip of panic on me. . . .

I reached the foot of the cliff. I believe I realized that if Angelos had gone to meet his cousin, he would have gone by the gateway, and not up the cliff. But this again was not a conscious thought. I only knew that I had to get up, out of the hot enclosing walls of rock, out onto the high open stretches above the cliff.

The afternoon sun shone full on the cliff where the path lay. The brightness of the white limestone splintered against the eyes. As I plunged up the steep, twisting little goat-track I felt the rock burn the soles of my shoes like hot metal. When I put a hand to the face of the cliff it seemed to scorch the flesh.

I climbed as fast as I dared, trying to make no sound. The dust hissed like sand under my feet. A pebble rolled and fell to the foot of the cliff with a crack like a pistol shot. My breathing was as loud in the still air as sobbing.

I was a little less than halfway up when I heard him coming back.

I stopped dead, pilloried against the naked rock, clamped to it, like a lizard on the bare stone. The rock burned through my thin dress. As soon as he got to the gateway he would see me. I couldn't possibly get to the top in time. If there were somewhere to hide. . . .

There was nowhere to hide. A bare zigzag of goat track; a couple of steep steps of natural rock open to the sun; a ledge holding a low tangle of brown scrub. . . .

Regardless now of noise I scrambled anyhow over the rocky steps, pulled myself off the path onto the ledge, and flung myself down behind the meagre shelter of the dead bushes.

There was one small holly oak, shining green, among a mass of foot-high tufted stuff like a tangle of rusty wire netting. This was prickly to the touch, but as I dragged myself nearer its shelter, pressing against it, it crumbled under my desperate hands. I remember that it seemed quite a natural part of the nightmare, that the barrier between me and murder should crumble as I touched it.

I drew back from the dead bushes and pressed myself deep into the dust of the ledge, as if like a mole I could dig myself into the ground for safety. I put my cheek to the hot dust and lay still. Above me an over-hang dealt a narrow shade, but where I lay the ledge was exposed to the sun. I could feel its cruel weight on my back and hand, but I hardly heeded it. Through the wiry scrub I was watching the corrie below me.

Angelos came up into the gateway and then walked quickly down the ramp and across the corrie. He didn't look up, but made straight for the cave, disappearing from my view in the corner.

I waited, pressed down in the burning dust. . . .

I was just getting ready to move, when I saw him again. He came out into the sunlight, moving very quietly now, and looking about him. He had brought his jacket out of the cave, and held it carefully over one arm. In the other hand he held something that shone in the sunlight. It was the torch I had dropped by Nigel's body. Angelos' own torch.

The black arched brows were drawn frowning over his eyes. The smile pulled the thick lips. He stopped in the centre of the corrie, turn-ing the torch over in his hand.

I lay still. Invisible, the mule moved restlessly, and metal clinked.

Angelos raised his head and sent one long look round the corrie. It raked the cliff, touched me, passed me by. Then the massive shoulders lifted in a tiny shrug, and he thrust the torch into a pocket of the jacket. I saw him slide his hand into the other pocket and bring out a gun. He weighed this for a moment in his hand, thoughtfully, and then turned back towards the cave.

My hands braced themselves in the dust. He would have recognized the torch, no doubt of that. He was going back into the cave to search for whoever had dropped it. And this time I didn't propose to linger till he came out again. I wasn't going to wait here, to be brushed off the cliff by that gun like a lizard off a wall.

I felt my muscles tighten up like vibrating wires. He was moving de-liberately across the corrie floor. Soon he would be out of sight.

Something fell onto my hand with a sharp little rap of pain that nearly made me cry out. A pebble. Then a shower of dust and small stones, dislodged from somewhere above me, rattled down the cliff like a charge of small shot.

Angelos stopped dead, turned, and stared upwards straight at me.

I didn't move. I didn't think he could see me at that angle. But my mind stampeded with another, and worse panic, as I heard the sounds approaching the top of the cliff. Dimitrios, as yet scatheless, with Simon behind him? Or Simon, coming cheerfully to tell me that justice had been done on "last night's marauder"? Any hope I had had that Dimitrios might have been forced into telling Simon himself about Angelos, vanished now as I listened to that incautious approach.

I saw Angelos stiffen, then he whipped out of sight behind a jut of rock.

The sounds came nearer. I turned my head till, by twisting my eyes in their sockets, I could see the cliff top. If it was Simon I must shout . . . my mouth opened ready for the cry, and I licked the dust off my dry lips. Then something moved suddenly against the sky at the brim of the cliff, and I saw what it was.

A goat. Another. Three big black goats, yellow-eyed, flop-eared, peacefully intent on the dry scrub at the cliff's head. . . . They turned aside at the brink of the cliff and moved slowly across above me, outlined against the deep blue of that translucent sky. As they went I thought I heard again the sweet faraway stave of the goat-herd's pipe. The coolly pastoral sound fell through the heat like the trickle of Apollo's spring.

The relief was dizzying. The rock swam in the dazzling light. I shut my eyes and put my head down beside the dusty scrub. Something smelt sweet and aromatic—some memory, wisping out of the dust, of potpourri and English gardens and bees among the thyme. . . .

I don't know how long it was before I realized that the afternoon held no sound at all.

When I looked again, Angelos had come out of concealment, and was standing where he had been before, in the centre of the corrie floor. He was standing very still, staring up, not at me, but at the edge of the cliff above me where the goats had been. Slowly I followed his gaze. I could feel the breath of the hot stone on my cheek.

The goats were still there. They, too, were standing stock-still, side by side, at the brink of the cliff. They were looking down, with ears forward and eyes intent and curious . . . six yellow satyrs' eyes, staring fixedly down at me, some forty feet below them.

Angelos dropped his coat onto a boulder beside him, and started for the foot of the cliff.

At his movement I heard the flurry of dust and pebbles as the goats fled. It echoed the quick jump and kick of my own heart. But I didn't move. Whether some instinct kept me clamped still like a hiding animal, or whether the flood of fear that washed and ebbed through my blood actually drained the power of movement from me, I can't tell. At any rate I lay flat for the few decisive moments during which the Greek crossed the corrie and plunged up the goat path towards me. And then it seemed that he was almost on me, and it was too late to escape. I remembered the gun and lay there, unbreathing, pressed flat to the hot earth.

I had a shelter of a sort from below, and from above the overhang might partly hide me. The path sloped sharply past the end of the ledge where I lay. It was possible—it was surely possible?—that he might hurry past it and never look back to see me lying there behind the crumbling scrub? My dress was of pale-coloured cotton, now sufficiently streaked with dust. Against the glaring rock and the red pebble-strewn dust he might miss me. He might yet—surely?—miss me.

He was just below me now. He stopped. His head was a few feet below the level of my ledge. I couldn't—daren't—look, but I heard the climbing steps stilled, and then his breathing close beneath me. He was looking up. My own breath hardly stirred the dust under my mouth.

He paused where he was for a few seconds, and then I heard the soft steps moving on. But they didn't come on up the track. They moved carefully away to the left, below my ledge.

Through the pathetic barrier of dead plants I could just see the top of his head. It was turned away now, and I knew that he must have left the track. I could hear loose pebbles slither and spatter down the rock, and the rustle of the dry plants he trod over. He went very carefully, with pauses almost between each step.

I had to know what he was doing. I moved my head slightly, and saw him better.

There was a ledge below mine, with a few sparse plants and a tumble of loose fragments of stone. I had noticed it in that second's wild glance round for shelter. It wouldn't have hidden anyone larger than a child. But he searched it, gun in hand, quartering it methodically, like a dog.

Then he left it, and came back carefully onto the track. He paused there briefly once again, so that for a silly moment I wondered if he was satisfied, and would go down again into the corrie, thinking perhaps that the goats had been watching a snake. . . . But he turned without further hesitation and started up the steep section that would bring him up to me.

I don't even think I was frightened; not now. It was as if fear had been raised to such a pitch that it killed itself, like a light that goes vividly

bright just before it goes out. I was back in that dim-lit, remote theatre of
unreality. This wasn't happening to me.

I suppose that nobody, in their heart of hearts, ever believes that they
themselves will die. Volumes of philosophies have been written out of
this belief alone. And I'm sure that nobody ever believes that a foul
thing like murder can overtake them. Something will stop it. It can't happen. To others, but not to them. Not to *me*.

I lay, almost relaxed, abandoned to fate and chance, in the hot dust,
and Angelos swiftly climbed the path towards me. In a moment now he
would reach the end of my ledge. He might see me straightaway, or he
might turn aside and beat the scrub till he flushed me, scared and filthy
with dust, from my hiding place. He was there now. He couldn't miss
me. . . .

I have read somewhere that when a man is hunted for his life, one of
the chief dangers he undergoes is the desperate urge to give himself up,
and have done. I had never believed it. I had thought that fear would
drive him till he dropped, like a hunted hare. But it's true. It may have
been that something forbade me to let the man find me crouching, dirty
and frightened, at his feet; it may simply have been the terrible blind instinct of the hunted. But the impulsion came and I didn't attempt to
resist it.

I stood up and began to brush the dirt off my frock.

I didn't look at him. He had stopped dead when I moved. He was
standing just where my ledge left the track. To get off it I would have to
pass him.

I walked forward through the scrub and stones as if I were walking in
my sleep. I didn't meet his eyes, but watched my feet on the rough going.
He moved a little to one side and I passed him. I went slowly down the
path again to the bottom of the corrie. He came just behind me.

When I got to the level ground I stumbled and nearly fell. His hand
took hold of my arm from behind, and my flesh seemed to wince and
shrink from the touch. I stopped.

The hand tightened, then with a jerk he pulled me round to face him.
I think if he had gone on touching me I would have screamed then and
there, but he let me go, so I kept silent. I knew that if I tried to scream I
would be killed out of hand. But I backed away from him a step or so
till a boulder touched the back of my legs. Without meaning to, I sat
down; I couldn't have stood. I put both hands flat on the hot surface of
the stone as if I could draw strength from it, and looked at Angelos.

He was standing perhaps five feet from me, his legs a little apart, one
hand thrust negligently into the belt of his trousers, the other arm hanging loose at his side with the gun dangling. His head was forward slightly,

like a bull's when it is deciding to charge. The heavy face was terrifying with its tight, curved smile, the perfect arch of the black brows and the cruel eyes that seemed to be solid, opaque black, without pupils, and without light from within. The thick nostrils were flared and he was breathing fast. The bulls' curls along his forehead were damp and tight with sweat.

He had recognized me, of course. I saw that as his slow stare raked me. He must have seen me distinctly last night in the light of the torch.

He said, "So it's my little friend of the studio, is it?" He was speaking in the quick guttural French he had used with Danielle.

I tried to say something, but no sound came. As I cleared my throat I saw the smile deepen. My voice came back. "I hope I hurt you," I said.

"That score," said Angelos, very pleasantly, "will soon be quite even." My hands pressed hard on the warm stone. I said nothing. He said abruptly, "Where's the Englishman?"

"I don't know."

He made a small movement towards me and I shrank back against the boulder. His expression didn't change but his voice did. "Don't be a fool. You didn't come up here alone. Where is he?"

I said hoarsely, "I—we were sitting up there on the cliff and we saw a man hanging about . . . that chap Dimitrios. He's a guide . . . I don't know if you know him. Simon . . . my friend . . . went off to speak to him. He—he thought it was him last night at the studio and I think—I think he wanted to find out what he'd been after."

It was so near the truth that I hoped he might be satisfied as far as Simon was concerned. But it wouldn't help me. Nothing would.

"And you've been up on the cliff all this time?"

"I—why, no. I went over the hill a little way, and then I thought Simon might have come back, so I—"

"And you haven't been in the cave?"

"Cave?" I said.

"That's what I said. The cave."

The sun was cold. The rock was cold. I suppose even till this I had been hoping against silly hope, but now I knew for certain. Of course I was going to die. Whatever I had seen or not seen—the mule, the cave, the treasure, Nigel, Danielle—it wouldn't help me in the least to play the innocent. None of these things mattered beside the one fact that now I had seen Angelos.

He had taken two paces away to where his coat lay over a boulder. He slipped a hand in the pocket and brought out the torch. "You left this, didn't you?"

"Yes."

A gleam of surprise in the black eyes showed that he had expected me to deny it. I said flatly, "I dropped it when I saw Nigel's body. And I was in the cave just now when you killed Danielle."

The metal of the torch flashed as he made a sudden little movement. At least I had startled him into interest. If I could keep him talking . . . if I could keep alive for just a few more minutes . . . perhaps the miracle would happen, and I wouldn't die. Murderers were conceited, weren't they? They talked about their murders? But then Angelos took murder so for granted that it had hardly seemed to interest him to commit, let alone to discuss. . . . But he was a sadist, too; perhaps he would enjoy talking to frighten me before he killed me. . . .

I said hoarsely, gripping the stone, "Why did you torture Nigel? Did you really mean to kill Danielle?"

It wasn't going to work. He dropped the torch back on top of the coat, and gave a quick glance round the encircling cliffs. Then he put the gun down gently beside the torch, and turned to me.

I did manage to move then, but the thrust of my hands that took me off the warm stone sent me a pace towards him. As I whirled to run he caught me from behind and pulled me back as easily as if I had been a rag doll. I suppose I fought him; I don't remember anything except the blind panic and the feel of his hands and the acrid smell of his sweat, and the appalling iron strength that held me as effortlessly as a man's hand holds a caught moth. One hand came hard over my mouth, crushing my lips against my teeth, but the palm was slimy with sweat; it slipped, and I wrenched my head away and managed at the same moment to kick him hard on the shinbone. I paid dearly for the moment of advantage, for as I twisted my body in a vain attempt to break away, he half-lunged forward to drag me close again and silence me, trod on a loose stone that rolled under his foot, and we fell together.

If I had fallen undermost I should probably have been badly hurt, if not stunned, for he was a heavy man; but he went down onto his side in a stumbling fall, dragging me with him. Even then the brutal grip never loosened, and as we hit the ground he moved like lightning, flinging himself over my body with a quick heave, and holding me down on the ground underneath him.

Then his grip shifted. I was on my back, my left arm twisted up under me, so that our double weight held it there, almost breaking. My right wrist was in his grip, clamped down against the rock beside me. His free hand flashed up to my throat. The heavy body held me down; I couldn't move, but frantic now with terror I screamed and twisted uselessly under him and jerked my head from side to side, trying to avoid the hand that slipped and groped on my throat for the hold he wanted. I screamed again. He cursed in Greek and hit me hard across the mouth and then as my head went back against the rock the hand gripped my throat at last, moved a little, tightened. . . .

I was still alive. It was years later and the boiling agonized black had cleared, and I was still alive. I was still lying on my back in the hot dust, and above me the sky arched in a great flashing, pulsating dome of blue. Angelos' weight was still on me. I could feel the heave of his heavy breathing; the smell of his sweat was rank; his hand was wet and sour and foul across my mouth; the other hand was still on my throat, but it lay loosely there, and now it lifted.

He didn't move away. He lay there quite still, with rigid muscles, looking up and away from me towards the entrance to the corrie. Then his hand slid from my face and went down onto the dusty rock beside my head, ready to thrust him to his feet. I remember that the hand was on my spread hair, and the tug as he put his weight on it hurt me. The tiny pain was like a spur. It pricked me back to consciousness. I stopped blinking up into the vibrating blue of the sky, and managed to move my head a fraction, to look where Angelos was looking.

He was staring straight into the sun. At first I could see nothing in the dazzle at the mouth of the corrie. Then I saw him.

I knew who it was straightaway, though he was only a shadow against the glare. But even so I felt the sharp cold thrill run up the marrow of my spine as I felt Angelos' heart jerk, once, in his body, and heard him say, thickly, "Michael?"

CHAPTER XIX

I am come,
Fresh from the cleansing of Apollo . . .
. . . To pay the bloody twain their debt
Of blood.

EURIPIDES: *Electra*
(*tr. Gilbert Murray*).

REALIZATION, SHOCK, recognition—it must only have taken a few seconds, but it seemed an age.

One moment Simon was silhouetted in fractional pause against the

glare of the gateway, the next, Angelos had swung himself off my body
and onto his feet as lightly as a dancer. He must have forgotten that his
gun had been laid aside, for I remember that his hand flashed, as if automatically, to his hip just as Simon, coming down the ramp with the
speed of a ski-jumper, brought up not five yards from him in a flurry of
dust and shale.

Angelos was standing right over me, hand still at hip, watching him.
Simon had stopped dead where he was. I couldn't see his expression,
but I could see Angelos', and fear seeped back into my blood as agoniz-
ingly as warmth after frostbite. I stirred in the dust and tried to say something, to tell Simon who and what he was, but my throat was swollen
and sore, and the brilliant light swam round me sickeningly as I moved,
and I couldn't make a sound. Angelos must have felt me move at his
feet, but he took no notice. Simon hadn't glanced at me either. The two
men watched one another, as wary and slow as two dogs circling before
a fight.

I waited for Simon to rush him as he had done last night. I didn't
notice then how hard he was breathing, fighting to get heart and lungs
under control after his rush up the steep track towards my terrified
screaming. Nor did I realize that he still thought the Greek might be
armed . . . and I was lying where knife or gun could reach me, seconds
before Simon could make contact. . . . None of this was I in any state
to realize. I only knew that Simon didn't move, and I remember wondering, with a sick cold little feeling, if he was afraid. Then he took two
paces forward, very slowly, and now that he was no longer between me
and the sun, I saw his face. The cold feeling went, and I wasn't afraid
any more. With the fear, the tenseness went out of my body, and I felt
myself relax and begin to tremble. The bruises the Greek had inflicted
began to hurt. I turned on my side and tried to pull myself a little further
away from him. I couldn't have got up, but I dragged myself a foot or
so away to crouch, shaking and still gasping for breath, against the base
of the boulder where I had sat before.

He took no notice of me. He had dealt with me, and thrown me aside,
and now he was going to deal with Simon. I could be finished after that.

Simon said pleasantly, "I take it you are Angelos?" His breathing was
still over-fast, but his voice was level.

"The same. And you are Michael's little brother."

"The same."

The Greek said, on a note between satisfaction and contempt, "You
are welcome."

Simon's lips thinned. "I doubt that. I believe, Angelos, that you and I
have met before."

"Last night."

"Yes." Simon looked at him for a few seconds in silence. His voice went flat and uninflected. Knowing him now, I felt my heart tighten and begin to race. He added, "I wish I had known—last night."

I turned my head painfully and managed to say, "He killed Nigel . . . and Danielle." It was some seconds before I realized that I had made no sound at all.

"You murdered my brother Michael." Simon hadn't even glanced at me. He was breathing evenly now, his face wiped clean of all expression but that light, watchful look. I recognized it for what it was. Just so must Michael have looked when he faced Angelos here all those years ago. Just so must this blazing sky have looked down, those indifferent rocks throwing back its blinding heat. Time had run back. Angelos faced Michael again, and this time the odds were on Michael.

It seemed that Angelos didn't think so. He laughed. "Yes, I killed Michael. And I shall kill you, little brother. In your country they do not teach men to be men. It is different here."

Simon was moving now, very slowly, forward a pace; another.

"How did you kill my brother, Angelos?"

"I broke his neck." I noticed with surprise that the Greek was giving ground. He had lowered his head in that characteristic way he had. I could see the contraction of the flat black eyes against the light. I saw him blink rapidly once or twice, and he moved his head as a bull does whose horns pain him. Then he took a slow step backwards, sidling a little. . . .

I thought for a moment that he was trying to get Simon out of line with him and the sun, and wondered fleetingly at the same time why he should have let the other play for time like this, when suddenly, like a flash out of a black night, I knew what he was doing. I remembered the gun, lying hidden from Simon in the tumble of Angelos' dropped coat.

Somehow I moved. It was like lifting a mattress stuffed with clay to lift my body from the scuffled dust, but I rolled over, kicked myself along the ground with one convulsive jack-knifing motion, like a fish, and grabbed at the dangling sleeve of the coat just as Angelos took a sudden, swift step aside, and stooped for the gun.

I had the sleeve. I yanked at it with all my strength. It caught at a bit of the rock, tore, and came with a jerk. The torch flashed over like a rocket and crashed on a stone by my head. The gun flew high and wide, hit a pile of stones three yards away, and slithered out of sight. It actually struck the Greek's hand as he reached to grab it. He whirled with a curse and kicked me and then went down sickeningly across the boulder as Simon hit him like a steam hammer.

Simon came in with the blow. The Greek's forearm, even as he went down over the rock, just managed to block the side-handed chop at the throat that followed it, and counter in the same movement with a wicked elbow punch that took Simon in the lower part of the stomach. I saw pain explode through him like a bursting shell, and as he recoiled the Greek, using the rock as a springboard, came away from it in a lunge with all his weight behind it. Simon's mouth disappeared in a smear of blood. His head snapped back in front of another blow that looked as if it had broken his neck, and he went down, but as he went he hooked one leg round Angelos' knee and, using the man's own momentum, brought him crashing down over him. Before the Greek hit the ground Simon had rolled aside and was above him. I saw the Greek lash out with a foot, miss, and aim a short chopping blow with the edge of a hand at Simon's neck; Simon hit him in the throat and then the two were locked, heaving and rolling in the dust that mushroomed up round them.

I couldn't see . . . couldn't make out . . . Angelos was on his back, and Simon seemed to be across him, trying to fix the man's arm in a lock, to drag it under him as Angelos had dragged mine; the Greek smashed again and again at his face; the shortened punches hadn't much force behind them but the blood was running from Simon's mouth. Then suddenly the flailing fist opened, clawed, came down onto Simon's cheekbone and slithered across it, the big spatulate thumb digging, digging, for his eye. . . .

I had dragged myself to my feet, holding on to the boulder beside me. He couldn't do it after all; he couldn't be expected to do it . . . he was the younger, and he knew how to fight, but Angelos had the weight, and all those desperate years behind him. . . . If I could help . . . if I could only help. . . .

I stooped giddily, and reached for a lump of rough rock, lifting it in hands that shook like leaves. I could hit him as I had last night . . . if I could find a weapon—perhaps the torch—

The gun.

I dropped the knob of rock and flung myself, with sobbing little breaths, at the pile of stones where the gun had gone. Here, surely, it had struck and slid out of sight? No sign. Then here? No. Here . . . oh, dear God, *here.* . . .

There, white on the limestone, a scratch had marked its passage . . . I drove a shaking hand down between the jammed rocks. They scraped the skin and it hurt me but I hardly noticed. I thrust my arm down as far as I could. My fingers, stretching, touched something cold and smooth . . . metal. I couldn't reach it; the tips of my fingers slipped over it, no more. I could feel my lips trembling as the tears spilt salt onto them. I lay down hard against the stones and thrust my arm further into the narrowing crack. The cruel stone rasped at the skin and I felt blood running down my wrist. My fingers slid further, curled, gripped. I had the gun. I tried to withdraw it. But with my hand now curved round the butt I couldn't pull it back between the stones. I dragged at it, hopelessly, stupidly, and my hand hurt till I cried out with the pain, but I couldn't drag the gun out. . . .

Simon had twisted back from that gouging thumb. The Greek lunged violently to one side as the other's hold slackened, and then, somehow, was free. With a movement incredibly quick for a man of his build he had rolled aside and was bunching to jump to his feet. As he went I saw his hand close, like mine, on a cruelly jagged chunk of rock. But Simon was as quick. The same movement that threw him back and away from the clawing hand had brought him to his feet. He saw the Greek clutch the rock. Even as the fist closed on it and the arm muscles tightened Simon jumped. His foot stamped down on the man's hand. The rock was undermost, and I heard the man make a dreadful sound as his hand was smashed down onto it. But he whipped over and brought his foot up with what looked like appalling force into Simon's groin. Simon saw it coming, and tried to sidestep. The foot grazed the inside of his thigh. Simon's hand came up under the lashing ankle; I saw a heave and a twist, and the Greek crashed back onto his side like a felled ox, and Simon plummeted down onto him again in the smother of dust. Another blow, a sick sound of flesh and bone smacking together, and then Angelos was uppermost, his fist smashing down like a hammer. . . .

I opened my hand and let the gun go. I dropped to the base of the pile of stones, and began to claw at them with those useless, shaking fingers, trying to pull the heavy stuff aside. From behind me came the thud and slither of their bodies on the ground, the torn dreadful breathing, and, again, the sudden sharp sound of pain. I thought it came from Simon.

The stone under my hands gave way, and I threw it down and tore at the next. And the next. And then a pile of dry earth and small jagged pebbles.

Then I saw the blue-dark gleam of the gun.

I thrust the last lump of rock aside and pushed my hand through. The muzzle was towards me. I grabbed it and dragged the thing out. I didn't even think once of the danger of holding it like that. I just dragged it out between the rough stones and turned, holding it in my aspen hands. I remember thinking with surprise how heavy it was. . . .

I'd never touched a gun before in my life. But of course it was quite easy. You simply pointed it and pressed the trigger: I knew that. Pro-

vided I got close enough . . . and if the men would only break apart for
a moment and let me see through that stifling dust. . . . One simply
pointed the thing and pulled the trigger, and Angelos would be dead,
blasted out of life in a fraction of time. It didn't occur to me that this was
in any way a wrong or a momentous thing to do. I took a couple of fal-
tering steps in the direction of the struggling bodies on the ground. . . .

It was funny, but it was difficult to walk. The ground was unsteady
and the dust dragged at my feet and the gun was too heavy and the sky
was far too bright but still I couldn't see properly. . . .

The locked bodies on the ground moved as the man underneath made
a seemingly titanic effort. Both men were covered with dust: I couldn't
see who it was lying prone with one arm twisted into that cruel lock behind his back . . . or who it was who lay astride him, shifting his grip
now, straining in some final agonizing effort. If only they would break
apart . . . if only I could see which was Angelos. . . .

The man uppermost lay clamped over the other, one hand hard round
the wrist of the locked arm, his own free arm flung round the prone
man's neck in a tight embrace. As I watched, the embrace tightened still
further. . . .

The prostrate man's head came painfully back. The red dust was thick
in the black curls. The broad cruel face was smeared red with it too, an
archaic mask carved grimacing in red sandstone. It was Angelos who lay
there in the dust, breath sobbing through the grinning lips, trying with
weaker and weaker movements to throw Simon off his body.

I stood there, the gun drooping in my hand, the driving purpose
snapped in me, staring like someone in a dream at the two bodies that
heaved, breathing as one, on the ground at my feet.

A muscle bunched in Simon's shoulder. The Greek's head moved
back another fraction. The grin was a rictus, fixed, horrible. His body
gave one last desperate heave to rid itself of its killer, threshing sideways
across the dusty rock. But Simon's grip didn't shift. Even as the two
bodies, still locked, slithered a yard or so across the dusty rock to fetch
up hard against the cairn where Michael had been murdered, I saw Simon's arm tense, and jerk tightly back, and heard Angelos' breath tear
out of his throat in a sort of whistling gasp that broke off short. . . .

I knew then that Simon didn't need me or the gun. I turned aside and
sat down on the boulder. I leaned back very wearily against the hot rock
and shut my eyes.

After a while there was silence.

Angelos lay still, sprawled face downward against the little cairn. Simon got very slowly to his feet. He stood for a moment looking down.

His face was filthy with dust and blood, and lined with fatigue. I could see how his muscles slumped with weariness as he stood there. He put up the back of his hand to wipe the blood from his face. His hands were bloody too.

Then he turned away and for the first time looked at me. He made as if to speak, and then I saw his tongue come out to wet the dust-caked lips. I answered his look quickly.

"I'm quite all right, Simon. He—he didn't hurt me." My voice had come back, hoarse and not too steady. But there was nothing to say. I whispered, "There's a rope on the mule. It's down by the cave."

"Rope?" His voice wasn't his own either. He was coming slowly towards me. "What for?"

"Him, of course. If he came round—"

"My dear Camilla," said Simon. And then, as he saw the look in my face, in a kind of anger, "What else did you expect me to do?"

"I don't know. Of course you had to kill him. It's just—of course you did."

His mouth twisted. It wasn't quite a smile, but nothing about him seemed, just at that moment, to be like himself. It was a stranger who stood in front of me in the blazing sunlight, with a stranger's voice, and something gone from his face that I remembered there. He stood there in silence, looking down at his hands. I still remember the blood on them.

The nausea had gone, and the world steadied. I said quickly, almost desperately, out of a rush of shame, "Simon. Forgive me. I—I guess I can't think straight yet. Of course you had to. It was only . . . coming so close to it. But you were right. There comes a time when one has to . . . accept . . . things like this. It was damnable of me."

He did smile then, a trace of genuine amusement showing through the weariness. "Not really. You were right too. But—just exactly what were you planning to do with that?"

"With what?" Following his look, I stared stupidly down at the gun in my hand.

He leaned forward and took it from me gently. The bloodstained fingers avoided mine. They were shaking a little. He laid the gun carefully to one side. "I think perhaps it's safer there."

Silence. He stood over me, looking down still with that stranger's look. "Camilla."

I met it then.

"If you hadn't got rid of that thing," he said, "I should be dead."

"And so should I. But you came."

"My dear, of course. But if he'd got to that gun . . ." A tiny pause, so slight it didn't seem that what he said could be important. "Would you have shot him, Camilla?"

Quite suddenly, I was shaking uncontrollably. I said, with a sort of violence, "Yes. Yes, I would. I was just going to, but then you . . . you killed him yourself. . . ."

I began to cry then, helplessly. I reached out blindly with both hands, and took his between them, blood and all.

He was sitting beside me on the boulder, with his arm round me. I don't remember what he said; I think part of the time he was swearing under his breath, and this seemed so unlike him that I had to fight harder to control the little spurts of laughter that shook me through the sobbing.

I managed to say, "I'm sorry. I'm all right. I'm not hysterical. It's—it's reaction or something."

He said with violence, the more shocking because it was the first time I had heard it from him, "I'll not forgive myself in a hurry for dragging you into this, by God! If I'd had any idea—"

"You didn't drag me in. I asked to be in, so I had to take what came, didn't I? It wasn't your fault it turned out as it did. A man does what he has to do, and since you *did* feel like that about Michael, after all, you did it. That's all."

"About Michael?"

"Yes. You said the tragedy was over, but of course once you knew Angelos was still alive—"

"My dear girl," said Simon, "you didn't imagine that I really killed him for Mick, did you?"

I looked up at him rather numbly. "No? But you told Angelos—"

"I was talking the language he'd understand. This is still Orestes' country, after all." He looked down at the scuffled dust between his feet. "Oh, I admit it was partly Mick—once I found myself here, and facing him. I felt murderous enough about him when I knew he was still alive, even before Dimitrios told me the rest."

"Dimitrios? Of course. He told you?"

"He was persuaded to, quite quickly. Niko turned up and helped me." A pause. "He told me what the two of them had done to Nigel."

"Then you know. . . ." The breath I drew was three parts relief. I remembered that look in Simon's eyes, and the smooth single-mindedness with which he had killed Angelos. I shivered a little. "I see."

"And then," he said, "there was you."

I said nothing. My eyes were on two—no, three specks in the bright air, circling slowly, high above the corrie. Simon sat beside me without moving, looking at the trampled dust. He looked all at once unutterably weary. If it hadn't been for the evidence sprawled across the stones one might almost have thought that he, not Angelos, had been beaten. "Any man's death diminishes me, . . ." I thought of Nigel, tumbled grotesquely behind the pile of dirt, and understood.

The silence drew out. Away somewhere on the mountain I thought I heard something, the clatter of stones, a breathless call. Simon didn't move. I said, "Tell me about Angelos. How did he get into it? Why did he wait till now to come back?"

"He's been before. We were right in our guesses about the search for the gold—the lights and voices, and Dimitrios' questions—but we were wrong about the name of the seeker. It wasn't Dimitrios himself. He knew nothing about the cache originally. When Angelos left Greece for Yugoslavia at the end of nineteen forty-four, he intended to come back as soon as he could. But he committed murder—political murder this time—in his adopted country, and was put away for 'life.' He was released two years ago, and came secretly back to look up his cousin. He let him into the secret, since he had to have somewhere to hide, and an agent to help him. They looked for the stuff—just as we guessed—but failed to find it. Dimitrios did his best to pump Stephanos, and the two of them must have searched desperately over the earthquake area at intervals through the spring and summer, then they gave up for the time being, and Angelos went back to live in Italy. I imagine he intended to come back again in the spring of this year, as soon as the snows had melted, but by then I had written to Stephanos, and the rumours were going about that I was coming to Delphi. He decided to wait and let us show him the place. That's all."

He glanced down at me. "And now, what happened to you? Why on earth did you come out of the cave? Surely he never found you in there, in sanctuary?"

"No." I told him then all that had happened since he had left me to follow Dimitrios. I found that I could tell it all quite calmly now, with that queer detachment I had felt in the cave, as if it were a play; as if these things had happened, not to me, but in some story I had read. But I remember being glad of the feel of Simon's arm round my shoulders, and of the heat of the sun.

He listened in silence, and when I had finished he still didn't speak for some minutes. Then he said, "I seem to have rather more to forgive myself for than just bringing you in on—that." For the first time his eyes went back to the cairn where the body lay. They were as I first remembered them, vivid and hard and cool. "Quite a score," he said. "Mick, Nigel, poor silly little Danielle. And then, of course, you. . . . It would almost take an Orestes, wouldn't it?" He took in his breath. "No, I doubt if the Furies, the Kindly Ones, will haunt me for this day's work, Camilla."

"No, I don't think they will."

There was a shout from the gateway behind us. With a clatter of stones, Niko hurled himself into the corrie and raced down towards us. "Beautiful miss!" he yelled. "*Kyrie* Simon! It's all right! I'm here!"

He slithered to a halt in front of us. His startled gaze took us both in —my torn and filthy dress, the bruises, my scraped wrists and hands, and Simon covered with blood and dust and marks of battle. "Mother of God, then he *was* here? Angelos was here? He got away? He—"

He stopped abruptly as he caught sight of the body lying against the cairn. He gulped, and flashed a look at Simon. He looked at me as if he were going to speak, but he just shut his mouth again, tightly, and then went—it seemed reluctantly—across to where Angelos lay. There was the sound of slower footsteps from the gateway of the corrie, and Stephanos came into sight. He paused there for a moment, just as Simon had done, then came deliberately down the ramp towards us. Simon got stiffly to his feet. The old man stopped at my elbow. His eyes, too, were on Angelos. Then he looked at Simon. He didn't speak, but he nodded, slowly. Then he smiled. I think he would have spoken to me then, but Niko had straightened up and now came running back. A flood of Greek was poured out at Simon, who answered, and presently seemed to be telling his story. I caught the name "Michael" several times, and then "the Englishman," and "the French girl," and the word "*speleos,*" which I took to mean "a cave." But I was suddenly too tired to pay any attention. I leaned back into a bar of shadow and waited, while the three of them talked across me. Presently, with a word from Simon, he and Stephanos left me and went towards the cave.

Niko lingered for a moment. "You are not well, beautiful miss?" he asked anxiously. "That one—that Bulgar—he hurt you?"

To call anyone a Bulgarian is the worst term of abuse a Greek can think up; and they have quite a range. "Not really, Niko," I said. "I'm a bit shaken, that's all." I smiled at him. "You should have been here."

"I wish I had been!" Niko's sidelong glance at the cairn was perhaps not as enthusiastic as his voice, but apparently it took more than murder really to dim his lights. He turned his look of dazzled admiration on me. "I should have dealt with him, me, and not on account of my grandfather's cousin Panos, but for *you*, beautiful miss. Though *Kyrie* Simon," he added generously, "did very well, not?"

"For an Englishman," I said deprecatingly.

"Indeed, for an Englishman." He caught my look and grinned, unabashed. "Of course," he added, "I help him with Dimitrios Dragoumis. I, Niko."

"He told me so. What did you do with him?"

The black eyes opened wide. He looked shocked. "I could not tell you *that*. You are a lady, and—oh, I *see*." The devastating smile flashed out. "Afterwards, you mean? I take him down to the road, but not to Delphi, because I want to get back and help *Kyrie* Simon, you understand. There is a truck, and I explain to the men, and they take him to Delphi to the police. The police will come. I shall go presently to meet them and guide them here. And so."

"And so." I said it very wearily. It seemed as good a period to the day as anything.

Beyond my bar of shadow the sun seemed white-hot. Niko had on a shirt of vivid electric blue, patterned with scarlet lozenges. The effect was blinding. He seemed to shimmer at the edges.

I heard him say cheerfully, "You are tired. You do not want to talk. And the other men will be needing me, not? I go."

As I shut my eyes and leaned back, I heard him crossing the corrie at his usual impetuous gallop.

It seemed a long time before the three of them came out of the cave again into the sunlight.

Niko came first, leading the mule. He seemed subdued now, and a little pale. He didn't come over to me again, but swung himself onto the mule's back, kicked it into reluctant motion, and, with a wave to me, clattered out of the corrie.

Stephanos and Simon stood talking for a few minutes longer. Stephanos looked sombre. I saw him nod to something Simon said, then he gestured upwards towards the blazing arch of sky where those black specks still hung and circled. Then he turned and trudged slowly across to a patch of shade near the body. He sat down there, and settled himself, as if to wait, leaning forward with his head against the hands clasped on his staff. He shut his eyes. He looked suddenly very old—with that Homeric head and the shut eyes as old as time itself.

It was a picture I was never to forget, that quiet tailpiece to tragedy. There was the blue arch of the brilliant sky; there the body that the Kindly Ones had hunted down and killed on the very spot where he himself had shed blood; there the old man, bearded like Zeus himself, nodding in the shade. At the head of the cliffs stood the black goats, staring.

From somewhere, not too far distant now, came the little stave of music; the goat-herd's pipe whose sound, drifting down through the light-well, had led me to the Apollo of the holy spring. At the sound the goats lifted their heads and, turning, moved off, black against the sky, an Attic frieze in slow procession.

Simon's shadow fell across me.

"Niko's gone to guide the police here. He wanted to escort you to Delphi, but I told him you wouldn't be fit for the trek quite yet. You and I have something still to do, haven't we?"

I hardly heard the question. I said, apprehensively, "The police?"

"Don't worry. There'll be no trouble for me. Apart from everything else, and God knows he's done plenty, he was trying to kill you." He smiled. "And now, are you coming? Stephanos is asleep, by the looks of it, so he won't wonder where we've gone."

"You didn't tell him and Niko about the shrine?"

"No. The question of what to do about the guns and gold is out of our hands now, thank heaven, but the other question's our own to answer. Do you know the answer?"

I looked at him inquiringly; perhaps a little doubtfully.

Then he nodded, and I said, slowly, "I suppose so."

He smiled and put down a hand to me.

We went into the cave in silence. Simon's torch was almost dead, but it showed the way. It was not strong enough to probe too far into the shadows. He paused just inside the entrance, and I saw him step aside and stoop over something that lay near the pile of rubble where the boxes had been. He straightened up with one of Angelos' crowbars in his hand. I didn't look further, but followed the mercifully dimming light through the pillared vaults until the slab barred the way.

The light paused on the old marks of tooling in the stone. "There," said Simon softly. "It should slide back easily enough. Even another three or four inches should block the entrance. . . . I'll leave this here for the moment."

He laid the crowbar down and we went through the cleft for the last time, and up the curving tunnel that led to the bright citadel.

He had stood there without move or change for more than two thousand years; now, it seemed a miracle that in the last hour he had remained untouched, unaltered. The sun had slid further towards the west and the light fell more slantingly through the leaves; that was all.

We knelt at his feet and drank. I cupped my hands under the spring and splashed the water over my face and neck, then held my wrists under the icy runnel. It stung on the bruises and the scraped flesh of my wrists, a sharp remedial stinging that seemed to signal my body's return from whatever numb borderlands of shock I had been straying in. I sat back, flicking the cool drops off my hands.

I noticed then that the mark had gone from the third finger of my left hand. There was no sign at all of the pale circle where Philip's ring had been.

I sat looking at my hands.

Simon was leaning forward, putting something on the stone plinth at the statue's feet. There was the gleam of gold.

He caught my look and smiled, a little wryly. "Gold for Apollo. I asked him to bring Angelos back, and he did it, even though it was done in that damned two-edged Delphic way that one always forgets to bargain for. However, there it is. It was a vow. Remember?"

"I remember."

"It comes to me that you made a vow too, in this very shrine."

"So I did. I'll have to share your coin, Simon. I've nothing here to give."

"Then we'll share," he said. That was all, in that casual easy voice with no change in it; but I turned quickly to look up at him. The vivid grey eyes held mine for a moment, then I turned from him almost at random and picked up Nigel's little water pot. "We'll leave this here too, shall we?"

Something glinted, deep in the grass, down beside the edge of the stone plinth. I smoothed the long stems aside and picked it up. It was another gold coin.

"Simon, look at this!"

"What is it? A talent? Don't tell me Apollo's provided a ram in the thicket for—" He stopped short as I held my hand out towards him.

I said, "It's a sovereign. That means Nigel did find the gold as well as the statue. He must have left this here."

"Must he?"

"Well, who else—?" Then I saw his face and stopped.

He nodded. "Yes. Of course. Michael made an offering, too."

He took it from me gently and laid it beside the water pot, at the feet of the god.